DEATH IN A WHITE TIE
OVERTURE TO DEATH
DEATH AT THE BAR

Dame Ngaio Marsh was born in New Zealand in 1895 and died in February 1982. She wrote over 30 detective novels and many of her stories have theatrical settings, for Ngaio Marsh's real passion was the theatre. Both actress and producer, she almost single-handedly revived the New Zealand public's interest in the theatre. It was for this work that she received what she called her 'damery' in 1966.

'The finest writer in the English language of the pure, classical puzzle whodunit. Among the crime queens, Ngaio Marsh stands out as an Empress.'   *The Sun*

'Ngaio Marsh transforms the detective story from a mere puzzle into a novel.'   *Daily Express*

'Her work is as nearly flawless as makes no odds. Character, plot, wit, good writing, and sound technique.'   *Sunday Times*

'She writes better than Christie!'   *New York Times*

'Brilliantly readable . . . first class detection.'   *Observer*

'Still, quite simply, the greatest exponent of the classical English detective story.'   *Daily Telegraph*

'Read just one of Ngaio Marsh's novels and you've got to read them all . . . '   *Daily Mail*

NGAIO MARSH

Death in a White Tie

Overture to Death

Death at the Bar

AND

The Figure Quoted

HARPER

HARPER

an imprint of HarperCollins*Publishers*
77-85 Fulham Palace Road
Hammersmith, London W6 8JB
www.harpercollins.co.uk

This omnibus edition 2009
1

Death in a White Tie first published in Great Britain by Geoffrey Bles 1938
Overture to Death first published in Great Britain by Collins 1939
Death at the Bar first published in Great Britain by Collins 1940
The Figure Quoted first published in Great Britain by Dent 1930

Ngaio Marsh asserts the moral right to
be identified as the author of these works

Copyright © Ngaio Marsh Ltd 1930, 1938, 1939, 1940

ISBN 978 0 00 732871 0

Mixed Sources
Product group from well-managed
forests and other controlled sources
www.fsc.org Cert no. SW-COC-1806
© 1996 Forest Stewardship Council

FSC is a non-profit international organisation established to promote the
responsible management of the world's forests. Products carrying the FSC
label are independently certified to assure consumers that they come
from forests that are managed to meet the social, economic and
ecological needs of present and future generations.

Find out more about HarperCollins and the environment at
www.harpercollins.co.uk/green

CONTENTS

Death in a White Tie

Contents

The Characters in the Tale

Chief Detective-Inspector
    Roderick Alleyn, CID
Lady Alleyn — *His mother*
Sarah Alleyn — *His débutante niece*
Miss Violet Harris — *Secretary to Lady Carrados*
Lady Evelyn Carrados — *A London hostess*
Bridget O'Brien — *Her daughter*
Sir Herbert Carrados — *Her husband*
Lord Robert Gospell
    ('Bunchy') — *A relic of Victorian days*
Sir Daniel Davidson — *A fashionable London physician*
Agatha Troy, RA — *A painter*
Lady Mildred Potter — *Lord Robert's widowed sister*
Donald Potter — *Her son – a medical student*
Mrs Halcut-Hackett — *A social climber*
General Halcut-Hackett — *Her husband*
Miss Rose Birnbaum — *Her protégée*
Captain Maurice Withers
    ('Wits') — *A man about town*
Colombo Dimitri — *A fashionable caterer*
Lucy, Dowager Marchioness
    of Lorrimer — *An eccentric old lady*
A Taxi-driver
Miss Smith — *A friend of Miss Harris*
Detective-Inspector Fox,
    CID
Percy Percival — *A young man about town*
Mr Trelawney-Caper — *His friend*
James d'Arcy Carewe — *A detective-constable*
François Dupont — *Dimitri's servant*
Mr Cuthbert — *Manager of the Matador*
Vassily — *Alleyn's servant*
The Reverend Walter Harris — *A retired clergyman*
Mrs Walter Harris — *His wife*
The Assistant Commissioner

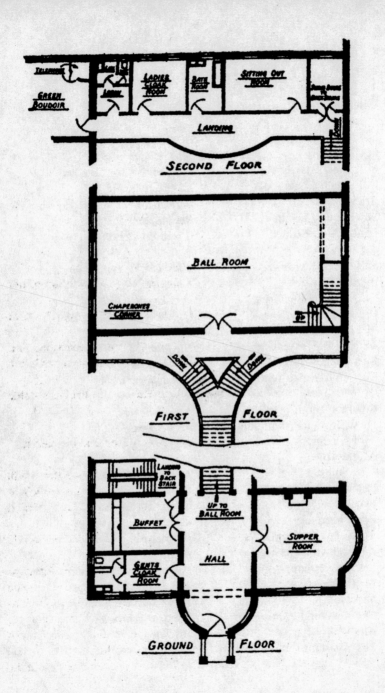

TELEPHONE

GREEN BOUDOIR

LADIES CLOAK ROOM

BATH ROOM

SITTING OUT ROOM

LANDING

SECOND FLOOR

BALL ROOM

CHAPERONES CORNER

WC

FIRST FLOOR

LANDING TO BACK STAIR

UP TO BALL ROOM

BUFFET

GENTS CLOAK ROOM

HALL

SUPPER ROOM

GROUND FLOOR

CHAPTER 1

The Protagonists

'Roderick,' said Lady Alleyn, looking at her son over the top of her spectacles, 'I am coming out.'

'Out?' repeated Chief Detective-Inspector Alleyn vaguely. 'Out where, mama? Out of what?'

'Out into the world. Out of retirement. Out into the season. Out. Dear me,' she added confusedly, 'how absurd a word becomes if one says it repeatedly. Out.'

Alleyn laid an official-looking document on the breakfast-table and stared at his mother.

'What can you be talking about?' he said.

'Don't be stupid, darling. I am going to do the London season.'

'Have you taken leave of your senses?'

'I think perhaps I have. I have told George and Grace that I will bring Sarah out this coming season. Here is a letter from George and here is another from Grace. Government House, Suva. They think it charming of me to offer.'

'Good Lord, mama,' said Alleyn, 'you must be demented. Do you know what this means?'

'I believe I do. It means that I must take a flat in London. It means that I must look up all sorts of people who will turn out to be dead or divorced or remarried. It means that I must give little luncheon-parties and cocktail-parties and exchange cutlets with hard-working mothers. It means that I must sit in ballrooms praising other women's grand-daughters and securing young men for my own. I shall be up until four o'clock five nights out of seven and I'm afraid, darling, that my black lace and my silver charmeuse will not be quite equal to the strain. So that in addition to buying clothes for Sarah I shall have to buy some for myself. And I should like to know what you think about that, Roderick?'

'I think it is all utterly preposterous. Why the devil can't George and Grace bring Sarah out themselves?'

'Because they are in Fiji, darling.'

'Well, why can't she stay in until they return?'

'George's appointment is for four years. In four years your niece will be twenty-two. An elderly sort of débutante.'

'*Why* has Sarah got to come out? Why can't she simply emerge?'

'That I cannot tell you, but George and Grace certainly could. I rather see it, I must say, Roderick. A girl has such fun doing her first season. There is nothing like it, ever again. And now we have gone back to chaperones and all the rest of it, it really does seem to have some of the old glamour.'

'You mean débutantes have gone back to being treated like hothouse flowers for three months and taking their chance as hardy perennials for the rest of their lives?'

'If you choose to put it like that. The system is not without merit, my dear.'

'It may be quite admirable, but isn't it going to be a bit too exhausting for you? Where is Sarah, by the way?'

'She is always rather late for breakfast. How wonderfully these children sleep, don't they? But we were talking about the season, weren't we? I think I shall enjoy it, Rory. And really and truly it won't be such hard work. I've heard this morning from Evelyn Carrados. She was Evelyn O'Brien, you know. Evelyn Curtis, of course, in the *first* instance, but that's so long ago nobody bothers about it. Not that she's as old as that, poor girl. She can't be forty yet. Quite a chicken, in fact. Her mother was my greatest friend. We did the season together when we came out. And now here's Evelyn bringing her own girl out and offering to help with Sarah. Could anything be more fortunate?'

'Nothing,' responded Alleyn dryly. 'I remember Evelyn O'Brien.'

'I should hope you do. I did my best to persuade you to fall in love with her.'

'Did I fall in love with her?'

'No. I could never imagine why, as she was quite lovely and very charming. Now I come to think of it, you hadn't much chance as she herself fell madly in love with Paddy O'Brien who returned suddenly from Australia.'

'I remember. A romantic sort of bloke, wasn't he?'

'Yes. They were married after a short engagement. Five months later he was killed in a motor accident. Wasn't it awful?'

'Awful.'

'And then in six months or so along came this girl, Bridget. Evelyn called her Bridget because Paddy was Irish. And then, poor Evelyn, she married Herbert Carrados. Nobody ever knew why.'

'I'm not surprised. He's a frightful bore. He must be a great deal older than Evelyn.'

'A thousand years and so pompous you can't believe he's true. You know him evidently.'

'Vaguely. He's something pretty grand in the City.'

Alleyn lit his mother's cigarette and his own. He walked over to the french window and looked across the lawn.

'Your garden is getting ready to come out, too,' he said. 'I wish I hadn't to go back to the Yard.'

'Now, darling? This minute?'

'Afraid so. It's this case.' He waved some papers in his hand. 'Fox rang up late last night. Something's cropped up.'

'What sort of case is it?'

'Blackmail, but you're not allowed to ask questions.'

'Rory, how exciting. Who's being blackmailed? Somebody frightfully important, I hope?'

'Do you remember Lord Robert Gospell?'

'*Bunchy* Gospell, do you mean? Surely he's not being blackmailed. A more innocent creature – '

'No, mama, he isn't. Nor is he a blackmailer.'

'He's a dear little man,' said Lady Alleyn emphatically. 'The nicest possible little man.'

'Not so little nowadays. He's very plump and wears a cloak and a sombrero like GKC.'

'Really?'

'You must have seen photographs of him in your horrible illustrated papers. They catch him when they can. "Lord Robert

('Bunchy') Gospell tells one of his famous stories." That sort of thing.'

'Yes, but what's he got to do with blackmail?'

'Nothing. He is, as you say, an extremely nice little man.'

'Roderick, don't be infuriating. Has Bunchy Gospell got anything to do with Scotland Yard?'

Alleyn was staring out into the garden.

'You might say,' he said at last, 'that we have a very great respect for him at the Yard. Not only is he charming – he is also, in his own way, a rather remarkable personage.'

Lady Alleyn looked at her son meditatively for some seconds.

'Are you meeting him today?' she asked.

'I think so.'

'Why?'

'Why, darling, to listen to one of his famous stories, I suppose.'

II

It was Miss Harris's first day in her new job. She was secretary to Lady Carrados and had been engaged for the London season. Miss Harris knew quite well what this meant. It was not, in a secretarial sense, by any means her first season. She was a competent young woman, almost frighteningly unimaginative, with a brain that was divided into neat pigeon-holes, and a mind that might be said to label all questions 'answered' or 'unanswered'. If a speculative or unconventional idea came Miss Harris's way, it was promptly dealt with or promptly shut up in a dark pigeon-hole and never taken out again. If Miss Harris had not been able to answer it immediately, it was unanswerable and therefore of no importance. Owing perhaps to her intensive training as a member of the large family of a Buckinghamshire clergyman she never for a moment asked herself why she should go through life organising fun for other people and having comparatively little herself. That would have seemed to Miss Harris an irrelevant and rather stupid speculation. One's job was a collection of neatly filed duties, suitable to one's station in life, and therefore respectable. It had no wider ethical interest of any sort at all. This is not to say Miss Harris was insensitive. On the contrary, she was rather touchy on all sorts of points of etiquette relating to her position in the houses in which she was employed. Where she had her lunch, with whom she had it, and who served it, were matters of great importance to her and she was painfully aware of the subtlest nuances in her employers' attitude towards herself. About her new job she was neatly optimistic. Lady Carrados had impressed her favourably, had treated her, in her own phrase, like a perfect lady. Miss Harris walked briskly along an upstairs passage and tapped twice, not too loud and not too timidly, on a white door.

'Come in,' cried a far-away voice.

Miss Harris obeyed and found herself in a large white bedroom. The carpet, the walls and the chairs were all white. A cedar-wood fire crackled beneath the white Adam mantelpiece, a white bearskin rug nearly tripped Miss Harris up as she crossed the floor to the large white bed where her employer sat propped up with pillows. The bed was strewn about with sheets of notepaper.

'Oh, good morning, Miss Harris,' said Lady Carrados. 'You can't think how glad I am to see you. *Do* you mind waiting a moment while I finish this note? Please sit down.'

Miss Harris sat discreetly on a small chair. Lady Carrados gave her a vague, brilliant smile, and turned again to her writing. Miss Harris with a single inoffensive glance had taken in every detail of her employer's appearance.

Evelyn Carrados was thirty-seven years old, and on her good days looked rather less. She was a dark, tall woman with little colour but a beautiful pallor. Paddy O'Brien had once shown her a copy of the Madonna di San Sisto and had told her that she was looking at herself. This was not quite true. Her face was longer and had more edge and character than Raphael's complacent virgin, but the large dark eyes were like and the sleek hair parted down the centre. Paddy had taken to calling her 'Donna' after that and she still had his letters beginning: 'Darling Donna.' Oddly enough, Bridget, his daughter, who had never seen him, called her mother 'Donna' too. She had come into the room on the day Miss Harris was interviewed and had sat on the arm of her mother's chair. A still girl with a lovely voice. Miss Harris looking straight in front of her remembered this interview now while she waited. '*He* hasn't appeared yet,' thought Miss Harris, meaning Sir Herbert Carrados, whose photograph faced her in a silver frame on his wife's dressing-table.

Lady Carrados signed her name and hunted about the counter-pane for blotting-paper. Miss Harris instantly placed her own pad on the bed.

'Oh,' said her employer with an air of pleased astonishment, 'you've got some! Thank you so much. There, that's settled *her*, hasn't it?'

Miss Harris smiled brightly. Lady Carrados licked the flap of an envelope and stared at her secretary over the top.

'I see you've brought up my mail,' she said.

'Yes, Lady Carrados. I did not know if you would prefer me to open all – '

'No, no. No, please not.'

Miss Harris did not visibly bridle, she was much too competent to do anything of the sort, but she was at once hurt in her feelings. A miserable, a hateful, little needle of mortification jabbed her thin skin. She had overstepped her mark.

'Very well, Lady Carrados,' said Miss Harris politely.

Lady Carrados bent forward.

'I know I'm all wrong,' she said quickly. 'I know I'm not behaving a bit as one should when one is lucky enough to have a secretary but, you see, I'm not used to such luxuries, and I still like to pretend I'm doing everything myself. So I shall have all the fun of opening my letters and all the joy of handing them over to you. Which is very unfair, but you'll have to put up with it, poor Miss Harris.'

She watched her secretary smile and replied with a charming look of understanding.

'And now,' she said, 'we may as well get it done, mayn't we?'

Miss Harris laid the letters in three neat heaps on the writing-pad and soon began to make shorthand notes of the answers she was to write for her employer. Lady Carrados kept up a sort of running commentary.

'Lucy Lorrimer. Who is Lucy Lorrimer, Miss Harris? *I* know, she's that old Lady Lorrimer who talks as if everybody was deaf. What does she want? "Hear you are bringing out your girl and would be so glad – " Well, we'll have to see about that, won't we? If it's a free afternoon we'd be delighted. There you are. Now, this one. Oh, *yes*, Miss Harris, now this is *most* important. It's from Lady Alleyn, who is a *great* friend of mine. Do you know who I mean? One of her sons is a deadly baronet and the other is a detective. Do you know?'

'Is it Chief Inspector Alleyn, Lady Carrados? The famous one?'

That's it. Terribly good-looking and remote. He was in the Foreign Office when the war broke out and then after the war he suddenly became a detective. I can't tell you why. Not that it matters,' continued Lady Carrados, glancing at the attentive face of her secretary, 'because this letter is nothing to do with him. It's about his brother George's girl whom his mother is bringing out and I said I'd help. So you must remember, Miss Harris, that Sarah Alleyn is to be asked to *everything*. And Lady Alleyn to the mothers' lunches and all those games. Have you got that? There's her address. And remind me to write personally. Now away we go again and – '

She stopped so suddenly that Miss Harris glanced up in surprise. Lady Carrados was staring at a letter which she held in her long white fingers. The fingers trembled slightly. Miss Harris with a sort of fascination looked at them and at the square envelope. There was a silence in the white room – a silence broken only by the hurried inconsequent ticking of a little china clock on the mantelpiece. With a sharp click the envelope fell on the heap of letters.

'Excuse me, Lady Carrados,' said Miss Harris, 'but are you feeling unwell?'

'What? No. No, thank you.'

She put the letter aside and picked up another. Soon Miss Harris's pen was travelling busily over her pad. She made notes for the acceptance, refusal and issuing of invitations. She made lists of names with notes beside them and she entered into a long discussion about Lady Carrados's ball.

'I'm getting Dimitri – the Shepherd Market caterer, you know – to do the whole thing,' explained Lady Carrados. 'It seems to be the – ' she paused oddly '– safest way.'

'Well, he *is* the best,' agreed Miss Harris. 'You were speaking of expense, Lady Carrados. Dimitri works out at about twenty-five shillings a head. But that's *everything*. You do know where you are and he is good.'

'Twenty-five? Four hundred, there'll be, I think. How much is that?'

'Five hundred pounds,' said Miss Harris calmly.

'Oh, dear, it is a lot, isn't it? And then there's the band. I do think we must have champagne at the buffet. It saves that endless procession to the supper-room which I always think is such a bore.'

'Champagne at the buffet,' said Miss Harris crisply. 'That will mean thirty shillings a head, I'm afraid.'

'*Oh*, how awful!'

'That makes Dimitri's bill six hundred. But, of course, as I say, Lady Carrados, that will be every penny you pay.'

Lady Carrados stared at her secretary without replying. For some reason Miss Harris felt as if she had made another *faux pas*. There was, she thought, such a very singular expression in her employer's eyes.

'I should think a thousand pounds would cover the whole of the expenses, band and everything,' she added hurriedly.

'Yes, I see,' said Lady Carrados. 'A thousand.'

There was a tap at the door and a voice called: 'Donna!'

'Come in, darling!'

A tall, dark girl carrying a pile of letters came into the room. Bridget was very like her mother but nobody would have thought of comparing her to the Sistine Madonna. She had inherited too much of Paddy O'Brien's brilliance for that. There was a fine-drawn look about her mouth. Her eyes, set wide apart, were deep under strongly marked brows. She had the quality of repose but when she smiled all the corners of her face tipped up and then she looked more like her father than her mother. 'Sensitive,' thought Miss Harris, with a mild flash of illumination. 'I hope she stands up to it all right. Nuisance when they get nerves.' She returned Bridget's punctilious 'Good morning' and watched her kiss her mother.

'Darling Donna,' said Bridget, 'you are so sweet.'

'Hullo, my darling,' said Lady Carrados, 'here we are plotting away for all we're worth. Miss Harris and I have decided on the eighth for your dance. Uncle Arthur writes that we may have his house on that date. That's General Marsdon, Miss Harris. I explained, didn't I, that he is lending us Marsdon House in Belgrave Square? Or did I?'

'Yes, thank you, Lady Carrados. I've got all that.'

'Of course you have.'

'It's a mausoleum,' said Bridget, 'but it'll do. I've got a letter from Sarah Alleyn, Donna. Her grandmother, your Lady Alleyn, you know, is taking a flat for the season. Donna, please, I want Sarah asked for *everything*. Does Miss Harris know?'

'Yes, thank you, Miss Carrados. I beg pardon,' said Miss Harris in some confusion, 'I should have said, Miss O'Brien, shouldn't I?'

'Help, yes! Don't fall into that trap whatever you do,' cried Bridget. 'Sorry, Donna darling, but really!'

'Ssh!' said Lady Carrados mildly. 'Are those your letters?'

'Yes. All the invitations. I've put a black mark against the ones I really do jib at and all the rest will just have to be sorted out. Oh, and I've put a big Y on the ones I want specially not to miss. And – '

The door opened again and the photograph on the dressing-table limped into the room.

Sir Herbert Carrados was just a little too good to be true. He was tall and soldierly and good-looking. He had thin sandy hair, a large guardsman's moustache, heavy eyebrows and rather foolish light eyes. You did not notice they were foolish because his eyebrows gave them a spurious fierceness. He was not, however, a stupid man but only a rather vain and pompous one. It was his pride that he looked like a soldier and not like a successful financier. During the Great War he had held down a staff appointment of bewildering unimportance which had kept him in Tunbridge Wells for the duration and which had not hampered his sound and at times brilliant activities in the City. He limped a little and used a stick. Most people took it as a matter of course that he had been wounded in the leg, and so he had – by a careless gamekeeper. He attended military reunions with the greatest assiduity and was about to stand for Parliament.

Bridget called him Bart, which he rather liked, but he occasionally surprised a look of irony in her eyes and that he did not at all enjoy.

This morning he had *The Times* under his arm and an expression of forbearance on his face. He kissed his wife, greeted Miss Harris with precisely the correct shade of cordiality, and raised his eyebrows at his stepdaughter.

'Good morning, Bridget. I thought you were still in bed.'

'Good morning, Bart,' said Bridget. 'Why?'

'You were not at breakfast. Don't you think perhaps it would be more considerate to the servants if you breakfasted before you started making plans?'

'I expect it would,' agreed Bridget and went as far as the door.

'What are your plans for today, darling?' continued Sir Herbert, smiling at his wife.

'Oh – everything. Bridget's dance. Miss Harris and I are – are going into expense, Herbert.'

'Ah, yes?' murmured Sir Herbert. 'I'm sure Miss Harris is a perfect dragon with figures. What's the total, Miss Harris?'

'For the ball, Sir Herbert?' Miss Harris glanced at Lady Carrados who nodded a little nervously. 'It's about a thousand pounds.'

'Good God!' exclaimed Sir Herbert and let his eyeglass fall.

'You see, darling,' began his wife in a hurry, 'it just *won't* come down to less. Even with Arthur's house. And if we have champagne at the buffet – '

'I cannot see the smallest necessity for champagne at the buffet, Evelyn. If these young cubs can't get enough to drink in the supper-room all I can say is, they drink a great deal too much. I must say,' continued Sir Herbert with an air of discovery, 'that I do not under-stand the mentality of modern youths. Gambling too much, drink-ing too much, no object in life – look at that young Potter.'

'If you mean Donald Potter,' said Bridget dangerously, ' I must – '

'Bridgie!' said her mother.

'You're wandering from the point, Bridget,' said her step-father.

'Me!'

'My point is,' said Sir Herbert with a martyred glance at his wife, 'that the young people expect a great deal too much nowadays. Champagne at every table – '

'It's not that – ' began Bridget from the door.

'It's only that it saves – ' interrupted her mother.

'However,' continued Sir Herbert with an air of patient courtesy, 'if you feel that you can afford to spend a thousand pounds on an evening, my dear – '

'But it isn't all Donna's money,' objected Bridget. 'It's half mine. Daddy left – '

'Bridget, darling,' said Lady Carrados, 'breakfast.'

'Sorry, Donna,' said Bridget. 'All right.' She went out.

Miss Harris wondered if she too had better go, but nobody seemed to remember she was in the room and she did not quite like to remind them of her presence by making a move. Lady Carrados with an odd mixture of nervousness and determination was talking rapidly.

'I know Paddy would have meant some of Bridgie's money to be used for her coming out, Herbert. It isn't as if – '

'My dear,' said Sir Herbert with an ineffable air of tactful reproach, and a glance at Miss Harris. 'Of course. It's entirely for you and Bridget to decide. Naturally. I wouldn't dream of interfering. I'm just rather an old fool and like to give any help I can. Don't pay any attention.'

Lady Carrados was saved the necessity of making any reply to this embarrassing speech by the entrance of the maid.

'Lord Robert Gospell has called, m'lady, and wonders if – '

''Morning, Evelyn,' said an extraordinarily high-pitched voice outside the door. 'I've come up. Do let me in.'

'Bunchy!' cried Lady Carrados in delight. 'How lovely! Come in!'

And Lord Robert Gospell, panting a little under the burden of an enormous bunch of daffodils, toddled into the room.

III

On the same day that Lord Robert Gospell called on Lady Carrados, Lady Carrados herself called on Sir Daniel Davidson in his consulting-rooms in Harley Street. She talked to him for a long time and at the end of half an hour sat staring rather desperately across the desk into his large black eyes.

'I'm frightfully anxious, naturally, that Bridgie shouldn't get the idea that there's anything the matter with me,' she said.

'There is nothing *specifically* wrong with you,' said Davidson, spreading out his long hands. 'Nothing, I mean, in the sense of your heart being overworked or your lungs at all unsound or any nonsense of that sort. I don't think you are anaemic. The blood test will clear all that up. But' – and he leant forward and pointed a finger at her – ' *but* you are very tired. You're altogether too tired. If I was an honest physician I'd tell you to go into a nursing-home and lead the life of a placid cow for three weeks.'

'I can't do that.'

'Can't your daughter come out next year? What about the little season?'

'Oh, no, it's impossible. Really. My uncle has lent us his house for the dance. She's planned everything. It would be almost as much trouble to put things off as it is to go on with them. I'll be all right, only I do rather feel as if I've got a jellyfish instead of a brain. A wobbly jellyfish. I get these curious giddy attacks. And I simply *can't* stop bothering about things.'

'I know. What about this ball? I suppose you're hard at it over that?'

'I'm handing it all over to my secretary and Dimitri. I hope you're coming. You'll get a card.'

'I shall be delighted, but I wish you'd give it up.'

'Truly I can't.'

'Have you got any particular worry?'

There was a long pause.

'Yes,' said Evelyn Carrados, 'but I can't tell you about that.'

'Ah, well,' said Sir Daniel, shrugging his shoulders. '*Les maladies suspendent nos vertus et nos vices.*'

She rose and he at once leapt to his feet as if she was royalty.

'You will get that prescription made up at once,' he said, glaring down at her. 'And, if you please, I should like to see you again. I suppose I had better not call?'

'No, please. I'll come here.'

'*C'est entendu,*'

Lady Carrados left him, wishing vaguely that he was a little less florid and longing devoutly for her bed.

IV

Agatha Troy hunched up her shoulders, pulled her smart new cap over one eye and walked into her one-man show at the Wiltshire Galleries in Bond Street. It always embarrassed her intensely to put in these duty appearances at her own exhibitions. People felt they had to say something to her about her pictures and they never knew what to say and she never knew how to reply. She became gruff with shyness and her incoherence was mistaken for intellectual snobbishness. Like most painters she was singularly inarticulate on the subject of her work. The careful phrases of literary appreciation showered upon her by highbrow critics threw Troy into an agony of embarrassment. She minded less the bland commonplaces of the philistines though for these also she had great difficulty in finding suitable replies.

She slipped in at the door, winked at the young man who sat at the reception desk and shied away as a large American woman bore down upon him with a white-gloved finger, firmly planted on a price in her catalogue.

Troy hurriedly looked away and in a corner of the crowded room, sitting on a chair that was not big enough for him, she saw a smallish round gentleman whose head was aslant, his eyes closed and his mouth peacefully open. Troy made for him.

'Bunchy!' she said.

Lord Robert Gospell opened his eyes very wide and moved his lips like a rabbit.

'Hullo!' he said. 'What a scrimmage, ain't it? Pretty good.'

'You were asleep.'

'May have been having a nap.'

'That's a pretty compliment,' said Troy without rancour.

'I had a good prowl first. Just thought I'd pop in,' explained Lord Robert. 'Enjoyed myself.' He balanced his glasses across his nose, flung his head back and with an air of placid approval contemplated a large landscape. Without any of her usual embarrassment Troy looked with him.

'Pretty good,' repeated Bunchy. 'Ain't it?'

He had an odd trick of using Victorian colloquialisms; legacies, he would explain, from his distinguished father. 'Lor'!' was his favourite ejaculation. He kept up little Victorian politenesses, always leaving cards after a ball and often sending flowers to the hostesses who dined him. His clothes were famous – a rather high, close-buttoned jacket and narrowish trousers by day, a soft wide hat and a cloak in the evening. Troy turned from her picture to her companion. He twinkled through his glasses and pointed a fat finger at the landscape.

'Nice and clean,' he said. 'I like 'em clean. Come and have tea.'

'I've only just arrived,' said Troy, 'but I'd love to.'

'I've got the Potters,' said Bunchy. 'My sister and her boy. Wait a bit. I'll fetch 'em.'

'Mildred and Donald?' asked Troy.

'Mildred and Donald. They live with me, you know, since poor
Potter died. Donald's just been sent down for some gambling scrape
or other. Nice young scamp. No harm in him. Only don't mention
Oxford.'

'I'll remember.'

'He'll probably save you the trouble by talking about it himself. I
like having young people about. Gay. Keeps one up to scratch. Can
you see 'em anywhere? Mildred's wearing a puce toque.'

'Not a *toque*, Bunchy,' said Troy. 'There she is. It's a very smart
purple beret. She's seen us. She's coming.'

Lord Robert's widowed sister came billowing through the crowd
followed by her extremely good-looking son. She greeted Troy
breathlessly but affectionately. Donald bowed, grinned and said: 'We
have been enjoying ourselves. Frightfully good!'

'Fat lot you know about it,' said Troy good-humouredly. 'Mildred,
Bunchy suggests tea.'

'I must say I should be glad of it,' said Lady Mildred Potter.
'Looking at pictures is the most exhausting pastime, even when they
are your pictures, dear.'

'There's a restaurant down below,' squeaked Lord Robert. 'Follow
me.'

They worked their way through the crowd and downstairs.
Donald who was separated from them by several strangers, shouted:
'I say, Troy, did you hear I was sent down?' This had the effect of
drawing everyone's attention first to himself and then to Troy.

'Yes, I did,' said Troy severely.

'Wasn't it awful?' continued Donald, coming alongside and
speaking more quietly. 'Uncle Bunch is *furious* and says I'm no
longer The Heir. It's not true, of course. He's leaving me a princely
fortune, aren't you, Uncle Bunch, my dear?'

'Here we are,' said Lord Robert thankfully as they reached the
door of the restaurant. 'Will you all sit down. I'm afraid I must be
rather quick.' He pulled out his watch and blinked at it. 'I've an
appointment in twenty minutes.'

'Where?' said Troy. 'I'll drive you.'

'Matter of fact,' said Lord Robert, 'it's at Scotland Yard. Meeting
an old friend of mine called Alleyn.'

CHAPTER 2

Bunchy

'Lord Robert Gospell to see you, Mr Alleyn,' said a voice in Alleyn's desk telephone.

'Bring him up, please,' said Alleyn.

He pulled a file out of the top drawer and laid it open before him. Then he rang through to his particular Assistant Commissioner.

'Lord Robert has just arrived, sir. You asked me to let you know.'

'All right, Rory, I'll leave him to you, on second thoughts. Fox is here with the report on the Temple case and it's urgent. Make my apologies. Say I'll call on him any time that suits him if he thinks it would be any good. You know him, don't you? Personally, I mean?'

'Yes. He's asked for me.'

'That's all right, then. Bring him along here if it's advisable, of course, but I'm snowed under.'

'Very good, sir,' said Alleyn. A police sergeant tapped, and opened the door. 'Lord Robert Gospell, sir.'

Lord Robert entered twinkling and a little breathless.

'Hullo, Roderick. How-de-do,' he said.

'Hullo, Bunchy. This is extraordinarily good of you.'

'Not a bit. Like to keep in touch. Enjoy having a finger in the pie, you know. Always did.' He sat down and clasped his little hands over his stomach. 'How's your mother?' he asked.

'She's very well. She knows we are meeting today and sent you her love.'

'Thank yer. Delightful woman, your mother. Afraid I'm a bit late. Took tea with another delightful woman.'

'Did you indeed?'

'Yes. Agatha Troy. Know her?'

There was a short silence.

'Yes,' said Alleyn.

'Lor', yes. Of course you do. Didn't you look after that case where her model was knifed?'

'Yes, I did.'

'Charming,' said Lord Robert. 'Ain't she?'

'Yes,' said Alleyn, 'she is.'

'I like her awfully. M'sister Mildred and her boy Donald and I had been to Troy's show. You know m'sister Mildred, don't you?'

'Yes,' said Alleyn, smiling.

'Yes. No end of a donkey in many ways but a good woman. The boy's a young dog.'

'Bunchy,' said Alleyn, 'you're better than Victorian, you're Regency.'

'Think so? Tell you what, Roderick, I've got to come out of my shell and do the season a bit.'

'You always do the season, don't you?'

'I get about a bit. Enjoy myself. Young Donald's paying his addresses to a gel called Bridget O'Brien. Know her?'

'That's funny,' said Alleyn. 'My mama is bringing out brother George's girl and it appears she's the bosom friend of Bridget O'Brien. She's Evelyn and Paddy O'Brien's daughter, you know.'

'I know. Called on Evelyn this morning. She married that ass Carrados. Pompous. Clever in the City, I'm told. I had a look at the gel. Nice gel, but there's something wrong somewhere in that family. Carrados, I suppose. D'you like the gel?'

'I don't know her. My niece Sarah likes her.'

'Look here,' said Lord Robert, spreading out his hands and staring at them in mild surprise. 'Look here. Dine with us for Lady C's dance. Will you? Do.'

'My dear Bunchy, I'm not asked.'

'Isn't your niece goin'?'

'Yes, I expect she is.'

'Get you a card. Easy as winking. Do come. Troy's dining too. Donald and I persuaded her.'

'Troy,' said Alleyn. 'Troy.'

Lord Robert looked sharply at him for about two seconds.

'Never mind if you'd rather not,' he said.

'I can't tell you how much I should like to come,' said Alleyn slowly, 'but you see I'm afraid I might remind Miss Troy of – of that very unpleasant case.'

'Oh. 'm. Well, leave it open. Think it over. You're sure to get a card. Now – what about business?'

He made a funny eager grimace, pursed his lips, and with a deft movement of his hand slung his glasses over his nose. 'What's up?' he asked.

'We rather think blackmail,' said Alleyn.

'Lor',' said Lord Robert. 'Where?'

'Here, there and everywhere in high society.'

'How d'yer know?'

'Well.' Alleyn laid a thin hand on the file. 'This is rather more than usually confidential, Bunchy.'

'Yes, yes, yes. All right. I'll be as silent,' said Lord Robert, 'as the grave. Mum's the word. Let's have the names and all the rest of it. None of your Mr and Mrs Xes.'

'All right. You know Mrs Halcut-Hackett? Old General Halcut-Hackett's wife?'

'Yes. American actress. Twenty years younger than H-H. Gorgeous creature.'

'That's the one. She came to us last week with a story of blackmail. Here it is in this file. I'll tell you briefly what she said, but I'm afraid you'll have to put up with one Madame X.'

'Phoo!' said Lord Robert.

'She told us that a very great woman-friend of hers had confided in her that she was being blackmailed. Mrs H-H wouldn't give this lady's name so there's your Mrs X.'

'Um,' said Lord Robert doubtfully. 'Otherwise Mrs 'Arris?'

'Possibly,' said Alleyn, 'but that's the story and I give it to you as Mrs H-H gave it to me. Mrs X, who has an important and imperious husband, received a blackmailing letter on the first of this month. It was written on Woolworth paper. The writer said he or she had possession of an extremely compromising letter written to Mrs X by a man-friend. The writer was willing to sell it for £500. Mrs X's account is gone into very thoroughly every month by her husband

and she was afraid to stump up. In her distress (so the story went) she flew to Mrs Halcut-Hackett who couldn't provide £500 but persuaded Mrs X to let her come to us with the whole affair. She gave us the letter. Here it is.'

Alleyn laid the file on Lord Robert's plump little knees. Lord Robert touched his glasses and stared for quite thirty seconds at the first page in the file. He opened his mouth, shut it again, darted a glance at Alleyn, touched his glasses again and finally read under his breath:

' "If you would care to buy a letter dated April 20th, written from the Bucks Club addressed to Darling Dodo and signed M., you may do so by leaving £500 in notes of small denomination in your purse behind the picture of the Dutch funeral above the fireplace in the ballroom of Comstock House on the evening of next Monday fortnight." '

Lord Robert looked up.

'That was the night the Comstocks ran their charity bridge-party,' he said. 'Big show. Thirty tables. Let's see, it was last Monday.'

'It was. On the strength of this letter we saw the Comstocks, told them a fairy-story and asked them to let us send in a man dressed as a waiter. We asked Mrs H-H to get her distressed friend to put the purse full of notes, which we dusted with the usual powder, behind the Dutch funeral. Mrs H-H said she would save her friend much agony and humiliation by doing this office for her.' Alleyn raised one eyebrow and bestowed a very slow wink upon Lord Robert.

'Poor thing,' said Lord Robert.

'Did she suppose she'd taken you in?'

'I don't know. I kept up a polite pretence. Our man, who I may say is a good man, attended the party, saw Mrs H-H tuck away the bag, and waited to see what would happen.'

'What did happen?'

'Nothing. Our man was there all night and saw a maid discover the bag next morning, put it unopened on the mantelpiece and call Mrs Comstock's attention to it. Mrs Comstock, in the presence of our man and the maid, opened it, saw the paper, was surprised, could find nothing to indicate the owner and told the maid to put it aside in case it was asked for.'

'And what,' asked Lord Robert, suddenly hugging himself with his short arms, 'what do you deduce from that, my dear Roderick?'

'They rumbled our man.'

'Is it one of the Comstocks' servants?'

'The whole show was done by Dimitri, the Shepherd Market caterer. You know who I mean, of course. He does most of the big parties nowadays. Supplies service, food and everything.'

'One of Dimitri's men?'

'We've made extremely careful enquiries. They've all got splendid references. I've actually spoken to Dimitri himself. I told him that there had been one or two thefts lately at large functions and we were bound to make enquiries. He got in no end of a tig, of course, and showed me a mass of references for all his people. We followed them up. They're genuine enough. He employs the best that can be found in the world. There's a strict rule that all objects left lying about at these shows should be brought at once to him. He then, himself, looks to see if he can find the owner and in the case of a lost purse or bag returns it in person or else, having seen the contents, sends it by one of his men. He explained that he did this to protect both his men and himself. He always asks the owner to examine a bag the moment it is handed to her.'

'Still – '

'I know it's by no means watertight but we've taken a lot of trouble over the Dimitri staff and in my opinion there's not a likely man among 'em.'

'Dimitri himself?'

Alleyn grimaced.

'Wonders will never cease, my dear Bunchy, but – '

'Yes, yes, of course, I quite see. He's a bit too damn grand for those capers, you'd imagine. Anything else?'

'We've been troubled by rumours of blackmail from other sources. You can see the file if you like. Briefly they all point to someone who works in the way suggested by Mrs Halcut-Hackett alias Mrs X. There's one anonymous letter sent to the Yard, presumably by a victim. It simply says that a blackmailer is at work among society people. Nothing more. We haven't been able to trace it. Then young

Kremorn shot himself the other day and we found out that he had been drawing very large sums in bank-notes for no known reason. His servant said he'd suspected blackmail for some time.' Alleyn rubbed his nose. 'It's the devil. And of all the filthy crimes this to my mind is the filthiest. I don't mind telling you we're in a great tig over it.'

'Bad!' said Lord Robert, opening his eyes very wide. 'Disgusting! Where do I come in?'

'Everywhere, if you will. You've helped us before and we'll be damn glad if you help us again. You go everywhere, Bunchy,' said Alleyn with a smile at his little friend. 'You toddle in and out of all the smart houses. Lovely ladies confide in you. Heavy colonels weep on your bosom. See what you can see.'

'Can't break confidences, you know, can I! Supposing I get 'em.'

'Of course you can't, but you can do a little quiet investigation on your own account and tell us as much as – ' Alleyn paused and added quickly: 'As much as a man of integrity may. Will you?'

'Love to!' said Lord Robert with a great deal of energy. 'Matter of fact, but it'd be a rum go if it was – coincidence.'

'What?'

'Well. Well, see here, Roderick, this is between ourselves. Thing is, as I told you, I called on Evelyn Carrados this morning. Passing that way and saw a feller selling daffodils so thought I'd take her some. Damn pretty woman, Evelyn, but – ' He screwed up his face. 'Saddish. Never got over Paddy's death, if you ask me. Devoted to the gel and the gel to her, but if you ask me Carrados comes the high horse a bit. Great pompous exacting touchy sort of feller, ain't he? Evelyn was in bed. Snowed under with letters. Secretary. Carrados on the hearth-rug looking injured. Bridget came in later on. Well now. Carrados said he'd be off to the City. Came over to the bed and gave her the sort of kiss a woman doesn't thank you for. Hand each side of her. Right hand under the pillow.'

Lord Robert's voice suddenly skipped an octave and became high-pitched. He leant forward with his hands on his knees, looking very earnestly at Alleyn. He moved his lips rather in the manner of a rabbit and then said explosively:

'It was singular. It was damned odd. He must have touched a letter under her pillow because when he straightened up it was in his right hand – a common-looking envelope addressed in a sort of script – letters like they print 'em only done by hand.'

Alleyn glanced quickly at the file but said nothing.

'Carrados said: "Oh, one of your letters, m'dear," squinting at it through his glass and then putting it down on the counterpane. "Beg pardon," or something. Thing is, she turned as white as the sheet. I promise you as white as anything, on my honour. And she said: "It's from one of my lame ducks. I must deal with it," and slid it under the others. Off he went, and that was that. I talked about their ball and so on and paid my respects and pretended I'd noticed nothing, of course, and, in short, I came away.'

Still Alleyn did not speak. Suddenly Lord Robert jabbed at the letter in the file with his fat finger.

'Thing is,' he said most emphatically. 'Same sort of script.'

'Exactly the same? I mean, would you swear to the same writer?'

'No, no! 'Course not. Only got a glimpse of the other, but I rather fancy myself on handwriting, you know.'

'We rather fancy you, too.'

'It was very similar,' said Lord Robert. 'It was exceedingly similar. On my honour.'

'Good Lord,' said Alleyn mildly. 'That's what the Americans call a break. Coincidence stretches out a long arm. So does the law. "Shake," says Coincidence. Not such a very long arm, after all, if this pretty fellow is working among one class only and it looks as if he is.' He shoved a box of cigarettes in Lord Robert's direction. 'We had an expert at that letter – the Mrs H-H one you've got there. Woolworth paper. She didn't show us the envelope, of course. Woolworth ink and the sort of nib they use for script writing. It's square with a feeder. You notice the letters are all neatly fitted between the ruled lines. That and the script nib and the fact that the letters are careful copies of ordinary print completely knocks out any sort of individuality. There were no finger-prints and Mrs Halcut-Hackett hadn't noticed the postmark. Come in!'

A police constable marched in with a packet of letters, laid them on the desk and marched out again.

'Half a moment while I have a look at my mail, Bunchy; there may just be – yes, by gum, there is!'

He opened an envelope, glanced at a short note, unfolded an enclosure, raised his eyebrows and handed it to Lord Robert.

'Wheeoo!' whistled Lord Robert.

It was a sheet of common ruled paper. Three or four rows of script were fitted neatly between the lines. Lord Robert read aloud:

' "Unforeseen circumstances prevented collection on Monday night. Please leave bag with same sum down between seat and left-hand arm of blue sofa in concert-room, 57 Constance Street, next Thursday afternoon." '

'Mrs Halcut-Hackett,' said Alleyn, holding out the note, 'explains that her unfortunate friend received this letter by yesterday evening's post. What's happening on Thursday at 57 Constance Street? Do you know?'

'Those new concert-rooms. Very smart. It's another charity show. Tickets on sale everywhere. Three guineas each. Chamber music. Bach. Sirmione Quartette. I'm going.'

'Bunchy,' said Alleyn, 'let nothing wean you from the blue sofa. Talk to Mrs Halcut-Hackett. Share the blue sofa with her and when the austere delights of Bach knock at your heart pay no attention but with the very comment of your soul – '

'Yes, yes, yes. Don't quote now, Roderick, or somebody may think you're a detective.'

'Blast you!' said Alleyn.

Lord Robert gave a little crowing laugh and rose from his chair.

'I'm off,' he said. Alleyn walked with him into the corridor. They shook hands. Alleyn stood looking after him as he walked away with small steps, a quaint out-of-date figure, black against a window at the end of the long passage. The figure grew smaller and smaller, paused for a second at the end of the passage, turned the corner and was gone.

CHAPTER 3

Sequence to a Cocktail-party

A few days after his visit to the Yard, Lord Robert Gospell attended
a cocktail-party given by Mrs Halcut-Hackett for her plain protégée.
Who this plain protégée was, nobody seemed to know, but it was
generally supposed that Mrs Halcut-Hackett's object in bringing her
out was not entirely philanthropic. At the moment nobody ever
remembered the girl's name but merely recognized her as a kind of
coda to Mrs Halcut-Hackett's social activities.

This was one of the first large cocktail-parties of the season and
there were as many as two hundred and fifty guests there. Lord
Robert adored parties of all kinds and was, as Alleyn had pointed
out, asked everywhere. He knew intimately that section of people to
whom the London season is a sort of colossal hurdle to be taken in
an exhilarating leap or floundered over as well as may be. He was
in tremendous demand as a chaperone's partner, could be depended
on to help with those unfortunate children of seventeen who, in
spite of all the efforts of finishing schools, dressmakers, hairdressers,
face-specialists and their unflagging mothers, were apt to be seen
standing alone nervously smiling on the outskirts of groups. With
these unhappy débutantes Lord Robert took infinite trouble. He
would tell them harmless little stories and when they laughed would
respond as if they themselves had said something amusing. His sharp
little eyes would search about for younger men than himself and he
would draw them into a group round himself and the girl. Because
of his reputation as a gentle wit, the wariest and most conceited
young men were always glad to be seen talking to Lord Robert, and

soon the débutante would find herself the only girl in a group of men who seemed to be enjoying themselves. Her nervous smile would vanish and a delicious feeling of confidence would inspire her. And when Lord Robert saw her eyes grow bright and her hands relax, he would slip away and join the cluster of chaperones where he told stories a little less harmless and equally diverting.

But in the plain protégée of General and Mrs Halcut-Hackett he met his Waterloo. She was not so very plain but only rather disastrously uneventful. Every inch of this unhappy child had been prepared for the cocktail-party with passionate care and at great expense by her chaperone – one of those important American women with lovely faces and cast-iron figures. Lord Robert was greeted by Mrs Halcut-Hackett, who looked a little older than usual, and by her husband the General, a notable fire-eater who bawled 'What!' two or three times and burst into loud surprising laughter which was his method of circulating massed gaiety. Lord Robert twinkled at him and passed on into the thick of the party. A servant whom he recognized as the Halcut-Hacketts' butler gave him a drink. 'Then they're not having Dimitri or anybody like that,' thought Lord Robert. He looked about him. On the right-hand side of the enormous room were collected the débutantes, and the young men who, in the last analysis, could make the antics of the best dance-bands in London, all the efforts of all the Dimitris, Miss Harrises, and Mrs Halcut-Hacketts to the tune of a thousand pounds, look like a single impotent gesture. Among them were the young men who were spoken of, in varying degrees of irony, as 'The Debs' Delight.' Lord Robert half suspected his nephew Donald of being a Debs' Delight. There he was in the middle of it all with Bridget O'Brien, making himself agreeable. Very popular, evidently. 'He'll have to settle down,' thought Lord Robert. 'He's altogether too irresponsible and he's beginning to look dissipated. Don't like it.'

Then he saw the plain protégée of Mrs Halcut-Hackett. She had just met a trio of incoming débutantes and had taken them to their right side of the room. He saw how they all spoke politely and pleasantly to her but without any air of intimacy. He saw her linger a moment while they were drawn into the whirlpool of high-pitched conversation. Then she turned away and stood looking towards the door where her chaperone dealt faithfully with the arrivals. She seemed utterly lost. Lord Robert crossed the room and greeted her with his old-fashioned bow.

'How-de-do. This *is* a good party,' he said, with a beaming smile.

'Oh! Oh – I'm so glad.'

'I'm an old hand, y'know,' continued Lord Robert, 'and I always judge a cocktail-party by the time that elapses between one's paying one's respects and getting a drink. Now this evening I was given this excellent drink within two minutes of shaking hands with the General. Being a thirsty, greedy old customer, I said to myself: "Good party." '

'I'm so glad,' repeated the child.

She was staring, he noticed, at her chaperone, and he saw that Mrs Halcut-Hackett was talking to a tall smooth man with a heavy face, lack-lustre eyes and a proprietary manner. Lord Robert looked fixedly at this individual.

'Do tell me,' he said, 'who is that man with our hostess?'

The girl started violently and without taking her gaze off Mrs Halcut-Hackett, said woodenly: 'It's Captain Withers.'

'Ah,' thought Lord Robert, 'I fancied it was.' Aloud he said: 'Withers? Then it's not the same feller. I rather thought I knew him.'

'Oh,' said the protégée. She had turned her head slightly and he saw that she now looked at the General. 'Like a frightened rabbit,' thought Lord Robert. 'For all the world like a frightened rabbit.' The General had borne down upon his wife and Captain Withers. Lord Robert now witnessed a curious little scene. General Halcut-Hackett glared for three seconds at Captain Withers who smiled, bowed, and moved away. The General then spoke to his wife and immediately, for a fraction of a second, the terror – Lord Robert decided that terror was not too strong a word – that shone in the protégée's eyes was reflected in the chaperone's. Only for a second, and then with her husband she turned to greet a new arrival who Lord Robert saw with pleasure was Lady Alleyn. She was followed by a thin girl with copper-coloured hair and slanting eyebrows that at once reminded him of his friend Roderick. 'Must be the niece,' he decided. The girl at his side suddenly murmured an excuse and hurried away to greet Sarah Alleyn. Lord Robert finished his drink and was given another. In a few minutes he was surrounded by acquaintances and was embarked upon one of his new stories. He made his point very neatly, drifted away on the wave of laughter that greeted it, and found Lady Alleyn.

'My dear Bunchy,' she said, 'you are the very person I hoped to see. Come and gossip with me. I feel like a phoenix.'

'You look like a princess,' he said. 'Why do we meet so seldom? Where shall we go?'

'If there is a corner reserved for grandmothers I ought to be in it. Good heavens, how everybody screams. How old are you, Bunchy?'

'Fifty-five, m'dear.'

'I'm sixty-five. Do you find people very noisy nowadays or are you still too much of a chicken?'

'I enjoy parties, awfully, but I agree that there ain't much repose in modern intercourse.'

'That's it,' said Lady Alleyn, settling herself in a chair. 'No repose. All the same I like the moderns, especially the fledgelings. As Roderick says, they finish their thoughts. *We* only did that in the privacy of our bedrooms and very often asked forgiveness of our Creator for doing it. What do you think of Sarah?'

'She looks a darling,' said Lord Robert emphatically.

'She's a pleasant creature. Amazingly casual but she's got character and, I think, looks,' said her grandmother. 'Who are those young things she's talking to?'

'Bridget O'Brien and my young scapegrace of a nephew.'

'So that's Evelyn Carrados's girl. She's like Paddy, isn't she?'

'She's very like both of 'em. Have you seen Evelyn lately?'

'We dined there last night for the play. What's the matter with Evelyn?'

'Eh?' exclaimed Lord Robert. 'You've spotted it, have you? You're a wise woman, m'dear.'

'She's all over the place. Does Carrados bully her?'

'Bully ain't quite the word. He's devilish grand and patient, though. But – '

'But there's something more. What was the reason for your meeting with Roderick the other day?'

'Hi!' expostulated Lord Robert in a hurry. 'What are you up to?'

'I shouldn't let you tell me if you tried. I trust,' said Lady Alleyn untruthfully but with great dignity, 'that I am not a curious woman.'

'That's pretty rich.'

'I don't know what you mean,' said Lady Alleyn grandly. 'But I tell you what, Bunchy. I've got neurotic women on the brain. Nervous women. Women that are on their guard. It's a most extraordinary thing,' she continued, rubbing her nose with a gesture that reminded Lord Robert of her son, 'but there's precisely the same look in our hostess's mascaraed eyes as Evelyn Carrados had in her naturally beautiful ones. Or has this extraordinary drink gone to my head?'

'The drink,' said Lord Robert firmly, 'has gone to your head.'

'Dear Bunchy,' murmured Lady Alleyn. Their eyes met and they exchanged smiles. The cocktail-party surged politely about them. The noise, the smoke, the festive smell of flowers and alcohol, seemed to increase every moment. Wandering parents eddied round Lady Alleyn's chair. Lord Robert remained beside her listening with pleasure to her cool light voice and looking out of the corner of his eye at Mrs Halcut-Hackett. Apparently all the guests had arrived. She was moving into the room. This was his chance. He turned round and suddenly found himself face to face with Captain Withers. For a moment they stood and looked at each other. Withers was a tall man and Lord Robert was obliged to tilt his head back a little. Withers was a fine arrogant figure, Lord Robert a plump and comical one. But oddly enough it was Lord Robert who seemed the more dominant and more dignified of these two men and before his mild glare the other suddenly looked furtive. His coarse, handsome face became quite white. Some seconds elapsed before he spoke.

'Oh – ah – how do you do?' said Captain Withers very heartily.

'Good evening,' said Lord Robert and turned back to Lady Alleyn. Captain Withers walked quickly away.

'Why, Bunchy,' said Lady Alleyn softly, 'I've never seen you snub anybody before.'

'D'you know who that was?'

'No.'

'Feller called Maurice Withers. He's a throw-back to my Foreign Office days.'

'He's frightened of you.'

'I hope so,' said Lord Robert. 'I'll trot along and pay my respects to my hostess. It's been charming seeing you. Will you dine with me one evening? Bring Roderick. Can you give me an evening? Now?'

'I'm so busy with Sarah. May we ring you up? If it can be managed – '

'It must be. *Au 'voir*, m'dear.'

'Good-bye, Bunchy.'

He made his little bow and picked his way through the crowd to Mrs Halcut-Hackett.

'I'm on my way out,' he said, 'but I hoped to get a word with you. Perfectly splendid party.'

She turned all the headlights of her social manner full on him. It was, he decided compassionately, a bogus manner. An imitation, but what a good imitation. She called him 'dear Lord Robert' like a grande dame in a slightly dated comedy. Her American voice, which he remembered thinking charming in her theatrical days, was now much disciplined and none the better for it. She asked him if he was doing the season very thoroughly and he replied with his usual twinkle that he got about a bit.

'Are you going to the show at the Constance Street Rooms on Thursday afternoon?' he asked. 'I'm looking forward to that awfully.'

Her eyes went blank but she scarcely paused before answering yes, she believed she was.

'It's the Sirmione Quartette,' said Lord Robert. 'Awfully good, ain't they? Real top-notchers.'

Mrs Halcut-Hackett said she adored music, especially classical music.

'Well,' said Lord Robert, 'I'll give myself the pleasure of looking out for you there if it wouldn't bore you. Not so many people nowadays enjoy Bach.'

Mrs Halcut-Hackett said she thought Bach was marvellous.

'Do tell me,' said Lord Robert with his engaging air of enjoying a gossip. 'I've just run into a feller whose face looked as familiar as anything, but I can't place him. Feller over there talking to the girl in red.'

He saw patches of rouge on her cheeks suddenly start up in hard isolation and he thought: 'That's shaken her, poor thing.'

She said: 'Do you mean Captain Maurice Withers?'

'Maybe. The name don't strike a chord, though. I've got a shocking memory. Better be getting along. May I look out for you on Thursday? Thank you so much. Good-bye.'

'Good-bye, dear Lord Robert,' said Mrs Halcut-Hackett.

He edged his way out and was waiting patiently for his hat and umbrella when someone at his elbow said:

'Hullo, Uncle Bunch, are you going home?'

Lord Robert turned slowly and saw his nephew.

'What? Oh, it's you, Donald! Yes, I am! Taking a cab. Want a lift?'

'Yes, please,' said Donald.

Lord Robert looked over his glasses at his nephew and remarked that he seemed rather agitated. He thought: 'What the deuce is the matter with everybody?' but he only said: 'Come along, then,' and together they went out into the street. Lord Robert held up his umbrella and a taxi drew in to the kerb.

''Evening, m'lord,' said the driver.

'Oh, it's you, is it?' said Lord Robert. ''Evening. We're going home.'

'Two hundred Cheyne Walk. Very good, m'lord,' wheezed the driver. He was a goggle-eyed, grey-haired, mottle-faced taximan with an air of good-humoured truculence about him. He slammed the door on them, jerked down the lever of his meter, and started up his engine.

'Everybody knows you, Uncle Bunch,' said Donald in a voice that was not quite natural. 'Even the casual taxi-driver.'

'This feller cruises about in our part of the world,' said Lord Robert. He twisted himself round in his seat and again looked at his nephew over the top of his glasses. 'What's up?' he asked.

'I – well – nothing. I mean, why do you think anything's up?'

'Now then,' said Lord Robert. 'No jiggery-pokery. What's up?'

'Well, as a matter of fact,' answered Donald, kicking the turned-up seat in front of him, 'I did rather want a word with you. I – I'm in a bit of a tight corner, Uncle Bunch.'

'Money?' asked his uncle.

'How did you guess?'

'Don't be an ass, my boy. What is it?'

'I – well, I was wondering if you would mind – I mean, I know I've been a bit extravagant. I'm damn sorry it's happened. I suppose I've been a fool but I'm simply draped in sackcloth and steeped in ashes. Never again!'

'Come, come, come,' said Lord Robert crisply. 'What is it? Gambling?'

'Well – yes. With a slight hint of riotous living. Gambling mostly.'

'Racing? Cards?'

'A bit, but actually I dropped the worst packet at roulette.'

'Good Gad!' exclaimed Lord Robert with surprising violence. 'Where the devil do you play roulette?'

'Well, actually it was at a house out at Leatherhead. It belongs to a man who was at that party. Some people I know took me there. It turned out to be a rather enterprising sort of gamble with a roulette-table and six fellows doing croupier. All in order, you know. I mean it's not run for anything but fun naturally, and Captain Withers simply takes on the bank – '

'*Who?*'

'The person's name is Withers.'

'When was this party?'

'Oh, a week or so ago. They have them fairly regularly. I paid all right, but – but it just about cleaned me up. I had the most amazing bad luck, actually. Would you believe it, there was a run of seventeen against me on the even chances? Bad. Very bad,' said Donald with an unconvincing return to his lighter manner. 'Disastrous, in fact.'

'You're shying about,' said Lord Robert. 'What's the real trouble?'

'One of my cheques has been returned R/D. I'm bust.'

'I paid your Oxford debts and started you off with five hundred as a yearly allowance. Are you telling me you've gone through five hundred since you came down?'

'I'm sorry,' said Donald. 'Yes.'

'Your mother gives you four pounds a week, don't she?'

'Yes.'

Lord Robert suddenly whisked out a notebook.

'How much was this returned cheque?'

'Fifty quid. Awful, isn't it?' He glanced at his uncle's profile and saw that his lips were pursed in a soundless whistle. Donald decided that it was not as bad as he had feared and said more hopefully: 'Isn't it a bore?'

Lord Robert, his pencil poised, said: 'Who was it made out to?'

'To Wits – Withers – everyone calls him Wits. You see, I had a side bet with him.'

Lord Robert wrote, turned, and looked over his spectacles at his nephew.

'I'll send Withers a cheque tonight,' he said.

'Thank you so much, Uncle Bunch.'

'What's the address?'

'Shackleton House, Leatherhead. He's got a flat in town but the Leatherhead address is all right.'

'Any other debts?'

'One or two shops. They seem to be getting rather testy about it. And a restaurant or two.'

'Here we are,' said Lord Robert abruptly.

The taxi drew up outside the house he shared with his sister. They got out. Lord Robert paid and tipped the driver.

'How's the lumbago?' he asked.

'Not too bad, m'lord, thank you, m'lord.'

'Good. 'Evening to you.'

'Good evening, m'lord.'

They entered the house in silence. Lord Robert said over his shoulder: 'Come to my room.'

He led the way, a small, comic, but somehow a rather resolute figure. Donald followed him into an old-fashioned study. Lord Robert sat at his desk and wrote a cheque with finicky movements of his fat hands. He blotted it meticulously and swung round in his chair to face his nephew.

'You still of the same mind about this doctoring?' he asked.

'Well, that's the big idea,' said Donald.

'Passed some examinations for it, didn't you?'

'Medical prelim,' said Donald easily. 'Yes, I've got that.'

'Before you were sent down for losing your mother's money. And mine.'

Donald was silent.

'I'll get you out of this mess on one condition. I don't know the way you set about working for a medical degree. Our family's been in the diplomatic for a good many generations. High time we did something else, I dare say. You'll start work at Edinburgh as soon as they'll have you. If that's not at once I'll get a coach and you'll go to Archery and work there. I'll show you as much as the usual medical student gets and I'll advise your mother to give you no more. That's all.'

'Edinburgh! Archery!' Donald's voice was shrill with dismay. 'But I don't want to go to Edinburgh for my training. I want to go to Thomas's.'

'You're better away from London. There's one other thing I must absolutely insist upon, Donald. You are to drop this feller Withers.'

'Why should I?'

'Because the feller's a bad 'un. I know something about him. I have never interfered in the matter of your friendships before, but I'd be neglectin' my duty like anything if I didn't step in here.'

'I won't give up a friend simply because you choose to say he's no good.'

'I give you my word of honour this man's a rotter – a criminal rotter. I was amazed when I recognized Withers this afternoon. My information dates from my Foreign Office days. It's unimpeachable. Very bad record. Come now, be sensible. Make a clean break and forget all about him. Archery's a nice old house. Your mother can use it as a *pied-à-terre* and see you sometimes. It's only ten miles out of Edinburgh.'

'But – '

'Afraid it's definite.'

'But – I don't want to leave London. I don't want to muck about with a lot of earnest Scots from God knows where. I mean the sort of people who go there are just simply The End!'

'Why?' asked Lord Robert.

'Well, because, I mean, you know what I mean. They'll be the most unspeakable curiosities. No doubt perfectly splendid but – '

'But not in the same class with young men who contract debts of honour which they cannot meet and do the London season on their mother's money?'

'That's not fair,' cried Donald hotly.

'Why?' repeated Lord Robert.

'I'll bet you got into the same sort of jams when you were my age.'

'You're wrong,' said Lord Robert mildly. 'I did as many silly things as most young men of my day. But I did not contract debts that I was unable to settle. It seemed to me that sort of thing amounted to theft. I didn't steal clothes from my tailor, drink from my hotel, or money from my friends.'

'But I knew it would be all right in the end.'

'You mean, you knew I'd pay?'

'I'm not ungrateful,' said Donald angrily.

'My dear fellow, I don't want you to be grateful.'

'But I won't go and stay in a deserted mausoleum of a Scotch house in the middle of the season. There's – there's Bridget.'

'Lady Carrados's gel? Is she fond of you?'

'Yes.'

'She seems a nice creature. You're fortunate. Not one of these screeching rattles. She'll wait for you.'

'I won't go.'

'M'dear boy, I'm sorry, but you've no alternative.'

Donald's face was white but two scarlet patches burned on his cheek-bones. His lips trembled. Suddenly he burst out violently.

'You can keep your filthy money,' he shouted. 'By God, I'll look after myself. I'll borrow from someone who's not a bloody complacent Edwardian relic and I'll get a job and pay them back as I can.'

'Jobs aren't to be had for the asking. Come now – '

'Oh, shut up!' bawled Donald and flung out of the room.

Lord Robert stared at the door which his nephew had not neglected to slam. The room was very quiet. The fire settled down with a small whisper of ashes and Lord Robert's clock ticked on the mantelpiece. It ticked very loudly. The plump figure, only half-lit by the lamp on the desk, was quite still, the head resting on the hand. Lord Robert sighed, a slight mournful sound. At last he pulled an envelope towards him and in his finicky writing addressed it to Captain Withers, Shackleton House, Leatherhead. Then he wrote a short note, folded a cheque into it and put them both in the envelope. He rang for his butler.

'Has Mr Donald gone out?'

'Yes, m'lord. He said he would not be returning.'

'I see,' said Lord Robert. 'Thank you. Will you see that this letter is posted immediately?'

CHAPTER 4

Blackmail to Music

Lord Robert had sat on the blue sofa since two-fifteen but he was not tired of it. He enjoyed watching the patrons of music arriving and he amused himself with idle speculations on the subject of intellectual snobbishness. He also explored the blue sofa, sliding his hands cautiously over the surface of the seat and down between the seat and the arms. He had taken the precaution of leaving his gloves on a chair on the left of the sofa and a little behind it. A number of people came and spoke to him, among them Lady Carrados, who was looking tired.

'You're overdoing it, Evelyn,' he told her. 'You look charming – that's a delightful gown, ain't it? – but you're too fragile, m'dear.'

'I'm all right, Bunchy,' she said. 'You've got a nice way of telling a woman she's getting older.'

'No, I say! It wasn't that. Matter of fact it rather suits you bein' so fine-drawn, but you are too thin, you know. Where's Bridgie?'

'At a matinee.'

'Evelyn, do you know if she sees anything of my nephew?'

'Donald Potter? Yes. We've heard all about it, Bunchy.'

'He's written to his mother who no doubt is giving him money. I suppose you know he's sharing rooms with some other feller?'

'Yes. Bridgie sees him.'

'Does Bridgie know where he is?'

'I think so. She hasn't told me.'

'Is she fond of the boy, Evelyn?'

'Yes.'

'What do you think of him?'

'I know. He's got a lot of charm, but I wish he'd settle down.'

'Is it botherin' you much?'

'That?' She caught her breath. 'A little, naturally. Oh, *there's* Lady Alleyn! We're supposed to be together.'

'Delightful woman, ain't she? I'm waiting for Mrs Halcut-Hackett.'

'I shouldn't have thought her quite your cup of tea,' said Lady Carrados vaguely.

Lord Robert made his rabbit-face and winked.

'We go into mutual raptures over Bach,' he said.

'I must join Lady Alleyn. Good-bye, Bunchy.'

'Good-bye, Evelyn. Don't worry too much – over anything.'

She gave him a startled look and went away. Lord Robert sat down again. The room was nearly full and in ten minutes the Sirmione Quartette would appear on the modern dais.

'Is she waiting for the lights to go down?' wondered Lord Robert. He saw Agatha Troy come in, tried to catch her eye, and failed. People were beginning to settle down in the rows of gilt chairs and in the odd armchairs and sofas round the walls. Lord Robert looked restlessly towards the door and saw Sir Daniel Davidson. Davidson made straight for him. Sir Daniel had once cured Lord Robert's sister of indigestion and Mildred, who was an emotional woman, had asked him to dinner. Lord Robert had been amused and interested by Davidson. His technique as a fashionable doctor was superb. 'If Disraeli had taken to medicine instead of primroses,' Lord Robert had said, 'he would have been just such another.' And he had encouraged Davidson to launch out on his favourite subject, The Arts, with rather emphatic capitals. He had capped Davidson's Latin tags, quoted Congreve against him, and listened with amusement to a preposterous parallel drawn between Rubens and Dürer. 'The extrovert and the introvert of Art,' Davidson had cried, waving his beautiful hands, and Lord Robert had twinkled and said: 'You are talking above my head.' 'I'm talking nonsense,' Davidson had replied abruptly, 'and you know it.' But in a minute or two he had been off again as flamboyantly as ever and had left at one o'clock in the morning, very pleased with himself and overflowing with phrases.

'Ah!' he said now as he shook hands. 'I might have guessed I should find you here. Doing the fashionable thing for the unfashionable reason. Music! My God!'

'What's wrong?' asked Lord Robert.

'My dear Lord Robert, how many of these people will know what they are listening to, or even listen? Not one in fifty.'

'Oh, come now!'

'Not one in fifty! There goes that fellow Withers whose aesthetic appreciation is less than that of a monkey on a barrel-organ. What's he here for? I repeat, not one in fifty of these humbugs knows what he's listening to. And how many of the forty-nine have the courage to confess themselves honest philistines?'

'Quite a number, I should have thought,' said Lord Robert cheerfully. 'Myself for one. I'm inclined to go to sleep.'

'Now, why say that? You know perfectly well – What's the matter?'

'Sorry. I was looking at Evelyn Carrados. She looks damn seedy,' said Lord Robert. Davidson followed his glance to where Lady Carrados sat beside Lady Alleyn. Davidson watched her for a moment and then said quietly:

'Yes. She's overdoing it. I shall have to scold her. My seat is somewhere over there, I believe.' He made an impatient gesture. 'They all overdo it, these mothers, and the girls overdo it, and the husbands get rattled and the young men neglect their work and then there are half a dozen smart weddings, as many nervous breakdowns and there's your London season.'

'Lor'!' said Lord Robert mildly.

'It's the truth. In my job one sees it over and over again. Yes, yes, yes, I know! I am a smart West End doctor and I encourage all these women to fancy themselves ill. That's what you may very well think, but I assure you, my dear Lord Robert, that one sees cases of nervous exhaustion that are enough to make a cynic of the youngest ingénue. And they are so charming, these mamas. I mean really charming. Women like Lady Carrados. They help each other so much. It is not all a cutlet for a cutlet. But' – he spread out his hands – 'what is it for? What is it all about? The same people meeting each other over and over again at great expense to the accompaniment of loud negroid noises of jazz bands. For what?'

'Damned if I know,' said Lord Robert cheerfully. 'Who's that feller who came in behind Withers? Tall, dark feller with the extraordinary hands. I seem to know him.'

'Where? Ah.' Davidson picked up his glasses which he wore on a wide black ribbon. 'Who is it, now! I'll tell you who it is. It's the catering fellow, Dimitri. He's having his three guineas' worth of Bach with the *haute monde* and, by God, I'll wager you anything you like that he's got more appreciation in his extraordinary little finger – you are very observant, it *is* an odd hand – than most of them have in the whole of their pampered carcasses. How do you do, Mrs Halcut-Hackett?'

She had come up so quietly that Lord Robert had actually missed her. She looked magnificent. Davidson, to Lord Robert's amusement, kissed her hand.

'Have you come to worship?' he asked.

'Why, certainly,' she said and turned to Lord Robert. 'I see you have not forgotten.'

'How could I?'

'Now isn't that nice?' asked Mrs Halcut-Hackett, looking slant-ways at the blue sofa. Lord Robert moved aside and she at once sat down, spreading her furs.

'I must find my seat,' said Davidson. 'They are going to begin.'

He went to a chair beside Lady Carrados on the far side of the room. Mrs Halcut-Hackett asked Lord Robert if he did not think Sir Daniel a delightful personality. He noticed that her American accent was not quite so strictly repressed as usual and that her hands moved restlessly. She motioned him to sit on her right.

'If you don't mind,' he said, 'I'll stick to my chair. I like straight backs.'

He saw her glance nervously at his chair which was a little behind the left arm of the sofa. Her bag was on her lap. It was a large bag and looked well filled. She settled her furs again so that they fell across it. Lord Robert perched on his hideously uncomfortable chair. He noticed that Dimitri had sat down at the end of a row of seats close by. He found himself idly watching Dimitri. 'Wonder what he thinks of us. Always arranging food for our parties and he could buy most of us up and not notice it, I shouldn't mind betting. They *are* rum hands and no mistake. The little finger's the same length as the third.'

A flutter of polite clapping broke out and the Sirmione String Quartette walked on to the dais. The concealed lights of the concert chamber were dimmed into darkness, leaving the performers brilliantly lit. Lord Robert experienced that familiar thrill that follows the glorious scrape of tuning strings. But he told himself he had not come to listen to music and he was careful not to look towards the dais lest his eyes should be blinded by the light. Instead he looked towards the left-hand arm of the blue sofa. The darkness gradually thinned and presently he could make out the dim sheen of brocade and the thick depth of blackness that was Mrs Halcut-Hackett's furs. The shape of this blackness shifted. Something glinted. He bent forward. Closer than the exquisite pattern of the music he caught the sound made by one fabric rubbed against another, a sliding rustle. The outline of the mass that was Mrs Halcut-Hackett went tense and then relaxed. 'She's stowed it away,' thought Lord Robert.

Nobody came near them until the lights went up for the interval and then Lord Robert realized how very well the blackmailer had chosen when he lit upon the blue sofa as a post-box, for the side door beyond it was thrown open during the interval and instead of going out into the lounge by the main entrance many people passed behind the blue sofa and out by this side door. And as the interval drew to a close people came in and stood behind the sofa gossiping. Lord Robert felt sure that his man had gone into the lounge. He would wait until the lights were lowered and come in with the rest of the stragglers, pass behind the sofa and slip his hand over the arm. Most of the men and many of the women had gone out to smoke, but Lord Robert remained uncomfortably wedded to his chair. He knew very well that Mrs Halcut-Hackett writhed under the pressure of conflicting desires. She wished to be alone when the bag was taken and she dearly loved a title. She was to have the title. Suddenly she murmured something about powdering her nose. She got up and left by the side door.

Lord Robert rested his head on his hand and devoted the last few minutes of the interval to a neat imitation of an elderly gentleman dropping off to sleep. The lights were lowered again. The stragglers, with mumbled apologies, came back. There was a little group of people still standing in the darkness behind the sofa. The performers returned to the dais.

Someone had advanced from behind Lord Robert and stood beside the sofa.

Lord Robert felt his heart jump. He had placed his chair carefully, leaving a space between himself and the left-hand arm of the sofa. Into this space the shadowy figure now moved. It was a man. He stood with his back to the lighted dais and he seemed to lean forward a little as though he searched the darkness for something. Lord Robert also leant forward. He emitted the most delicate hint of a snore. His right hand propped his head. Through the cracks of his fat fingers he watched the left arm of the sofa. Into this small realm of twilight came the shape of a hand. It was a curiously thin hand and he could see quite clearly that the little finger was as long as the third.

Lord Robert snored.

The hand slid over into the darkness and when it came back it held Mrs Halcut-Hackett's bag.

As if in ironic appreciation the music on the dais swept up a sharp crescendo into a triumphant blare. Mrs Halcut-Hackett returned from powdering her nose.

CHAPTER 5

Unqualified Success

The ball given by Lady Carrados for her daughter Bridget O'Brien was an unqualified success. That is to say that from half-past ten when Sir Herbert and Lady Carrados took up their stand at the head of the double staircase and shook hands with the first guests until half-past three the next morning when the band, white about the gills and faintly glistening, played the National Anthem, there was not a moment when it was not difficult for a young man to find the débutantes with whom he wished to dance and easy for him to avoid those by whom he was not attracted. There was no ominous aftermath when the guests began to slide away to other parties, to slip through the doors with the uncontrollable heartlessness of the unamused. The elaborate structure, built to pattern by Lady Carrados, Miss Harris and Dimitri, did not slide away like a sand-castle before a wave of unpopularity, but held up bravely till the end. It was, therefore, an unqualified success.

In the matter of champagne Lady Carrados and Miss Harris had triumphed. It flowed not only in the supper-room but also at the buffet. In spite of the undoubted fact that débutantes did not drink, Dimitri's men opened two hundred bottles of Heidsieck '28 that night, and Sir Herbert afterwards took a sort of well-bred pride in the rows of empty bottles he happened to see in a glimpse behind the scenes.

Outside the house it was unseasonably chilly. The mist made by the breathing of the watchers mingled with drifts of light fog. As the guests walked up the strip of red carpet from their cars to the great door they passed between two wavering masses of dim faces. And while the warmth and festive smell of flowers and expensive scents reached the noses of the watchers, through the great doors was driven the smell of mist so that footmen in the hall told each other from time to time that for June it was an uncommonly thickish night outside.

By midnight everybody knew the ball was a success and was able when an opportunity presented itself to say so to Lady Carrados. Leaving her post at the stairhead she came into the ballroom looking very beautiful and made her way towards the far end where most of the chaperones were assembled. On her way she passed her daughter dancing with Donald Potter. Bridget smiled brilliantly at her mother, and raised her left hand in gay salute. Her right hand was crushed against Donald's chest and round the misty white nonsense of her dress was his black arm and his hard masculine hand was pressed against her ribs. 'She's in love with him,' thought Lady Carrados. And up through the maze of troubled thoughts that kept her company came the remembrance of her conversation with Donald's uncle. She wondered suddenly if women ever fainted from worry alone and as she smiled and bowed her way along the ballroom she saw herself suddenly crumpling down among the dancers. She would lie there while the band played on and presently she would open her eyes and see people's legs and then someone would help her to her feet and she would beg them to get her away quickly before anything was noticed. Her fingers tightened on her bag. Five hundred pounds! She had told the man at the bank that she wanted to pay some of the expenses of the ball in cash. That had been a mistake. She should have sent Miss Harris with the cheque and made no explanation to anybody. It was twelve o'clock. She would do it on her way to supper. There was that plain Halcut-Hackett protégée without a partner again. Lady Carrados looked round desperately and to her relief saw her husband making his way towards the girl. She felt a sudden wave of affection for her husband. Should she go to him tonight and tell him everything? And just sit back and take the blow? She must be very ill indeed to dream of such a thing. Here she was in the chaperones' corner and there, thank God, was Lady Alleyn with an empty chair beside her.

'Evelyn!' cried Lady Alleyn. 'Come and sit down, my dear, in all your triumph. My granddaughter has just told me this is the very pinnacle of all balls. Everybody is saying so.'

'I'm so thankful. It's such a toss-up nowadays. One never knows.'

'Of course one doesn't. Last Tuesday at the Gainscotts' by one o'clock there were only the three Gainscott girls, a few desperate couples who hadn't the heart to escape, and my Sarah and her partner whom I had kept there by sheer terrorism. Of course, they didn't have Dimitri, and I must say I think he *is* a perfect magician. Dear me,' said Lady Alleyn, 'I *am* enjoying myself.'

'I'm so glad.'

'I hope you are enjoying yourself, too, Evelyn. They say the secret of being a good hostess is to enjoy yourself at your own parties. I have never believed it. Mine always were a nightmare to me and I refuse to admit they were failures. But they are so exhausting. I suppose you wouldn't come down to Danes Court with me and turn yourself into an amiable cow for the weekend?'

'Oh,' said Lady Carrados, 'I wish I could.'

'Do.'

'That's what Sir Daniel Davidson said I should do – lead the life of a placid cow for a bit.'

'It's settled, then.'

'But – '

'Nonsense. There is Davidson, isn't it? That dark flamboyant-looking man talking to Lucy Lorrimer. On my left.'

'Yes.'

'Is he clever? Everyone seems to go to him. I might show him my leg one of these days. If you don't promise to come, Evelyn, I shall call him over here and make a scene. Here comes Bunchy Gospell,' continued Lady Alleyn with a quick glance at her hostess's trembling fingers, 'and I feel sure he's going to ask you to sup with him. Why, if that isn't Agatha Troy with him!'

'The painter?' said Lady Carrados faintly. 'Yes. Bridgie knows her. She's going to paint Bridgie.'

'She did a sketch portrait of my son Roderick. It's amazingly good.'

Lord Robert, looking, with so large an expanse of white under his chin, rather like Mr Pickwick, came beaming towards them with Troy at his side. Lady Alleyn held out her hand and drew Troy down to a stool beside her. She looked at the short dark hair, the long neck and the spare grace that was Troy's and wished, not for the first time, that it was her daughter-in-law that sat at her feet. Troy was the very wife she would have chosen for her son, and, so she believed, the wife that he would have chosen for himself. She rubbed her nose vexedly. 'If it hadn't been for that wretched case!' she thought. And she said:

'I'm so pleased to see you, my dear. I hear the exhibition is the greatest success.'

Troy gave her a sideways smile.

'I wonder,' continued Lady Alleyn, 'which of us is the most surprised at seeing the other. I have bounced out of retirement to launch my granddaughter.'

'I was brought by Bunchy Gospell,' said Troy. 'I'm so seldom smart and gay that I'm rather enjoying it.'

'Roderick had actually consented to come but he's got a tricky case on his hands and has to go away again tomorrow at the crack of dawn.'

'Oh,' said Troy.

Lord Robert began to talk excitedly to Lady Carrados.

'Gorgeous!' he cried, pitching his voice very high in order to top the band which had suddenly begun to make a terrific din. 'Gorgeous, Evelyn! Haven't enjoyed anything – ages – superb!' He bent his knees and placed his face rather close to Lady Carrados's. 'Supper!' he squeaked. 'Do say you will! In half an hour or so. Will you?'

She smiled and nodded. He sat down between Lady Carrados and Lady Alleyn and gave them each a little pat. His hand alighted on Lady Carrados's bag. She moved it quickly. He was beaming out into the ballroom and seemed lost in a mild ecstasy.

'Champagne!' he said. 'Can't beat it! I'm not inebriated, my dears, but I am, I proudly confess, a little exalted. What I believe is nowadays called nicely thank you. How-de-do? Gorgeous, ain't it?'

General and Mrs Halcut-Hackett bowed. Their smiling lips moved in a soundless assent. They sat down between Lady Alleyn and Sir Daniel Davidson and his partner, Lady Lorrimer.

Lucy, Dowager Marchioness of Lorrimer, was a woman of eighty. She dressed almost entirely in veils and untidy jewellery. She was enormously rich and not a little eccentric. Sir Daniel attended to her lumbago. She was now talking to him earnestly and confusedly and he listened with an air of enraptured attention. Lord Robert turned with a small bounce and made two bobs in their direction.

'There's Davidson,' he said delightedly, 'and Lucy Lorrimer. How are you, Lucy?'

'What?' shouted Lucy Lorrimer.

'How are yer?'

'Busy. I thought you were in Australia.'

'Why?'

'What?'

'Why?'

'Don't interrupt,' shouted Lucy Lorrimer. 'I'm talking.'

'Never been there,' said Lord Robert; 'the woman's mad.'

The Halcut-Hacketts smiled uncomfortably. Lucy Lorrimer leant across Davidson and bawled: 'Don't forget tomorrow night!'

'Who? Me?' asked Lord Robert. 'Of course not.'

'Eight-thirty sharp.'

'I know. Though how you could think I was in Australia – '

'I didn't see it was you,' screamed Lucy Lorrimer. 'Don't forget now.' The band stopped as abruptly as it had begun and her voice rang out piercingly. 'It wouldn't be the first night you had disappointed me.'

She leant back chuckling and fanning herself. Lord Robert took the rest of the party in with a comical glance.

'Honestly, Lucy!' said Lady Alleyn.

'He's the most absent-minded creature in the world,' added Lucy Lorrimer.

'Now to that,' said Lord Robert, 'I do take exception. I am above all things a creature of habit, upon my honour. I could tell you, if it wasn't a very boring sort of story, exactly to the minute what I shall do with myself tomorrow evening and how I shall ensure my punctual arrival at Lucy Lorrimer's party.'

'Suddenly remember it at a quarter to nine and take a cab,' said Lucy Lorrimer.

'Not a bit of it.'

Mrs Halcut-Hackett suddenly joined in the conversation.

'I can vouch for Lord Robert's punctuality,' she said loudly. 'He always keeps his appointments.' She laughed a little too shrilly and for some unaccountable reason created an uncomfortable atmosphere. Lady Alleyn glanced sharply at her. Lucy Lorrimer stopped short in the middle of a hopelessly involved sentence; Davidson put up his glass and stared. General Halcut-Hackett said, 'What!' loudly and uneasily.

Lord Robert examined his fat little hands with an air of complacent astonishment. The inexplicable tension was relieved by the arrival of Sir Herbert Carrados with the plain protégée of the Halcut-Hacketts. She held her long chiffon handkerchief to her face and she looked a little desperately at her chaperone. Carrados who had her by the elbow was the very picture of British chivalry.

'A casualty!' he said archly. 'Mrs Halcut-Hackett, I'm afraid you are going to be very angry with me!'

'Why, Sir Herbert!' said Mrs Halcut-Hackett; 'that's surely an impossibility.'

The General said 'What!'

'This young lady,' continued Carrados, squeezing her elbow, 'no sooner began to dance with me than she developed toothache. Frightfully bad luck – for both of us.'

Mrs Halcut-Hackett eyed her charge with something very like angry despair.

What's the matter,' she said, 'darling?'

'I'm afraid I'd better go home.'

Lady Carrados took her hand.

'That *is* bad luck,' she said. 'Shall we see if we can find something to – '

'No, no, please,' said the child. 'I think really, I'd better go home. I – I'm sure I'd better. Really.'

The General suddenly became human. He stood up, took the girl by the shoulders, and addressed Lady Carrados.

'Better at home,' he said. 'What? Brandy and oil of cloves. Damn bad show. Will you excuse us?' He addressed his wife. 'I'll take her home. You stay on. Come back for you.' He addressed his charge: 'Come on, child. Get your wrap.'

'You need not come back for me, dear,' said Mrs Halcut-Hackett. 'I shall be quite all right. Stay with Rose.'

'If I may,' squeaked Lord Robert, 'I'll give myself the pleasure of driving your wife home, Halcut-Hackett.'

'No, no,' began Mrs Halcut-Hackett, 'I – please – '

'Well,' said the General. 'Suit splendidly. What? Say good night. What?' They bowed and shook hands. Sir Herbert walked away with both of them. Mrs Halcut-Hackett embarked on a long polite explanation and apology to Lady Carrados.

'Poor child!' whispered Lady Alleyn.

'Poor child, indeed,' murmured Troy.

Mrs Halcut-Hackett had made no further reply to Lord Robert's offer. Now, as he turned to her, she hurriedly addressed herself to Davidson.

'I must take the poor lamb to a dentist,' she said. 'Too awful if her face should swell half-way through the season. Her mother is my dearest friend but she'd never forgive me. A major tragedy.'

'Quite,' said Sir Daniel rather dryly.

'Well,' said Lucy Lorrimer beginning to collect her scarves, 'I shall expect you at eight twenty-seven. It's only me and my brother, you know. The one that got into difficulties. I want some supper. Where is Mrs Halcut-Hackett? I suppose I must congratulate her on her ball, though I must say I always think it's the greatest mistake – '

Sir Daniel Davidson hurriedly shouted her down.

'Let me take you down and give you some supper,' he suggested loudly with an agonized glance at Mrs Halcut-Hackett and Lady Carrados. He carried Lucy Lorrimer away.

'Poor Lucy!' said Lady Alleyn. 'She never has the remotest idea where she is. I wish, Evelyn, that he hadn't stopped her. What fault do you suppose she was about to find in your hospitality?'

'Let's follow them, Evelyn,' said Lord Robert, 'and no doubt we shall find out. Troy, m'dear, there's a young man making for you. May we dance again?'

'Yes, of course, Bunchy dear,' said Troy, and went off with her partner.

Lady Carrados said she would meet Lord Robert in the supper-room in ten minutes. She left them, threading her way down the ballroom, her fingers clutching her bag. At the far end she overtook Sir Daniel and Lucy Lorrimer.

Lady Alleyn, looking anxiously after her, saw her sway a little. Davidson stepped up to her quickly and took her arm, steadying her. Lady Alleyn saw him speak to her with a quick look of concern. She saw Evelyn Carrados shake her head, smiling at him. He spoke again with emphasis and then Lucy Lorrimer shouted at him and he shrugged his shoulders and moved away. After a moment Lady Carrados, too, left the ballroom.

Lord Robert asked Mrs Halcut-Hackett if she would 'take a turn' with him once round the room. She excused herself, making rather an awkward business of it:

'I fancy I said that I would keep this one for – I'm so sorry – Oh, yes – here he comes right now.'

Captain Withers had come from the farther side of the ballroom. Mrs Halcut-Hackett hurriedly got up and went to meet him. Without a word he placed his arm round her and they moved off together, Withers looking straight in front of him.

'Where's Rory?' Lord Robert asked Lady Alleyn. 'I expected to find him here tonight. He refused to dine with us.'

'Working at the Yard. He's going north early tomorrow. Bunchy, that was your Captain Withers, wasn't it? The man we saw at the Halcut-Hacketts' cocktail-party?'

'Yes.'

'Is she having an affair with him, do you suppose? They've got that sort of look.'

Lord Robert pursed his lips and contemplated his hands.

'It's *not* malicious curiosity,' said Lady Alleyn. 'I'm worried about those women. Especially Evelyn.'

'You don't suggest Evelyn – ?'

'Of course not. But they've both got the same haunted look. And if I'm not mistaken Evelyn nearly fainted just then. Your friend Davidson noticed it and I think he gave her the scolding she needs. She's at the end of her tether, Bunchy.'

'I'll get hold of her and take her into the supper-room.'

'Do. Go after her now, like a dear man. There comes my Sarah.'

Lord Robert hurried away. It took him some time to get round the ballroom and as he edged past dancing couples and over the feet of sitting chaperones he suddenly felt as if an intruder had thrust open all the windows of this neat little world and let in a flood of uncompromising light. In this cruel light he saw the people he liked best and they were changed and belittled. He saw his nephew Donald, who had turned aside when they met in the hall, as a spoilt, selfish boy with no honesty or ambition. He saw Evelyn Carrados as a woman haunted by some memory that was discreditable, and hag-ridden by a blackmailer. His imagination leapt into extravagance, and in many of the men he fancied he saw something of the unscrupulousness of Withers, the pomposity of Carrados, and the stupidity of old General Halcut-Hackett. He was plunged into a violent depression that had a sort of nightmarish quality. How many of these women were what he still thought of as 'virtuous'? And the débutantes? They had gone back to chaperones and were guided and guarded by women, many of whose own private lives would look ugly in this flood of hard light that had been let in on Lord Robert's world. The girls were sheltered by a convention for three months but at the same time they heard all sorts of things that would have horrified and bewildered his sister Mildred at their age. And he wondered if the Victorian and Edwardian eras had been no more than freakish incidents in the history of society and if their proprieties had been as artificial as the paint on a modern woman's lips. This idea seemed abominable to Lord Robert and he felt old and lonely for the first time in his life. 'It's the business with Donald and this blackmailing game,' he thought as he twisted aside to avoid a couple who were dancing the rumba. He had reached the door. He went into the lounge which opened off the ballroom, saw that Evelyn Carrados was not there, and made for the staircase. The stairs were covered with couples sitting out. He picked his way down and passed his nephew Donald who looked at him as if they were strangers.

'No good trying to break that down,' thought Lord Robert. 'Not here. He'd only cut me and someone would notice.' He felt wretchedly depressed and tired, and was filled with a premonition of disaster that quite astonished himself. 'Good God,' he thought suddenly, 'I must be going to be ill.' And oddly enough this comforted him a little. In the lower hall he found Bridget O'Brien with a neat, competent-looking young woman whose face he dimly remembered.

'Now, Miss Harris,' Bridgie was saying, 'are you sure you're getting on all right? Have you had supper?'

'Well, thank you so much, Miss O'Brien, but really it doesn't matter – '

Of course, it was Evelyn's secretary. Nice of Evelyn to ask her. Nice of Bridgie to take trouble. He said:

'Hullo, m'dear. What a grand ball. Has your mother come this way?'

'She's in the supper-room,' said Bridget without looking at him, and he realized that of course she had heard Donald's side of their quarrel. He said:

'Thank you, Bridgie, I'll find her.' He saw Miss Harris was looking a little like a lost child so he said: 'Wonder if you'd be very nice and give me a dance later on? Would you?'

Miss Harris turned scarlet and said she would be very pleased thank you, Lord – Lord Gospell.

'Got it wrong,' thought Lord Robert. 'Poor things, they don't get much fun. Wonder what *they* think of it all. Not much, you may depend upon it.'

He found Lady Carrados in the supper-room. He took her to a corner table, made her drink champagne and tried to persuade her to eat.

'I know what you're all like,' he told her. 'Nothing all day in your tummies and then get through the night on your nerves. I remember mama used to have the vapours whenever she gave a big party. She always came round in time to receive the guests.'

He chattered away, eating a good deal himself and getting over his own unaccountable fit of depression in his effort to help Lady Carrados. He looked round and saw that the supper-room was inhabited by only a few chaperones and their partners. Poor Davidson was still in Lucy Lorrimer's toils. Withers and Mrs Halcut-Hackett were tucked away in a corner. She was talking to him earnestly and apparently with great emphasis. He glowered at the table and laughed unpleasantly.

'Lor'!' thought Lord Robert, 'she's giving him his marching orders. Now why's that? Afraid of the General or of – what? Of the blackmailer? I wonder if Withers is the subject of those letters. I wonder if Dimitri has seen her with him some time. I'll swear it was Dimitri's hand. But what does he know about Evelyn? The least likely woman in the world to have a guilty secret. And, damme, there is the fellow as large as you please, running the whole show.'

Dimitri had come into the supper-room. He gave a professional look round, spoke to one of his waiters, came across to Lady Carrados and bowed tentatively and then went out again.

'Dimitri is a great blessing to all of us,' said Lady Carrados. She said it so simply that he knew at once that if Dimitri was blackmailing her she had no idea of it. He was hunting in his mind for something to reply when Bridget came into the supper-room.

She was carrying her mother's bag.

Everything seemed to happen at the same moment. Bridget calling gaily: 'Really, Donna darling, you're *hopeless*. There was your bag, simply preggy with banknotes, lying on the writing-table in the green boudoir. And I *bet* you didn't know where you'd left it.' Then Bridget, seeing her mother's face and crying out: 'Darling, what's the matter?' Lord Robert himself getting up and interposing his bulk between Lady Carrados and the other tables. Lady Carrados half-laughing, half-crying and reaching out frantically for the bag. Himself saying: 'Run away, Bridget, I'll look after your mother.' And Lady Carrados, in a whisper: 'I'm all right. Run upstairs, darling, and get my smelling-salts.'

Somehow they persuaded Bridget to go. The next thing that happened was Sir Daniel Davidson, who stood over Evelyn Carrados like an elegant dragon.

'You're all right,' he said. 'Lord Robert, see if you can open that window.'

Lord Robert succeeded in opening the window. A damp hand seemed to be laid on his face. He caught sight of street lamps blurred by impalpable mist.

Davidson held Lady Carrados's wrist in his long fingers and looked at her with a sort of compassionate exasperation.

'You women,' he said. 'You impossible women.'

'I'm all right. I simply felt giddy.'

'You ought to lie down. You'll faint and make an exhibition of yourself.'

'No I won't. Has anybody – ?'

'Nobody's noticed anything. Will you go up to your room for half an hour?'

'I haven't got a room. It's not my house.'

'Of course it's not. The cloakroom, then.'

'I – yes. Yes, I'll do that.'

'Sir Daniel!' shouted Lucy Lorrimer in the corner. 'For Heaven's sake go back to her,' implored Lady Carrados, 'or she'll be here.'

'*Sir Daniel!*'

'Damn!' whispered Davidson. 'Very well, I'll go back to her. I expect your maid's here, isn't she? Good. Lord Robert, will you take Lady Carrados?'

'I'd rather go alone. Please!'

'Very well. But *please* go.'

He made a grimace and returned to Lucy Lorrimer.

Lady Carrados stood up, holding her bag. 'Come on,' said Lord Robert. 'Nobody's paying any attention.'

He took her elbow and they went out into the hall. It was deserted. Two men stood just in the entrance to the cloakroom. They were Captain Withers and Donald Potter. Donald glanced round, saw his uncle, and at once began to move upstairs. Withers followed him. Dimitri came out of the buffet and also went upstairs. The hall was filled with the sound of the band and with the thick confusion of voices and sliding feet.

'Bunchy,' whispered Lady Carrados. 'You must do as I ask you. Leave me for three minutes. I – '

'I know what's up, m'dear. Don't do it. Don't leave your bag. Face it and let him go to the devil.'

She pressed her hand against her mouth and looked wildly at him.

'You *know*?'

'Yes, and I'll help. I know who it is. You don't, do you? See here – there's a man at the Yard – whatever it is – '

A look of something like relief came into her eyes. 'But you don't know what it's about. Let me go. I've *got* to do it. Just this once more.'

She pulled her arm away and he watched her cross the hall and slowly climb the stairs.

After a moment's hesitation he followed her.

CHAPTER 6

Bunchy Goes Back to the Yard

Alleyn closed his file and looked at his watch. Two minutes to one. Time for him to pack up and go home. He yawned, stretched his cramped fingers, walked over to the window and pulled aside the blind. The row of lamps hung like a necklace of misty globes along the margin of the Embankment.

'Fog in June,' muttered Alleyn. 'This England!'

Out there in the cold, Big Ben tolled one. At that moment three miles away at Lady Carrados's ball, Lord Robert Gospell was slowly climbing the stairs to the top landing and the little drawing-room.

Alleyn filled his pipe slowly and lit it. An early start tomorrow, a long journey, and a piece of dull routine at the end of it. He held his fingers to the heater and fell into a long meditation. Sarah had told him Troy was going to the ball. She was there now, no doubt.

'Oh, well!' he thought and turned off his heater.

The desk telephone rang. He answered it.

'Hullo?'

'Mr Alleyn? I thought you were still there, sir. Lord Robert Gospell.'

'Right.'

A pause and then a squeaky voice:

'Rory?'

'Bunchy?'

'You said you'd be at it till late. I'm in a room by myself at the Carrados's show. Thing is, I think I've got him. Are you working for much longer?'

'I can.'

'May I come round to the Yard?'

'Do!'

'I'll go home first, get out of this boiled shirt and pick up my notes.'

'Right. I'll wait.'

'It's the cakes-and-ale feller.'

'Good Lord! No names, Bunchy.'

''Course not. I'll come round to the Yard. Upon my soul it's worse than murder. Might as well mix his damn' brews with poison. And he's working with – Hullo! Didn't hear you come in.'

'Is someone there?' asked Alleyn sharply.

'Yes.'

'Good-bye,' said Alleyn, 'I'll wait for you.'

'Thank you so much,' squeaked the voice. 'Much obliged. Wouldn't have lost it for anything. Very smart work, officer. See you get the reward.'

Alleyn smiled and hung up his receiver.

II

Up in the ballroom Hughie Bronx's Band packed up. Their faces were the colour of raw cod and shone with a fishy glitter, but the hair on their heads remained as smooth as patent leather. The four experts who only ten minutes ago had jigged together with linked arms in a hot rhythm argued wearily about the way to go home. Hughie Bronx himself wiped his celebrated face with a beautiful handkerchief and lit a cigarette.

'OK, boys,' he sighed. 'Eight-thirty tomorrow and if any – calls for "My Girl's Cutie" more than six times running we'll quit and learn anthems.'

Dimitri crossed the ballroom.

'Her ladyship particularly asked me to tell you,' he said, 'that there is something for you gentlemen at the buffet.'

'Thanks a lot, Dim,' said Mr Bronx. 'We'll be there.'

Dimitri glanced round the ballroom, walked out and descended the stairs.

Down in the entrance hall the last of the guests were collected. They looked wan and a little raffish but they shouted cheerfully, telling each other what a good party it had been. Among them, blinking sleepily through his glasses, was Lord Robert. His celebrated cape hung from his shoulders and in his hands he clasped his broad-brimmed black hat. Through the open doors came wreaths of mist. The sound of people coughing as they went into the raw air was mingled with the noise of taxi engines in low gear and the voices of departing guests.

Lord Robert was among the last to go.

He asked several people, rather plaintively, if they had seen Mrs Halcut-Hackett. 'I'm supposed to be taking her home.'

Dimitri came up to him.

'Excuse me, my lord, I think Mrs Halcut-Hackett has just left. She asked me if I had seen you, my lord.'

Lord Robert blinked up at him. For a moment their eyes met.

'Oh. Thank you,' said Lord Robert. 'I'll see if I can find her.' Dimitri bowed.

Lord Robert walked out into the mist.

His figure, looking a little like a plump antic from one of Verlaine's poems, moved down the broad steps. He passed a crowd of stragglers who were entering their taxis. He peered at them, watched them go off, and looked up and down the street. Lord Robert walked slowly down the street, seemed to turn into an insubstantial wraith, was hidden for a moment by a drift of mist, reappeared much farther away, walking steadily into nothingness, and was gone.

III

In his room at the Yard Alleyn woke with a start, rushing up on a wave of clamour from the darkness of profound sleep. The desk telephone was pealing. He reached out for it, caught sight of his watch and exclaimed aloud. Four o'clock! He spoke into the receiver.

'Hullo?'

'Mr Alleyn?'

'Yes.'

He thought: 'It's Bunchy. What the devil – !'

But the voice in the receiver said:

'There's a case come in, sir. I thought I'd better report to you at once. Taxi with a fare. Says the fare's been murdered and has driven straight here with the body.'

'I'll come down,' said Alleyn.

He went down thinking with dismay that another case would be most unwelcome and hoping that it would be handed on to someone else. His mind was full of the blackmail business. Bunchy Gospell wouldn't have said he'd found his man unless he was damn certain of him. The cakes-and-ale fellow. Dimitri. Well, he'd have opportunities, but what sort of evidence had Bunchy got? And where the devil was Bunchy? A uniformed sergeant waited for Alleyn in the entrance hall.

'Funny sort of business, Mr Alleyn. The gentleman's dead all right. Looks to me as if he'd had a heart attack or something, but the cabby insists it was murder and won't say a word till he sees you. Didn't want me to open the door. I did, though, just to make sure. Held my watch-glass to the mouth and listened to the heart. Nothing! The old cabby didn't half go off pop. He's a character.'

'Where's the taxi?'

'In the yard, sir. I told him to drive through.'

They went out to the yard.

'Dampish,' said the sergeant and coughed.

It was very misty down there near the river. Wreaths of mist that were almost rain drifted round them and changed on their faces into cold spangles of moisture. A corpse-like pallor had crept into the darkness and the vague shapes of roofs and chimneys waited for the dawn. Far down the river a steamer hooted. The air smelt dank and unwholesome.

A vague huge melancholy possessed Alleyn. He felt at once nerveless and over-sensitized. His spirit seemed to rise thinly and separate itself from his body. He saw himself as a stranger. It was a familiar experience and he had grown to regard it as a precursor of evil. 'I must get back,' cried his mind and with the thought the return was accomplished. He was in the yard. The stones rang under his feet. A taxi loomed up vaguely with the overcoated figure of its driver standing motionless by the door as if on guard.

'Cold,' said the sergeant.

'It's the dead hour of the night,' said Alleyn.

The taxi-driver did not move until they came right up to him.

'Hullo,' said Alleyn, 'what's it all about?'

''Morning, governor.' It was the traditional hoarse voice. He sounded like a cabby in a play. 'Are you one of the inspectors?'

'I am.'

'I won't make no report to any copper. I got to look after meself, see? What's more, the little gent was a friend of mine, see?'

'This is Chief Detective-Inspector Alleyn, daddy,' said the sergeant.

'All right. That's the stuff. I got to protect meself, ain't I? Wiv a blinking stiff for a fare.'

He suddenly reached out a gloved hand and with a quick turn flung open the door.

'I ain't disturbed 'im,' he said. 'Will you switch on the glim?'

Alleyn's hand reached out into the darkness of the cab. He smelt leather, cigars and petrol. His fingers touched a button and a dim light came to life in the roof of the taxi.

He was motionless and silent for so long that at last the sergeant said loudly:

'Mr Alleyn?'

But Alleyn did not answer. He was alone with his friend. The small fat hands were limp. The feet were turned in pathetically, like the feet of a child. The head leant sideways, languidly, as a sick child will lean its head. He could see the bare patch on the crown and the thin ruffled hair.

'If you look froo the other winder,' said the driver, 'you'll see 'is face. 'E's dead all right. Murdered!'

Alleyn said: 'I can see his face.'

He had leant forward and for a minute or two he was busy. Then he drew back. He stretched out his hand as if to close the lids over the congested eyes. His fingers trembled.

He said: 'I mustn't touch him any more.' He drew his hand away and backed out of the taxi. The sergeant was staring in astonishment at his face.

'Dead,' said the taxi-driver. 'Ain't he?'

'– you!' said Alleyn with a violent oath. 'Can't I see he's dead without –'

He broke off and took three or four uncertain steps away from them. He passed his hand over his face and then stared at his fingers with an air of bewilderment.

'Wait a moment, will you?' he said.

'I'm sorry,' said Alleyn at last. 'Give me a moment.'

'Shall I get someone else, sir?' asked the sergeant. 'It's a friend of yours, isn't it?'

'Yes,' said Alleyn. 'It's a friend of mine.'

He turned on the taxi-driver and took him fiercely by the arm.

'Come here,' he said and marched him to the front of the car.

'Switch on the headlights,' he said.

The sergeant reached inside the taxi and in a moment the driver stood blinking in a white flood of light.

'Now,' said Alleyn. 'Why are you so certain it was murder?'

'Gorblimy, governor,' said the driver, 'ain't I seen wiv me own eyes 'ow the ovver bloke gets in wiv 'im, and ain't I seen wiv me own eyes 'ow the ovver bloke gets out at 'is lordship's 'ouse dressed up in 'is lordship's cloak and 'at and squeaks at me in a rum little voice same as 'is lordship: "Sixty-three Jobbers Row, Queens Gate"? Ain't I driven 'is corpse all the way there, not knowing? 'Ere! You say 'is lordship was a friend of yours. So 'e was o' mine. This is bloody murder, this is, and I want to see this Mr Clever, what's diddled me and done in as nice a little gent as ever I see, swing for it. That's me.'

'I see,' said Alleyn. 'All right. I'll get a statement from you. We must get to work. Call up the usual lot. Get them all here. Get Dr Curtis. Photograph the body from every angle. Note the position of the head. Look for signs of violence. Routine. Case of homicide. Take the name, will you? Lord Robert Gospell, two hundred Cheyne Walk – '

CHAPTER 7

Stop Press News

LORD ROBERT GOSPELL DIES IN TAXI
Society Shocked. Foul Play Suspected
Full Story of Ball on Page 5

Evelyn Carrados let the paper fall on the counterpane and stared at her husband.

'The papers are full of it,' she said woodenly.

'Good God, my dear Evelyn, of course they are! And this is only the ten o'clock racing edition brought in by a damn pup of a footman with my breakfast. Wait till we see the evening papers! Isn't it enough, my God, that I should be rung up by some jack-in-office from Scotland Yard at five o'clock in the morning and cross-examined about my own guests without having the whole thing thrust under my nose in some insulting bloody broadsheet!'

He limped angrily about the room.

'It's perfectly obvious that the man has been murdered. Do you realize that at any moment we'll have some damned fellow from Scotland Yard cross-questioning us and that all the scavengers in Fleet Street will be hanging about our door for days together? Do you realize – '

'I think he was perhaps my greatest friend,' said Evelyn Carrados.

'If you look at their damned impertinent drivel on page five you will see the friendship well advertised. My God, it's intolerable. Do you realize that the police rang up Marsdon House at quarter-past four – five minutes after we'd gone, thank God! – and asked when

Robert Gospell left? Some fellow of Dimitri's answered them and now a blasted snivelling journalist has got hold of it. Do you realize – '

'I only realize,' said Evelyn Carrados, 'that Bunchy Gospell is dead.'

Bridget burst into the room, a paper in her hands.

'Donna! Oh, Donna – it's our funny little Bunchy. Our funny little Bunchy's dead! Donna!'

'Darling – I know.'

'But, Donna – *Bunchy*!'

'Bridget,' said her stepfather, 'please don't be hysterical. The point we have to consider is – '

Bridget's arm went round her mother's shoulders.

'But we *mind*' she said. 'Can't you see – Donna minds *awfully*.'

Her mother said: 'Of course we mind, darling, but Bart's thinking about something else. You see, Bart thinks there will be dreadful trouble – '

'About what?'

Bridget's eyes blazed in her white face as she turned on Carrados.

'Do you mean Donald? *Do you?* Do you dare to suggest that Donald would – would – '

'Bridgie!' cried her mother, 'what are you saying!'

'Wait a moment, Evelyn,' said Carrados. 'What is all this about young Potter?'

Bridget pressed the back of her hand against her mouth, looked distractedly from her mother to her stepfather, burst into tears and ran out of the room.

II

'BUNCHY' GOSPELL DEAD
Mysterious death in Taxi
Sequel to the Carrados Ball

Mrs Halcut-Hackett's beautifully manicured hands closed like claws on the newspaper. Her lips were stretched in a smile that emphasized the carefully suppressed lines from her nostrils to the corners of her mouth. She stared at nothing.

General Halcut-Hackett's dressing-room door was flung open and the General, wearing a dressing-gown but few teeth, marched into the room. He carried a copy of a ten o'clock sporting edition.

'What!' he shouted indistinctly. 'See here! By God!'

'I know,' said Mrs Halcut-Hackett. 'Sad, isn't it?'

'Sad! Bloody outrage! What!'

'Shocking,' said Mrs Halcut-Hackett.

'Shocking!' echoed the General. 'Preposterous!' and the explosive consonants pronounced through the gap in his teeth blew his moustache out like a banner. His bloodshot eyes goggled at his wife. He pointed a stubby forefinger at her.

'He said he'd bring you home,' he spluttered.

'He didn't do so.'

'When did you come home?'

'I didn't notice. Late.'

'Alone?'

Her face was white but she looked steadily at him. 'Yes,' she said. 'Don't be a fool.'

III

STRANGE FATALITY
Lord Robert Gospell dies
after Ball
Full Story

Donald Potter read the four headlines over and over again. From the centre of the page his uncle's face twinkled at him. Donald's cigarette-butt burnt his lips. He spat it into his empty cup, and lit another. He was shivering as if he had a rigor. He read the four lines again. In the next room somebody yawned horribly.

Donald's head jerked back.

'Wits!' he said. 'Wits! Come here!'

'What's wrong?'

'*Come here*!'

Captain Withers, clad in an orange silk dressing-gown, appeared in the doorway. 'What the hell's the matter with you?' he enquired. 'Look here.'

Captain Withers, whistling between his teeth, strolled up and looked over Donald's shoulder. His whistling stopped. He reached out his hand, took the newspaper, and began to read. Donald watched him.

'Dead!' said Donald. 'Uncle Bunch! Dead!'

Withers glanced at him and returned to the paper. Presently he began again to whistle through his teeth.

IV

DEATH OF LORD ROBERT GOSPELL
Tragic end to a distinguished career
Suspicious Circumstances

Lady Mildred Potter beat her plump hands on the proofs of the *Evening Chronicle* obituary notice and turned upon Alleyn a face streaming with tears.

'But who could have *wanted* to hurt Bunchy, Roderick? Everyone adored him. He hadn't an enemy in the world. Look what the *Chronicle* says – and I must say I think it charming of them to let me see the things they propose to say about him – but look what it says. "Beloved by all his friends!" And so he was. So he was. By all his friends.'

'He must have had one enemy, Mildred,' said Alleyn.

'I can't believe it. I'll never believe it. It must be an escaped lunatic.' She pressed her handkerchief to her eyes and sobbed violently. 'I shall never be able to face all this dreadful publicity. The police! I don't mean you, Roderick, naturally. But everything – the papers, everyone poking and prying. Bunchy would have detested it. I can't face it. I can't.'

'Where's Donald?'

'He rang up. He's coming.'

'From where?'

'From this friend's flat, wherever it is.'

'He's away from home?'

'Didn't Bunchy tell you? Ever since that awful afternoon when he was so cross with Donald. Bunchy didn't understand.'

'Why was Bunchy cross with him?'

'He had run into debt rather. And now, poor boy, he is no doubt feeling too dreadfully remorseful.'

Alleyn did not answer immediately. He walked over to the window and looked out.

'It will be easier for you,' he said at last, 'when Donald gets here. I suppose the rest of the family will come too?'

'Yes. All our old cousins and aunts. They have already rung up. Broomfield – Bunchy's eldest nephew, you know – I mean my eldest brothers son is away on the Continent. He's the head of the family, of course. I suppose I shall have to make all the arrangements and – and I'm so dreadfully shaken.'

'I'll do as much as I can. There are some things that I must do. I'm afraid, Mildred, I shall have to ask you to let me look at Bunchy's things. His papers and so on.'

'I'm sure,' said Lady Mildred, 'he would have preferred you to anyone else, Roderick.'

'You make it very easy for me. Shall I get it done now?'

Lady Mildred looked helplessly about her.

'Yes. Yes, please. You'll want his keys, won't you?'

'I've got the keys, Mildred,' said Alleyn gently.

'But – where – ?' She gave a little cry. 'Oh, poor darling. He always took them with him everywhere.' She broke down completely. Alleyn waited for a moment and then he said:

'I shan't attempt the impertinence of condoling phrases. There is small comfort in scavenging in this mess for crumbs of consolation. But I tell you this, Mildred, if it takes me the rest of my life, and if it costs me my job, by God! if I have to do the killing myself, I'll get this murderer and see him suffer for it.' He paused and made a grimace. 'Good Lord, what a speech! Bunchy *would* have laughed at it. It's a curious thing that when one speaks from the heart it is invariably in the worst of taste.'

He looked at her grey hair arranged neatly and unfashionably and enclosed in a net. She peered at him over the top of her drenched handkerchief and he saw that she had not listened to him.

'I'll get on with it,' said Alleyn, and made his way alone to Lord Robert's study.

V

LORD ROBERT GOSPELL
DIES IN TAXI
Last night's shocking Fatality
Who was the Second Passenger?

Sir Daniel Davidson arrived at his consulting-rooms at half-past ten. At his front door he caught sight of the news placard and, for the first time in his life, bought a sporting edition. He now folded the paper carefully and laid it on top of his desk. He lit a cigarette, and glanced at his servant.

'I shan't see any patients,' he said. 'If anybody rings up – I'm out. Thank you.'

'Thank you, sir,' said the servant and removed himself.

Sir Daniel sat thinking, He had trained himself to think methodically and he hated slipshod ideas as much as he despised a vague diagnosis. He was, he liked to tell his friends, above all things, a creature of method and routine. He prided himself upon his memory. His memory was busy now with events only seven hours old. He closed his eyes and saw himself in the entrance-hall of Marsdon House at four o'clock that morning. The last guests, wrapped in coats and furs, shouted cheerfully to each other and passed through the great doors in groups of twos and threes. Dimitri stood at the foot of the stairs. He himself was near the entrance to the men's cloakroom. He was bent on avoiding Lucy Lorrimer, who had stayed to the bitter end, and would offer to drive him home if she saw him. There she was, just going through the double doors. He hung back. Drifts of fog were blown in from the street. He remembered that he had wrapped his scarf over his mouth when he noticed the fog. It was at that precise moment he had seen Mrs Halcut-Hackett, embedded in furs, slip through the entrance alone. He had thought there was something a little odd about this. The collar of her fur wrap turned up, no doubt against the fog, and the manner in which she slipped, if so majestic a woman could be said to slip, round the outside of the group! There was something furtive about it. And then he himself had been jostled by that fellow Withers, coming out of the cloakroom. Withers had scarcely apologized, but had looked quickly round the melting group in the hall and up the stairs.

It was at that moment that Lord Robert Gospell had come downstairs. Sir Daniel twisted the heavy signet ring on his little finger and still with closed eyes he peered back into his memory. Withers had seen Lord Robert. There was no doubt of that. Sir Daniel heard again that swift intake of breath and noticed the quick glance before the fellow unceremoniously shoved his way through the crowd and disappeared into the fog. Then Lord Robert's nephew, young Donald Potter, came out of the buffet near the stairs. Bridget O'Brien was with him. They almost ran into Lord Robert, but when Donald saw his uncle he sheered off, said something to Bridget, and then went out by the front entrance. One more picture remained.

Bunchy Gospell speaking to Dimitri at the foot of the stairs. This was the last thing Sir Daniel saw before he, too, went out into the fog.

He supposed that those moments in the hall would be regarded by the police as highly significant. The papers said that the police wished to establish the identity of the second fare. Naturally, since he was obviously the murderer! The taxi-driver had described him as a well-dressed gentleman who, with Lord Robert, had entered the cab about two hundred yards up the street from Marsdon House. 'Was it one of the guests?' asked the paper. That meant the police would get statements from everyone who left the house about the same time as Lord Robert. The last thing in the world that Sir Daniel wanted was to appear as a principal witness at the inquest. That sort of publicity did a fashionable physician no good. His name in block capitals, as likely as not, across the front sheets of the penny press and before you knew where you were some fool would say: 'Davidson? Wasn't he mixed up in that murder case?' He might even have to say he saw the Halcut-Hackett woman go out, with Withers in hot pursuit. Mrs Halcut-Hackett was one of his most lucrative patients. On the other hand, he would look extremely undignified if they found out that he was one of the last to leave and had not come forward to say so. It might even look suspicious. Sir Daniel swore picturesquely in French, reached for his telephone and dialled WHI1212.

VI

MYSTERY IN MAYFAIR
Lord Robert Gospell suffocated in Taxi
Who was the second fare?

Colombo Dimitri in his smart flat in the Cromwell Road drew the attention of his confidential servant to the headlines.

'What a tragedy,' he said. 'It may be bad for us at the beginning of the season. Nobody feels very gay after a murder. He was so popular, too. It is most unfortunate.'

'Yes, monsieur,' said the confidential servant.

'I must have been almost the last person to speak with him,' continued Dimitri, 'unless, of course, this dastardly assassin addressed him. Lord Robert came to me in the hall and asked me if I had seen Mrs Halcut-Hackett. I told him I had just seen her go away. He thanked me and left. I, of course, remained in the hall. Several of the guests spoke to me after that, I recollect. And then, an hour later, when I had left, but my men were still busy, the police rang up. He was a charming personality. I am very, very sorry.'

'Yes, monsieur.'

'It would be a pleasant gesture for us to send flowers. Remind me of it. In the meantime, if you please, no gossip. I must instruct the staff on this point. I absolutely insist upon it. The affair must not be discussed.'

'*C'est entendu, monsieur.*'

'In respect of malicious tittle-tattle,' said Dimitri virtuously, 'our firm is in the well-known position of Caesar's wife.' He glanced at his servant's face. It wore a puzzled expression. 'She did not appear in gossip columns,' explained Dimitri.

VII

MYSTERY OF UNKNOWN FARE
'Bunchy' Gospell dead
Who was the Man in Dress Clothes?

Miss Harris finished her cup of tea but her bread and butter remained untasted on her plate. She told herself she did not fancy it. Miss Harris was gravely upset. She had encountered a question to which she did not know the answer and she found herself unable to stuff it away in one of her pigeon-holes. The truth was Miss Harris's heart was touched. She had seen Lord Robert several times in Lady Carrados's house and last night Lord Robert had danced with her. When Lady Carrados asked Miss Harris if she would like to come to the ball she had never for a moment expected to dance at it. She had expected to spend a gratifying but exceedingly lonely night watching the fruits of her own labours. Her expectations had been realized until the moment when Lord Robert asked her to dance, and from then onwards Miss Harris had known a sort of respectable rapture. He had found her on the upper landing where she was sitting by herself outside the little green boudoir. She had just come out of the 'Ladies' and had had an embarrassing experience practically in the doorway. So she had sat on a chair on the landing to recover her poise and because there did not seem to be anywhere else much to go. Then she had pulled herself together and gone down to the ballroom. She was trying to look happy and not lost when Lord Robert came up and remembered his request that they should dance. And dance they did, round and round in the fast Viennese waltz, and Lord Robert had said he hadn't enjoyed himself so much for ages. They had joined a group of dizzily 'right' people and one of them, Miss Agatha Troy the famous painter it was, had talked to her as if they had been introduced. And then, when the band played another fast Viennese waltz because they were fashionable, Miss Harris and Lord Robert had danced again and had afterwards taken champagne at the buffet. That had been quite late – not long before the ball ended. How charming he had been, making her laugh a great deal and feel like a human young woman of thirty and not a dependent young lady of no age at all.

And now, here he was, murdered.

Miss Harris was so upset that she could not eat her breakfast. She glanced automatically at her watch. Twelve o'clock. She was to be at Lady Carrados's house by two in case she was needed. If she was quick she would have time to write an exciting letter home to the Buckinghamshire vicarage. The girl-friend with whom she shared the flatlet was still asleep. She was a night operator in a telephone exchange. But Miss Harris's bosom could contain this dreadful news no longer. She rose, opened the bedroom door and said:

'Smithy!'

'Uh!'

'Smithy, something awful has happened. Listen!'

'Uh?'

'The girl has just brought in a paper. It's about Lord Gospell. I mean Lord Robert Gospell. You know. I told you about him last night – '

'For God's sake!' said Miss Smith. 'Did you have to wake me up again to hear all about your social successes?'

'No, but Smithy, *listen!* It's simply frightful! He's murdered.'

Miss Smith sat up in bed looking like a sort of fabulous goddess in her mass of tin curling-pins.

'My dear, he isn't,' said Miss Smith.

'My dear, he is!' said Miss Harris.

CHAPTER 8

Troy and Alleyn

When Alleyn had finished his examination of the study he sat at Lord Robert's desk and telephoned to Marsdon House. He was answered by one of his own men.

'Is Mr Fox there, Bailey?'

'Yes, sir. He's upstairs. I'll just tell him.'

Alleyn waited. Before him on the desk was a small, fat notebook and upon the opened page he read again in Lord Robert's finicky writing the notes he had made on his case:

'*Saturday, May 8th.* Cocktail-party at Mrs H-H's house in Halkin Street. Arrived 6.15. Mrs H-H *distraite*. Arranged to meet her June 3rd, Constance Street Hall. Saw Maurice Withers, ref. drug affair 1924. Bad lot. Seems thick with Mrs H-H. Shied off me. *Mem.* Tell Alleyn about W's gambling hell at L.

'*Thursday, June 3rd.* Constance Street Hall. Recital by Sirmione Quartette. Arrived 2.15. Met Mrs H-H 2.30. Mrs H-H sat on left-hand end of blue sofa (occupant's left). Sofa about 7 feet inside main entrance and 8 feet to right as you enter. Sofa placed at right angles to right-hand corner of room. Side entrance on right-hand wall about ten feet behind sofa. My position in chair behind left arm of sofa. At 3.35 immediately after interval observed Mrs H-H's bag taken from left end of sofa where previously I watched her place it. She had left the room during interval and returned after bag had gone. Will swear that hand taking the bag was that of Dimitri of Shepherd

Market Catering Company. Saw him there. Seat nearby. Little finger same length as next and markedly crooked. Withers was there. *N.B.* Think Mrs H-H suspects me of blackmail. R.G.'

Fox's voice came through the receiver. 'Hullo, sir?'

'Hullo, Fox. Have you seen the room where he telephoned to me?'

'Yes. It's a room on the top landing. One of Dimitri's waiters saw him go in. The room hasn't been touched.'

'Right. Anything else?'

'Nothing much. The house is pretty well as it was when the guests left. You saw to that, sir.'

'Is Dimitri there?'

'No.'

'Get him, Fox. I'll see him at the Yard at twelve o'clock. That'll do him for the moment. Tell Bailey to go all over the telephone room for prints. We've got to find out who interrupted that call to the Yard. And, Fox – '

'Sir?'

'Can you come round here? I'd like a word with you.'

'I'll be there.'

'Thank you,' said Alleyn, and hung up the receiver.

He looked again at the document he had found in the central drawer of Lord Robert's desk. It was his will. A very simple little will. After one or two legacies he left all his possessions and the life interest on £40,000 to his sister, Lady Mildred Potter, to revert to her son on her death and the remainder of his estate, £20,000, to that same son, his nephew, Donald Potter. The will was dated January 1st of that year.

'His good deed for the New Year,' thought Alleyn.

He looked at the two photographs in leather frames that stood on Lord Robert's desk. One was of Lady Mildred Potter in the presentation dress of her girlhood. Mildred had been rather pretty in those days. The other was of a young man of about twenty. Alleyn noted the short Gospell nose and wide-set eyes. The mouth was pleasant and weak, the chin one of those jutting affairs that look determined and are too often merely obstinate. It was rather an attractive face. Donald had written his name across the corner with the date, January 1st.

'I hope to God,' thought Alleyn, 'that he can give a good account of himself.'

'Good morning,' said a voice from the doorway.

He swung round in his chair and saw Agatha Troy. She was dressed in green and had a little velvet cap on her dark head and green gloves on her hands.

'Troy!'

'I came in to see if there was anything I could do for Mildred.'

'You didn't know I was here?'

'Not till she told me. She asked me to see if you had everything you wanted.'

'Everything I wanted,' repeated Alleyn.

'If you have,' said Troy, 'that's all right. I won't interrupt.'

'Please,' said Alleyn, 'could you *not* go just for a second?'

'What is it?'

'Nothing. I mean, I've no excuse for asking you to stay, unless, if you will forgive me, the excuse of wanting to look at you and listen for a moment to your voice.' He held up his hand. 'No more than that. You liked Bunchy and so did I. He talked about you the last time I saw him.'

'A few hours ago,' said Troy. 'I was dancing with him.'

Alleyn moved to the tall windows . . . They looked out over the charming little garden to the Chelsea reaches of the Thames.

'A few hours ago' – he repeated her words slowly – ' the river was breathing mist. The air was threaded with mist and as cold as the grave. That was before dawn broke. It was beginning to get light when I saw him. And look at it now. Not a cloud. The damned river's positively sparkling in the sunlight. Come here, Troy.'

She stood beside him.

'Look down there into the street. Through the side window. At half-past three this morning the river mist lay like a pall along Cheyne Walk. If anybody was awake at that mongrel hour or abroad in the deserted streets they would have heard a taxi come along Cheyne Walk and stop outside this gate. If anybody in this house had had the curiosity to look out of one of the top windows they would have seen the door of the taxi open and a quaint figure in a cloak and wide-brimmed hat get out.'

'What do you mean? *He got out?* '

'The watcher would have seen this figure wave a gloved hand and heard him call to the driver in a shrill voice: "Sixty-three Jobbers Row, Queens Gate." He would have seen the taxi drive away into the mist – and then – what? What did the figure do? Did it run like a grotesque with flapping cloak towards the river to be swallowed up in vapour? Or did it walk off sedately into Chelsea? Did it wait for a moment, staring after the taxi? Did Bunchy's murderer pull off his cloak, fold it and walk away with it over his arm? Did he hide his own tall hat under the cloak before he got out of the taxi, and afterwards change back into it? And where are Bunchy's cloak and hat, Troy? Where are they?'

'What did the taxi-driver say?' asked Troy. 'There's nothing coherent in the papers. I don't understand.'

'I'll tell you. Fox will be here soon. Before he comes I can allow myself a few minutes to unload my mind, if you'll let me. I've done that before – once – haven't I?'

'Yes,' murmured Troy. 'Once.'

'There is nobody in the world who can listen as you can. I wish I had something better to tell you. Well, here it is. The taxi-driver brought Bunchy to the Yard at four o'clock this morning, saying he was murdered. This was his story. He picked Bunchy up at three-thirty some two hundred yards from the doors of Marsdon House. There was a shortage of taxis and we suppose Bunchy had walked so far, hoping to pick one up in a side street, when this fellow came along. The unnatural mist that hung over London last night was thick in Belgrave Square. As the taximan drove towards Bunchy he saw another figure in an overcoat and top-hat loom through the mist and stand beside him. They appeared to speak together. Bunchy held up his stick. The cabby knew him by sight and addressed him:

' "'Morning, m'lord. Two hundred Cheyne Walk?"

' "Please," said Bunchy.

'The two men got into the taxi. The cabby never had a clear view of the second man. He had his back turned as the taxi approached and when it stopped he stood towards the rear in shadow. Before the door was slammed the cabby heard Bunchy say: "You can take him on." The cabby drove to Cheyne Walk by way of Chesham Place, Cliveden Place, Lower Sloane Street and Chelsea Hospital and across Tite Street. He says it took about twelve minutes. He stopped here at Bunchy's gate and in a few moments Lord Robert, as he supposed him to be, got out and slammed the door. A voice squeaked through a muffler: "Sixty-three Jobbers Row, Queens Gate," and the cabby drove away. He arrived at Jobbers Row ten minutes later, waited for his fare to get out and at last got out himself and opened the door. He found Bunchy.'

Alleyn waited for a moment, looked gravely at Troy's white face. She said:

'There was no doubt – '

'None. The cabby is an obstinate, opinionated, cantankerous old oddity, but he's no fool. He satisfied himself. He explained that he once drove an ambulance and knew certain things. He headed as far as he could for the Yard. A sergeant saw him; saw everything; made sure it was – what it was, and got me. I made sure, too.'

'What had been done to Bunchy?'

'You want to know? Yes, of course you do. You're too intelligent to nurse your sensibilities.'

'Mildred will ask me about it. What happened?'

'We think he was struck on the temple, stunned and then suffocated,' said Alleyn, without emphasis. 'We shall know more when the doctors have finished.'

'Struck?'

'Yes. With something that had a pretty sharp edge. About as sharp as the back of a thick knife-blade.'

'Did he suffer?'

'Not very much. Hardly at all. He wouldn't know what happened.'

'His heart was weak,' said Troy suddenly.

'His heart? Are you sure of that?'

'Mildred told me the other day. She tried to persuade him to see a specialist.'

'I wonder,' said Alleyn, 'if that made it easier – for both of them.' Troy said:

'I haven't seen you look like that before.'

'What do you mean, Troy?'

He turned to her a face so suddenly translated into gentleness that she could not answer him.

'I – it's gone now.'

'When I look at you I suppose all other expression is lost in an effect of general besottedness.'

'How can I answer that?' said Troy.

'Don't. I'm sorry. What *did* you mean?'

'You looked savage.'

'I feel it when I think of Bunchy.'

'I can understand that.'

The hunt is up,' said Alleyn. 'Have you ever read in the crime books about the relentless detective who swears he'll get his man if it takes him the rest of his life? That's me, Troy, and I always thought it rather a bogus idea. It is bogus in a way, too. The real heroes of criminal investigation are Detective-Constables X, Y and Z – the men in the ranks who follow up all the dreary threads of routine without any personal feeling or interest, who swear no full round oaths, but who, nevertheless, *do* get their men in the end; and with a bit of luck and the infinite capacity for taking pains. Detective-Constables X, Y and Z are going to be kept damned busy until this gentleman is laid by the heels. I can promise them that.'

'I don't feel like that,' said Troy. 'I mean, I don't feel anything in particular about this murderer except that I think he must be mad. I know he should be found but I can't feel savage about him. It's simply Bunchy who did no harm in this world; no harm at all, lying dead and lonely. I must go now, and see what I can do for Mildred. Has Donald come in?'

'Not yet. Do you know where he is staying?'

'He wouldn't tell Mildred because he thought she would tell Bunchy, and he wanted to be independent. She's got the telephone number. I've seen it written on the memorandum in her room. I suppose you heard about the difference?'

'Yes, from Mildred. It was his debts, wasn't it?'

'Yes. Mildred has always spoilt Donald. He's not a bad child really. He will be terribly upset.'

Alleyn looked at the photograph.

'Did you see him at the dance?'

'Yes. He danced a lot with Bridgie O'Brien.'

'Did he stay until the end, do you know?'

'I didn't stay till the end myself. Mildred and I left at half-past one. She dropped me at my club. Bunchy – Bunchy – was seeing us home, but he came and asked us if we'd mind going without him. He said he was feeling gay.'

'Did you see much of him, please?'

'I danced three times with him. He *was* very gay.'

'Troy, did you notice anything? Anything at all?'

'What sort of things?'

'Did there seem to be any hint of something behind his gaiety? As if, do you know, he was thinking in the back of his head?'

Troy sat on the edge of the desk and pulled off her cap. The morning sun came through the window and dappled her short dark hair with blue lights. It caught the fine angle of her jaw and her cheek-bone. It shone into her eyes, making her screw them up as she did when she painted. She drew off her green gloves and Alleyn watched her thin intelligent hands slide out of their sheaths and lie delicately in the fur of her green jacket. He wondered if he would ever recover from the love of her.

He said: 'Tell me everything that happened last night while you were with Bunchy. Look back into your memory before it loses its edge and see if there is anything there that seemed a little out of the ordinary. Anything, no matter how insignificant.'

'I'll try,' said Troy. 'There was nothing when we danced except – yes. We collided once with another couple. It was a Mrs Halcut-Hackett. Do you know her?'

'Yes. Well?'

'It's a tiny thing, but you say that doesn't matter. She was dancing with a tall coarse-looking man. Bunchy apologized before he saw who they were. He danced very bouncily, you know, and always apologized when there were collisions. Then we swung round and he saw them. I felt his hand tighten suddenly and I looked over his shoulder at them. The man's red face had gone quite pale and Mrs Halcut-Hackett looked very odd. Frightened. I asked Bunchy who the man was and he said: "Feller called Withers," in a queer frozen little voice. I said: "Don't you like him?" and he said: "Not much, m'dear," and then began to talk about something else.'

'Yes,' said Alleyn. 'That's interesting. Anything more?'

'Later on, Bunchy and I went to chaperones' corner. You know, the end of the ballroom where they all sit. Your mother was there. Mrs Halcut-Hackett came up with her husband and then the girl she's bringing out arrived with that old ass Carrados. The girl had toothache, she said, but I'm afraid the wretched child was really not

having a great success. There's something so blasted cruel and barbaric about this season game,' said Troy vigorously.

'I know.'

'Your mother noticed it. We said something to each other. Well,
General Halcut-Hackett said he'd take the girl home and Bunchy
offered to take Mrs Halcut-Hackett home later on. The General
thanked him but *she* looked extraordinarily put out and seemed to
me to avoid answering. I got the impression that she hated the idea.
There was one other thing just about then. Wait a second! Bunchy
started a conversation about punctuality with old Lucy Lorrimer.
You know?'

'Lord, yes. She's a friend of my mama's. Dotty.'

'That's her. She twitted Bunchy about being late or something
and Mrs Halcut-Hackett suddenly said in a loud, high voice that she
knew all about Bunchy's punctual habits and could vouch for them.
It sounds nothing, but for some extraordinary reason it made everybody feel uncomfortable.'

'Can you remember exactly what she said?'

Troy ran her fingers through her hair and scowled thoughtfully.

'No, not exactly. It was just that she knew he always kept
appointments. Your mother might remember. I went away to dance
soon after that. Evelyn Carrados was there but – '

'But what?'

'You'll think I'm inventing vague mysteries but I thought she
seemed very upset, too. Nothing to do with Bunchy. She looked ill.
I heard someone say afterwards that she nearly fainted in the supper-room. She looked rather as if she might when I saw her. I
noticed her hands were tense. I've often thought I'd like to paint
Evelyn's hands. They're beautiful. I watched them last night. She
kept clutching a great fat bag in her lap. Bunchy sat between her and
your mother and he gave each of them a little pat – you know
Bunchy's way. His hand touched Evelyn's bag and she started as if
he'd hurt her and her fingers tightened. I can see them now, white,
with highlights on the knuckles, dug into the gold stuff of the bag. I
thought again I'd like to paint them and call the thing: "Hands of a
frightened woman." And then later on – but look here,' said Troy,
'I'm simply maundering.'

'God bless your good painter's eyes, you're not. Go on.'

'Well, some time after supper when I'd danced again with Bunchy, I sat out with him in the ballroom. We were talking away and he was telling me one of his little stories, a ridiculous one about Lucy Lorrimer sending a wreath to a wedding and a toasting-fork to a funeral, when he suddenly stopped dead and stared over my shoulder. I turned and saw he was looking at Evelyn Carrados. There was nothing much to stare at. She still looked shaken, but that was all. Dimitri, the catering man you know, was giving her back that bag. I suppose she'd left it somewhere. What's the matter?'

Alleyn had made a little exclamation.

He said: 'That great fat bag you had noticed earlier in the evening?'

'Yes. But it wasn't so fat this time,' said Troy quickly. 'Now I think of it, it was quite limp and flat. You see, I was looking at her hands again. I remember thinking subconsciously that it seemed such a large bag for a ball-dress. Mildred came up and we left soon after that. I'm afraid that's all.'

'Afraid? Troy, you don't know what an important person you are.'

'Don't I?'

She looked at him with an air of bewildered friendliness and at once his whole face was lit by his fierce awareness of her. Troy's eyes suddenly filled with tears. She reached out her hand and touched him.

'I'll go,' she said. 'I'm so sorry.'

Alleyn drew back. He struck one hand against the palm of the other and said violently:

'For God's sake, don't be kind! What is this intolerable love that forces me to do the very things I wish with all my soul to avoid? Yes, Troy, please go now.'

Troy went without another word.

CHAPTER 9

Report from Mr Fox

Alleyn walked about the room swearing under his breath. He was found at this employment by Detective-Inspector Fox, who arrived looking solid and respectable. 'Good morning, sir,' said Fox.

'Hullo, Fox. Sit down. I've found the will. Everything goes to his sister and her son. The boy's in debt and has quarrelled with his uncle. He's living away from home but will be in any moment. I've found Lord Robert's notes on the blackmail case. He told me when he rang up at one o'clock this morning that he'd call here first to get out of his boiled shirt and collect the notes. There they are. Look at 'em.'

Fox put on his spectacles and took the little notebook in his enormous fist. He read solemnly with his head thrown back a little and his eyebrows raised.

'Yes,' he said when he had finished. 'Well now, Mr Alleyn, that's quite an interesting little bit of evidence, isn't it? It puts this Mr Dimitri in what you might call a very unfavourable light. We can get him for blackmail on this information if the lady doesn't let us down. This Mrs Halcut-Hackett, I mean.'

'You notice Lord Robert thought she suspected him himself of taking the bag at the concert.'

'Yes. That's awkward. You might say it gives her a motive for the murder.'

'If you can conceive of Mrs Halcut-Hackett, who is what the drapers call a queenly woman, dressing up as a man during the ball, accosting Lord Robert in the street, getting him to give her a lift, knocking him out, smothering him, and striding home in the light of dawn in somebody's trousers.'

That's right,' said Fox. 'I can't. She might have an accomplice.'

'So she might.'

'Still, I must say Dimitri looks likelier,' Fox plodded on thoughtfully. 'If he found out Lord Robert had a line on him. But how would he find out?'

'See here,' said Alleyn. 'I want you to listen while I go over that telephone call. I was working late at the Yard on the Temple case. I would have gone north today, as you know, if this hadn't happened. At one o'clock Lord Robert rang me up from a room at Marsdon House. He told me he had proof positive that Dimitri was our man. Then he said he'd come round to the Yard. And then – ' Alleyn shut his eyes and screwed his face sideways. 'I want to get his exact words,' he said. 'I'm my own witness here. Wait, now, wait. Yes. He said: "I'll come round to the Yard. Upon my soul, it's worse than murder. Might as well mix his damn brews with poison," and then, Fox, he added this phrase: "And he's working with – " He never finished it. He broke off and said: "Hallo, I didn't hear you come in." I asked if anyone was there and he said yes and pretended he'd rung up about lost property. He must have done that because he realized this new arrival had overheard him mention the Yard. See here, Fox, we've got to get the man or woman who overheard that call.'

'If it was Dimitri,' began Fox.

'Yes, I know. If it was Dimitri! And yet, somehow, he sounded as if he was speaking to a friend. "Hallo, I didn't hear you come in." Might well have been. But we've got to get at it, Fox.'

' "And he's working with – " ' quoted Fox. 'What do you reckon he was going to say? Name an accomplice?'

'No. He was too old a hand to use names on the telephone. It might have been "with somebody else", or it might have been "with devilish ingenuity". I wish to God we knew. And now what have you done?'

Fox unhooked his glasses.

'Following your instructions,' he said, 'I went to Marsdon House. I got there at eight o'clock. I found two of our chaps in charge, and got a report from them. They arrived there at four-twenty, a quarter of an hour after the taxi got to the Yard and five minutes after you rang up. Dimitri had left the house, but our chaps, having the office from you, sir, telephoned him at his flat to make sure he was there and sent a plain-clothes man round to watch it. He's being relieved at ten o'clock by that new chap, Carewe. I thought he might take it on. He's a bit too fanciful for my liking. Well, to go back to Marsdon House. They took statements from the men Dimitri had left to clear up the house, sent them away, and remained in charge until I got there at eight. We've located the room where Lord Robert rang you up. The telephone was left switched through there for the whole evening. We've sealed it up. I've got a guest list. Bit of luck, that. We found it in the buffet. Names and addresses all typed out, very methodical. It's a carbon copy. I suppose Lady Carrados's secretary must have done it. I found out from Dimitri's men some of the people who had left early. The men's cloakroom attendant was still there and could remember about twenty of them. He managed to recollect most of the men who were the last to go. I started off on them. Rang them up and asked if they noticed Lord Robert Gospell. Several of them remembered him standing in the hall at the very end. Most of the people left in parties and we were able to check up on these at once. We found that Dimitri was in the hall at this time. I called in at his flat just now before I came here. You'll notice he's a witness of some importance as well as, on the strength of what you've told me, a prime suspect. I've got a list, very likely incomplete, of the guests who left alone about the same time as Lord Robert. Here it is. A bit rough. I've put it together from notes on my way here.'

Fox took out a fat notebook, opened it and handed it to Alleyn, who read:

'*Mrs Halcut-Hackett*. Seen leaving alone by footman at door, Dimitri, and linkman, who offered to call a taxi for her. She refused and walked away, Lord Robert had not left. Dimitri says he thinks Lord Robert came downstairs about this time.

'*Captain Maurice Withers*. Seen leaving alone by Dimitri, footman and by several members of a party whom he passed on the steps outside the house. Refused a lift. Footman thinks Capt W left after Mrs H-H. Impression confirmed by Dimitri. Lord Robert at foot of stairs.

'*Mr Donald Potter*. Seen saying good-bye to Miss O'Brien by Dimitri and by two servants near door into buffet at foot of stairs. Dimitri noticed him meet Lord Robert, appear to avoid him, and go away hurriedly.

'*Sir Daniel Davidson*. Seen leaving alone immediately after this by Dimitri and two of the servants.

'*Miss Violet Harris*. Secretary to Lady Carrados, seen leaving alone by cloakroom attendant standing at door, to whom she said good night. Unnoticed by anyone else.

'*Mr Trelawney-Caper*. Young gentleman who had lost Mr Percy Percival. Asked repeatedly for him. Handed a ten-shilling note to footman who remembers him. Described by footman as being "nicely decorated but not drunk."

'*Lord Robert Gospell*. Both footmen and a linkman saw him go. One footman places his departure immediately after Sir Daniel Davidson's. The other says it was some minutes later. The cloakroom attendant says it was about two minutes after Miss Harris and five after Sir DD.'

Alleyn looked up.

'Where was Dimitri, then?' he asked. 'He seems to have faded out.'

'I asked him,' said Fox. 'He said he went into the buffet about the time Sir Daniel left and was kept there for some time. The buffet's at the foot of the stairs.'

'Any confirmation of that?'

'One of his men remembers him there but can't say exactly when or for how long. He was talking to Sir Herbert Carrados.'

'To Carrados? I see. How did Dimitri shape when you saw him?'

'Well,' said Fox slowly, 'he's a pretty cool customer, isn't he? Foreign, half-Italian, half-Greek, but that's hardly noticeable in his speech. He answered everything very smoothly and kept saying it was all very regrettable.'

'I trust he'll find it even more so,' said Alleyn and returned to the notebook.

'The rest,' said Fox, 'left after Lord Robert and as far as we can make out, some time after. There are only three names and I don't fancy they'll amount to much, but I thought we'd better have them.'

'When did the Carrados party go? Last of all, of course?'

'Yes. Sir Herbert and Lady Carrados were at the head of the stairs on the ballroom landing saying good-bye most of this time, but Sir Herbert must have come down to the buffet if it's right that Dimitri talked to him there. I've left Sir Herbert to you, Mr Alleyn. From what I hear of him he'll need handling.'

'Extraordinarily kind of you,' said Alleyn grimly. 'Is there any exit from the buffet other than the one into the hall?'

'Yes, there is. A door that gives on to the back stairs down to the basement.'

'So it's conceivable that Dimitri might have gone out into the street that way?'

'Yes,' agreed Fox. 'It's possible, all right. And come back.'

'He would have been away at least forty minutes,' said Alleyn, 'if he's our man. If, if, if! Would he be able to get hold of a topper? The murderer wore one. What would he say to Bunchy to persuade him to give him a lift? "I want to talk to you about blackmail?" Well – that might work.'

'For all we know,' said Fox, 'it may not have been any of the guests or Dimitri.'

'True enough. For all we know. All the same, Fox, it looks as if it was. It's not easy to fit an outsider into what facts we've got. Try. An unknown in full evening dress wearing an overcoat and a top-hat stands outside Marsdon House waiting for Lord Robert to come out and on the off-chance of getting a lift. He doesn't know when Lord Robert will leave, so he has to hang about for three hours. He doesn't know if he'll get a chance to speak to Lord Robert, whether Lord Robert will leave in a party or alone, in a private car or a taxi. He does-n't know a heavy mist is going to crawl over London at one o'clock.'

'He might have just happened to come up,' said Fox and added immediately: 'All right, all right, sir. I won't press it. We've got plenty to go on from inside and it's a bit far-fetched, I will allow.'

'The whole thing's too damn far-fetched, in my opinion,' said Alleyn. 'We're up against a murder that was very nearly unpremeditated.'

'How do you make that out?'

'Why, Fox, for the reasons we've just ticked off. Lord Robert's movements could not be anticipated. I have just learned that he had intended to leave much earlier with his sister, Lady Mildred Potter, and Miss Troy.'

'Miss Agatha Troy?'

'Yes, Fox.' Alleyn turned aside and looked out of the window. 'She's a friend of the family. I've spoken to her. She's here.'

'Fancy that, now,' said Fox comfortably.

'I think,' continued Alleyn after a pause, 'that when the murderer went out from the lighted house into that unwholesome air he perhaps knew that Bunchy – Lord Robert – was returning alone. He may have seen him alone in the hall. That's why your little list is important. If the man was Dimitri he went out with the deliberate intention of accomplishing his crime. If it was one of the guests he may have made up his mind only when he caught a glimpse of Bunchy standing alone in the mist, waiting for a taxi. He may have meant to threaten, or reason, or plead. He may have found Bunchy obdurate, and on an impulse killed him.'

'How do you reckon he brought it off? With what?'

'Back to the jurists' maxim,' said Alleyn with a slight smile: *'Quis, quid, ubi, quibus auxiliis, cur, quomodo, quando?'*

'I never can remember it that way,' said Fox, 'knowing no Latin. But I've got old Gross's rhyme all right:

'What was the crime, who did it, when was it done, and where?
How done, and with what motive, who in the deed did share?'

'Yes,' said Alleyn. 'We've got *quid, quomodo* and *ubi,* but we're not so sure of *quibus auxiliis.* Dr Curtis says the abrasion on the temple is two and a half inches long and one-twelfth of an inch across. The blow, he thinks, was not necessarily very heavy, but sharp and extremely accurate. What sort of implement does that suggest to you, Fox?'

'I've been thinking that – '

The desk telephone rang. Alleyn answered it.

'Hullo?'

'Mr Alleyn? The Yard here. Sir Daniel Davidson has rung up and says he may have something to tell you. He'll be in all day.'

'Where is he?'

'In his rooms, number fifty St. Luke's Chambers, Harley Street.'

'Say I'll call at two o'clock. Thank him.' Alleyn put the receiver down.

'Davidson,' he said, 'thinks he may have something to relate. I bet he had a heart-to-heart talk with himself before he decided to ring up.'

'Why?' asked Fox. 'Do you mean he feels shaky?'

'I mean he's a fashionable doctor and they don't care for the kind of publicity you get from criminal investigations. If he's a clever fellow, and I imagine he must be to have got where he is, he's realized he was one of the last people to see Lord Robert. He's decided to come to us before we go to him. According to your notes, Fox, Sir Daniel was the first of the last three people to leave before Lord Robert. The other two were a tight young gentleman and a female secretary. Sir Daniel would have seen Lord Robert was alone and about to leave. He could have waited outside in the mist and asked for a lift in the taxi as easily as anybody. I wonder if he realizes that.'

'No motive,' said Fox.

'None, I should imagine. I mustn't get fantastic, must I? Damn young Potter, why doesn't he come?'

'Have you finished here, sir?'

'Yes. I got here at five o'clock this morning, broke the news to Lady Mildred, and settled down to Lord Robert's dressing-room, bedroom and this study. There's nothing at all to be found except his notes and the will. From seven until ten I looked in their garden, the neighbouring gardens and up and down the Embankment for a cloak and a soft hat. With no success. I've got a squad of men at it now.'

'He may not have got rid of them.'

'No. He may have been afraid of leaving some trace of himself. If that's the case he'll want to destroy or lose them. It was low tide at three o'clock this morning. To drop them in the river he'd have to get to a bridge. What sort of house is Dimitri's?'

'It's a small two-roomed flat in the Cromwell Road. He keeps a servant. French, I should say.'

'We'll go round there at noon when he's due at the Yard, and see if we can find anything. You've seen the flat. Where's his telephone?'

'On the landing.'

'Right. You'd better ring from the nearest call-box as soon as I've gone in. Keep the servant on the telephone as long as possible. You can put a string of questions about the time Dimitri got in, ask for the names of some of the men, anything. I'll have a quick look round for a possible spot to hide a largish parcel. We must get the dust-bins watched, though he's not likely to risk that. Blast this nephew. Fox, go and do your stuff with the maids. Don't disturb Lady Mildred, but ask for Mr Donald's telephone number. It's written on a memorandum in her room, but they may have it, too.'

Fox went out and returned in a few minutes.

'Sloane 8405.'

Alleyn reached for the telephone and dialled a number. 'Chief Detective-Inspector Alleyn, Scotland Yard. I want you to trace Sloane 8405 at once, please. I'll hang on.'

He waited, staring absently at Fox, who was reading his own notes with an air of complacent detachment.

'What?' said Alleyn suddenly. 'Yes. Will you repeat that. Thank you very much. Good-bye.'

He put back the receiver.

'Mr Donald Potter's telephone number,' he said, 'is that of Captain Maurice Withers, one hundred and ten Grandison Mansions, Sling Street, Chelsea. Captain Maurice Withers, as you will have noticed, appears in Lord Robert's notes. He was at the cocktail-party at Mrs Halcut-Hackett's and "seemed thick with her". He was at the concert when Dimitri took her bag. Now look at this – '

Alleyn took a cheque book from a drawer in the desk and handed it to Fox.

'Look at the heel of the book. Turn up June 8th, last Saturday.'

Fox thumbed over the leaves of the heel until he found it.

'Fifty pounds. M Withers. (D) Shackleton House, Leatherhead.'

'That's the day of the cocktail-party at Mrs Halcut-Hackett's. This case is beginning to make a pattern.'

Fox, who had returned to Lord Robert's notes, asked:

'What's this he says about Captain Withers being mixed up in a drug affair in 1924?'

'It was rather in my salad days at the Yard, Fox, but I remember, and so will you. The Bouchier-Watson lot. They had their headquarters at

Marseilles and Port Said, but they operated all over, the shop. Heroin mostly. The FO took a hand. Bunchy was there in those days and helped us enormously. Captain Withers was undoubtedly up to his nasty neck in it, but we never quite got enough to pull him in. A very dubious person. And young Donald's flown to him for sanctuary. Besotted young ninny! Oh, blast! Fox, blast!'

'Do you know the young gentleman, sir?'

'What? Yes. Oh, yes, I know him vaguely. What's going to come of this? I'll have to probe. A filthy crime-dentist! And quite possibly I'll haul up young Potter wriggling like a nerve on the end of a wire. These people are supposed to be my friends! Fun, isn't it? All right, Fox, don't look perturbed. But if Donald Potter doesn't show up here before – '

The door was suddenly flung open and Donald walked into the room.

He took half a dozen steps, pulled up short, and glared at Alleyn and Fox. He looked awful. His eyes were bloodshot and his face pallid.

He said: 'Where's my mother?'

Alleyn said: 'Agatha Troy's looking after her. I want to speak to you.'

'I want to see my mother.'

'You'll have to wait,' said Alleyn.

CHAPTER 10

Donald

Donald Potter sat on a chair facing the window. Alleyn was at Lord Robert's desk. Fox sat in the window, his notebook on his knee, his pencil in his hand. Donald lit one cigarette from the butt of another. His fingers shook.

'Before we begin,' said Alleyn, 'I should like to make one point quite clear to you. Your uncle has been murdered. The circumstances under which he was murdered oblige us to go most thoroughly into the movements of every person who was near to him within an hour of his death. We shall also find it necessary to make exhaustive enquiries into his private affairs, his relationship with members of his own family, and his movements, conversation and interests during the last weeks or perhaps months of his life. Nothing will be sacred. You, of course, are most anxious that his murderer should be arrested?'

Alleyn paused. Donald wetted his lips and said:

'Naturally.'

'Naturally. You will therefore give us all the help you can at no matter what cost to yourself?'

'Of course.'

'You will understand, I am sure, that everything the police do is done with one purpose only. If some of our enquiries seem impertinent or irrelevant that cannot be helped. We must do our job.'

'Need we go into all this?' said Donald.

'I hope it has been quite unnecessary. When did you last speak to your uncle?'

'About ten days ago.'

'When did you leave this house?'

'On the same day,' said Donald breathlessly.

'You left as the result of a misunderstanding with your uncle?'

'Yes.'

'I'm afraid I shall have to ask you to tell me about it.'

'I – it's got nothing to do with this – this awful business. It's not too pleasant to remember. I'd rather not – '

'You see,' said Alleyn, 'there was some point in my solemn opening speech.' He got up and reached out a long hand, and touched Donald's shoulder. 'Come,' he said. 'I know it's not easy.'

'It wasn't that I didn't like him.'

'I can't believe anyone could dislike him. What was the trouble? Your debts?'

'Yes.'

'Then why did you quarrel?'

'He wanted me to go to Edinburgh to take my medical.'

'And you didn't want to go?'

'No.'

'Why?'

'I thought it would be so damned dull. I wanted to go to Thomas's. He had agreed to that.'

Alleyn returned to his seat at the desk. 'What made him change his mind?' he asked.

'This business about my debts.'

'Nothing else?'

Donald ground out his cigarette with a trembling hand and shook his head.

'Did he object to any of your friends, for instance?' Alleyn asked.

'I – well, he may have thought – I mean, it wasn't that.'

'Did he know you were acquainted with Captain Maurice Withers?'

Donald darted a glance of profound astonishment at Alleyn, opened his mouth, shut it again, and finally said:

'I think so.'

'Aren't you certain?'

'He knew I was friendly with Withers. Yes.'

'Did he object to this friendship?'

'He did say something, now I come to think about it.'

'It didn't leave any particular impression on you?'

'Oh, no,' said Donald.

Alleyn brought his hand down sharply on Lord Robert's cheque book.

'Then, I take it,' he said, 'you have forgotten a certain cheque for fifty pounds.'

Donald stared at the long thin hand lying across the blue cover. A dull flush mounted to the roots of his hair.

'No,' he said, 'I remember.'

'Did he pay this amount to Withers on your behalf?'

'Yes.'

'And yet it left no particular impression on you?'

'There were,' said Donald, 'so many debts.'

'Your uncle knew you were friendly with this man. He had certain information about him. I know that. I ask you whether, in fact, he did not object most strongly to your connection with Withers?'

'If you like to put it that way.'

'For God's sake,' said Alleyn, 'don't hedge with me. I want to give you every chance.'

'*You – don't – think – I*'

'You're his heir. You quarrelled with him. You've been in debt. You are sharing rooms with a man against whom he warned you. You're in no position to try and save your face over smaller matters. You want to spare your mother as much as possible, don't you? Of course you do, and so do I. I ask you most earnestly as a friend, which I should not do, to tell me the whole truth.'

'Very well,' said Donald.

'You're living in the same flat as Captain Withers. What have you been doing there?'

'I – we – I was waiting to see if I couldn't perhaps go to Thomas's, after all.'

'How could you afford to do that?'

'My mother would have helped me. I've got my prelim, and I thought if I read a bit and tried to earn a bit, later on I could start.'

'How did you propose to earn a bit?'

'Wits was helping me – Captain Withers, I mean. He's been perfectly splendid. I don't care what anybody says about him, he's not a crook.'

'What suggestions did he make?'

Donald fidgeted.

'Oh, nothing definite. We were going to talk it over.'

'I see. Is Captain Withers doing a job of work himself?'

'Well, not exactly. He's got a pretty decent income, but he's thinking of doing something one of these days. He hates being idle, really.'

'Will you tell me, please, why you were in debt to him for fifty pounds?'

'I – simply owed it to him.'

'Evidently. For what? Was it a bet?'

'Yes. Well, one or two side bets, actually.'

'On what – horses?'

'Yes,' said Donald quickly.

'Anything else?'

Silence.

'Anything else?'

'No. I mean . . . I can't remember exactly.'

'You must remember. Was it at poker? Cards of any sort?'

'Yes, poker.'

'There's something else,' said Alleyn. 'Donald, I can't exaggerate the harm you may do if you insist on hedging with us. Don't you see that with every fresh evasion you put your friend in an even more dubious light than the one in which he already appears? For God's sake think of your uncle's death and your mother's sensibilities and your own foolish skin. How else did you lose money to Captain Withers?'

Alleyn watched Donald raise his head, knit his brows, and put his fingers to his lips. His eyes were blank but they were fixed on Alleyn's and presently an expression of doubtful astonishment crept into them.

'I don't know what to do,' he said naïvely.

'You mean you owe something to Withers. You have made some promise, I suppose. Is that it?'

'Yes.'

'To me the young men of your generation are rather bewildering. You seem to be a great deal more knowing than we were and yet I swear I would never have been taken in by a flashy gentleman with persuasive manners and no occupation, unless running an illicit hole-and-corner casino may be called an occupation.'

'I never mentioned roulette,' said Donald in a hurry.

'It is indeed a shame to take your money,' rejoined Alleyn.

Fox gave a curious little cough and turned a page of his notebook.

Alleyn said: 'Has Captain Withers, by any chance, suggested that you should earn an honest penny by assisting him?'

'I can't answer any more questions about him,' said Donald in a high voice. He looked as if he would either fly into a violent rage or burst into tears.

'Very well,' said Alleyn. 'When did you hear of this tragedy?'

'This morning when the sporting edition came in.'

'About an hour and a half ago?'

'Yes.'

'How long does it take to get here from Captain Withers's flat? It's in Sling Street, Chelsea, isn't it? About five minutes' walk. Why were you so long coming here?'

'I wasn't dressed, and though you may not believe it, I got a shock when I heard of my uncle's death.'

'No doubt. So did your mother. I wonder she didn't ring you up.'

'The telephone's disconnected,' said Donald.

'Indeed? Why is that?'

'I forgot to pay the bloody bill. Wits left it to me. I rang her from a call-box.'

'I see. Fox, one of our men is out there. Ask him to go to one hundred and ten Grandison Mansions, Sling Street, and tell Captain Withers I shall call on him in a few minutes and will be obliged if he remains indoors.'

'Very good, Mr Alleyn,' said Fox, and went out.

'Now then,' Alleyn continued. 'I understand you were among the last to leave Marsdon House this morning. Correct?'

'Yes.'

'I want you to tell me exactly what happened just before you left. Come now, will you try to give me a clear account?'

Donald looked slightly more at his ease. Fox came back and resumed his seat.

'I'll try, certainly,' said Donald. 'Where do you want me to begin?'

'From the moment when you came into the hall to go out.'

'I was with Bridget O'Brien. I had the last dance with her and then we went into the buffet downstairs for soup.'

'Anybody else there?'

'Her stepfather. I said good night to him and then Bridgie and I went into the hall.'

'Who was in the hall?'

'I don't remember except – '

'Yes?'

'Uncle Bunch was there.'

'Did you speak to him?'

'No, I wish to God I had.'

'What was he doing?'

'He had his cloak on. You know that extraordinary garment he wears? I think I heard him asking people if they'd seen Mrs Halcut-Hackett.'

'Had you seen her?'

'Not for some time, I think.'

'So you remember nobody in the hall except your uncle and Miss O'Brien?'

That's right. I said good night to Bridgie and went away.'

'Alone?'

'Yes.'

'Captain Withers was not at the ball?'

'Yes, but he'd gone.'

'Why did you not go away together?'

'Wits was going on somewhere. He had a date.'

'Do you know where he went and with whom?'

'No.'

'When you left Marsdon House what did you do?'

'Some people waiting outside for a taxi asked me to go on with them to the Sauce Boat, but I didn't want to. To get rid of them I walked to the corner to look for a taxi.'

'Which corner?'

'First on the left as you come out of Marsdon House. Belgrave Road, I think it is.'

'Anyone see you?'

'I don't know. Shouldn't think so. There was a damned heavy mist lying like a blanket over everything.'

'We'll have to find your taxi.'

'But I didn't get a taxi.'

'What!'

Donald began to speak rapidly, his words tumbling over each other, as though he had suddenly opened all the doors of his thoughts.

'There wasn't a taxi at the corner, so I walked. I walked on and on through Eaton Square. It was late – after three o'clock. Lots of taxis passed me, of course, but they were all engaged. I was thinking about things. About Bridget. I meant to keep her out of this but I suppose you'll hear everything now. Everything will be dragged out and – and made to look awful. Bridgie, and – and Uncle Bunch – and taking my medical – and everything. I hardly noticed where I was going. It's queer walking through mist. Your footsteps sound odd. Everything seemed thin and simple. I can't describe it. I went on and on and presently there weren't any more taxis and I was in the Kings Road so I just walked home. Past the Chelsea Palace and then off to the right into Sling Street. That's all.'

'Did you meet anyone?'

'I suppose I must have met a few people. I didn't notice.'

'What time did you get home?'

'I didn't notice.'

Alleyn looked gravely at him.

'I want you, please, to try very hard to remember if you met any-body on that walk, particularly in the early stages, just after you left Marsdon House. I see no reason why I should not point out the importance of this. As far as we can make out your uncle left the house a few minutes after you did. He, too, walked a short way round the square. He hailed a taxi and was joined at the last minute by a man in evening dress who got into the taxi with him. It is the identity of this man that we are anxious to establish.'

'You can't think I would do it!' Donald said. 'You can't! You've been our friend. You can't treat me like this, as though I was just anybody under suspicion. You *know* us! Surely to God – ! '

Alleyn's voice cut coldly across his protestations.

'I am an investigating officer employed by the police. I must behave as if I had no friends while I am working on this case. If you think for a little you will see that this must be so. At the risk of sounding pompous I must go a bit further and tell you that if I found my friendship with your uncle, your mother, or yourself, was in any way influencing my conduct of this case I should be obliged to give up. Ask to be relieved of the job. Already I have spoken to you as a friend – I should not have done this. If you are innocent, you are in no danger unless you prevaricate or shift ground, particularly in matters relating to your acquaintance with Captain Withers.'

'You can't suspect Withers! Why should he want to kill Uncle Bunch? It's got nothing to do with him.'

'In that case he has nothing to fear.'

'On that account, of course, he hasn't. I mean – oh, hell!'

'Where were you when you lost this money to him?'

'In a private house.'

'Where was it?'

'Somewhere near Leatherhead. Shackleton House, I think it's called.'

'Was it his house?'

'Ask him. *Ask him*. Why do you badger me with all this! My God, isn't it enough that I should be faced with the other business! I can't stand any more. Let me out of this.'

'You may go, certainly. There will be a statement for you to sign later on.'

Donald got up and walked to the door. He turned and faced Alleyn.

'I'm as anxious as you,' he said, 'that the man should be caught. Naturally, I'm as anxious as anybody.'

'Good,' said Alleyn.

Donald's face was puckered into the sort of grimace a small boy makes when he is trying not to cry. For some reason this gave him a strong look of his uncle. Alleyn felt his heart turn over. He got up, crossed the room in six long strides, and took Donald roughly by the arm.

'There!' he said, 'if you're innocent you're safe. As for this other mess you've got yourself into, stick to the truth and we'll do what we can for you. Tell your mama the house is rid of us for the time being. Now, march!'

He turned Donald round, shoved him through the door, and slammed it behind him.

'Come on, Fox,' he said. 'Pack up those things – the will and the notes. Ring up the Yard and see if the postmortem report is through, tell them to look Withers up in the record, and if one of my men is free, send him straight off to Shackleton House, Leatherhead. He'd better take a search-warrant, but he's not to use it without ringing me up first. If the place is locked up he's to stay there and report to me by telephone. Tell him we want evidence of a gambling hell. Fix that while I see the men outside and then we'll be off.'

'To see Withers?'

'Yes. To see Captain Maurice Withers who, unless I'm much mistaken, has added a gambling hell to his list of iniquitous sources of livelihood. My God, Fox, as someone was out for blood, why the hell couldn't they widen their field to include Captain Maurice Withers? Come on.'

CHAPTER 11

Captain Withers at Home

The report on the post-mortem was ready. Fox took it down over the telephone and he and Alleyn discussed it on their way to Sling Street.

'Dr Curtis,' said Fox, 'says there's no doubt that he was suffocated. They've found' – and here Fox consulted his book – 'Tardieu's ecchymosis on the congested lungs and on the heart. There were signs of fatty degeneration in the heart. The blood was dark-coloured and very liquid – '

'All right,' said Alleyn violently. 'Never mind that. Sorry, Fox. On you go.'

'Well, sir, they seem to think that the condition of the heart would make everything much more rapid. That's what you might call a merciful thing, isn't it?'

'Yes.'

'Yes. Barring the scar on the temple, Dr Curtis says there are no marks on the face. The mucous membrane in the fore-part of the palate is slightly congested. Posteriorly it is rather bleached. But there are no marks of violence.'

'I noticed that. There was no struggle. He was unconscious after the blow on the temple,' said Alleyn.

'That's what Dr Curtis thinks.'

'This murderer knew what he was about,' said Alleyn. 'Usually your asphyxiating homicide merchant goes in for a lot of unnecessary violence. You get marks round the mouth. Has Curtis any idea what was used?'

'He says possibly a plug of soft material introduced into the mouth and held over the nostrils.'

'Yes. Not Bunchy's handkerchief. That was quite uncreased.'

'Perhaps his own handkerchief.'

'I don't think so, Fox. I found a trace of fine black woollen fluff in the mouth.'

'The cloak?'

'Looks like it. It might be. One of the reasons why the cloak was got out of the way. By the way, Fox, did you get a report from that PC in Belgrave Square last night?'

'Yes. Nothing suspicious.'

They plodded on, working out lines to take in the endless interviews. They correlated, sorted and discussed each fragment of information. 'Finding the pattern of the case,' Alleyn called it. A five minutes' walk brought them to Sling Street and to a large block of rather pretentious service flats. They took the lift up to 110 and rang the bell.

'I'm going to take some risks here,' said Alleyn.

The door was opened by Captain Withers himself.

He said: 'Good morning. Want to see me?'

'Good morning, sir,' said Alleyn. 'Yes. You had our message just now, I hope. May we come in?'

'Certainly,' said Withers and walked away from the door with his hands in his pockets.

Alleyn and Fox went in. They found themselves in a mass-production furnished sitting-room with a divan bed against one wall, three uniform armchairs, a desk, a table and built-in cupboards. It had started off by being an almost exact replica of all the other 'bachelor flats' in Grandison Mansions, but since it is impossible to live in any place without leaving some print of yourself upon it, this room bore the impress of Captain Maurice Withers. It smelt of hairwash, cigars and whisky. On one wall hung a framed photograph of the sort advertised in magazines as 'artistic studio studies from the nude'. On the bookshelves guides to the Turf stood between shabby copies of novels Captain Withers had bought on the Riviera and, for some reason, troubled to smuggle into England. On a table by the divan bed were three or four medical text-books. 'Donald Potter's,' thought Alleyn. Through a half-open door Alleyn caught a glimpse of a small bedroom and a second masterpiece that may have been a studio study but appeared to be an exercise in pornographic photography.

Captain Withers caught Fox's bland gaze directed at this picture and shut the bedroom door.

'Have a drink?' he said.

'No, thank you,' said Alleyn.

'Well, sit down then.'

Alleyn and Fox sat down, Fox with extreme propriety, Alleyn with an air of leisurely fastidiousness. He crossed one long leg over the other, hung his hat on his knee, pulled off his gloves, and contemplated Captain Withers. They made a curious contrast. Withers was the sort of man who breathes vulgarity into good clothes. His neck was too thick, his fingers too flat and pale and his hair shone too much; his eyes were baggy and his eyelashes were white. Yet in spite of these defects he was a powerful dominant animal with a certain coarse arrogance that was effective. Alleyn, by contrast, looked fine-drawn, a cross between a monk and a grandee. The planes of Alleyn's face and head were emphatically defined, the bony structure showed clearly. There was a certain austerity in the chilly blue of his eyes and in the sharp blackness of his hair. Albrecht Dürer would have made a magnificent drawing of him, and Agatha Troy's sketch portrait of Alleyn is one of the best things she has ever done.

Withers lit a cigarette, blew the smoke down his nose and said:

'What's it all about?'

Fox produced his official notebook. Captain Withers eyed the letters MP on the cover and then looked at the carpet.

'First, if I may,' said Alleyn, 'I should like your full name and address.'

'Maurice Withers and this address.'

'May we have the address of your Leatherhead house as well, please?'

'What the hell d'you mean?' asked Withers quite pleasantly. He looked quickly at the table by the divan and then full in Alleyn's face.

'My information,' lied Alleyn, 'does not come from the source you suppose, Captain Withers. The address, please.'

'If you mean Shackleton House, it is not mine. It was lent to me.'

'By whom?'

'For personal reasons, I'm afraid I can't tell you that.'

'I see. Do you use it much?'

'Borrow it for weekends sometimes.'

'Thank you,' said Alleyn, 'Now, if you please, I want to ask you one or two questions about this morning. The early hours of this morning.'

'Oh, yes,' said Withers, 'I suppose you're thinking of the murder.'

'Whose murder?'

'Why, Bunchy Gospell's.'

'Was Lord Robert Gospell a personal friend of yours, Captain Withers?'

'I didn't know him.'

'I see. Why do you think he was murdered?'

'Well, wasn't he?'

'I think so. Evidently you think so. Why?'

'Judging from the papers it looks like it.'

'Yes, doesn't it?' said Alleyn. 'Won't you sit down, Captain Withers?'

'No, thanks. What about this morning?'

'When did you leave Marsdon House?'

'After the ball was over.'

'Did you leave alone?'

Withers threw his cigarette with great accuracy into a tin waste-paper bin.

'Yes,' he said.

'Can you remember who was in the hall when you went away?'

'What? I don't know that I can. Oh, yes. I bumped into Dan Davidson. You know. The fashionable quack.'

'Is Sir Daniel Davidson a friend of yours?'

'Not really. I just know him.'

'Did you notice Lord Robert in the hall as you left?'

'Can't say I did.'

'You went out alone. Did you take a taxi?'

'No. I had my own car. It was parked in Belgrave Road.'

'So you turned to the left when you went away from Marsdon House. That,' said Alleyn, 'is what the murderer, if there is, as you say, a murderer, must have done.'

'Better choose your words a bit more carefully, hadn't you?' enquired Captain Withers.

'I don't think so. As far as I can see my remark was well within the rules. Did you see any solitary man in evening dress as you walked from Marsdon House to Belgrave Road? Did you overtake or pass any such person?'

Withers sat on the edge of the table and swung his foot. The fat on his thighs bulged through his plaid trouser leg.

'I might have. I don't remember. It was misty.'

'Where did you go in your car?'

'To the Matador.'

'The night club in Sampler Street?'

'That's right.'

'Did you meet anybody there?'

'About a hundred and fifty people.'

'I mean,' said Alleyn with perfect courtesy, 'did you meet a partner there by arrangement?'

'Yes.'

'May I have her name?'

'No.'

'I shall have to find out by the usual routine,' murmured Alleyn. 'Make a note of it will you, Fox?'

'Very good, Mr Alleyn,' said Fox.

'You can produce no witness to support your statement that you drove to the Matador from Marsdon House?'

The swinging foot was suddenly motionless. Withers waited a moment and then said: 'No.'

'Perhaps your partner was waiting in your car, Captain Withers. Are you sure you did not drive her there? Remember there is a commissionaire at the Matador.'

'Is there?'

'Well?'

'All right,' said Withers. 'I did drive my partner to the Matador but I shan't give you her name.'

'Why not?'

'You seem to be a gentleman. One of the new breed at the Yard, aren't you? I should have thought you'd have understood.'

'You are very good,' said Alleyn, 'but I am afraid you are mistaken. We shall have to use other methods, but we shall find out the name of your partner. Have you ever studied wrestling, Captain Withers?'

'What? What the hell has that got to do with it?'

'I should be obliged if you would answer.'

'I've never taken it up. Seen a bit out East.'

'Ju-jitsu?'

'Yes.'

'Do they ever use the side of the hand to knock a man out? On one of the vulnerable points or whatever you call them? Such as the temple?'

'I've no idea.'

'Have you any medical knowledge?'

'No.'

'I see some text-books over there by the bed.'

'They don't belong to me.'

'To Mr Donald Potter?'

'That's right.'

'He is living here?'

'You've been talking to him, haven't you? You must be a bloody bad detective if you haven't nosed that out.'

'Do you consider that you have a strong influence over Mr Potter?'

'I'm not a bear leader!'

'You prefer fleecing lambs, perhaps?'

'Is that where we laugh?' asked Withers.

'Only, I am afraid, on the wrong side of our faces. Captain Withers, do you recollect the Bouchier-Watson drug-running affair of 1924?'

'No.'

'You are fortunate. We have longer memories at the Yard. I am reminded of it this morning by certain notes left in his private papers by Lord Robert Gospell. He mentions the case in connection with recent information he gleaned about an illicit gambling club at Leatherhead.'

The coarse white hands made a convulsive movement which was immediately checked. Alleyn rose to his feet.

'There is only one other point,' he said. 'I believe your telephone is disconnected. Inspector Fox will fix that. Fox, will you go out to the post office at the corner? Wait a second.'

Alleyn took out his notebook, scribbled: 'Get Thompson to tail W at once,' and showed it to Fox. 'Give that message, will you, and see that Captain Withers's telephone is reconnected immediately. As soon as it's through, ring me here. What's the number?'

'Sloane 8405,' said Withers.

'Right. I'll join you, Fox.'

'Very good, sir,' said Fox. 'Good morning, sir.'

Withers did not answer. Fox departed.

'When your telephone is working again,' Alleyn said, 'I would be glad if you'd ring up Mr Donald Potter to suggest that as his mother is in great distress, you think it would be well if he stayed with her for the time being. You will send his property to Cheyne Walk in a taxi.'

'Are you threatening me?'

'No. I am warning you. You are in rather uncertain country at the moment, you know.'

Alleyn walked over to the divan bed and looked at the books.

'Taylor's *Medical Jurisprudence*,' he murmured. 'Is Mr Potter thinking of becoming a medical jurist?'

'I haven't the slightest idea.'

Alleyn ruffled the pages of a large blue volume.

'Here we have the fullest information on asphyxia. Very interesting. May I borrow this book? I'll return it to Mr Potter.'

'I've no objection. Nothing to do with me.'

'Splendid. Have you any objection to my looking at your dress clothes?'

'None,' said Withers.

'Thank you so much. If you wouldn't mind showing them to me.'

Withers walked into the bedroom and Alleyn followed him. While Withers opened his wardrobe and pulled open drawers Alleyn had a quick look round the room. Apart from the photograph, which was frankly infamous, the only item of interest was a row of paperbound banned novels of peculiar indecency and no literary merit whatsoever.

Withers threw a tail coat, a white waistcoat and a pair of trousers on the bed. Alleyn examined them with great care, smelt the coat and turned out the pockets, which were empty.

'Had you a cigarette-case?' he asked.

'Yes.'

'May I see it?'

'It's in the next room.'

Withers went into the sitting-room. Alleyn, with a catlike swiftness, looked under the bed and in at a cupboard door.

Withers produced a small, flat silver case. 'Is this the only case you possess?'

'It is.'

Alleyn opened it. The inside lid was inscribed: 'Maurice from Estelle.' He returned it and took another from his pocket.

'Will you look at this case carefully, please, and tell me if you have seen it before?'

Withers took it. It was a thin, smooth, gold case, uninscribed, but with a small crest in one corner.

'Open it, will you, please?'

Withers opened it.

'Do you know it?'

'No.'

'You don't by any chance recognize the crest?'

'No.'

'It is not Mr Donald Potter's crest, for instance?'

Withers made a quick movement, opened his mouth, shut it again and said:

'It isn't his. I've seen his. It's on his links. They're here somewhere.'

'May I see them?' said Alleyn, taking the case.

Withers crossed to the dressing-table. Alleyn rapidly wrapped his silk handkerchief round the case and put it in his pocket.

'Here they are,' said Withers.

Alleyn solemnly inspected Donald's links and returned them.

The telephone rang in the next room.

'Will you answer it, please?' said Alleyn.

Withers went into the sitting-room. Alleyn whipped off the dust jacket from one of the banned novels and coolly slipped it in his overcoat pocket. He then followed Withers.

'It's for you,' Withers said, 'if you're Alleyn.'

'Thank you.'

It was Fox; to say in an extremely low voice that Thompson was well on his way.

'Splendid,' said Alleyn. 'Captain Withers wanted to use it at once.'

He hung up the receiver and turned to Withers.

'Now, please,' he said. 'Will you telephone Mr Potter? I'd be glad if you would not mention that it was my suggestion. It would come more gracefully from you.'

Withers dialled the number with as bad a grace as well might be. He got Donald, whose voice came over in an audible quack.

'Hullo.'

'Hullo, Don, it's Wits.'

'Oh, God, Wits, I'm most frightfully worried, I – '

'You'd better not talk about your worries on the telephone. I rang up to say I thought it might be as well if you stayed with your mother for a bit. She'll want you there with all this trouble. I'll send your things round.'

'Yes, but listen, Wits. About the house at – '

Captain Withers said: 'You stay where you are,' and rang off.

'Thank you,' said Alleyn. 'That will do nicely. How tall are you, Captain Withers?'

'Five foot eight and a half in my socks.'

'Just about Lord Robert's height,' said Alleyn, watching him.

Withers stared blankly at him.

'I suppose there must be some sense in a few of the things you say,' he said.

'I hope so. Can you remember what Lord Robert was saying on the telephone when you walked into the room at one o'clock this morning?'

'What room?'

'At Marsdon House.'

'You're talking through your hat. I never heard him on any telephone.'

'That's all right then,' said Alleyn. 'Were you on the top landing near the telephone-room round about one o'clock?'

'How the devil should I know? I was up there quite a bit.'

'Alone?'

'No. I was there with Don sometime during the supper dances. We were in the first sitting-out room. Old Carrados was up there then.'

'Did you hear anyone using a telephone?'

'Fancy I did, now you mention it.'

'Ah well, that's the best we can do at the moment, I suppose,' said Alleyn, collecting Taylor's *Medical Jurisprudence*. 'By the way, would you object to my searching these rooms? Just to clear your good name, you know.'

'You can crawl over them with a microscope, if you like.'

'I see. Thank you very much. Some other time, perhaps. Good morning.' He'd got as far as the door when Withers said: 'Here! Stop!'

'Yes?'

Alleyn turned and saw a flat white finger pointed at his face.

'If you think,' said Captain Withers, 'that I had anything to do with the death of this buffoon you're wasting your time. I didn't. I'm not a murderer and if I was I'd go for big game – not domestic pigs.'

Alleyn said: 'You are fortunate. In my job we often have to hunt the most unpleasant quarry. A matter of routine. Good morning.'

CHAPTER 12

Report from a Waiter

In the street outside Alleyn met Detective-Sergeant Thompson, who did not look like a detective-sergeant. As Captain Withers's windows enjoyed an uninterrupted view of Sling Street Alleyn did not pause to speak to Thompson, but he remarked to the air as they passed:

'Don't lose him.'

Fox was waiting outside the post office.

'He's a nasty customer, I should say,' he remarked as they fell into step.

'Who? Withers? I believe you, my old – '

'You were pretty well down on him, Mr Alleyn.'

'I was in a fix,' said Alleyn. 'I'd have liked to raid this place at Leatherhead without giving him any warning, but the wretched Donald is sure to let him know what he told us and Withers will close down his gambling activities. The best we can hope for in that direction is that our man will find something conclusive if he gets into the house. We'd better take a taxi to Dimitri's. What time was he to be at the Yard?'

'Midday.'

'It's a quarter to twelve. He ought to have left. Come on.'

They got a taxi.

'How about Withers?' asked Fox, staring solemnly at the driver's back.

'For a likely suspect? He's the right height to within an inch. Good enough in the cloak and hat to diddle the taxi-man. By the way, there's nowhere in the bedroom where he could have stowed them.

I saw inside the wardrobe and had a quick look under the bed and in the cupboard while he was on the telephone. Anyway, he said I could crawl over the flat with a microscope if I liked and he wasn't calling my bluff either. If he's got anything to hide it's at the house at Leatherhead.'

'The motive's not so hot,' said Fox.

'What is the motive?'

'He knew Lord Robert had recognized him and thought he was on his trail. He wants to get hold of the money and knows young Potter is the heir.'

'That's two of his motives. But well? Damn,' said Alleyn, 'nearly a quotation! Bunchy warned me against 'em. Associating with the peerage, that's what it is. There's a further complication. Mrs Halcut-Hackett may think Bunchy was a blackmailer. From his notes Bunchy seems to have got that impression. He was close to her when her bag was taken and had stuck to her persistently. If Withers is having an affair with the woman, she probably confided the blackmail stunt to him. Withers is possibly the subject of the Halcut-Hackett blackmail. The letter the blackmailer has got hold of may be one from Mrs H-H to Withers or t'other way round. If she told him she thought Lord Robert was the blackmailer – '

'That's three of his motives,' said Fox.

'You may say so. On the other hand Withers may be the blackmailer. It's quite in his line.'

'Best motive of all,' said Fox, 'if he thought Lord Robert was on to him.'

'How you do drone on, you old devil. Well, if we want to, we can pull him in for having dirty novels in his beastly flat. Look at this.'

Alleyn pulled the book jacket out of his pocket. It displayed in primary colours a picture of a terrible young woman with no clothes on, a florid gentleman and a lurking harridan. It was entitled: *The Confessions of a Procuress*.

'Lor'!' said Fox. 'You oughtn't to have taken it.'

'What a stickler you are to be sure.' Alleyn pulled a fastidious grimace. 'Can't you see him goggling over it in some bolt-hole on the Cote d'Azur! I've got his nasty flat prints on my own cigarette-case. We'll see if he's handled Donald Potter's "Taylor". Particularly the sections that deal with suffocation and asphyxia. I fancy, Fox, that a

Captain Withers who was uninstructed in the art of smothering would have made the customary mistake of using too much violence. We'll have to see if he's left any prints in this telephone room at Marsdon House.'

'The interruption,' said Fox thoughtfully. 'As I see it, we've got to get at the identity of the individual who came in while Lord Robert was talking to you on the telephone. If the party's innocent, well, there'll be no difficulty.'

'And contrariwise. I tried to bounce Withers into an admission. Took it for granted he was the man.'

'Any good?'

'Complete wash-out. He never batted an eyelid. Seemed genuinely astonished.'

'It may have been Dimitri. At least,' said Fox, 'we know Dimitri collects the boodle. What we want to find out is whether he's on his own or working for someone else.'

'Time enough. Which brings us back to Bunchy's broken sentence. "And he's working with – " With whom? Or is it with what? Hullo, one arrives.'

The taxi pulled up at a respectable old apartment house in the Cromwell Road. On the opposite pavement sat a young man mending the seat of a wicker chair.

'That's Master James D'Arcy Carewe, detective-constable,' said Alleyn.

'What him!' cried Fox in a scandalized voice. 'So it is. What's he want to go dolling himself up in that rig for?'

'He's being a detective,' Alleyn explained. 'His father's a parson and he learnt wicker-work with the Women's Institute or something. He's been pining to disguise himself ever since he took the oath.'

'Silly young chap,' said Fox.

'He's quite a bright boy really, you know.'

'Why's he still there, anyway?'

'Dimitri hasn't left yet, evidently. Wait a moment.'

Alleyn slid back the glass partition of the taxi and addressed the driver:

'We're police officers. In a minute or two a man will come out of this house and want a cab. Hang about for him. He will probably ask you to drive him to Scotland Yard. If he gives any other address I want you to write it quickly on this card while he is getting into the cab. Drop the card through the gear lever slit in the floor. Here's a pencil. Can you do this?'

'Right you are, governor,' said the taximan.

'I want you to turn your car and pass that fellow mending a chair seat. Go as slow as you can, drive two hundred yards up the road and let us out. Then wait for your man. Here's your fare and all the rest of it.'

'Thank you sir. OK, sir,' said the taximan.

He turned, Alleyn lowered the window and, as they passed the wicker expert, leant out and said:

'Carewe! Pick us up.'

The expert paid no attention.

'I told you he's not as silly as he looks,' said Alleyn. 'There we are.'

They got out. The taxi turned once more. They heard the driver's hoarse: 'Taxi, sir?' heard him pull up, heard the door slam, heard the cab drive away. 'He hasn't dropped his card,' said Alleyn staring after the taxi. They continued to walk up the Cromwell Road. Presently a cry broke out behind them.

Chairs to mend! Chairs to mend!'

'There!' said Fox in exasperation. 'Listen to him making an exhibition of himself! It's disgraceful. That's what it is. Disgraceful.'

They turned and found the wicker-worker hard at their heels, followed by long trails of withy.

'Sir!' said the wicker-worker in consternation.

'Tell me,' Alleyn went on, 'why are you presenting the Cries of London to an astonished world?'

'Well, sir,' said the chair-mender, 'following your instructions, I proceeded – '

'Quite. But you should understand by this time that the art of disguise is very often unnecessary and is to be attained by simpler means than those which embrace a great outlay in willow wands, envious slivers, and cabriole legs. What, may I ask, would you have done with all this gear when the hunt was up?'

'There's a taxi rank round the corner, sir. If I whistled – '

'And a pretty sight you'd have looked,' said Fox indignantly, 'whistling cabs in that rig-out. By the time you'd wound yourself in and out of that muck and got yourself aboard, your man would have been half-way to Lord knows where. If that's the sort of stuff they teach you at – '

'Yes, all right, Fox,' said Alleyn hastily. 'Very true. Now, look here, Carewe, you go away and undress and report to me at the Yard. You can go back by Underground. Don't look so miserable or the old ladies will start giving you coppers.'

Carewe departed.

'Now then, Fox,' Alleyn continued, 'give me a few minutes in that flat and then ring up as if from the Yard and keep Dimitri's servant on the telephone as long as possible. You'd better have a list of names and places. Say Dimitri has given them to you and say you will be able to confirm them. All right?'

'Right oh, Mr Alleyn.'

'You can use the call-box at the taxi rank. Then away with you to the Yard and keep Dimitri going until I come. Arrange to have him tailed when he leaves.'

Alleyn returned to Dimitri's flat which was on the ground floor. The door was opened by a thin dark man who exuded quintessence of waiter.

'Is Mr Dimitri in?' asked Alleyn.

'Monsieur has just left, sir. May I take a message?'

'He's gone, has he?' said Alleyn very pleasantly. 'What a bore, I've just missed him. Do you know if he was going to Scotland Yard?'

The man hesitated.

'I'm not sure, sir. I think – '

'Look here,' said Alleyn, 'I'm Chief Inspector Alleyn. Here's my card. I was in this part of the world and I thought I'd save Mr Dimitri the trouble of moving if I called. As I am here I may as well get you to clear up one or two points for me. Do you mind?'

'Please, sir! Not at all, but it is a little difficult – '

'It is rather, out here. May I come in?' asked Alleyn, and walked in without waiting for the answer.

He found himself in a sitting-room that had an air of wearing a touch of black satin at the neck and wrists but was otherwise unremarkable. The servant followed him and stood looking uneasi-ly at his own hands.

'You will have guessed,' Alleyn began, 'that I am here on business connected with the death of Lord Robert Gospell.'

'Yes, sir.'

'The first thing I have to say is that we would be glad if you'd use great discretion in discussing this affair. Indeed it would be better if you did not discuss it at all, with anybody. Except of course, Mr Dimitri himself.'

The man looked relieved.

'But it is understood perfectly, sir. Monsieur has already warned me of this himself. I shall be most discreet.'

'Splendid. We feel it our duty to protect Mr Dimitri and any other person of position from the unpleasant notoriety that unfortunately accompanies such accidents as these.'

'Yes, certainly, sir. Monsier himself was most emphatic.'

'I'm sure he was. You will understand,' Alleyn went on, 'that it is also necessary to have before us a clear account of the movements of many persons. What is your name?'

'François, sir, François Dupont.'

'Were you at Marsdon House last night?'

'Yes, sir. By an unusual chance I was there.'

'How did that happen?'

'An important member of our staff failed M. Dimitri yesterday afternoon. It seems that he was afflicted suddenly with appendicitis. M. Dimitri was unable to replace him satisfactorily at so short notice and I took his place.'

'This was unusual?'

'Yes, sir. I am M. Dimitri's personal servant.'

'Where were you stationed at Marsdon House?' A telephone rang in the entrance passage. 'Excuse me, sir,' said the servant. 'The tele-phone.'

'That's all right,' said Alleyn.

The man went out closing the door softly behind him.

Alleyn darted into an adjoining bedroom, leaving the door ajar. He opened built-in cupboards, ran his hands between hanging suits, amongst neatly stacked shirts and under-garments, disturbing nothing, exploring everywhere. Thanking his stars that the drawers ran easily he moved with economy, swiftness and extreme precision. The adjoining bedroom was innocently naked. Dimitri's servant looked after him well. There was no hiding-place anywhere for a bulky cloth cloak. Everything was decently ordered. Alleyn returned silently to the sitting-room. He could hear the servant's voice:

'Hullo? Hullo? Yes, sir. I am still here. Yes, sir, that is quite correct. It is as Monsieur Dimitri says, sir. We returned together at three-thirty in a taxi. At three-thirty. No, sir, no. At three-thirty. I am sorry, sir, I will repeat. At three-thirty we return – '

The sideboard contained only bottles and glasses, the bookcases only books. The desk was locked but it was a small one. Dimitri and his servant were tidy men with few possessions. Alleyn opened the last cupboard. It contained two suitcases. He tipped them gingerly. No sound of anything. He opened them. They were empty. Alleyn shut the cupboard door tenderly and returned to the middle of the sitting-room where he stood with his head slanted, listening to Dimitri's servant whose voice had risen to a painful falsetto.

'But I am telling you. Permit me to speak. Your colleague is here. He is about to ask me all these questions himself. He has given me his card. It is the Chief Inspector All-eyne. Ah, *mon Dieu! Mon Dieu!*'

Alleyn went into the passage. He found François with his shoulders up to his ears and his unoccupied hand sketching desperation to the air.

'What is it?' asked Alleyn. 'Is it for me?'

'Here is M. l'Inspecteur!' screamed François into the receiver. 'Will you have the goodness – '

Alleyn addressed the telephone.

'Hullo!'

'Hullo there!' Fox's voice in accents of exasperation.

'Is that you, Fox? What's the matter?'

'Nothing, I hope, Mr Alleyn,' said Fox, falling back on an indistinct mumble.

'It's Alleyn, here. There's been a slight misunderstanding. I have missed Mr Dimitri but will come along as soon as possible. Will you ask him to wait? Apologize for me.'

'I hope there *was* time. I'll get along to the Yard now.'

'Very well. That's perfectly all right,' said Alleyn and rang off.

He returned to the sitting-room followed by François.

'A slight misunderstanding,' explained Alleyn blandly. 'My colleague did not quite follow you. He is unfortunately rather deaf and is about to retire.'

François muttered.

'To resume,' said Alleyn. 'You were going to tell me where you were stationed last night.'

'By the top landing, sir. The gallery above the ballroom. My duties were to keep the ash-trays emptied and to attend to the wishes of the guests who sat out dances on this floor.'

'What are the rooms on this gallery?'

'At the stairhead, sir, one finds a green baize door leading to the servants' quarters, the back stairs and so on. Next to this door is a room which last night was employed as a sitting-room. One finds next a bathroom, bedroom and toilet used last night for ladies. Last at the end of the gallery, a green boudoir also used as a sitting-room for the ball.'

'Was there a telephone in any of these rooms?'

'In the green boudoir, sir. It was used several times during the evening.'

'You are an excellent witness, François. I compliment you. Now tell me. You were stationed on this landing. Do you remember the names of the persons who used the telephone?'

François pinched his lower lip.

'It was used by Lady Jennifer Trueman to enquire for her little girl who is ill. Her ladyship requested me to get the number for her. It was used by a young gentleman who called a toll number to say that he would not be returning to the country. Early in the evening it was answered by Sir Daniel Davidson, who, I think, is a doctor. He spoke about a patient who had had an operation. It was also used, sir, by Lord Robert Gospell.'

Alleyn waited a moment. With a sort of astonishment he realized his heart had quickened.

'Could you hear what Lord Robert said?'

'No, sir.'

'Did you notice if anyone went into the room while Lord Robert was at the telephone?'

'No, sir. Immediately after Lord Robert entered this room I was summoned by Sir Herbert Carrados who came out of the other sitting-room and spoke to me about the lack of matches. Sir Herbert was annoyed. He sent me into this room to see for myself and ordered me to go at once and fetch more matches. There did not appear to me to be any lack of matches but I did not, of course, say so. I fetched more matches from downstairs. When I returned I went to the telephone-room and found it empty. I attended to the ash-tray and the matches in the telephone-room, also.'

Alleyn sighed.

'Yes, I see. I've no doubt you made a good job of it. Any cigar-stumps in the telephone-room? You wouldn't remember, of course.'

'No, sir.'

'No. François – who was in the other sitting-room and who was on the landing before Lord Robert telephoned? Before Sir Herbert Carrados sent you away. Can you remember?'

'I will try, sir. There were two gentlemen who also sent me away.'

'What?'

'I mean, sir, that one of them asked me to fetch two whiskies-and-sodas. That is not at all a usual request under the circumstances. It is not even *comme il faut* at a ball of this sort, where there is champagne at the buffet and also whisky, to order drinks as if it were an hotel. I received the impression that these two gentlemen wished to be alone on the landing. I obtained their drinks, using the back stairs. When I returned I gave them the drinks. At that time, sir, Lord Robert Gospell had just come up the stairs and when they saw him these two gentlemen moved into the first sitting-room which was unoccupied.'

'Do you mean that they seemed to avoid him?'

'I received the impression, sir, that these gentlemen wished to be alone. That is why I remember them.'

'Their names?'

'I do not know their names.'

'Can you describe them?'

'One, sir, was a man perhaps forty-five or fifty years of age. He was a big man with a red face and thick neck. His voice was an unsympathetic voice. The other was a young gentleman, dark, rather nervous. I observed that he danced repeatedly with Miss Bridget O'Brien.'

'Thank you,' said Alleyn. 'That is excellent. Any others?'

'I cannot recall any others, sir. Wait! There *was* someone who was there for some time.'

François put his first finger to his chin like a sort of male dairymaid and cast his eyes to the ceiling.

'*Tiens!*' he exclaimed, 'who could it have been? *Alors*, I have it. It is of no importance at all, sir. It was the little mademoiselle, the secretary, who was known to few and therefore retired often to the gallery. I have remembered too that Sir Daniel Davidson, the physician, came upstairs. That was earlier. Before Lord Robert appeared. I think Sir Daniel looked for a partner because he went quickly in and out of both rooms and looked about the landing. I have remembered now that it was for Lady Carrados he enquired but she had gone downstairs a few minutes earlier. I told Sir Daniel this and he returned downstairs.'

Alleyn looked over his notes.

'See now,' he said. 'I am right in saying this? The persons who, as far as you know, could have gone into the telephone-room while Lord Robert was using the telephone were Sir Herbert Carrados and the two gentlemen who sent you for whisky.'

'Yes, sir. And the mademoiselle. Miss Harris is her name. I believe she entered the ladies' toilet just as Lord Robert went into the telephone-room. I have remarked that when ladies are much disengaged at balls they frequently enter the dressing-room. It is,' added François with an unexpected flash of humanity, 'a circumstance that I find rather pathetic.'

'Yes,' said Alleyn. 'Very pathetic I am right, then, in saying that before Lord Robert went to telephone, you fetched drinks for these two men and immediately after that he began to telephone. You were sent away by Sir Herbert Carrados, leaving him, Miss Harris and possibly others, whom you have forgotten, on the landing, and the two gentlemen in the other sitting-out room. Sir Daniel Davidson had gone downstairs some minutes previously. Lady Carrados before Sir Daniel, who was looking for her. You're sure of that?'

'Yes, sir. It is in my memory because after her ladyship had gone I entered the telephone-room and saw she had left her bag there. Monsieur – Mr Dimitri – came up at that time, saw it, and said he would return it to her ladyship. I told him she had gone downstairs and he returned, I think, by the back stairs.'

'He fits in between Lady Carrados and Sir Daniel. Did he return?'

'No, sir. I believe, sir, that I have mentioned everyone who was on the landing. At that time nearly all the guests were at supper. Later, of course, many ladies used the cloakroom toilet.'

'I see. Now for the rest of the evening. Did you see Lord Robert again?'

'No, sir. I remained on the top landing until the guests had gone, I then took a tray to Monsieur in the butler's pantry.'

'Was this long after the last guest had left?'

'No, sir. To be correct, sir, I fancy there may still have been one or two left in the hall. Monsieur was in the buffet when I came down.'

'Was Sir Herbert Carrados in the buffet?'

'He left as I entered. It was after he left that Monsieur ordered his little supper.'

'When did you go home?'

'As I have explained to your colleague, at three-thirty, with Monsieur. The police rang up this flat before Monsieur had gone to bed.'

'You carried Monsieur Dimitri's luggage for him, no doubt?'

'His luggage, sir? He had no luggage.'

'Right. I think that is all. You have been very helpful and obliging.'

François took his tip with a waiter's grace and showed Alleyn out.

Alleyn got a taxi. He looked at his watch. Twenty past twelve. He hoped Fox was keeping Dimitri for him. Dimitri! Unless François lied, it looked as if the odds against Dimitri being the murderer were lengthening.

'And the worst of it is,' muttered Alleyn, rubbing his nose, 'that I think François, blast his virtue, spoke nothing but the truth.'

CHAPTER 13

Dimitri Cuts His Fingers

In his room at the Yard Alleyn found Dimitri closeted with Fox. Fox introduced them solemnly.

'This is Mr Dimitri; Chief Detective-Inspector Alleyn, who is in charge of this case.'

'Ah, yes?' said Dimitri bowing. 'I believe we have met before.'

Alleyn said: 'I have just come from your flat, Mr Dimitri. I was up that way and hoped to save you a journey. I was, however, too late. I saw your servant and ventured to ask him one or two questions. He was most obliging.'

He smiled pleasantly at Dimitri and thought: 'He's looking sulky. Not a good head. Everything's a bit too narrow. He's got a mean look. No fool, though. Expensive clothes, fishy hands, uses a lot of hair oil. Honey and flowers. Ears set very low. No lobes to them. Less than an eye's width between the two eyes. I fancy the monocle is a dummy. Dents by the nostrils. False teeth. A smooth gentleman.'

Dimitri said: 'Your colleague has already rung my servant, Mr Alleyn.'

'Yes,' said Fox. 'I just checked up the time Mr Dimitri left. I've been explaining, sir, that we realize Mr Dimitri doesn't want to appear more than can be avoided.'

'In my position, Chief Inspector,' said Dimitri, 'it is most undesirable. I have been seven years building up my business and it is a specialized business. You understand that I have an extremely good clientele. I may say the very best. It is essential to my business that my clients should have complete faith in my discretion. But essential! In my position one sees and hears many things.'

'I have no doubt of that,' said Alleyn, looking steadily at him. 'Things that with a less discreet, less scrupulous person, might be turned to advantage.'

'That is a dreadful thought, Mr Alleyn. One cannot with equanimity contemplate such a base idea. But I must tell you that in my business the finest shades of discretion must be observed.'

'As in ours. I shall not ask you to repeat any scandals, Mr Dimitri. We will confine ourselves to the simplest facts. Your own movements, for instance.'

'Mine?' asked Dimitri, raising his eyebrows.

'If you please. We are anxious to get a little information about a small green boudoir on the top gallery at Marsdon House. It has a telephone in it. Do you know the room I mean?'

'Certainly.' The sharp eyes were veiled, the mouth set in a thin line.

'Did you at any time visit this room?'

'Repeatedly. I make it my business to inspect all the rooms continually.'

'The time in which we are interested is about one o'clock this morning. Most of Lady Carrados's guests were at supper. Captain Maurice Withers and Mr Donald Potter were on this top landing. So was your servant, François. Do you remember going upstairs at this time?'

Dimitri spread out his hands.

'It is impossible for me to remember, I am so very sorry.' He removed his rimless eyeglass and began to turn it between the fingers and thumb of his left hand.

'Let me try to help you. I learnt that at about this time you returned Lady Carrados's bag to her. One of the guests noticed you. Where did you find this bag, Mr Dimitri? Perhaps that will help.'

Dimitri suddenly put his hands in his pockets and Alleyn knew that it was an unfamiliar gesture. He could see that the left hand was still secretly busy with the eyeglass.

'That is correct. I seem to think the bag was in the room you mention. I am very particular about such things. My servants may not touch any bags that are left lying about the rooms. It is incredible how careless many ladies are with their bags, Mr Alleyn. I make it a rule that only I myself return them. Thus,' said Dimitri virtuously, 'am I solely responsible.'

'It might be quite a grave responsibility. So the bag was in the green room. Anybody there?'

'My servant François. I trust there was nothing missing from this bag?' asked Dimitri with an air of alarm. 'I asked her ladyship to be good enough to look at it.'

'Her ladyship,' said Alleyn, 'has made no complaint.'

'I am extremely relieved. For a moment I wondered – however.'

'The point is this,' said Alleyn, 'At one o'clock Lord Robert telephoned from this little green room. My informant is not your servant, Mr Dimitri. I must make that clear. At this time I think he was downstairs. My informant tells me that you were on the landing. Perhaps it was shortly after you collected Lady Carrados's bag.'

'If it was I did not hear anything of it,' said Dimitri instantly. 'Your informant is himself misinformed. I did not see Lord Robert on this gallery. I did not notice him at all until he was leaving.'

'You saw him then?'

'Yes. He enquired if I had seen Mrs Halcut-Hackett. I informed his lordship that she had left.'

'This was in the hall?'

'Yes.'

'Did you see Lord Robert leave?'

There was a marked pause and then Dimitri said:

'I have already explained all this to your colleague. After speaking to his lordship I went to the buffet on the ground floor. I remained there for a time speaking to Sir Herbert Carrados.'

Alleyn took a piece of paper from his pocket-book and handed it to Dimitri.

'This is the order of departure amongst the last guests. We have got our information from several sources. Mr Fox was greatly helped in compiling it by his interview with you earlier this morning. Would you mind glancing at it?'

Dimitri surveyed the list.

'It is correct, as far as I can remember, up to the time I left the hall.'

'I believe you saw the encounter at the foot of the stairs between Lord Robert and his nephew, Mr Donald Potter?'

'It was scarcely an encounter. They did not speak.'

'Did you get the impression that they avoided each other?'

'Mr Alleyn, we have already spoken of the need for discretion. Of course, one understands this is a serious matter. Yes. I did receive this impression.'

'Right. Then before you went to the buffet you noticed Mrs Halcut-Hackett, Captain Withers, Mr Potter and Sir Daniel Davidson leave separately, and in that order?'

'Yes.'

'Do you know Captain Withers?'

'Professionally? No. He does not entertain, I imagine.'

'Who left the buffet first, you or Sir Herbert?'

'I really do not remember. I did not remain very long in the buffet.'

'Where did you go?'

'I was fatigued. I made certain that my staff was working smoothly and then my servant brought me a light supper to the butler's pantry which I had reserved for my office.'

'How long was this after Lord Robert left?'

'I really do not know. Not long.'

'Did François remain in the butler's pantry?'

'Certainly not.'

'Did anyone come in while you were there?'

'I do not remember.'

'If, on reflection, you do recall any witness to your solitary supper-party it would help us in our work and free you from further embarrassment.'

'I do not understand you. Do you attempt to establish my alibi in this most regrettable and distressing fatality? Surely it is obvious that I could not have been in a taxi-cab with Lord Robert Gospell and in the buffet at Marsdon House at the same moment.'

'What makes you think that this crime was committed during the short time you spent in the buffet, Mr Dimitri?'

'Then or later, it is all the same. Still I am ready to help you, Chief Inspector. I will try to remember if I was seen in the pantry.'

'Thank you. I believe you attended the Bach recital by the Sirmione Quartette in the Constance Street Hall on June 3rd?'

The silence that followed Alleyn's question was so complete that the rapid tick of his desk clock came out of obscurity to break it. Alleyn was visited by a fantastic idea. There were four clocks in the room: Fox, Dimitri, himself and that small mechanical pulse on the writing desk.

Dimitri said: 'I attended the concert, yes. I am greatly attached to the music of Bach.'

'Did you happen to notice Lord Robert at this concert?'

It was as if the clock that was Dimitri was opened, and the feverish little pulse of the brain revealed. Should he say yes; should he say no?

'I am trying to remember. I think I do remember that his lordship was present.'

'You are quite correct, Mr Dimitri. He was not far away from you.'

'I pay little attention to externals when I listen to beautiful music.'

'Did you return her bag to Mrs Halcut-Hackett?'

Dimitri gave a sharp cry. Fox's pencil skidded across the page of his notebook. Dimitri drew his left hand out of his pocket and stared at his fingers. Three drops of blood fell from them to his striped trouser leg.

'Blood on your hand, Mr Dimitri,' said Alleyn.

Dimitri said: 'I have broken my glass.'

'Is the cut deep? Fox, my bag is in the cupboard there. I think there is some lint and strapping in it.'

'No,' said Dimitri, 'it is nothing.' He wrapped his fine silk handkerchief round his fingers and nursed them in his right hand. He was white to the lips.

'The sight of blood,' he said, 'affects me unpleasantly.'

'I insist that you allow me to bandage your hand,' said Alleyn. Dimitri did not answer. Fox produced iodine, lint and strapping. Alleyn unwrapped the hand. Two of the fingers were cut and bled freely. Dimitri shut his eyes while Alleyn dressed them. The hand was icy cold and clammy.

'There,' said Alleyn. 'And your handkerchief to hide the blood-stains which upset you so much. You are quite pale, Mr Dimitri. Would you like some brandy?'

'No. No, thank you.'

'You are recovered?'

'I do not feel well. I must ask you to excuse me.'

'Certainly. When you have answered my last question. Did you ever return Mrs Halcut-Hackett's bag?'

'I do not understand you. We spoke of Lady Carrados's bag.'

'We speak now of Mrs Halcut-Hackett's bag which you took from the sofa at the Sirmione Concert. Do you deny that you took it?'

'I refuse to prolong this interview. I shall answer no more questions without the advice of my solicitor. That is final.'

He rose to his feet. So did Alleyn and Fox.

'Very well,' said Alleyn. 'I shall have to see you again, Mr Dimitri; and again, and I daresay again. Fox, will you show Mr Dimitri down?'

When the door had closed Alleyn spoke into his telephone.

'My man is leaving. He'll probably take a taxi. Who's tailing him?'

'Anderson relieving Carewe, sir.'

'Ask him to report when he gets a chance, but not to take too big a chance. It's important.'

'Right, Mr Alleyn.'

Alleyn waited for Fox's return. Fox came in grinning.

'He's shaken up a fair treat to see, Mr Alleyn. Doesn't know if he's Mayfair, Soho, or Wandsworth.'

'We've a long way to go before he's Wandsworth. How are we ever going to persuade women like Mrs Halcut-Hackett to charge their blackmailers? Not in a lifetime, unless – '

'Unless what?'

'Unless the alternative is even more terrifying. Fox, do you think it within the bounds of possibility that Dimitri ordered his trifle of caviare and champagne at Sir Herbert's expense, that François departed and Dimitri, hurriedly acquiring a silk hat and overcoat, darted out by the back door just in time to catch Lord Robert in the mist, ask him preposterously for a lift and drive away? Can you swallow this camel of unlikelihood and if so, can you open your ponderous and massy jaws still farther and engulf the idea of Dimitri performing his murder and subsequent masquerade, returning to Marsdon House, and settling down to his supper without anybody noticing anything out of the ordinary?'

'When you put it that way, sir, it does sound funny. But we don't know it's impossible.'

'No, we don't. He's about the right height. I've a strong feeling, Fox, that Dimitri is not working this blackmail game on his own. We're not allowed strong feelings, so ignore it. If there is another scoundrel in the game they'll try to get into touch. We'll have to do something about that. What's the time? One o'clock, I'm due at Sir Daniel's at two and I'll have to see the AC before then. Coming?'

'I'll do a bit of work on the file first. We ought to hear from the fellow at Leatherhead any time now. You go to lunch, Mr Alleyn. When did you last eat anything?'

'I don't know. Look here – '

'Did you have any breakfast?' asked Fox, putting on his spectacles and opening the file.

'Good Lord, Fox, I'm not a hothouse lily.'

'This isn't a usual case, sir, for you. It's a personal matter, say what you like, and you'll do no good if you try and work it on your nerves.'

Fox glanced at Alleyn over the top of his spectacles, wetted his thumb, and turned a page.

'Oh God,' said Alleyn, 'once the wheels begin to turn, it's easier to forget the other side. If only I didn't see him so often. He looked like a child, Fox. Just like a child.'

'Yes,' said Fox. 'It's a nasty case, personal feelings aside. If you see the Assistant Commissioner now, Mr Alleyn, I'll be ready to join you for a bite of lunch before we go to Sir Daniel Davidson's.'

'All right, blast you. Meet me downstairs in a quarter of an hour.'

'Thank you, sir,' said Fox. 'I'll be pleased.'

About twenty minutes later he presided over Alleyn's lunch with all the tranquil superiority of a nannie. They arrived at St. Luke's Chambers, Harley Street, at two o'clock precisely. They sat in a waiting-room lavishly strewn with new periodicals. Fox solemnly read *Punch*, while Alleyn, with every appearance of the politest attention, looked at a brochure appealing for clothes and money for the Central Chinese Medical Mission. In a minute or two a secretary told them that Sir Daniel would see them and showed them into his consulting-room.

'The gentlemen from Scotland Yard, Sir Daniel. Mr Alleyn and Mr Fox.'

Davidson, who had apparently been staring out of the window, came forward and shook hands.

'It's very good of you to come to me,' he said. 'I said on the telephone that I was quite ready to report at Scotland Yard whenever it suited you. Do sit down.'

They sat down. Alleyn glanced round the room and what he saw pleased him. It was a charming room with apple-green walls, an Adam fireplace and silver-starred curtains. Above the mantelpiece hung a sunny landscape by a famous painter. A silk praying-mat that would not have disgraced a collector's walls did workaday service before the fireplace. Sir Daniel's desk was an adapted spinet, his inkwell recalled the days when sanded paper was inscribed with high-sounding phrases in quill-scratched calligraphy. As he sat at his desk Sir Daniel saw before him in Chinese ceramic, a little rose-red horse. A beautiful and expensive room, crying in devious tones of the gratitude of wealthy patients. The most exalted, if not the richest, of these stared with blank magnificence from a silver frame.

Sir Daniel himself, neat, exquisite in London clothes and a slightly flamboyant tie, with something a little exotic about his fine dark head, looked as though he could have no other setting than this. He seated himself at his desk, joined his hands and contemplated Alleyn with frank curiosity.

'Surely you are Roderick Alleyn?' he said.

'Yes.'

'I have read your book.'

'Are you interested in criminology?' asked Alleyn with a smile.

'Enormously! I hardly dare to tell you this because you must so often fall a victim to the enthusiasm of fools. I, too! "Oh, Sir Daniel, it must be *too* marvellous to be able to look into the minds of people as you do." Their minds! My God! Their stomachs are enough. But I often think quite seriously that I should have liked to follow medical jurisprudence.'

'We have lost a great figure then,' said Alleyn.

'That's very graceful. But it's untrue, I'm afraid. I am too impatient and altogether too much of a partisan. As in this case. Lord Robert was a friend of mine. It would be impossible for me to look at this case with an equal eye.'

'If you mean,' said Alleyn, 'that you do not feel kindly disposed towards his murderer, no more do we. Do we, Fox?'

'No, sir, that we do not,' said Fox.

Davidson's brilliant eyes rested for a moment on Fox. With a single glance he seemed to draw him into the warm circle of his confidence and regard. 'All the same,' thought Alleyn, 'he's uneasy. He doesn't quite know where to begin.' And he said:

'You very kindly rang up to say you might be able to help us.'

'Yes,' said Davidson, 'yes, I did.' He lifted a very beautiful jade paperweight and put it down. 'I don't know how to begin.' He darted a shrewd and somehow impish glance at Alleyn. 'I find myself in the unenviable position of being one of the last people to see Lord Robert.'

Fox took out his notebook. Davidson looked distastefully at it.

'When did you see him?' Alleyn asked.

'In the hall. Just before I left.'

'You left, I understand, after Mrs Halcut-Hackett, Captain Withers and Mr Donald Potter, who went away severally about three-thirty.'

Davidson's jaw dropped. He flung up his beautiful hands.

'Believe it or not,' he said, 'I had a definite struggle with my conscience before I made up my mind to admit it.'

'Why was that?' asked Alleyn.

Again that sideways impish glance.

'I didn't want to come forward at all. Not a bit. It's very bad for us parasites to appear in murder trials. In the long run, it is very bad indeed. By the way, I suppose it *is* a case of homicide. No doubt about it? Or shouldn't I ask?'

'Of course you can ask. There seems to be no doubt at all. He was smothered.'

'Smothered!' Davidson leant forward, his hands clasped on the desk. Alleyn read in his face the subtle change that comes upon all men when they embark on their own subject. 'Good God!' he said, 'he wasn't a Desdemona! Why didn't he make a rumpus? Is he marked?'

'There are no marks of violence.'

'None? Who did the autopsy?'

'Curtis. He's our expert.'

'Curtis, Curtis? – yes, of course. How does he account for the absence of violence? Heart? His heart was in a poor condition.'

'How do you know that, Sir Daniel?'

'My dear fellow, I examined him most thoroughly three weeks ago.'

'Did you!' exclaimed Alleyn. 'That's very interesting. What did you find?'

'I found a very unpleasant condition. Evidence of fatty degeneration. I ordered him to avoid cigars like the plague, to deny himself his port and to rest for two hours every day. I am firmly persuaded that he paid no attention whatsoever. Nevertheless, my dear Mr Alleyn, it was not a condition under which I would expect an unprovoked heart attack. A struggle certainly might induce it and you tell me there is no evidence of a struggle.'

'He was knocked out.'

'Knocked out! Why didn't you say so before? Because I gave you no opportunity, of course. I see. And quietly asphyxiated? How very horrible and how ingenious.'

'Would the condition of the heart make it quicker?'

'I should say so, undoubtedly.'

Davidson suddenly ran his fingers through his picturesque hair.

'I am more distressed by this abominable, this unspeakable crime than I would have thought possible. Mr Alleyn, I had the deepest regard for Lord Robert. It would be impossible to exaggerate my regard for him. He seemed a comic figure, an aristocratic droll with an unusual amount of charm. He was much more than that. He had a keen brain. In conversation, he understood everything that one left unsaid, his mind was both subtle and firm. I am a man of the people. I adore all my smart friends and I understand – *Cristo Mio*, do I not understand! – my smart patients! But I am not, deep in my heart, at ease with them. With Lord Robert I was at ease. I showed off and was not ashamed afterwards that I had done so.'

'You pay him a great compliment when you confess as much,' said Alleyn.

'Do I not? Listen. If it had been anyone else, do you know what I should have done? I should have kept quiet and I should have said to myself *il ne faut pas réveiller le chat qui dort*, and hoped nobody would remember that I stood in the hall this morning at Marsdon House and watched Lord Robert at the foot of the stairs. But as it is I have screwed myself up to making the superb gesture of coming to you with information you have already received. *Gros-Jean en remontre à son curé!*'

'Not altogether,' said Alleyn. 'It is not entirely *une vieille histoire*. You may yet glow with conscious virtue. I am longing for a precise account of those last minutes in the hall. We have the order of the going but not the nature of it. If you don't mind giving us a microscopically exact version?'

'Ah!' Davidson frowned. 'You must give me a moment to arrange my facts. A microscopically exact version! Wait now.' He closed his eyes and his right hand explored the surface of the carved jade paperweight. The deliberate movement of the fingers arrested Alleyn's attention. The piece of jade might have been warm and living, so sensitively did the fingertips caress it. Alleyn thought: 'He loves his beautiful possessions.' He determined to learn more of this *poseur* who called himself a man of the people and spattered his conversation with French and Italian tags, who was at once so frankly theatrical and so theatrically frank.

Davidson opened his eyes. The effect was quite startling. They were such remarkable eyes. The light grey iris, unusually large, was ringed with black, the pupil a sharp black accent. 'I bet he uses that trick on his patients to some effect,' thought Alleyn, and then realized that Davidson was smiling. 'Blast him, he's read my thoughts.' And he found himself returning the smile as if he and Davidson shared an amusing secret.

'Take this down, Fox,' said Alleyn.

'Very good, sir,' said Fox.

'As you have noticed,' Davidson began, 'I have a taste for the theatrical. Let me present this little scene to you as if we watched it take place behind the footlights. I have shaken hands with my host and hostess where the double flight of stairs meet in a gallery outside the ballroom. I come down the left-hand flight of stairs, thinking of my advancing years and longing for my bed. In the hall are scattered groups of people; coated, cloaked, ready for departure. Already the great house seems exhausted and a little raffish. One feels the presence of drooping flowers, one seems to smell the dregs of champagne. It is indeed time to be gone. Among the departing guests I notice an old lady whom I wish to avoid. She's rich, one of my best patients, but her chief complaint is a condition of chronic, complicated and acute verbal diarrhoea. I have ministered to this complaint already this evening and as I have no wish to be offered a lift in her car I dart into the men's cloakroom. I spend some minutes there, marking time. It is a little awkward as the only other men in the cloakroom are obviously engaged in an extremely private conversation.'

'Who are they?' asked Alleyn.

'A certain Captain Withers who is newly come upon the town and that pleasant youth, Donald Potter. They both pause and stare at me. I make a great business of getting my coat and hat. I chat with the cloakroom attendant after I have tipped him. I speak to Donald Potter, but am so poorly received that in sheer decency I am forced to leave. Lucy Lorrimer – *tiens*, there I go!'

'It's all right,' said Alleyn, 'I know all about Lucy Lorrimer.'

'What a woman! She is still screaming out there. I pull up my scarf and lurk in the doorway, waiting for her to go. Having nothing else to do I watch the other people in the hall. The *grand seigneur* of the stomach stands at the foot of the stairs.'

'Who?'

'The man who presides over all these affairs. What is his name?'

'Dimitri?'

'Yes, Dimitri. He stand there like an imitation host. A group of young people go out. Then an older woman, alone, comes down the stairs and slips through the doors into the misty street. It was very strange, all that mist.'

'Was this older woman Mrs Halcut-Hackett?'

'Yes. That is who it was,' said Davidson a little too casually.

'Is Mrs Halcut-Hackett a patient of yours, Sir Daniel?'

'It so happens that she is.'

'Why did she leave alone? What about her husband and – hasn't she got a débutante attached to her?'

'The protégée, who is unfortunately *une jeune fille un peu farouche*, fell a prey to toothache earlier in the evening and was removed by the General. I heard Lord Robert offer to escort Mrs Halcut-Hackett home.'

'Why did he not do so?'

'Perhaps because they missed each other.'

'Come now, Sir Daniel, that's not your real opinion.'

'Of course it's not, but I don't gossip about my patients.'

'I needn't assure you that we shall be very discreet. Remember what you said about your attitude towards this case.'

'I do remember. Very well. Only please, if you can avoid my name in subsequent interviews, I shall be more than grateful. I'll go on with my recital. Mrs Halcut-Hackett, embedded in ermine, gives a swift look round the hail and slips out through the doors into the night. My attention is arrested by something in her manner, and while I stare after her somebody jostles me so violently that I actually stumble forward and only just save myself from falling. It is Captain Withers, who has come out of the cloakroom behind me. I turn to receive his apologies and find him with his mouth set and his unpleasant eyes – I mistrust people with white lashes – goggling at the stairhead. He does not even realize his own incivility, his attention is fixed on Lord Robert Gospell, who has begun to descend the stairs. This Captain Withers's expression is so singular that I, too, forget our encounter. I hear him draw in his breath. There is a second's pause and then he, too, thrusts his way through a party of chattering youngsters and goes out.'

'Do you think Withers was following Mrs Halcut-Hackett?'

'I have no reason to think so, but I do think so.'

'Next?'

'Next? Why, Mr Alleyn, I pull myself together and start for the door. Before I have taken three steps young Donald Potter comes out of the buffet with Bridget O'Brien. They meet Lord Robert at the foot of the stairs.'

'Yes?' said Alleyn, as Davidson paused.

'Donald Potter,' he said at last, 'says what is no doubt a word of farewell to Bridget, and then he too goes out by the front entrance.'

'Without speaking to his uncle?'

'Yes.'

'And Lord Robert?'

'Lord Robert is asking in that very penetrating high-pitched voice of his if Dimitri has seen Mrs Halcut-Hackett. I see him now and hear him – the last thing I do see or hear before the double doors close behind me.'

CHAPTER 14

Davidson Digresses

'That was a very vivid little scene,' said Alleyn.

'Well, it was not so long ago, after all,' said Davidson.

'When you got outside the house, did you see any of the others, or had they all gone?'

'The party of young people came out as I did. There was the usual bustle for taxis with linkmen and porters. Those linkmen! They are indeed a link with past glories. When one sees the lights from their torches flicker on the pale, almost wanton faces of guests half-dazed with dancing, one expects Millamant herself to come down the steps and all the taxis to turn into sedan chairs. However, I must not indulge my passion for elaboration. The party of young people surged into the three taxis that had been summoned by the porter. He was about to call one for me when, to my horror, I saw a Rolls-Royce on the other side of the road. The window was down and there, like some Sybil, mopping and mowing, was Lucy Lorrimer. "Sir Daniel! Sir Daniel." I shrank further into my scarf, but all in vain. An officious flunkey cries out: "The lady is calling you, sir." Nothing for it but to cross the road. "Sir Daniel! Sir Daniel! I have waited for you. Something most important! I shall drive you home and on the way I can tell you – " An impossible woman. I know what it means. She is suffering from a curious internal pain that has just seized her and now is the moment for me to make an examination. I must come in. She is in agony. I think furiously and by the time I reach her window I am prepared. "Lady Lorrimer – forgive me – not a moment to spare –

the Prime Minister – a sudden indisposition – !" and while she still gapes I turn and bolt like a rabbit into the mist!'

For the first time since the tragedy of last night Alleyn laughed. Davidson gave him a droll look and went on with his story.

'I ran as I have not done since I was a boy in Grenoble, pursued by that voice offering, no doubt, to drive me like the wind to Downing Street. Mercifully the mist thickened. On I went, looking in vain for a taxi. I heard a car and shrank into the shadows. The Rolls-Royce passed. I crept out. At last a taxi! It was coming behind me. I could just see the two misted headlights. Then voices, but indistinguishable. The taxi stopped, came on towards me. Engaged! *Mon Dieu*, what a night! I walked on, telling myself that sooner or later I must find a cab. Not a bit of it! By this time, I suppose, the last guest had gone. It was God knows what time of the morning and the few cabs I did meet were all engaged. I walked from Belgrave Square to Cadogan Gardens, and I assure you, my dear Mr Alleyn, I have never enjoyed a walk more. I felt like a middle-aged harlequin in search of adventure. That I found none made not the smallest matter.'

'Unless I'm much mistaken,' said Alleyn, 'you missed it by a very narrow margin. Adventure is perhaps not the right word. I fancy tragedy passed you by, Sir Daniel, and you did not recognize it.'

'Yes,' said Davidson, and his voice was suddenly sombre. 'Yes, I believe you may be right. It is not so amusing, after all.'

'That taxi-cab. Which way did you turn when you fled from Lady Lorrimer?'

'To my right.'

'How far had you run when you heard the taxi?'

'I don't know. It is almost impossible to judge. Perhaps four hundred yards. Not far, because I had stopped and hidden from Lucy Lorrimer.'

'You tell us you heard voices. Did you recognize them?'

Davidson waited, staring thoughtfully at Alleyn.

'I realize how important this is,' he said at last. 'I am almost afraid to answer. Mr Alleyn, I can only tell you that when those voices – I could hear no words, remember – reached me through the mist, I thought at first that one was a woman's voice and then I changed my mind and thought it was a man's. It was a high-pitched voice.'

'And the other?'

'Definitely a man's.'

'Can you remember anything else, anything at all, about this incident?'

'Nothing. Except that when the taxi passed me I thought the occupants were men.'

'Yes. Will you give us a signed statement?'

'About the taxi incident? Certainly.'

'Can you tell me who was left behind at Marsdon House when you went away?'

'After the noisy party that went when I did, very few remained. Let me think. There was a very drunk young man. I think his name is Percival and he came out of the buffet just before I left and went into the cloakroom. There was somebody else. Who was it? Ah, yes, it was a curious little lady who seemed to be rather a fish out of water. I had noticed her before. She was quite unremarkable and one would never have seen her if she had not almost always been alone. She wore glasses. That is all I can tell you about her except – yes – I saw her dancing with Lord Robert. I remember now that she was looking at him as he came downstairs. Perhaps she felt some sort of gratitude towards him. She would have been pathetic if she had not looked so composed. I shouldn't be surprised if she was a dependant of the house. Perhaps Bridget's ex-governess, or Lady Carrados's companion. I fancy I encountered her myself somewhere during the evening. Where was it? I forget!'

'The ball was a great success, I believe?'

'Yes. Lady Carrados was born under a star of hospitality. It is always a source of wonderment to me why one ball should be a great success and another offering the same band, caterer and guests an equally great failure. Lady Carrados, one would have said, was at a disadvantage last night.'

'You mean she was unwell?'

'So you've heard about that. We tried to keep it quiet. Yes, like all these mothers, she's overdone herself.'

'Worrying about something, do you imagine?' asked Alleyn, and then in reply to Davidson's raised brows, he said: 'I wouldn't ask if it was not relevant.'

'I can't imagine, I must confess, how Lady Carrados's indisposition can have any possible connection with Lord Robert Gospell's death.

She is nervously exhausted and felt the strain of her duties.' Davidson added as if to himself: 'This business will do her no good, either.'

'You see,' said Alleyn, 'in a case of this sort we have to look for any departure from the ordinary or the expected. I agree that this particular departure seems quite irrelevant. So, alas, will many of the other facts we bring to light. If they cannot be correlated they will be discarded. That is routine.'

'No doubt. Well, all I can tell you is that I noticed Lady Carrados was unwell, told her to go and lie down in the ladies' cloakroom, which I understand was on the top landing, and to send her maid for me if she needed me. Getting no message, I tried to find her, but couldn't. She reappeared later on and told me she felt a little better and not to worry about her.'

'Sir Daniel, did you happen to see the caterer, Dimitri, return her bag to Lady Carrados?'

'I don't think so. Why?'

'I've heard that for a time last night she thought she had lost it and was very distressed.'

'She said nothing to me about it. It might account for her upset. I noticed that bag. It has a very lovely emerald and ruby clasp – an old Italian setting and much too choice a piece to bedizen a bit of tinsel nonsense. But nowadays people have no sense of congruity in ornament. None.'

'I have been looking at your horse. You, at least, have an appreciation of the beautiful. Forgive me for forgetting my job for a moment but – a ray of sunshine has caught that little horse. Rose red and ochre! I've a passion for ceramics.'

Davidson's face was lit from within. He embarked eagerly on the story of how he acquired his little horse. His hands touched it as delicately as if it was a rose. He and Alleyn stepped back three thousand centuries into the golden age of pottery and Inspector Fox sat as silent as stout Cortez with his official notebook open on his knees and an expression of patient tolerance on his large solemn face.

'– and speaking of Benvenuto,' said Davidson who had talked himself into the Italian Renaissance, 'I saw in a room at Marsdon House last night, unless I am a complete nincompoop, an authentic Cellini medallion. And where, my dear Alleyn, do you suppose it was? To what base use do you imagine it had been put?'

'I've no idea,' said Alleyn, smiling.

'It had been sunk; sunk, mark you, in a machine-turned gold case with a devilish diamond clasp and it was surrounded with brilliants. Doubtless this sacrilegious abortion was intended as a receptacle for cigarettes.'

'Where was this horror?' asked Alleyn.

'In an otherwise charming green sitting-room.'

'On the top landing?'

'That's the one. Look for this case yourself. It's worth seeing in a horrible sort of way.'

'When did you visit this room?'

'When? Let me see. It must have been about half-past eleven. I had an urgent case yesterday and the assistant surgeon rang me up to report.'

'You didn't go there again?'

'No. I don't think so. No, I didn't.'

'You didn't,' persisted Alleyn, 'happen to hear Lord Robert telephone from that room?'

'No. No, I didn't return to it at all. But it was a charming room. A Greuze above the mantelpiece and three or four really nice little pieces on a pie-crust table and with them this hell-inspired crime. I could not imagine a person with enough taste to choose the other pieces, allowing such a horror as a Benvenuto medallion – and a very lovely one – sunk, no doubt cemented, by its perfect reverse, to this filthy cigarette-case.'

'Awful,' agreed Alleyn. 'Speaking of cigarettes, what sort of case did you carry last night?'

'Hullo!' Davidson's extraordinary eyes bored into his. 'What sort of – ' He stopped and then muttered to himself: 'Knocked out, you said. Yes, I see. On the temple.'

'That's it,' said Alleyn.

Davidson pulled a flat silver case from his pocket. It was beautifully made with a sliding action and bevelled edges. Its smooth surface shone like a mirror between the delicately tooled margins. He handed it to Alleyn.

'I don't despise frank modernity, you see.'

Alleyn examined the case, rubbing his fingers over the tooling. Davidson said abruptly:

'One could strike a sharp blow with it.'

'One could,' said Alleyn, 'but it's got traces of plate-powder in the tooling and it's not the right kind, I fancy.'

'I wouldn't have believed it possible that I could have been so profoundly relieved,' said Davidson. He waited for a moment and then with a nervous glance at Fox, he added: 'I suppose I've no alibi?'

'Well, no,' said Alleyn, 'I suppose you haven't, but I shouldn't let it worry you. The taximan may remember passing you.'

'It was filthily misty,' said Davidson peevishly. 'He may not have noticed.'

'Come,' said Alleyn, 'you mustn't get investigation nerves. There's always Lucy Lorrimer.'

'There is indeed always Lucy Lorrimer. She has rung up three times this morning.'

'There you are. I'll have to see her myself. Don't worry; you've given us some very useful information, hasn't he, Fox?'

'Yes, sir. It's kind of solidified what we had already.'

'Anything you'd like to ask Sir Daniel, Fox?'

'No, Mr Alleyn, thank you. I think you've covered the ground very thoroughly. Unless – '

'Yes?' asked Davidson. 'Come on, Mr Fox.'

'Well, Sir Daniel, I was wondering if you could give us an opinion on how long it would take a man in Lord Robert Gospell's condition to die under these circumstances.'

'Yes,' said Davidson, and again that professional note sounded in his voice. 'Yes. It's not easy to give you the sort of answer you want. A healthy man would go in about four minutes if the murderer completely stopped all access of air to the lungs. A man with a condition of the heart which I believe to have obtained in this instance would be most unlikely to live for four minutes. Life might become extinct within less than two. He might die almost immediately.'

'Yes. Thank you' sir.'

Alleyn said: 'Suppose the murderer had some slight knowledge of medicine and was aware of Lord Robert's condition, would he be likely to realize how little time he needed?'

'That is rather a difficult question to answer. His slight knowledge might not embrace asphyxia. I should say that any first-year student would probably realize that a diseased heart would give out very rapidly under these conditions. A nurse would know. Indeed, I should have thought most laymen would think it probable. The actual time to within two or three minutes might not be appreciated.'

'Yes. Thank you.'

Alleyn got up.

'I think that really is everything. We'll get out a statement for you to sign, if you will. Believe me, we do realize that it has been very difficult for you to speak of your patients under these extremely disagreeable circumstances. We'll word the beastly document as discreetly as may be.'

'I'm sure you will. Mr Alleyn, I think I remember Lord Robert telling me he had a great friend at Scotland Yard. Are you this friend? I see you are. Please don't think my question impertinent. I am sure that you have suffered, with all his friends, a great loss. You should not draw too much upon your nervous energy, you know, in investigating this case. It is quite useless for me to tell you this, but I am a physician and I do know something about nerves. You are subjecting yourself to a very severe discipline at the moment. Don't overdo it.'

'Just what I'd like to tell him, sir,' said Fox unexpectedly.

Davidson turned on him a face cordial with appreciation. 'I see we understand each other, Mr Fox.'

'It's very kind of you both,' said Alleyn with a grin, 'but I'm not altogether a hothouse flower. Good-bye, Sir Daniel. Thank you so much.'

They shook hands and Fox and Alleyn went out.

'Where do we go now?' asked Fox.

'I think we'd better take a look at Marsden House. Bailey ought to have finished by now. I'll ring up from there and see if I can get an appointment with the Carrados family en masse. It's going to be difficult, that. There seems to be no doubt that Lady Carrados is one of the blackmailing victims. Carrados himself is a difficult type, a frightful old snob he is, and as vain as a peacock. Police investigation will undoubtedly stimulate all his worst qualities. He's the sort of man who'd go to any lengths to avoid the wrong kind of publicity. We'll have go to warily if we don't want him to make fools of us and a confounded nuisance of himself.'

On the way to Marsdon House they went over Davidson's evidence.

'It's a rum thing, when you come to think of it,' ruminated Fox. 'There was Sir Daniel looking at that taxi and wishing it wasn't booked and there inside it were Lord Robert and the man who had made up his mind to kill him. He must have started in to do it almost at once. He hadn't got much time, after all.'

'No,' said Alleyn, 'the time factor is important.'

'How exactly d'you reckon he set about it, sir?'

'I imagine them sitting side by side. The murderer takes out his cigarette-case, if indeed it was a cigarette-case. Perhaps he says something to make Lord Robert lean forward and look through the window. He draws back his hand and hits Lord Robert sharply on the temple with the edge and point of the case – the wound seems to indicate that. Lord Robert slumps back. The murderer presses his muffled hand over the nose and mouth, not too hard but carefully. As the mouth opens he pushes the material he is using between the teeth and further and further back towards the throat. With his other hand he keeps the nostrils closed. And so he sits until they are nearly at Cheyne Walk. When he removes his hands the pulse is still, there is no attempt at respiration. The head falls sideways and he knows it is all over.' Alleyn clenched his hands. 'He might have been saved even then, Fox. Artificial respiration might have saved him. But there was the rest of the drive to Queens Gate and then on to the Yard. Hopeless!'

'The interview with Sir Herbert Carrados ought to clear up this business of Dimitri,' Fox said. 'If Sir Herbert was any length of time in the buffet with Dimitri.'

'We'll have to go delicately with Carrados. I wonder if the obscure lady will be there. The lady that nobody noticed but who, since she did not dance very much, may have fulfilled the traditional office of the onlooker. Then there's the Halcut-Hackett game. We'll have to get on with that as soon as possible. It links up with Withers.'

'What sort of a lady is Mrs Halcut-Hackett? She came and saw you at the Yard, didn't she, about the blackmail business?'

'Yes, Fox, she did. She played the old, old game of pretending to be the friend of the victim. Still she had the pluck to come. That visit of hers marked the beginning of the whole miserable affair. You may be sure that I do not forget this. I asked Bunchy to help us find the black-mailer. If I hadn't done that he'd be alive now, I suppose, unless . . . unless, my God! Donald killed his uncle for what he'd get out of it. If blackmail's at the bottom of the murder, I'm directly responsible.'

'Well, sir, if you'll excuse me, I don't think that's a remark to get you or anyone else much further. Lord Robert wouldn't have thanked you for it and that's a fact. We don't feel obliged to warn everybody who helps in a blackmail case that it's liable to turn to murder. And why?' continued Fox with the nearest approach to animation that Alleyn had ever seen in him. 'Because up to now it never has.'

'All right, Brer Fox,' said Alleyn. 'I'll pipe down.'

And for the rest of the way to Marsdon House they were both silent.

CHAPTER 15

Simple Soldier-man

Marsdon House had been put into a sort of cold-storage by the police. Dimitri's men had done a certain amount of clearing up before Alleyn's men arrived, but for the most part the great house seemed to be suffering from a severe form of carry-over. It smelt of stale cigarette butts. They were everywhere, bent double, stained red, stained brown, in ash-trays, fireplaces and waste-paper boxes; ground into the ballroom floor, dropped behind chairs, lurking in dirty cups and floating in a miserable state of disintegration among the stalks of dying flowers. Upstairs in the ladies' dressing-room they lay in drifts of spilt powder, and in the green boudoir someone had allowed a cigarette to eat a charred track across the margin of a pie-crust table.

Alleyn and Fox stood in the green boudoir and looked at the telephone.

'There he sat,' said Alleyn, and once more he quoted: '"The cakes-and-ale feller. Might as well mix his damn brews with poison. And he's working with – " Look, Fox, he must have sat in this chair, facing the door. He wouldn't see anybody coming because of that very charming screen. Imagine our interloper sneaking through the door. He catches a word that arrests his attention, stops for a second and then, realising what Lord Robert is doing, comes round the screen. Lord Robert looks up: "Hullo, I didn't see you," and knowing he has just mentioned the Yard, pitches his lost property story and rings off. I've left word at the Yard that every name on that guest list is to be traced and each guest asked as soon as possible if he or she butted in on that conversation. I'm using a lot of men on this case, but the AC's behaving very prettily, thank the Lord. Get that PC, will you?'

The constable who had been left in charge reported that Detective-Sergeant Bailey had been all over the room for prints and had gone to the Yard before lunch.

'Is the telephone still switched through to this room?'

'I believe so, sir. Nothing's been touched.'

'Fox, ring up the Yard and see if there's anything new.'

While Fox was at the telephone Alleyn prowled about the room looking with something like despair at the evidence of so many visitors. It was useless to hope that anything conclusive would be deduced from Bailey's efforts. They might find Lord Robert's prints on the telephone but what was the good of that? If they could separate and classify every print that had been left in the room it would lead them exactly nowhere.

Fox turned away from the telephone.

'They've got through the list of guests, sir. Very smart work. Five men on five telephones. None of the guests admit to having overheard Lord Robert, and none of the servants.'

'That's our line, then. Find the interloper. Somehow I thought it would come to that.' Alleyn wandered about the room. 'Davidson was right; it's a pleasant room.'

'The house belongs to an uncle of Lady Carrados, doesn't it?'

'Yes, General Marsdon. He would appear to be a fellow of taste. The Greuze is charming. And these enamels. Where's the offensive Cellini conversion, I wonder.' He bent over the pie-crust table. 'Nothing like it here. That's funny. Davidson said it was on this table, didn't he? It's neither here nor anywhere else in the room. Rum! Must have belonged to one of the guests. Nothing much in it. Still, we'd better check it. What a hellish bore! All through the guests again, unless we strike it lucky! François might have noticed it sometime when he was doing the ash-trays. Better ask him.'

He rang up François, who said he knew nothing of any stray cigarette-case. Alleyn sighed and took out his notes. Fox cruised solemnly about the top landing.

'Hi!' called Alleyn after ten minutes. 'Hi! Fox!'

'Hullo, sir?'

'I've been trying to piece these people's movements together. As far as I can see, it goes something like this. Now pay attention, because it's very muddly and half the time I won't know what I'm talking about. Some time during the supper interlude Lady Carrados left her bag in this room. François saw Dimitri collect it and go downstairs. Miss Troy, who was dancing with Bunchy, saw him return the bag to Lady Carrados in the ballroom. Miss Troy noticed it looked much emptier than before. We don't know if there were any witnesses to the actual moment when she left the bag, but it doesn't matter. Bunchy saw her receive it from Dimitri. At one o'clock he rang me up to say he had a strong line on the blackmailer and the crucial conversation took place. Now, according to François, there were four people who might have overheard this conversation. Withers, Donald Potter, Sir Herbert Carrados, and the colourless Miss Harris, who may or may not have been in the lavatory, but was certainly on this landing. Someone else may have come and gone while François was getting matches for the enraged Carrados. On François's return he went into the telephone-room and found it empty. Sounds easier when you condense it. All right. Our job is to find out if anyone else could have come upstairs, listened to the telephone, and gone down again while François was in the servants' quarters. Withers says he heard the telephone when he was in the other sitting-room. He also says Carrados was up here at that time so, liar though no doubt he is, it looks as if he spoke the truth about that. Come on, Fox, let's prowl.'

The gallery was typical of most large, old-fashioned London houses. The room with the telephone was at the far end, next it was a lavatory. This turned out to be a Victorian affair with a small ante-room and a general air of varnish and gloom. The inner door was half-panelled with thick clouded glass which let through a little murky daylight. Beyond it was a bedroom that had been used as a ladies' cloakroom and last, at the top of the stairs, the second sitting-out room. Beside the door of this room was another green baize door leading to servants' quarters and back stairs. The other side of the gallery was open and looked over the great well of the house. Alleyn leant on the balustrade and stared down the steep perspective of twisting stairs into the hall two storeys below.

'A good vantage spot this,' he said. 'We'll go down, now.'

On the next landing was the ballroom. Nothing could have looked more desolate than the great empty floor, the chairs that wore that disconcerting air of talking to each other, the musicians' platform, littered with cigarette butts and programmes. A fine dust lay over everything and the great room echoed to their footsteps. The walls sighed a little as though the air imprisoned behind them sought endlessly for escape. Alleyn and Fox hunted about but found nothing to help them and went down the great stairs to the hall.

'Here he stood,' said Alleyn, 'at the foot of the left-hand flight of stairs. Dimitri is not far off. Sir Daniel came out of the cloakroom over there on the left. The group of noisy young people was nearer the front entrance. And through this door, next the men's cloak-room, was the buffet. Let's have a look at it. You've seen all this before, Brer Fox, but you must allow me to maunder on.'

They went into the buffet.

'It stinks like a pot-house, doesn't it? Look at Dimitri's neat boxes of empty champagne bottles under the tables. Gaiety at ten pounds a dozen. This is where Donald and Bridget came from in the penultimate scene and where Dimitri and Carrados spoke together just before Lord Robert left. And for how long afterwards? Look, Fox, here's a Sherlock Holmes touch. A cigar stump lying by a long trace of its own ash. A damn good cigar and has been carefully smoked. Here's the gentleman's glass beside it and here, on the floor, is the broken band. A Corona-Corona.' Alleyn sniffed at the glass. 'Brandy. Here's the bottle, Courvoisier '87. I'll wager that wasn't broadcast among the guests. More likely to have been kept for old Carrados. Fox, ring up Dimitri and find out if Sir Herbert drank brandy and smoked a cigar when he came in here after the party. And at the same time you might ask if we can see the Carrados family in about half an hour. Then we'll have to go on to the Halcut-Hackett group. Their house is close by here, Halkin Street. We'll have to come back. I want to see Carrados first. See if General and Mrs Halcut-Hackett will see us in about two hours, will you, Fox?'

Fox padded off to the telephone and Alleyn went through the second door of the buffet into a back passage. Here he found the but-ler's pantry. Dimitri's supper tray was still there. 'He did himself very well,' thought Alleyn, noticing three or four little green-black pellets on a smeared plate. 'Caviare. And here's the wing of a bird picked clean. Champagne, too. Sleek Mr Dimitri, eating away like a well-fed cat behind the scenes.'

He rejoined Fox in the hall. 'Mr Dimitri,' said Fox, 'remembered giving Sir Herbert Carrados brandy from a special bottle reserved for him. He thought that Sir Herbert smoked a cigar while he took his brandy, but would not swear to it.'

'We'd better print the brandy-glass,' said Alleyn. 'I'll get Bailey to attend to it and then, I think, they can clean up here. How did you get on?'

'All right, sir. The Halcut-Hacketts will see us any time later on this afternoon.'

'What about Carrados?'

'He came to the telephone,' said Fox. 'He'll see us if we go round now.'

'How did he sound? Bloody-minded?'

'If you like to put it that way, sir. He seemed to be sort of long-suffering, more than angry, I thought, and said something about hoping he knew his duty. He mentioned that he is a great personal friend of the chief commissioner.'

'Oh, Lord, Lord! Huff and grandeur! Uncertain, coy, and hard to please. Don't I know it. Fox, we must continue to combine deference with a suggestion of high office. Out with the best butter and lay it on in slabs. Miserable old article, he is. Straighten your tie, harden your heart, and away we go.'

Sir Herbert and Lady Carrados lived in Green Street. A footman opened the door to Alleyn.

'Sir Herbert is not at home, sir. Would you care to leave a message?'

'He has an appointment with me,' said Alleyn pleasantly, 'so I expect he is at home really. Here's my card.'

'I beg pardon, sir,' said the footman, looking at Alleyn's clothes, which were admirable. 'I understood it was the police who were calling.'

'We are the police,' said Alleyn.

Fox, who had been dealing with their taxi, advanced. The footman's eye lit on his bowler and boots.

'I beg pardon, sir,' he said, 'will you come this way, please?'

He showed them into a library. Three past Carradoses, full length, in oils, stared coldly into space from the walls. The firelight wavered on a multitude of books uniformly bound, behind glass doors. Sir Herbert, in staff-officer's uniform with shiny boots and wonderful breeches, appeared in a group taken at Tunbridge Wells, the centre of his wartime activities. Alleyn looked at it closely, but the handsome face was as expressionless as the tightly-breeched knees which were separated by gloved hands resting with embarrassing importance on the inside of the thighs. A dumb photograph. It was flanked by two illuminated addresses of which Sir Herbert was the subject. A magnificent cigar box stood on a side table. Alleyn opened it and noted that the cigars were the brothers of the one that had been smoked in the buffet. He gently closed the lid and turned to inspect a miniature French writing-cabinet.

Fox, completely at his ease, stood like a rock in the middle of the room. He appeared to be lost in a mild abstraction, but he could have gone away and described the library with the accuracy of an expert far-gone in Pelmanism.

The door opened and Carrados came in. Alleyn found himself unaccountably reminded of bereaved royalty. Sir Herbert limped rather more perceptibly than usual and employed a black stick. He paused, screwed his glass in his eye, and said:

'Mr Alleyn?'

Alleyn stepped forward and bowed.

'It is extremely kind of you to see us, sir,' he said.

'No, no,' said Carrados, 'one must do one's duty however hard one is hit. One has to keep a stiff upper lip. I was talking to your chief commissioner just now, Mr Alleyn. He happens to be a very old friend of mine – er – won't you sit down both of you? Mr – er – ?'

'This is Inspector Fox, sir.'

'Oh, yes,' said Carrados, extending his hand. 'Do sit down, Fox. Yes – ' he turned again to Alleyn when they were all seated. 'Your CO tells me you are a son of another old friend. I knew your mother very well years ago and she sees quite a lot of my wife, I believe. She was at Marsdon House last night.' He placed his hand over his eyes and repeated in an irritating whisper: 'At Marsdon House. Ah, well!'

Alleyn said: 'We are very sorry indeed, sir, to bother you after what has happened. This tragedy has been a great shock to you, I'm afraid.'

Carrados gave him an injured smile.

'Yes,' he said, 'I cannot pretend that it has not. Lord Robert was one of our dearest friends. Not only have we a great sense of personal bereavement but I cannot help thinking that my hospitality has been cruelly abused.'

This reduction of homicide to terms of the social amenities left Alleyn speechless. Sir Herbert appeared to regard murder as a sort of inexcusable *faux pas*.

'I suppose,' he continued, 'that you have come here armed with a list of questions. If that is so I am afraid you are doomed to disappointment. I am a simple soldier-man, Mr Alleyn, and this sort of thing is quite beyond my understanding. I may say that ever since this morning we have been pestered by a crew of insolent young pups from Fleet Street. I have been forced to ask Scotland Yard, where I believe my name is not unknown, if we had no redress from this sort of damnable persecution. I talked about it to your chief who, as I think I told you, is a personal friend of mine. He agrees with me that the behaviour of journalists nowadays is intolerable.'

'I am sorry you have been badgered,' said Alleyn. 'I will be as quick as I can with our business. There *are* one or two questions, I'm afraid, but only one or two and none of them at all formidable.'

'I can assure you I am not in the least afraid of police investigation,' said Carrados with an injured laugh. His hand still covered his eyes.

'Of course not, sir. I wanted first of all to ask you if you spoke to Lord Robert last night. I mean something more than hail and farewell. I thought that if there was anything at all unusual in his manner it would not escape your notice as it would the notice of, I am afraid, the majority of people.'

Carrados looked slightly less huffy.

'I don't pretend to be any more observant than the next fellow,' he said, 'but as a soldier-man I've had to use my eyes a bit and I think if there's anything wrong anywhere I'm not likely to miss it. Yes, I spoke to Lord Robert Gospell once or twice last night and I can assure you he was perfectly normal in every possible way. He was nice enough to tell me he thought our ball the most successful of the season. Perfectly normal.'

Alleyn leant forward and fixed Carrados with a reverent glare.

'Sir Herbert,' he said, 'I'm going to do a very unconventional thing and I hope you won't get me my dismissal as I'm sure you very easily could. I'm going to take you wholly into our confidence.'

It was pleasant to see the trappings of sorrow fall softly away from Carrados, and to watch his posture change from that of a stricken soldier-man to an exact replica of the Tunbridge Wells photograph. Up came his head. The knees were spread apart, the hands went involuntarily to the inside of the thighs. Only the gloves and breeches were lacking. A wise son of Empire sat confessed.

'It would not be the first time,' said Carrados modestly, 'that confidence has been reposed in me.'

'I'm sure it wouldn't. This is our difficulty. We have reason to believe that the key to this mystery lies in a single sentence spoken by Lord Robert on the telephone from Marsdon House. If we could get a true report of the conversation that Lord Robert held with an unknown person at one o'clock this morning I believe we would have gone a long way towards making an arrest.'

'Ah!' Carrados positively beamed. 'This bears out my own theory, Mr Alleyn. It was an outside job. You see I am conversant with your phraseology. From the moment we heard of this tragedy I said to my wife that I was perfectly satisfied that none of our guests could be in any way implicated. A telephone message from outside! There you are!'

'I had half-hoped,' said Alleyn modestly, 'that you might have heard about this call. I suppose it was stupid of me.'

'When was it?'

'At one o'clock. We've got so far.'

'At one o'clock. One o'clock. Let me see!' Carrados drew his heavy brows down over his foolish eyes and scowled importantly. 'At the moment I must confess I cannot quite recall – '

'Most of your guests were still at supper, I think,' said Alleyn. 'I've spoken to the servant on duty on the top landing and he fancies he can remember that you came upstairs round about that time.'

The purple veins in Sir Herbert's red cheeks suddenly started up.

'By God, I should think the fellow did remember, confound his impudence. Certainly, I went on to the top landing and it *was* one o'clock. You are perfectly right, Mr Alleyn. I pay these damn caterers a fortune to organize the whole affair and I expect, not unreasonably I hope, a certain standard of efficiency. And what do I find? No matches! No matches in the sitting-out room at the head of the stairs and the damn place smothered in ash. A lighted cigarette burning the mantelpiece! It was underneath the clock. That's how I remember the time. Just on one o'clock, as you say. I trust I'm a reasonable sort of fellow, Alleyn, but I don't mind telling you I saw red. I went out on to the landing and I gave that fellow a dressing-down he won't forget in a hurry. Sent him haring off downstairs with a flea in his ear. Damn, spoon-fed dago!'

'Were you on the landing all this time, sir?'

'Of course I wasn't on the landing all the time! I was in and out of the blasted sitting-room, damn it. I went upstairs at, I suppose, about five to one, walked into this room and found it in the condition I've described. I would have looked at the other room, the one with the telephone, but I saw there was a couple sitting out in there. Behaving, I may say, more like a footman and a housemaid than the sort of people one is accustomed to receive as one's guests. However! The man came sneaking out just as I was blasting this damned waiter-fellow. He hung about the landing. This fellow Withers, I mean. Don't know if I gave you his name before. Then the lady came out and scuttled into the cloakroom. Yes, by God, sir, and Robert Gospell came upstairs and went into the telephone room.'

Carrados blew out his moustache triumphantly. 'There you are!' he said. 'Into the room to telephone.'

'Splendid, sir. Now may I just go over this to make sure I've got it right? You came out of the first sitting-room and spoke to the waiter. Captain Withers came out of the second room (the telephone-room) followed in a moment by Mrs Halcut-Hackett, who went into the cloakroom.'

'Here!' ejaculated Carrados, 'I didn't mention the lady's name, Alleyn. By God, I hope I know my manners better than to use a lady's name out of turn.'

Alleyn achieved an expression of gentlemanly cunning.

'I'm afraid, sir, I rather jumped to conclusions.'

'Really? D'you mean it's common talk? An American, wasn't she? Well, well, well, I'm sorry to hear that. Halcut-Hackett's a very old friend of mine. I'm very sorry to hear that.'

Alleyn reflected acidly that Sir Herbert was enjoying himself thoroughly and hurried on.

'At this moment, just as you return to the sitting-room, having sent the waiter downstairs, and Mrs Halcut-Hackett dives into the cloakroom, Lord Robert comes upstairs. What does Withers do?'

'Sheers off and comes sloping into the sitting-room after me. I had to make conversation with the fellow. Young Potter was sulking about in there too. I hope I've got as much tolerance for the youngsters as any other old fogey, Alleyn, but I must confess I – '

He stopped and looked uncomfortable.

'Yes?' murmured Alleyn.

'I – it doesn't matter. Stick to the point, eh? Withers, eh? Yes. Well now, I flatter myself, Alleyn, that I can get along with most people, but I freely confess I did not enjoy Withers's company. Calls himself Captain. What was his regiment?'

'I don't know at all. Could you, by any chance, hear Lord Robert from the other room?'

'No. No, I couldn't. Now you mention it, I believe I heard the extension bell doing that damned dialling tinkle. The fact is I couldn't stand any more of that confounded outsider's conversation. I made my excuses and went downstairs.'

'Did you meet anybody coming up?'

'I don't think so. Mrs Halcut-Hackett was going down ahead of me.'

'So while you were still in the sitting-room, sir, anybody might have come upstairs and gone into the room where Lord Robert sat telephoning?'

'I suppose so.'

'Mrs Halcut-Hackett might have gone in before you went downstairs. Captain Withers or Donald Potter might have done it afterwards?'

'Yes, by Gad, they might. If you want to get an account of this telephone conversation you might ask 'em. I don't like to make the suggestion about one of my guests, but upon my soul I wouldn't put it past Withers to listen to a private conversation. What's young Potter doing, cottoning on to a cad twenty years his senior, I'd like to know? However! Anything more?'

'Yes, sir. Did you by any chance notice a Miss Harris while you were upstairs? The man said something – '

'Harris? D'you mean m'wife's secretary? Yes, of course I saw her. She bolted into the lavatory when I came up. I didn't see her come out.'

'I see. Perhaps I might have a word with her before I go.'

'Certainly, but you'll find her a bit difficult. She's a shy little thing – pity there aren't more like her. Nowadays they don't give a damn who sees them coming out of any door.'

Sir Herbert suddenly made up his mind he had said something amusing and broke into loud baying laughter in which Alleyn was careful to join.

'Poor little Harris,' Carrados said. 'Well, well, well!'

'Now,' continued Alleyn when the laughter had died away, 'about the end of the ball. We would like to trace Lord Robert's movements, of course. I don't know, sir, if you can give us any help at all.'

'Ah! Yes. Well, let me see. My wife and I stood on the ballroom gallery at the head of the stairs saying goodbye to our guests – those of them who were old-fashioned enough to think it necessary to thank their hosts. Some of the young cubs didn't take the trouble, I may tell you. Lord Robert came, of course, and was perfectly charming. Let me see, now. He went downstairs, into the cloakroom and out again wearing that extraordinary cloak of his. I remember this because I came down and passed him. I went into the buffet.'

'Did you come out again before Lord Robert left?'

'No.' Carrados returned for a moment to the stricken soldier-man. 'No. That was the last I shall ever see of Robert Gospell. Ah, well! I don't mind admitting, Alleyn, that this thing has hit me pretty hard. Pretty hard! Still, we've got to bite on the bullet, haven't we? What were we saying? Oh yes. I stayed in the buffet for some time. I don't mind admitting I was about all in. I smoked a cigar and had a peg of brandy. I had a word with that fellow Dimitri and then I went home.'

'With Lady Carrados and Miss O'Brien?'

'What? No. No, I packed them off earlier in the other car. My wife was absolutely fagged out. I wanted to have a look round. Make sure everything was all right. I wouldn't trust anybody else. These people are so damned careless, leaving lighted cigarettes all over the place. I satisfied myself everything was all right and then I went home. The chauffeur came back for me. Daresay you'd like to see him.'

'No, sir, thank you. I think we may take that as read.'

'I've no wish to be treated differently from anyone else, but that's as you please, of course. Anything else?'

'If I might have a word with Lady Carrados, sir?'

'I don't think my wife can give you any information, Alleyn. She's absolutely prostrated by this business. Robert Gospell was a very great friend of hers and she's taken it damn hard. Matter of fact, she's not up.'

Alleyn paused.

'I am so sorry,' he said at last. 'That's most unfortunate. I wanted if possible to save her appearing at the inquest.'

'When is the inquest?'

'Tomorrow morning, sir.'

Carrados glared at him.

'She will certainly be too unwell for any such thing. I shall see that her doctor forbids it. And it is equally impossible for her to see you this afternoon. I know that if I were to disturb her, which I have no intention of doing as she is asleep in bed, she would refuse. That's definite.'

The door opened and the footman came in.

'Her ladyship, sir, wishes me to say that if Mr Alleyn has a few minutes to spare she would be very pleased to see him.'

He waited, gently closing the door on an extremely uncomfortable silence.

CHAPTER 16

Lady Carrados Looks Back

Alleyn followed the footman upstairs, leaving Fox in the library to make the best of a sticky situation.

The footman handed Alleyn over to a maid who took him to Lady Carrados. She was not in bed. She was in her boudoir erect in a tall blue chair and wearing the look that had prompted Paddy O'Brien to compare her with a Madonna. She held out her hands when she saw Alleyn and as he took them a phrase came into his mind. He thought: 'She is an English lady and these are an English lady's hands, thin, unsensual, on the end of delicate thin arms.'

She said: 'Roderick! I do call you Roderick, don't I?'

Alleyn said: 'I hope so. It's a long time since we met, Evelyn.'

'Too long. Your mother tells me about you sometimes. We spoke to each other today on the telephone. She was so very kind and understanding, Roderick, and she told me that you would be too. Do sit down and smoke. I should like to feel that you are not a great detective but an old friend.'

'I should like to feel that too,' said Alleyn. 'I must tell you, Evelyn, that I was on the point of asking to see you when I got your message.'

'An official call?'

'Yes, bad luck to it. You've made everything much pleasanter by asking for me.'

She pressed the thin hands together and Alleyn, noticing the bluish lights on the knuckles, remembered how Troy had wanted to paint them.

Lady Carrados said, 'I suppose Herbert didn't want you to see me?'

'He wasn't very pleased with the idea. He thought you were too tired and distressed.'

She smiled faintly: 'Yes,' she said, and it was impossible to be sure that she spoke ironically. 'Yes, he is very thoughtful. What do you want to ask me, Roderick?'

'All sorts of dreary questions, I'm afraid. I'm sorry about it. I know you were one of Bunchy's friends.'

'So were you.'

'Yes.'

'What is your first question?'

Alleyn went over the final scene in the hall and found she had nothing new to tell him. She answered him quickly and concisely. He could see that his questions held no particular significance for her and that her thoughts were lying in wait, anxiously, for what was yet to come. As soon as he began to speak of the green room on the top landing he knew that he touched her more nearly. He felt a profound distaste for his task. He went on steadily, without emphasis.

'The green sitting-room with the telephone. We know that he used the telephone and are anxious to find out if he was overheard. Someone says you left your bag there, Evelyn. Did you?'

'Yes.'

'Dimitri returned it to you?'

'Yes.'

'When was this?'

'Soon after I had come up from supper – about half-past twelve or a quarter to one.'

'Not as late as one o'clock?'

'No.'

'Why are you so certain of this, please?'

'Because,' said Lady Carrados, 'I was watching the time rather carefully.'

'Were you? Does the peak of a successful ball come at a specific moment?'

'Well, one rather watches the time. If they don't begin to drift away after supper it looks as if it will be a success.'

'Where were you when Dimitri returned your bag?'

'In the ballroom.'

'Did you notice Bunchy at about this time?'

'I – don't think – I remember.'

The hands were pressed closer together as if she held her secret between them; as if it might escape. Her lips were quite white.

The door opened and Bridget came in. She looked as if she had been crying.

'Oh, Donna,' she said, 'I'm sorry, I didn't know – '

'This is my girl, Roderick. Bridget, this is Sarah's uncle.'

'How do you do,' said Bridget. 'The detective one?'

'The detective one.'

'Sarah says you're quite human really.'

'That's very kind of Sarah,' said her uncle drily.

'I hope you're not heckling my mother,' said Bridget, sitting on the arm of the chair. She had an air of determined sprightliness.

'I'm trying not to. Perhaps you could help us both. We are talking about last night.'

'Well, I might be able to tell you something frightfully important without knowing it myself, sort of, mightn't I?'

'It's happened before now,' said Alleyn with a smile. 'We were talking about your mother's bag.'

'The one she left upstairs and that I found?'

'Bridgie!' whispered Lady Carrados. 'Oh, Bridgie!'

'It's all right, Donna, my sweet. That had nothing to do with Bunchy. Oh – he was there, wasn't he? In the supper-room when I brought it to you?'

Bridget, perched on the arm of the wing chair, could not see her mother's face and Alleyn thought: 'Now we're in for it.'

He said: '*You* returned the bag in the *supper-room*, did you?'

Lady Carrados suddenly leant back and closed her eyes.

'Yes,' Bridget said, 'and it was simply squashed full of money. But why the bag? Does it fit somewhere frightfully subtle? I mean was the motive really money and did the murderer think Donna gave Bunchy the money, sort of? Or something?'

Lady Carrados said: 'Bridgie, darling. I'm by way of talking privately to Mr Alleyn.'

'Oh, are you, darling? I'm sorry. I'll whizz off. Shall I see you again before you go, Mr Alleyn?'

'Please, Miss Bridget.'

'Well, come along to the old nursery. I'll be there.'

Bridget looked round the corner of the chair at her mother, who actually managed to give her a smile. She went out and Lady Carrados covered her face with her hands.

'Don't try to tell me, Evelyn,' said Alleyn gently. 'I'll see if I can tell you. Come now, it may not be so dreadful, after all. Listen. Someone has been blackmailing you. You have had letters written in script on Woolworth paper. One of them came on the morning Bunchy brought you spring flowers. You put it under your pillow. Last night you left your bag in the green room, because you had been told to leave it there. It contained the money the blackmailer demanded. It now appears that Bridget returned your bag, still full of notes, while you were in the supper-room with Bunchy. Did you replace it in the green sitting-room? You did . . . and later it was returned to you, empty – while you were in the ballroom?'

'But – you *know* all this! Roderick, do you also know what they have found out?'

'No. I have no idea what they found out. Had Bunchy?'

'That is what horrifies me. Bunchy knew, at least, that I was being persecuted. When Bridgie brought back that hideous bag last night I nearly collapsed. I can't tell you what a shock it was to me. You are quite right, a letter, like the one you described, came a few days ago. There had been others. I didn't answer them. I destroyed them all and tried to put them out of my mind. I thought perhaps they wouldn't go on with it if I paid no attention. But this one threatened dreadful things, things that would hurt Bridgie so much – so much. It said that if I didn't do as I was ordered Herbert and Bridgie would be told about – everything. I couldn't face that. I did what they said. I put five hundred pounds in green notes in the bag and left it on the little table in the green sitting-room before one o'clock. And then Bridgie must have seen it. I shall never forget her coming into the supper-room, laughing and holding out that bag. I suppose I must have looked frightful. It's all muddled in my mind now, like the memory of a terrible dream. Somehow we got rid of Bridgie. Bunchy must have been splendid. Sir Daniel Davidson was there. I've been to see him lately about my health and he had said something to me before that evening. I got rid of him, too, and then Bunchy and I went out into the hall and Bunchy said he knew what I wanted to do with my bag and begged me not to do it. I was frantic. I broke away from him and went back again to the green sitting-room. Nobody was there. I put the bag back on the table. It was then twenty to one. I put it behind a big ormolu and enamel box on the table. Then I went down to the ballroom. I don't know how much later it was when I saw Dimitri coming through the room with the bag. At first I thought the same thing had happened again, but when I took it in my hand I knew the money had gone. Dimitri had found the bag, he said, and recognized it as mine. That's all.'

'That's all,' repeated Alleyn. 'It's a good deal. Look here, Evelyn, I'm going to ask you point-blank, is it possible that Dimitri is the man who is blackmailing you?

'Dimitri!' Her eyes opened wide. 'Good heavens, no! No, no, it's out of the question. He couldn't possibly have any idea, any means of knowing. Not possibly.'

'Are you sure of that? He is in and out of people's houses and has free access to their rooms. He has opportunities of overhearing conversations, of watching people when they are off their guard.'

'How long has he been doing this work?'

'He told me seven years.'

'My secret is more than twice as old as that. "Lady Audley's Secret"! But it's not so amusing, Roderick, when you carry it about with you. And yet, do you know, there have been times when I have almost forgotten my secret. It all happened so very long ago. The years have sifted past and mounted like sand into smooth unremark-able shapes and they have gradually hidden the old times. I thought I should never be able to speak of this to anyone in the world, but, oddly enough, it is rather a relief to talk about it.'

'You realize, don't you, that I am here to investigate a murder? It's my job to work out the circumstances surrounding it. I must have no consideration for anybody's feelings if they come between me and the end of the job. Bunchy knew you were the victim of a blackmailer. You are not the only victim. He was actually working with us on information we had from another source but which points directly to the same individual. It's quite possible, and to us it seems probable, that the blackmailing may be linked with the murder. So we have a double incentive to get at the blackmailer's identity.'

'I know what you are going to ask me. I have no idea who it is. None. I've asked myself over and over again who it could be.'

'Yes. Now see here, Evelyn, I could get up to all the old tricks, and with any luck I'd probably get a line on this secret of yours. I'd trap you into little admissions and when I got away from here I'd write them all down, add them up, and see what I could make of the answer. Probably there wouldn't be an answer so we'd begin to dig and dig. Back through those years that have sifted over your trouble and hidden it. And sooner or later we would find something. It would all be very disagreeable and I should hate it and the final result would be exactly the same as if you told me your whole story now.'

'I can't. I can't tell you.'

'You are thinking of the consequences. Newspaper publicity. Court proceedings. You know it wouldn't be nearly as bad as you imagine. Your name would probably never appear.'

'Madame X,' said Lady Carrados with a faint smile, 'and everybody in court knowing perfectly well who I was. Oh, it's not for myself I mind. It's Bridgie. And Herbert. You've met Herbert and you must realize how he'd take a blow of this sort. I can think of nobody who would mind more.'

'And how is he going to take it if we find out for ourselves? Evelyn, think! You're one of Bunchy's friends.'

'I'm not a revengeful woman.'

'Good God, it's not a question of revenge. It's a question of leaving a blackmailing murderer at large.'

'You needn't go on, Roderick. I know quite well what I ought to do.'

'And I know quite well that you're going to do it.'

They looked squarely at each other. Her hands made a gesture of surrender.

'Very well,' said Lady Carrados. 'I give in. How much more dignified it would have been, wouldn't it, if I had accepted my duty at first?'

'I had no doubt about what you'd do. It's quite possible, you know, that your side of the business need never come out. Of course, I can't promise this, but it is possible we'll work on your information without putting it in as evidence.'

'That's very kind of you,' she said faintly.

'You're being ironical,' said Alleyn with a grin, 'and that shows you're not going to mind as much as you feared, or I hope it does.

Now then. It's something about Bridget, isn't it, and it happened more than fourteen years ago. Bridget's how old? Seventeen?'

Lady Carrados nodded.

'I don't believe I ever met your first husband, Evelyn. Is Bridget very like him?'

'Yes. She's got all Paddy's gaiety.'

'My mother told me that. Bridget doesn't remember him, of course. Ought we to begin with him?'

'Yes. You needn't go on being delicate, Roderick. I think you've guessed, haven't you? Paddy and I were not married.'

'Bless my soul,' said Alleyn, 'how very courageous of you, Evelyn.'

'I think it was now but it didn't seem so then. Nobody knew. It's the *Jane Eyre* theme but I hadn't Miss Eyre's moral integrity. Paddy left a wife in an Australian lunatic asylum, came home, and fell in love with me. As you would say in your report, we went through a form of marriage and lived happily and bigamously together. Then Paddy died.'

'Weren't you afraid it would come out?'

'No. Paddy's wife had no relations.' Lady Carrados waited for a moment. She seemed to be gravely contemplating the story she had decided to relate. When she spoke again it was with composure and even, or so Alleyn fancied, an air of relaxation. He wondered if she had often marshalled the facts in her own mind and rehearsed her story to an imaginary listener. The quiet voice went on sedately: 'She was a music-hall comedienne who had been left stranded in a little town in New South Wales. He married her there and took her to Sydney. Six weeks later she became hopelessly insane. He found out that her mother was in a lunatic asylum somewhere in America. Paddy had not told anybody of his marriage and he had not looked up any of his acquaintances in Sydney. When he arranged to have her put away it was under her maiden name. He invested a sum of money, the interest on which was enough to pay the fees and expenses. He left the whole thing in the hands of the only man who knew the truth. He was Anthony Banks, Paddy's greatest friend, and was absolutely above suspicion, I am sure. He lived in Sydney and helped Paddy all through that time. He held Paddy's power of attorney. Even he did not know Paddy had remarried. Nobody knew that.'

'What about the parson who married them?'

'I remember that Paddy said he was a very old man. The witnesses were his wife and sister. You see, we talked it all over very carefully and Paddy was quite certain there was no possibility of discovery.'

'There is something more, isn't there?'

'Yes. Something that I find much more difficult.' The even voice faltered for a moment. Alleyn saw that she mustered up all her fortitude before she went on. 'Five months after we were married he was killed. I had started Bridgie and came up to London to stay with my mother and to see my doctor. Paddy was to motor up from our house at Ripplecote and drive me back. In the morning I had a telegram from him. It said: "The best possible news from Anthony Banks." On the way the car skidded and crashed into the wall of a bridge. It was in a little village. He was taken into the vicarage and then to the cottage hospital. When I got there he was unconscious and he didn't know that I was with him when he died.'

'And the news?'

'I felt certain that it could only be one thing. His wife must have died. But we could find no letters or cables at all, so he must have destroyed whatever message he had been sent by Anthony Banks. The next thing that happened was that Paddy's solicitors received five thousand pounds from Australia and a letter from Anthony Banks to say it was forwarded in accordance with Paddy's instructions. In the meantime I had written to Anthony Banks. I told him of Paddy's death but wrote as a cousin of Paddy's. He replied with the usual sort of letter. He didn't, of course, say anything about Paddy's wife, but he did say that a letter from him must have reached Paddy just before he died and that if it had been found he would like it to be destroyed unopened. You see, Roderick, Anthony Banks must have been honest because he could have kept that five thousand pounds himself quite easily, when she died. And he didn't know Paddy had remarried.'

'Yes, that's quite true. Are you certain from what you knew of Paddy that he would have destroyed Banks's letter?'

'No. I've always thought he would have kept it to show me.'

'Do you think he asked the people in the vicarage or at the hospital to destroy his letters?'

'They had found his name and address on other letters in his wallet, so it wasn't that.' For the first time the quiet voice faltered a little. 'He only spoke once, they said. He asked for me.'

'Do you remember the name of the people at the vicarage?'

'I don't. I wrote and thanked them for what they had done. It was some very ordinary sort of name.'

'And the cottage hospital?'

'It was at Falconbridge in Buckinghamshire. Quite a big hospital. I saw the superintendent doctor. He was an elderly man with a face like a sheep. I think his name was Bletherley. I'm perfectly certain that he was not a blackmailer, Roderick. And the nurses were charming.'

'Do you think that he could possibly have left the letter in the case, or that it could have dropped out of his pocket?'

'I simply cannot believe that if he kept it at all it would be anywhere but in his wallet. And I was given the wallet. It was in the breast pocket of his coat. You see, Roderick, it's not as if I didn't try to trace the letter. I was desperately anxious to see the message from Anthony Banks. I asked again and again if anything could have been overlooked at the hospital and endless enquiries were made.'

She stopped for a moment and looked steadily at Alleyn.

'You can see now,' she said, 'why I would go almost to any length to keep this from Bridget.'

'Yes,' said Alleyn, 'I can see.'

CHAPTER 17

The Element of Youth

Alleyn saw Bridget in her old nursery which had been converted into a very human sitting-room. She made him take a large armchair and jiggled a box of cigarettes under his nose.

'It's no good being official and pretending you don't. I can see you do.'

'Really!' exclaimed Alleyn with a look at his fingers which were not stained with nicotine. 'How?'

'The outline of your case shows through your coat. You should take up detection, Mr Alleyn, it's *too* interesting.'

Alleyn took a cigarette.

'Got me there,' he said. 'Have you yourself any ideas about being a policewoman?' He fingered the outline that showed through his breast-pocket.

'I suppose one has to begin at the bottom,' said Bridget. 'What's the first duty of a policewoman?'

'I don't know. We are not allowed to hang around the girls in the force.'

'What a shame!' said Bridget. 'I won't join. I should like you to hang round me, Mr Alleyn.'

Alleyn thought: 'She's being just a bit too deliberately the audacious young charmer. What's up with her? Young Donald, damn his eyes!'

He said: 'Well, so I must for the moment. I want to talk to you about last night, if I may.'

'I'm afraid I won't be much good,' said Bridget. 'I hope you find whoever it was. It's worrying Donna to death, and Bart's being absolutely lethal over it. Bart's my stepfather. You've met him, haven't you? All pukka sahib and horsewhips. Is a horsewhip any worse than an ordinary one, do you know?'

'You knew Lord Robert pretty well, didn't you?' asked Alleyn.

'Yes. He was a great friend of Donna's. I suppose you think I'm being hard and modern about him. I'd have been sorrier if it had happened longer ago.'

'That's rather cryptic,' said Alleyn. 'What does it mean?'

'It doesn't mean I'm not sorry now. I am. We all loved him and I mind most dreadfully. But I found out I didn't really know him well. He was harder than you'd ever believe. In a way that makes it worse; having been out of friends with him. I feel I'd give anything to be able to tell him I – I – I – I'm sorry.'

'Sorry for what?'

'For not being nice to him last night. I snubbed him.'

'Why did you snub poor Bunchy?'

'Because he was beastly to his nephew who happens to be rather a particular friend of mine.'

'Donald Potter? Yes, I know about that. Don't you think it's possible that Donald was rather hard on his uncle?'

'No, I don't. Donald's a man now. He's got to stand on his own feet and decide things for himself. Bunchy simply wouldn't understand that. He wanted to choose Donald's friends, settle his career, and treat him exactly as if he was a schoolboy. Bunchy was just hopelessly Victorian and conventional.'

'Do you like Captain Withers?' asked Alleyn suddenly.

'What?' Bridget became rather pink. 'I can't say he's exactly my cup of tea. I suppose he is rather ghastly in a way, but he's a marvellous dancer and he can be quite fun. I can forgive anybody almost anything if they're amusing, can't you?'

'What sort of amusement does Captain Withers provide?'

'Well, I mean he's gay. Not exactly gay but he goes everywhere and everybody knows him, so he's always quite good value. Donald says Wits is a terribly good business man. He's been frightfully nice about advising Donald and he knows all sorts of people who could be useful.'

'Useful in what way? Donald is going in for medicine, isn't he?'

'Well – ' Bridget hesitated. 'Yes. That was the original idea, but Wits rather advises him not to. Donald says there's not much in medicine nowadays and, anyway, a doctor is rather a dreary sort of thing to be.'

'Is he?' asked Alleyn. 'You mean not very smart?'

'No, of course I don't mean that,' said Bridget. She glared at Alleyn. 'You *are* a pig,' she said. 'I suppose I do. I hate drab, worthy sort of things and, anyway, it's got nothing to with the case.'

'I should like to know what career Captain Withers has suggested for Donald.'

'There's nothing definite yet. They've thought of starting a new night club. Wits has got wonderfully original ideas.'

'Yes,' agreed Alleyn. 'I can quite imagine it. He's doing quite well with the place at Leatherhead, isn't he? Why doesn't he take Donald in there?'

Bridget looked surprised.

'How did you know about that?' she asked.

'You must never say that to policemen,' said Alleyn. 'It steals their thunder. As a matter of fact, I have been talking to Withers and the Leatherhead venture cropped up.'

'Well, I dare say you know more about it than I do,' said Bridget. 'Donald says it's just a small men's club. More for fun than to make money. They play bridge and things. I don't think there's any opening there.'

'Have you spoken to Donald since his uncle died?' Bridget clenched her hands and thumped them angrily on her knees.

'Of course, he rang me up. I'd just got to the telephone when Bart came in looking like a beastly old Cochin China rooster and took the receiver from me. I could have killed him, he was so infuriating! He was all sort of patient and old-world. He sympathized with Donald and then he said: "If you don't mind old fellow speaking frankly, I think it would be better if you didn't communicate with my stepdaughter for the time being!" I said: "No! Give it to me," but he simply turned his back on me and went on: "You understand. I'm afraid I must forbid it," and put the receiver down. I stormed at him but we were in Donna's room and she was so upset I had to give in and promise I wouldn't write or anything. It's so beastly, *beastly* unfair. And it's all because Bart's such a filthy old snob and is afraid of all the reporters and scandal and everything. Horrid bogus old man. And he's absolutely *filthy* to darling Donna. How she ever married him! After daddy, who must have been so gay, and charming, and who loved her so much. How she could! And if Bart thinks I'm going to give Donald up he's jolly well got another think coming.'

'Are you engaged?'

'No. We're waiting till Donald begins to earn.'

'And how much must Donald earn before he is marriageable?'

'You don't put it very nicely, do you? I suppose you think I'm hard and modern and beastly. I dare say I am, but I can't bear the idea of everything getting squalid and drab because we have to worry about money. A horrid little flat, second-rate restaurants, whitewood furniture painted to look fresh and nice. Ugh! I've seen these sorts of marriages,' said Bridget looking worldly-wise, 'and I *know*.'

'Donald is his uncle's heir, you know.'

Bridget was on her feet, her eyes flashing.

'Don't you dare,' she said, 'don't you dare to say that because Donald gets the money he had anything to do with this. Don't you dare.'

'And don't you go putting ideas into people's heads by getting on the defensive before you've been given cause,' said Alleyn very firmly indeed. He put his hand inside his breast-pocket. The slight bulge disappeared and out came Alleyn's notebook. In the midst of her fury Bridget's glance fell on it. She looked from the notebook to Alleyn. He raised one eyebrow and screwed his face into an apologetic grimace.

'The idea was perfectly magnificent,' he said. 'It did look like a cigarette-case. The edges of the bulge weren't quite sharp enough.'

'Pig!' said Bridget.

'Sorry,' said Alleyn. 'Now then. Three or four offical questions, if you please. And look here, Miss Bridget, will you let me offer you a very dreary piece of advice? It's our set-piece for innocent witnesses. Don't prevaricate. Don't lose your temper. And don't try any downright thumping lies, because if you do, as sure as eggs is eggs, you'll be caught out and it'll look very nasty indeed for anyone whom you thought you were going to protect. You think Donald is innocent, don't you?'

'I *know* he is innocent.'

'Right. Then you have nothing in the wide world to fear. Away we go. Did you sit out in the green sitting-room on the top gallery?'

'Yes. Lots of times.'

'During the supper hour? Between twelve and one?'

Bridget pondered. As he watched her Alleyn looked back at youth and marvelled at its buoyancy. Bridget's mind bounced from thoughts of death to thoughts of love. She was sorry Bunchy was murdered, but as long as Donald was not suspected she was also rather thrilled at the idea of police investigation. She was sincerely concerned at her mother's distress and ready to make sacrifices on Lady Carrados's behalf. But ready to meet all sorrow, anger or fright was her youth, like a sort of pneumatic armour that received momentary impressions of these things but instantly filled out again. Now, when she came to her mother's indisposition she spoke soberly, but it was impossible to escape the impression that on the whole she was stimulated rather than unnerved by tragedy.

'I was up there with Donald until after most people had gone into the supper-room. We both came down together. That was when I returned her bag to Donna. Donna wasn't well. She's awfully tired. She nearly fainted when I found her in the supper-room. She said afterwards it was the stuffiness.'

'Yes?'

'It was a queer sort of night, hot indoors, but when any of the windows were opened the mist came in and it brought a kind of dank chilliness. Donna asked me to fetch. her smelling-salts. I ran upstairs to the ladies' cloakroom. Donna's maid Sophie was there. I got the smelling-salts from Sophie and ran downstairs. I couldn't find Donna but I ran into Bunchy who said she was all right again. I had booked that dance with Percy Percival. He was a bit drunk and was making a scene about my having cut him out. So I danced with him to keep him quiet.'

'Did you go up to the green sitting-room again?'

'Not for some time. Donald and I went up there towards the end of the party.'

'Did you at any stage of the proceedings leave your cigarette-case on the pie-crust table in that room?'

Bridget stared at him.

'I haven't got a cigarette-case; I don't smoke. Is there something about a cigarette-case in the green sitting-room?'

'There may be. Do you know if anybody overheard Bunchy telephone from that room at about one o'clock?'

'I haven't heard of it,' said Bridget. He saw that her curiosity was aroused. 'Have you asked Miss Harris?' she said. 'She was on the top landing a good deal last night. She's somewhere in the house now.'

'I'll have a word with her. There's just one other point. Lord Robert was with your mother when you returned her bag, wasn't he? He was there when she felt faint?'

'Yes. Why?'

'Did he seem upset in any way?'

'He seemed very concerned about Donna but that was all. Sir Daniel – Donna's doctor – came up. Bunchy opened a window. They all seemed to want me out of the way. Donna asked for her smelling-salts, so I went and got them. That's all. What about a cigarette-case? Do tell me.'

'It's gold with a medallion sunk in the lid and surrounded by brilliants. Do you know it?'

'It sounds horribly grand. No, I don't think I do.'

Alleyn got up.

'That's all, then,' he said. Thank you so much, Miss Bridget. Good-bye.' He had got as far as the door before she stopped him.

'Mr Alleyn!'

'Yes?'

She was standing very erect in the middle of the room, her chin up and a lock of hair falling across her forehead.

'You seem to be very interested in the fact that my mother was not well last night. Why?'

'Lord Robert was with her at the time – ' Alleyn began.

'You seem equally interested in the fact that I returned my mother's bag to her. Why? Neither of these incidents had anything to do with Bunchy Gospell. My mother's not well and I won't have her worried.'

'Quite right,' said Alleyn. 'I won't either if I can help it.'

She seemed to accept that, but he could see that she had something else to say. Her young, beautifully made-up face in its frame of careful curls had a frightened look.

'I want you to tell me,' said Bridget, 'if you suspect Donald of anything.'

'It is much too soon for us to form any definite suspicion of anybody,' Alleyn said. 'You shouldn't attach too much significance to any one question in police interrogations. Many of our questions are nothing but routine. As Lord Robert's heir – no, don't storm at me again, you asked me and I tell you – as Lord Robert's heir Donald is bound to come in for his share of questions. If you are worrying about him, and I see you are, may I give you a tip? Encourage him to return to medicine. If he starts running night clubs the chances are that sooner or later he will fall into our clutches. And then what?'

'Of course,' said Bridget thoughtfully, 'it'll be different now. We could get married quite soon, even if he was at a hospital or something all day. He will have *some* money.'

'Yes,' agreed Alleyn, 'yes.'

'I mean I don't want to be heartless,' continued Bridget looking at him quite frankly, 'but naturally one can't help thinking of that. We're terribly, terribly sorry about Bunchy. We couldn't be sorrier. But he wasn't young like us.'

Into Alleyn's mind came suddenly the memory of a thinning head, leant sideways, of fat hands, of small feet turned inwards.

'No,' he said, 'he wasn't young like you.'

'I think he was stupid and tiresome over Donald,' Bridget went on in a high voice, 'and I'm not going to pretend I don't, although I am sorry I wasn't friends with him last night. But all the same I don't believe he'd have minded us thinking about the difference the money would make. I believe he would have understood that.'

'I'm sure he would have understood.'

'Well then, don't look as if you're thinking I'm hard and beastly.'

'I don't think you're beastly and I don't believe you are really very hard.'

'Thank you for nothing,' said Bridget and added immediately: 'Oh, damn, I'm sorry.'

'That's all right,' said Alleyn. 'Good-bye.'

'Yes, but – '

'Well?'

'Nothing. Only, you make me feel shabby and it's not fair. If there was anything I could do for Bunchy I'd do it. So would Donald, of course. But he's dead. You can't do anything for dead people.'

'If they have been murdered you can try to catch the man that killed them.'

' "An eye for an eye." It doesn't do them any good. It's only savagery.'

'Let the murderer asphyxiate someone else if it's going to suit his book,' said Alleyn. 'Is that the idea?'

'If there was any real thing we could do – '

'How about Donald doing what his uncle wanted so much? Taking his medical? That is,' said Alleyn quickly, 'unless he really has got a genuine ambition in another direction. Not by way of Captain Withers's night clubs.'

'I've just said he might be a doctor, now, haven't I?'

'Yes,' said Alleyn, 'you have. So we're talking in circles.' His hand was on the door-knob.

'I should have thought,' said Bridget, 'that as a detective you would have wanted to make me talk.'

Alleyn laughed outright.

'You little egoist,' he said, 'I've listened to you for the last ten minutes and all you want to talk about is yourself and your young man. Quite right too, but not the policeman's cup of tea. You take care of your mother who needs you rather badly just now, encourage your young man to renew his studies and, if you can, wean him from Withers. Good-bye, now, I'm off.'

CHAPTER 18

Predicament of a Secretary

When he had closed the nursery door behind him, Alleyn made for the stairs. If Fox was still closeted in the library with Carrados conversation must be getting a bit strained. He passed Lady Carrados's room and heard a distant noise.

'It's insufferable, my dear Evelyn, that – '

Alleyn grimaced and went on downstairs.

He found Fox alone in the library.

'Hullo, Brer Fox,' said Alleyn. 'Lost the simple soldier-man?'

'Gone upstairs,' said Fox. 'I can't say I'm sorry. I had a job to keep him here at all after you went.'

'How did you manage it?'

'Asked him if he had any experience of police investigation. That did it. We went from there to how he helped the police catch a footman that stole somebody's pearls in Tunbridge and how if he just hadn't happened to notice the man watching the vase on the piano nobody would ever have thought of looking in the Duchess's potpourri. Funny how vain some of these old gentlemen get, isn't it?'

'Screamingly. As we seem to have this important room all to ourselves we'd better see if we can get hold of Miss Harris. You might go and ask – '

But before Fox got as far as the door it opened and Miss Harris herself walked in.

'Good afternoon,' she said crisply, 'I believe you wished to see me. Lady Carrados's secretary.'

'We were on the point of asking for you, Miss Harris,' said Alleyn. 'Won't you sit down? My name is Alleyn and this is Inspector Fox.'

'Good afternoon,' repeated Miss Harris and sat down.

She was neither plain nor beautiful, short nor tall, dark nor fair. It crossed his mind that she might have won a newspaper competition for the average woman, that she represented the dead norm of femininity. Her clothes were perfectly adequate and completely without character. She was steeped in nonentity. No wonder that few people had noticed her at Marsdon House. She might have gone everywhere, heard everything like a sort of upper middle-class Oberon at Theseus's party. Unless, indeed, nonentity itself was conspicuous at Marsdon House last night.

He noticed that she was not in the least nervous. Her hands rested quietly in her lap. She had laid a pad and pencil on the arm of her chair exactly as if she was about to take notes at his dictation. Fox took his own notebook out and waited.

'May we have your name and address?' asked Alleyn.

'Certainly, Mr Alleyn,' said Miss Harris crisply. 'Dorothea Violet Harris. Address – town or country?'

'Both, please.'

'Town: fifty-seven Ebury Mews, S.W. Country: The Rectory, Barbicon-Bramley, Bucks.' She glanced at Fox. 'B-a-r-b-i – '

'Thank you, miss, I think I've got it,' said Fox.

'Now, Miss Harris,' Alleyn began, 'I wonder if you can give me any help at all in this business.'

To his tense astonishment Miss Harris at once opened her pad on which he could see a column of shorthand hieroglyphics. She drew out from her bosom on a spring extension a pair of rimless pince-nez. She placed them on her nose and waited with composure for Alleyn's next remark.

He said: 'Have you some notes there, Miss Harris?'

'Yes, Mr Alleyn. I saw Miss O'Brien just now and she told me you would be requiring any information I could give about Lord Gospell's movements last night and this morning. I thought it better to prepare what I have to say. So I just jotted down one or two little memos.'

'Admirable! Let's have 'em.'

Miss Harris cleared her throat.

'At about twelve-thirty,' she began in an incisive monotone, 'I met Lord Robert Gospell in the hall. I was speaking to Miss O'Brien. He asked me to dance with him later in the evening. I remained in the hall until a quarter to one. I happened to glance at my watch. I then went downstairs to top landing. Remained there. Period of time unknown but I went down to the ballroom landing before one-thirty. Lord Gospell – I mean Lord Robert Gospell then asked me to dance.'

Miss Harris's voice stopped for a moment. She moved her writing-pad on the arm of her chair.

'We danced,' she continued. 'Three successive dances with repeats. Lord Robert introduced me to several of his friends and then he took me into the buffet on the street-level. We drank champagne. He then remembered that he had promised to dance with the Duchess of Dorminster – ' Here Miss Harris appeared to lose her place for a moment. She repeated: 'Had promised to dance with the Duchess of Dorminster,' and cleared her throat again. 'He took me to the ballroom and asked me for the next Viennese waltz. I remained in the ballroom. Lord Robert danced with the Duchess and then with Miss Agatha Troy, the portrait painter, and then with two ladies whose names I do not know. Not at once, of course,' said Miss Harris in parenthesis. 'That would be ridiculous. I still remained in the ballroom. The band played the "Blue Danube". Lord Robert was standing in a group of his friends close to where I sat. He saw me. We danced the "Blue Danube" together and revisited the buffet. I noticed the time. I had intended leaving much earlier and was surprised to find that it was nearly three o'clock. So I stayed till the end.'

She glanced up at Alleyn with the impersonal attentive air proper to her position. He felt so precisely that she was indeed his secretary that there was no need for him to repress a smile. But he did glance at Fox, who for the first time in Alleyn's memory, looked really at a loss. His large hand hovered uncertainly over his own notebook. Alleyn realized that Fox did not know whether to take down Miss Harris's shorthand in his own shorthand.

Alleyn said: Thank you, Miss Harris. Anything else?'

Miss Harris turned a page.

'Details of conversation,' she began. 'I have not made memos of *all* the remarks I have remembered. Many of them were merely light comments on suitable subjects. For instance, Lord Robert spoke of Lady Carrados and expressed regret that she seemed to be tired. That sort of thing.'

'Let us have his remarks under this heading,' said Alleyn with perfect gravity.

'Certainly, Mr Alleyn. Lord Robert asked me if I had noticed that Lady Carrados had been tired for some time. I said yes I had, and that I was sorry because she was so nice to everybody. He asked if I thought it was entirely due to the season. I said I expected it was, because many ladies I have had posts with have found the season very exhausting, although in a way Lady Carrados took the entertaining side very lightly. Lord Robert asked me if I liked being with Lady Carrados. I replied that I did, very much. Lord Robert asked me several questions about myself. He was very easy to talk to. I told him about the old days at the rectory and how we ought to have been much better off, and he was very nice, and I told about my father's people in Bucks and he seemed quite interested in so many of them being parsons and what an old Buckinghamshire family we really are.'

'Oh, God,' thought Alleyn on a sudden wave of painful compassion. 'And so they probably are and because for the last two or three generations they've had to haul down the social flag inch by inch their children are all going to talk like this and nobody's going to feel anything but uncomfortably incredulous.'

He said: 'You come from Barbicon-Bramley? That's not far from Bassicote, is it? I know that part of Bucks fairly well. Is your father's rectory anywhere near Falconbridge?'

'Oh, no. Falconbridge is thirty miles away. My uncle Walter was rector at Falconbridge.'

Alleyn said: 'Really? Long ago?'

'When I was a small girl. He's retired now and lives in Barbicon-Bramley. All the Harrises live to ripe old ages. Lord Robert remarked that many of the clergy do. He said longevity was one of the more dubious rewards of virtue,' said Miss Harris with a glance at her notes.

Alleyn could hear the squeaky voice uttering this gentle epigram.

'He *was* amusing,' added Miss Harris.

'Yes. Now look here, Miss Harris, we're coming to something rather important. You tell me you went up to the top landing between, say, a quarter to one and one-fifteen. Do you think you were up there all that time?'

'Yes, Mr Alleyn, I think I was.'

'Whereabouts were you?'

Miss Harris turned purple with the rapidity of a pantomime fairy under a coloured spotlight.

'Well, I mean to say, I sat on the gallery, I went into the ladies' cloakroom on the landing to tidy and see if everything was quite nice, and then I sat on the gallery again and – I mean I was just about.'

'You were on the gallery at one o'clock, you think?'

'I – really I'm not sure if I – '

'Let's see if we can get at it this way. Did you go into the cloak-room immediately after you got to the landing?'

'Yes. Yes, I did.'

'How long were you in the cloakroom?'

'Only a few minutes.'

'So you were back on the gallery again well before one.'

'Yes,' said Miss Harris without enthusiasm, 'but – '

'At about the time I am trying to get at, Captain Withers and Mr Donald Potter were on the gallery, from where they moved into the sitting-room on that landing. Sir Herbert Carrados was in and out of the sitting-room and you may have heard him order the servant on duty up there to attend to the ash-trays and matches. Do you remember this?'

'No. Not exactly. I think I remember seeing Captain Withers and Mr Potter through the sitting-room door as I passed to go down-stairs. The larger sitting-room – not the one with the telephone. Lord Robert was in the telephone-room.'

'How do you know that?'

'I – heard him.'

'From the cloakroom?'

'The – I mean – '

'The room between the cloakroom and the telephone-room, perhaps,' said Alleyn, mentally cursing the extreme modesty of Miss Harris.

'Yes,' said Miss Harris looking straight in front of her. Her discomfiture was so evident that Alleyn himself almost began to feel shy.

'Please don't mind if I ask for very exact information,' he said. 'Policemen are rather like doctors in these instances. Things don't count. When did you go into this ladies' room?'

'As soon as I got upstairs,' said Miss Harris. 'Hem!'

'Right. Now let's see if we can get things straight, shall we? You came upstairs at, say, about ten or fifteen minutes to one. You went straight to this door next the green sitting-room with the telephone. Did you see anyone?'

'Captain Withers was just coming out of the green sitting-room. I think there was a lady in there. I saw her through the open door as I – as I opened the other.'

'Yes. Anyone else?'

'I think I noticed Sir Herbert in the other sitting-room, the first one, as I passed the door. That's all.'

'And then you went into the ladies' room?'

'Yes,' admitted Miss Harris, shutting her eyes for a moment and opening them again to stare with something like horror at Fox's pencil and notebook. Alleyn felt that already she saw herself being forced to answer these and worse questions shouted at her by celebrated counsel at the Old Bailey.

'How long did you remain in this room?' he asked.

White to the lips Miss Harris gave a rather mad little laugh. 'Oh,' she said, 'oh, quayte a tayme. You know.'

'And while you were there you heard Lord Robert telephoning in the next room?'

'Yes, I did,' said Miss Harris loudly with an air of defiance.

'She's looking at me,' thought Alleyn, 'exactly like a trapped rabbit.'

'So Lord Robert probably came upstairs after you. Do you suppose the lady you had noticed was still in the green room when he began telephoning?'

'No. I heard her come out and – and she – I mean she tried to – tried to – '

'Yes, yes,' said Alleyn, 'quite. And went away?'

'Definitely.'

'And then Lord Robert began to telephone? I see. Could you hear what he said?'

'Oh, no. He spoke in a low tone, of course. I made no attempt to listen.'

'Of course not.'

'I could not have heard if I had tried,' continued Miss Harris. 'I could only hear the tone of the voice and that was quite unmistakable.'

'Yes?' said Alleyn encouragingly. 'Now,' he thought, 'now at last are we getting to it?' Miss Harris did not go on, however, but sat with her mouth done up in a maddening button of conscious rectitude.

'Did you hear the end of the conversation?' he said at last.

'Oh, yes! The end. Yes. At least someone came into the room. I heard Lord Robert say: "Oh, hello!" Those were the only words I did distinguish, and almost immediately I heard the telephone tinkle, so I knew he had rung off.'

'And the other person? Was it a man?'

'Yes. Yes, a man.'

'Could you,' said Alleyn in a level voice, 'could you recognize this man?'

'Oh, *no*,' cried Miss Harris with an air of relief. 'No *indeed*, Mr Alleyn, I haven't the faintest idea. You see, after that I didn't really hear anything at all in the next room. Nothing at all. Really.'

'You returned to the landing?'

'Not immediately. No.'

'Oh!' said Alleyn. He could think of nothing else to say. Even Fox seemed to have caught the infection of extreme embarrassment. He cleared his throat loudly. Miss Harris, astonishingly, broke into a high-pitched prattle, keeping her eyes fixed on the opposite wall and clenching and unclenching her hands.

'No. Not for some minutes and then, of course, when I did return they had both gone. I mean when I finally returned. Of course Lord Robert went before then and – and – so that was perfectly all right. Perfectly.'

'And the other man?'

'He – it was most unfortunate. A little mistake. I assure you I did not see who it was. I mean as soon as he realized it was the wrong door he went out again. Naturally. The inner door being half-glass made it even more unfortunate though of course there being two rooms was – was better for all concerned than if it was the usual arrangement. And I mean that he didn't see me so that in a way it didn't matter. It didn't really matter a scrap. Not a scrap.'

Alleyn, listening to this rigmarole, sent his memory back to the top gallery of Marsdon House. He remembered the Victorian ante-room that opened off the landing, the inner gloomy sanctum beyond. The chaotic fragments of Miss Harris's remarks joggled together in his brain and then clicked into a definite pattern.

'Not a scrap, really,' Miss Harris still repeated.

'Of course not,' agreed Alleyn cheerfully. 'I think I understand what happened. Tell me if I go wrong. While you were still in the inner room the man who had interrupted Lord Robert's telephone conversation came out of the green sitting-room and blundered through the wrong door into the ante-room of the ladies' lavatory. That it?'

Miss Harris blanched at the unfortunate word but nodded her head.

'Why are you so sure it was this same man, Miss Harris?'

'Well, because, because I heard their voices as they came to the door of the next room and then Lord Robert's voice on the landing and then – then it happened. I just knew that was who it was.'

Alleyn leant forward.

'The inner door,' he said, 'is half-glass. Could you see this intruder?'

'Dimly, dimly,' cried Miss Harris. 'Greatly obscured, I assure you. I'm sorry to say I forgot for some seconds to switch off my light. The other was on.'

'So you actually could see the shape of this person, however shadowy, through the clouded glass?'

'Yes. For a second or two. Before he went away. I think perhaps he was feeling unwell.'

'Drunk?'

'No, no. Certainly not. It was not a bit like that. He looked more as if he'd had a shock.'

'Why?'

'He – the shape of him put its hands to its face and it swayed towards the glass partition and for a moment leant against it. Thank God,' said Miss Harris with real fervour, 'I had locked the door.'

'The silhouette would be clearer, more sharply defined, as it came closer to the door?'

'I suppose so. Yes, it was.'

'Still you did not recognize it?'

'No. Never for an instant.'

'Suppose – for the sake of argument, I were to say this man was either Sir Herbert Carrados, Captain Withers, the waiter on the landing, Mr Donald Potter, or Dimitri the caterer. Which would you think most likely?'

'I don't know. Perhaps Dimitri. I don't know.'

'What height?'

'Medium.'

'Well,' said Alleyn, 'what happened next?'

'He took his hands from his face. He had turned away with his back against the door. I – I got the impression he suddenly realized where he was. Then the shape moved away and turned misty and then disappeared. I heard the outer door shut.'

'And at last you were able to escape?'

'I waited for a moment.' Miss Harris looked carefully at Alleyn. Perhaps she saw something in his eye that made her feel, after all, her recital had not been such a terrible affair.

'It *was* awkward,' she said, 'wasn't it? Honestly?'

'Honestly,' said Alleyn, 'it was.'

CHAPTER 19

The General

'Then your idea is,' said Fox as they headed again for Belgrave Square, 'that this chap in the WC was the murderer.'

'Yes, Fox, that *is* my idea. There's no earthly reason why an innocent person should not admit to interrupting the telephone call and nobody has admitted to it. I'm afraid we'll have to go again through the whole damn boiling, guests, servants and all, to make sure of our ground. *And* we'll have to ask every man jack of 'em if they burst across the threshold of Miss Harris's outer sanctuary. Every *man* jack. Thank the Lord there's no need for the women, though from what I know of my niece Sarah we wouldn't meet with many mantling cheeks and conscious looks among the débutantes. If nobody admits to the telephone incident, or to the sequel in the usual offices, then we can plot another joint in our pattern. We can say there is a strong probability that our man overheard Bunchy telephone to me, interrupted the sentence: "and he's working with – " waited in the green sitting-room until Bunchy had gone and then blundered into the ante-room.'

'But why would he do that?' said Fox. 'Did he think it was a man's, or was he trying to avoid somebody? Or what?'

'It's a curious picture, isn't it? That dim figure seen through the thick glass. Even in her mortal shame Miss Harris noticed that he seemed to be agitated. The hands over the face, the body leaning for a moment against the door. And then suddenly he pulls himself together and goes out. He looked, said Miss Harris, as though he'd had a shock. He'd just intercepted a telephone call to the Yard from a man who apparently knew all there was to know about his blackmailing activities. He might well feel he must blunder through the first door he came to and have a moment alone to pull himself together.'

'Yes,' agreed Fox, 'so he might. I'd like something a bit more definite to hinge it on, though.'

'And so, I promise you, would I. The detestable realms of conjecture! How I hate them.'

'Miss Harris didn't get us any further with the business down in the hall.'

'The final departures? No, she didn't. She simply bore out everything we'd already been told.'

'She's an observant little lady, isn't she?' said Fox.

'Yes, Fox, she's no fool, for all her tender qualms. And now we have a delightful job ahead of us. We've got to try to bamboozle, cajole, or bully Mrs Halcut-Hackett into giving away her best young man. A charming occupation.'

'Will we be seeing the General, too? I suppose we'll have to. I don't think the other chaps will have tackled him. I told them not to touch any of our lot.'

'Quite right,' said Alleyn, with a sigh. 'We shall be seeing the General. And here we are at Halkin Street. The Halcut-Hacketts of Halkin Street! An important collection of aspirates and rending consonants. The General first, I suppose.'

The General was expecting them. They walked through a hall which, though it had no tongue, yet it did speak of the most expensive and most fashionable house decorator in London. They were shown into a study smelling of leather and cigars and decorated with that pleasant sequence of prints of the Nightcap Steeplechase. Alleyn wondered if the General had stood with his cavalry sabre on the threshold of this room, daring the fashionable decorator to come on and see what he would get. Or possibly Mrs Halcut-Hackett, being an American, caused her husband's study to be aggressively British. Alleyn and Fox waited for five minutes before they heard a very firm step and a loud cough. General Halcut-Hackett walked into the room.

'Hullo! Afternoon! What!' he shouted.

His face was terra-cotta, his moustache formidable, his eyes china blue. He was the original ramrod brass-hat, the subject of all army jokes kindly or malicious. It was impossible to believe his mind was as blank as his face would seem to confess. So true to type was he that he would have seemed unreal, a two-dimensional figure that had stepped from a coloured cartoon of a regimental dinner, had it not been for a certain air of solidity and a kind of childlike constancy that was rather appealing. Alleyn thought: 'Now, *he* really *is* a simple soldier-man.'

'Sit down,' said General Halcut-Hackett. 'Bad business! Damn blackguardly killer. Place is getting no better than Chicago. What are you fellows doing about it? What? Going to get the feller? What?'

'I hope so, sir,' said Alleyn.

'Hope so! By Gad, I should hope you hope so. Well, what can I do for you?'

'Answer one or two questions, if you will, sir.'

''Course I will. Bloody outrage. The country's going to pieces in my opinion and this is only another proof of it. Men like Robert Gospell can't take a cab without gettin' the life choked out of them. What it amounts to. Well?'

'Well, sir, the first point is this. Did you walk into the green sitting-room on the top landing at one o'clock this morning while Lord Robert Gospell was using the telephone?'

'No. Never went near the place. Next!'

'What time did you leave Marsden House?'

'Between twelve and one.'

'Early,' remarked Alleyn.

'My wife's charge had toothache. Brought her home. Whole damn business had been too much for her. Poodle-faking and racketing! All people think of nowadays. Goin' through her paces from morning till night. Enough to kill a horse.'

'Yes,' said Alleyn. 'One wonders how they get through it.'

'Is your name Alleyn?'

'Yes, sir.'

'George Alleyn's son, are you? You're like him. He was in my regiment. I'm sixty-seven,' added General Halcut-Hackett with considerable force. 'Sixty-seven. Why didn't you go into your father's regiment? Because you preferred this? What?'

'That's it, sir. The next point is – '

'What? Get on with the job, eh? Quite right.'

'Did you return to Marsden House?'

'Why the devil should I do that?'

'I thought perhaps your wife was – '

The General glared at the second print in the Nightcap series and said:

'M'wife preferred to stay on. Matter of fact, Robert Gospell offered to see her home.'

'He didn't do so, however?'

'Damn it, sir, my wife is not a murderess.'

'Lord Robert might have crossed the square as escort to your wife, sir, and returned.'

'Well, he didn't. She tells me they missed each other.'

'And you, sir. You saw your daughter in and then – '

'She's not my daughter!' said the General with a good deal of emphasis. 'She's the daughter of some friend of my wife's.' He glowered and then muttered half to himself: 'Unheard of in my day, that sort of thing. Makes a woman look like a damn trainer. Girl's no more than a miserable scared filly. Pah!'

Alleyn said: 'Yes, sir. Well, then, you saw Miss –'

'Birnbaum. Rose Birnbaum, poor little devil. Call her Poppet.'

'– Miss Birnbaum in and then – '

'Well?'

'Did you stay up?'

To Alleyn's astonishment the General's face turned from terracotta to purple, not, it seemed, with anger, but with embarrassment. He blew out his moustache several times, pouted like a baby, and blinked. At last he said:

'Upon my soul, I can't see what the devil it matters whether I went to bed at twelve or one.'

'The question may sound impertinent,' said Alleyn. 'If it does I'm sorry. But, as a matter of police routine, we want to establish alibis – '

'*Alibis!*' roared the General. '*Alibis!* Good God, sir, are you going to sit there and tell me I'm in need of an alibi? Hell blast it, sir – '

'But, General Halcut-Hackett,' said Alleyn quickly, while the empurpled General sucked in his breath, 'every guest at Marsdon House is in need of an alibi.'

'Every guest! Every guest! But, damn it, sir, the man was murdered in a bloody cab, not a bloody ballroom. Some filthy bolshevistic fascist,' shouted the General, having a good deal of difficulty with this strange collection of sibilants. He slightly dislodged his upper plate but impatiently champed it back into position. 'They're all alike!' he added confusedly. 'The whole damn boiling.'

Alleyn hunted for a suitable phrase in a language that General Halcut-Hackett would understand. He glanced at Fox who was staring solemnly at the General over the top of his spectacles.

'I'm sure you'll realize, sir,' said Alleyn, 'that we are simply obeying orders.'

'What!'

'That's done it,' thought Alleyn.

'Orders! I can toe the line as well as the next fellow,' said the General, and Alleyn, remembering Carrados had used the same phrase, reflected that in this instance it was probably true. The General, he saw, *was* preparing to toe the line.

'I apologize,' said the General. 'Lost me temper. Always doing it nowadays. Indigestion.'

'It's enough to make anybody lose their temper, sir.'

'Well,' said the General, 'you've kept yours. Come on, then.'

'It's just a statement, sir, that you didn't go out again after you got back here and, if possible, someone to support the statement.'

Once again the General looked strangely embarrassed.

'I can't give you a witness,' he said. 'Nobody saw me go to bed.'

'I see. Well then, sir, if you'll just give me your word that you didn't go out again.'

'But, damme, I did take a – take a – take a turn round the Square before I went to bed. Always do.'

'What time was this?'

'I don't know.'

'You can't give me an idea? Was it long after you got home?'

'Some time. I saw the child to her room and stirred up my wife's maid to look after her. Then I came down here and got myself a drink. I read for a bit. I dare say I dozed for a bit. Couldn't make up my mind to turn in.'

'You didn't glance at the clock on the mantelpiece there?'

Again the General became acutely self-conscious.

'I may have done so. I fancy I did. Matter of fact, I remember now I did doze off and woke with a bit of a start. The fire had gone out. It was devilish chilly.' He glared at Alleyn and then said abruptly: 'I felt wretchedly down in the mouth. I'm getting an old fellow nowadays and I don't enjoy the small hours. As you say, I looked at the clock. It was half-past two. I sat there in this chair trying to make up my mind to go to bed. Couldn't. So I took a walk round the Square.'

'Now that's excellent, sir. You may be able to give us the very piece of information we're after. Did you by chance notice anybody hanging about in the Square?'

'No.'

'Did you meet anybody at all?'

'Constable.'

Alleyn glanced at Fox.

'PC Titheridge,' said Fox. 'We've got his report, sir.'

'All right,' said Alleyn. 'Were people beginning to leave Marsdon House when you passed, sir?'

The General muttered something about 'might have been,' paused for a moment and then said: 'It was devilish murky. Couldn't see anything.'

'A misty night; yes,' said Alleyn. 'Did you happen to notice Captain Maurice Withers in the mist?'

'No!' yelled the General with extraordinary vehemence. 'No, I did not. I don't know the feller. No!'

There was an uncomfortable pause and then the General said: 'Afraid that's all I can tell you. When I got in again I went straight to bed.'

'Your wife had not returned?'

'No,' said the General very loudly. 'She had not.'

Alleyn waited for a moment and then he said:

'Thank you very much, sir. Now, we'll prepare a statement from the notes Inspector Fox has taken, and if you've no objection, we'll get you to sign it.'

'I – um – um – um – I'll have a look at it.'

'Yes. And now, if I may, I'd like to have a word with Mrs Halcut-Hackett.'

Up went the General's chin again. For a moment Alleyn wondered if they were in for another outburst. But the General said: 'Very good. I'll tell her,' and marched out of the room.

'Crikey!' said Fox.

'That's Halcut-Hackett, that was,' said Alleyn. 'Why the devil,' he added rubbing his nose, 'why the devil is the funny old article in such a stew over his walk round the Square?'

'Seems a natural thing for a gentleman of his kind to do,' Fox ruminated. 'I'm sure I don't know. I should have thought he's the sort that breaks the ice on the Serpentine every morning as well as walking round the Square every night.'

'He's a damn bad liar, poor old boy. Or is he a poor old boy? Is he not perhaps a naughty old boy? Blast! Why the devil couldn't he give us a nice straight cast-iron alibi? Poking his nose into Belgrave Square; can't tell us exactly when or exactly why or for exactly how long. What did the PC say?'

'Said he'd noticed nothing at all suspicious. Never mentioned the General. I'll have a word with Mr PC Titheridge about this.'

'The General is probably a stock piece if he walks round Belgrave Square every night,' said Alleyn.

'Yes, but not at half-past two in the morning,' objected Fox.

'Quite right, Fox, quite right. Titheridge must be blasted. What the devil was old Halcut-Hackett up to last night! We can't let it go, you know, because, after all, if he suspects – '

Alleyn broke off. He and Fox stood up as Mrs Halcut-Hackett made her entrance.

Alleyn, of course, had met her before, on the day she came to his office with the story of Mrs X and the blackmailing letters. He reflected now that in a sense she had started the whole miserable business. 'If it hadn't been for this hard, wary, stupid woman's visit,' he thought, 'I shouldn't have asked Bunchy to poke his head into a deathtrap. Oh, God!' Mrs Halcut-Hackett said:

'Why, Inspector, they didn't tell me it was you. Now, do you know I never realized, that day I called about my poor friend's troubles, that I was speaking to Lady Alleyn's famous son.'

Inwardly writhing under this blatant recognition of his snob-value Alleyn shook hands and instantly introduced Fox to whom Mrs Halcut-Hackett was insufferably cordial. They all sat down. Alleyn deliberately waited for a moment or two before he spoke. He looked at Mrs Halcut-Hackett. He saw that under its thick patina of cream and rouge her face was sagging from the bones of her skull. He saw that her eyes and her hands were frightened.

He said: 'I think we may as well begin with that same visit to the Yard. The business we talked about on that occasion seems to be linked with the death of Lord Robert Gospell.'

She sat there, bolt upright in her expensive stays and he knew she was terrified.

'But,' she said, 'that's absurd. No, honestly, Mr Alleyn, I just can't believe there could be any possible connection. Why, my friend – '

'Mrs Halcut-Hackett,' said Alleyn, 'I am afraid we must abandon your friend.'

She shot a horrified glance at Fox, and Alleyn answered it.

'Mr Fox is fully acquainted with the whole story,' he said. 'He agrees with me that your friend had better dissolve. We realize that beyond all doubt you yourself were the victim of these blackmailing letters. There is no need for you to feel particularly distressed over this. It is much better to tackle this sort of thing without the aid of an imaginary Mrs X. She makes for unnecessary confusion. We now have the facts – '

'But – how do you – ?'

Alleyn decided to take a risk. It was a grave risk.

'I have already spoken to Captain Withers,' he said.

'My God, has Maurice confessed?'

Fox's notebook dropped to the floor.

Alleyn, still watching the gaping mouth with its wet red margin, said: 'Captain Withers has confessed nothing.' And he thought: 'Does she realize the damage she's done?'

'But I don't mean that,' Mrs Halcut-Hackett gabbled. 'I don't mean that. It's not that. You must be crazy. He couldn't have done it.' She clenched her hands and drummed with her fists on the arms of the chair. 'What did he tell you?'

'Very little I'm afraid. Still we learned at least that it was not impossible – '

'You must be crazy to think he did it. I tell you he couldn't do it.'

'He couldn't do what, Mrs Halcut-Hackett?' asked Alleyn.

'The thing – Lord Robert . . .' She gaped horridly and then with a quick and vulgar gesture, covered her mouth with her ringed hand. Horrified intelligence looked out of her eyes.

'What did you think Captain Withers had confessed?'

'Nothing to do with this. Nothing that matters to anyone but me. I didn't mean a thing by it. You've trapped me. It's not fair.'

'For your own sake,' said Alleyn, 'you would be wise to try to answer me. You say you did not mean to ask if Captain Withers had confessed to murder. Very well, I accept that for the moment. What might he have confessed? That he was the author of the letter your blackmailer had threatened to use. Is that it?'

'I won't answer. I won't say anything more. You're trying to trap me.'

'What conclusion am I likely to draw from your refusal to answer? Believe me, you take a very grave risk if you refuse.'

'Have you told my husband about the letter?'

'No. Nor shall I do so if it can be avoided. Come now.' Alleyn deliberately drew all his power of concentration to a fine point. He saw his dominance drill like a sort of mental gimlet through her flabby resistance. 'Come now. Captain Withers is the author of this letter. Isn't he?'

'Yes, but – '

'Did you think he had confessed as much?'

'Why, yes, but – '

'And you suppose Lord Robert Gospell to have been the blackmailer? Ever since that afternoon when he sat behind you at the concert?'

'Then it was Robert Gospell!' Her head jerked back. She looked venomously triumphant.

'No,' said Alleyn. 'That was a mistake. Lord Robert was not a blackmailer.'

'He was. I know he was. Do you think I didn't see him last night, watching us. Why did he ask me about Maurice? Why did Maurice warn me against him?'

'Did Captain Withers suggest that Lord Robert was a blackmailer?' In spite of himself a kind of cold disgust deadened Alleyn's voice. She must have heard it because she cried out:

'Why do you speak of him like that? Of Captain Withers, I mean. You've no right to insult him.'

'My God, this is a stupid woman,' thought Alleyn. Aloud he said: 'Have I insulted him? If so I have gone very far beyond my duty. Mrs Halcut-Hackett, when did you first miss this letter?'

'About six months ago. After my charade party in the little season.'

'Where did you keep it?'

'In a trinket-box on my dressing-table.'

'A locked box?'

'Yes. But the key was sometimes left with others in the drawer of the dressing-table.'

'Did you suspect your maid?'

'No. I can't suspect her. She has been with me for fifteen years. She's my old dresser. I know she wouldn't do it.'

'Have you any idea who could have taken it?'

'I can't think, except that for my charade party I turned my room into a buffet, and the men moved everything round.'

'What men?'

'The caterer's men. Dimitri. But Dimitri superintended them the whole time. I don't believe they had an opportunity.'

'I see,' said Alleyn.

He saw she now watched him with a different kind of awareness. Alleyn had interviewed a great number of Mrs Halcut-Hacketts in his day. He knew very well that with such women he carried a weapon that he was loath to use, but which nevertheless fought for him. This was the weapon of his sex. He saw with violent distaste that some taint of pleasure threaded her fear of him. And the inexorable logic of thought presented him to himself, side by side with her lover.

He said: 'Suppose we get the position clear. In your own interest I may tell you that we have already gathered a great deal of information. Lord Robert was helping us on the blackmail case, and he has left us his notes. From them and from our subsequent enquiries we have pieced this much together. In your own case Captain Withers was the subject of the blackmailing letters. Following our advice you carried out the blackmailer's instruction and left your bag in the corner of the sofa at the Constance Street Hall. It was taken. Because Lord Robert deliberately sat next to you and because Captain Withers had, as you put it, warned you against him, you came to the conclusion that Lord Robert took the bag and was therefore your blackmailer. Why did you not report to the police the circumstances of the affair at the concert? You had agreed to do so. Were you advised to let the case drop as far as the Yard was concerned?'

'Yes.'

'By Captain Withers? I see. That brings us to last night. You say you noticed that Lord Robert watched you both during the ball. I must ask you again if Captain Withers agrees with your theory that Lord Robert was a blackmailer.'

'He – he simply warned me against Lord Robert.'

'In view of these letters and the sums of money the blackmailer demanded, did you think it advisable to keep up your friendship with Captain Withers?'

'We – there was nothing anybody could – I mean –'

'What do you mean?' asked Alleyn sternly.

She wetted her lips. Again he saw that look of subservience and thought that of all traits in an ageing woman this was the unloveliest and most pitiable.

She said: 'Our friendship is partly a business relationship.'

'A business relationship?' Alleyn repeated the words blankly.

'Yes. You see Maurice – Captain Withers – has very kindly offered to advise me and – I mean right now Captain Withers has in mind a little business venture in which I am interested, and I naturally require to talk things over so – you see – ?'

'Yes,' said Alleyn gently, 'I do see. This venture of Captain Withers is of course the club at Leatherhead, isn't it?'

'Why, yes, but – '

'Now then,' said Alleyn quickly, 'about last night. Lord Robert offered to see you home, didn't he? You refused or avoided giving an answer. Did you go home alone?'

She might as well have asked him how much he knew, so clearly did he read the question in her eyes. He thanked his stars that he had made such a fuss over Withers's telephone. Evidently Withers had not rung her up to warn her what to say. Frightened his call would be tapped, thought Alleyn with satisfaction, and decided to risk a further assumption. He said:

'You saw Captain Withers again after the ball, didn't you?'

'What makes you think that?'

'I have every reason to believe it. Captain Withers's car was parked in a side street off Belgrave Square. How long did you sit there waiting for him?'

'I don't admit I sat there.'

'Then if Captain Withers tells me he took a partner to the Matador last night after the ball I am to conclude that it was not you?'

'Captain Withers would want to protect me. He's very, very thoughtful.'

'Can you not understand,' said Alleyn, 'that it is greatly to your advantage and his, if you can prove that you both got into his car and drove to the Matador last night?'

'Why? I don't want it said that – '

'Mrs Halcut-Hackett,' said Alleyn: 'Do you want an alibi for yourself and Captain Withers or don't you?'

She opened her mouth once or twice like a gaping fish, looked wildly at Fox and burst into tears.

Fox got up, walked to the far end of the room, and stared with heavy tact at the second print in the Nightcap series. Alleyn waited while scarlet claws scuffled in an elaborate handbag. Out came a long piece of monogrammed tulle. She jerked at it violently.

Something clattered to the floor. Alleyn darted forward and picked it up.

It was a gold cigarette-case with a medallion set in the lid and surrounded by brilliants.

CHAPTER 20

Rose Birnbaum

Mrs Halcut-Hackett dabbed at the pouches under her eyes as if her handkerchief was made of blotting-paper.

'You frighten me,' she said. 'You frighten me so. I'm just terrified.'

Alleyn turned the cigarette-case over in his long hands.

'But there is no need to be terrified, none at all. Don't you see that if you can give me proof that you and Captain Withers motored straight from Marsdon House to the Matador, it clears you at once from any hint of complicity in Lord Robert's death?'

He waited. She began to rock backwards and forwards, beating her hands together and moving her head from side to side like a well-preserved automaton.

'I can't. I just can't. I won't say anything more. I just won't say another thing. It's no good. I won't say another thing.'

'Very well,' said Alleyn, not too unkindly. 'Don't try. I'll get at it another way. This is a very magnificent case. The medallion is an old one. Italian Renaissance, I should think. It's most exquisitely worked. It might almost be Benvenuto himself who formed those minute scrolls. Do you know its history?'

'No. Maurice picked it up somewhere and had it put on the case. I'm crazy about old things,' said Mrs Halcut-Hackett with a dry sob. 'Crazy about them.'

Alleyn opened the lid. An inscription read 'E from M W' He shut the case but did not return it to her.

'Don't lose it, Mrs Halcut-Hackett. The medal is a collector's piece. Aren't you afraid to carry it about with you?'

She seemed to take heart of grace at his interest. She dabbed again at her eyes and said: 'I'm just terribly careless with my things. Perhaps I ought not to use it. Only last night I left it lying about.'

'Did you? Where?'

She looked terrified again the moment he asked her a question.

'Some place at the ball,' she said.

'Was it in the green sitting-room on the top landing?'

'I – yes – I think maybe it was.'

'At what time?'

'I don't know.'

'During the supper hour didn't you sit in that room with Captain Withers?'

'Yes. Why not? Why shouldn't I?' She twisted the handkerchief round her hands and said: 'How do you know that? My husband – I'm not – *he's not having me watched?*'

'I don't for a moment suppose so. I simply happened to know that you sat in this room some time just before one o'clock. You tell me you left your cigarette-case there. Now when you came out of that room what did you do?'

'I went into the cloakroom to tidy. I missed the case when I opened my bag in the cloakroom.'

'Right. Now as you went from the green sitting-room to the cloakroom two doors away, did you happen to notice Lord Robert on the landing? Please don't think I am trying to entrap you. I simply want to know if you saw him.'

'He was coming upstairs,' she said. Her voice and manner were more controlled now.

'Good. Did you hear the dialling sound on the telephone extension while you were in the cloakroom?'

'Yes. Now you remind me I did hear it.'

'When you came out of the cloakroom did you go back for your case?'

'No. No, I didn't.'

'Why not?'

'Why? Because I forgot.'

'You forgot it again!'

'I didn't just forget but I went to the head of the stairs and Maurice was in the other sitting-out room at the stairhead, waiting for me. I went in there, and then I remembered my case and he got it for me.'

'Had the telephone rung off?' asked Alleyn.

'I don't know.'

'Was anyone else on the landing?'

'I guess not.'

'Not, by any chance, a short rather inconspicuous lady sitting alone?'

'No. There wasn't anybody on the landing. Donald Potter was in the sitting-room.'

'Was Captain Withers long fetching your case?'

'I don't think so,' she said nervously. 'I don't remember. I talked to Donald. Then we all went downstairs.'

'Captain Withers did not say whether there was anyone else in the telephone-room when he got the cigarette-case?'

'No, he didn't say anything about it.'

'Will you be very kind and let me keep this case for twenty-four hours?'

'Why? Why do you want it?'

Alleyn hesitated and at last he said: 'I want to see if anybody else recognizes it. Will you trust me with it?'

'Very well,' she said. 'I can't refuse, can I?'

'I'll take great care of it,' said Alleyn. He dropped it in his pocket and turned to Fox who had remained at the far end of the room. Fox's notebook was open in his hand.

'I think that's all, isn't it?' asked Alleyn. 'Have I missed anything, Fox?'

'I don't fancy so, sir.'

'Then we'll bother you no longer, Mrs Halcut-Hackett,' said Alleyn, standing before her. She rose from her chair. He saw that there was a sort of question in her eyes. 'Is there anything you would like to add to what you have said?' he asked.

'No. No. But you said a little while ago that you would find out about what you asked me before. You said you'd trace it another way.'

'Oh,' said Alleyn cheerfully, 'you mean whether you went from Marsdon House to the Matador in Captain Withers's car, and if so,

how long it took. Yes, we'll ask the commissionaire and the man in
the office at the Matador. They may be able to help.'

'My God, you mustn't do that!'

'Why not?'

'You can't do that. For God's sake say you won't. For God's sake . . .'

Her voice rose to a stifled, hysterical scream, ending in a sort of
gasp. Fox sighed heavily and gave Alleyn a look of patient
endurance. Mrs Halcut-Hackett drew breath. The door opened.

A plain girl, dressed to go out, walked into the room.

'Oh, I'm sorry,' she said, 'I didn't know – '

Mrs Halcut-Hackett stared round her with the air of a trapped
mastodon and finally blundered from the room as fast as her French
heels would carry her.

The door slammed behind her.

The plain girl, who was most beautifully curled, painted and
dressed, looked from Alleyn to Fox.

'I'm so sorry,' she repeated nervously. 'I'm afraid I shouldn't have
come in. Ought I to go and see if there's anything I can do?'

'If I were you,' said Alleyn, 'I don't think I should. Mrs Halcut-
Hackett is very much distressed over last night's tragedy and I expect
she would rather be alone. Are you Miss Birnbaum?'

'Yes, I am. You're detectives, aren't you?'

'That's us. My name is Alleyn and this is Mr Fox.'

'Oh, how d'you do?' said Miss Birnbaum hurriedly. She hesitated
and then gave them her hand. She looked doubtfully into Alleyn's
face. He felt the chilly little fingers tighten their grip like those of a
frightened child.

'I expect you've found it rather upsetting too, haven't you?'

'Yes,' she said dutifully. 'It's dreadful, isn't it?' She twisted her
fingers together. 'Lord Robert was very kind, wasn't he? He was very
kind to me.'

'I hope your toothache's better,' said Alleyn.

She looked at her hands and then up into his face.

'I didn't have toothache,' she said.

'No?'

'No. I just wanted to go home. I *hate* coming out,' added Miss
Birnbaum with extraordinary vigour. 'I knew I would and I do.'

'That's bad luck. Why do you do it?'

'Because,' said Miss Birnbaum with devastating frankness, 'my mother paid Mrs Hackett, I mean Mrs Halcut-Hackett, five hundred pounds to bring me out.'

'Hi!' said Alleyn, 'aren't you talking out of school?'

'You won't tell anybody I said that, will you? I've never breathed a word about it before. Not to a single soul. But you look my kind of person. And I'm absolutely fed up. I'm simply not the social kind. Golly, what a relief to get that off my chest!'

'What would you like to do?'

'I want to be an art student. My grandfather was a painter, Joseph Birnbaum. Have you ever heard of him?'

'I think I have. Didn't he paint a thing called "Jewish Sabbath"?'

'That's right. He was a Jew, of course. I'm a Jewess. My mother isn't, but I am. That's another thing I'm not supposed to say. I'm only sixteen. Would you have thought I was older?'

'I think I should.'

'That,' said Miss Birnbaum, 'is because I'm a Jewess. They mature very quickly, you know. Well, I suppose I mustn't keep you.'

'I should like to keep *you* for a minute, if I may.'

'That's all right then,' said Miss Birnbaum and sat down. 'I suppose Mrs Halcut-Hackett won't come back, will she?'

'I don't think so.'

'I don't mind so much about the General. He's stupid, of course, but he's quite kind. But I'm *terrified* of Mrs Halcut-Hackett. I'm such a failure and she hates it.'

'Are you sure you're such a failure?'

'Oh, yes. Last night only four people asked me to dance. Lord Robert, when I first got there, and a fat man, and the General, and Sir Herbert Carrados.'

She looked away for a moment and her lips trembled.

'I tried to pretend I had a soul above social success,' she said, 'but I haven't at all. I minded awfully. If I could paint and get out of it all it wouldn't matter, but when you're in a thing it's beastly to be a failure. So I got toothache. I must say it *is* queer me saying all this to you.'

'The General took you home, didn't he?'

'Yes. He *was* very. kind. He got Mrs Halcut-Hackett's maid, whom I hate worse than poison, to give me oil of cloves and Ovaltine. *She* knew all right.'

'Did you go to sleep?'

'No. I tried to think of a way to write to mother so that she would let me give it up. And then everything began to go through and through my head. I tried to think of other things but all the failure-parties kept coming up.'

'Did you hear the others return?'

'I heard Mrs Halcut-Hackett come in. It was frightfully late. She goes past my door to her room and she's got diamante shoe buckles that make a clicking noise with every step. I had heard the clock strike four. Did the General go back to the dance?'

'He went out again, I think.'

'Well, then it must have been the General I heard come along the passage at a quarter-past three. Just after. I heard every clock chime from one till six. Then I fell asleep. It was quite light then.'

'Yes.'

Alleyn took a turn up and down the room.

'Have you met Agatha Troy?' he asked.

'The painter? She was there last night. I wanted awfully for some-one to introduce us but I didn't like to ask. I think she's the best liv-ing English painter, don't you?'

'Yes, I believe I do. She teaches, you know.'

'Does she? Only geniuses, I suppose.'

'I think only students who have gone a certain distance.'

'If I were allowed to go a certain distance first, I wonder if she would ever have me.'

'Do you think you would be good?' asked Alleyn.

'I'm sure I would be able to draw. I'm not so sure of paint. I see everything in line. I say.'

'Hallo?'

'D'you think this will make any difference to the coming-out game? Is she going to be ill? I've thought so lots of times lately. She's so bloody-minded.'

'Don't say "she" and don't say "bloody-minded". The one's com-mon and you're too young for the other.'

Miss Birnbaum grinned delightedly.

'Well,' she said, 'it's what I think anyway. And she's not even virtuous. Do you know the Withers person?'

'Yes.'

'He's her boy-friend. Don't pretend to be shocked. I wrote and told mother about it. I hoped it'd shake her a bit. My father wrote and asked me if he was called Maurice and was like a red pig – that's a frightful insult, you know – because if he was I wasn't to stay. I like my father. But mother said if he was a friend of Mrs Halcut-Hackett he must be all right. I thought that frightfully funny. It's about the only thing that is at all funny in the whole business. I don't think it can be very amusing to be frightened of your boy-friend and your husband, do you?'

Alleyn rubbed his head and stared at Miss Birnbaum.

'Look here,' he said, 'you're giving us a good deal of information, you know. There's Mr Fox with his notebook. What about that?'

The dark face was lit with an inward smouldering fire. Two sharp lines appeared at the corners of the thick lips.

'Do you mean she may get into trouble? I hope she does. I hate her. She's a wicked woman. She'd murder anyone if she wanted them out of the way. She's felt like murdering me pretty often. She says things to me that twist me up inside, they hurt so. "My dear child, how can you expect me to do anything with you if you stare like a fish and never utter?" "My God, what have I done to be sad-dled with a burden like this?" "My dear child, I suppose you can't help looking what you are, but at least you might make some effort to sound a little less like Soho." And then she imitates my voice. Yesterday she told me there was a good deal to be said for the German point of view, and asked me if I had any relations among the refugees because she heard quite a number of English people were taking them as maids. I hope she is a murderess. I hope you catch her. I hope they hang her by her beastly old neck until she's dead.'

The thick soft voice stopped. Miss Birnbaum was trembling very slightly. A thin line of damp appeared above her upper lip.

Alleyn grimaced, rubbed his nose and said:

'Do you feel any better for that?'

'Yes.'

'Vindictive little devil! Can't you get on top of it all and see it as something intensely disagreeable that won't last for ever? Have you tried drawing as a counter-irritant?'

'I've done a caricature of Her. When I get away from here I'll send it to her if she's not in gaol by that time.'

'Do you know Sarah Alleyn?'

'She's one of the successes. Yes, I know her.'

'Do you like her?'

'She's not bad. She actually remembers who I am when she sees me.'

Alleyn decided to abandon his niece for the moment.

'Well,' he said, 'I dare say you're nearer to escape than you imagine. I'll be off now. I hope we meet again.'

'So do I. I suppose you think I'm pretty ghastly.'

'That's all right. Make up your mind everybody hates you and you'll always be happy.'

Miss Birnbaum grinned.

'You think you're clever,' she said, 'don't you? Goodbye.'

They shook hands in a friendly manner, and she saw them out into the hall. Alleyn had a last glimpse of her standing stocky, dark and truculent against a background of restrained and decorous half-tones and beautiful pseudo-Empire curtains.

CHAPTER 21

Statement by Lucy Lorrimer

It was nearly six o'clock in the evening when Alleyn and Fox returned to Scotland Yard. They went to Alleyn's room. Fox got to work on his notes, Alleyn tackled the reports that had come in while they were away. They both lit pipes and between them was established that pleasant feeling of unexpressed intimacy that comes to two people working in silence at the same job.

Presently Alleyn put down the reports and looked across at his friend. He thought: 'How often we have sat like this, Fox and I, working like a couple of obscure clerks in the offices of the Last Judgment concern, filing and correlating the misdeeds of men. Fox is getting quite grizzled and there are elderly purple veins in his cheeks. I shall go home later on, a solitary fellow, to my own hole.' And into his thoughts came the image of a woman who sat in a tall blue chair by his fire, but that was too domestic a picture. Rather, she would sit on the hearthrug. Her hands would be stained with charcoal and they would sweep beautiful lines across a white surface. When he came in she would look up from her drawing and Troy's eyes would smile or scowl. He jerked the image away and found that Fox was looking at him with his usual air of bland expectancy.

'Finished?' said Alleyn.

'Yes, sir. I've been trying to sort things out. There's the report on the silver cleaning. Young Carewe took that on and he seems to have made a fair job of it. Got himself up as a Rat and Mice Destruction Officer and went round all the houses and palled up with the servants. All the Carrados silver was cleaned this morning including

Sir Herbert's cigar-case which isn't the right shape anyway, because he saw it in the butler's pantry. Sir Daniel's man does his silver cleaning on Mondays and Fridays, so it was all cleaned up yesterday. François does Dimitri's stuff every day or says he does. Young Potter and Withers are looked after by the flat service and only their table silver is kept polished. The Halcut-Hacketts' cases are cleaned once a week – Fridays – and rubbed up every morning. That's that. How's the report from Bailey?'

'Bailey hasn't much. There's nothing in the taxi. He got Withers's prints from my cigarette-case but, as we expected, the green sitting-room was simply a mess. He *has* found Withers's and young Potter's prints on the pages of Taylor's *Medical Jurisprudence*. The pages that refer to asphyxiation.'

'By gum, that's something.'

'Not such a great deal, Fox. They will tell us that when the newspaper report came out they were interested and turned up Taylor on suffocation; and who is to call them liars? The man who went to Leatherhead had a success. Apparently Withers keeps a married couple there. Our man pitched a yarn that he had been sent by the borough to inspect the electrical wiring in the house, and got in. What's more he seems to have had a good look round. He found a roulette wheel and had the intelligence to examine it pretty closely. The middle dozen slots had been very slightly opened. I expect the idea is that Master Donald or some other satellite of Withers should back the middle dozen. The wheel seems brand new. There was an older one that showed no signs of irregularity. There were also several packs of cards which had been lightly treated with the favourite pumice-stone. Luckily for us the married couple had a violent row with the gallant Captain and were prepared to talk. I think we've got enough to pull him in on a gambling-hell charge. Thompson reports that Withers has stayed in all day. The telephone was disconnected as soon as we left. Donald Potter's clothes were returned to him by taxi. Nobody has visited Withers. Dimitri comes next. Dimitri went home after he left here, visiting a chemist on the way to get his hand bandaged. He, too, has remained indoors, and has made no telephone calls. Most exemplary behaviour. How the blazes are we going to get any of these victims to charge Dimitri?'

'You're asking me!' said Fox.

'Yes. Not a hope in a hundred. Well now, Fox, I've been over this damnable, dreary, involved, addling business of the green sitting-room. It boils down to this. The people who could have overheard Lord Robert's telephone conversation were Withers, Sir Herbert Carrados, Miss Harris, Mrs Halcut-Hackett and Donald. They were all on or about the top landing and wouldn't have to lie particularly freely in avoiding any reference to a brief dart in and out of the tele-phone-room. But, but, but, and a blasted but it is, it is quite possible that while Lord Robert telephoned, someone came upstairs and walked into the telephone-room. Mrs Halcut-Hackett was in the cloakroom; Withers, Donald and Carrados in the other sitting-room, Miss Harris in the lavatory. Dimitri says he was downstairs but who the devil's to prove it? If the others are speaking the truth, anybody might have come up and gone down again unseen.'

'The gentleman who burst into the lavatory?'

'Precisely. He may even have hidden in there till the coast was clear, though I can't see why. There's nothing particularly fishy in coming out of a sitting-room.'

'Ugh,' said Fox.

'As I see the case now, Fox, it presents one or two highlights. Most of them seem to be concentrated on cigarette-cases. Two cigarette-cases. The murderer's and Mrs Halcut-Hackett's.'

'Yes,' said Fox.

'After the cigarette-cases comes the lost letter. The letter written by Paddy O'Brien's friend in Australia. The letter that somebody seems to have stolen eighteen years ago in Buckinghamshire. It's odd, isn't it, that Miss Harris's uncle was sometime rector of Falconbridge, the village where Paddy O'Brien met with his accident? I wonder if either Miss Harris or Lady Carrados realizes there is this vague connection. I think our next move after the inquest is to go down to Barbicon-Bramley where we may disturb the retirement of Miss Harris's uncle. Then we'll have to dive into the past history of the hospital in Falconbridge. But what a cold trail! A chance in a thousand.'

'It's a bit of a coincidence Miss Harris linking up in this way, isn't it?' ruminated Fox.

'Are you building up a picture with Miss Harris as the agent of an infamous old parson who had treasured a compromising letter for eighteen years, and now uses it? Well, I suppose it's not so impossible.

But I don't regard it as a *very* great coincidence that Miss Harris has drifted into Lady Carrados's household. Coincidences become increasingly surprising as they gain in importance. One can imagine someone telling Miss Harris about Paddy O'Brien's accident and Miss Harris saying the parson at Falconbridge was her uncle. Everybody exclaims tiresomely at the smallness of the world and nobody thinks much more of it. Mix a missing letter up in the story and we instantly incline to regard Miss Harris's remote connection with Falconbridge as a perfectly astonishing coincidence.'

'She'd hardly have mentioned it so freely,' admitted Fox, 'if she'd had anything to do with the letter.'

'Exactly. Still, we'll have to follow it up. And, talking of following things up, Fox, there's Lady Lorrimer. We'll have to check Sir Daniel Davidson's account of himself.'

'That's right, sir.'

Fox unhooked his spectacles and put them in their case.

'On what we've got,' he asked, 'have you any particular leaning to anyone?'

'Yes. I've left it until we had a moment's respite to discuss it with you. I wanted to see if you'd arrived independently at the same conclusion yourself.'

'The cigarette-case and the telephone call.'

'Yes. Very well, Fox: "in a contemplative fashion and a tranquil frame of mind," let us discuss the cigarette-cases. Point one.'

They discussed the cigarette-cases.

At seven o'clock Fox said:

'We're not within sight of making an arrest. Not on that evidence.'

Alleyn said: 'And don't forget we haven't found the cloak and hat.'

Fox said: 'It seems to me, Mr Alleyn, we'll have to ask every blasted soul that hasn't got an alibi if we can search their house. Clumsy.'

'Carrados,' began Alleyn, 'Halcut-Hackett, Davidson, Miss Harris. Withers and Potter go together. I swear the hat and cloak aren't in that flat. Same goes for Dimitri.'

'The garbage-tins,' said Fox gloomily. 'I've told the chaps about the garbage-tins. They're so unlikely they're enough to make you cry. What would anybody do with a cloak and hat, Mr Alleyn, if they wanted to get rid of 'em? We know all the old dodges. You couldn't burn 'em in any of these London flats. It was low tide, as you've pointed out, and they'd have had to be dropped off the bridge which would have been a pretty risky thing to do. D'you reckon they'll try leaving 'em at a railway office?'

'We'll have to watch for it. We'll have to keep a good man to tail our fancy. I don't somehow feel it'll be a left-luggage affair, Brer Fox. They've been given a little too much publicity of late years. Limbs and torsos have bobbed up in corded boxes with dreary insistence, not only up and down the LNER and kindred offices, but throughout the pages of detective fiction. I rather fancy the parcels post myself. I've sent out the usual request. If they were posted it was probably during the rush hour at one of the big central offices, and how the suffering cats we're to catch up with that is more than I can tell. Still, we'll hope for a lucky break, whatever that may be.'

The desk telephone rang. Alleyn, suddenly and painfully reminded of Lord Robert's call, answered it.

His mother's voice asked if he would dine with her.

'I don't suppose you can get away, my dear, but as this flat is only five minutes in a taxi it might suit you to come in.'

'I'd like to,' said Alleyn. 'When?'

'Eight, but we can have it earlier if you like. I'm all alone.'

'I'll come now, mama, and we'll have it at eight. All right?'

'Quite all right,' said the clear little voice. 'So glad, darling.'

Alleyn left his mother's telephone number in case anybody should want him, and went by taxi to the flat she had taken in Catherine Street for the London season. He found Lady Alleyn surrounded by newspapers and wearing horn-rimmed glasses.

'Hullo, darling,' she said. 'I shan't pretend I'm not reading about poor Bunchy, but we won't discuss it if you don't want to.'

'To tell you the truth,' said Alleyn, 'I rather feel I want to sit in an armchair, stare at nothing, and scarcely speak. Charming company for you, mama.'

'Why not have a bath?' suggested Lady Alleyn without looking up from her paper.

'Do I smell?' asked her son.

'No. But I always think a bath is rather a good idea when you've got to the staring stage. What time did you get up this morning?'

'*Yesterday* morning. But I have bathed and shaved since then.'

'No bed at all last night? I should have a bath. I'll run it for you. Use my room. I've sent for a change of clothes.'

'Good Lord!' said Alleyn, and then: 'You're something rather special in the maternal line, aren't you?'

He bathed. The solace of steaming water wrapped him in a sort of luxurious trance. His thoughts, that for sixteen hours had been so sharply concentrated, became blurred and nebulous. Was it only 'this morning' that he had crossed the courtyard to a taxi, half-hidden by wreaths of mist? This morning! Their footsteps had sounded hollow on the stone pavement. 'I got to look after meself, see?' A door opened with a huge slow movement that was full of horror. 'Dead, ain't 'e? *Dead, ain't 'e?* DEAD, AIN'T 'E?' 'Suffocated!' gasped Alleyn and woke with his nose full of bath-water.

His man had sent clean linen and a dinner-suit. He dressed slowly, feeling rarefied, and rejoined his mother in the sitting-room.

'Help yourself to a drink,' she said from behind her newspaper.

He got his drink and sat down. He wondered vaguely why he should feel so dog-tired. He was used to missing a night's sleep and working straight through the twenty-four hours. It must be because it was Bunchy. And the thought came into his mind that there must be a great many people at this hour who with him remembered that comic figure and regretted it.

'He had a great deal of charm,' said Alleyn aloud and his mother's voice answered him tranquilly.

'Yes, a great deal of charm. The most unfair of all the attributes.'

'You don't add: "I sometimes think," ' said Alleyn.

'Why should I?'

'People so often use that phrase to water down their ideas. You are too positive to use it.'

'In Bunchy's case the charm was one of character and then it is not unfair,' said Lady Alleyn. 'Shall we dine? It's been announced.'

'Good Lord,' said Alleyn, 'I never noticed.'

Over their coffee he asked: 'Where's Sarah?'

'She's dining and going to a play with a suitably chaperoned party.'

'Does she see anything of Rose Birnbaum?'

'My dear Roderick, who on earth is Rose Birnbaum?'

'She's Mrs Halcut-Hackett's burden for the season. Her professional burden.'

'Oh, that gel! Poor little thing, yes. I've noticed her. I don't know if Sarah pays much attention. Why?'

'I wish you'd ask her here some time. Not a seasonable party. She's got an inferiority complex about them. She's one of the more unfortunate by-products of the season.'

'I see. I wonder why that singularly hard woman has involved herself with a paying protégée. Are the Halcut-Hacketts short of money?'

'I don't know. I should think she might be at the moment.'

'Withers,' said Lady Alleyn.

'Hullo. You know all about Withers, do you?'

'My dear Rory, you forget I sit in chaperones' corner.'

'Gossip,' said Alleyn.

'The gossip is not as malicious as you may think. I always maintain that men are just as avid scandalmongers as women.'

'I know you do.'

'Mrs Halcut-Hackett is not very popular, so they don't mind talking about her in chaperones' corner. She's an opportunist. She never gives an invitation that will not bring its reward and she never accepts one that is likely to lower her prestige. She is not a kind woman. She's extremely common, but that doesn't matter. Lots of common people are charming. Like bounders. I believe no woman ever falls passionately in love with a man unless he has just the least touch of the bounder somewhere in his composition.'

'Really, mama!'

'I mean in a very rarified sense. A touch of arrogance. There's nothing like it, my dear. If you're too delicately considerate of a woman's feelings she may begin by being grateful, but the chances are she'll end by despising you.'

Alleyn made a wry face. 'Treat 'em rough?'

'Not actually, but let them think you *might*. It's humiliating but true that ninety-nine women out of a hundred like to feel their lover is capable of bullying them. Eighty of them would deny it. How often does one not hear a married woman say with a sort of satisfaction that her husband won't let her do this or that? Why do abominably written books with strong silent heroes still find a large female public? What do you suppose attracts thousands of women to a cinema actor with the brains of a mosquito?'

'His ability as a cinema actor.'

'That, yes. Don't be tiresome, Roderick. Above all, his arrogant masculinity. That's what attracts ninety-nine out of a hundred, you may depend upon it.'

'There is, perhaps fortunately, always the hundredth woman.'

'And don't be too sure of her. I am *not*, I hope, one of those abominable women who cries down her own sex. I'm by way of being a feminist, but I refuse to allow the ninety-nine (dear me, this begins to sound like a hymn) to pull the wool over the elderly eyes.'

'You're an opinionated little party, mama, and you know it. But don't suppose you can pull the wool over my eyes either. Do you suggest that I go to Miss Agatha Troy, haul her about her studio by her hair, tuck her under my arrogant masculine arm, and lug her off to the nearest registry office?'

'Church, if you please. The Church knows what I'm talking about. Look at the marriage service. A direct and embarrassing expression of the savagery inherent in our ideas of mating.'

'Would you say the season came under the same heading?'

'In a way I would say so. And why not? As long as one recognizes the more savage aspects of the season, one keeps one's sense of proportion and enjoys it. As I do. Thoroughly. And as Bunchy Gospell did. When I think of him,' said Lady Alleyn, her eyes shining with tears, 'when I think of him this morning, gossiping away to all of us, so pleased with Evelyn's ball, so gay and – and *real*, I simply cannot realize – '

'I know.'

'I suppose Mrs Halcut-Hackett comes into the picture, doesn't she? And Withers?'

'What makes you think so?'

'He had his eye on them. Both there and at the Halcut-Hacketts' cocktail-party. Bunchy knew something about Captain Withers, Roderick. I saw that and I remarked on it to him. He told me not to be inquisitive, bless him, but he admitted I was right. Is there anything more in it than that?'

'A good deal. Withers has a bad record and Bunchy knew it.'

'Is that a motive for murder?' asked Lady Alleyn.

'It might be. There are several discrepancies. I've got to try to settle one of them tonight.'

'Tonight? My dear, you'll fall asleep with the customary warning on your lips.'

'Not I. And I'm afraid there's no occasion as yet for the customary warning.'

'Does Evelyn Carrados come into the picture at all?'

Alleyn sat up.

'Why do you ask that?'

'Because I could see that Bunchy had his eye on her too.'

'We'd better change jobs, darling. You can go into the Yard and watch people having their eyes on each other and I'll sit in chaperones' corner, pounce at young men for Sarah, and make conversation with Lady Lorrimer. I've got to see her some time soon, by the way.'

'Lucy Lorrimer! You don't mean to tell me she's in this business. I can well understand somebody murdering *her*, but I don't see her on the other side of the picture. Of course she *is* mad.'

'She's got to supply half an alibi for Sir Daniel Davidson.'

'Good heavens, who next! Why Davidson?'

'Because he was the last man to leave before Bunchy.'

'Well, I hope it's not Sir Daniel. I was thinking of showing him my leg. Roderick, I suppose I can't help you with Lucy Lorrimer. I can easily ring her up and ask her to tea. She must be seething with excitement and longing to talk to everybody. Bunchy was to dine with her tonight.'

'Why?'

'For no particular reason. But she kept saying she knew he wouldn't come, that he'd forget. I can easily ring her up and she shouts so loudly you need only sit beside me to hear every word.'

'All right,' said Alleyn, 'let's try. Ask her if she saw anything of Bunchy as she was leaving. You sit in the chair here, darling, and I'll perch on the arm. We can have the receiver between us.'

Lady Lorrimer's telephone was persistently engaged but at last they got through. Her ladyship, said a voice, was at home.

'Will you say it's Lady Alleyn? Thank you.'

During the pause that followed Lady Alleyn eyed her son with a conspiratorial air and asked him to give her a cigarette. He did so and provided himself with pencil and paper.

'We'll be *ages*,' she whispered, waving the receiver to and fro rather as if it were a fan. Suddenly it emitted a loud crackling sound and Lady Alleyn raised it gingerly to within four inches of her right ear.

'Is that you, Lucy?'

'My *dear*,' shouted the receiver, 'I'm *so* glad. I've been *longing to* speak to you for, of course, you can tell us *everything*. I've always thought it was *such* a pity that good-looking son of yours turning himself into a policeman because, say what you will, it must be frightfully bad for them so long in the one position only moving their arms and the internal organs taking *all* the strain which Sir Daniel tells me is the cause of half the diseases of women, though I must own I think his practice is getting rather beyond him. Of course in the case of the Prime Minister everything must be excused.'

Lady Alleyn looked an inquiry at her son who nodded his comprehension of this amazing tarradiddle.

'Yes, Lucy?' murmured Lady Alleyn.

'Which brings me to this *frightful* calamity,' continued the telephone in a series of cracks and splutters. '*Too* awful! And you know he was to dine with me tonight. I put my brother off because I felt I could never accustom myself to the idea that there but for the Grace of God sat Bunchy Gospell. Not perhaps the Grace of God but His ways are inscrutable indeed and when I saw him come down the staircase humming to himself I little thought that he was going to his grave. I shall *never* forgive myself, of course, that I did not offer to drive him and as it turned out with the Prime Minister being so ill I might have done so.'

'Why do you keep introducing the Prime Minister into this story, Lucy?' asked Lady Alleyn. She clapped her hand over the mouthpiece and said crossly: 'But *I* want to know, Roderick.'

'It's all right,' said Alleyn. 'Davidson pretended – do listen, darling, she's telling you.'

'– I can't describe the agony, Helena,' quacked the telephone, 'I really thought I should *swoon* with it. I felt Sir Daniel must examine me without losing a moment, so I told my chauffeur to look out for him because I promise you *I* was too ill to distinguish one man from another. Then I saw him coming out of the door. "Sir Daniel, Sir Daniel!" He did not hear me and all would have been lost if one of

the linkmen had not seen my distress and drawn Sir Daniel's attention to me. He crossed the street and as a very old patient I don't
mind admitting to you, Helena, I *was* rather *disappointed* but of
course with the country in the state it is one must make sacrifices.
He was extremely agitated. The Prime Minister had developed some
terrible complaint. Please tell nobody of this, Helena. I know you are
as silent as the grave but Sir Daniel would no doubt be gravely compromised if it were ever to leak out. Under those conditions I could
do nothing but bear my cross in silence and it was not until he had
positively *run* away that I thought of driving him to Downing Street.
By the time my fool of a chauffeur had started the car, of course, it
was too late. No doubt Sir Daniel had raced to the nearest taxi-cab
and, although I have rung up to inquire tactfully, he is continually
engaged, so that one fears the worst.'

'Mad!' said Lady Alleyn to her son.

'– I can't tell you how much it has upset me but I hope I know
my duty, Helena, and having just recollected that your boy was a
constable I said to myself that he should learn of this extraordinary
man whom I am firmly persuaded is an assassin. What other explanation can there be?'

'Sir Daniel Davidson!' exclaimed Lady Alleyn.

'Good heavens, Helena, are you mad! For pity's sake tell your son
to come and see me himself in order that there may be no mistake.
How could it be my poor Sir Daniel, who was already on his way to
Downing Street? I attribute my appalling condition at this moment
to the shock I received. Do you remember a play called *The Face at
the Window?* I was reminded of it. I assure you I screamed aloud – my
chauffeur will bear witness. The nose was flat and white and the
moustache quite frightful, like some hairy monster gummed to the
window-pane. The eyes rolled, I could do nothing but clutch my
pearls. "Go away!" I screamed. My chauffeur, fool that he is, had
seen nothing and by the time he roused himself it had disappeared.'

Alleyn held a sheet of paper before his mother's nose. On it he
had written: 'Ask her who it was.'

'Have you any idea who it was, Lucy?' asked Lady Alleyn.

'There is no doubt whatsoever in my mind, Helena, and I should
have thought little in yours. These appalling cases that have
occurred! The papers are full of them. The Peeping Tom of Peckham,

though how he has managed to go there every night from Halkin Street – '

Alleyn gave a stifled exclamation.

'From Halkin Street?' repeated Lady Alleyn.

'There is no doubt that his wife's appalling behaviour has turned his head. He suspected poor Robert Gospell. You must have heard, as I did, how he asked her to let him take her home. No doubt he was searching for them. The jury will bring in a strong recommendation for mercy or perhaps they will find him guilty but insane, as no doubt he is.'

'But, Lucy! Lucy, listen. *Whom are you talking about?*'

'Don't be a fool, Helena, who should it be but George Halcut-Hackett?'

CHAPTER 22

Night Club

'Well Roderick,' said Lady Alleyn when she had at last got rid of Lucy Lorrimer, 'you may be able to make something of this but it seems to me that Lucy has at last gone completely insane. Do you for an instant suppose that poor old General Halcut-Hackett is the Peeping Tom of Peckham?'

'Some case the Press had made into a front-page story – no, of course, it's completely irrelevant. But all the same it does look as though old Halcut-Hackett flattened his face against the window of Lucy Lorrimer's car.'

'But Lucy stayed till the end, she says, and I know he took that unfortunate child away soon after midnight. What was the poor creature doing in Belgrave Square at half-past three?'

'He told me he went for a constitutional,' murmured Alleyn.

'Rubbish. One doesn't peer into old ladies' cars when one takes constitutionals at half-past three in the morning. The whole thing's preposterous.'

'It's so preposterous that I'm afraid it must be included in my dreary programme. Would you care to come to a night club with me, mama?'

'No thank you, Rory.'

'I thought not. I must go alone to the Matador. I imagine they open at about eleven.'

'Nobody goes until after midnight or later,' said Lady Alleyn.

'How do you know?'

'Sarah is forever pestering me to allow her to "go on to the Matador". She now hopes to produce a chaperone, but I imagine it is scarcely the haunt of chaperones. I have no intention of letting her go.'

'It's one of those places that offer the attractions of a tiny dancing-floor, a superlative band and a crowd so dense that you spend the night dancing cheek-to-cheek with somebody else's partner. It is so dimly lit that the most innocent visitor takes on an air of intrigue and the guiltiest has at least a sporting chance of going unrecognized.'

'You seem to be remarkably familiar with its amenities,' said his mother dryly.

'We've had our eye on the Matador for some time. It will meet with one of three fates. The smartest people will get tired of it and it will try to hold them by relaxing its vigilance in the matter of drink; or the smartest people will get tired of it and it will gradually lose its prestige and continue to make money out of the less exclusive but equally rich; or the smartest people will get tired of it and it will go bust. We are interested in the first contingency and they know it. They are extremely polite to me at the Matador.'

'Shall you be long there?'

'No. I only want to see the commissionaire and the secretary. Then I'll go home and to bed. May I use your telephone?'

Alleyn rang up Fox and asked him if he had seen the constable on night duty in Belgrave Square.

'Yes,' said Fox. 'I've talked to him. He says he didn't report having seen the General, you know who – double aitch – because he didn't think anything of it, knowing him so well. He says he thought the General had been at the ball and was on his way home.'

'When was this?'

'About three-twenty when most of the guests were leaving Marsdon House. Our chap says he didn't notice the General earlier in the evening when he took the young lady home. He says he still had his eye on the crowd outside the front door at that time and might easily have missed him. He says it's right enough that the old gentleman generally takes a turn round the Square of an evening but he's never noticed him as late as this before. I've told him a few things about what's expected of him and why sergeants lose their stripes,' added Fox. 'The fact of the matter is he spent most of his time round about the front door of Marsdon House. Now there's one other thing, sir. One of these linkmen has reported he noticed a man in a black overcoat with a white scarf pulled up to his mouth, and a black trilby hat, standing for a long time in the shadow on the outskirts of the crowd. The linkman says he was tall and looked like a gentleman. Thinks he wore evening clothes under his overcoat. Thinks he had a white moustache. He says this man seemed anxious to avoid notice and hung about in the shadows, but he looked at him several times and wondered what he was up to. The linkman reckons this man was hanging about on the other side of the street in the shadow of the trees, when the last guests went away. Now, sir, I reckon that's important.'

'Yes, Fox. Are you suggesting that this lurker was the General?'

'The description tallies, sir. I thought I'd arrange for this chap, who's still here at the Yard, to get a look at the General and see if he can swear to him.'

'You do. Better take your linkman off to the Square. See if you can catch the General doing his evening march. He'll be able to see him in the same light under the same conditions as last night's.'

'That's right.'

'I'm going to the Matador and then home. Ring me up if there's anything.'

'Very good, Mr Alleyn. Good night.'

'Good night, Brer Fox.'

Alleyn turned from the telephone and stared at his mother.

'It looks as if Lucy Lorrimer isn't altogether dotty,' he said. 'Old Halcut-Hackett seems to have behaved in a very curious manner last night. If, indeed, it was the General, and I fancy it must have been. He was so remarkably evasive about his own movements. Do you know him at all well?'

'Not very, darling. He was a brother-officer of your father's. I rather think he was one of those large men whom regimental humour decrees shall be called "Tiny". I can't remember ever hearing that he had a violent temper or took drugs or seduced his colonel's wife or indeed did anything at all remarkable. He didn't marry this rather dreadful lady of his until he was about fifty.'

'Was he rich?'

'I rather think he was fairly rich. Still is, I should have thought from that house. He's got a country place too, I believe, somewhere in Kent.'

'Then why on earth does she bother with paying débutantes?'

'Well, you know, Rory, if she's anxious to be asked everywhere and do everything she's more likely to succeed with something young behind her. Far more invitations would come rolling in.'

'Yes. I rather think there's more to it than that. Good night, darling. You are the best sort of mama. Too astringent to be sweet, thank God, but nevertheless comfortable.'

'Thank you, my dear. Come in again if you want to. Good night.'

She saw him out with an air of jauntiness, but when she returned to her drawing-room she sat still for a long time thinking of the past of her son, of Troy, and of her own fixed determination never to meddle.

Alleyn took a taxi to the Matador in Soho. The Matador commissionaire was a disillusioned giant in a plum-coloured uniform. He wore beautiful gloves, a row of medals, and an expression of worldly wisdom. He stood under a representation in red neon lights of a capering bull-fighter, and he paid the management twenty pounds a year for his job. Alleyn gave him good evening and walked into the entrance-hall of the Matador. The pulsation of saxophones and percussion instruments hung on the air, deadened in this ante-room by draperies of plum-coloured silk caught up into classic folds by rows of silvered tin sunflowers. A lounge porter came forward and directed Alleyn to the cloakroom.

'I wonder if you know Captain Maurice Withers by sight,' asked Alleyn. 'I'm supposed to join his party and I'm not sure if I've come to the right place. He's a member here.'

'I'm sorry, sir. I've only just taken this job myself and I don't know the members by sight. If you ask at the office, sir, they'll tell you.'

With a silent anathema on this ill chance Alleyn thanked the man and looked for the box-office. He found it beneath a large sunflower and surrounded by richer folds of silk. Alleyn peered into it and saw a young man in a beautiful dinner-jacket, morosely picking his teeth.

'Good evening,' said Alleyn.

The young man abandoned the toothpick with lightning sleight-of-hand.

'Good evening, sir,' he said brightly in a cultured voice.

'May I speak to you for a moment – Mr – ?'

The young man instantly looked very wary.

'Well – ah – I am the manager. My name is Cuthbert.'

Alleyn slid his card through the peep-hole. The young man looked at it, turned even more wary, and said:

'Perhaps if you wouldn't mind walking round to the side door, Mr – Oh! – Inspector – ah! – Alleyn. Simmons!'

A cloakroom attendant appeared. On the way to the side door Alleyn tried his story again but neither the cloakroom attendant nor the commissionaire, who was recalled, knew Withers by sight. The attendant conducted Alleyn by devious ways into a little dim room behind the box-office. Here he found the manager.

'It's nothing very momentous,' said Alleyn. 'I want you to tell me, if you can, about what time Captain Maurice Withers arrived at this club last night – or rather this morning?'

He saw Mr Cuthbert glance quickly at an evening paper on which appeared a quarter-page photograph of Robert Gospell. During the second or two that elapsed before he replied, Alleyn heard again that heavy insistent thudding of the band.

'I'm afraid I have no idea at all,' said Mr Cuthbert at last.

'That's a pity,' said Alleyn. 'If you can't tell me I suppose I'll have to make rather a business of it. I'll have to ask all your guests if they saw him and when and so on. I'm afraid I shall have to insist on see-ing the book. I'm sorry. What a bore for you!'

Mr Cuthbert looked at him with the liveliest distaste.

'You can understand,' he began, 'that in our position we have to be extremely tactful. Our guests expect it of us.'

'Oh, rather,' agreed Alleyn. 'But there's not going to be nearly such a fluster if you give me the information I want quietly, as there will be if I have to start asking all sorts of people all sorts of questions.'

Mr Cuthbert stared at his first finger-nail and then bit it savagely.

'But if I don't know,' he said peevishly.

'Then we're just out of luck. I'll try your commissionaire and – Simmons, is it? If that fails we'll have to start on the guests.'

'Oh, damn!' ejaculated Mr Cuthbert. 'Well, he came in late. I do remember that.'

'How do you remember that, please?'

'Because we had a crowd of people who came from – from the Marsdon House Ball at about half-past three or a quarter to four. And then there was a bit of a lull.'

'Yes?'

'Yes, well, and then a good deal later Captain Withers signed in. He ordered a fresh bottle of gin.'

'Mrs Halcut-Hackett arrived with him, didn't she?'

'I don't know the name of his partner.'

'A tall, big, blonde woman of about forty to forty-five, with an American accent. Perhaps you wouldn't mind calling – '

'All right, then, all right. She did.'

'Was it as late as half-past four when they arrived?'

'I don't – look here, I mean – '

'It's quite possible you may hear no more of this. The more exact your information, you know, the less troublesome our subsequent enquiries.'

'Yes, I know, but we owe a DUTY to our guests.'

'Do you know actually to within say ten minutes when this couple arrived? I think you do. If so, I most strongly advise you to tell me.'

'Oh, all right. As a matter of fact it was a quarter-past four. There'd been such a long gap with nobody coming in – we were practically full anyway of course – that I *did* happen to notice the time.'

'That's perfectly splendid. Now if you'll sign a statement to this effect I don't think I need bother you any more.'

Mr Cuthbert fell into a profound meditation. Alleyn lit a cigarette and waited with an air of amiability. At last Mr Cuthbert said:

'Am I likely to be called as a witness to anything?'

'Not very. We'll spare you if we can.'

'I could refuse.'

'And I,' said Alleyn, 'could become a member of your club. You couldn't refuse that.'

'Delighted, I'm sure,' said Mr Cuthbert unhappily. 'All right. I'll sign.'

Alleyn wrote out a short statement and Mr Cuthbert signed it. Mr Cuthbert became more friendly and offered Alleyn a drink, which he refused with the greatest amiability. Mr Cuthbert embarked on a long eulogistic account of the Matador and the way it was run and the foolishness of night-club proprietors who attempted to elude the lawful restriction imposed on the sale of alcoholic beverages.

'It never pays,' cried Mr Cuthbert. 'Sooner or later they get caught. It's just damn silly.'

A waiter burst into the room, observed something in Mr Cuthbert's eye, and flew out again. Mr Cuthbert cordially invited Alleyn to accompany him into the dance-room. He was so insistent that Alleyn allowed himself to be ushered through the entrance-hall and down a plum-coloured tunnel. The sound of the band swelled into a rhythmic all-pervading rumpus. Alleyn was aware of more silver sunflowers; of closely ranked tables and faces dimly lit from below, of a more distant huddle of people ululating and sliding in time to the band. He stood just inside the entrance, trying to accustom his eyes to this scene, while Mr Cuthbert prattled innocently 'Ruddigore' – 'We only cut respectable capers.' He was about to turn away when he knew abruptly that someone was watching him. His eyes followed this intangible summons. He turned slowly to the left and there at a corner table sat Bridget O'Brien and Donald Potter.

They were both staring at him and with such intensity that he could not escape the feeling that they had wished to attract his attention. He deliberately met their gaze and returned it. For a second or two they looked at each other and then Bridget made a quick gesture, inviting him to join them.

He said: 'I see some friends. Do you mind if I speak to them for a moment?'

Mr Cuthbert was delighted and melted away on a wave of tactfulness. Alleyn walked over to the table and bowed.

'Good evening.'

'Will you sit down for a minute?' said Bridget. 'We want to speak to you.'

One of Mr Cuthbert's waiters instantly produced a chair.

'What is it?' asked Alleyn.

'It's Bridgie's idea,' said Donald. 'I can't stand it any longer. I've said I'll do whatever Bridgie says. I suppose I'm a fool but I give in. In a way I want to.'

'He's got nothing to fear,' said Bridget. 'I've told him – '

'Look here,' said Alleyn, 'this doesn't seem a particularly well-chosen spot for the kind of conversation that's indicated.'

'I know,' said Bridget. 'If Donna or Bart ever finds out I've been here there'll be a row of absolutely horrific proportions. The Matador! Unchaperoned! With Donald! But we were desperate – we *had* to see each other. Bart has driven me stark ravers, he's been so awful. I managed to ring Donald up from an outside telephone and we arranged to meet here. Donald's a member. We've talked it all over and we were coming to see you.'

'Suppose you do so now. The manager here knows I'm a policeman so we'd better not leave together. Here's my address. Come along in about fifteen minutes. That do?'

'Yes, thank you,' said Bridget, 'won't it, Donald?'

'All right, all right,' said Donald. 'It's your idea, darling. If it lands me in – '

'It won't land you anywhere but in my flat,' said Alleyn. 'You've both come to a very sensible decision.'

He rose and looked down at them. 'Good Lord,' he thought, 'they *are* young.' He said: 'Don't weaken. *Au revoir,*' and walked out of the Matador.

On the way to his flat he wondered if the loss of the best part of another night's sleep was going to get him any nearer a solution.

CHAPTER 23

Donald on Wits

Alleyn walked restlessly about his sitting-room. He had sent Vassily, his old servant, off to bed. The flat, at the end of a cul-de-sac behind Coventry Street, was very silent. He was fond of this room. It had a contradictory air of monastic comfort that was, if he had realized it, a direct expression of himself. Dürer's praying hands were raised above his mantelpiece. At the other end of the room Troy's painting of the wharf at Suva uttered, in sharp cool colours, a simple phrase of beauty. He had bought this picture secretly from one of her exhibitions and Troy did not know that it hung there in his room. Three comfortable elderly chairs from his mother's house at Bossicote, his father's desk and, waist-high all round the walls, a company of friendly books. But this June night his room seemed chilly. He put a match to the wood fire and drew three armchairs into the circle of its radiance. Time those two arrived. A taxi came up the cul-de-sac and stopped. The door banged. He heard Bridget's voice and went to let them in.

He was reminded vividly of two small children entering a dentist's waiting-room. Donald was the victim, Bridget the not very confident escort. Alleyn tried to dispel this atmosphere, settled them in front of the fire, produced ciagrettes, and remembering they were grown-up offered them drinks. Bridget refused. Donald with an air of grandeur accepted a whisky and soda.

'Now then,' said Alleyn, 'What's it all about?' He felt he ought to add: 'Open wide!' and as he handed Donald his drink: 'Rinse, please.'

'It's about Donald,' said Bridget in a high determined voice. 'He's promised to let me tell you. He doesn't like it but I say I won't marry him unless he does, so he's going to. And besides, he really thinks he ought to do it.'

'It's a damn fool thing to do,' said Donald. 'There's no reason actually why I should come into it at all. I've made up my mind but all the same I don't see – '

'All the same, you are in it, darling, so it doesn't much matter if you see why or not, as the case may be.'

'All right. That's settled anyway, isn't it? We needn't go on argu-ing. Let's tell Mr Alleyn and get it over.'

'Yes, Let's. Shall I?'

'If you like.'

Bridget turned to Alleyn.

'When we met tonight,' she began, 'I asked Donald about Captain Withers, because the way you talked about him this afternoon made me think perhaps he's not a good idea. I made Donald tell me *exact-ly* what he knows about Wits.'

'Yes?'

'Yes. Well, Wits is a crook. Isn't he Donald?'

'I suppose so.'

'He's a crook because he runs a gambling hell at Leatherhead. Don says you know that or anyway you suspect it. Well, he does. And Donald said he'd go in with him only he didn't know then how crooked Wits was. And then Donald lost money to Wits and could-n't pay him back and Wits said he'd better stand in with him because he'd make it pretty hot for Donald if he didn't. What with Bunchy and everything.'

'But Bunchy paid your debts to Withers,' said Alleyn.

'Not all,' said Donald with a scarlet face but a look of desperate determination ('First extraction,' thought Alleyn.) 'I didn't tell him about all of it.'

'I see.'

'So Donald said he'd go in with Wits. And then when he quar-relled with Bunchy and went to live with Wits he found out that Wits was worse of a crook than ever. Don found out that Wits was getting money from a woman. Do I have to tell you who she was?'

'Was it Mrs Halcut-Hackett?'

'Yes.'

'Was it much?' Alleyn asked Donald.

'Yes, sir,' said Donald. 'I don't know how much. But she – he told me she had an interest in the Leatherhead club. I thought at first it was all right. Really I did. It's hard to explain. I just got sort of used to the way Wits talked. Everything is a ramp nowadays – a racket – that's what Wits said and I began rather to think the same way. I suppose I lost my eye. Bridget says I did.'

'I expect she's right, isn't she?'

'I suppose so. But – I don't know. It was all rather fun in a way until – well, until today.'

'You mean since Bunchy was murdered?'

'Yes. I do. But – you see – '

'Let me,' said Bridget. 'You see, Mr Alleyn, Donald got rather desperate. Wits rang up and told him to keep away. That was this morning.'

'I know. It was at my instigation,' said Alleyn. 'I was there.'

'Oh,' said Donald.

'Well, anyway,' said Bridget, 'Donald got a bit of a shock. What with your questions and Wits always rubbing it in that Donald was going to be quite well off when his uncle died.'

'Did Captain Withers make a lot of that?'

Bridget took Donald's hand.

'Yes,' she said, 'he did. Didn't he, Donald?'

'Anyone would think, Bridget, that you wanted to hang one of us, Wits or me,' said Donald and raised her hand to his cheek.

Bridget said: 'I'm going to tell *everything*. You're innocent, and if you're innocent you're safe. My mother would say that. You say it, don't you, Mr Alleyn?'

'Yes,' said Alleyn.

'Well, this afternoon,' Bridget went on, 'Donald's things came back from Wits' flat. His clothes and his books. When he unpacked them he saw one book was missing.'

'The first volume of Taylor's *Medical Jurisprudence*?'

Donald wetted his lips and nodded.

'That upset Donald awfully,' Bridget continued, growing rather white in the face, 'because of one chapter in the book. After they read the papers this morning Donald and Wits had an argument about how long it took to – to – '

'Oh God!' said Donald suddenly.

'To asphyxiate anybody?' asked Alleyn.

'Yes. And Donald looked it up in this book.'

'Did Captain Withers handle the book?'

Donald looked quickly at Bridget and said: 'Yes, he did. He read a bit of it and then lost interest. He thought it would have taken longer, he said.'

'Donald was puzzled about the book not arriving, and about Wits telling him not to come to the flat,' said Bridget. 'He thought about it all the afternoon, and the more he thought the less he liked it. So he rang up. Wits answered but when he heard Donald's voice he simply cut him off without another word. Didn't he, darling?'

'Yes,' said Donald. 'I rang again and he didn't answer. I – I couldn't think clearly at all. I felt stone cold in the pit of my stomach. It was simply ghastly to find myself cut dead like that. *Why* shouldn't he answer me, *why?* Why hadn't he sent the book? Only this morning we'd been together in his flat, perfectly friendly. Until the news came – after that I didn't listen to anything Wits said. As soon as I knew Uncle Bunch had been murdered I couldn't think of anything else. I wasn't dressed when the papers came. Mother had known for hours but, the telephone being disconnected then, she couldn't get hold of me. I hadn't told her my address. Wits kept talking. I didn't listen. And then, when I did get home, you were there, getting at me, getting at me. And then my mother crying, and the flowers, and everything. And on top of it all this business of Wits not wanting to speak to me. I couldn't think. I just *had* to see Bridget.'

'Yes,' said Bridget, 'he had to see me. But you're muddling things, Donald. We ought to keep them in their right order. Mr Alleyn, we've got as far as this afternoon. Well, Donald got so rattled about the telephone and the missing book that in spite of what Wits had said, he felt he *had* to see him. So after dinner he took a taxi to Wits's flat and he could see a light under the blind, so he knew Wits was in. Donald still had his own latch-key so he went straight in and up to the flat. Now you go on, Donald.'

Donald finished his whisky and soda and with unsteady fingers lit a fresh cigarette. 'All right,' he said. 'I'll tell you. When I walked into the sitting-room he was lying on the divan bed. I stood in the middle of the room looking at him. He didn't move, and he didn't speak at all loudly. He called me a foul name and told me to get out. I said

I wanted to know why he'd behaved as he did. He just lay there and looked at me. I said something about you, sir – I don't know what – and in a split second he was on his feet. I thought he was going to start a fight. He asked me what the bloody hell I'd said to you about him. I said I'd avoided speaking about him as much as possible. But he began to ask all sorts of questions. God, he did look ugly. You often read about the veins swelling with rage in people's faces. They did in his. He sat on the edge of the table swinging one foot and his face got sort of dark.'

'Yes,' said Alleyn. 'I can see Captain Withers. Go on.'

'He said – ' Donald caught his breath. Alleyn saw his fingers tighten round Bridget's. 'He said that unless I kept my head and held my tongue he'd begin to talk himself. He said that after all I had quarrelled with Uncle Bunch and I had been in debt and I was Uncle Bunch's heir. He said if he was in this thing up to his knees I was in it up to my neck. He pulled his hand out of his pocket and pointed his flat finger at my neck. Then he told me to remember, if I didn't want to commit suicide, that when he left Marsdon House he went to his car and drove to the Matador. I was to say that I'd seen him drive off with his partner.'

'Did you see this?'

'No. I left after him. I did think I saw him walking ahead of me towards his car. It was parked in Belgrave Road.'

'Why, do you suppose, did Withers take this extraordinary attitude when you saw him tonight?'

'He thought I'd given him away to you. He told me so.'

'About Leatherhead?'

'Yes. You said something about – about – '

'Fleecing lambs,' said Bridget.

'Yes. So I did,' admitted Alleyn cheerfully.

'He thought I'd lost my nerve and talked too much.'

'And now you are prepared to talk?'

'Yes.'

'Why?'

'We've told you – ' Bridget began.

'Yes, I know. You've told me that you persuaded Donald to come to me because you thought it better for him to explain his association with Withers. But I rather think there's something more behind it than that. Would I be wrong, Donald, if I said that you were at least encouraged to take this decision by the fear that Withers himself might get in first and suggest that you had killed your uncle?'

Bridget cried out: 'No! *No!* How can you be so cruel? How can you think that of Donald! Donald!'

But Donald looked steadily at Alleyn and when he spoke again it was gravely and with a certain dignity that became him very well.

He said: 'Don't, Bridget. It's perfectly natural Mr Alleyn should think that I'm afraid of Wits accusing me. I *am* afraid of it. I didn't kill Uncle Bunch. I think I was fonder of him than anyone else in the world except you, Bridgie. But I had quarrelled with him. I wish to God I hadn't. I didn't kill him. The reason I'm quite ready now to answer any questions about Wits, even if it means implicating myself – ' He stopped and took a deep breath.

'Yes?' asked Alleyn.

'– is that after seeing Wits this evening I believe he murdered my uncle.'

There was a long silence.

'Motive?' asked Alleyn at last.

'He thought he had a big enough hold over me to get control of the money.'

'Proof?'

'I've none. Only the way he spoke tonight. He's afraid I believe he'd murder anyone if he'd enough incentive.'

'That's not proof, nor anything like it.'

'No. It seemed good enough,' said Donald, 'to bring me here When I might have kept quiet.'

The telephone rang. Alleyn went over to the desk and answered it.

'Hullo?'

'Roderick, is that you?'

'Yes. Who is it, please?'

'Evelyn Carrados.'

Alleyn looked across to the fireplace. He saw Bridget bend forward swiftly and kiss Donald.

'Hullo!' he said. 'Anything the matter?'

'Roderick, I'm so worried. I don't know what to do. Bridgie has gone out without saying a word to anyone. I've rung up as many people as I dared and I haven't an inkling where she is. I'm so terrified she's done something wild and foolish. I thought she might be with Donald Potter and I wondered if you could tell me his telephone number. Thank Heaven Herbert is out at a regimental dinner, at Tunbridge. I'm distraught with anxiety.'

'It's all right, Evelyn,' said Alleyn. 'Bridget's here with me.'

'With you?'

'Yes. She wanted to talk to me. She's quite all right. I'll bring her back – '

'Is Donald Potter there?'

'Yes.'

'*But why?* What have they *done* it for? Roderick, I want to see you. I'll come and get Bridget, may I?'

'Yes, do,' said Alleyn and gave her his address.

He hung up the receiver and turned to find Bridget and Donald looking very startled.

'*Donna!*' whispered Bridget. 'Oh, golly!'

'Had I better go?' asked Donald.

'I think perhaps you'd better,' said Alleyn.

'If Bridgie's going to be hauled over the coals I'd rather stay.'

'No, darling,' said Bridget, 'it will be better not, honestly. As long as Bart doesn't find out I'll be all right.'

'Your mother won't be here for ten minutes,' said Alleyn. 'Look here, Donald, I want a full account of this gambling business at Leatherhead. If I put you in another room will you write one for me? It will save us a great deal of time and trouble. It must be as clear as possible with no trimmings and as many dates as you can conjure up. It will, I hope, lead to Captain Withers's conviction.'

Donald looked uncomfortable.

'It seems rather a ghastly sort of thing to do. I mean – '

'Good heavens, you have just told me you think the man's a murderer and you apparently know he's a blackguard. He's used you as a cat's-paw and I understand his idea has been to swindle you out of your money!'

'All right,' said Donald. 'I'll do it.'

Alleyn took him into the dining-room and settled him there with pen and paper.

'I'll come in later on and see what sort of fist you've made of it. There will have to be witnesses to your signature.'

'Shall I be had up as an accomplice?'

'I hardly think so. How old are you?'

'Twenty-one in August. It's not that I mind for myself. At least it would be pretty bloody, wouldn't it? But I've said I'll go through with it.'

'So you have. Don't make too big a sainted martyr of yourself,' said Alleyn good-naturedly. Donald looked up at him and suddenly the ghost of Lord Robert's twinkle came into his eyes.

'All right,' he said. 'I won't.'

Alleyn returned to Bridget and found her sitting on the hearth-rug. She looked very frightened.

'Does Bart know?'

'No, but your mother's been very worried.'

'Well, that's not all me. Bart's nearly driving her dotty. I can't tell you what he's like. Honestly it would never astonish me if Bart had an apoplectic fit and went crazy.'

'Dear me,' said Alleyn,

'No, honestly. I don't know what he told you when you inter-viewed him but I suppose you saw through the famous Carrados pose, didn't you? Of course you did. But you may not have realized what a temper he's got. I didn't for a long time. I mean not until I was about fifteen.'

'Two years ago?' asked Alleyn with a smile. 'Tell me about it.'

'It was simply frightful. Donna had been ill and she was sleeping very badly. Bart was asked if he'd mind going into his dressing-room. I didn't realize then, but I do now, that that was what annoyed him. He always gets the huff when Donna's ill. He takes it as a sort of per-sonal insult and being a beastly old Victorian Turk the dressing-room idea absolutely put the tin cupola on it. Are you shocked?'

'I suppose not,' said Alleyn cautiously. 'Anyway, go on.'

'Well, you're not. And so he went into his dressing-room. And then Donna got really ill and I said we must have Sir Daniel because she *was* so ill and he's an angel. And Bart rang him up. Well, I want-ed to get hold of Sir Daniel first to tell him about Donna before Bart did. So I went downstairs into Bart's study because I told the butler to show Sir Daniel in there. Bart was up with Donna telling her how "seedy" he felt, and it didn't matter, she wasn't to notice. And then Sir Dan came in and was angelic and I told him about Donna.

Did you notice in the study there's a French escritoire thing on a table?'

'Yes.'

'Well, Sir Dan adores old things and he saw it and raved about it and said it was a beautiful piece and told me when it was made and how they used sometimes to put little secret drawers in them and you just touch a screw and they fly out. He said it was a museum piece and asked me if I didn't think some of the vanished ladies might come back and open the secret drawer with ghostly fingers. So I thought I'd like to see, and when Sir Dan had gone up to Donna I tried prodding the screws with a pencil and at last a little drawer did fly out triangularly, sort of. There was a letter in it. I didn't touch it, naturally, but while I was looking at the drawer, Bart must have come in. What did you say?'

'Nothing,' said Alleyn. 'Go on.'

'I can't *tell* you what he was like. He went absolutely stark *ravers*, honestly. He took hold of my arm and twisted it so much I screamed before I could stop myself. And then he turned as white as the washing and called me a little bastard. I believed he'd have actually hit me if Sir Dan hadn't come down. I think Sir Dan had heard me yell and he must have guessed what had happened because he had one glance at my arm – I had short sleeves – and then he said in a lovely *dangerous* sort of voice: "Are you producing *another* patient for me, Carrados?" Bart banged the little drawer shut, began to splutter and try to get up some sort of explanation. Sir Daniel just looked at him through his glasses – the ones with the black ribbon. Bart tried to pretend I'd slipped on the polished floor and he'd caught me by the arm. Sir Daniel said: "Very curious indeed," and went on look-ing at my arm. He gave me a prescription for some stuff to put on it and was frightfully nice to me, and didn't ask questions, but just ignored Bart. It made me absolutely *crawl* with shame to hear Bart trying to do his simple-soldier stuff and sort of ingratiate himself with Sir Dan. And when he'd gone Bart apologized to me and said he was really terribly nervy and ill and had never recovered from the war, which was pretty good as he spent it in Tunbridge Wells. That was the worst of all, having to hear him apologize. He said there was a letter from his mother in the drawer and it was very sacred. Of course I felt simply *lousy*. He's never forgiven me and I've never forgotten. My private belief is there was something about his miserable past in that drawer.'

Bridget's voice at last stopped. Alleyn, who had sat in his chair, was silent for so long that at last she turned from the fire and looked into his face.

'It's a queer story, isn't it?' she said.

'Very queer, indeed,' said Alleyn. 'Have you ever told anyone else about it?'

'No. Well, only Donald.' She wriggled across the hearthrug. 'It's funny,' she said. 'I suppose I ought to be frightened of you, but I'm not. Why's Donna coming?'

'She wants to collect you, and see me,' said Alleyn absently.

'Everybody wants to see you.' She clasped her hands over her knees. 'Don't they?' insisted Bridget.

'For no very flattering reason, I'm afraid.'

'Well, I think you're really rather a lamb,' said Bridget.

'Tell me,' said Alleyn, 'do you think anyone else knows the secret of that French writing-case?'

'I shouldn't think so. You'd never know unless somebody showed you.'

'None of the servants?'

'I'm not sure. Bart slammed the drawer shut as soon as Sir Daniel came in.'

'Has Sir Daniel ever been alone in that room?'

'Sir Dan? Good heavens, you don't think my angelic Sir Dan had anything to do with Bart's beastly letter?'

'I simply want to clear things up.'

'Well, as a matter of fact I don't think he's been in the study before or since and he was never alone there that day. When Sir Dan comes, the servants always show him straight upstairs. Bart hates his room to be used for visitors.'

'Has Dimitri, the catering man, ever been alone in that room?'

'Why – I don't know. Yes, now you come to mention it he *did* interview Donna there, about a month before our ball-dance. I went down first and he was alone in the room.'

'When was this? Can you remember the date?'

'Let me see. I'll try. Yes. Yes, I can. It was on the tenth of May. We were going to Newmarket and Dimitri came early in the morning because of that.'

'Would you swear he was alone in the room?'

'Yes, yes, I would. But, please, what does it mean?'

'See here,' said Alleyn. 'I want you to forget all about this. Don't speak of it to anyone, not even to Donald. Understood?'

'Yes, but – '

'I want your promise.'

'All right, I promise.'

'Solemnly?'

'Solemnly.'

The front-door bell rang.

'Here's your mother,' said Alleyn.

CHAPTER 24

The Dance Is Wound Up

When Alleyn opened the door to Evelyn Carrados, he saw her as a dark still figure against the lighted street. Her face was completely shadowed and it was impossible for him to glean anything from it. So that when she walked into the sitting-room he was not prepared for her extraordinary pallor, her haunted eyes and the drawn nervousness of her mouth. He remembered that she had gone to her room before she missed Bridget, and he realized with compassion that she had removed her complexion and neglected to replace it. Perhaps Bridget felt something of the same compassion, for she uttered a little cry and ran to her mother. Lady Carrados, using that painful gesture of all distracted mothers, held Bridget in her arms. Her thin hands were extraordinarily expressive.

'Darling,' she murmured. With a sort of hurried intensity she kissed Bridget's hair. 'How could you frighten me like this, Bridgie, how *could* you?'

'I thought you wouldn't know. Donna, *don't*. It's all right, really it is. It was only about Donald. I didn't want to worry you. I'm so sorry, *dear* Donna.' Lady Carrados gently disengaged herself and turned to Alleyn.

'Come and sit down, Evelyn,' he said. 'There's nothing to worry about. I would have brought your daughter home, but she had some interesting news and I thought you would trust her with me for half an hour.'

'Yes, Roderick, of course. If only I had known. Where's Donald? I thought he was here.'

'He's in the next room. Shall we send Bridget to join him for a minute or two?'

'Please.'

'Don't interrupt him,' said Alleyn as Bridget went out.

'All right.'

The door closed behind her.

Alleyn said: 'Do you ever drink brandy, Evelyn?'

'Never, why?'

'You're going to do so now. You're quite done up. Warm your hands at my fire while I get it for you.'

He actually persuaded her to drink a little brandy, and laughed at her convulsive shudder.

'Now then,' he said, 'there's no need for you to fuss about Bridget. She's been, on the whole, a very sensible young person and her only fault is in giving a commonplace visit the air of a secret elopement.'

'My nerves have gone, I think. I began to imagine all sorts of horrible things. I even wondered if she suspected Donald of this crime.'

'She is, on the contrary, absolutely assured of Donald's innocence.'

'Then why did she do this?'

'I'd better tell you the whole story. The truth is, Evelyn, they were longing for each other's bright eyes. Bridget wanted to convince me of Donald's innocence. She also wanted him to tell me this and that about a third person who doesn't matter at the moment. They met, most reprehensibly, at the Matador.'

'The Matador! Roderick, how naughty of them! It just simply isn't done by débutantes. No, really that was very naughty.'

Alleyn was both relieved and surprised to find that this departure from débutantes' etiquette took momentary precedence over Lady Carrados's other troubles.

'They had only just arrived, I imagine, when I ran into them there. The place was only half-full, Evelyn. It was too early for the smart people. I shouldn't think anyone else saw them. I brought them on here.'

'I'm very glad you did,' she said doubtfully.

'Was that all that worried you?'

'No. It's Herbert. He's been so extraordinary, Roderick, since this tragedy. He's stayed indoors all day and he never takes his eyes off me. I was afraid he would give up this dinner tonight, but, thank Heaven, he didn't. It is followed by the annual regimental dance and he has to present trophies or something so it will keep him quite late. I should have gone too, but I couldn't face it. I couldn't face another hour with him. He keeps making curious hints as if he – Roderick, almost as if he suspected me of something.'

'Tell me what he says.'

She leant back in her chair and relaxed. He saw that, not for the first time, he was to play the part of confidant. 'An odd rôle for a CID man,' he thought, 'and a damn useful one.' He settled himself to listen.

'It began soon after you left. While we were at tea. We had tea in my boudoir. I asked my secretary, Miss Harris, to join us, because I thought if she was there it might be a little easier. Naturally enough, but most unfortunately, poor Miss Harris began to speak to Bridget about Bunchy. She said she'd been reading a book on famous trials and somehow or other the word "blackmail" cropped up. I – I'm afraid I was startled and showed it. The very word was enough as you may imagine. I looked up to find Herbert's eyes fixed on me with an expression of – how can I describe it? – of knowing terror. He didn't go with the others after tea but hung about the room watching me. Suddenly he said: "You were very friendly with Robert Gospell, weren't you?" I said: "Of course I was." Then he asked me to show him my bank-book. It sounded perfectly insane, right on top of his other question. Almost funny – as if he suspected I'd been keeping poor Bunchy. But it wasn't very funny. It terrified me. He never worries about my money as a rule. He generally makes rather a point of not doing so, because, apart from the allowance he gives me, I've got my own, and what Paddy left me. I knew if he saw my bank-book it would show that I had been drawing large sums – five hundred pounds, to meet the demands of – to – '

'The five hundred that went into that big bag of yours last night. How did you draw it out, Evelyn?'

'I drew some myself. I cashed a cheque for five hundred, I can't think that Herbert knew, or that he could have suspected the truth, if he did know. It's all so terribly disturbing. I put him off by saying I couldn't find the book, that I thought I had sent it back to the bank.

He hardly seemed to listen. Suddenly he asked me if Bunchy had ever called when I was out? It seemed a perfectly inane question. I said I didn't know. He sat glaring at me till I could have screamed, and then he said: "Did he know anything about old furniture?" '

Alleyn glanced up quickly: 'Old furniture?'

'I know! It sounds demented, doesn't it? I repeated it like you, and Herbert said: "Well antiques. Pieces like the escritoire in my study." And then he leaned forward and said: "Do you think he knew anything about that?" I said: "Herbert, what *are* you talking about?" and he said: "I suppose I'm going to pieces. I feel I have been surrounded by treachery all my life!" It sounds just silly, but it frightened me. I rather lost my head, and asked him how he could talk like that. I began to say that Bridget was always loyal, when he burst out laughing. "Your daughter," he said, "loyal! How far do you suppose her loyalty would take her? Would you care to put it to the test?" '

Lady Carrados pressed her hands together.

'He's always disliked Bridgie. He's always been jealous of her. I remember once, it must be two years ago now, they had some sort of quarrel, and Herbert actually hurt her. He hurt her arm. I should never have found out if I hadn't gone to her room and seen the marks. I think he sees some reflection of Paddy in her. Roderick, do you think Herbert can know about Paddy and me? Is there the smallest possibility that the blackmailer has written to him?'

'It is possible, of course,' said Alleyn slowly, 'but I don't think it quite fits in. You say this extraordinary change in Carrados began after Miss Harris and Bridget talked of blackmail, and you showed you were startled?'

'Yes.'

'Do you think your obvious dismay could have suggested to him that you yourself were the victim of blackmail?'

'I don't know. It certainly suggested something pretty ominous,' said Lady Carrados, with the ghost of a smile. 'He's in the most extraordinary state of mind, it terrifies me.'

'When did you marry him, Evelyn?'

'When? Two years after Paddy died. He had wanted me to marry him before. Herbert was a very old friend of my family's. He had always been rather attached to me.'

'He's never given any sign of this sort of behaviour before?'

'Not *this* sort. Of course, he's rather difficult sometimes. He's very touchy. He's eighteen years older than I am, and he hates to be reminded of it. One has to be rather tactful. I suppose he's vain. Bridgie thinks so, I know.'

The gentle voice, with its tranquil, level note, faltered for a moment, and then went on steadily. 'I suppose you wonder why I married him, don't you?'

'A little, yes. Perhaps you felt that you needed security. You had had your great adventure.'

'It was exactly that. But it wasn't right, I see that now. It wasn't fair. Although Herbert knew quite well that he was not my great love, and was very chivalrous and humble about it, he couldn't really resign himself to the knowledge, and he grew more and more inclined to be rather a martyr. It's pathetically childish sometimes. He tries to draw my attention to his little ailments. He gets a sort of patient look. It irritates Bridgie dreadfully, which is such a pity. And yet, although Herbert seems simple, he's not. He's a mass of repressions, and queer twisted thoughts. Do you know, I think he is still intensely jealous of Paddy's memory.'

'Did you see much of him before Paddy died?'

'Yes. I'm afraid, poor Herbert, that he rather saw himself as the faithful, chivalrous friend who continued to adore me quite honourably after I was – married. You see, I still think of myself as Paddy's wife. We used to ask Herbert to dine quite often. He bored Paddy dreadfully but – well, I'm afraid Paddy rather gloried in some of Herbert's peculiarities. He almost dined out on them. It was very naughty of him, but he was so gay always and so charming that he was forgiven everything. Everything.'

'I know.'

'Herbert rather emphasized the sacrificial note in his friendship, and of course Paddy saw that, and used to tease me about him. But I was very attached to him. No, he wasn't quite so touchy in those days, poor fellow. He was always very kind indeed. I'm afraid both Paddy and I rather got into the way of making use of him.'

'You are sure he suspected nothing?'

'Absolutely. In a way he was our greatest friend. I told you that I was staying with my mother when Paddy was hurt. She rang Herbert up when the news came through. Almost instinctively we turned to him. He was with us in a few minutes. Why, I suppose in a way I owe it to Herbert that I was in time to see Paddy before he died.'

Alleyn opened his mouth, and shut it again. Lady Carrados was staring into the fire, and gave no sign that she realized the significance of this last statement. At last Alleyn said: 'How did that come about?'

'Didn't I tell you this afternoon? It was Herbert who drove me down to the Vicarage at Falconbridge on the day Paddy died.'

It was one o'clock in the morning when Alleyn saw Lady Carrados, Bridget and Donald into a taxi, thankfully shut his door and went to bed. Less than twenty-four hours had passed since Robert Gospell met with his death, yet in that short time all the threads but one of the most complicated homicide cases he had ever dealt with had been put into his hands. As he waited for sleep, so long delayed, he saw the protagonists as a company of dancers moving in a figure so elaborate that the pattern of their message was almost lost in the confusion of individual gestures. Now it was Donald and Bridget who met and advanced through the centre of the maze; now Withers, marching on the outskirts of the dance, who turned to encounter Mrs Halcut-Hackett. Evelyn Carrados and her husband danced back to back into the very heart of the measure. Sir Daniel Davidson, like a sort of village master of ceremonies, with a gigantic rosette streaming from his buttonhole, gyrated slowly across and across. Dimitri slipped like a thief into the dance, offering a glass of champagne to each protagonist. Miss Harris skipped in a decorous fashion round the inner figure, but old General Halcut-Hackett, peering anxiously into every face, seemed to search for his partner. To and fro the figures swam more and more dizzily, faster and faster, until the confusion was intolerable. And then, with terrifying abruptness, they were stricken into immobility, and before he sank into oblivion, Alleyn, in a single flash, saw the pattern of the dance.

CHAPTER 25

Benefit of Clergy

The inquest on Lord Robert Gospell was held at eleven o'clock the next morning. It was chiefly remarkable for the circumstance that more people were turned away from it than had ever been turned away from any previous inquest in the same building. The coroner was a cross-grained man with the poorest possible opinion of society with a small 's' and a perfectly venomous hatred of Society with a large one. He suffered from chronic dyspepsia and an indeterminate but savage conviction that somebody was trying to get the better of him. The proceedings were coloured by his efforts to belittle the whole affair when he thought of the fashionable spectators, and to make the very most of it when he reflected that this sort of thing was the direct outcome of the behaviour of those sorts of people. However, apart from this personal idiosyncrasy, he was a good coroner. He called Donald, who, very white-faced, gave formal evidence of identification. He then heard the evidence of the taxi-driver, was particular about time, place and route, and called Alleyn.

Alleyn described his first view and examination of the body. In formal phrases he gave a precise account of the injuries he had found on the body of his friend. Dr Curtis followed with his report on the post-mortem. One of Dimitri's men gave evidence on the time Lord Robert left Marsdon House. The coroner with a vindictive glance at the audience said he saw no reason to call further evidence, addressed the jury in words that left them in no possible doubt as to the verdict they should return and when they had duly returned it, ordered an adjournment. He then fixed a baleful blue eye on the farthest wall and pronounced an expression of sympathy with the relatives. The whole proceedings had lasted twenty minutes.

'Swish!' said Fox when he met Alleyn in the street outside. 'That's old "Slap-Bang, Here-we-are-again." You can't beat him for speed, can you, sir?'

'Mercifully, you can't. Fox, we're off to Barbicon-Bramley. I've borrowed my mother's car and I've a hell of a lot to tell you, and I rather think the spell is wound up.'

'Sir?'

'You are quite right, Fox. Never quote, and if you do certainly not from Macbeth.'

Lady Alleyn's car was parked in a side street. Fox and Alleyn got into it and headed for the Uxbridge Road. On the way Alleyn related Bridget's and Donald's and Lady Carrados's stories. When he had finished Fox grunted and they were both silent for ten minutes.

'Well,' said Fox at last, 'it all points to the same thing doesn't it, Mr Alleyn?'

'Yes, Fox. In a dubious sort of way it does.'

'Still, I don't see how we can exclude the others.'

'Nor do I unless we get something definite from these people. If necessary we'll have to go on to Falconbridge and visit the hospital, but I'm in hopes that Miss Harris's uncle will come out of his retirement and go back to his gay young rectorish days seventeen years ago.'

'What a hope!' said Fox.

'As you indicate, the chances are thin.'

'If they couldn't find this chap O'Brien's letter on the premises then how can we expect to trace it now, seventeen years later?'

'Well urged, Brer Fox, well urged. But I fancy we know something now that they didn't know then.'

'Oh, well,' conceded Fox. 'Maybe. But all the same I wouldn't give you a tuppenny damn for our chances and that's flat.'

'I'm a little more sanguine than that. Well, if we fail here we'll have to peg away somewhere else.'

'There's the missing cloak and hat.'

'Yes. Any report come in this morning from the postal people?'

'No. I've followed your suggestion and asked them to try to check yesterday's overseas parcels post. Our chaps have gone into the rubbish-bin game and there's nothing there. The Chelsea and Belgrave bins were emptied this morning and there's no cloaks or hats in any of them. Of course something may come in from farther afield.'

'I don't fancy the rubbish-bins, Fox. Too risky. For some reason he wanted those things to be lost completely. Hair oil, perhaps. Yes, it might be hair oil. I'm afraid, you know, that we *shall* have to ask all these people if we may search their houses.'

'Carrados is sure to object, sir, and you don't want to have to get search warrants yet, do you?'

'I think we can scare him by saying that Dimitri, Withers, Davidson, Halcut-Hackett and Lady Potter are all going to be asked to allow a search of their houses. He'll look a bit silly if he refuses on top of that.'

'Do you think the cloak and hat may still be hidden away in – well, in the guilty party's house?'

'No, blast it. I think he got rid of them yesterday before we had covered the first phase of investigation.'

'By post?'

'Well, can you think of a better method? In London? We've decided the river's barred because of the tide. We've advertised the damn thing well enough – they haven't been shoved down anyone's area. We've searched all the way along the Embankment. The men are still at it but I don't think they'll find them. The murderer wouldn't have time to do anything very elaborate in the way of hiding them and anyway, if we're right, it's off his beat.'

'Where would he send them?' ruminated Fox.

'Put yourself in his place. What address would you put on an incriminating parcel?'

'Care of Private Hoo Flung Dung, forty-second battalion, Chop Suey, Mah Jongg, Manchuria, to wait till called for,' suggested Fox irritably.

'Something like that,' said Alleyn. 'Something very like that, Brer Fox.'

They drove in silence for the rest of the way to Barbicon-Bramley.

Miss Harris's natal village proved to be small and rather self-consciously picturesque. There was a preponderance of ye olde-ness about the few shops and a good deal of pseudo-Tudor half-timbering on the outlying houses. They stopped at the post office and Alleyn asked to be directed to the Reverend Mr Walter Harris's house.

'I understand he is not the rector but his brother.'

'Oo, yes,' agreed the post office lady rattling her basket cuffs and flashing a smile. 'That will be the old gentleman. Quayte an aydentity in the district. First to the left into Oakapple Lane and straight on to the end. "The Thatch." It's ever so unmistakable. The last residence on the left, standing back in its own grounds.'

'Thank you so much,' said Alleyn.

They found 'The Thatch' as she had predicted, without any difficulty. The grounds of its own in which it stood back were an eighth of an acre of charming cottage garden. Alleyn and Fox had only got half-way up the cobbled path when they came upon two rumps up-ended behind a tall border of rosemary and lavender. The first was clad in patched trousers of clerical grey, the second in the navy blue decency of a serge skirt. Fragrant herbs hid the rest of these two gardeners from view.

'Good afternoon, sir,' said Alleyn, removing his hat.

With a slow upheaving movement, the Reverend and Mrs Walter Harris became wholly vertical and turned about.

'Oh!' they said gently. 'Good afternoon.'

They were very old indeed and had the strange marital likeness that so often comes upon a man and woman who have worked together all their lives. Their faces, though they differed in conformation, echoed each other in expression. They both had mild grey eyes surrounded by a network of kindly lines; they were both weather-beaten, and each of their mouths in repose, curved into a doubtful smile. Upon Mrs Harris's hair rather than her head was a wide garden hat with quite a large rent in the crown through which straggled a straight grey lock or two. Her husband also wore well over his nose a garden hat, an ancient panama with a faded green ribbon. His long crêpey neck was encircled by a low clerical collar, but instead of the usual grey jacket an incredibly faded All Souls blazer hung from his sharp shoulder-blades. He now tilted his head backwards in order to look at Alleyn under his hat-brim and through his glasses which were clipped half-way down his nose.

Alleyn said: 'I'm so sorry to bother you, sir.'

'No matter,' said Mr Harris, 'no matter.' His voice had the authentic parsonic ring.

'There's nothing more maddening than to be interrupted when you've settled down to a good afternoon's gardening,' Alleyn added.

'Twitch!' said Mr Harris violently.

'I beg your pardon?'

'Twitch! It's the bane of my existence. It springs up like veritable dragon's teeth and I assure you if s a great deal more difficult to extract. Three wheelbarrow loads since last Thursday forenoon.'

'Walter,' said his wife, 'these gentlemen want to speak to you.'

'We won't keep you more than a few minutes, sir,' said Alleyn.

'Yes, dear. Where shall I take them?'

'Into your den,' said Mrs Harris, as if her husband was a carnivorous ravager.

'Certainly, certainly. Come along. Come along,' said Mr Harris in the patient voice of vicarage hospitality. 'Come along.'

He took them through a french window into a little faded red room where old dim photographs of young men in cassocks hung beside old dim photographs of famous cathedrals. The shelves were full of dusty volumes of sermons and the works of Mrs Humphry Ward, Charles Kingsley, Charlotte M. Yonge, Dickens and Sir Walter Scott. Between a commentary and an *Imitation of Christ* was a copy of *The Martyrdom of Man*, truculently solid. For Mr Harris had once been an earnest undergraduate and had faced things. It was a shabby, friendly old room.

'Sit down, sit down,' said Mr Harris.

He hurriedly gathered up from the chairs, parish magazines, *Church Times* and seed catalogues. With his arms full of these papers, he wandered vaguely about his den.

Alleyn and Fox sat down on the horsehair chairs.

'That's right,' said Mr Harris. He incontinently dropped all his papers on the floor and sat down.

'Now, what can I have the pleasure – ? Um?'

'First, sir, I must tell you we are police officers.'

'Dear me,' said Mr Harris, 'not young Hockley again, I hope. Are you sure it's not my brother you want? The rector of Barbicon-Bramley? He's been very interested in the case and he told me that if the poor lad was not charged he could find a post for him with some kind souls who are prepared to overlook – '

'No, sir,' interrupted Alleyn gently, 'it's you we want to see.'

'But I'm retired,' said Mr Harris opening his eyes very wide. 'I'm quite retired, you know.'

'I am going to ask you to go back to the days when you were rector of Falconbridge.'

'Of Falconbridge!' Mr Harris beamed at them. 'Now this is really the greatest pleasure. You come from dear old Falconbridge! Let me see, I don't recollect either of your faces though, of course, I have been retired now for fifteen years and I'm afraid my memory is not what it used to be. Now tell me your names.'

'Mr Harris, we don't come from Falconbridge, we are from Scotland Yard. My name is Alleyn and this is Inspector Fox.'

'How do you do? I hope nothing has gone wrong in the dear old village,' ejaculated Mr Harris anxiously. He suddenly remembered his panama hat and snatched it from his head revealing a shining pink pate with an aura of astonished white fluff.

'No, no,' said Alleyn hastily. 'At least, not recently.' He darted a venomous glance at Fox who was grinning broadly. 'We are investigating a case, sir, and are anxious to trace a letter which we believe to have been lost in Falconbridge between seventeen and eighteen years ago.'

'A letter! Dear me, I'm afraid if it was addressed to me there is very little hope of recovery. Only this morning I found I had mislaid a most important letter from a very dear old friend, Canon Worsley of All Saints, Chipton. It's a most *extraordinary* thing where that letter has gone. I distinctly remember that I put it in the pocket of this jacket and – '

He thrust his hands in the side pockets of his blazer and pulled out a collection of string, seed-packets, pencils and pieces of paper.

'Why, there it is!' he exclaimed, staring at an envelope that had fallen to the floor. 'There, after all, it is! I am ASTOUNDED.'

'Mr Harris,' said Alleyn loudly. Mr Harris instantly threw his head back and looked at Alleyn through his glasses.

'Eighteen years ago,' continued Alleyn very rapidly, 'there was a motor accident on the bridge outside the rectory at Falconbridge.

The driver, Captain O'Brien, was severely injured and was taken into the rectory. Do you remember?'

Mr Harris had opened his mouth in astonishment but he said nothing. He merely continued to gape at Alleyn.

'You were very kind to him,' Alleyn went on; 'you kept him at the rectory and sent for help. He was taken to the hospital and died there a few hours later.'

He paused, but Mr Harris's expression had not changed. There was something intensely embarrassing in his posture and his unexpected silence.

'Do you remember?' asked Alleyn.

Without closing his mouth Mr Harris slowly shook his head from side to side.

'But it was such a serious accident. His young wife motored down from London. She went to the hospital but he died without regaining consciousness.'

'Poor fellow!' said Mr Harris in his deepest voice. 'Poor fell-oh!'

'Can't you remember, now?'

Mr Harris made no reply but got to his feet, went to the french window, and called into the garden.

'Edith! Edith!'

'Hoo-ee?' replied a wavering voice close at hand.

'Can you spare-ah a moment?'

'Coming.'

He turned away from the window and beamed at them.

'Now we shan't be long,' he announced.

But when Alleyn saw Mrs Harris amiably blunder up the garden path he scarcely shared in this optimistic view. They all stood up. She accepted Alleyn's chair and drew her gardening gloves from her old hands. Mr Harris contemplated her as if she was some rare achievement of his own.

'Edith, my dear,' he said loudly, 'would you tell these gentlemen about an accident?'

'Which accident?'

'That, I'm afraid, I don't know, dear. Indeed we are depending upon you to inform us.'

'I don't understand you, Walter.'

'I don't understand myself very well, I must admit, Edith. I find it all very puzzling.'

'What?' said his wife. Alleyn now realized that she was slightly deaf.

'Puzzling,' shouted Mr Harris.

'My husband's memory is not very good,' explained Mrs Harris smiling gently at Alleyn and Fox. 'He was greatly shaken by his cycling accident some months ago. I suppose you have called about the insurance.'

Raising his voice Alleyn embarked once more on his recital. This time he was not interrupted, but as neither of the Harrises gave any sign of understanding, it was impossible to tell whether or not he spoke in vain. By the time he had finished, Mr Harris had adopted his former disconcerting glare. Mrs Harris, however, turned to her husband and said:

'You remember the blood on the carpet, Walter? At dear old Falconbridge?'

'Dear me, yes. Now *that's* what I was trying to recollect. Of course it was. Poor fellow. Poor fell-oh!'

'Then you *do* remember?' Alleyn cried.

'Indeed I do,' said Mrs Harris reproachfully. 'The poor young wife wrote us such a charming letter, thanking us for the little we had been able to do for him. I would have liked to answer it but unfortunately my husband lost it.'

'Edith, I have discovered dear old Worsley's letter. It was in my pocket. Fancy!'

'Fancy, dear, yes.'

'Talking of letters,' said Alleyn to Mrs Harris. 'Can you by any chance remember anything about a letter that was lost on the occasion of Captain O'Brien's accident? I think you were asked if it had been found in the vicarage.'

'I'm afraid I didn't catch – '

Alleyn repeated it.

'To be sure I do,' said Mrs Harris. 'Perfectly.'

'You were unable to give any information about this letter?'

'On the contrary.'

'What!'

'On the contrary,' repeated Mrs Harris firmly. 'I sent it after him.'

'*After who?*' roared Fox so loudly that even Mrs Harris gave a little jump. 'I'm sure I beg pardon, sir,' said Fox hastily, 'I don't know what came over me.' He opened his notebook in some confusion.

'Mrs Harris,' said Alleyn, 'will you please tell us everything you can remember about this letter?'

'Yes, please do, Edith,' said her husband unexpectedly. 'She'll find it for you,' he added in an aside. 'Don't distress yourselves.'

'Well,' began Mrs Harris. 'It's a long time ago now and I'm afraid I'm rather hazy. It was after they had taken him away, I fancy, that we found it under the couch in the study. That was when we noticed the stain on the carpet you remember, Walter. At first, of course, I thought it was one of my husband's letters – it was not in an envelope. But when I glanced at it I realized at once that it was not, as it began "Dear Daddy" and we have no children.'

' "Dear Daddy," ' repeated Alleyn.

'I decided afterwards that it was perhaps "Dear Paddy" but as my husband's name is Walter Bernard it didn't signify. "Why," I said, or something of that sort. "Why, it must have dropped out of that poor fellow's coat when the ambulance man examined him." And – of course, I remember it now as clearly as if it was yesterday – and I said to little Violet: "Pop on your bicycle and take it to the hospital as quickly as you can, dear, because they may be looking for it." So little Violet – '

'Who was she, please?' asked Alleyn rather breathlessly.

'I beg your pardon?'

'*Who was little Violet?*' shouted Alleyn.

'My small niece. My husband's brother's third daughter. She was spending her holidays with us. She is grown up now and has a delightful post in London with a Lady Carrados.'

'Thank you,' said Alleyn. 'Please go on.'

CHAPTER 26

Alleyn Plots a Dénouement

But there was not much more to tell. Apparently Violet Harris had
bicycled off with Paddy O'Brien's letter and had returned to say she
had given it to the gentleman who had brought the lady in the
motor-car. The gentleman had been sitting in the motor-car outside
the hospital. As far as Mrs Harris could state, and she and her
husband went into a mazed avuncular family history to prove their
point, little Violet had been fifteen years old at the time. Alleyn
wrote out her statement, shorn of its interminable parentheses, and
she signed it. Throughout the interview neither she nor her husband
gave the faintest sign of any form of curiosity. Apparently it did not
strike either of them as singular that the interest in a letter lost
eighteen years ago should suddenly be excited to such a pitch that
CID officers thought it necessary to seek for signed statements in the
heart of Buckinghamshire.

They insisted on taking Alleyn and Fox round their garden.
Alleyn hadn't the heart to refuse and besides he had a liking for gardens. Mrs Harris gave them each a bunch of lavender and rosemary,
which flowers, she said, were less conspicuous for gentlemen to
carry than the gayer blossoms of summer. The sight of Fox solemnly grasping a posy in his enormous fist and examining a border of
transplanted pansies was almost too much for his superior officer. It
was two o'clock when the tour of the garden was completed.

'You must come in whenever you are passing,' said Mrs Harris,
blinking cordially at Alleyn, 'and I shall remember what you say
about your mother's herb garden.'

'Yes, yes,' agreed Mr Harris. 'Whenever you are passing. Of course. Anybody from dear old Falconbridge is doubly welcome.'

They stood side by side at the gate and waved, rather in the manner of children, as Alleyn turned the car and drove away down Oakapple Lane.

'Well!' ejaculated Fox. 'Well!'

'Not another word,' said Alleyn, 'until we get to that pub outside Barbicon-Bramley. Do you realize we've had no lunch? I refuse to utter another word until I've drunk a pint of bitter.'

'And some bread and cheese and pickles,' said Fox. 'Pickles with plenty of onions in them.'

'Lord! Lord! Fox, what a choice! Now I come to think of it, though, it sounds damn good. "Bread and cheese and pickles," Fox, it's what we need. New white bread, mouse-trap cheese, home-made pickles and bitter.'

'That's the idea, Mr Alleyn. You're a great gourmet,' said Fox who had taught himself French, 'and don't think I haven't enjoyed some of those dinners you've given me when everything seemed to sort of slide into something else. I have. But when you're famished and in the English countryside you can't beat bread and cheese and pickles.'

The pub provided them with these delicacies. They took about a quarter of an hour over their meal and then set out again.

'Now then,' said Alleyn.

'The thing that beats me,' said Fox, wiping his short moustache with his handkerchief, 'is little Violet. We knew she was a niece of this old gentleman's but, by gum, we didn't know she was staying there at the time, now, did we?'

'No, Brer Fox, we didn't.'

'I suppose she may not know it herself,' continued Fox. 'I mean to say, Miss Violet Harris may not realize that Lady Carrados was this Mrs O'Brien whose husband was brought into her uncle's vicarage when she was a kid of fifteen.'

'Quite possible. I hope she remembers the bicycle ride. We'll have to jog her memory, I dare say.'

'Yes. Now I reckon, on what we've heard, that it was Carrados who took that letter from little Violet. Carrados, sitting in the car outside the hospital, while the poor chap who'd got the letter from

Australia was dying inside. And then, later on, when there's all the fuss about a missing letter, what does he do?'

Alleyn knew this question was purely rhetorical and didn't interrupt.

'He tells the widow,' said Fox; 'he tells the widow that he's made every inquiry and there isn't a letter to be found.'

'Yes,' agreed Alleyn. 'No doubt he tells her that.'

'Right. Now, why does he do that? I reckon it's because Sir Herbert Carrados is what you might call a bit of a moral coward with a kind of mental twist. What these psycho-johnnies call a repression or some such thing. As I see it he didn't want to admit to having seen the letter because he'd actually read it. This Australian bloke knew Captain O'Brien had married a loony and wrote to tell him he was now a widower. If what Lady Carrados told you was correct and he'd fancied her for a long time, that letter must have shaken him up a bit. Now perhaps he says to himself, being a proud, snobbish sort of chap and yet having set his heart on her, that he'll let sleeping dogs lie.'

'Cut the whole thing dead? Yes. That's sound enough. It's in character.'

'That's what I mean,' said Fox in a gratified voice. 'But all the same he doesn't destroy the letter. Or does he?'

'That,' said Alleyn, 'is exactly what we've got to find out.'

'Well, sir, we've got our suspicions, haven't we?'

'Yes. Before this evening, Fox, I want to make certainties of our suspicions.'

'By gum, Mr Alleyn, if we can do that we'll have made a tidy job of this case. Don't count your chickens, as well I know, but if we can get an arrest within two days after the crime, in a complicated case like this, we're not doing too badly, now are we?'

'I suppose not, you old warrior, I suppose not.' Alleyn gave a short sigh. 'I wish – ' he said. 'Oh God, Fox, I do wish he hadn't died. No good maundering. I also wish very much that we'd been able to find some trace of something, just *something* in the taxi. But not a thing.'

'The funeral's at three o'clock tomorrow, isn't it?' asked Fox.

'Yes. Lady Mildred has asked me to be one of the bearers. It's pretty strange under the circumstances, but I'd like to do it. And I'd like to think we had our killer locked up before then. When we get back, Fox, we'll have to arrange for these people to come round to the Yard. We'll want Miss Harris, Bridget O'Brien, her mother, Carrados himself, Davidson, Withers, Dimitri and Mrs Halcut-Hackett. I'll see Lady Carrados alone first. I want to soften the shock a little if it's possible.'

'When shall we get them to come, sir?'

'It'll be four o'clock by the time we're back to the Yard. I think we'll make it this evening. Say nine o'clock. It's going to be devilish tricky. I'm counting on Dimitri losing his head. It's a cool head, blast it, and he may keep his wits about him. Talking of wits, there's the gallant Captain to be reckoned with. Unless I'm a Dutchman, Donald Potter's given me enough in his statement to lock the gallant Captain up for a nice long stretch. That's some comfort.'

They were silent until they got as far as the Cromwell Road and then Fox said: 'I suppose we are right, Mr Alleyn. I know that seems a pretty funny thing to say at this stage, but it's a worrying business and that's a fact. It's the trickiest line of evidence I've *ever* come across. We seem to be hanging our case on the sort of things you usually treat with a good deal of suspicion.'

'Don't I know it. No, Fox, I think it'll hold firm. It depends on what these people say in their second interviews tonight, of course. If we can establish the facts about the two cigarette-cases, the secret drawer, the telephone conversation and the stolen letter, we're right. Good Lord, that sounds like a list of titles from the old Sherlock Holmes stories. I think part of the charm of those excellent tales lies in Watson's casual but enthralling references to cases we never hear of again.'

'The two cigarette-cases,' repeated Fox slowly, 'the secret drawer, the telephone conversation, and the stolen letter. Yes. Yes, that's right. You may say we hang our case on those four hooks.'

'The word "hang," ' said Alleyn grimly, 'is exceedingly apposite. You may.'

He drove Fox to the Yard.

'I'll come up with you and see if anything fresh has come in,' he said.

They found reports from officers who were out on the job. Dimitri's men reported that Francois had gone to the local stationers and bought a copy of this morning's *Times*. The stationer had told the Yard man that Dimitri as a rule took the *Daily Express*.

Alleyn laid the report down.

'Beat up a *Times*, Brer Fox.'

Fox went out. He was away for some time. Alleyn brought his file up to date and lit his pipe. Then he rang up Lady Carrados.

'Evelyn? I've rung you up to ask if you and your husband and Bridget will come to my office at the Yard tonight. It's some more tidying up of this affair. If possible I'd like to have a word with you first. Would you rather it was here or in your house?'

'In your office, *please*, Roderick. It would be easier. Shall I come now?'

'If you will. Don't be fussed. I'm so sorry to bother you.'

'I'll come at once,' said the faint voice.

Fox returned with a *Times* which he laid on Alleyn's desk. He pointed a stubby finger at the personal column.

'What about the third from the top?' he said.

Alleyn read it aloud.

' "Childie Darling. Living in exile. Longing. Only want Daughter. Daddy." '

'Um,' said Alleyn. 'Has daddy had anything else to say to Childie during the last week or so?'

'Not during the last fortnight, anyway. I've looked up the files.'

'There's nothing else in the agony column. The others are old friends, aren't they?'

'That's right.'

'We'd better ask Father *Times* about Daddy.'

'I'll do that,' said Fox, 'and I'll get going on these people for tonight.'

'Thank you, Fox. I've tackled Lady Carrados who is coming to see me now. If you've time I'd be glad if you'd fix the others. I ought to go and see Lady Mildred about the arrangements for tomorrow.'

'You'll have time for that later on.'

'Yes. I must report to the AC before this evening. I'll go along now, I think, and see if he's free. Ask them to show Lady Carrados up here, Fox, and ring through when she arrives.'

'Very good, Mr Alleyn.'

Alleyn saw the Assistant Commissioner's secretary, who sent him in to the great man. Alleyn laid the file on the desk. The AC disregarded it.

'Well, Rory, how goes it? I hear you've got half the Yard mudlark-ing on Chelsea Embankment and the other half tailing the aristocra-cy. What's it all about?' asked the AC, who had been kept perfectly *au fait* with the case but whose favourite pose was one of ignorance. 'I suppose you want me to read this damn nonsense?' he added, laying his hand on the file.

'If you will, sir. I've summed-up at the end. With your approval I'm collecting the relevant people here tonight and if the interviews go the right way I hope to be able to make an arrest. If you agree, I'd like a blank warrant.'

'You're a pretty cool customer, aren't you?' grunted the AC. 'And if the interviews go all wrong you return the warrant and think of something else? That it?'

'Yes, sir. That's it.'

'See here, Rory, our position in this affair is that we've got to have a conviction. If your customer gets off on this sort of evidence, opposing counsel is going to make us look like so many Aunt Sallies. It's so damn shaky. Can't you hear what old Harrington-Barr will do with you if he's briefed? Make you look a boiled egg, my good man, unless you've got a damning admission or two to shove at the jury. *And* all this blackmail stuff. How are you going to get any of these people to charge their blackmailer? You know what people are over blackmail.'

'Yes, sir. I do rather hope for a damning admission.'

'Do you, by Gad! All right, all right. See them in here. In my room. I'd better know the worst at once, I suppose.' He scowled at Alleyn. 'This goes a bit close to you, doesn't it? Lord Robert was a friend of yours, wasn't he?'

'He was, sir, yes.'

'Ugh! He was a nice little chap. I understand the FO is making tender enquiries. In case a foreign power remembers him pottering about twenty years ago and has decided to assassinate him. Silly asses. Well, I'm sorry you've had this knock, Rory. It doesn't seem to have cramped your style. Quick work, if it's accurate.'

'If!' said Alleyn. 'I hope to Heaven we haven't gone wrong.'

'What time's the dénouement tonight?'

'Nine o'clock, sir.'

'All right. Trot 'em along here. Thank you, Rory.'

'Thank you, sir.'

On his return to his own room he found Fox was waiting for him.

'Lady Carrados is downstairs, sir.'

'Go and bring her up, Fox, will you?'

Fox turned in the doorway.

'I've got on to *The Times*' he said. 'They were a bit dignified about it but I know one of the chaps who deals with the agony-column notices and got hold of him. He told me the Childie Darling thing came by mail with a postal order for double rates and a request that it should appear, very particular, in this morning's edition. The note said the advertiser would call to collect the change, if any, and was signed W.A.K. Smith, address GPO, Erith.'

'Postmark?'

'They'd lost the envelope but he'll look for it. The writing,' said Fox, 'was in script on common notepaper.'

'Was it indeed?' murmured Alleyn.

'There's one other thing,' said Fox. 'The reports have come through from the post offices. A clerk at the Main Western District says that during the rush hour yesterday someone left a parcel on the counter. He found it later on in the day. It was soft, about the right weight and had five bob in tuppenny stamps on it, one and fivepence more than was necessary. He remembers the address was to somewhere in China and it was written in script. So my Private Hoo Flung Dung may have been a fair guess. We've got on to Mount Pleasant and it's too late. A parcels post went out to China this afternoon.'

'Blast!' said Alleyn.

'I'll be off,' said Fox, 'and get her ladyship.'

While he waited for Lady Carrados, Alleyn cut the little notice out of *The Times*. After a moment's consideration he unlocked a drawer in his desk and took out Mrs Halcut-Hackett's gold cigarette-case. He opened it and neatly gummed the notice inside the lid.

Fox showed Lady Carrados in and went away.

'I'm so sorry, Evelyn,' said Alleyn. 'I've been closeted with my superior. Have you been here long?'

'No. What is it now, please, Roderick?'

'It's this. I want you to allow what may seem a rather drastic step. I want you to give me permission to talk to your husband, in front of you, about Paddy O'Brien.'

'You mean – tell him that we were not married?'

'If it seems necessary.'

'I can't.'

'I shouldn't do it if it wasn't vitally necessary. I do not believe, Evelyn, that he would' – Alleyn hesitated – ' that he would be as shocked as you imagine.'

'But I *know* he would be terribly shocked. Of course he would.'

'I think I can promise you that you have nothing to fear from this decision. I mean that Carrados's attitude to yourself and Bridget will not be materially affected by it.'

'I cannot believe that. I cannot believe that he will not be dreadfully wounded. Even violent.'

'I promise you that I honestly believe that it may help you both to a better understanding.'

'If only I could think that!'

'It will certainly help us to see justice done on your blackmailer. Evelyn, I don't want to be intolerably priggish, but I do believe it is your duty to do this.'

'I had almost made up my mind to tell him.'

'All the better. Come now. Look at me! Will you let me deal with it?'

She looked at him. Quite deliberately he used the whole force of that thing people call personality and of which he knew – how could he not know? – he had his share. He imposed his will on hers as surely as if it was a tangible instrument. And he saw her give way.

She raised her hands and let them fall limply back on her lap.

'Very well, I'm so bemused and puzzled, I don't know, I give up. My house is falling about my ears. I'll do whatever you think best, Roderick.'

'You need say very little.' He went into details. She listened attentively and repeated his instructions. When that was over he rose and looked down at her. 'I'm sorry,' he said. 'It's no good my trying to make light of this. It *is* a very upsetting business for you. But take heart of grace. Bridget need not know, although I think if I were you I should tell her. She's got plenty of courage and the moderns don't make nearly such heavy weather of that sort of thing as we did. My niece Sarah prattles away about people born in and out of wedlock as if it was a fifty-fifty chance. Upon my word, Evelyn, I wouldn't be surprised if your daughter found a certain amount of romantic satisfaction in the story you have been at such pains to hide from her.'

'That would be almost funny, wouldn't it?' Lady Carrados looked into Alleyn's compassionate eyes. She reached out her hand and he took it firmly between both of his.

'Roderick,' she said, 'how old are you?'

'Forty-three, my dear.'

'I'm nearly forty,' and absent-mindedly she added, as women do: 'Isn't it awful?'

'Dreadful,' agreed Alleyn, smiling at her,

'Why haven't you married?'

'My mother says she tried to make a match of it between you and me. But Paddy O'Brien came along and I hadn't a chance.'

'That seems odd, now, doesn't it? If it's true. I don't remember that you ever paid me any particular attention.'

He saw that she had reached the lull in the sensibilities that sometimes follows extreme emotional tension. She spoke idly with an echo of her customary gentle gaiety. She sounded as if her mind had gone as limp as the thin hand he still held.

'You ought to marry,' she said vaguely and added: 'I must go.'

'I'm coming down. I'll see you to your car.'

As she drove away he stood looking after her for a second or two, and then shook his head doubtfully and set out for Cheyne Walk.

CHAPTER 27

Interlude for Love

Alleyn wondered if it was only because he knew the body of his friend had come home that he felt its presence. Perhaps the house was not more quiet than it had been that morning. Perhaps the dead did not in truth cast about them so deep a spell. And then he smelt lilies and all the hushed chill of ceremonial death closed about his heart. He turned to Bunchy's old butler who was in the condition so often found in the faithful retainers of Victorian melodrama. He had been weeping. His eyes were red and his face blotted with tears, and his lips trembled. He showed Alleyn into Mildred's sitting-room. When she came forward in her lustreless black clothes, he found in her face the same unlovely reflection of sorrow. Mildred wore the customary expression of bereavement, and though he knew it to be the stamp of sincere grief, he felt a kind of impatience. He felt a profound loathing of the formalities of death. A dead body was nothing, nothing but an intolerable caricature of something someone had loved. It was a reminder of unspeakable indignities, and yet people surrounded their dead with owlish circumstances, asked you, as Mildred was asking him now, in a special muted voice, to look at them.

'I know you'd like to see him, Roderick.'

He followed her into a room on the ground floor. The merciless scent of flowers was so heavy here that it hung like mist on the cold air. The room was crowded with flowers. In the centre, on three shrouded trestles, Robert Gospell's body lay in its coffin.

It was the face of an elderly baby, dignified by the possession of some terrific secret. Alleyn was not troubled by the face. All dead faces looked like that. But the small fat hands, which in life had moved with staccato emphasis, were obediently folded, and when he saw these his eyes were blinded by tears. He groped in his overcoat pocket for a handkerchief and his fingers found the bunch of rosemary from Mr Harris's garden. The grey-green spikes were crisp and unsentimental and they smelt of the sun. When Mildred turned aside, he gave them to the dead.

He followed her back to her drawing-room and she began to tell him about the arrangements for the funeral.

'Broomfield, who as you know is the head of the family, is only sixteen. He's abroad with his tutor and can't get back in time. We are not going to alter his plans. So that Donald and I are the nearest. Donald is perfectly splendid. He has been such a comfort all day. Quite different. And then dear Troy has come to stay with me and has answered all the letters and done everything.'

Her voice, still with that special muted note, droned on, but Alleyn's thoughts had been arrested by this news of Troy and he had to force himself to listen to Mildred. When she had finished he asked her if she wished to know anything about his side of the picture and discovered that she was putting all the circumstances of her brother's death away from her. Mildred had adopted an ostrich attitude towards the murder and he got the impression that she rather hoped the murderer would never be caught. She wished to cut the whole thing dead and he thought it was rather clever and rather nice of her to be able to welcome him so cordially as a friend and pay no attention to him as a policeman.

After a minute or two there seemed to be nothing more to say to Mildred. Alleyn said good-bye to her, promised to attend the memorial service at eleven and to do his part at the funeral. He went out into the hall.

In the doorway he met Troy.

He heard his own voice saying: 'Hullo, you're just in time. You're going to save my life.'

'Whatever do you mean?'

'It's nearly five. I've had six hours' sleep in the last fifty-eight hours. That's nothing for us hardy coppers but for some reason I'm feeling sorry for myself. Will you take tea or a drink or possibly both with me? For God's sake say you will.'

'Very well, where shall we go?'

'I thought,' said Alleyn, who up to that moment had thought nothing of the sort, 'that we might have tea at my flat. Unless you object to my flat.'

'I'm not a débutante,' said Troy. 'I don't think I need coddle my reputation. Your flat let it be.'

'Good,' said Alleyn.'I've got mother's car. I'll just warn my servant and tell the Yard where to find me. Do you think I may use the telephone.'

'I'm sure you may.'

He darted to telephone and was back in a minute.

'Vassily is tremendously excited,' he said. 'A lady to tea! Come on.'

On the way Alleyn was so filled with astonishment at finding himself agreeably alone with Troy that he fell into a trance from which he only woke when he pulled the car up outside his own flat. He did not apologize for his silence: he felt a tranquillity in Troy that had accepted it, and when they were indoors he was delighted to hear her say: 'This is peaceful,' and to see her pull off her cap and sit on a low stool before the fireplace.

'Shall we have a fire?' asked Alleyn. 'Do say yes. It's not a warm day, really.'

'Yes, let's,' agreed Troy.

'Will you light it while I see about tea?'

He went out of the room to give Vassily a series of rather confused orders, and when he returned there was Troy before the fire, bare-headed, strangely familiar.

'So you're still here,' said Alleyn.

'It's a nice room, this.'

He put a box of cigarettes on the floor beside her and took out his pipe. Troy turned and saw her own picture of Suva at the far end of the room.

'Oh, yes,' said Alleyn, 'there's that.'

'How did you get hold of it?'

'I got someone to buy it for me.'

'But why – '

'I don't know why I was so disingenuous about it except that I wanted it so very badly for reasons that were not purely aesthetic

and I thought you would see through them if I made a personal
business of it.'

'I should have been rather embarrassed, I suppose.'

'Yes.' Alleyn waited for a moment and then said: 'Do you remember how I found you that day, painting and cursing? It was just as
the ship moved out of Suva. Those sulky hills and that ominous sky
were behind you.'

'We had a row, didn't we?'

'We did.'

Troy's face became rather pink.

'In fact,' said Alleyn, 'there is scarcely an occasion on which
we have met when we have not had a row. Why is that, do you
suppose?'

'I've always been on the defensive.'

'Have you? For a long time I thought you merely disliked me.'

'No. You got under my guard.'

'If it hadn't been for that damned case, things might have gone
better,' said Alleyn. 'What a pity it is that we cannot sometimes react
to situations like characters in the less honest form of novel. The
setting should have been ideal, you know. A murder in your house.
You with just enough motive to make a "strong situation" and not
enough seriously to implicate you. Me, as the grim detective finding
time for a bit of Rochester stuff. You should have found yourself
drawn unwillingly into love, Troy. Instead of which I merely
acquired a sort of post-mortem disagreeableness. If you painted a
surrealist picture of me I would be made of Metropolitan Police
notebooks, one eye would be set in a keyhole, my hands would be
occupied with somebody else's private correspondence. The background would be a morgue and the whole pretty conceit wreathed
with festoons of blue tape and hangman's rope. What?'

'Nonsense,' said Troy.

'I suppose so. Yes. The vanity of the male trying to find extraordinary reasons for a perfectly natural phenomenon. You don't happen
to love me. And why the devil should you?'

'You don't happen to understand,' said Troy shortly, 'and why the
devil should you.'

She took a cigarette and tilted her face up for him to give her a
light. A lock of her short dark hair had fallen across her forehead.

Alleyn lit the cigarette, threw the match into the fire and tweaked the lock of hair.

'Abominable woman,' he said abruptly. 'I'm so glad you've come to see me.'

'I tell you what,' said Troy more amiably. 'I've always been frightened of the whole business. Love and so on.'

'The physical side?'

'Yes, that, but much more than that. The whole business. The breaking down of all one's reserves. The mental as well as the physical intimacy.'

'My mind to me a kingdom is.'

'I feel it wouldn't be,' said Troy.

'I feel it rather terrifyingly still would be. Don't you think that in the closest possible union there must always be moments when one feels oneself completely separate, completely alone? Surely it must be so, otherwise we would not be so astonished on the rare occasions when we read each other's thoughts.'

Troy looked at him with a sort of shy determination that made his heart turn over.

'Do you read my thoughts?' she asked.

'Not very clearly, Troy. I dare not wish I could.'

'I do yours, sometimes. That is one of the things that sends my defences up.'

'If you could read them now,' said Alleyn, 'you might well be frightened.'

Vassily came in with tea. He had, Alleyn saw at a glance, excitedly rushed out to his favourite delicatessen shop round the corner and purchased caviare. He had made a stack of buttered toast, he had cut up many lemons, and he had made tea in an enormous Stuart pot of Lady Alleyn's which her son had merely borrowed to show to a collector. Vassily had also found time to put on his best coat. His face was wreathed in smiles of embarrassing significance. He whispered to himself as he set this extraordinary feast out on a low table in front of Troy.

'Please, please,' said Vassily. 'If there is anysink more, sir. Should I not perhaps – ?'

'No, no,' said Alleyn hastily, 'that will do admirably.'

'Caviare!' said Troy. 'Oh, how glad I am – a heavenly tea.'

Vassily broke into a loud laugh, excused and bowed himself out, and shut the doors behind him with the stealth of a soubrette in a French comedy.

'You've transported the old fool,' said Alleyn.

'What is he?'

'A Russian carry-over from a former case of mine. He very nearly got himself arrested. Can you really eat caviare and drink Russian tea? He's put some milk there.'

'I don't want milk and I shall eat any quantity of caviare,' said Troy.

When they had finished and Vassily had taken away the tea things, Troy said: 'I must go.'

'Not yet.'

'Oughtn't you to be at Scotland Yard?'

'They'll ring me up if I'm wanted. I'm due there later on.'

'We've never once mentioned Bunchy,' said Troy.

'No.'

'Shall you get an early night tonight?'

'I don't know, Troy.'

Alleyn sat on the footstool by her chair. Troy looked down on his head propped between his long thin hands.

'Don't talk about the case if you'd rather not. I only wanted to let you know that if you'd like to, I'm here.'

'You're here. I'm trying to get used to it. Shall you ever come again, do you think? Do you know I swore to myself I would not utter one word of love this blessed afternoon? Well, perhaps we'd better talk about the case. I shall commit a heinous impropriety and tell you I may make an arrest this evening.'

'You *know* who killed Bunchy?'

'We believe we do. If tonight's show goes the right way we shall be in a position to make the arrest.'

He turned and looked into her face.

'Ah,' he said, 'my job again! Why does it revolt you so much?'

Troy said: 'It's nothing reasonable – nothing I can attempt to justify. It's simply that I've got an absolute horror of capital punishment. I don't even know that I agree with the stock arguments against it. It's just one of those nightmare things. Like claustrophobia. I used to adore the Ingoldsby Legends when I was a child. One day I came across the one about my Lord Tomnoddy and the hanging. It made the most extraordinary impression on me. I dreamt about it. I couldn't get it out of my head. I used to turn the pages of the book, knowing that I would come to it, dreading it, and yet – I had to read it. I even made a drawing of it.'

'That should have helped.'

'I don't think it did. I suppose most people, even the least imaginative, have got a bogey man in the back of their minds. That has always been mine. I've never spoken of it before. And so you see when you and I met in that other business and it ended in your arrest of someone I knew – ' Her voice wavered. 'And then there was the trial and – the end – '

With a nervous movement she touched his head.

'It's not you. And yet I mind so much that it is you.'

Alleyn pulled her hand down against his lips.

There was complete silence. Everything he had ever felt; every *frisson,* the most profound sorrow, the least annoyance, the greatest joy and the smallest pleasure had been but preparation for this moment when her hand melted against his lips. Presently he found himself leaning over her. He still held her hand like a talisman and he spoke against the palm.

'This must be right. I swear it must be right. I can't be feeling this alone. Troy?'

'Not now,' Troy whispered. 'No more, now. Please.'

'Yes.'

'Please.'

He stooped, took her face between his hands, and kissed her hard on the mouth. He felt her come to life beneath his lips. Then he let her go.

'And don't think I shall ask you to forgive me,' he said. 'You've no right to let this go by. You're too damn particular by half, my girl. I'm your man and you know it.'

They stared at each other.

'That's the stuff to give the troops,' Alleyn added. 'The arrogant male.'

'The arrogant turkey-cock,' said Troy shakily.

'I know, I know. But at least you didn't find it unendurable. Troy, for God's sake can't we be honest with each other? When I kissed you just then you seemed to meet me like a flame. Could I have imagined that?'

'No.'

'It was as if you shouted with your whole body that you loved me. How can I not be arrogant?'

'How can I not be shaken?'

When he saw that she was indeed greatly shaken an intolerable wave of compassion drowned his thoughts. He stammered. 'I'm sorry, I'm sorry.'

Troy began to speak slowly.

'Let me go away now. I want to think. I will try to be honest. I promise you I did not believe I loved you. It seemed to me that I couldn't love you when I resented so much the feeling that you made some sort of demand whenever we met. I don't understand physical love. I don't know how much it means. I'm just plain frightened, and that's a fact.'

'You shall go. I'll get a taxi. Wait a moment.'

He ran out and got a taxi. When he returned she was standing in front of the fire holding her cap in her hand and looked rather small and lost. He brought her coat and dropped it lightly across her shoulders.

'I've been very weak,' said Troy. 'When I said I'd come I thought I would keep it all very peaceful and impersonal. You looked so worn and troubled and it was so easy just to do this. And now see what's happened?'

'The skies have opened and the stars have fallen. I feel as if I'd run the world in the last hour. And now you must leave me.'

He took her to the taxi. Before he shut the door he said: 'Your most devoted turkey-cock.'

CHAPTER 28

Alleyn Marshals the Protagonists

The Assistant Commissioner's clock struck a quarter to nine as Alleyn walked into the room.

'Hello, Rory.'

'Good evening, sir.'

'As you have no doubt observed with your trained eye, my secretary is not present. So you may come off the official rocks. Sit down and light your pipe.'

'Thank you,' said Alleyn.

'Feeling a bit shaky?'

'A bit. I shall look such an egregious ass if they don't come up to scratch.'

'No doubt. It's a big case, Chief Inspector.'

'Don't I know it, sir!'

'Who comes first?'

'Sir Herbert and Lady Carrados.'

'Any of 'em arrived yet?'

'All except Dimitri. Fox has dotted them about the place. His room, mine, the waiting-room and the charge-room. As soon as Dimitri arrives, Fox'll come and report.'

'Right. In the meantime, we'll go over the plan of action again.'

They went over the plan of action.

'Well,' said the Assistant Commissioner, 'it's ticklish, but it may work. As I see it, everything depends on the way you handle them.'

'Thank you, sir,' said Alleyn grimly, 'for those few reassuring words.'

The Assistant Commissioner's clock struck nine. Alleyn knocked
out his pipe. There was a tap on the door and Fox came in.

'We are all ready, sir,' he said.

'All right, Mr Fox. Show them in.'

Fox went out. Alleyn glanced at the two chairs under the central
lamp, and then at the Assistant Commissioner sitting motionless in
the green-shaded light from his desk. Alleyn himself stood before
the mantelpiece.

'Stage set,' said the quiet voice beyond the green lamp. 'And now
the curtain rises.'

There was a brief silence, and then once more the door opened.

'Sir Herbert and Lady Carrados, sir.'

They came in. Alleyn moved forward, greeted them formally,
and then introduced them to the Assistant Commissioner.
Carrados's manner as he shook hands was a remarkable mixture of
the condescension of a viceroy and the fortitude of an early
Christian martyr.

The Assistant Commissioner was crisp with them.

'Good evening, Lady Carrados. Good evening, Sir Herbert. In
view of certain information he has received, Chief Detective-
Inspector Alleyn and I decided to invite you to come and see us. As
the case is in Mr Alleyn's hands, I shall leave it to him to conduct the
conversation. Will you both sit down?'

They sat. The light from the overhead lamp beat down on their
faces, throwing strong shadows under the eyes and cheek-bones.
The two heads turned in unison to Alleyn.

Alleyn said: 'Most of what I have to say is addressed to you, Sir
Herbert.'

'Indeed?' said Carrados. 'Well, Alleyn, as I fancy I told you yesterday afternoon, I am only too anxious to help you to clear up the
wretched business. As Lord Robert's host on that fatal night – '

'Yes, we quite realize that, sir. Your attitude encourages one to
hope that you will understand, or at any rate excuse, my going over
old ground, and also breaking into new. I am in a position to tell you
that we have followed a very strange trail since yesterday – a trail
that has led us to some remarkable conclusions.'

Carrados turned his eyes, but not his head, towards his wife. He
did not speak.

'We have reason to believe,' Alleyn went on, 'that the murder of Lord Robert Gospell is the outcome of blackmail. Did you speak, sir?'

'No. No! I cannot see, I fail to understand – '

'I'll make myself clearer in a moment, I hope. Now, for reasons into which I need not go at the moment, the connection between this crime and blackmail leads us to one of two conclusions. Either Lord Robert was a blackmailer, and was killed by one of his victims, or possibly someone wishing to protect his victim – '

'What makes you say that?' asked Carrados hoarsely. 'It's impossible!'

'Impossible? Why, please?'

'Because, Lord Robert, Lord Robert was not – it's impossible to imagine – have you any proof that he was a blackmailer?'

'The alternative is that Lord Robert had discovered the identity of the blackmailer, and was murdered before he could reveal it.'

'You say this,' said Carrados, breathlessly, 'but you give no proof.'

'I ask you, sir, simply to accept my statement that rightly or wrongly we believe our case to rest on one or the other of those alternatives.'

'I don't pretend to be a detective, Alleyn, but – '

'Just a minute, sir, if you don't mind. I want you now to go back with me to a day nearly eighteen years ago, when you motored Lady Carrados down to a village called Falconbridge in Buckinghamshire. You were not married then.'

'I frequently motored her into the country in those days.'

'You will have no difficulty in remembering this occasion. It was the day on which Captain Paddy O'Brien met with his accident.'

Alleyn waited. He saw the sweat round Carrados's eyes shine in the strong lamplight.

'Well?' said Carrados.

'You do remember that day?' Alleyn asked.

'But Herbert,' said Lady Carrados, 'of course you do.'

'I remember, yes. But I fail to see – '

'Please, sir! I shall fire point-blank in a moment. You remember?'

'Naturally.'

'You remember that Captain O'Brien was taken first to the vicarage and from there, in an ambulance, to the hospital, where he died a few hours later?'

'Yes.'

'You remember that, after he died, your wife, as she is now, was very distressed because she believed that a certain letter which Captain O'Brien carried had been lost?'

'I have no recollection of this.'

'Let me help you. She said that he had probably carried it in his pocket, that it must have fallen out, that she was most anxious to recover it. Am I right, Lady Carrados?'

'Yes – quite right.'

Her voice was low, but perfectly steady. She was looking at Alleyn with an air of shocked bewilderment.

'Did you ask Sir Herbert if he had enquired everywhere for this missing letter?'

'Yes.'

'Do you remember now, Sir Herbert?'

'I think – I remember – something. It was all very distressing. I tried to be of some use; I think I may have been of some use.'

'Did you succeed in finding the letter?'

'I – don't think so.'

'Are you sure?'

A little runnel of sweat trickled down each side of his nose into that fine moustache.

'I am tolerably certain.'

'Do you remember sitting in your car outside the hospital while Lady Carrados was with Captain O'Brien?'

Carrados did not speak for a long time. Then he swung round in his chair, and addressed that silent figure in the green lamplight.

'I can see no possible reason for this extraordinary procedure. It is most distressing for my wife, and I may say, sir, it strikes me as being damnably offensive and outside the duties of your office.'

'I don't think it is, Sir Herbert,' said the Assistant Commissioner. 'I advise you to answer Mr Alleyn, you know.'

'I may tell you,' Carrados began, 'that I am an intimate friend of your chief's. He shall hear about this.'

'I expect so,' said the Assistant Commissioner. 'Go on, Mr Alleyn.'

'Lady Carrados,' said Alleyn, 'did you, in point of fact, leave Sir Herbert in the car when you went into the hospital?'

'Yes.'

'Yes. Now, Sir Herbert, while you waited there, do you remember a schoolgirl of fifteen or so coming up on her bicycle?'

'How the devil can I remember a schoolgirl on a bicycle eighteen years ago?'

'Only because she gave you the letter that we have been discussing.'

Evelyn Carrados uttered a stifled cry. She turned and looked at her husband, as though she saw him for the first time. He met her with what Alleyn thought one of the most extraordinary glances he had ever seen – accusation, abasement, even a sort of triumphant misery, were all expressed in it; it was the face of a mean martyr. 'The mask of jealousy,' thought Alleyn. 'There's nothing more pitiable or more degrading. My God, if ever I – ' He thrust the thought from him, and began again.

'Sir Herbert, did you take that letter from the schoolgirl on the bicycle?'

Still with a sort of smile on his mouth, Carrados turned to Alleyn.

'I have no recollection of it,' he said.

Alleyn nodded to Fox, who went out. He was away for perhaps two minutes. Nobody spoke. Lady Carrados had bent her head, and seemed to look with profound attention at her gloved hands, clasped tightly together in her lap. Carrados suddenly wiped his face with his palm, and then drew out his handkerchief. Fox came back.

He ushered in Miss Harris.

'Good evening, Miss Harris,' said Alleyn.

'Good evening, Mr Alleyn. Good evening, Lady Carrados. Good evening, Sir Herbert. Good evening,' concluded Miss Harris with a collected glance at the Assistant Commissioner.

'Miss Harris,' said Alleyn, 'do you remember staying with your uncle, Mr Walter Harris, when he was vicar at Falconbridge? You were fifteen at the time I mean.'

'Yes Mr Alleyn, certainly,' said Miss Harris.

Carrados uttered some sort of oath. Lady Carrados said: ' But – what do you mean, Miss Harris?'

'Certainly, Lady Carrados,' said Miss Harris brightly.

'At that time,' said Alleyn, 'there was a fatal motor accident.'

'To Captain O'Brien. Pardon me, Lady Carrados. Yes, Mr Alleyn.'

'Good Lord!' ejaculated Alleyn, involuntarily. 'Do you mean to say that you have realized that – '

'I knew Captain "Paddy" O'Brien was Lady Carrados's first husband, naturally.'

'But,' said Alleyn, 'did you never think of telling Lady Carrados that there was this, well, this link, between you?'

'Oh, no,' said Miss Harris, 'naturally not, Mr Alleyn. It would not have been at all my place to bring it up. When I was given the list of vacant posts at the Friendly Cousins Registry Office I thought this seemed the most suitable, and I – please excuse me, Lady Carrados – I made enquiries, as one does, you know. And I said to my friend Miss Smith: "What an extraordinary coincidence," because when I learned of Lady Carrados's former name I realized it must be the same, and I said to Smithy: "I think that must be an omen," so I applied for the post.'

'I see,' said Alleyn, 'and do you remember Sir Herbert, too?'

'Oh, yes. At least, I wasn't quite sure at first, but afterwards I was. Sir Herbert was the gentleman in the car. Perhaps I should explain?'

'Please do.'

'I had actually spoken to him.' She looked apologetically at Carrados. 'I'm quite sure Sir Herbert has quite forgotten, because I was just a gawky schoolgirl at the time.'

'That will do, Miss Harris,' said Carrados violently. 'You will please not answer any further questions.'

Miss Harris looked extremely startled, turned bright pink, and opened her eyes very wide indeed. She closed her lips in a prudent button.

'Go on, Miss Harris,' said Alleyn.

'Which do you wish me to do, Lady Carrados?' asked her secretary.

'I think you had better go on,' said the faint voice.

'Very well, Lady Carrados. You see, I had the pleasure of returning a letter that had been left behind at the vicarage.'

'That is an absolute lie,' said Carrados, loudly.

'Pardon me,' said Miss Harris, 'but I cannot let that pass. I am speaking the truth.'

'Thank you, Miss Harris,' said Alleyn quickly. 'Would you mind waiting outside for a moment? Fox.'

Fox shepherded her out.

'By God!' began Carrados. 'If you take the word of a – '

'Wait a moment,' said Alleyn, 'I think I shall go on with my story. Our case, Sir Herbert, is that you did, in fact, take this letter, and for some reason never gave it to the lady who afterwards married you. Our case is that, having read the letter, you kept it for eighteen years, in the drawer of a miniature writing-desk in your study.'

'I protest. I absolutely deny – '

'You deny this, too?'

'It is outrageous! I tell you this, sir, if I have any influence – '

'Just a moment,' said Alleyn, 'Lady Carrados is speaking.'

The focus of attention shifted to the woman. She sat there as if she attended a meeting of some society in which she was interested. Her furs, her expensive, unnoticeable clothes, her gloves, her discreet make-up, might have been taken as symbols of controlled good breeding. It was the fierce rigidity of her figure that gave expression to her emotion. Her voice scarcely wavered. Alleyn realized that she was oblivious to her surroundings, and to the presence of other people in the room, and that seemed to him to be the most significant indication of her distress. She spoke directly to her husband.

'You knew! All these years you have watched me, and known how much I suffered. Why did you hide the letter? Why did you marry me, knowing my past history? It seems to me you must be mad. I understand now why you have watched me, why, since this awful business, you have never taken your eyes off me. You knew. You knew I was being blackmailed.' She caught her breath, and moved round stiffly until she faced her husband. 'You've done it,' she whispered. 'It's you. You're mad, and you've done it to torture me. You've always been jealous of Paddy. Ever since I told you it could never be the same with anyone else. You were jealous of dead Paddy.'

'Evelyn,' said Alleyn gently. She made a slight impatient gesture, but she spoke only to Carrados.

'You wrote those letters. It's you.'

Carrados stared at her like an idiot. His mouth was open. His eyebrows were raised in a sort of imbecile astonishment. He shook his head from side to side.

'No,' he said. 'No, Evelyn, no.'

'Make him tell you, Roderick,' she said, without turning her head.

'Sir Herbert,' said Alleyn. 'Do you deny you kept this letter in the secret drawer of that desk?'

'Yes.'

Fox glanced at Alleyn, went out, and returned, after another deadly silence, with Bridget.

Lady Carrados gave a little moaning cry, and caught at her daughter's hand.

'Miss O'Brien,' said Alleyn, 'I've asked you to come here in order that the Assistant Commissioner may hear of an incident you related to me yesterday. You told me that on one occasion, when you were alone in the study of your stepfather's house, you examined the miniature writing-cabinet in that room. You told me that when you pressed a tiny screw a triangular drawer opened out of the cabinet, and that there was a letter in it. Is this true?'

'Donna?' Bridget looked anxiously at her mother.

'Yes, yes, darling. Tell them. Whatever it is, tell them.'

'It's quite true,' said Bridget.

'Your stepfather came into the study at this juncture?'

'Yes.'

'What was his attitude when he saw what you had done?'

'He was very angry indeed.'

'What did he do?'

'He twisted my arm, and bruised it.'

'A lie. The child has always hated me. Everything I have tried to do for her – a lie, a wicked spiteful lie!'

'Fox,' said Alleyn, 'will you ask Sir Daniel to come in?'

Sir Daniel had evidently been sitting in the secretary's office, as he came in almost immediately. When he saw the two Carradoses and Bridget, he greeted them exactly as if they were fellow guests at a party. He then shook hands with the Assistant Commissioner, and turned to Alleyn.

'Sir Daniel,' said Alleyn. 'I've asked you to come in as I understand you were witness to a scene which Miss O'Brien has just described to us. It took place about two years ago. Do you remember that Miss O'Brien rang you up and asked you to come and see her mother who was unwell?'

'That has happened more than once,' said Davidson.

'On this particular visit you went into the study and talked to Miss O'Brien about a small French writing-cabinet.'

Davidson moved his eyebrows.

'Oh, yes?'

'Do you remember it?'

'I do. Very well.'

'You told her that there was probably a secret drawer in the box. Then you went upstairs to see Lady Carrados.'

'Yes. That's how it was, I think.'

'When you returned, were Miss O'Brien and Sir Herbert together in the study?'

'Yes,' said Davidson, and set his lips in an extremely firm line.

'Will you describe the scene that followed?'

'I am afraid not, Mr Alleyn.'

'Why not?'

'Let us say, for reasons of professional etiquette.'

Lady Carrados said: 'Sir Daniel, if you are thinking of me, I implore you to tell them what they want to know. I want the truth as much as anyone here. If I don't know the truth now, I shall go to pieces.'

Davidson looked at her in astonishment.

'*You* want me to tell them about that afternoon?'

'Yes, yes, I do.'

'And you, Carrados?' Davidson stared at Carrados, as if he were a sort of curiosity.

'Davidson, I implore you to keep your head. I am sure you saw nothing that could be construed – that could be regarded as evidence – that – Davidson, you know me. You know that I'm not a vindictive man. You know.'

'Come,' said Alleyn, 'we can cut this short. Sir Daniel, did you examine Miss O'Brien's arm when you returned to the study?'

'I did,' said Davidson, turning his back on Carrados.

'What did you find?'

'A certain amount of contusion, for which I prescribed a lotion.'

'To what cause did you' attribute these bruises?'

'They suggested that the arm had been tightly held, and twisted.'

'What were the relative positions of Sir Herbert and his step-daughter when you came into the study?'

'He held her by the arm.'

'Would it be correct to say he was storming at her?'

Davidson looked thoughtfully at Bridget. They exchanged half-smiles. 'He was shouting a good deal, certainly,' said Davidson dryly.

'Did you notice the writing-desk?'

'I don't think I noticed it the second time I went into the room. I realized that Sir Herbert Carrados was talking about it when I came in.'

'Yes. Thank you, Sir Daniel. Will you and Miss O'Brien wait out-side? We'll see Mr Dimitri, if you please, Fox.'

Davidson and Bridget both went out. Dimitri was ushered in by Fox. He was very sleek, with a clean bandage round his cut finger, oil on his hair, scent on his person. He looked out of the corners of his eyes, and bowed extensively.

'Good evening, my lady. Good evening, gentlemen.'

'Mr Dimitri,' Alleyn began, 'I have – '

'Stop.'

Carrados had got to his feet. He stood with his hand raised before his face in a curious gesture, half-defensive, half-declamatory. Then he slowly extended his arm, and pointed to Dimitri. The action was both ridiculous and alarming.

'What's the matter, Sir Herbert?' asked Alleyn.

'What's he doing here? My God, now I know – I know – '

'Well, Sir Herbert? What do you know?'

'Stop! I'll tell you. I did it! I did it! I confess. I confess everything. I did it!'

CHAPTER 29

Climax

'You did what, Sir Herbert?'

It was the AC's voice, very quiet and matter-of-fact.

'I kept the letter.' Carrados looked directly at his wife. 'You know why. If ever you had spoken of him, if ever you had compared me to that fellow, if I had found you – You know why.'

'Yes,' said Lady Carrados. 'I know why.'

'For God's sake,' Carrados said, 'for God's sake, gentlemen, let this go no further. It's a private matter between my wife and myself.'

'It has gone much further than that,' said Alleyn. 'Did you not in fact write blackmailing letters to your wife purely in order to torture her mind? Did you not do this?'

'You fool,' shouted Carrados. 'You fool! It's I who have suffered. It's I who have dreaded what might happen. The letter was stolen. It was stolen. It was stolen.'

'Now,' said Alleyn, 'it seems we are going to get the truth. When did you miss the letter?'

Carrados looked from one face to the other. For a frightful moment Alleyn thought he was going to burst into tears. His lips were shaking. He seemed an old man. He began to speak.

'It was when we came back from Newmarket. That evening I was alone in my study. Bridget had been very inconsiderate all day, leaving us and going off with a young man of whom I could not approve. My wife had taken her part against me. I was alone in my study. I found myself looking at the French writing-cabinet. There was something different in the arrangement of the pieces in front of it. I went to re-arrange them, and being there I tried the hidden drawer. It was empty! I tell you the letter was there the day before. I saw it there. The day before I had been very angry with my wife. She had been cruel to me. I am very sensitive and my nerves are shattered. I am alone. Terribly lonely. Nobody cares what becomes of me. She was so thoughtless and cruel. So I looked at the letter because the letter gave me comfort. It was there the night before. And do you know who was alone in my room on May the ninth?'

'Yes,' said Alleyn. 'I am glad you, too, remember. It was Mr Colombo Dimitri.'

'Ah,' said Carrados shakily. 'Ah, now we're getting at it. Now, we're getting at it.'

'I aim afraid I do not understand,' said Dimitri. 'Is Sir Herbert perhaps ill?'

Carrados slewed round and again he pointed at Dimitri.

'You stole it, you filthy dago. I know you stole it. I have suspected it from the first. I could do nothing – nothing.'

'Excuse me, Mr Alleyn,' said Dimitri, 'but I believe that I may charge Sir Herbert Carrados with libel on this statement. Is it not so?'

'I don't think I advise you to do so, Mr Dimitri. On the other hand I shall very strongly advise Lady Carrados to charge you with blackmail. Lady Carrados, is it a fact that on the morning of May twenty-fifth, when Lord Robert Gospell paid you a visit, you received a blackmailing letter?'

'Yes.'

'Do you believe that the only source from which the blackmailer could have got his information was the letter lost on the day of Captain O'Brien's accident?'

'Yes.'

Alleyn took an envelope from his pocket, handed it to her.

'Was the blackmailing letter written in a similar style to this?'

She glanced at it and turned her head away.

'It was exactly like that.'

'If I tell you that the lady to whom this letter is addressed had been blackmailed as you have been blackmailed and that we have positive evidence that the man who wrote this address was Colombo Dimitri, are you prepared to charge him with blackmail?'

'Yes.'

'It is completely false,' said Dimitri. 'I shall certainly sue for libel.'

His face was ashen. He put his bandaged hand to his lips and pressed it against them.

'Before we go any further,' said Alleyn, 'I think I should explain that Lord Robert Gospell was in the confidence of Scotland Yard as regards these blackmailing letters. He was working for us on the case. We've got his signed statement that leaves no doubt at all that Mr Dimitri collected a sum of money at a concert held at the Constance Street Hall on Thursday, June the third. Lord Robert actually watched Mr Dimitri collect his money.'

'He – ' Dimitri caught his breath, his lips were drawn back from his teeth in a sort of grin. 'I deny everything,' he said. 'Everything. I wish to send for my lawyer.'

'You shall do so, Mr Dimitri, when I have finished. On June the eighth, two nights ago, Lady Carrados gave a ball at Marsden House. Lord Robert was there. As he knew so much about Mr Dimitri already, he thought he would find out a little more. He watched Mr Dimitri. He now knew the method employed. He also knew that Lady Carrados was the victim of blackmail. Is that right, Lady Carrados?'

'Yes. I had a conversation with him about it. He knew what I was going to do.'

'What were you going to do?'

'Put my bag containing five hundred pounds in a certain place in the green sitting-room upstairs.'

'Yes,' said Alleyn. 'Now, Lord Robert saw Mr Dimitri return her empty bag to Lady Carrados shortly before one o'clock. At one o'clock he rang me up and told me he now had enough evidence. The conversation was interrupted by someone who must have overheard at least one very significant phrase. Two and a half hours later Lord Robert was murdered.'

The quiet of the room was blown into piercing clamour. Dimitri had screamed like a woman, his mouth wide open. This shocking rumpus lasted for a second and stopped. Alleyn had a picture of an engine-driver pulling a string and then letting it go. Dimitri stood, still with a gaping mouth, wagging his finger at Alleyn.

'Now then, now then,' said Fox and stepped up to him.

'False!' said Dimitri, frantically snapping his fingers in Fox's face and then shaking them as if they were scorched. 'False! You accuse me of murder. I am not an assassin. I am innocent. *Cristo mio,* I am innocent, innocent, innocent!'

For a moment it looked as if he'd try to bolt from the room. He might have been a tenor giving an excruciatingly bad performance in a second-rate Italian opera. He mouthed at Alleyn, tore his hair, crumpled on to a chair, and burst into tears. Upon the five English people in the office there descended a heavy aura of embarrassment.

'I am innocent,' sobbed Dimitri. 'As innocent as a child. The blessed saints bear witness to my innocence. The blessed saints bear witness – '

'Unfortunately,' said Alleyn, 'their evidence is not acceptable in a court of law. If you will keep quiet for a moment, Mr Dimitri, we can get on with our business. Will you ask Mrs Halcut-Hackett to come in, please, Fox?'

The interval was enlivened by the sound of Dimitri biting his nails and sobbing.

Mrs Halcut-Hackett, dressed as if she was going to a Continental restaurant and looking like a beauty specialist's mistake, came into the office. Fox followed with an extra chair which he placed for her. She sat down and drew up her bust until it seemed to perch like some super-structure on a rigid foundation. Then she saw Lady Carrados. An extraordinary look passed between the two women. It was as if they had said to each other: 'You, too?'

'Mrs Halcut-Hackett,' said Alleyn. 'You have told me that after a charade party you gave in December you found that a document which you valued was missing from a box on your dressing-table. Had this man, Colombo Dimitri, an opportunity of being alone in this room?'

She turned her head and looked at Dimitri who flapped his hands at her.

'Why, yes,' she said. 'He certainly had.'

'Did Lord Robert sit near you at the Sirmione Quartette's concert on June the third?'

'You know he did.'

'Do you remember that this man, Colombo Dimitri, sat not very far away from you?'

'Why – yes.'

'Your bag was stolen that afternoon?'

'Yes.' She looked again at Lady Carrados who suddenly leant forward and touched her hand.

'I'm so sorry,' she said. 'I, too. Indeed you have nothing to fear from us. We have suffered, too. I have made up my mind to hide nothing now. Will you help by also hiding – nothing?'

'Oh, my dear!' said Mrs Halcut-Hackett in a whisper.

'We need not ask for very much more,' said Alleyn. 'Would it have been possible for Dimitri to have taken your bag while you were out of the concert-room?'

'Lord Robert might have seen,' said Mrs Halcut-Hackett.

'Lord Robert did see,' said Alleyn.

'The dead!' cried Dimitri. 'I cannot be accused by the dead.'

'If that was true,' said Alleyn, 'as it often is, what a motive for murder! I tell you we have a statement, written and signed by the dead.'

Dimitri uttered a sort of moan and shrank back in his chair.

Alleyn took from his pocket the cigarette-case with the medallion.

'This is yours, isn't it?' he asked Mrs Halcut-Hackett. 'Yes. I've told you so.'

'You left it in the green sitting-room at Marsdon House?'

'Yes – only a few minutes.'

'A minute or two, not more, after you came out of that room you heard the dialling tinkle of the telephone?'

'Yes.'

'You had seen Lord Robert coming upstairs?'

'Yes.'

Alleyn nodded to Fox who again left the room.

'After you had joined your partner in the other sitting-out room, you discovered the loss of your case?'

'Yes, I did.'

'Your partner fetched it.'

She wetted her lips. Dimitri was listening avidly. Carrados had slumped down in his chair with his chin on his chest. Alleyn felt he was giving, for anybody that had time to notice it, a quiet performance of a broken man. Lady Carrados sat upright, her hands folded in her lap, her face looked exhausted. The AC was motionless behind the green lamp.

'Well, Mrs Halcut-Hackett? Your partner fetched your case from the green sitting-room, didn't he?'

'Yes.'

The door opened and Withers walked in after Fox. He stood with his hands in his pockets and blinked his white eyelashes.

'Hallo,' he said. 'What's the idea?'

'I have invited you to come here, Captain Withers, in order that the Assistant Commissioner may hear your statement about your movements on the night of the ball at Marsdon House. I have discovered that although you left Marsdon House at three-thirty you did not arrive at the Matador Night Club until four-fifteen. You therefore have no alibi for the murder of Lord Robert Gospell.'

Withers looked at Mrs Halcut-Hackett with a sort of sneer.

'She can give me one,' he said.

She looked at him and spoke to Alleyn. Her voice was quite expressionless.

'I'd made up my mind it would have to come out. Between the time we left the ball and the time we got to the Matador, Captain Withers drove me about in his car. I was afraid of my husband. I had seen him watching me. I wanted to talk to Captain Withers. I was afraid to say this before.'

'I see,' said Alleyn. 'You accept that, Captain Withers?'

'It's true enough.'

'Very well. Now, to return to Marsdon House. You told me that at one o'clock you were in the sitting-room at the head of the stairs.'

'So I was.'

'You did not tell me you were also in the telephone-room.'

Withers stared at Mrs Halcut-Hackett. She had been watching him like a frightened animal but as soon as his eyes turned towards her she looked away from him.

'Why should I?' said Withers

'You were in the telephone room with Mrs Halcut-Hackett before you went to the other room. You returned to it from the other room to fetch this.'

Alleyn's long arm shot up. Seven heads followed the movement. Seven pairs of eyes were concentrated on the gold cigarette-case with the jewelled medallion.

'And what if I did?'

'Where did you find this case?'

'On a table in the room with the telephone.'

'When I asked you yesterday if you overheard Lord Robert telephoning in this room, as we know he did at one o'clock, you denied it.'

'There wasn't anybody in the room when I fetched the case. I told you I heard the dialling tinkle on the extension a bit before then. If it was Gospell I suppose he'd gone when I got there.'

'Is there any reason why anybody, say Mr Dimitri in the corner there, should not have gone into the telephone-room after you left it with Mrs Halcut-Hackett, and before you returned for the case?'

'No reason at all as far as I'm concerned.'

'Dimitri,' said Alleyn, 'have you seen this case before? Look at it. Have you seen it before?'

'Never. I have never seen it. I do not know why you ask. I have never seen it.'

'Take it in your hands. Look at it.'

Dimitri took the case.

'Open it.'

Dimitri opened it. From where Alleyn stood he could see the little cutting taken from *The Times*. Dimitri saw it too. His eyes dilated. The case dropped through his hands to the floor. He pointed a shaking finger at Alleyn.

'I think you must be the devil himself,' he whispered.

'Fox,' said Alleyn, 'will you pass the case round?'

It passed from hand to hand. Withers, Evelyn Carrados and Carrados all looked at it. Withers handled it as if he had done so before, but seemed quite unmoved by the cutting. The Carradoses both looked blankly at it and passed it on. Mrs Halcut-Hackett opened the case and stared at the scrap of paper.

This wasn't here before,' she said. 'What is it? Who put it here?'

'I'm sorry,' said Alleyn. 'It's done no damage. It will come off quite easily.'

He took the case from her.

Dimitri suddenly leapt to his feet. Fox who had never taken his eyes off him moved in front of the door.

'Sit down, Mr Dimitri,' said Alleyn.

'I am going. You can keep me here no longer against my will. You accuse, you threaten, you lie! I say I can endure it no longer. I am an innocent man, a man of standing with a clientéle of great excellence. I will see a lawyer. My God, let me pass!'

He plunged forward. Alleyn caught him by one arm. Fox by the other. He struggled violently. The AC pressed a bell on his desk, the door was opened from the outside and two plain-clothes men walked into the room. Beyond, in the brightly lit secretary's room three startled faces, Bridget's, Davidson's and Miss Harris's, peered over the shoulders of more Yard men, and through the doorway.

Dimitri, mouthing and panting, was taken over by the two officers.

'Now then,' they said. 'Now then.'

'Lady Carrados,' said Alleyn, 'will you formally charge this man?'

'I do charge him.'

'In a moment,' said Alleyn to Dimitri, 'you will be taken to the charge-room, but before we talk about the exact nature of the charge – ' He looked through the door: 'Sir Daniel? I see you're still there. May I trouble you again for a moment?'

Davidson, looking very startled, came through.

'Good God, Alleyn!' he said, staring at Dimitri. 'What's this?'

Alleyn said: 'You can, I believe, give me the final piece of evidence in an extremely involved affair. You see this cigarette-case?'

Davidson took it.

'My dear fellow,' he said, 'that's the abortion. I told you about it. It's part of the collection at Marsdon House. You remember?'

He moved to the light and after another startled glance at Dimitri, who had gone perfectly still and stared at him like a lost soul, Davidson put up his glasses and examined the case.

'You know, I believe it *is* Benvenuto,' he said, looking over his glasses at Alleyn.

'Yes, yes, I dare say. Will you tell us where you saw it?'

'Among a collection of *objets d'art* on a pie-crust table in an upstairs room at Marsdon House.'

'At what time, Sir Daniel?'

'My dear Alleyn, I told you. About eleven-thirty or so. Perhaps earlier.'

'Would you swear you noticed it no later than eleven-thirty?' insisted Alleyn.

'But of course I would,' said Davidson. 'I did not return to that room. I am quite ready to swear it.'

He held the cigarette-case up in his beautifully shaped hand.

'I swear I saw this case on the table in the green sitting-room not later than eleven-thirty. That do?'

The silence was broken only by Dimitri's laboured breathing.

And then, surprisingly clear and firm, Mrs Halcut-Hackett's voice: 'But that can't be true.'

Alleyn said: 'Will you open the case?'

Davidson, who was gazing in amazement at Mrs Halcut-Hackett, opened the cigarette-case and saw the notice.

'Will you read that press cutting?' said Alleyn. 'Aloud, please.'

The deep expressive voice read the absurd message.

'Childie Darling. Living in exile. Longing. Only want Daughter. Daddy.'

'What in the name of all wonders is this?'

'We believe it to be a murderer's message,' said Alleyn. 'We think this man, Dimitri, can translate it.'

Davidson shut the case with a snap.

Something had gone wrong with his hands. They shook so violently that the diamonds on the gold case seemed to have a separate flashing life of their own.

'So Dimitri is a murderer,' he said.

'Look out!' said Alleyn loudly.

Dimitri flung himself forward with such extreme and sudden violence that the men who held him were taken off their guard and his hands were at Davidson's throat before they had regained their hold on him. In a moment the room was full of struggling men. Chairs crashed to the floor, a woman screamed. Fox's voice shouted urgently: 'Get to it. What are you *doing?*' There was a concerted upheaval against the edge of the desk. The green-shaded lamp smashed into oblivion.

'That's better,' said Alleyn's voice. 'Now then. Hands together.'

A sharp click, a cry from Dimitri, and then the figures resolved themselves into a sort of tableau: Dimitri, handcuffed and held by three men, against the desk; Davidson in the centre of the room with Alleyn, Fox and a plain-clothes man grasping his arms behind his back; the Assistant Commissioner, between the two groups, like a distinguished sort of referee.

'Murderer!' screamed Dimitri. 'Treacherous, filthy assassin! I confess! Gentlemen, I confess! I have worked for him for seven years and now, now, *now* he will stand aside and let me go to the gallows for the crime he has himself committed. I will tell you everything. *Everything.*'

'Speak up, Rory,' said the AC.

'Daniel Davidson,' said Alleyn, 'I arrest you for the murder of Lord Robert Gospell, and I warn you . . .'

CHAPTER 30

Confessions from Troy

'I thought,' said Alleyn, 'that you would like to know at once, Mildred.'

Lady Mildred Potter shook her head, not so much in disagreement as from a sort of general hopelessness.

'It was nice of you to come, Roderick. But I'm afraid I simply cannot take it in. Sir Daniel has always been perfectly charming to both of us. Bunchy liked him very much. He told me so. And there's no doubt Sir Daniel did wonders with my indigestion. Quite cured it. Are you sure you are not mistaken?'

'Quite sure, I am afraid, Mildred. You see, Dimitri has confessed that Davidson has been in a sort of infamous partnership with him for seven years. Davidson knew something about Dimitri in the first instance, I think. That's probably how he managed to get his hold over Dimitri. Davidson has been extremely careful. He has found the data but he has left Dimitri to carry out the practical work. Davidson saw the open drawer and the letter in Carrados's writing-cabinet. Davidson came in on the scene between Carrados and Bridget. He was careful never to be left alone in the room himself, but he told Dimitri about the secret drawer and instructed Dimitri how to steal the letter. He told Dimitri that there might be something interesting there. Dimitri did all the dirty work. He collected the handbags of the blackmailed ladies. He wrote the letters. Sometimes he got the ideas. Mrs Halcut-Hackett's trinket-box was one of Dimitri's brightest ideas, I imagine.'

'I'm lost in it, Roderick. Troy, darling, do *you* understand?'

Alleyn looked at Troy, sitting on the floor at Mildred's feet.

'I think I'm beginning to understand,' said Troy.

'Well, go on, Roderick,' said Mildred drearily.

'There were three things that I could not fit into the pattern,' said Alleyn, and he spoke more to Troy than to Mildred. 'It seemed at first that if Dimitri overheard the telephone call he had an overwhelming motive. We knew he was a blackmailer, and we knew Bunchy was on his track. But we found that Dimitri literally could not have done the murder. His alibi stood up to the time factor and came out on top.

'Withers is a bad lot, and Bunchy knew that too, but somehow I could not see Withers as the killer. He's hard, wary and completely unscrupulous. If he did ever murder it would be deliberately, and with forethought. The whole thing would be worked out to the last second. This job was, we believed, unpremeditated until within two and a half hours of its execution. Still Withers had to be considered. There was a gap in his alibi. I now know that he spent that gap driving his woman-dupe about in his car in order to discuss a situation which had become acute. Into this department, and again I implore your silence because I certainly shouldn't tell you about it, came old General Halcut-Hackett like an elderly harlequin dodging about in the fog of Belgrave Square at the crucial time when the guests left Marsdon House. He, of course, was looking for his wife. Next came Carrados. Old Carrados was an infernal bore. His alibi, which overlapped Dimitri's, held good, but his behaviour was rum in the extreme. It was not until I heard of an incident eighteen years old that I managed to fit him into the pattern. And all the time there were three things about Davidson for which I could find only one explanation. He told me he saw a certain cigarette-case in the green sitting-room at about eleven-thirty. Certainly not later. We found that the cigarette-case in question was only in this room for about four minutes round about one o'clock during which the telephone conversation took place. Why should Davidson lie? He had thought the case was a set-piece – one of the Marsdon House possessions; he had *not* realized that it was the personal property of one of the guests. He stated most emphatically that he did not overhear the conversation and indeed did not return to the room after eleven-thirty. But there is a curious point about the telephone conversation.

Bunchy said to me: "He might as well mix his damn brews with poison." Davidson must have overheard that sentence because it came just before Bunchy broke off. Bunchy was talking about Dimitri, of course, but I believe Davidson thought he was talking about him. The broken sentence: "with such filthy ingenuity," or something of that sort. Davidson probably thought the next word Bunchy spoke would be his (Davidson's) name. That's odd, isn't it?

'As for the figure Miss Harris saw beyond the glass panel, undoubtedly it was Davidson's. At his wits' end he must have dived through the nearest door and there, I suppose, pulled himself together and decided to murder Bunchy.'

'Then there is the other cigarette-case.'

Alleyn looked at Lady Mildred. Her head nodded like a mandarin's. He turned back to Troy and spoke softly.

'I mean the weapon. On the morning after the murder I asked to see Davidson's case. He showed me a cigarette-case that was certainly too small for the job and said it was the one he had carried last night. I noticed how immaculate it was, looked closely at it, and found traces of plate-powder in the tooling. We learnt that Davidson's cases were cleaned the morning before the ball and had not been touched after the ball. It seemed to me that this case had certainly not been out all night. It shone like a mirror and I would have sworn had not been used since it was put in his pocket. It was a thin bit of evidence but it did look as if he had lied when he said it was the case he took to Marsden House. And then there was the condition – is Mildred asleep?'

'Yes,' said Lady Mildred. 'Do you mind very much, dear Roderick, if I go to bed? I'm afraid I shall never understand, you see, and I am really so very tired. I think sorrow is one of the most tiring things, don't you? Troy, my dear, you will look after poor Roderick, won't you? Donald will be in late and I don't know where he is just now.'

'I think he took Bridget Carrados home,' said Alleyn, opening the door for Mildred. 'Evelyn and her husband wanted to be alone and Donald was in the waiting-room looking hopeful.'

'He seems to be very attached to her,' said Mildred, pausing at the door and looking at Alleyn with tear-stained eyes. 'Is she a nice girl, Roderick?'

'Very nice. I think she'll look after him. Good night, Mildred.'

'Good night.'

Alleyn shut the door after her and returned to Troy.

'May I stay for a little longer?'

'Yes, please. I want to hear the end of it all.' Troy looked sideways at him. 'How extraordinarily well-trained your eye must be! To notice the grains of plate-powder in the tooling of a cigarette-case; could anything be more admirable? What else did you notice?'

'I notice that although your eyes are grey there are little flecks of green in them and that the iris is ringed with black. I notice that when you smile your face goes crooked. I notice that the third fin-ger of your left hand has a little spot of vermillion on the inside where a ring should hide it; and from that, Miss Troy, I deduce that you are a painter in oils and are not so proud as you should be of your lovely fingers.'

'Please tell me the end of the case.'

'I would rather tell you that since this afternoon in the few spare moments I have had to spend upon it I have considered your case and that I have decided to take out a warrant for your arrest. The charge is impeding an officer of the law in the execution of his duty.'

'Don't be so damned facetious,' said Troy.

'All right. Where was I?'

'You had got to the third point against Davidson.'

'Yes. The third point was in the method used in committing the crime. I don't think Bunchy would mind if he knew that even while I described his poor little body I was thinking of the woman to whom I spoke. Do you? He was such an understanding person, was-n't he, with just the right salty flavour of irony? I'm sure he knew how short-lived the first pang of sorrow really is if only people would confess as much. Well, Troy, the man who killed him knew how easy it was to asphyxiate people and I didn't think many killers would know that. The only real mark of violence was the scar made by the cigarette-case. A doctor would realize how little force was needed and Bunchy's doctor would know how great an ally that weak heart would be. Davidson told me about the condition of the heart because he knew I would discover he had examined Bunchy. He kept his head marvellously when I interviewed him, did Sir Daniel. He's as clever as paint. We're searching his house tonight. Fox is there now. I don't think we'll find anything except perhaps the lethal cigarette-case, but I've more hopes of Dimitri's desk. I couldn't get into that yesterday.'

'What about the cloak and hat?'

'That brings us to a very curious episode. We have searched for the cloak and hat ever since four o'clock yesterday morning and we have not found them. We did our usual routine stuff, going round all the dust-bin experts and so on and we also notified the parcels-post offices. This afternoon we heard of a parcel that had been dumped at the Main Western office during the rush hour yesterday. It was over-stamped with tuppenny stamps and addressed to somewhere in China. The writing was script which was our blackmailer's favourite medium of expression. It's gone, alas, but I think there's just a chance we may trace it. It's a very long chance. Now who is likely to have an unlimited supply of tuppenny stamps, my girl?'

'Somebody who gives receipts?'

'Bless me, if you're not a clever old thing. Right as usual, said the Duchess. And who should give receipts but Sir Daniel, the fashionable physician? Who but he?'

'Dimitri for one.'

'I'm sorry to say that is perfectly true, darling. But when I was in Davidson's waiting-room, I saw several of those things that I think are called illustrated brochures. They appealed for old clothes for the Central Chinese Medical Mission at God knows where. It is our purpose, my dear Troy, to get one of those brochures and write to the Central Chinese Mission asking for further information.'

'I wonder,' murmured Troy.

'And so, you may depend upon it, do I. There's one other point which has been kindly elucidated by the gibbering Dimitri. This morning he sent his servant out for a *Times*. When we heard of this we had a look at *The Times*, too. We found the agony-column notice that I talked about when poor Mildred was trying not to go to sleep, and before I could tell you how much I approve of the solemn way you knit your brows when you listen to me. Now, this notice read like this: "Childie Darling. Living in exile. Longing. Only want Daughter. Daddy." A rum affair, we thought, and we noticed in our brilliant way that the initial letters read "CD. Lie low. D.D." which might not be too fancifully elaborated into "Colombo Dimitri, lie low, Daniel Davidson." And, in fact, Mr Dimitri confessed to this

artless device. It was arranged, he says, that if anything unprece-
dented, untoward, unanticipated, ever occurred, Davidson would
communicate with Dimitri in precisely this manner. It was a poor
effort, but Sir Daniel hadn't much time. He must have composed it
as soon as he got home after his night's work. Anything more?'

'What about Dimitri and Withers?'

'They were taken to the charge-room, and duly charged. The one
with blackmail, the other with running a gaming-house. I'll explain
the gaming-house some other time. They are extremely nasty fellows, but if Dimitri hadn't been quite such a nasty fellow, we would-
n't have stood as good a chance of scaring him into fits and getting
the whole story about Davidson. I gambled on that, and by jingo,
Troy, it *was* a gamble.'

'What would have happened if Dimitri had kept quiet even
though he did think you were going to arrest him for murder?'

'We would still have arrested him for blackmail, and would have
had to plug away at Davidson on what we'd got. But Dimitri saw we
had a clear case on the blackmail charge. He'd nothing to gain in
protecting Davidson.'

'Do you think he really *knows* Davidson did the murder?'

'I think we shall find that Davidson tried to warn him against collecting Evelyn Carrados's bag at the ball. Davidson saw Bunchy was
with Evelyn, when Bridget returned her bag the first time.'

'You didn't tell me about that.'

Alleyn told her about it.

'And isn't that really all?' he asked.

'Yes. That's all.'

'Troy, I love you more than anything in life. I've tried humility;
God knows, I am humble. And I've tried effrontery. If you can't love
me, tell me so, and please let us not meet again because I can't manage meeting you unless it is to love you.'

Troy raised a white face and looked solemnly at him.

'I know my mind at last,' she said. 'I couldn't be parked.'

'Darling, darling Troy.'

'I do love you. Very much indeed.'

'Wonder of the world!' cried Alleyn, and took her in his arms.

Epilogue

Down a sun-baked mud track that ran through the middle of the most remote of all the Chinese Medical mission's settlements in Northern Manchuria walked a short, plump celestial. He was followed by six yellow urchins upon each of whose faces was an expression of rapt devotion, and liveliest envy. If his face and legs had been visible, it would have been seen that sweat poured down them in runnels. But his face was hidden by a black hat, and his legs by the voluminous folds of a swashbuckling cloak. There was glory in his gait.

In the receiving office of the mission, a jaded young Englishman gazed in perplexity at a telegram a month old. It had been forwarded from the head depot and had done the rounds of most of the settlements. It was from New Scotland Yard, London.

The young Englishman gazed blankly through the open door at the little procession in the sun-baked track outside.

Overture to Death

For the Sunday Morning Party:
G. M. LESTER
DUNDAS AND CECIL WALKER
NORMAN AND MILES STACPOOLE BATCHELOR
& My Father

Contents

Cast of Characters

Jocelyn Jernigham	*Of Pen Cuckoo*
Henry Jernigham	*His son*
Eleanor Prentice	*His cousin*
Taylor	*His butler*
Walter Copeland, B.A. OXON.	*Rector of Winton St Giles*
Dinah Copeland	*His daughter*
Idris Campanula	*Of the Red House, Chipping*
Dr William Templett	*Of Chippingwood*
Selia Ross	*Of Duck Cottage, Cloudyfold*
Superintendent Blandish	*Of the Great Chipping Constabulary*
Sergeant Roper	*Of the Great Chipping Constabulary*
Mrs Biggins	
Georgie Biggins	*Her son*
Gibson	*Miss Campanula's Chauffeur*
Gladys Wright	*Of the Y.P.F.C.*
Saul Tranter	*Poacher*
Chief Detective-Inspector Alleyn	*Of the Criminal Investigation Department*
Detective-Inspector Fox	*His assistant*
Detective-Sergeant Bailey	*His finger print expert*
Detective-Sergeant Thompson	*His camera expert*
Nigel Bathgate	*Journalist, his Watson*

CHAPTER 1

The Meet at Pen Cuckoo

Jocelyn Jernigham was a good name. The seventh Jocelyn thought so as he stood at his study window and looked down the vale of Pen Cuckoo toward that precise spot where the spire of Salisbury Cathedral could be seen through field-glasses on a clear day.

'Here I stand,' he said without turning his head, 'and here my forebears have stood, generation after generation, and looked over their own tilth and tillage. Seven Jocelyn Jernighams.'

'I'm never quite sure,' said his son Henry Jocelyn, 'what tilth and tillage are. What precisely, Father, is tilth?'

'There's no feeling for that sort of thing,' said Jocelyn, angrily, 'among the present generation. Cheap sneers and clever talk that mean nothing.'

'But I assure you I like words to mean something. That is why I ask you to define a tilth. And you say, "the present generation." You mean my generation, don't you? But I'm twenty-three. There is a newer generation than mine. If I marry Dinah – '

'You quibble deliberately in order to lead our conversation back to this absurd suggestion. If I had known – '

Henry uttered an impatient noise and moved away from the fire-place. He joined his father in the window and he too looked down into the darkling vale of Pen Cuckoo. He saw an austere landscape, adamant beneath drifts of winter mist. The naked trees slept soundly, the fields were dumb with cold; the few stone cottages, with their comfortable signals of blue smoke, were the only waking things in all the valley.

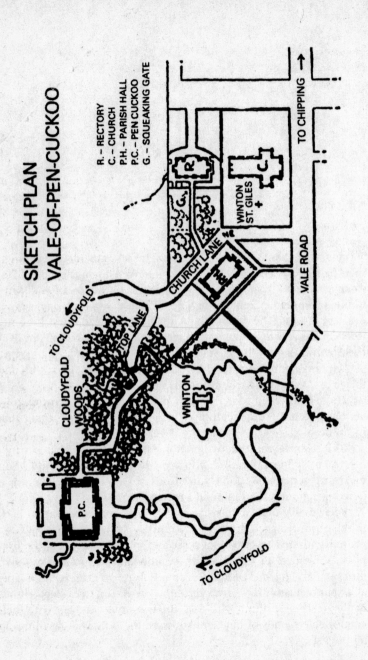

SKETCH PLAN
VALE-OF-PEN-CUCKOO

R. – RECTORY
C. – CHURCH
P.H. – PARISH HALL
P.C. – PEN CUCKOO
G. – SQUEAKING GATE

TO CHIPPING

WINTON
ST. GILES

VALE ROAD

CHURCH LANE

TO CLOUDYFOLD

CLOUDYFOLD
WOODS

TOP LANE

WINTON

P.C.

TO CLOUDYFOLD

'I too love Pen Cuckoo,' said Henry, and he added, with that tinge of irony which Jocelyn, who did not understand it, found so irritating: 'I have all the pride of prospective ownership. But I refuse to be bully-ragged by Pen Cuckoo. I refuse to play the part of a Victorian young gentleman with a touch of Cophetua thrown in. I refuse to allow this conversation to run along the lines of ancient lineage. The proud father and self-willed heir stuff simply doesn't fit. We are not discussing a possible misalliance. Dinah is not a blushing maid of inferior station. She is part of the country, rooted equally with us. If we are going to talk about her in country terms, I can strike a suitable attitude and say there have been Copelands at the rectory for as many generations as there have been Jernighams at Pen Cuckoo.'

'You are both much too young – ' began Jocelyn.

'No, really, sir, that won't do. What you mean is that Dinah is too poor. If it had been somebody smarter and richer, you and my dear cousin Eleanor wouldn't have talked about youth. Don't let's pretend.'

'And don't you talk to me like a damned sententious young puppy, Henry, because I won't have it.'

'I'm sorry,' said Henry, 'I know I'm being tiresome.'

'You're being extremely tiresome. Very well, I'll speak as plainly as you like. Pen Cuckoo means more to me and should mean more to you, than anything else in life. You know as well as I do that we're damned hard up. There are all sorts of things that should be done to the place. Those cottages up at Cloudyfold! Winton! Rumbold tells me that Winton'll leak like a basket if we don't fix up the roof. The point is – '

'I can't afford to make a poor marriage?'

'If you choose to put it like that.'

'How else can one put it?'

'Very well, then.'

'Well, since we must speak in terms of hard cash, which I assure you I don't enjoy, Dinah won't always be the poor parson's one ewe lamb.'

'What d'you mean?' asked Jocelyn, uneasily, but with a certain air of pricking up his ears.

'I thought everyone knew Miss Campanula has left all her filthy lucre, or most of it, to the rector. Don't pretend, Father; you must have heard that piece of gossip. The cook and housemaid witnessed the will and the housemaid overheard Miss C. bawling about it to her lawyer. Dinah doesn't want the money and nor do I – much – but that's what'll happen to it eventually.'

'Servant's gossip,' muttered the squire. 'Most distasteful. Anyway, it may not – she may change her mind. It's *now* we're so damned hard-up.'

'Let me find a job of work,' Henry said.

'Your job of work is here.'

'What! with a perfectly good agent who looks upon me as a sort of impediment in his agricultural speech?'

'Nonsense!'

'Look here, Father,' said Henry gently, 'how much of this has been inspired by Eleanor?'

'Eleanor is as anxious as I am that you shouldn't make a bloody fool of yourself. If your mother had been alive – '

'No, no,' cried Henry, 'let us not put ideas into the minds of the dead. That is so grossly unfair. Let's recognize Eleanor's hand in this. Eleanor has been too clever by half. I didn't mean to tell you about Dinah until I was sure that she loved me. I am not sure. The scene, which Eleanor so conveniently overheard yesterday at the rectory, was purely tentative.' He broke off, turned away from his father, and pressed his cheek against the window pane.

'It is intolerable,' said Henry, 'that Eleanor should have spoilt the memory of my first – my first approach to Dinah. To stand in the hall, as she must have done, and to listen! To come clucking back to you like a vulgar hen, agog with her news! As if Dinah was a house-maid with a follower. No, it's too much!'

'You've never been fair to Eleanor. She's done her best to take your mother's place.'

'For God's sake,' said Henry violently, 'don't use that detestable phrase! Cousin Eleanor has never taken my mother's place. She is an ageing spinster cousin of the worst type. It was not particularly kind of her to come to Pen Cuckoo. Indeed, it was her golden opportunity. She left the Cromwell Road for the glories of "county." It was the great moment of her life. She's a vulgarian.'

'On her mother's side,' said Jocelyn, 'she's a Jernigham.'

'Oh, my dear father!' said Henry, and burst out laughing.

Jocelyn glared at his son, turned purple in the face, and began to stammer.

'You may laugh, but Eleanor – Eleanor – in bringing this information – unavoidably overheard – no question of eavesdropping – only doing what she believed to be her duty.'

'I'm sure she told you that.'

'She did and I agreed with her. I am most strongly opposed to this affair with Dinah, and I am most relieved to hear that so far it is, as you put it, purely tentative.'

'If Dinah loves me,' said Henry, setting the Jernigham jaw, 'I shall marry her. And that's flat. If Eleanor wasn't here to jog at your pride, Father, you would at least try to see my side. But Eleanor won't let you. She dramatizes herself as the first lady of the district. The squiress. The chatelaine of Pen Cuckoo. She sees Dinah as a sort of rival. What's more, I believe she's genuinely jealous of Dinah. It's the jealousy of a woman of her age and disposition, a jealousy rooted in sex.'

'Disgusting balderdash!' said Jocelyn, angrily, but he looked uncomfortable.

'No!' cried Henry. 'No, it's not. I'm not talking highbrow pornography. You must have seen what Eleanor is. She's an avid woman. She was in love with you until she found it was a hopeless proposition. Now she and her girl friend the Campanula are rivals for the rector. Dinah says all old maids always fall in love with her father. Everybody sees it. It's a recognized phenomenon with women of Eleanor's and Idris Campanula's type. Have you heard her on the subject of Dr Templett and Selia Ross? She's nosed out a scandal there. The next thing that happens will be Eleanor feeling it her duty to warn poor Mrs Templett that her husband is too fond of the widow. That is, if Idris Campanula doesn't get in first. Women like Eleanor and Miss Campanula are pathological. Dinah says – '

'Do you and Dinah discuss my cousin's attachment, which I don't admit, for the rector? If you do, I consider it shows an extraordinary lack of manners and taste.'

'Dinah and I,' said Henry, 'discuss everything.'

'And this is modern love-making!'

'Don't let's start abusing each other's generations, Father. We've never done that. You've been so extraordinarily understanding in so many ways. It's Eleanor!' said Henry. 'It's Eleanor, Eleanor, Eleanor who is to blame for this!'

The door at the far end of the room was opened and against the lamplit hall beyond appeared a woman's figure.

'Did I hear you call me, Henry?' asked a quiet voice.

II

Miss Eleanor Prentice came into the room. She reached out a thin hand and switched on the lights.

'It's past five o'clock,' said Miss Prentice. 'Almost time for our little meeting. I asked them all for half-past five.'

She walked with small mimbling steps towards the cherrywood table which, Henry noticed, had been moved from the wall into the centre of the study. Miss Prentice began to place pencils and sheets of paper at intervals round the table. As she did this she produced, from between her thin closed lips, a deary flat humming which irritated Henry almost beyond endurance. More to stop this noise than because he wanted to know the answer, Henry asked:

'What meeting, Cousin Eleanor?'

'Have you forgotten, dear? The entertainment committee. The rector and Dinah, Dr Templett, Idris Campanula, and ourselves. We are counting on you. And on Dinah, of course.'

She uttered this last phrase with additional sweetness. Henry thought, 'She knows we've been talking about Dinah.' As she fiddled with her pieces of paper Henry watched her with that peculiar intensity that people sometimes lavish on a particularly loathed individual.

Eleanor Prentice was a thin, colourless woman of perhaps forty-nine years. She disseminated the odour of sanctity to an extent that Henry found intolerable. Her perpetual half-smile suggested that she was of a gentle and sweet disposition. This faint smile caused many people to overlook the strength of her face, and that was a mistake, for its strength was considerable. Miss Prentice was indeed a Jernigham. Henry suddenly thought that it was rather hard on Jocelyn that both his cousin and his son should look so much more like the family portraits than he did. Henry and Eleanor had each got the nose and jaw proper to the family. The squire had inherited his mother's round chin and indeterminate nose. Miss Prentice's prominent grey eyes stared coldly upon the world through rimless pince-nez. The squire's blue eyes, even when inspired by his frequent twists of ineffectual temper, looked vulnerable and slightly surprised. Henry, still watching her, thought it strange that he himself should resemble this woman whom he disliked so cordially. Without a taste in common, with violently opposed views on almost all ethical issues, and with a profound mutual distrust, they yet shared a certain hard determination which each recognized in the other. In Henry this quality was tempered by courtesy and by a generous mind. She was merely polite and long-suffering. It was typical of her that although she had evidently overheard Henry's angry reiteration of her name, she accepted his silence and did not ask again why he had called her. Probably, he thought, because she had stood outside the door listening. She now began to pull forward the chairs.

'I think we must give the rector your arm-chair, Jocelyn,' she said. 'Henry, dear, would you mind? It's rather heavy.'

Henry and Jocelyn helped her with the chair and, at her instruction, threw more logs of wood on the fire. These arrangements completed, Miss Prentice settled herself at the table.

'I think your study is almost my favourite corner of Pen Cuckoo, Jocelyn,' she said brightly.

The squire muttered something, and Henry said, 'But you are very fond of every corner of the house, aren't you, Cousin Eleanor?'

'Yes,' she said softly. 'Ever since my childhood days when I used to spend my holidays here (you remember, Jocelyn?) I've loved the dear old home.'

'Estate agents,' Henry said, 'have cast a permanent opprobrium on the word "home." It has come to mean nothing. It is a pity that when I marry, Cousin Eleanor, I shall not be able to take my wife to Winton. I can't afford to mend the roof, you know.'

Jocelyn cleared his throat, darted an angry glance at his son, and returned to the window.

'Winton is the dower-house, of course,' murmured Miss Prentice.

'As you already know,' Henry continued, 'I have begun to pay my addresses to Dinah Copeland. From what you overheard at the rectory do you think it likely that she will accept me?'

He saw her eyes narrow but she smiled a little more widely, showing her prominent and unlovely teeth. 'She's like a French caricature of an English spinster,' thought Henry.

'I'm quite sure, dear,' said Miss Prentice, 'that you do not think I willingly overheard your little talk with Dinah. Far from it. It was very distressing when I caught the few words that – '

'That you repeated to Father? I'm sure you were.'

'I thought it my duty to speak to your father, Henry.'

'Why?'

'Because I think, dear, that you two young people are in need of a little wise guidance.'

'Do you like Dinah?' asked Henry abruptly.

'She has many excellent qualities, I am sure,' said Miss Prentice.

'I asked you if you liked her, Cousin Eleanor.'

'I like her for those qualities. I am afraid, dear, that I think it better not to go any further just at the moment.'

'I agree,' said Jocelyn from the window. 'Henry, I won't have any more of this. These people will be here in a moment. There's the rectory car, now, coming round Cloudyfold bend. There'll be here in five minutes. You'd better tell us what it's all about, Eleanor.'

Miss Prentice seated herself at the foot of the table. 'It's the YPFC,' she said. 'We badly want funds and the rector suggested that perhaps we might get up a little play. You remember, Jocelyn. It was the night we dined there.'

'I remember something about it,' said the squire.

'Just among ourselves,' continued Miss Prentice, 'I know you've always loved acting, Jocelyn, and you're so good at it. So natural. Do you remember *Ici on Parle Français* in the old days? I've talked it all over with the rector and he agrees it's a splendid idea. Dr Templett is *very* good at theatricals, especially in funny parts, and dear Idris Campanula, of course, is all enthusiasm.'

'Good Lord!' ejaculated Henry and his father together.

'What on earth is *she* going to do in the play?' asked Jocelyn.

'Now, Jocelyn, we mustn't be uncharitable,' said Miss Prentice, with a cold glint of satisfaction in her eye. 'I dare say poor Idris would make quite a success of a small part.'

'I'm too old,' said Jocelyn.

'What nonsense, dear. Of course you're not. We'll find something that suits you.'

'I'm damned if I'll make love to the Campanula,' said the squire ungallantly. Eleanor assumed her usual expression for the reception of bad language, but it was coloured by that glint of complacency.

'Please, Jocelyn,' she said.

'What's Dinah going to do?' asked Henry.

'Well, as dear Dinah is almost a professional – '

'She *is* a professional,' said Henry.

'Such a pity, yes,' said Miss Prentice.

'Why?'

'I'm old-fashioned enough to think that the stage is not a very nice profession for a gentlewoman, Henry. But of course Dinah must act in our little piece. If she isn't too grand for such humble efforts.'

Henry opened his mouth and shut it again. The squire said, 'Here they are.'

There was the sound of a car pulling up on the gravel drive outside, and two cheerful toots on an out-of-date klaxon.

'I'll go and bring them in,' offered Henry.

III

Henry went out through the hall. When he opened the great front door the upland air laid its cold hand on his face. He smelt frost, dank earth, and dead leaves. The light from the house showed him three figures climbing out of a small car. The rector, his daughter Dinah, and a tall woman in a shapeless fur coat – Idris Campanula. Henry produced the right welcoming noises and ushered them into the house. Taylor, the butler, appeared, and laid expert hands on the rector's shabby overcoat. Henry, his eyes on Dinah, dealt with Miss Campanula's furs. The hall rang with Miss Campanula's conversation. She was a large arrogant spinster with a firm bust, a high-coloured complexion, coarse grey hair, and enormous bony hands. Her clothes were hideous but expensive, for Miss Campanula was extremely wealthy. She was supposed to be Eleanor Prentice's great friend. Their alliance was based on mutual antipathies and interests. Each adored scandal and each cloaked her passion in a mantle of conscious rectitude. Neither trusted the other an inch, but there was no doubt that they enjoyed each other's company. In conversation their technique varied widely. Eleanor never relinquished her air of charity and when she struck, the blow always fell obliquely. But Idris was one of those women who pride themselves on their outspokenness. Repeatedly did she announce that she was a downright sort of person. She was particularly fond of saying that she called a spade a spade, and in her more daring moments would add that her cousin, General Campanula, had once told her that she went further than that and called it a 'B shovel.' She cultivated an air of bluff forthrightness that should have deceived nobody, but actually passed as true currency among the simpler of her acquaintances. The truth was that she reserved to her self the right of broad speech, but would have been livid with rage if anybody had replied in kind.

The rector, a widower whose classic handsomeness made him the prey of such women, was, so Dinah had told Henry, secretly terrified of both these ladies who loomed so large in parochial affairs. Eleanor Prentice had a sort of coy bedside manner with the rector. She spoke to him in a dove-smooth voice and frequently uttered little musical laughs. Idris Campanula was bluff and proprietary, called him 'my dear man' and watched him with an intensity that made him blink, and aroused in his daughter a conflicting fury of disgust and compassion.

Henry laid aside the fur coat and hurried to Dinah. He had known Dinah all his life, but while he was at Oxford and later, when he did a course with a volunteer air-reserve unit, he had seen little of her. When he returned to Pen Cuckoo, Dinah had finished her dramatic course, and had managed to get into the tail end of a small repertory company where she remained for six weeks. The small repertory company then fell to pieces and Dinah returned home, an actress. Three weeks ago he had met her unexpectedly on the hills above Cloudyfold, and with that encounter came love. He had felt as if he saw her for the first time. The bewildered rapture of discovery was still upon him. To meet her gaze, to speak to her, to stand near her, launched him upon a flood of bliss. His sleep was tinged with the colour of his love and when he woke he found her already waiting in his thoughts. 'She is my whole desire,' he said to himself. And, because he was not quite certain that she loved him in return, he had been afraid to declare himself until yesterday, in the shabby, charming old drawing-room at the rectory, when Dinah had looked so transparently into his eyes that he began to speak of love. And then, through the open door, he had seen Eleanor, a still figure, in the dark hall beyond. Dinah saw Eleanor a moment later and, without a word to Henry, went out and welcomed her. Henry himself had rushed out of the rectory and driven home to Pen Cuckoo in a white rage. He had not spoken to Dinah since then, and now he looked anxiously at her. Her wide eyes smiled at him.

'Dinah?'

'Henry?'

'When can I see you?'

'You see me now,' said Dinah.

'Alone. Please?'

'I don't know. Is anything wrong?'

'Eleanor.'

'Oh, Lord!' said Dinah.

'I must talk to you. Above Cloudyfold where we met that morning? Tomorrow, before breakfast. Dinah, will you?'

'All right,' said Dinah. 'If I can.'

Idris Campanula's conversation flowed in upon their consciousness. Henry was suddenly aware that she had asked him some sort of question.

'I'm so sorry,' he began. 'I'm afraid I – '

'Now, Henry,' she interrupted, 'where are we to go? You're forgetting your duties, gossiping there with Dinah.' And she laughed her loud rocketing bray.

'The study, please,' said Henry. 'Will you lead the way?'

She marched into the study, shook hands with Jocelyn and exchanged pecks with Eleanor Prentice.

'Where's Dr Templett?' she asked.

'He hasn't arrived yet,' answered Miss Prentice. 'We must always make allowances for our medical men, mustn't we?'

'He's up beyond Cloudyfold,' said the rector. 'Old Mrs Thrinne is much worse. The third Cain boy has managed to run a nail through his big toe. I met Templett in the village and he told me. He said I was to ask you not to wait.'

'Beyond Cloudyfold?' asked Miss Prentice sweetly. Henry saw her exchange a glance with Miss Campanula.

'Mrs Ross doesn't have tea till five,' said Miss Campanula, 'which I consider a silly ostentation. We certainly will *not* wait for Dr Templett. Ha!'

'Templett didn't say anything about going to Mrs Ross's,' said the rector, innocently, 'though to be sure it is on his way.'

'My dear good man,' said Miss Campanula, 'if you weren't a saint – however! I only hope he doesn't try and get her into our play.'

'Idris dear,' said Miss Prentice. 'May I?'

She collected their attention and then said very quietly:

'I think we are all agreed, aren't we, that this little experiment is to be just among ourselves? I have got several little plays here for five and six people and I fancy Dinah has found some too.'

'Six,' said Miss Campanula very firmly. 'Five characters won't do, Eleanor. We've three ladies and three men. And if the rector – '

'No,' said the rector, 'I shall not appear. If there's any help I can give behind the scenes, I shall be only too delighted, but I really don't want to appear.'

'Three ladies and three men, then,' said Miss Campanula. 'Six.'

'Certainly no more,' said Miss Prentice.

'Well,' said the squire, 'if Mrs Ross is very good at acting, and I must say she's an uncommonly attractive little thing – '

'No, Jocelyn,' said Miss Prentice.

'She is very attractive,' said Henry.

'She's got a good figure,' said Dinah. 'Has she had any experience?'

'My dear child,' said Miss Campanula loudly, 'she's as common as dirt and we certainly don't want her. I may say that I myself have seen Eleanor's plays and I fully approve of *Simple Susan*. There are six characters: three men and three ladies. There is no change of scene, and the theme is suitable.'

'It's rather old,' said Dinah dubiously.

'My dear child,' repeated Miss Campanula, 'if you think we're going to do one of your modern questionable problem-plays you're very greatly mistaken.'

'I think some of the modern pieces are really *not* quite suitable,' agreed Miss Prentice gently.

Henry and Dinah smiled.

'And as for Miss Selia Ross,' said Miss Campanula, 'I believe in calling a spade a spade and I have no hesitation in saying I think we'll be doing a Christian service to poor Mrs Templett, who we all know is too much an invalid to look after herself, if we give Dr Templett something to think about besides – '

'Come,' said the rector desperately, 'aren't we jumping our fences before we meet them? We haven't appointed a chairman yet and so far nobody has suggested that Mrs Ross be asked to take part.'

'They'd better not,' said Miss Campanula.

The door was thrown open by Taylor, who announced:

'Mrs Ross and Dr Templett, sir.'

'What!' exclaimed the squire involuntarily.

An extremely well-dressed woman and a short rubicund man walked into the room.

'Hullo! Hullo!' shouted Dr Templett. 'I've brought Mrs Ross along by sheer force. She's a perfectly magnificent actress and I tell her she's got to come off her high horse and show us all how to set about it. I know you'll be delighted.'

CHAPTER 2

Six Parts and Seven Actors

It was Henry who rescued the situation when it was on the verge of becoming a scene. Neither Miss Campanula nor Miss Prentice made the slightest attempt at cordiality. The squire uttered incoherent noises, shouted 'What!' and broke out into uncomfortable social laughter. Dinah greeted Mrs Ross with nervous civility. The rector blinked and followed his daughter's example. But on Henry the presence of Dinah acted like a particularly strong stimulant and filled him with a vague desire to be nice to the entire population of the world. He shook Mrs Ross warmly by the hand, complimented Dr Templett on his side, and suggested, with a beaming smile, that they should at once elect a chairman and decide on a play.

The squire, Dinah, and the rector confusedly supported Henry. Miss Campanula gave a ringing sniff. Miss Prentice, smiling a little more widely than usual, said:

'I'm afraid we are short of one chair. We expected to be only seven. Henry dear, you will have to get one from the dining-room. I'm so sorry to bother you.'

'I'll share Dinah's chair,' said Henry happily.

'Please don't get one for me,' said Mrs Ross. 'Billy can perch on my arm.'

She settled herself composedly in a chair on the rector's left and Dr Templett at once sat on the arm. Miss Prentice had already made sure of her place on the rector's right hand and Miss Campanula, defeated, uttered a short laugh and marched to the far end of the table.

'I don't know whether this is where I am bidden, Eleanor,' she said, 'but the meeting seems to be delightfully informal, so this is where I shall sit. Ha!'

Henry, his father, and Dinah took the remaining chairs.

From the old chandelier a strong light was cast down on the eight faces round the table; on the squire, pink with embarrassment; on Miss Prentice, smiling; on Miss Campanula, like an angry mare, breathing hard through her nostrils; on Henry's dark Jernigham features; on Dinah's crisp and vivid beauty; on the rector's coin-sharp priestliness and on Dr Templett's hearty undistinguished normality. It shone on Selia Ross. She was a straw-coloured woman of perhaps thirty-eight. She was not beautiful but she was exquisitely neat. Her hair curved back from her forehead in pale waves. The thick white skin of her face was beautifully made-up and her clothes were admirable. There was a kind of sharpness about her so that she nearly looked haggard. Her eyes were pale and you would have guessed that the lashes were white when left to themselves. Almost every human being bears some sort of resemblance to an animal and Mrs Ross was a little like a ferret. But for all that she had a quality that arrested the attention of many woman and most men. She had a trick of widening her eyes, and looking slant ways. Though she gave the impression of fineness she was in reality so determined that any sensibilities she possessed were held in the vice of her will. She was a coarse-grained woman but she seemed fragile. Her manner was gay and good natured, but though she went out of her way to do kindnesses, her tongue was quietly malicious. It was clear to all women who met her that her chief interest was men. Dinah watched her now and could not help admiring the cool assurance with which she met her frigid reception. It was impossible to guess whether Mrs Ross was determined not to show her hurts or was merely so insensitive that she felt none. 'She *has* got a cheek,' thought Dinah. She looked at Henry and saw her own thoughts reflected in his face. Henry's rather startlingly fierce eyes were fixed on Mrs Ross and in them Dinah read both awareness and appraisal. He turned his head, met Dinah's glance, and at once his expression changed into one of such vivid tenderness that her heart turned over. She was drowned in a wave of emotion and was brought back to the world by the sound of Miss Prentice's voice.

'– to elect a chairman for our little meeting. I should like to propose the rector.'

'Second that,' said Miss Campanula, in her deepest voice.

'There you are, Copeland,' said the squire, 'everybody says "Aye"
and away we go.' He laughed loudly and cast a terrified glance at his
cousin.

The rector looked amiably round the table. With the exception of
Henry, of all the company he seemed the least embarrassed by the
arrival of Mrs Ross. If Mr Copeland had been given a round gentle
face with unremarkable features and kind shortsighted eyes it would
have been a perfect expression of his temperament. But ironical
nature had made him magnificently with a head so beautiful that to
most observers it seemed that his character must also be on a grand
scale. With that head he might have gone far and become an important dignitary of the church, but he was unambitious and sincere,
and he loved Pen Cuckoo. He was quite content to live at the rectory as his forebears had lived, to deal with parish affairs, to give what
spiritual and bodily comfort he could to his people, and to fend off
the advances of Idris Campanula and Eleanor Prentice. He knew
very well that both these ladies bitterly resented the presence of Mrs
Ross, and that he was in for one of those hideously boring situations
when he felt exactly as if he was holding down with his thumb the
cork of a bottle filled with seething ginger-pop.

He said, 'Thank you very much. I don't feel that my duties as
chairman will be very heavy as we have only met to settle the date
and nature of this entertainment, and when that is decided all I shall
have to do is to hand everything over to the kind people who take
part. Perhaps I should explain a little about the object we have in
mind. The Young People's Friendly Circle, which has done such
splendid work in Pen Cuckoo and the neighbouring parishes, is
badly in need of funds. Miss Prentice as president and Miss
Campanula as secretary, will tell you all about that. What we want
more than anything else is a new piano. The present instrument was
given by your father, wasn't it, squire?'

'Yes,' said Jocelyn. 'I remember quite well. It was when I was about
twelve. It wasn't new then. I can imagine it's pretty well a dead horse.'

'We had a tuner up from Great Chipping,' said Miss Campanula,
'and he says he can't do anything more with it. I blame the scouts.

Ever since the eldest Cain boy was made scout master they have gone from bad to worse. He's got no idea of discipline, that young man. On Saturday I found Georgie Biggins trampling up and down the keyboard in his boots and whanging the wires inside with the end of his pole. "If I were your scout-master," I said, "I'd give you a beating that you'd not forget in a twelvemonth." His reply was grossly impertinent. I told the eldest Cain that if he couldn't control his boys himself he'd better hand them over to someone who could.'

'Dear me, yes,' said the rector hurriedly. 'Young barbarians they are sometimes. Well now, the piano is of course not the sole property of the YPFC. It was a gift to the parish. But I have suggested that, as they use it a great deal, perhaps it would be well to devote whatever funds result from this entertainment to a piano fund, rather than to a general YPFC fund. I don't know what you all think about this.'

'How much would a new piano cost?' asked Dr Templett.

'There's a very good instrument at Preece's in Great Chipping,' said the rector. 'The price is £50.'

'We can't hope to make that at our show, can we?' asked Dinah.

'I tell you what,' said the squire. 'I'll make up the difference. The piano seems to be a Pen Cuckoo affair.'

There was a general gratified murmur.

'Damned good of you squire,' said Dr Templett. 'Very generous.'

'Very good indeed,' agreed the rector.

Miss Prentice, without moving, seemed to preen herself. Henry saw Miss Campanula look at her friend and was startled by the singularly venomous glint in her eye. He thought, 'She's jealous of Eleanor taking reflected glory from Father's offer.' And suddenly he was appalled by the thought of these two ageing women united in so profound a dissonance.

'Perhaps,' said the rector, 'we had better have a formal motion.'

They had a formal motion. The rector hurried them on. A date was fixed three weeks ahead for the performance in the parish hall. Miss Prentice who seemed to have become a secretary by virtue of her seat on the rector's right hand, made quantities of notes. And all the time each of these eight people knew very well that they merely moved in a circle round the true matter of their meeting. What Miss Prentice called 'the nature of our little entertainment' had yet to be determined. Every now and then someone would steal a covert glance at the small pile of modern plays in front of Dinah and the larger pile of elderly French's acting editions in front of Miss Prentice. And while they discussed prices of admission, and dates, through each of their minds raced their secret thoughts.

II

The rector thought, 'I cannot believe it of Templett. A medical man with an invalid wife! Besides, there's his professional position. But what persuaded him to bring her here? He must have known how they would talk. I wish Miss Campanula wouldn't look at me like that. She wants to see me alone again. I wish I'd never said confession was recognized by the church, but how could I not? I wish she wouldn't confess. I wish that I didn't get the impression that she and Miss Prentice merely use the confessional as a means of informing against each other. Six parts and seven people. Oh, dear!'

The squire thought, 'Eleanor's quite right, I was good in *Ici on Parle Française*. Funny how some people take to the stage naturally. Now, if Dinah and Henry try to suggest one of those modern things, as likely as not there will be nothing that suits me. What I'd like is one of those charming not-so-young men in a Marie Tempest comedy. Mrs Ross could play the Marie Tempest part. Eleanor and old Idris wouldn't have that at any price. I wonder if it's true that they don't really kiss on the stage because of the grease paint. Still, at rehearsals . . . I wonder if it's true about Templett and Mrs Ross. I'm as young as ever I was. What the devil am I going to do about Henry and Dinah Copeland? Dinah's a pretty girl. Hard, though. Modern. If only the Copelands were a bit better off it wouldn't matter. I suppose they'll talk about me, both of them. Henry will say something clever. Blast and damn Eleanor! Why the devil couldn't she hold her tongue, and then I shouldn't have had to deal with it. Six parts and seven people. Why shouldn't she be in it, After all? I suppose Templett would want the charming not-so-young part and they'd turn me into some bloody comic old dodderer.'

Eleanor Prentice thought, 'If I take care and manage this well it will look as if it's Idris who is making all the trouble and he will think her uncharitable. Six parts and seven people. Idris is determined to stop that Ross woman at all costs. I can see one of Idris's tantrums coming. That's all to the good. I shall be forty-nine next month. Idris is more than forty-nine. Dinah should work in the parish. I wonder what goes on among actors and actresses. Dressing and undressing behind the scenes and travelling about together. If I could find out that Dinah had – If I married, Jocelyn would make me an allowance. To see that woman look at Templett like that and he at her! Dinah and Henry! I can't bear it. I can't endure it. Never show you're hurt. I want to look at him, but I mustn't. Henry might be watching. Henry knows. A parish priest should be married. His head is like an angel's head. No. Not an angel's. A Greek God. Prostrate before Thy throne to lie and gaze and gaze on thee. Oh, God, let him love me!'

Henry thought, 'Tomorrow morning if it's fine I shall meet Dinah above Cloudyfold and tell her that I love her. Why shouldn't Templett have his Selia Ross in the play? Six parts and seven people to the devil! Let's find a new play. I'm in love for the first time. I've crossed the border into a strange country and never again will there be a moment quite like this. Tomorrow morning, if it's fine, Dinah and I will be up on Cloudyfold.'

Dinah thought, 'Tomorrow morning, if it's fine, Henry will be waiting for me above Cloudyfold and I think he will tell me he loves me. There will be nobody in the whole wide world but Henry and me.'

Templett thought, 'I'll have to be careful. I suppose I was a fool to suggest her coming, but after she said she was so keen on acting it seemed the only thing to do. If those two starved spinsters get their teeth into us it'll be all up with the practice. I wish to God I was made differently. I wish to God my wife wasn't what she is. Perhaps it'd be all the same if she wasn't. Selia's got me. It's like an infection. I'm eaten up with it.'

Selia Ross thought, 'So far so good. I've got here. I can manage the squire easily enough, but he's got his eye on me already. The boy's in love with the girl, but he's a man and I think he'll be generous. He's no fool, though, and I rather fancy he's summed me up. Attractive, with those light grey eyes and black lashes. It might be amusing to take him from her. I doubt if I could. He's past the age when they fall for women a good deal older than themselves. I feel equal to the whole of them. It was fun coming in with Billy and seeing those two frost-bitten old virgins with their eyes popping out of their heads. They know I'm too much for them with my good common streak of hard sense and determination. They're both trying to see if Billy's arm is touching my shoulders. The Campanula is staring quite openly and the Poor Relation's looking out of the corner of her eyes. I'll lean back a little. There! Now have a good look. It's a bore about Billy's professional reputation and having to be so careful. I want like hell to show them he's all mine. I've never felt like this about any other man, never. It's as if we'd engulfed each other. I suppose it's love. I won't have him in their bogus school-room play without me. He might have a love scene with the girl. I couldn't stand that. Seven people and six parts. Now, then!'

And Idris Campanula thought, 'If I could in decency lay my hands on that straw-coloured wanton I'd shake the very life out of her. The infamous brazen effrontery! To force her way into Pen Cuckoo, without an invitation, under the protection of that man! I always suspected Dr Templett of that sort of thing. If Eleanor had the gumption of a rabbit she'd have forbidden them the house. Sitting on the arm of her chair! A fine excuse! He's practically got his arm round her. I'll look straight at them and let her see what I think of her. There! She's smiling. She knows, and she doesn't care. It amounts to lying in open sin with him. The rector *can't* let it pass. It's an open insult to me, making me sit at the same table with them. Every hand against me. I've no friends. They only want my money. Eleanor's as bad as the rest. She's tried to poison the rector's mind against me. She's jealous of me. The play was *my* idea and now she's talking as if it was hers. The rector must be warned. I'll ask him to hear my confession on Friday. I'll confess the unkind thoughts I've had of Eleanor Prentice and before he can stop me I'll tell him what they were and then perhaps he'll begin to see through Eleanor. Then I'll say I've been uncharitable about Mrs Ross and Dr Templett. I'll say I'm an outspoken woman and believe in looking facts in the face. He *must* prefer me to Eleanor. I ought to have married. With my ability and my money and my brains I'd make a success of it. I'd do the Rectory up and get rid of that impertinent old maid. Dinah could go back to the stage as soon as she liked, or if Eleanor's gossip is true, she could marry Henry Jernigham. Eleanor wouldn't care much for that. She'll fight tooth and nail before she sees another chatelaine at

Pen Cuckoo. I'll back Eleanor up as far as Dr Templett and his common little light-of-love are concerned, but if she tries to come
between me and Walter Copeland she'll regret it. Now then, I'll
speak.'

And bringing her large, ugly hand down sharply on the table she
said:

'May I have a word?'

'Please do,' said Mr Copeland nervously.

'As secretary,' began Miss Campanula loudly, 'I have discussed
this matter with the YPFC members individually. They plan an
entertainment of their own later on in the year and they are *most*
anxious that this little affair should be arranged *entirely* by ourselves.
Just five or six, they said, of the people who are really interested in
the Circle. They mentioned you, of course, rector, and the squire, as
patron, and you, Eleanor, naturally, as president. They said they
hoped Dinah would not feel that our humble efforts were beneath
her dignity and that she would grace our little performance. And
you, Henry, they particularly mentioned you.'

'Thank you,' said Henry solemnly. Miss Campanula darted a suspicious glance at him and went on:

'They seem to think they'd like to see me making an exhibition of
myself with all the rest of you. Of course, I don't pretend to histrionic talent – '

'Of *course* you must have a part, Idris,' said Miss Prentice. 'We
depend upon you.'

'Thank you, Eleanor,' said Miss Campanula; and between the two
ladies there flashed the signal of an alliance.

'That makes five, doesn't it?' asked Miss Prentice sweetly.

'Five,' said Miss Campanula.

'Six, with Dr Templett,' said Henry.

'We should be very glad to have Dr Templett,' rejoined Miss
Prentice, with so cunningly balanced an inflection that her rejection
of Mrs Ross was implicit in every syllable.

'Well, a GP's an awkward sort of fellow when it comes to
rehearsals,' said Dr Templett. 'Never know when an urgent case may
crop up. Still, if you don't mind risking it I'd like to take part.'

'We'll certainly risk it,' said the rector. There was a murmur of
assent followed by a deadly little silence. The rector drew in his

breath, looked at his daughter who gave him a heartening nod, and said:

'Now, before we go any further with the number of performers, I think we should decide on the form of the entertainment. If it is going to be a play, so much will depend upon the piece chosen. Has anybody any suggestion?'

'I move,' said Miss Campanula, 'that we do a play, and I suggest *Simple Susan* as a suitable piece.'

'I should like to second that,' said Miss Prentice.

'What sort of play is it?' asked Dr Templett. 'I haven't heard of it. Is it new?'

'It's a contemporary of *East Lynne* and *The Silver King* I should think,' said Dinah.

Henry and Dr Templett laughed. Miss Campanula thrust out her bosom, turned scarlet in the face, and said:

'In my humble opinion, Dinah, it is none the worse for that.'

'It's so amusing,' said Miss Prentice. 'You remember it, Jocelyn, don't you? There's that little bit where Lord Sylvester pretends to be his own tailor and proposes to Lady Maude, thinking she's her own lady's maid. Such an original notion and so ludicrous.'

'It has thrown generations of audiences into convulsions,' agreed Henry.

'Henry,' said the squire.

'Sorry, Father. But honestly, as a dramatic device – '

'*Simple Susan*,' said Miss Campanula hotly, 'may be old-fashioned in the sense that it contains no disgusting innuendos. It does not depend on vulgarity for its fun, and that's more than can be said for most of your modern comedies.'

'How far does Lord Sylvester go – ' began Dinah.

'Dinah!' said the rector quietly.

'All right, Daddy. Sorry. I only – '

'How old is Lord Sylvester?' interrupted the squire suddenly.

'Oh, about forty-five or fifty,' murmured Miss Prentice.

'Why not do *The Private Secretary*?' inquired Henry.

'I never thought *The Private Secretary* was a very nice play,' said Miss Prentice. 'I expect I'm prejudiced.' And she gave the rector a reverent smile.

'I agree,' said Miss Campanula. 'I always thought it in the worst of taste. I may be old fashioned but I don't like jokes about the cloth.'

'I don't think *The Private Secretary* ever did us much harm,' said the rector mildly. 'But aren't we wandering from the point? Miss Campanula has moved that we do a play called *Simple Susan*. Miss Prentice has seconded her. Has anybody else a suggestion to make?'

'Yes,' said Selia Ross, 'I have.'

CHAPTER 3

They Choose a Play

If Mrs Ross had taken a ticking bomb from her handbag and placed it on the table, the effect could have been scarcely more devastating. What she did produce was a small green book. Seven pairs of eyes followed the movements of her thin scarlet-tipped hands. Seven pairs of eyes fastened, as if mesmerized, on the black letters of the book cover. Mrs Ross folded her hands over the book and addressed the meeting.

'I do hope you'll all forgive me for making my suggestion,' she said, 'but it's the result of a rather odd coincidence. I'd no idea of your meeting until Dr Templett called in this afternoon, but I happened to be reading this play and when he appeared the first thing I said was, "Some time or other we simply *must* do this thing," Didn't I, Billy? I mean, it's absolutely marvellous. All the time I was reading it I kept thinking how perfect it would be for some of you to do it in aid of one of the local charities. There are two parts in it that would be simply ideal for Miss Prentice and Miss Campanula. The Duchess and her sister. The scene they have with General Talbot is one of the best in the play. It simply couldn't be funnier and you'd be magnificent as the General, Mr Jernigham.'

She paused composedly and looked sideways at the squire. Nobody spoke, though Miss Campanula wetted her lips. Selia Ross waited for a moment, smiling frankly, and then she said:

'Of course, I didn't realize you had already chosen a play. Naturally I wouldn't have dreamt of coming if I had known. It's all this man's fault.' She gave Dr Templett a sort of a comradely jog with her elbow. 'He bullied me into it. I ought to have apologized and crept away at once, but I just couldn't resist telling you about my discovery.' She opened her eyes a little wider and turned them on the rector. 'Perhaps if I left it with you, Mr Copeland, the committee might just like to glance at it before they quite decide. *Please* don't think I want a part in it or anything frightful like that. It's just that it *is* so good and I'd be delighted to lend it.'

'That's very kind of you,' said the rector.

'It's not a bit kind. I'm being thoroughly selfish. I just long to see you all doing it and I'm secretly hoping you won't be able to resist it. It's so difficult to find modern plays that aren't offensive,' continued Mrs Ross, with an air of great frankness, 'but this really is charming.'

'But what is the play?' asked Henry, who had been craning his neck in a useless attempt to read the title.

'*Shop Windows*, by Jacob Hunt.'

'Good Lord!' ejaculated Dinah. 'Of course! I never thought of it. It's the very thing.'

'Have you read it?' asked Mrs Ross, with a friendly glance at her.

'I saw the London production,' said Dinah. 'You're quite right, it would be grand. But what about the royalties? Hunt charges the earth for amateur rights, and anyway he'd probably refuse them to us.'

'I was coming to that,' said Mrs Ross. 'If you should decide to do it I'd like to stand the royalties if you'd let me.'

There was another silence, broken by the rector.

'Now, that's very generous indeed,' he said.

'No, honestly it's not. I've told you I'm longing to see it done.'

'How many characters are there?' asked the squire suddenly.

'Let me see, I think there are six.' She opened the play and counted prettily on her fingers.

'Five, six – no, there seem to be seven! Stupid of me.'

'Ha!' said Miss Campanula.

'But I'm sure you could find a seventh. What about the Moorton people?'

'What about you?' asked Dr Templett.

'No, no!' said Mrs Ross quickly. 'I don't come into the picture. Don't be silly.'

'It's a damn' good play,' said Henry. 'I saw the London show too, Dinah. D'you think we could do it?'

'I don't see why not. The situations would carry it through. The three character parts are really the stars.'

'Which are they?' demanded the squire.

'The General and the Duchess and her sister,' said Mrs Ross.

'They don't come on till the second act,' continued Dinah, 'but from then on they carry the show.'

'May I have a look at it?' asked the squire.

Mrs Ross opened the book and passed it across to him.

'Do read the opening of the act,' she said, 'and then go on to page forty-eight.'

'May I speak?' demanded Miss Campanula loudly.

'Please!' said the rector hurriedly. 'Please do. Ah – order!'

II

Miss Campanula gripped the edge of the table with her large hands and spoke at some length. She said that she didn't know how everybody else was feeling but that she herself was somewhat bewildered. She was surprised to learn that such eminent authorities as Dinah and Henry and Mrs Ross considered poor Pen Cuckoo capable of producing a modern play that met with their approval. She thought that perhaps this clever play might be a little too clever for poor Pen Cuckoo and the Young People's Friendly Circle. She asked the meeting if it did not think it would make a great mistake if it was overambitious. 'I must confess,' she said, with an angry laugh, 'that I had a much simpler plan in mind. I did not propose to fly as high as West End successes and I don't mind saying I think we would be in a fair way to making fools of ourselves. And that's that.'

'But, Miss Campanula,' objected Dinah, 'it's such a mistake to think that because the cast is not very experienced it will be better in a bad play than in a good one.'

'I'm sorry you think *Simple Susan* a bad play, Dinah,' said Miss Prentice sweetly.

'Well I think it's very dated and I'm afraid I think it's rather silly,' said Dinah doggedly.

Miss Prentice gave a silvery laugh in which Miss Campanula joined.

'I agree with Dinah,' said Henry quickly.

'Suppose we all read both plays,' suggested the rector.

'I have read *Shop Windows*,' said Dr Templett. 'I must say I don't see how we could do better.'

'We seem to be at a disadvantage, Eleanor,' said Miss Campanula unpleasantly, and Miss Prentice laughed again. So, astonishingly, did the squire. He broke out in a loud choking snort. They all turned to look at him. Tears coursed each other down his cheeks and he dabbed at them absentmindedly with the back of his hand. His shoulders quivered, his brows were raised in an ecstasy of merriment, and his cheeks were purple. He was lost in the second act of Mrs Ross's play.

'Oh! Lord!' he said, 'this is funny.'

'Jocelyn!' cried Miss Prentice.

'Eh?' said the squire, and he turned a page, read half-a-dozen lines, laid the book on the table and gave himself up to paroxysms of unbridled laughter.

'Jocelyn!' repeated Miss Prentice. 'Really!'

'What?' gasped the squire. 'Eh? All right, I'm quite willing. Damn' good! When do we begin?'

'Hi!' said Henry. 'Steady, Father! The meeting hasn't decided on the play.'

'Well, we'd better decide on this,' said the squire, and he leant towards Selia Ross. 'When he starts telling her he's got the garter,' he said, 'and she thinks he's talking about the other affair! And then when she says she won't take no for an answer. Oh, Lord!'

'It's heavenly, isn't it?' agreed Mrs Ross, and she and Henry and Dinah suddenly burst out laughing at the recollection of this scene, and for a minute or two they all reminded each other of the exquisite facetiæ in the second act of *Shop Windows*. The rector listened with a nervous smile; Miss Prentice and Miss Campanula with tightly-set lips. At last the squire looked round the table with brimming eyes and asked what they were all waiting for.

'I'll move we do *Shop Windows*,' he said. 'That in order?'

'I'll second it,' said Dr Templett.

'No doubt I am in error,' said Miss Campanula, 'but I was under the impression that my poor suggestion was before the meeting, seconded by Miss Prentice.'

The rector was obliged to put this motion to the meeting.

'It is moved by Miss Campanula,' he said unhappily, 'and seconded by Miss Prentice, that *Simple Susan* be the play chosen for the production. Those in favour – '

'Aye,' said Miss Campanula and Miss Prentice.

'And the contrary?'

'No,' said the rest of the meeting with perfect good humour.

'Thank you,' said Miss Campanula. '*Thank you*. Now we know where we are.'

'You wait till you start learning your parts in this thing,' said Jocelyn cheerfully, 'and you won't know whether you're on your head or your heels. There's an awful lot of us three, isn't there?' he continued, turning the pages. 'I suppose Eleanor will do the Duchess and Miss Campanula will be the other one – Mrs Thing or whoever she is! Gertrude! That the idea?'

'That was my idea,' said Mrs Ross.

'If I may be allowed to speak,' said Miss Campanula, 'I should like to say that it is just within the bounds of possibility that it may not be ours.'

'Perhaps, Jernigham,' said the rector, 'you had better put your motion.'

But of course the squire's motion was carried. Miss Campanula and Miss Prentice did not open their lips. Their thoughts were alike in confusion and intensity. Both seethed under the insult done to *Simple Susan*, each longed to rise and, with a few well-chosen words, withdraw from the meeting. Each was checked by a sensible reluctance to cut off her nose to spite her face. It was obvious that *Shop Windows* would be performed whether they stayed in or flounced out. Unless all the others were barefaced liars, it seemed that there were two outstandingly good parts ready for them to snap up. They hung off and on, ruffled their plumage, and secretly examined each other's face.

III

Meanwhile with the enthusiasm that all Jernighams brought to a new project Jocelyn and his son began to cast the play. Almost a century ago there had been what Eleanor, when cornered called an 'incident' in the family history. The Mrs Jernigham of that time was a plain silly woman and barren into the bargain. Her Jocelyn, the fourth of that name, had lived openly with a very beautiful and accomplished actress and had succeeded in getting the world to pretend that his son by her was his lawful scion, and had jockeyed his wife into bringing the boy up as her own. By this piece of effrontery he brought to Pen Cuckoo a dram of mummery, and ever since those days most of the Jernighams had had a passion for theatricals. It was as if the lovely actress had touched up the family portraits with a stick of rouge. Jocelyn and Henry had both played in the OUDS. They both had the trick of moving about a stage as if they grew out of the boards, and they both instinctively bridged that colossal gap between the stage and the front row of the stalls. Jocelyn thought himself a better actor than he was, but Henry did not realize how good he might be. Even Miss Prentice, a Jernigham, as the squire had pointed out, on her mother's side, had not escaped that dram of player's blood. Although she knew nothing about theatre, mistrusted and disliked the very notion of the stage as a career for gentle people, and had no sort of judgement for the merit of a play, yet in amateur theatricals she was surprisingly composed and perfectly audible, and she loved acting. She knew now that Idris Campanula expected her to refuse to take part in *Shop Windows*, and more than half her inclination was so to refuse. 'What,' she thought. 'To have my own play put aside for something chosen by that woman! To have to look on while they parcel out the parts!' But even as she pondered on the words with which she would offer her resignation, she pictured Lady Appleby of Moorton Grange accepting the part that Jocelyn said was so good. And what was more, the rector would think Eleanor herself uncharitable. That decided her. She waited for a pause in the chatter round Jocelyn, and then she turned to the rector.

'May I say just one little word?' she asked.

'Yes, yes, of course,' said Mr Copeland. 'Please, everybody. Order!'

'It's only this,' said Miss Prentice, avoiding the eye of Miss Campanula. 'I do hope nobody will think I am going to be disappointed or hurt about my little play. I expect it *is* rather out-of-date, and I am only too pleased to think that you have found one that is more suitable. If there is anything I can do to help, I shall be only too glad. Of course.'

She received, and revelled in, the rector's beaming smile, and met Idris Campanula's glare with a smile of her own. Then she saw Selia Ross watching her out of the corners of her eyes and suddenly she knew that Selia Ross understood her.

'That's perfectly splendid,' exclaimed Mr Copeland. 'I think it is no more than we expected of Miss Prentice's generosity, but we are none the less grateful.' And he added confusedly, 'A very graceful gesture.'

Miss Prentice preened and Miss Campanula glowered. The others, vaguely, aware that something was expected of them, made small appreciative noises.

'Now, how about casting the play?' said Dr Templett.

IV

There was no doubt that the play had been well chosen. With the exception of one character, it practically cast itself. The squire was to play the General; Miss Prentice, the Duchess; Miss Campanula, of whom everybody felt extremely frightened, was cast for Mrs Arbuthnot, a good character part. Miss Campanula, when offered this part, replied ambiguously:

'Who knows?' she looked darkly. 'Obviously, it is not for me to say.'

'But you will do it, Idris?' murmured Miss Prentice.

'I have but one comment,' rejoined Miss Campanula. 'Wait and see.' She laughed shortly, and the rector, in a hurry, wrote her name down opposite the part. Dinah and Henry were given the two young lovers, and Dr Templett said he would undertake the French Ambassador. He began to read some of the lines in violently broken English. There remained the part of Hélène, a mysterious lady who had lost her memory and who turned up in the middle of the first act at a country house-party.

'Obviously, Selia,' said Dr Templett, 'you must be Hélène.'

'No, *no*,' said Mrs Ross, 'that isn't a bit what I meant. Now do be quiet, Billy, or they'll think I came here with an ulterior motive.'

With the possible exception of the squire, that was precisely what they all did think, but not even Miss Campanula had the courage to say so. Having accepted Mrs Ross's play they could do nothing but offer her the part, which as far as lines went, was not a long one. Perhaps only Dinah realized quite how good Hélène was. Mrs Ross protested and demurred.

'If you are quite sure you want me,' she said, and looked sideways at the squire. Jocelyn, who had glanced through the play and found that the General had a love scene with Hélène, said heartily that they wanted her very much indeed. Henry and Dinah, conscious of their own love-scenes, agreed, and the rector formally asked Mrs Ross if she would take the part. She accepted with the prettiest air in the world. Miss Prentice managed to maintain her gentle smile and Miss Campanula's behaviour merely became a degree more darkly ominous. The rector put on his glasses and read his notes.

'To sum up,' he said loudly. 'We propose to do this play in the Parish Hall on Saturday 27th. Three weeks from tonight. The proceeds are to be devoted to the piano-fund and the balance of the sum needed will be made up most generously by Mr Jocelyn Jernigham. The Committee and members of the YPFC will organize the sale of tickets and will make themselves responsible for the – what is the correct expression, Dinah?'

'The front of the house, Daddy.'

'For the front of the house, yes. Do you think we can leave these affairs to your young folks, Miss Campanula? I know you can answer for them.'

'My dear man,' said Miss Campanula, 'I can't answer for the behaviour of thirty village louts and maidens, but they usually do what I tell them to. Ha!'

Everybody laughed sycophantically.

'My *friend*,' added Miss Campanula, with a ghastly smile, 'my *friend* Miss Prentice is president. No doubt, if they pay no attention to me, they will do anything in the world for her.'

'Dear Idris!' murmured Miss Prentice.

'Who's going to produce the play?' asked Henry. 'I think Dinah ought. She's a professional.'

'Hear, hear!' said Dr Templett, Selia Ross and the squire. Miss Prentice added rather a tepid little, 'Of course, yes.' Miss Campanula said nothing. Dinah grinned shyly and looked into her lap. She was elected producer. Dinah had not passed the early stages of theatrical experience when the tyro lards his conversation with professional phrases. She accepted her honours with an air of great seriousness and called her first rehearsal for Tuesday night, November 9th.

'I'll get all your sides typed by then,' she explained. 'I'm sure Gladys Wright will do them, because she's learning and wants experience. I'll give her a proper part so that she gets the cues right. We'll have a reading and if there's time I'll set positions for the first act.'

'Dear me,' said Miss Prentice, 'sounds very alarming. I'm afraid, Dinah dear, that you will find us all very amateurish.'

'Oh, no!' cried Dinah gaily. 'I know it's going to be marvellous.' She looked uncertainly at her father and added, 'I should like to say, thank you all very much for asking me to produce. I do hope I'll manage it all right.'

'Well, you know a dashed sight more about it than any of us,' said Selia Ross bluntly.

But somehow Dinah didn't quite want Mrs Ross so frankly on her side. She was aware in herself of a strong antagonism to Mrs Ross and this discovery surprised and confused her, because she believed herself to be a rebel. As a rebel, she should have applauded Selia Ross. To Dinah, Miss Prentice and Miss Campanula were the hated symbols of all that was mean, stupid, and antediluvian. Selia Ross had deliberately given battle to these two ladies and had won the first round. Why, then, could Dinah not welcome her as an ally after her own heart? She supposed it was because, in her own heart, she mistrusted and disliked Mrs Ross. This feeling was entirely instinctive and it upset and bewildered her. It was as if some dictator in her blood refused an allegiance that she should have welcomed. She could not reply with the correct comradely smile. She felt her face turning pink with embarrassment and she said hurriedly:

'What about music? We'll want an overture and an entr'acte.'

And with those words Dinah unconsciously rang up the curtain on a theme that was to engulf Pen Cuckoo and turn *Shop Windows* from polite comedy into outlandish, shameless melodrama.

CHAPTER 4

Cue for Music

As soon as Dinah had spoken those fatal words everybody round the table in the study at Pen Cuckoo thought of 'Rachmaninoff's Prelude in C sharp Minor,' and with the exception of Miss Campanula, everybody's heart sank into his or her boots. For the Prelude was Miss Campanula's speciality. In Pen Cuckoo she had the sole rights in this composition. She played it at all church concerts, she played it on her own piano after her own dinner parties, and, unless her hostess was particularly courageous, she played it after other people's dinner parties, too. Whenever there was any question of music sounding at Pen Cuckoo, Miss Campanula offered her services, and the three pretentious chords would boom out once again: 'Pom, *Pom,* POM.' And then down would go Miss Campanula's foot on the left pedal and the next passage would follow in a series of woolly but determined jerks. She even played it as a voluntary when Mr Withers, the organist, went on his holidays and Miss Campanula took his place. She had had her photograph taken, seated at the instrument, with the Prelude on the rack. Each of her friends had received a copy at Christmas. The rector's was framed, and he had not known quite what to do with it. Until three years ago when Eleanor Prentice had come to live at Pen Cuckoo, Idris Campanula and her Prelude had had it all their own way. But Miss Prentice also belonged to a generation when girls learnt the pianoforte from their governesses, and she, too, liked to be expected to perform. Her *pièce de résistance* was Ethelbert Nevin's 'Venetian Suite', which she rendered with muffled insecurity, the chords of the accompaniment never quite synchronizing with the saccharine notes of the melody. Between the two ladies the battle had raged at parish entertainments, Sunday School services, and private parties. They only united in deploring the radio and in falsely pretending that music was a bond between them.

So that when Dinah in her flurry asked, 'What about music?' Miss Campanula and Miss Prentice both became alert.

Miss Prentice said, 'Yes, of course. Now, couldn't we manage that amongst ourselves somehow? It's *so* much pleasanter, isn't it, if we keep to our own small circle?'

'I'm afraid my poor wits are rather confused,' began Miss Campanula. 'Everything seems to have been decided out of hand. You must correct me if I'm wrong, but it appears that several of the characters in this delightful comedy – by the way, is it a comedy?'

'Yes,' said Henry.

'Thank you. It appears that some of the characters do not appear until somewhere in the second act. I don't know which of the characters, naturally, as I have not yet looked between the covers.'

With hasty mumbled apologies they handed the play to Miss Campanula. She said:

'Oh thank you. Don't let me be selfish. I'm a patient body.'

When Idris Campanula alluded to herself jocularly as a 'body' it usually meant that she was in a temper. They all said, 'No, no! Please have it.' She drew her pince-nez out from her bosom by a patent extension and slung them across her nose. She opened the play and amidst dead silence she began to inspect it. First she read the cast of characters. She checked each one with a large bony forefinger, and paused to look round the table until she found the person who had been cast for it. Her expression, which was forbidding, did not change. She then applied herself to the first page of the dialogue. Still everybody waited. The silence was broken only by the sound of Miss Campanula turning a page. Henry began to feel desperate. It seemed almost as if they would continue to sit dumbly round the table until Miss Campanula reached the end of the play. He gave Dinah a cigarette and lit one himself. Miss Campanula raised her eyes and watched them until the match was blown out, and then returned to her reading. She had reached the fourth page of the first act. Mrs Ross looked up at Dr Templett who had bent his head and whispered. Again Miss Campanula raised her eyes and stared at the offenders. The squire cleared his throat and said:

'Read the middle bit of Act II. Page forty-eight, it begins. Funniest thing I've come across for ages. It'll make you laugh like anything.'

Miss Campanula did not reply, but she turned to Act II. Dinah, Henry, Dr Templett, and Jocelyn waited with anxious smiles for her to give some evidence of amusement, but her lips remained firmly pursed, her brows raised, and her eyes fishy. Presently she looked up.

'I've reached the end of the scene,' she said. 'Was that the funny one?'

'Don't you think it's funny?' asked the squire.

'My object was to find out if there was anybody free to play the entr'acte,' said Miss Campanula coldly. 'I gather that there is. I *gather* that the Arbuthnot individual does not make her first appearance until halfway through the second act.'

'Didn't somebody say that Miss Arbuthnot and the Duchess appeared together?' asked Miss Prentice to the accompaniment, every one felt, of the 'Venetian Suite'.

'Possibly,' said Miss Campanula. 'Do I understand that I am expected to take this Mrs Arbuthnot upon myself?'

'If you will,' rejoined the rector. 'And we hope very much indeed that you will.'

'I wanted to be quite clear. I dare say I'm making a great to-do about nothing but I'm a person that likes to know where she is. Now I *gather*, and you must correct me if I'm wrong, that if I do this part there is no just cause or impediment,' and here Miss Campanula threw a jocular glance at the rector, 'why I should not take a little more upon myself and seat myself at the instrument. You *may* have other plans. You *may* wish to hire Mr Joe Hopkins and his friends from Great Chipping, though on a Saturday night I gather they are rather more undependable and tipsy than usual. *If* you have other plans then no more need be said. If not, I place myself at the committee's disposal.'

'Well, that seems a most excellent offer,' the poor rector began. 'If Miss Campanula – '

'May I?' interrupted Miss Prentice sweetly. 'May I say that I think it very kind indeed of dear Idris to offer herself, but may I add that I do also think we are a little too inclined to take advantage of her generosity. She will have all the young folk to manage and she has a large part to learn. I do feel that we should be a little selfish if we also expected her to play for us on that dreadful old piano. Now, as the new instrument is to be in part, as my cousin says, a Pen Cuckoo affair, I think the very least I can do is to offer to relieve poor Idris of this unwelcome task. If you think my little efforts will pass muster I shall be very pleased to play the overture and entr'acte.'

'Very thoughtful of you, Eleanor, but I am quite capable – '

'Of course you are, Idris, but at the same time – '

They both stopped short. The antagonism that had sprung up between them was so obvious and so disproportionate that the others were aghast. The rector abruptly brought his palm down on the table and then, as if ashamed of a gesture that betrayed his thoughts, clasped his hands together and looked straight before him.

He said, 'I think this matter can be decided later.'

The two women glanced quickly at him and were silent.

'That is all, I believe,' said Mr Copeland. 'Thank you, everybody.'

II

The meeting broke up. Henry went to Dinah who had moved over to the fire.

'Ructions!' he said under his breath.

'Awful!' agreed Dinah. 'You'd hardly believe it possible, would you?'

They smiled secretly and when the others crowded about Dinah, asking if they could have their parts before Monday, what sort of clothes would be needed and whether she thought they would be all right, neither she nor Henry minded very much. It did not matter to them that they were unable to speak to each other, for their thoughts went forward to the morning, and their hearts trembled with happiness. They were isolated by their youth, two scatheless figures. It would have seemed impossible to them that their love for each other could hold reflection, however faint, of the emotions that drew Dr Templett to Selia Ross, or those two ageing women to the rector. They would not have believed that there was a reverse side to love, or that the twin-opposites of love lay dormant in their own hearts. Nor were they to guess that never again, as long as they lived, would they know the rapturous expectancy that now possessed them.

Miss Prentice and Miss Campanula carefully avoided each other. Miss Prentice had seized her opportunity and had cornered Mr Copeland. She could be heard offering flowers from the Pen Cuckoo greenhouses for a special service next Sunday. Miss Campanula had tackled Jocelyn about some enormity committed on her property by the local fox-hounds. Dr Templett, a keen follower of hounds, was lugged into the controversy. Mrs Ross was therefore left alone. She stood a little to one side, completely relaxed, her head slanted, a half-smile on her lips. The squire looked over Idris Campanula's shoulder, and caught that half-smile.

'Can't have that sort of thing,' he said vaguely. 'I'll have a word with Appleby. Will you forgive me? I just want – '

He escaped thankfully and joined Mrs Ross. She welcomed him with an air that flattered him. Her eyes brightened and her smile was intimate. It was years since any woman had smiled in that way at Jocelyn, and he responded with Edwardian gallantry. His hand went to his moustache and his eyes brightened.

'You know, you're a very alarming person,' said Jocelyn.

'Now what precisely do you mean by that?' asked Mrs Ross.

He was delighted. This was the way a conversation with a pretty woman ought to start. Forgotten phrases returned to his lips, waggishly nonsensical phrases that one uttered with just the right air of significance. One laughed a good deal and let her know one noticed how damned well-turned-out she was.

'I see that we have a most important scene together,' said Jocelyn, 'and I shall insist on a private rehearsal.'

'I don't know that I shall agree to that,' said Selia Ross.

'Oh, come now, it's perfectly safe.'

'Why?'

'Because you are to be the very charming lady who has lost her memory. Ha, ha, ha! Damn' convenient, what!' shouted Jocelyn, wondering if this remark was as daring as it sounded. Mrs Ross laughed very heartily and the squire glanced in a gratified manner round the room, and encountered the astonished gaze of his son.

'This'll show Henry,' thought Jocelyn. 'These modern pups don't know how to flirt with an attractive woman.' But there was an unmistakably sardonic glint in Henry's eye, and the squire, slightly shaken, turned back to Mrs Ross. She still looked roguishly expectant and he thought, 'Anyway, if Henry's noticed *her*, he'll know I'm doing pretty well.' And then Dr Templett managed to escape Miss Campanula and joined them.

'Well, Selia,' he said, 'if you're ready I think I'd better take you home.'

'Doesn't like me talking to her!' thought the squire in triumph. 'The little man's jealous.'

When Mrs Ross silently gave him her hand, he deliberately squeezed it.

'*Au revoir*,' he said. 'This is your first visit to Pen Cuckoo, isn't it? Don't let it be the last.'

'I shouldn't be here at all,' she answered. 'There have been no official calls, you know.'

Jocelyn made a slightly silly gesture and bowed.

'We'll waive all that sort of nonsense,' he said. 'Ha, ha, ha!'

Mrs Ross turned to say good-bye to Eleanor Prentice.

'I have just told your cousin,' she said, 'that I've no business here. We haven't exchanged calls, have we?'

If Miss Prentice was at all taken aback, she did not show it. She gave her musical laugh and said, 'I'm afraid I am very remiss about these things.'

'Miss Campanula hasn't called on me either,' said Mrs Ross. 'You must come together. Goodbye.'

'Goodbye, everybody,' said Mrs Ross.

'I'll see you to your car,' said the squire. 'Henry!'

Henry hastened to the door. Jocelyn escorted Mrs Ross out of the room and, as Dr Templett followed them, the rector shouted after them:

'Just a minute, Templett. About the youngest Cain.'

'Oh, yes. Silly little fool! Look here, rector – '

'I'll come out with you,' said the rector.

Henry followed and shut the door behind them.

'Well!' said Miss Campanula. 'Well!'

'*Isn't it?*' said Miss Prentice. '*Isn't it?*'

III

Dinah, left alone with them, knew that the battle of the music was postponed in order that the two ladies might unite in the abuse of Mrs Ross. That it was postponed and not abandoned was evident in their manner, which reminded Dinah of stewed fruit on the turn. Its sweetness was impregnated by acidity.

'Of course, Eleanor,' said Miss Campanula, 'I can't for the life of me see why you didn't show her the door. I should have refused to receive her. I should!'

'I was simply dumbfounded,' said Miss Prentice. 'When Taylor announced them, I really couldn't believe my senses. I am deeply disappointed in Dr Templett.'

'Disappointed! The greatest piece of brazen effrontery I have ever encountered. He shan't have my lumbago! I can promise him that.'

'I really should have thought he'd have known better,' continued Miss Prentice. 'It isn't as if we don't know who he is. He should be a gentleman. I always thought he took up medicine as a *vocation*. After all, there have been Templetts at Chippingwood for – '

'For as long as there have been Jernighams at Pen Cuckoo,' said Miss Campanula. 'But of course, you wouldn't know that.'

This was an oblique hit. It reminded Miss Prentice that she was a new-comer and not, strictly speaking, a Jernigham of Pen Cuckoo. Miss Campanula followed it up by saying, 'I suppose in your position you could do nothing but receive her; but I must say I was astonished that you leapt at her play as you did.'

'I did not leap, Idris,' said Miss Prentice. 'I hope I took the dignified course. It was obvious that everybody but you and me was in favour of her play.'

'Well, it's a jolly good play,' said Dinah.

'So we have been told,' said Miss Campanula. 'Repeatedly.'

'I was helpless,' continued Miss Prentice. 'What could I do? One can do nothing against sheer common persistence. Of course she has triumphed.'

'She's gone off now, taking every man in the room with her,' said Miss Campanula. 'Ha!'

'Ah, well,' added Miss Prentice, 'I suppose it's always the case when one deals with people who are *not quite*. Did you hear what she said about our not calling?'

'I was within an ace of telling her that I understood she received men only.'

'But, Miss Campanula,' said Dinah, 'we don't know there's anything more than friendship between them, do we? And even if there is, it's their business.'

'Dinah, *dear*!' said Miss Prentice.

'As a priest's daughter, Dinah – ' began Miss Campanula.

'As a priest's daughter,' said Dinah, 'I've got a sort of idea charity is supposed to be a virtue. And, anyway, I think when you talk about a person's family it's better not to call him a priest. It sounds so scandalous, somehow.'

There was dead silence. At last Miss Campanula rose to her feet.

'I fancy my car is waiting for me, Eleanor,' she said. 'So I shall make my adieux. I am afraid we are neither of us intelligent enough to appreciate modern humour. Good-night.'

'Aren't we driving you home?' asked Dinah.

'Thank you, Dinah, no. I ordered my car for six, and it is already half-past. Good-night.'

CHAPTER 5

Above Cloudyfold

The next morning was fine. Henry woke up at six and looked out of his window at a clear, cold sky with paling stars. In another hour it would begin to get light. Henry wide awake, his mind sharp with anticipation, leapt back into bed and sat with the blankets caught between his chin and his knees, hugging himself. A fine winter's dawn with a light frost and then the thin, pale sunlight. Down in the stables they would soon be moving about with lanthorns to the sound of clanking pails, shrill whistling, and boots on cobblestone. Hounds met up at Moorton Park today, and Jocelyn's two mounts would be taken over by his groom to wait for his arrival by car. Henry spared a moment to regret his own decision to give up hunting. He had loved it so much: the sound, the smell, the sight of the hunt. It had all seemed so perfectly splendid until one day, quite suddenly as if a new pair of eyes had been put into his head, he had seen a mob of well-fed expensive people, with red faces, astraddle shiny quadrupeds, all whooping ceremoniously after a very small creature which later on was torn to pieces while the lucky ones sat on their horses and looked on, well satisfied. To his violent annoyance, he had found that he could not rid himself of this unlovely picture and, as it made him feel slightly sick, he had given up everything but drag-hunting. Jocelyn had been greatly upset and had instantly accused Henry of pacifism. Henry had just left off being a pacifist, however, and assured his father that if England was invaded he would strike a shrewd blow before he would see Cousin Eleanor raped by a foreign mercenary. Hugging his knees, he chuckled at the memory of

Jocelyn's face. Then he gave himself four minutes to revise the conversation he had planned to have with Dinah. He found that the thought of Dinah sent his heart pounding, just as it used to pound in the old days before he took his first fence. 'I suppose I'm hunting again,' he thought, and this primitive idea gave him a curiously exalted sensation. He jumped out of bed, bathed, shaved and dressed by lamplight, then he stole downstairs out into the dawn.

It's a fine thing to be abroad on Dorset hills on a clear winter's dawn. Henry went round the west wing of Pen Cuckoo. The gravel crunched under his shoes and the dim box-borders smelt in a garden that was oddly remote. Familiar things seemed mysterious as if the experience of the night had made strangers of them. The field was rimmed with silver, the spinney on the far side was a company of naked trees locked in a deep sleep from which the sound of footsteps among the dead leaves and twigs could not awaken them. The hillside smelt of cold earth and frosty stones. As Henry climbed steeply upwards, it was as if he left the night behind him down in Pen Cuckoo. On Cloudyfold, the dim shapes took on some resolute form and became rocks, bushes and posts, expectant of the day. The clamour of faraway cock-crows rose vaguely from the valley like the overlapping echoes of dreams, and with this sound came the human smell of woodsmoke.

Henry reached the top of Cloudyfold and looked down the vale of Pen Cuckoo. His breath a small cold mist in front of his face, his fingers were cold and his eyes watered, but he felt like a god as he surveyed his own little world. Half-way down, and almost sheer beneath him, was the house he had left. He looked down into the chimney-tops, already wreathed in thin drifts of blue. The servants were up and about. Farther down, and still drenched in shadow, were the roofs of Winton. Henry wondered if they really leaked badly and if he and Dinah could ever afford to repair them. Beyond Winton his father's land spread out into low hills and came to an end at Selwood Brook. Here, half-screened by trees, he could see the stone façade of Chippingwood which Dr Templett had inherited from his elder brother who had died in the Great War. And separated from Chippingwood by the hamlet of Chipping was Miss Campanula's Georgian mansion, on the skirts of the village but not of it. Farther away, and only just visible over the downlands that separated it from the Vale, was Great

Chipping, the largest town in that part of Dorset. Half-way up the slope, below Winton and Pen Cuckoo, was the church, Winton St Giles, with the rectory hidden behind it. Dinah would strike straight through their home copse and come up the ridge of Cloudyfold. If she came! Please God make it happen, said Henry's thoughts as they used to do when he was a little boy. He crossed the brow of the hill. Below him, on the far side, was Moorton Park Road and Cloudyfold village, and there, tucked into a bend in the road, Duck Cottage, with its scarlet door and window frames, newly done up by Mrs Ross. Henry wondered why Selia Ross had decided to live in a place like Cloudyfold. She seemed to him so thoroughly urban. For a minute or two he thought of her, still snugly asleep in her renovated cottage, dreaming perhaps of Dr Templett. Farther away over the brow of the hill was the Cains' farm, where Dr Templett must drive to minister to the youngest Cain's big toe.

'They're all down there,' thought Henry, 'tucked up in their warm houses, fast asleep; and none of them knows I'm up here in the cold dawn waiting for Dinah Copeland.'

He felt a faint warmth on the back of his neck. The stivered grass was washed with colour, and before him his attenuated shadow appeared. He turned to the east and saw the sun. Quite near at hand he heard his name called, and there, coming over the brow of Cloudyfold, was Dinah, dressed in blue with a scarlet handkerchief round her neck.

Henry could make no answering call. His voice stuck in his throat. He raised his arm, and the shadow before him set a long blue pointer over the grass. Dinah made an answering gesture. Because he could not stand dumbly and smile until she came up with him, he lit a cigarette, making a long business of it, his hands cupped over his face. He could hear her footsteps on the frozen hill, and his own heart thumped with them. When he looked up she was beside him.

'Good-morning,' said Henry.

'I've no breath left,' said Dinah; 'but good-morning to you, Henry. Your cigarette smells like heaven.'

He gave her one.

'It's grand up here,' said Dinah. 'I'm glad I came. You wouldn't believe you could be hot, would you? But I am. My hands and face are icy and the rest of me's like a hot-cross bun.'

'I'm glad you came, too,' said Henry. There was a short silence. Henry set the Jernigham jaw, fixed his gaze on Miss Campanula's chimneys, and said, 'Do you feel at all shy?'

'Yes,' said Dinah. 'If I start talking I shall go on and on talking, rather badly. That's a sure sign I'm shy.'

'It takes me differently. I can hardly speak. I expect I'm turning purple, and my top lip seems to be twitching.'

'It'll go off in a minute,' said Dinah. 'Henry, what would you do if you suddenly knew you had dominion over all you survey? That sounds Biblical. I mean, suppose you could alter the minds – and that means the destinies – of all the people living down there – what would you do?'

'Put it into Cousin Eleanor's heart to be a missionary in Polynesia.'

'Or into Miss Campanula's to start a nudist circle in Chipping.'

'Or my father might go surrealist.'

'No, but honestly, what would you do?' Dinah insisted.

'I don't know. I suppose I would try and simplify them. People seem to me to be much too busy and complicated.'

'Make them kinder?'

'Well, that might do it, certainly.'

'It would do it. If Miss Campanula and your Cousin Eleanor left off being jealous of each other, and if Dr Templett was sorrier for his wife, and if Mrs Ross minded more about upsetting other people's apple-carts, we wouldn't have any more scenes like the one last night.'

'Perhaps not,' Henry agreed. 'But you wouldn't stop them falling in love, if you can call whatever they feel for each other, falling in love. I'm in love with you, as I suppose you know. It makes me feel all noble minded and generous and kind; but, just the same, if I had a harem of invalid wives, they wouldn't stop me telling you I loved you, Dinah. Dinah, I love you so desperately.'

'Do you, Henry?'

'You'd never believe how desperately. This is all wrong. I'd thought out the way I'd tell you. First we were to have a nice conversation and then, when we'd got to the right place, I was going to tell you.'

'All elegant like?'

'Yes. But it's too much for me.'

'It's too much for me, too,' said Dinah.

They faced each other, two solitary figures. All their lives they were to remember this moment, and yet they did not see each other's face very clearly, for their sight was blurred by the agitation in their hearts.

'Oh, Dinah,' said Henry. 'Darling, darling Dinah, I do love you so much.'

He reached out his hand blindly and touched her arm. It was a curious tentative gesture. Dinah cried out: 'Henry, my dear.'

She raised his hand to her cold cheek.

'Oh, God!' said Henry, and pulled her into his arms.

Jocelyn's groom, hacking quietly along the road to Cloudyfold, looked up and saw two figures locked together against the winter sky.

II

'We must come back to earth,' said Dinah. 'There's the church clock. It must be eight.'

'I'll kiss you eight times to wind up the spell,' said Henry. He kissed her eyes, her cheeks, the tips of her ears, and he kissed her twice on the mouth.

'There!' he muttered. 'The spell's wound up.'

'Don't!' cried Dinah.

'What, my darling?'

'Don't quote from Macbeth. It couldn't be more unlucky!'

'Who says so?'

'In the theatre everybody says so.'

'I cock a snook at them! We're not in the theatre: we're on top of the world.'

'All the same, I'm crossing my thumbs.'

'When shall we be married?'

'Married?' Dinah caught her breath, and Henry's pure happiness was threaded with a sort of wonder when he saw that she was no longer lost in bliss.

'What is it?' he said. 'What has happened? Does it frighten you to think of our marriage?'

'It's only that we *have* come back to earth,' Dinah said sombrely. 'I don't know when we'll be married. You see, something pretty difficult has happened.'

'Good Lord, darling, what are you going to falter in my ear? Not a family curse, or dozens of blood relations stark ravers in lunatic asylums?'

'Not quite. It's your Cousin Eleanor.'

'Eleanor!' cried Henry. 'She scarcely exists.'

'Wait till you hear. I've got to tell you now. I'll tell you as we go down.'

'Say first that you're as happy as I am.'

'I couldn't be happier.'

'I love you, Dinah.'

'I love you, Henry.'

'The world is ours,' said Henry. 'Let us go down and take it.'

III

They followed the shoulder of the hill by a path that led down to the rectory garden. Dinah went in front, and their conversation led to repeated halts.

'I'm afraid,' Dinah began, 'that I don't much care for your Cousin Eleanor.'

'You astonish me, darling,' said Henry. 'For myself, I regard her as a prize bitch.'

'That's all right, then. I couldn't mention this before you'd declared yourself, because it's all about us.'

'You mean the day before yesterday when she lurked outside your drawing-room door? Dinah, if she hadn't been there, what would you have done?'

This led to a prolonged halt.

'The thing is,' said Dinah presently, 'she must have told your father.'

'So she did.'

'He's spoken to you?'

'He has.'

'Oh, Henry!'

'That sounds as if you were setting a quotation. Yes, we had a grand interview. "What is this I hear, sir, of your attentions to Miss Dinah Copeland?" "Forgive me, sir, but I refuse to answer you." "Do you defy me, Henry?" "With all respect, sir, I do!" "That sort of thing."'

'He doesn't want it?'

'Eleanor has told him he doesn't, blast her goggling eyes!'

'Why? Because I'm the poor parson's daughter, or because I'm on the stage, or just because he hates the sight of me?'

'I don't think he hates the sight of you.'

'I suppose he wants you to marry a proud heiress.'

'I suppose he does. It doesn't matter a tuppenny button, my sweet Dinah, what he thinks.'

'But it does. You haven't heard. Miss Prentice came to see Daddy last night.'

Henry stopped dead and stared at her.

'She said – she said – '

'Go on.'

'She told him we were meeting, and that you were keeping it from your father, but he'd found out and was terribly upset and felt we'd both been very underhand and – oh, she must have been absolutely foul! She must have sort of hinted that we were – ' Dinah boggled at this and fell silent.

'That we were living in roaring sin?' Henry suggested.

'Yes.'

'My God, the minds of these women! Surely the rector didn't pay any attention.'

'She's so loathsomely plausible. Do you remember the autumn day, weeks ago, soon after I came back, when you drove me to Moorton Bridge and we picnicked and didn't come back till the evening?'

'Every second of it.'

'She'd found out about that. There was no reason why the whole world shouldn't know, but I hadn't told Daddy about it. It had been such a glowing, marvellous day that I didn't want to talk about it.'

'Me, too.'

'Well, now, you see, it looks all fishy and dubious, and Daddy feels I have been behaving in an underhand manner. When Miss Prentice had gone he took me into his study. He was wearing his beretta, a

sure sign that he's feeling his responsibilities. He spoke more in sorrow than in anger, which is always rather toxic, and worst of it is, he
really was upset. He got more and more feudal and said we'd always
been – I forget what – almost fiefs or vassals of this-man's-man of the
Jernighams, and had never done anything disloyal, and here I was
behaving like a housemaid having clandestine assignations with you.
On and on and on; and Henry, my darling, my dear darling, ridiculous though it sounds, I began to feel shabby and common.'

'He didn't believe – ?'

'No, of course he didn't believe that. But all the same, you know
he's frightfully muddled about sex.'

'They all are,' said Henry, with youthful gloom. 'And with
Eleanor and Idris hurling their inhibitions in his teeth – '

'I know. Well, anyway, the upshot was, he forbade me to see you
alone. I said I wouldn't promise. It was the first really deadly row
we've ever had. I fancy he prayed about it for hours after I'd gone to
bed. It's very vexing to lie in bed knowing that somebody in the
room below is praying away like mad about you. And, you see, I
adore the man. At one moment I thought I would say my own
prayers, but the only thing I could think of was the old
Commination Service. You know: "Cursed is he that smiteth his
neighbour secretly. Amen."'

'One for Eleanor,' said Henry appreciatively.

'That's what I thought, but I didn't say it. But what I've been trying to come to is this: I can't bear to upset Daddy permanently, and
I'm afraid that's just what would happen. No, please wait, Henry.
You see, I'm only nineteen, and he can forbid the banns – and,
what's more, he'd do it.'

'But why?' said Henry. 'Why? Why? Why?'

'Because he thinks that we shouldn't oppose your father and
because, secretly, he's got a social inferiority complex. He's a snob,
poor sweet. He thinks if he smiled on us it would look as if he was
all agog to make a grand match for me, and was going behind the
squire's back to do it.'

'Absolutely drivelling bilge!'

'I know, but that's how it goes. It's just one of those things. And
it's all due to Miss Prentice. Honestly, Henry I think she's positively
evil. *Why* should she mind about us?'

'Jealousy,' said Henry. 'She's starved and twisted and a bit dotty. I dare say it's physiological as well as psychological. I imagine she thinks you'll sort of dethrone her when you're my wife. And, as likely, as not, she's jealous of your father's affection for you.'

They shook their heads wisely.

'Daddy's terrified of her,' said Dinah. '*and* of Miss Campanula. They *will* ask him to hear their confessions, and when they go away he's a perfect wreck.'

'I'm not surprised, if they tell the truth. I expect what they really do is to try to inform against the rest of the district. Listen to me, Dinah. I refuse to have our love for each other messed up by Eleanor. You're mine. I'll tell your father I've asked you to marry me, and I'll tell mine. I'll *make* them see reason: and if Eleanor comes creeping in – my God, I'll, I'll, I'll – '

'Henry,' said Dinah, 'how magnificent!'

Henry grinned.

'It'd be more magnificent,' he said, 'if she wasn't just an unhappy, warped, middle-aged spinster.'

'It must be awful to be like that,' agreed Dinah. 'I hope it never happens to me.'

'You!'

There was another halt.

'Henry,' said Dinah suddenly. 'Let's ask them to call an armistice until after the play.'

'But we must see each other like this. Alone.'

'I shall die if we can't; but all the same I feel, somehow, if we said we'd wait until then, that Daddy might sort of begin to understand. Weil meet at rehearsals, and we won't pretend we're not in love, but I'll promise him I won't meet you alone. It'll be – it'll be kind of dignified. Henry, *do* you see?'

'I suppose so,' said Henry unwillingly.

'It'd stop those hateful old women talking.'

'My dear, nothing would stop them talking.'

'Please, darling Henry.'

'Oh, Dinah.'

'Please.'

'All right. It's insufferable, though, that Eleanor should be able to spoil a really miraculous thing like Us.'

'Insufferable.'

'She's so completely insignificant.'

Dinah shook her head.

'All the same,' she said, 'she's a bad enemy. She creeps and creeps, and she's simply brimful of poison. She'll drop some of it into our cup of happiness if she can.'

'Not if I know it,' said Henry.

CHAPTER 6

Rehearsal

The rehearsals were not going too well. For all Dinah's efforts, she hadn't been able to get very much concerted work out of her company. For one thing, with the exception of Selia Ross and Henry, they would *not* learn their lines. Dr Templett even took a sort of pride in it. He was forever talking about his experiences in amateur productions when he was a medical student.

'I never knew what I was going to say,' he said cheerfully. 'I'm capable of saying almost anything. It was always all right on the night. A bit of cheek goes a long way. One can bluff it out with a gag or two. The great thing is not to be nervous.'

He himself was not at all nervous. He uttered such lines of the French Ambassador's as he remembered, in a high-pitched voice, made a great many grimaces, waved his hands in a foreign manner, and was never still for an instant.

'I leave it to the spur of the moment,' he told them. 'It's wonderful what a difference it makes when you're all made-up, with funny clothes on. I never know where I ought to be. You can't do it in cold blood.'

'But, Dr Templett, you've got to,' Dinah lamented. 'How can we get the timing right or the positions, if at one rehearsal you're on the prompt and at the next on the o.p.?'

'Don't you worry,' said Dr Templett. 'We'll be all right. Eet vill be – 'ow you say? – so, so charmante.'

Off-stage he continually spoke his lamentable broken English, and when he dried up, as he did incessantly, he interpolated his: ''ow you say?'

'If I forget,' he said to the rector, who was prompting, 'I'll just walk over to your side and say, "'ow you say?" like that, and then you'll know.'

Selia Ross and he had an irritating trick of turning up late for rehearsals. Apparently the youngest Cain's big toe still needed Dr Templett's attention, and he explained that he picked up Mrs Ross and brought her to rehearsal on his way back from Cloudyfold. They would walk in with singularly complacent smiles, half an hour late, while Dinah was reading both their parts and trying to play her own. Sometimes she got her father to read their bits, but the rector intoned them so carefully and slowly that everybody else was thrown into a state of deadly confusion.

Miss Campanula, in a different way, was equally troublesome. She refused to give up her typewritten part. She carried it about with her and read each of her speeches in an undertone during the preceding dialogue, so that whenever she was on the stage the others spoke through a distressing mutter. When her cue came she seldom failed to say, 'Oh. Now it's me,' before she began. She would often rattle off her lines without any inflexion, and apparently without the slightest regard for their meaning. She was forever telling Dinah that she was open to correction, but she received all suggestions in huffy grandeur, and they made not the smallest difference to her performance. Worse than all these peculiarities were Miss Campanula's attempts at characterization. She made all sorts of clumsy and ineffective movements over which she herself seemed to have little control. She continually shifted her weight from one large foot to the other, rather in the manner of a penguin. She wandered about the stage and she made embarrassing grimaces. In addition to all this she had developed a frightful cold in her nose, and rehearsals were made hideous by her catarrhal difficulties.

Jocelyn was the type of amateur performer who learns his lines from the prompter. Unlike Miss Campanula, he did not hold his part in his hand. Indeed, he had lost it irrevocably immediately after the first rehearsal. He said that it did not matter, as he had already memorized his lines. This was a lie. He merely had the vague idea of their sense. His performance reminded Dinah of divine service, as he was obliged to repeat all his lines, like responses, after the rector. However, in spite of this defect, the squire had an instinctive sense of theatre. He did not fidget or gesticulate. With Dr Templett tearing about the stage like a wasp, this was particularly refreshing.

Miss Prentice did not know her part either, but she was a cunning bluffer. She had a long scene in which she held a newspaper open in her hands. Dinah discovered that Miss Prentice had pinned several of her sides to *The Times*. Others were left in handy places about the stage. When, in spite of these manoeuvres, she dried up, Miss Prentice stared in a gently reproachful manner at the person who spoke after her, so that everybody thought it was her *vis-à-vis* who was at fault.

Mrs Ross had learnt her part. Her clear, hard voice had plenty of edge. Once there, she worked, tried to follow Dinah's suggestions, and was very good-humoured and obliging. If ever anything was wanted, Mrs Ross would get it. She brought down to the Parish Hall her cushions, her cocktail glasses and her bridge table. Dinah found herself depending more and more on Mrs Ross for 'hand props' and odds and ends of furniture. But, for all that, she did not like Mrs Ross, whose peals of laughter at all Dr Templett's regrettable antics were extremely irritating. The determined rudeness with which Miss Prentice and Miss Campanula met all Mrs Ross's advances forced Dinah into making friendly gestures which she continually regretted. She saw, with something like horror, that her father had innocently succumbed to Mrs Ross's charm, and to her sudden interest in his church. This, more than anything else she did, inflamed Miss Campanula and Eleanor Prentice against Selia Ross. Dinah felt that her rehearsals were shot through and through with a mass of ugly suppressions. To complete her discomfort, the squire's attitude towards Mrs Ross, being ripe with Edwardian naughtiness, obviously irritated Henry and the two ladies almost to breaking point.

Henry had learnt his part and shaped well. He and Dinah were the only members of the cast who gave any evidence of team work. The others scarcely even so much as looked at each other, and treated their speeches as if they were a string of interrupted recitations.

II

The battle of the music had raged for three weeks. Miss Prentice and Miss Campanula, together and alternately, had pretended to altruistic motives, and accused each other of selfishness, sulked, denied all desire to perform on the piano, given up their parts, relented, and offered their services anew. In the end Dinah, with her father's moral support behind her, seized upon a moment when Miss Campanula had said she'd no wish to play on an instrument with five dumb notes in the treble and six in the bass.

'All right, Miss Campanula,' said Dinah, 'we'll have it like that. Miss Prentice has kindly volunteered, and I shall appoint her as pianist. As you've got the additional responsibility of the YPFC girls in the front of the house, it really does seem the best idea.'

After that Miss Campanula was barely civil to anybody but the rector and the squire.

Five days before the performance, Eleanor Prentice developed a condition which Miss Campanula called 'a Place' on the index finger of the left hand. Everybody noticed it. Miss Campanula did not fail to point out that it would probably be much worse on the night of the performance.

'You'd better take care of that Place on your finger Eleanor,' she said. 'It's gathering, and to me it looks very nasty. Your blood must be out of order.'

Miss Prentice denied this with an air of martyrdom, but there was no doubt that the Place grew increasingly ugly. Three days before the performance it was hidden by an obviously professional bandage, and everybody knew that she had consulted Dr Templett. A rumour sprang up that Miss Campanula had begun to practise her Prelude every morning after breakfast.

Dinah had a private conversation with Dr Templett.

'What about Miss Prentice's finger? Will she be able to play the piano?'

'I've told her she'd better give up all idea of it,' he said. 'There's a good deal of inflammation, and it's very painful. It'll hurt like the devil if she attempts to use it, and it's not at all advisable that she should.'

'What did she say?'

Dr Templett grinned.

'She said she wouldn't disappoint her audience, and that she could rearrange the fingering of her piece. It's the "Venetian Suite", as usual, of course?'

'It is,' said Dinah grimly, '"Dawn" and "On the Canal" for the overture, and the "Nocturne" for the entr'acte. She'll never give way.'

'Selia says she wouldn't mind betting old Idris has put poison in her girl friend's gloves like the Borgias,' said Dr Templett, and added: 'Good Lord, I oughtn't to have repeated that! It's the sort of thing that's quoted against you in a place like this.'

'I won't repeat it,' said Dinah.

She asked Miss Prentice if she would rather not appear at the piano.

'How thoughtful of you, Dinah, my dear,' rejoined Miss Prentice, with her holiest smile. 'But I shall do my little best. You may depend upon me.'

'But, Miss Prentice, your finger!'

'Ever so much better,' said Eleanor in a voice that somehow suggested that there was something slightly improper in mentioning her finger.

'They are waiting to print the programmes. Your name – '

'Please don't worry, dear. My name may appear in safety. Shall we just not say any more about it, but consider it settled?'

'Very well,' said Dinah uneasily. 'It's very heroic of you.'

'Silly child!' said Eleanor playfully.

III

And now, on Thursday, November the 25th, two nights before the performance, Dinah stood beside the paraffin heater in the aisle of the parish hall, and with dismay in her heart prepared to watch the opening scenes in which she herself did not appear. There was to be no music at the dress rehearsal.

'Just to give my silly old finger time to get *quite* well,' said Miss Prentice.

But Henry had told Dinah that both he and his father had seen Eleanor turn so white after knocking her finger against a chair that they thought she was going to faint.

'You won't stop her,' said Henry. 'If she has to play the bass with her feet, she'll do it.'

Dinah gloomily agreed.

She had made them up for the dress rehearsal and had attempted to create a professional atmosphere in a building that reeked of parochial endeavour. Even now her father's unmistakably clerical voice could be heard beyond the green serge curtain, crying obediently:

'Beginners, please.'

In front of Dinah, six privileged Friendly Young Girls, who were to sell programmes and act as ushers at the performance, sat in a giggling row to watch the dress rehearsal. Dr Templett and Henry were their chief interest. Dr Templett was aware of this and repeatedly looked round the curtain. He had insisted on making himself up, and looked as if he had pressed his face against a gridiron and then garnished his chin with the hearth-brush. Just as Dinah was about to bring up the curtain, his head again bobbed round the corner.

'Vy do you, 'ow you say, gargle so mooch?' he asked the helpers. A renewed paroxysm broke out.

'Dr Templett!' shouted Dinah. 'Clear stage, *please*.'

'Ten thousand pardons, Mademoiselle,' said Dr Templett. 'I vaneesh.' He made a comic face and disappeared.

'All ready behind, Daddy?' shouted Dinah.

'I think so,' said the rector's voice doubtfully.

'Positions, everybody. House lights, please.' Dinah was obliged to execute this last order herself, as the house lights switch was in the auditorium. She turned it off and the six onlookers yelped maddeningly.

'Ssh, please! Curtain!'

'Just a minute,' said the rector dimly.

The curtain rose in a series of uneven jerks, and the squire, who should have been at the telephone, was discovered gesticulating violently to someone in the wings. He started, glared into the house, and finally took up his position.

'Where's that telephone bell?' demanded Dinah.

'Oh, dear!' said the rector's voice dismally. He could be heard scuffling about in the prompt-corner and presently an unmistakable bicycle bell pealed. But Jocelyn had already lifted the receiver and, although the bell, which was supposed to summon him to the telephone, continued to ring off-stage, he embarked firmly on his opening lines:

'Hallo! Hallo! Well, who is it?'

The dress rehearsal had begun.

Actors say that a good dress rehearsal means a bad performance. Dinah hoped desperately that the reverse would prove true. Everything seemed to go wrong. She suspected that there were terrific rows in the dressing-rooms, but as she herself had no change to make, she stayed in front whenever she was not actually on the stage. Before the entrance of the two ladies in the second act, Henry came down and joined her.

'Frightful, isn't it?' he asked.

'It's the end,' said Dinah.

'My poor darling, it's pretty bad luck for you. Perhaps it'll pull through tomorrow.'

'I don't see how – Dr Templett!' roared Dinah. 'What are you doing? You ought to be up by the fireplace. Go back, please.'

Miss Prentice suddenly walked straight across the stage, in front of Jocelyn, Selia Ross and Dr Templett, and out at the opposite door.

'*Miss Prentice!*'

But she had gone, and could be heard in angry conversation with Georgie Biggins, the call-boy, and Miss Campanula.

'You're a very naughty little boy, and I shall ask the rector to forbid you to attend the performance.'

'You deserve a sound whipping,' said Miss Campanula's voice. 'And if I had my way – '

The squire and Dr Templett stopped short and stared into the wings.

'What is it?' Dinah demanded.

Georgie Biggins was thrust on the stage. He had painted his nose carmine, and Miss Prentice's hat for the third act was on his head. He had a water pistol in his hand. The girls in the front row screamed delightedly.

'Georgie,' said Dinah with more than a suspicion of tears in her voice, 'take that hat off and go home.'

'I never – ' began Georgie.

'Do what I tell you.'

'Yaas, Miss.'

Miss Prentice's arm shot through the door. The hat was removed. Dr Templett took Georgie Biggins by the slack of his pants and dropped him over the footlights.

'Gatcha!' said Georgie and bolted to the back of the hall.

'Go on, please,' said poor Dinah.

Somehow or another they got through. Dinah took them back over the scenes that had been outstandingly bad. This annoyed and bored them all very much, but she was adamant.

'It'll be all right on the night,' said Dr Templett.

'Saturday's the night,' said Dinah, 'and it won't.'

At midnight she sat down in the third bench and said she supposed they had better stop. They all assembled in one of the Sunday School rooms behind the stage and gathered round a heater, while Mrs Ross gave them a very good supper. She had insisted on making this gesture and had provided beer, whisky, coffee and sandwiches. Miss Campanula and Miss Prentice had both offered to make themselves responsible for this supper, and were furious that Mrs Ross had got in first.

Dinah was astounded to learn from their conversation that they thought they had done quite well. The squire was delighted with himself; Dr Templett still retained his character as a French man; and Selia Ross said repeatedly that she thought both of them had been marvellous. The other two ladies spoke only to Mr Copeland, and each waited until she could speak alone. Dinah saw that her father was bewildered and troubled.

'Oh, Lord!' thought Dinah. 'What's brewing now?' She wished that her father was a stronger character, that he would bully or frighten those two venomous women into holding their tongues. And suddenly, with a cold pang, she thought: 'If he should lose his head and marry one of them!'

Henry brought her a cup of black coffee.

'I've put some whisky in it,' he said. 'You're as pale as a star, and look frightened. What is it?'

'Nothing. I'm just tired.'

Henry bent his dark head and whispered:

'Dinah?'

'Yes.'

'I'll talk to Father on Saturday night when he's flushed with his dubious triumphs. Did you get my letter?'

Dinah's hand floated to her breast.

'Darling,' whispered Henry. 'Yours, too. We can't wait any longer. After tomorrow?'

'After tomorrow,' murmured Dinah.

CHAPTER 7

Vignettes

'I have sinned,' said Miss Prentice, 'in thought, word and deed by my fault, by my own fault, by my most grievous fault. Especially I accuse myself that since that last confession, which was a month ago, I have sinned against my neighbour. I have harboured evil suspicions of those with whom I have come in contact, accusing them in my heart of adultery, unfaithfulness and disobedience to their parents. I have judged my sister-woman in my heart and condemned her. I have listened many times to evil reports of a woman, and because I could not in truth say that I did not believe them – '

'Do not seek to excuse rather than to condemn yourself,' said the rector from behind the Norman confessional that his bishop allowed him to use. 'Condemn only your own erring heart. You have encouraged and connived at scandal. Go on.'

There was a brief silence.

'I accuse myself that I have committed sins of omission, not performing what I believed to be my bounden Christian duty to the sick, not warning one whom I believe to be in danger of great unhappiness.'

The rector heard Miss Prentice turn a page of the notebook where she wrote her confessions. 'I know what she's getting at,' he thought miserably. But because he was a sincere and humble man, he prayed: 'Oh, God, give me the strength of mind to tackle this woman. Amen.'

Miss Prentice cleared her throat in a subdued manner and began again. 'I have consorted with a woman whom I believe to be of evil nature, knowing that by doing so I may have seemed to connive in sin.'

'Our Lord consorted with sinners and was sinless. Judge not that you be not judged. The sin of another should excite only compassion in your heart. Go on.'

'I have had angry and bitter thoughts of two young people who have injured someone who is – '

'Stop!' said the rector. 'Do not accuse others. Accuse only your-self. Examine your conscience. Be sure that you have come here with a contrite and humble heart. If it holds any uncharitable thoughts, repent and confess them. Do not try to justify your anger by relating the cause. God will judge how greatly you have been tempted.'

He waited. There was no response at all from his penitent. The church, beyond the confessional, seemed to listen with him for the next whisper.

'My daughter, I am waiting,' said the rector, and was horrified when he was answered by a harsh, angry sobbing.

II

In spite of her cold, Miss Campanula was happy. She was about to make her confession, and she felt at peace with the world and quite youthful and exalted. The terrible black mood that had come upon her when she woke up that morning had vanished completely. She even felt fairly good-humoured when she thought of Eleanor play-ing her 'Venetian Suite' at the performance tomorrow evening. With that Place on her finger, Eleanor was likely enough to make a hash of the music, and then everybody would think it was a pity that she, Idris Campanula, had not been chosen. That thought gave her a happy, warm feeling. Nowadays she was never sure what her mood would be. It changed in the most curious fashion from something like ecstasy to a dreadful irritation that came upon her with such violence and with so little provocation that it quite frightened her. It was as if, like the people in the New Testament, she had a devil in her, a beast that could send her thoughts black and make her trem-ble with anger. She had confessed these fits of rage to Father

Copeland (she and Eleanor called him that when they spoke of him together), and he had been kind and had prayed for her. He had also, rather to her surprise suggested that she should see a doctor. But there was nothing wrong with her health, she reflected, except lumbago and the natural processes attached to getting a little bit older. She pushed that thought away quickly, as it was inclined to make her depressed, and when she was depressed the beast took advantage of her.

Her chauffeur drove her to church, but she was a few minutes early, so she decided that she would look in at the parish hall and see if the committee of the YPFC had begun to get it ready for tomorrow night. The decorating, of course, would all be done in the morning under her supervision; but there were floors to be swept, forms shifted and tables moved. Perhaps Eleanor would be there – or even Father Copeland on his way to church. Another wave of ecstasy swept over her. She knew why she was so happy. He would perhaps be at Pen Cuckoo for this ridiculous 'run through for words' at five o'clock; but, better than that, it was Reading Circle night in the rectory dining-room, and her turn to preside. After it was over she would look in at the study, and Father Copeland would be there alone and would talk to her for a little.

Telling her chauffeur to wait, she marched up the gravelled path to the hall.

It was locked. This was irritating. She supposed those young people imagined they had done enough for one day. You might depend upon it, they had made off leaving half the work for tomorrow. She was just going away again when dimly, from within, she heard the sound of strumming. Someone was playing 'Chop-sticks' very badly, with the loud pedal on. Miss Campanula felt a sudden desire to know who had remained inside the hall to strum. She rattled the doors. The maddening noise stopped immediately.

'Who's in there?' shouted Miss Campanula, in a cold-infected voice, and rattled again.

There was no answer.

'The back door!' she thought. 'It may be open.' And she marched round the building. But the back door was shut, and although she pounded angrily on it, splitting her black kid gloves, nobody came to open it. Her face burned with exertion and rising fury. She started off again and completed the circuit of the hall. The frosted windows were all above the level of her eyes. The last one she came to was open at the bottom. Miss Campanula returned to the lane and saw that her chauffeur had followed her in the car from the church.

'Gibson!' she shouted. 'Gibson, come here!'

He got out of the car and came towards her. He was a wooden-faced man with a fine physique; very smart in his dark maroon livery and shiny gaiters. He followed his mistress round the front of the hall to the far side.

'I want you to look inside that window,' said Miss Campanula. 'There's somebody in there who's behaving suspiciously.'

'Very good, miss,' said Gibson.

He gripped the window sill. The muscles under his smart tunic swelled as he raised himself until his eyes were aboove the sill.

Miss Campanula sneezed violently, blew her nose on her enormous handkerchief drenched in eucalyptus, and said, 'Cad you see anddythingk?'

'No, miss. There's nobody there.'

'But there *bust* be,' insisted Miss Campanula.

'I can't see any one, miss. The place is all tidied up, like, for tomorrow.'

'Where's the piano?'

'Down on the floor, miss, in front of the stage.'

Gibson lowered himself.

'They bust have gone into one of the back rooms,' muttered Miss Campanula.

'Could whoever it was have come out at the front door, miss, while you were round at the back?'

'Did you see addybody?'

'Can't say I did, miss. Not round the hall. But I was turning the car. They would have gone round the bend in the lane before I would notice.'

'I consider it bost peculiar and suspicious.'

'Yes, miss. There's Miss Prentice just coming out of church, miss.'

'Is she?' Miss Campanula peered short-sightedly down the lane. She could see the south porch of St Giles and a figure in the doorway.

'I mustn't be late,' she thought. 'Eleanor has got in first as usual.' And she ordered Gibson to wait for her outside the church. She crossed the lane and strode down to the lych-gate. Eleanor was still in the porch. One did not stop to gossip when going to confession, but she gave Eleanor her usual nod and was astonished to see that she looked ghastly.

'There's something wrong with her,' thought Miss Campanula, and somewhere, in the shifting hinterland between her conscious and unconscious thoughts, lay the warm hope that the rector had been displeased with Eleanor at confession.

Miss Campanula entered the church with joy in her heart.

III

At the precise moment when Miss Prentice and Miss Campanula passed each other in the south porch, Henry, up at Pen Cuckoo, decided that he could remain indoors no longer. He was restless and impatient. He and Dinah had kept their pact, and since their morning on Cloudyfold had not met alone. Henry had announced their intention to his father at breakfast while Eleanor Prentice was in the room.

'It's Dinah's idea,' he had said. 'She calls it an armistice. As our affairs seem to be so much in the public eye, and as her father has been upset by the conversation you had with him last night, Cousin Eleanor, Dinah thinks it would be a good thing if we promised him we would postpone what you have described as our clandestine meetings for three weeks. After that I shall speak to the rector myself.' He had looked directly at Miss Prentice and added: 'I shall be very grateful if you would not discuss the matter with him in the meantime. After all, it is primarily our affair.'

'I shall do what I believe to be my duty, Henry,' Miss Prentice had said; and Henry had answered, 'I'm afraid you will,' and walked out of the room.

He and Dinah had written to each other. Henry had found Miss Prentice eyeing Dinah's first letter as it lay beside his plate at breakfast. He had put it in the breast pocket of his coat, rather shocked at the look he had surprised in her face. After that morning he had come down early to breakfast.

During the three weeks' truce, Jocelyn never spoke to his son of Dinah, but Henry knew very well that Miss Prentice nagged at the squire whenever a chance presented itself. Several times Henry had walked into the study to find Eleanor closeted with Jocelyn. The silence that invariably followed his entrance, his father's uncomfortable attempts to break it, and Miss Prentice's tight smile as she glided away, left Henry in no doubt as to the subject of their conversation.

This afternoon, Jocelyn was hunting. Miss Prentice would come back from church before three, and Henry could not face the prospect of tea alone with his cousin. She had refused a car, and would return tired and martyred. Although Jocelyn had taught her to drive, it was her infuriating custom to refuse a car. She would walk to church after dark, on pouring wet nights, and give herself maddening colds in the head. Today, however, was fine with glints of watery sunlight. He took a stick and went out.

Henry walked through the trees into a lane that came out near the church. Perhaps there would be a job of work to be done at the hall. If Dinah was there she would be surrounded by helpers, so that would be all right.

But about half-way down he walked round a sharp bend in the lane and found himself face to face and alone with Dinah.

For a moment they stood and stared at each other. Then Henry said, 'I thought I might be able to help in the hall.'

'We finished for today at two o'clock.'

'Where are you going?'

'Just for a walk. I didn't know you'd – I thought you'd be – '

'I didn't know either. It was bound to happen sooner or later.'

'Yes, I suppose so.'

'Your face is white,' said Henry, and his voice shook. 'Are you all right?'

'Yes. It's only the shock. Yours is white, too.'

'Dinah!'

'No, no. Not till tomorrow. We promised.'

As if moved by some compulsion outside themselves, they moved like automatons into each other's arms.

When Miss Prentice, dry-eyed but still raging, came round the bend in the lane Henry was kissing Dinah's throat.

IV

'I can't see,' said Selia Ross, 'that it matters what a couple of shock-ing, nasty old church-hens choose to say.'

'But it does,' answered Dr Templett. He kicked a log on the fire. 'Mine is one of the few jobs where your private life affects your prac-tice. Why it should be so, the Lord alone knows. And I can't afford to lose my practice, Selia. My brother went through most of what was left when my father died. I don't want to sell Chippingwood, but it takes me all my time to keep it up. It's a beastly situation, I know. Other things being equal, I still couldn't ask Freda to divorce me. Lying there from one year's end to another! Spinal paralysis isn't much fun and – she's still fond of me.'

'My poor darling,' said Mrs Ross softly. Templett's back was towards her. She looked at him speculatively. Perhaps she wondered if she should go to him. If so, she decided against it and remained, exquisitely neat and expensive in a high-backed chair.

'Only just now,' muttered Templett, 'old Mrs Cain said something about seeing my car outside. I've noticed things. They're beginning to talk, damn their eyes. And with this new fellow over at Penmoor I can't afford to take chances. It's all due to those two women. Nobody would have thought anything about it if they hadn't got their claws into me. The other day, when I fixed up old Prentice's finger she asked after Freda, and in almost the same breath she began to talk about you. My God, I wish she'd get gangrene! And now this!'

'I'm sorry I told you.'

'No, it was much better you should. I'd better see the damn' thing.'

Mrs Ross went to her writing-desk and unlocked a drawer. She took out a sheet of note-paper and gave it to him. He stared at six lines of black capitals.

'You are given notice to leave the district. If you disregard this warning, your lover will suffer.'

'When did it come?'

'This morning. The postmark was Chipping.'

'What makes you think it's her?'

'Smell it.'

'Eucalyptus, my God!'

'She's drenched in it.'

'She probably carried it in her bag?'

'That's it. You'd better burn it, Billy.'

Dr Templett dropped the paper on the smouldering log and then snatched it up again.

'No,' he said. 'I've got a note from her at home. I'll compare the paper.'

'Surely hers has a printed address.'

'This might be a plain sheet for the following on. It's good paper.'

'She'd never be such a fool.'

'The woman's pathological, my dear. She might do anything. Anyway. I'll see.'

He put the paper in his pocket.

'In my opinion,' said Selia Ross, 'she's green with jealousy because I've rather got off with the parson and the squire.'

'So am I.'

'Darling,' said Mrs Ross, 'you can't think how pure I am with them.'

Templett suddenly burst out laughing.

CHAPTER 8

Catastrophe

At ten minutes to eight on the night of Saturday, November 27th, the parish hall at Winton St Giles smelt of evergreens, wet mackintoshes, and humanity. Members of the Young People's Friendly Circle, harried and dragooned by Miss Campanula, had sold all the tickets in advance, so in spite of the appalling weather, every seat was occupied. Even the Moorton Park people had come over with their house-party, and sat in the front row of less uncomfortable chairs at two shillings a head. Behind them were ranged the church workers including Mr Prosser, chemist of Chipping, and Mr Blandish, the police superintendent, both churchwardens. The Women's Institute was there with its husband and children. Farther back, in a gaggling phalanx, were those girls of the Friendly Circle who were not acting as ushers, and behind them, on the back benches, the young men of the farms and villages, smelling of hair-grease and animal warmth. In the entrance, Miss Campanula had posted Sergeant Roper, of the Chipping Constabulary, and sidesman of St Giles. His duties were to collect tickets and subdue the backbenchers, who were inclined to guffaw and throw paper pellets at their girls. At the end of the fourth row from the front, on the left side of the centre aisle, sat Georgie Biggins with his parents. He seemed strangely untroubled by his dethronement from the position of call-boy. His hair was plastered down with water on his bullet-shaped head, his head shone rosily, and there was an unholy light in his black boot-button eyes, which were fixed on the piano.

The piano, soon to achieve a world-wide notoriety, stood beneath the stage and facing the centre aisle. One of the innumerable photographs that appeared in the newspapers on Monday, November 29th, shows a museum piece, a cottage pianoforte of the nineties, with a tucked silk panel, badly torn, in front. It has a hardbitten look. It would be too fanciful to compare it to a spinster, dressed in dilapidated moth-eaten finery, still retaining an air of shabby gentility, but given over to some very dubious employment. This air is enhanced by the presence of five aspidistras, placed in a row on the top of the bunting, which has been stretched across the top over the opening and the turned-back lid, tightly fixed to the edges with drawing pins, and allowed to fall in artistic festoons down the sides and in a sort of valance-like effect across the front. At ten to eight on the night of the concert, there on the fretwork rack under the valance of bunting was Miss Prentice's 'Venetian Suite', rather the worse for wear, but ready for her attention.

There was a notice in the programmes about the object of the performance, a short history of the old piano, a word of thanks to Jocelyn Jernigham, Esq., of Pen Cuckoo, for his generous offer to make up the sum of money needed for a new instrument. The old piano came in for a lot of attention that evening.

At eight o'clock Dinah, sick with apprehension in the prompt corner, turned on the stage lights. Sergeant Roper, observing this signal, leant across the row of boys on the back bench and switched off the house lights. The audience made noises of pleasurable anticipation.

Improvised footlights shone upwards on the faded green curtain. After a moment's pause, during which many people in the audience said, 'Ssh!' an invisible hand drew the curtain aside and the rector walked through. There was a great burst of applause in the second row, and the reporter from the *Chipping Courier* took out his pad and pencil.

Mr Copeland's best cassock was green about the seams, the toes of his boots turned up because he always neglected to put trees in them. He was actually a good-looking, rather shabbily-dressed parish priest. But, lit dramatically from beneath, he looked magnificent. It was the head of a mediæval saint, austere and beautiful, sharp as a cameo against its own black shadow.

'He ought to be a bishop,' said old Mrs Cain to her daughter.

Behind the curtain, Dinah took a final look at the set. The squire, satisfactory in plus-fours and a good clean make-up, was in his right position up-stage, with a telegram in his hand. Henry stood off-stage at the prompt entrance, very nervous. Dinah moved into the wings with the bicycle bell in her hand.

'Don't answer the telephone till it's rung twice,' she hissed at Jocelyn.

'All right, all right, all right.'

'Clear, please,' said Dinah severely. 'Stand by.'

She went into the prompt box, seized the curtain lines and listened to her father.

'– So you see,' the rector was saying, 'the present piano is almost a historical piece, and I'm sure you will be glad to hear that this old friend will be given an honourable place in the small recreation room at the back of the stage.'

Sentimental applause.

'I have one other announcement. You will see on your programmes that Miss Prentice of Pen Cuckoo, in addition to taking part, was to play the overture and entr'acte this evening. I am sorry to say that Miss Prentice has – ah – has – ah – an injured finger which has given – and I am sorry to say it is still giving her – a great deal of pain. Miss Prentice, with her customary pluck and unselfishness' – Mr Copeland paused hopefully and was awarded a tentative outbreak of clapping – 'was anxious not to disappoint us and was prepared, up to a minute or two ago, to play the piano. However, as she has an important rôle to fill later on in the evening, and as her hand is really not fit, she – ah – Dr Templett has – ah – has taken matters in hand and ordered her not to – to play.'

The rector paused again while the audience wondered if it should applaud Dr Templett's efficiency, but decided that, on the whole, it had better not.

'Now, although you will be disappointed and will sympathize, I am sure, with Miss Prentice, we all know we mustn't disobey doctor's orders. I am happy to say that we shall still have our music – and very good music, too. Miss Idris Campanula, at literally a moment's notice, has consented to play for us. Now, I think this is particularly generous and sporting of Miss Campanula, and I'll ask you all to show your appreciation in a really – '

Deafening applause.

'Miss Campanula,' ended Mr Copeland, 'will play Rachmaninoff's "Prelude in C Sharp Minor". Miss Campanula.'

He led her from the wings, handed her down the steps to the piano, and returned to the stage through the side curtains.

It was wonderful to see Idris Campanula acknowledge the applause with an austere bend, smile more intimately at the rector, descend the steps carefully and, with her back to the aisle, seat herself at the instrument. It was wonderful to see her remove the 'Venetian Suite', and place her famous Prelude on the music rack, open it with a masterly flip, deal it a jocular slap, and then draw out her pince-nez from the tucked silk bosom that so closely resembled the tucked silk bosom of the instrument. Miss Campanula and the old piano seemed to face each other with an air of understanding and affinity. Miss Campanula's back hollowed as she drew up her bosom until it perched on the top of her stays. She leant forward until her nose was within three inches of the music, and she held her left hand poised over the bass. Down it came.

Pom. *Pom*. POM.

The three familiar chords.

Miss Campanula paused, lifted her big left foot and planked it down on the soft pedal.

II

The air was blown into splinters of atrocious clamour. For a second nothing existed but noise – hard, racketing noise. The hall, suddenly thick with dust, was also thick with a cloud of intolerable sound. And, as the dust fell, so the pandemonium abated and separated into recognizable sources. Women were screaming. Chair legs scraped the floor, branches of ever-greens fell from the walls, the piano hummed like a gigantic top.

Miss Campanula fell forward. Her face slid down the sheet of music which stuck to it. Very slowly and stealthily she slipped sideways to the keys of the piano, striking a final discord in the bass. She remained there, quite still, in a posture that seemed to parody the antics of an affected virtuoso. She was dead.

III

Lady Appleby in her chair by the piano turned to her husband as if to ask him a question and fainted.

Georgie Biggins screamed like a whistle.

The rector came through the curtain and ran down the steps to the piano. He looked at that figure leaning on the keys, wrung his hands and faced the audience. His lips moved, but he could not be heard.

Dinah came out of the prompt corner and stood transfixed. Her head was bent as if in profound meditation. Then she turned, stumbled past the curtain, calling 'Henry! Henry!' and disappeared.

Dr Templett, in his appalling make-up, came through from the opposite side of the curtain. He went up to the rector, touched his arm and then descended to the piano. He bent down with his back to the audience, stayed so for a moment and then straightened up. He shook his head slightly at the rector.

Mr Blandish, in the third row, pushed his way to the aisle and walked up to the stage.

He said, 'What's all this?' in a loud, constabulary tone, and was heard. The hall went suddenly quiet. The voice of Mr Prosser, the Chipping organist, said all by itself: 'It was a gun. That's what it was. It was a gun.'

Mr Blandish was not in uniform, but he was dressed in authority. He examined the piano and spoke to Dr Templett. There was a screen masking the corner on the prompt side between the stage and the wall. The two men fetched it and put it round the piano.

The rector mounted the steps to the stage and faced his parishioners.

'My dear people,' he said in a trembling voice, 'there has been a terrible accident. I beg of you all to go away quietly to your homes. Roper, will you open the door?'

'Just a minute,' said Mr Blandish. 'Just a minute, if *you please*, sir. This is an affair for the police. Charlie Roper, you stay by that door. Have you got your note-book on you?'

'Yes sir,' said Sergeant Roper.

'All right.' Mr Blandish raised his voice. 'As you pass out,' he roared, 'I'll ask you to leave your names and addresses with the sergeant on duty at the door. Anybody who had had anything to do with this entertainment,' continued Mr Blandish with no trace of irony in his voice, 'either in the way of taking part or decorating the hall or so forth, will kindly remain behind. Now move along quietly, please, there's no need to rush. The back benches first. Keep your seats till your turn comes.'

To the rector he said, 'I'd be much obliged if you'd go to the back door, sir, and see nobody leaves that way. If it can be locked and you've got the key, lock it. We'll have this curtain up, if you please. I'm going to the telephone. It's in the back room, isn't it? Much obliged.'

He went through the back of the stage, passing Dinah and Henry, who stood side by side in the wings.

'Good-evening, Mr Jernigham,' said the superintendent. 'Do you mind raising the curtain?'

'Certainly,' said Henry.

The curtain rose in a series of uneven jerks, revealing to the people still left in the hall a group of four persons: Jocelyn Jernigham, Selia Ross, Eleanor Prentice and the rector, who had returned from the back door with the key in his hand.

'I can't believe it,' said the rector. 'I simply cannot believe that it has happened.'

'Is it murder?' asked Mrs Ross sharply. Her voice pitched a note too high, sounded shockingly loud.

'I – I can't believe – ' repeated Mr Copeland.

'But see here, Copeland,' interrupted the squire, 'I don't know what the devil everybody's driving at. Shot through the head! What d'you mean? Somebody must have seen something. You can't shoot people through the head in a crowded hall without being spotted.'

'The shot seems to have come from – from – '

'From where, for heaven's sake?'

'From inside the piano,' said the rector unhappily. 'We mustn't touch anything; but it seems to come from inside the piano. You can see through the torn silk.'

'Good God!' said Jocelyn. He looked irritably at Miss Prentice, who rocked to and fro like a middle-aged marionette and moaned repeatedly.

'Do be quiet, Eleanor,' said the squire. 'Here! Templett!'

Dr Templett had again gone behind the screen, but he came out and said, 'What?' in an irascible voice.

'Has she been shot through the head?'

'Yes.'

'How?'

'From inside the piano.'

'I never heard of such a thing,' said Jocelyn. 'I'm coming to look.'

'Yes. But I say,' objected Dr Templett, 'I don't think you ought to, you know. It's a matter for the police.'

'Well, you've just been in there.'

'I'm police surgeon for the district.'

'Well, by God,' said the squire, suddenly remembering it, 'I'm Acting Chief Constable for the county.'

'Sorry,' said Dr Templett. 'I'd forgotten.'

But the squire was prevented from looking behind the screen by the return of Mr Blandish.

'That's all right,' said the superintendent peaceably. He turned to the squire. 'I've just rung up the station and asked for two chaps to come along, sir.'

'Oh, yes. Yes. Very sensible,' said Jocelyn.

'Just a minute, Blandish,' said Dr Templett. 'Come down here, would you?'

They disappeared behind the screen. The others waited in silence. Miss Prentice buried her face in her hands. The squire walked to the edge of the stage, looked over the top of the piano, turned aside, and suddenly mopped his face with his handkerchief.

Blandish and Templett came out and joined the party on the stage.

'Lucky, in a way, your being here on the spot, sir,' Blandish said to Jocelyn. 'Your first case of this sort since your appointment, I believe.'

'Yes.'

'Very nasty affair.'

'It is.'

'Yes. Well now, with your approval, Mr Jernigham, I'd just like to get a few notes down. I fancy Mr Henry Jernigham and Miss Copeland are with us.'

He peered into the shadows beyond the stage.

'We're here,' said Henry.

He and Dinah came on the stage.

'Ah, yes. Good-evening, Miss Copeland.'

'Good-evening,' said Dinah faintly.

'Now,' said Blandish, looking round the stage, 'this is the whole company of performers, I take it. *With* the exception of the deceased, of course.'

'Yes,' said Jocelyn.

'I'll just make a note of the names.'

They sat round the stage while Blandish wrote in his note-book. A group of ushers and two youths were huddled on a bench at the far end of the hall under the eyes of Sergeant Roper. Dinah fixed her gaze on this group, on Blandish, on the floor, anywhere but on the top of the piano jutting above the footlights and topped with pots of aspidistra. For down through the aspidistras, heavily shadowed by the screen, and not quite covered by the green and yellow bunting they had thrown over it, was Miss Campanula's body, face down on the keys of the piano. Dinah found herself wondering who was responsible for the aspidistras. She had meant to have them removed. They must mask quite a lot of the stage from the front rows.

'*Don't look at them,*' said her mind. She turned quickly to Henry. He took her hands and pulled her round with her back to the footlights.

'It's all right, Dinah,' he whispered, 'it's all right, darling.'

'I'm not panicked or anything,' said Dinah.

'Yes,' said Blandish, 'that all the names. Now, sir – well, what is it?'

A uniformed constable had come in from the front door and stood waiting in the hall.

'Excuse me,' said Blandish, and went down to him. There was a short rumbling conversation. Blandish turned and called to the squire.

'Can you spare a moment, sir?'

'Certainly,' said Jocelyn, and joined them.

'Can you beat this, sir?' said Blandish, in an infuriated whisper. 'We've had nothing better than a few old drunks and speed merchants in this place for the last six months or more, and now, tonight, there's got to be a breaking and entering job at Moorton Park with five thousand pounds' worth of her ladyship's jewellery gone and Lord knows what else besides. Their butler rang up the station five minutes ago, and this chap's come along on his motor bike and he says the whole place is upside down. Sir George and her ladyship and the party haven't got back yet. It looks like the work of the gang that cleaned up a couple of jobs in Somerset a fortnight back. It'll be a big thing to tackle. Now what am I to do, sir?'

Jocelyn and Blandish stared at each other.

'Well,' said Jocelyn at last, 'you can't be in two places at once.'

'That's right, sir,' said Blandish. 'It goes against the grain we've scarcely got started, but it looks as if it'll have to be the Yard.'

CHAPTER 9

CID

Five hours after Miss Campanula struck the third chord of the Prelude, put her foot on the soft pedal, and died, a police car arrived at the parish hall of Winton St Giles. It had come from Scotland Yard. It contained Chief Detective-Inspector Alleyn, Detective-Inspector Fox, Detective-Sergeant Bailey, and Detective-Sergeant Thompson.

Alleyn, looking up from his road map, saw a church spire against a frosty, moonlit hill, trees against stars, and nearer at hand the lighted windows of a stone building.

'This looks like the hidden treasure,' he said to Thompson who was driving. 'What's the time?'

'One o'clock, sir.'

As if in confirmation a clock, outside in the night, chimed for an hour and tolled one.

'Out we get,' said Alleyn.

The upland air was cold after the stuffiness of the car. It smelt of dead leaves and frost. They walked up a gravelled path to the front door of the building. Fox flashed a torch on a brass plate.

'Winton St Giles Parish Hall. The Gift of Jocelyn Jernigham Esquire of Pen Cuckoo, 1805. To the Glory of God. In memory of his wife Prudence Jernigham who passed away on May 7th, 1801.'

'This is the place, sir,' said Fox.

'Sure enough,' said Alleyn, and rapped smartly on the door.

It was opened by Sergeant Roper, bleary-eyed after a five hours' vigil.

'Yard,' said Alleyn.

'Thank Gawd,' said Sergeant Roper.

They walked in.

'The super asked me to say, sir,' said Sergeant Roper, 'that he was very sorry not to be here when you arrived, but seeing as how there's been a first-class breaking and entering up to Moorton Park – '

'That's all right,' said Alleyn. 'What's it all about?'

'Murder,' said Roper. 'Will I show you?'

'Do.'

They walked up the centre aisle between rows of empty benches and chairs. The floor was littered with programmes.

'I'll just turn on the other lights, sir,' said Roper. 'Deceased's behind the screen.'

He trudged up the steps to the stage. A switch clicked and Dinah's improvised foot- and proscenium-lights flooded the stage. Bailey and Thompson pulled the screen to one side.

There was Miss Campanula with her face on the keyboard on the piano, waiting for the expert, the camera, and the pathologist.

'Good Lord!' said Alleyn.

Rachmaninoff's (and Miss Campanula's) Prelude was crushed between her face and the keys. A dark crimson patch seeped out towards the margin of the music, but the title showed clearly. A hole had been blown through the centre. Without touching the music, Alleyn could see several pencilled reminders. After the last of the opening chords was an emphatic 'SP.' The left hand had been pinned down by the face but the right had fallen, and hung inconsequently at the end of a long purple arm. The face itself was hidden. They stared down at the back of the head. Its pitiful knot of grey hair, broken and loosened, hung over a dark hole. Weepers of stained hair stuck to the thin neck.

'Through the back of the skull,' said Fox.

'That's the wound of exit,' said Alleyn. 'We shall have to find the bullet.'

Bailey turnd away and began to search along the aisle.

Alleyn shone his torch on the tucked silk front of the piano. There was a rent exactly in the centre, extending above and below the central hole made by the bullet. Inside the hole, but quite close to the surface, the light picked up a shining circle. Alleyn leaned forward, peering, and uttered a soft exclamation.

'That's the gun that did the job, sir,' said Roper. 'Inside the piano.'

'Has it been touched?'

'No, sir, no. The super was in the audience and he took over immediately, did super. Except for doctor, not a soul's been near.'

'The doctor. Where is he?'

'He's gone home, sir. Dr Templett it is, up to Chippingwood. He's police surgeon. He was here when it happened. He said would I ring him up when you came and if you wanted him he'd be over. It's only a couple of miles off.'

'I think he'd better come. Ring him up now, will you?'

When Roper had gone, Alleyn said, 'This is a rum go, Fox.'

'Very peculiar, Mr Alleyn. How's it been worked?'

'We'll take a look-see when we've got some pictures. Take every angle, Thompson.'

Thompson had already begun to set up his paraphernalia. Soon the flashlight threw Miss Campanula into startling relief. For the second and last time she was photographed, seated at the instrument.

Roper came back from the telephone and watched the experts with avid interest.

'Funniest go you ever did see,' he said to Bailey, who had moved to the end of the aisle. 'I was on the spot. The old lady sits down at the piano in her bold way and wades into it. Biff, biff, plonk, and before you know where you are the whole works go off like a packet of crackers and she's lying there a corpse.'

'Cuh!' said Bailey and stooped swiftly to the floor. 'Here we are, sir,' he said. 'Here's the bullet.'

'Got it? I'll look at it in a minute.'

Alleyn marked the position of the head and arm and squatted on the floor to run a chalk line round the feet.

'Size eight,' he murmured. 'The left foot looks as if it's slipped on the soft pedal. Now, I wonder. Well, we'll soon find out. Got gloves on, all of you? Good. Go carefully, I should, and keep away from the front. Will you, sergeant – what is your name, by the way?'

'Roper, sir.'

'Right. Will you clear the stuff off the top?'

Roper shifted the aspidistra and began to unpin the bunting. Alleyn went up to the stage and squatted over the footlights like a sort of presiding deity.

'Gently does it, the thing's tottering. Look at that!'

He pointed at the inside of the top lid, which was turned back.

'Wood-rot. No wonder they wanted a new one. Good Lord!'

'What, sir?'

'Come and look at this, Fox.'

Alleyn shone his torch in at the top. The light glinted on a steel barrel. He slipped in his gloved fingers. There was a sharp click.

'I've just snicked over the safety-catch on a perfectly good automatic. Now, then.'

Roper pulled away the bunting.

'Well, I'll be damned!' said Fox.

II

'Very fancy, isn't it?' said Alleyn.

'A bit too fancy for me, sir. How does it work?'

'It's a Colt. The butt's jammed between the pegs, where the wires are made fast, and the front of the piano. The nozzle fits into a hole in this fretwork horror in front of the silk bib. The bib's rotten with age and bulging. It could be tweaked in front of the nozzle. Anyway, the music would hide it. Of course the top was smothered in bunting and vegetables.'

'But what pulled the trigger?'

'Half a second. There's a loop of string round the butt and over the trigger. The string goes on to an absurd little pulley in the back of the inner case. Then forward to another pulley on a front strut. Then it goes down.' He moved his torch. 'Yes, now you can see. The other end of the string is fixed to the batten that's part of the soft pedal action. When you use the pedal the batten goes backwards. Moves about two inches, I fancy. Quite enough to give a sharp jerk to the string. We'll have some shots of this, Thompson. It's a bit tricky. Can you manage?'

'I think so, Mr Alleyn.'

'It looks like a practical joke,' said Fox.

Alleyn looked up quickly.

'Funny you should say that,' he said. 'You spoke my thoughts. A small boy's practical joke. The Heath Robinson touch with the string and pulleys is quite in character. I believe I even recognize those little pulleys, Fox. Notice how very firmly they've been anchored. My godson's got their doubles in one of those building sets, an infernal dithering affair that's supposed to improve the mind, and nearly sent me out of mine. "Twiddletoy," it's called. Yes, and by George, Brer Fox, that's the sort of cord they provide: thin green twine, very tough, like fishing line, and fits nicely into the groove of the pulley.'

'D'you reckon some kid's gone wild and rigged this for the old girl?' asked Fox.

'A child with a Colt .32?'

'Hardly. Still, he might have got hold of one.'

Alleyn swore softly.

'What's up, sir?' asked Fox.

'It's the whole damn' lay-out of the thing! It's exactly like a contraption they give in the book of the words of these toys. "Fig. 1. Signal." It's no more like a signal than your nose. Less, if anything. But you build it on this principle. I made the thing for my godson. The cord goes up in three steps to pulleys that are fixed to a couple of uprights. At the bottom it's tied to a little arm and at the top to a bigger one. When you push down the lower arm, the upper one waggles. I'll swear it inspired this job. You see how there's just room for the pulley in the waist of the Colt at the back? They're fiddling little brutes, these pulleys, as I know to my cost. Not much bigger than the end of a cigarette. Hole through the middle. Once you've threaded the twine it can't slip out. It's guarded by the curved lips of the groove. You see, the top one's anchored to the wires above that strip of steel. The bottom one's tied to a strut in the fretwork. All right, Thompson, your witness.'

Thompson manœuvred his camera.

A car drew up outside the hall. A door slammed.

'That'll be the doctor, sir,' said Roper.

'Ah, yes. Let him in, will you?'

Dr Templett came in. He had removed his make-up and his beard and had changed the striped trousers and morning coat proper to a French Ambassador, for a tweed suit and sweater.

'Hullo,' he said. 'Sorry if I kept you waiting. Car wouldn't start.'

'Dr Templett?'

'Yes, and you're from Scotland Yard, aren't you? Didn't lose much time. This is a nasty business.'

'Beastly,' said Alleyn. 'I think we might move her now.'

They brought a long table from the back of the hall and on it they laid Miss Campanula. She had been shot between the eyes.

'Smell of eucalyptus,' said Alleyn.

'She had a cold.'

Dr Templett examined the wounds while the others looked on. At last he straightened up, took a bottle of ether from his pocket, and used a little to clean his hands.

'There's a sheet in one of the dressing-rooms, Roper,' he said. Roper went off to get it.

'What've you got there?' Templett asked Alleyn.

Alleyn had found Miss Prentice's Venetian Suite behind the piano. He turned it over in his hands. Like the Prelude, it was a very jaded affair. The red back of the cover had a discoloured circular patch in the centre. Alleyn touched it. It was damp. Roper returned with the sheet.

'Can't make her look very presentable, I'm afraid,' said Dr Templett. 'Rigor's fairly well advanced in the jaw and neck. Rather quick after five hours. She fell at an odd angle. I didn't do more than look at her. The exit wound showed clearly enough what had happened. Of course, I assured myself she was dead.'

'Did you realize at once that it was a wound of exit?'

'What? Yes. Well, after a second or two I did. Thought at first she'd been shot through the back of the head and then I noticed characteristics of an exit wound, direction of the matted hair and so on. I bent down and tried to see the face. I could just see the blood. Then I noticed the hole in the music. The frilling round the edge of the hole showed clearly enough which way the bullet had come.'

'Very sound observation,' said Alleyn. 'You knew, then, what had happened?'

'I was damn' puzzled and still am. When we'd rigged up the screen I had another look and spotted the nozzle of the revolver of whatever it is, behind the silk trimmings. I told Blandish, the local superintendent, and he had a look too. How the devil was it done?'

'A mechanical device that she worked herself.'

'Not suicide?'

'No, murder. You'll see when we open the piano.'

'Extraordinary business.'

'Very,' agreed Alleyn. 'Bailey, you might get along with your department now. When Thompson's finished, you can go over the whole thing for prints and then dismantle it. In the meantime, I'd better produce my note-book and get a few hard facts.'

They carried the table into a corner and put the screen round it. Roper came down with a sheet and covered the body.

'Let's sit down somewhere,' suggested Dr Templett. 'I want a pipe. It's given me a shock, this business.'

They sat in the front row of stalls. Alleyn raised an eyebrow at Fox who came and joined them. Roper stood in the offing. Dr Templett filled his pipe. Alleyn and Fox opened their note-books.

'To begin with,' said Alleyn, 'who was this lady?'

'Idris Campanula,' said Dr Templett. 'Spinster of this parish.'

'Address?'

'The Red House, Chipping. You passed it on your way up.'

'Have the right people been told about this?'

'Yes. The rector did that. Only the three maids. I don't know about the next-of-kin. Somebody said it was a second cousin in Kenya. We'll have to find that out. Look here, shall I tell you the story in my own words?'

'I wish you would.'

'I thought I'd find myself in the double rôle of police surgeon and eye-witness, so I tried to sort it out while I waited for your telephone call. Here goes. Idris Campanula was about fifty years of age. She came to the Red House as a child of twelve to live with her uncle, General Campanula, who adopted her on the death of her parents. He was an old bachelor and the girl was brought up by his acidulated sister, whom my father used to call one of the nastiest women he'd ever met. When Idris was about thirty, the general died, and his sister only survived him a couple of years. The house and money, a lot of money by the way, were left to Idris, who by that time was shaping pretty much like her aunt. Nil nisi and all that, but it's a fact. She never had a chance. Starved and repressed and hung about with a mass of shibboleths and Victorian conversation. Well, here she's stayed for the last twenty years, living on rich food, good works and local scandal. Upon my word, it's incredible that she's gone. Look here, I'm being too diffuse, aren't I?'

'Not a bit. You're giving us a picture in the round which is what we like.'

'Well, there she was until tonight. I don't know if you've heard from Roper about the play.'

'We haven't had time,' said Alleyn, 'but I hope to get volumes from him before dawn.'

Roper looked gratified and drew nearer.

'The play was got up by a group of local people.'

'Of whom you were one,' said Alleyn.

'Hullo!' Dr Templett took his pipe out of his mouth and stared at Alleyn. 'Now, did anyone tell you that, or is this the real stuff?'

'I'm afraid it's not even up to Form 1 at Hendon. There's a trace of grease paint in your hair. I wish I could add that I have written a short monograph on grease paint.'

Dr Templett grinned.

'I'd lay you ten to one,' he said, 'that you can't deduce what sort of part I had.'

Alleyn glanced sideways at him.

'We are not allowed to show off,' he said, 'but with Inspector Fox's austere eye on me, I venture to have a pot-shot. A character part, possibly a Frenchman, wearing a rimless eyeglass. Any good?'

'Did we bet shillings?'

'It was no bet,' said Alleyn apologetically.

'Well, let's have the explanation,' said Templett. 'I enjoy feeling a fool.'

'I'm afraid I'll feel rather a fool making it,' said Alleyn. 'It's a small beer indeed. In the words of all detective heroes, you only need to consider. You removed your make-up in a hurry. Spirit gum, on which I have not written a monograph, leaves its mark unless removed with care and alcohol. Your chin and upper lips show signs of having been plucked and there's a very remote trace of black crêpe hairiness. Only on the tip of your chin and not your cheeks. Ha! A black imperial. The foreign ambassadorial touch. A sticky reddish dint by the left eye suggests a rimless glass, fixed with more spirit gum. The remains of the heated line across the brow suggested a top-hat. And, when you mentioned your part, you moved your shoulders very slightly. You were thinking subconsciously of your performance. Broken English. "'Ow you say?" with a shrug. That sort of thing. For heaven's sake say I'm right.'

'By gum!' said Sergeant Roper devoutly.

'Amen,' said Dr Templett. 'In the words of Mr Holmes – '

'– of whom nobody shall make mock in my presence. Pray continue your most interesting narrative,' said Alleyn.

CHAPTER 10

According to Templett

'– and so you see,' concluded Templett, 'there is absolutely nothing about any of us that is at all out of the ordinary. You might find the same group of people in almost any of the more isolated bits of English countryside. The parson, the squire, the parson's daughter, the squire's son, the two church hens and the local medico.'

'And the lady from outside,' added Alleyn, looking at his notes. 'You have forgotten Mrs Ross.'

'So I have. Well, she's simply a rather charming newcomer. That's all. I'm blessed if I can see who, by the wildest flight of imagination, could have wanted to kill this very dull middle-aged frumpish spinster. I shouldn't have thought she had an enemy in the world.'

'I wouldn't say that,' said Sergeant Roper, unexpectedly. Alleyn looked up at him.

'No?'

'No, sir, I wouldn't say that. To speak frankly, she was a very sharp-tongued lady. Mischievous like. Well, overbearing. Very curious, too. Proper nosey-parker. My missus always says you couldn't change your mind without it being overheard at the Red House. My missus is friendly with the cook up to Red House, but she never says anything she doesn't want everybody in the village to hear about. Miss Campanula used to order the meals and then wait for the news, as you might say. They call her the Receiving Set in Chipping.'

'Do they, indeed,' murmured Alleyn.

'You don't murder people for being curious,' said Templett.

'You do sometimes, I reckon, doctor,' said Roper.

'I can't imagine it with Miss Campanula.'

'I don't reckon anybody *did* want to murder Miss Campanula,' said Roper, stolidly.

'Hullo!' Alleyn ejaculated. 'What's all this?'

'I reckon they wanted to murder Miss Prentice.'

'Good God!' said Templett. 'I never thought of that!'

'Never thought of what?' said Alleyn.

'I forgot to tell you. Good Lord, what a fool! Why didn't you remind me, Roper? Good Lord!'

'May we hear now?' asked Alleyn patiently.

'Yes, of course.'

In considerable confusion, Templett explained about Miss Prentice's finger and the change of pianists.

'This is altogether another kettle of fish,' said Alleyn. 'Let's get a clear picture. You say that up to twenty minutes to eight Miss Prentice insisted that she was going to do the overture and entr'acte?'

'Yes. I told her three days ago she'd better give it up. There was this whitlow in her middle finger and she mucked about with it and got some sort of infection. It was very painful. D'you think she'd give in? Not a bit of it. Said she'd alter the fingering of her piece. Wouldn't hear of giving it up. I asked her tonight if she'd let me look at it. Oh, no! It was "much easier"! She'd got a surgical stall over it. At about twenty to eight I passed the ladies' dressing-room. The door was half-open and I heard a sound like somebody crying. I could see her in there alone, rocking backwards and forwards holding this damned finger. I went in and insisted on looking at it. All puffed up and as fiery as hell! She was in floods of tears but she still said she'd manage. I put my foot down. Dinah Copeland came in, saw what was up, and fetched her father who's got more authority over these women than anybody else. He made her give in. Old Idris, poor old girl, had turned up by then and was all agog to play the famous Prelude. She's played it in and out of season for the last twenty years, if it's been written as long as that. Somebody was sent off to the Red House for the music and a dress; she was dressed up for her part, you see. The rector said he'd make an announcement about it. By that time Miss Prentice had settled down to being a martyr and – but, look here, I'm being most amazingly indiscreet. Now, don't go and write all this down in that note-book and quote me as having said it.'

Dr Templett looked anxiously at Fox whose note-book was flattened out on his enormous knee.

'That's all right, sir,' said Fox blandly. 'We only want the essentials.'

'And I'm giving you all the inessentials. Sorry.'

'I didn't say that, now, doctor.'

'We can take it,' Alleyn said, 'that, in your opinion up to twenty to eight everybody, including Miss Campanula and Miss Prentice, believed the music would be provided by Miss Prentice.'

'Certainly.'

'And this "Venetian Suite" was Miss Prentice's music?'

'Yes.'

'Nobody could have rigged this apparatus inside the piano after seven-forty?'

'Lord, no! The audience began to arrive at about half-past seven, didn't it, Roper? You were on the door.'

'The Cains turned up at seven-twenty,' said Roper, 'and Mr and Mrs Biggins and that young limit Georgie were soon after them. I was on duty at seven. Must have been done before then, sir.'

'Yes. What about the afternoon and morning? Anybody here?'

'We were all in and out during the morning,' said Dr Templett. 'The YPFC girls did the decorating and fixed up the supper arrangements and so on, and we got our stuff ready behind the screens. Masses of people.'

'You'd been rehearsing here, I suppose?'

'Latterly. We did most of the rehearsing up in the study at Pen Cuckoo. It was too cold here until they got extra heaters in. We had our dress rehearsal here on Thursday night. Yesterday afternoon at five, Friday I mean, we went up to Pen Cuckoo and had what Dinah calls a run-through for words.'

'What about this afternoon before the performance?'

'It was shut up during the afternoon. I called in at about three o'clock to drop some of my gear. The place was closed then and the key hung up between the wall of the outside place and the main building. We'd arranged that with Dinah.'

'Did you notice the piano?'

'Now, did I? Yes. Yes, I did. It was where it is now, with bunting all over the top and a row of pot plants. They'd fixed it up like that in the morning.'

'Did anybody else look in at three o'clock while you were here?'

'Let me think. Yes, Mrs Ross was there with some foodstuff. She left it in the supper-room at the back of the stage.'

'How long were you both in the place?'

'Oh, not long. We – talked for a minute or two and then came away.'

'Together?'

'No. I left Mrs Ross arranging sandwiches on plates. By the way, if you want anything to eat, do help yourselves. And there's some beer under the table. I provided it, so don't hesitate.'

'Very kind of you,' said Alleyn.

'Not a bit. Be delighted. Where were we? Oh, yes. I had a case over near Moorton and I wanted to look in at the cottage hospital. I wasn't here long.'

'Nobody else came in?'

'Not then.'

'Who was the first to arrive in the evening?'

'I don't know. I was the last. Had an emergency case at six. When I got home I found my wife not so well again. We didn't get here till half-past seven. Dinah Copeland thought I wasn't going to turn up and had worked herself into a frightful stew. She'd be able to tell you all about times of arrival. I bet she got here long before the rest of the cast. Dinah Copeland. That's the parson's daughter. She produced the play.'

'Yes. Thank you.'

'Well, I suppose you don't want me any longer. Good Lord, it's nearly two o'clock!'

'Awful, isn't it? We shall be here all night, I expect. No, we won't bother you any more, Dr Templett.'

'What about moving the body. Shall I fix up for the mortuary van to come along as early as possible?'

'I wish you would.'

'I have to do the PM, I suppose?'

'Yes. Yes, of course.'

'Pretty plain sailing, it'll be, poor old girl. Well, goodnight or good-morning, er – I don't know your name, do I?'

'Alleyn.'

'What, Roderick Alleyn?'

'Yes.'

'By George, I've read your book of criminal investigation. Damned good. Fascinating subject, isn't it?'

'Enthralling.'

'For the layman, what? Not such fun for the expert.'

'Not quite such fun.'

Dr Templett shook hands, turned to go, and then paused.

'I tell you what,' he said. 'I'd like to see how this booby-trap worked.'

'Yes, of course. Come and have a look.'

Bailey was at the piano with an insufflator and a strong lamp. Thompson stood by with his cameras.

'How's it going, Bailey?' asked Alleyn.

'Finished the case, sir. Not much doing. Somebody must have dusted the whole show. We may get some latent prints but I don't think there's a chance, myself. Same with the Colt. We're ready to take it down.'

'All right. Go warily, we don't want to lose any prints if they're there. I'll move the front of the piano off and you hold the gun.'

Bailey reached a gloved hand inside the top.

'I'll take off the pulley on the front panel, sir.'

'Yes. That'll give us a better picture than if you dismantled the twine altogther.'

Fox undid the side catches and Alleyn lifted away the front of the piano and put it on one side.

'Hullo,' he said, 'this silk panelling seems as though it's had water spilt on it. It's still dampish. Round the central hole.'

'Blood?' Suggested Dr Templett.

'No. There's a little blood. This was water. A circular patch of it. Now, I wonder. Well, let's have a look at the works.'

The Colt, supported at the end of the barrel by Bailey's thumb and forefinger, was revealed with its green twine attachments. The butt was still jammed against the pegs at the back. Alleyn picked up the detached pulley and held it in position.

'Good God!' said Dr Templett.

'Ingenious, isn't it?' Alleyn said. 'I think we'll have a shot of it like this, Thompson. It'll look nice and clear for the twelve good men and true.'

'Is the safety catch on?' demanded Dr Templett, suddenly stepping aside.

'It is. You've dealt with the soft pedal, haven't you, Bailey?' He stooped and pressed the left pedal down with his hand. The batten with its row of hammers moved towards the string. The green twine tightened in the minute pulleys.

'That's how it worked. You can see where the pressure comes on the trigger.'

'A very neat-fingered person, wouldn't you say, Mr Alleyn?' said Fox.

'Yes,' said Alleyn. 'Neat and sure fingers.'

'Oh, I don't know,' said Templett. 'It's amazingly simple really. The only tricky bit would be passing the twine through the trigger guard, round the butt, and through the top pulley. That could be done before the gun was jammed in position. No, it's simpler than it looks.'

'It's like one of these affairs in books,' said Bailey disgustedly. 'Someone trying to think up a new way to murder. Silly, I call it.'

'What do you say, Roper?' said Alleyn.

'To my way of thinking, sir,' said Sergeant Roper, 'these thrillers are ruining our criminal classes.'

Dr Templett gave a shout of laughter. Roper turned scarlet and stared doggedly at the wall.

'What d'you mean by that, my lad?' asked Fox, who was on his knees, staring into the piano.

Thompson, grinning to himself, touched off his flashlight.

'What I mean to say, Mr Fox,' said Roper. 'It puts ideas in their foolish heads. And the talkies, too. Especially young chaps. They get round the place talking down their noses and making believe they're gangsters. Look at this affair! I bet the chap that did this got the idea of it out of print.'

'That's right, Roper, stick to it,' said Dr Templett. Roper disregarded him. Templett repeated his good-nights and went away.

'Go on, Roper. It's an idea,' said Alleyn when the door had slammed. 'What sort of print do you imagine would inspire this thing?'

'One of those funny drawings with bits of string and cogs and umbrellas and so forth?' suggested Thompson.

'Heath Robinson? Yes.'

'Or more likely, sir,' said Roper, 'one of they four-penny boys' yarns in paper covers like you buy at the store in Chipping. I used to buy them myself as a youngster. There's always a fat lad and a comic lad and the comical chap plays off the fat one. Puts lighted crackers in his pants and all that. I recollect trying the cracker dodge under the rector's seat at Bible class, and he gave me a proper tanning for it, too, did the rector.'

'The practical joke idea, you see, Fox,' said Alleyn.

'Well,' said Fox, stolidly. 'Do we start off reading the back numbers of a boys' paper, or what ?'

'You never know, Brer Fox. Have you noticed the back of the piano where the bunting's pinned down? There are four holes in the centre drawing-pin and three to each of the others. Will you take the Colt out now, and all the rest of the paraphernalia? I'm going to take a look round the premises. We'll have to start seeing these people in the morning. Who the devil's that?'

There was a loud knock at the front entrance.

'Will I see?' asked Sergeant Roper.

'Do.'

Roper tramped off down the centre aisle and threw open the doors.

'Good-morning,' said a man's voice outside. 'I wonder if I can come in for a moment. It's raining like Noah's half-holiday and I'd like to have a word with – '

'Afraid not, sir,' said Roper.

'But I assure you I want to see the representative from Scotland Yard. I've come all the way from London,' continued the voice plaintively. 'I have, indeed. I represent the *Evening Mirror*. He'll be delighted to see me. Is it by any chance – '

'Yes, it is,' said Alleyn loudly and ungraciously. 'You can let him in, Roper.'

A figure in a dripping machintosh and streaming hat made a quick rush past Roper, gave a loud exclamation expressive of delight, and hurried forward with outstretched hand.

'I am *not* pleased to see you,' said Alleyn.

'Good-morning, Mr Bathgate,' said Fox. 'Fancy it being you.'

'Yes, just fancy!' agreed Nigel Bathgate. 'Well, well, well! I never expected to find the old gang. Bailey, too, and Thompson.

It's like the chiming of old bells to see you all happily employed together.'

'How the blue hell did you get wind of this?' inquired Alleyn.

'The gentleman who does market and social notes for the *Chipping Courier* was in the audience tonight and like a bright young pressman he rang up the Central News. I was in the office when it came through and you couldn't see my rudder for foam. Down here in four hours with one puncture. God bless my soul, now, what's it all about?'

'Sergeant Roper will perhaps spare a moment to throw you a bone or two. I'm busy. How are you?'

'Grand. Angela would send her love if she knew I was here, and your godson wants you to put him down for Hendon. He's three on Monday. Is it too late?'

'I'll inquire. Roper, you will allow Mr Bathgate to sit quietly in a corner somewhere. I'll be back in a few minutes. Coming Fox?'

Alleyn and Fox went up on the stage, looked round the box-set, and explored the wings.

'We'll have to go over this with a tooth-comb,' Alleyn said, 'looking for Lord knows what, as usual. Miss Dinah Copeland seems to have gone to a lot of trouble. The scenery's been patched up. Improvised footlights, you see, and I should think the two big overheads are introduced.'

He went into the prompt corner.

'Here's the play. *Shop Window,* by Hunt. Rather a good comedy. Very professional, with all the calls marked and so on. A bicycle bell. Probably an adjunct of the telephone on the stage. Let's have a look behind.'

A short flight of steps on each side of the back wall led down into a narrow room that ran the length of the stage.

'Mrs Ross's supper arrangements all laid out on the table. Lord, Fox, those sandwiches look good.'

'There's a lot more in this basket,' said Fox. 'Dr Templett did say – '

'And beer under the table,' murmured Alleyn. 'Brer Fox?'

'A keg of it,' said Fox, who was exploring. 'Dorset draught beer. Very good, Dorset draught.'

'You're right,' said Alleyn after an interval. 'It's excellent. Hullo!'

He stooped and picked something out of a box on the floor.

'Half a Spanish onion. Any onion in your sandwiches?'

'No.'

'Nor in mine. It's got flour or something on it.' He put the onion on the table and began to examine the plates of sandwiches. 'Two kinds only, Fox. Ham and lettuce on the one hand, cucumber on the other. Hullo, here's a tray all set out for a stage tea. Nobody ate a thing. Wait a bit.'

He lifted the lid of the empty teapot and sniffed at the inside.

'The onion appears to have lived in the teapot. Quaint conceit, isn't it? Very rum, indeed. Come on.'

They explored the dressing-rooms. There were two on each side of the supper-room.

'Gents to the right, ladies to the left,' said Alleyn. He led the way into the first room on the left. He and Fox began a methodical search through the suitcases and pockets.

'Not quite according to Cocker, perhaps,' Alleyn remarked, peering at Miss Prentice's black Marocain on the wall. 'But I think we'll ask afterwards. Anyway I'm provided with a blank search-warrant so we're all right. Damn this onion, my hand stinks of it. This must be the two spinsters' room, judging by the garments.'

'Judging by the pictures,' said Fox, 'it's a Bible classroom in the ordinary way.'

'Yes. The Infant Samuel. What about next door? Ah, rather more skittish dresses. This will be Dinah Copeland and Mrs Ross. Dr Templett seemed rather self-conscious about Mrs Ross, I thought. Miss Copeland's grease paints are in a cardboard box with her name on it. They've been used a lot. Mrs Ross's, in a brand new japanned tin affair and brand new themselves, from which, inspired by Dorset draught, I deduce that Miss Copeland may be a professional, but Mrs Ross undoubtedly is not. Here's a card in the new tin box. "Best luck for tonight, B." A present, by gum! Who's B., I wonder. Now for the men's rooms.'

They found nothing of interest in the men's rooms until Alleyn came to a Donegal tweed suit.

'This is the doctor's professional suit,' he said. 'It reeks of surgery. Evidently the black jacket is not done in a country practice. I suppose, in the hubbub, he didn't change but went home looking like a comic-opera Frenchman. He must have – '

Alleyn stopped short. Fox looked up to see him staring at a piece of paper.

'Found something, sir?'

'Look.'

It was a thin piece of plain blue paper. Fox read the lines of capitals:

YOU ARE GIVEN NOTICE TO LEAVE THIS DISTRICT.
IF YOU DISREGARD THIS WARNING YOUR LOVER SHALL
SUFFER.

'Where did you find this, Mr Alleyn?'

'In a wallet. Inside breast pocket of the police surgeon's suit,' said Alleyn. He dropped it on the dressing-table and then bent down and sniffed at it.

'It smells of eucalyptus,' he said.

CHAPTER 11

According to Roper

'That's awkward,' grunted Fox, after a pause.

'Couldn't be more awkward.'

'"Your *lover* shall suffer,"' quoted Fox. 'That looks as if it was written to a woman, doesn't it?'

'It's not common usuage nowadays the other way round, but it's English. Common enough in the mixed plural.'

'He's a married man,' Fox remembered.

'Yes, it sounded as if his wife's an invalid, didn't it? This may have been written to his mistress or possibly to him, or it may have been shown to him by a third person who is threatened and wants advice.'

'Or he may have done it himself.'

'Yes, it's possible, of course. Or it may be the relic of a parlour game. Telegrams, for instance. You make a sentence from a string of letters. He'd hardly carry that about next to his heart, though, would he? Damn! I'm afraid we're in for a nasty run, Brer Fox.'

'How did the doctor strike you, Mr Alleyn?'

'What? Rather jumpy. Bit too anxious to please. Couldn't stop talking.'

'That's right,' agreed Fox.

'Well have to flourish the search-warrant a bit if we work on this,' said Alleyn. 'It'll be interesting to see if he misses it before we tackle him about it.'

'He's doing the PM.'

'I know. We shall be present. Anyway, the lady was shot through the head. We've got the weapon and we've got the projectile. The post-mortem is not likely to be very illuminating. Hullo, Bailey, what is it?'

Bailey had come down the steps from the stage.

'I thought you'd better know, sir. This chap Roper's recognized the automatic. Mr Bathgate ran him down to the station and they've checked up the number.'

'Where is he?'

'Out in the hall.' A reluctant grin appeared on Bailey's face. 'I reckon he still thinks it's great to be a policeman. He wants to tell you himself.'

'Very touching. All right, Bailey, I want you to test this paper for prints. Do it at once, will you, and put it between glass when you've finished. And, Bailey, have a shot at the teapot there. Inside and out.'

'Teapot, sir?'

'Yes. Also the powdered onion on the table. I dare say it's quite immaterial, but it's queer, so we'd better tackle it.'

They returned to the hall where they found Roper standing over the automatic with something of the air of a clever retriever.

'Well, Roper,' said Alleyn, 'I hear you've done a bit of investigation for us.'

'Yes, sir, I have so. I've recognized the lethal weapon, sir.'

'Well, whose is it?'

'I says to myself when I see it,' said Roper, 'I know you, my friend, I've had you in my hands, I said. And then I remembered it. It was when we checked up on firearms licences six months ago. Now, I suppose a hundred weapons must have passed under my notice that time, this being a sporting part of the world, so I reckon it's not surprising I didn't pick this affair as soon as I clapped eyes on her. I reckon that's not surprising, and yet she looked familiar, you understand?'

'Yes, Roper, I quite understand. Who is the owner?'

'This weapon, sir, is a Colt .32 automatic, the property of Jocelyn Jernigham, Esquire, of Pen Cuckoo.'

'Is it indeed?' murmured Alleyn.

'This gentleman, Mr Bathgate, ran me down to the station, sir, and it didn't take me over and above five minutes to lay my finger on the files. You can take a look at the files, sir, and – '

'I shall do so. Now, Roper, see if you can give me some modal answers. Short, crisp, and to the point. When did you see the automatic? Can you give me the date?'

'In the files!' shouted Sergeant Roper, triumphantly. 'May 31st of the current year.'

'Where was it?'

'In the study at Pen Cuckoo, sir, that being the room at the extreme end of the west wing facing the Vale.'

'Who showed it to you?'

'Squire, himself, showed it to me. We'd checked up all the weapons in the gun-room, of which there was a number, and squire takes me into his study and says, "There's one more," he says, and he lays his hand on a wooden box on the table and opens the lid. There was this lethal masterpiece laying on her side, with a notice written clear in block letters. "Loaded." "It's all right," says Mr Jernigham, seeing me step aside as he takes her out. "The safety catch is on," he says. And he showed me. And he says, "It went all through the war with me," he says, "and there's half a clip left in it. I'd fired two shots when I got my Blighty one," he says, "and I've kept it like this ever since. I let it be known there's a loaded automatic waiting at Pen Cuckoo for anybody that feels like coming in uninvited." We'd had some thieving in the district at that time, same as we've got now. He told me this weapon had lain in that box for twenty years, did squire.'

'Was the box locked?'

'No, sir. But he said all the maids was warned about it.'

'Anybody else in the room?'

'Yes, sir. Mr Henry was there and Miss Prentice, sitting quietly by the fire and smiling, pussy-like, same as she always does.'

'Don't you like Miss Prentice?'

'I think she's all right, but my missus says she's proper sly. My missus is a great one for the institute and Miss Prentice is president of same.'

'I see. Any local gossip about Miss Prentice?'

Roper expanded. He placed his hands in his belt with the classic heaving movement of all policemen. He then appeared to remember he was in the presence of authority and rearranged himself in an attitude of attention.

'Aye,' he said, 'they talk all right, sir. You see, Miss Prentice, she came along, new to the Vale, on three years back when Mrs Jernigham died. I reckon the late Mrs Jernigham was nigh-on the best liked lady in this part of Dorset. A Grey of Stourminster-Weston she was, Dorset born and bred, and a proper lady. Now, this Miss Prentice, for all she's half a Jernigham, is a foreigner as you might say, and she doesn't know our ways here. Mrs Jernigham was welcome everywhere, cottage and big houses alike, and wherever she went she was the same. Never asking questions or if she did, out of real niceness and not nosey-parkishness. Now, folk about here say Miss Prentice is the other way round. Sly. Makes trouble between cottages and rectory, or would if she could. Cor!' said Roper, passing his ham of a hand over his face. 'The way that old maiden got after rector! My missus says – well, my missus is an outspoken woman and come off a farm.'

Alleyn did not press for a repetition of Mrs Roper's agricultural similes.

'There was only one worse than her,' continued Roper, 'and that was the deceased. She was a dragon after rector. And before Miss Prentice came, Miss Campanula had it all her own way, but I reckon Miss Campanula kind of lost driving power when t'other lady got going with her insinuating antics.'

'How did they get on together?'

'Fast as glue,' said Roper. 'Thick as thieves. My missus says they knew too much about each other to be anything else. Cook up to Red House, she says Miss Campanula was jealous fair-to-bust of Miss Prentice, but she was no match for her, however, being the type of woman that lets her anger be seen and rages out in the open, whereas Miss Prentice, with her foxy ways, goes quiet to work. Cook told my missus that deceased was losing ground daily and well-nigh desperate over it.'

'How do you mean, losing ground?'

'With rector.'

'Dear me,' murmured Alleyn. 'How alarming for the rector.'

'Reckon he picks his way like that chap in Bible,' said Roper. 'He's a simple sort of chap but he's a Vale man and he suits us. His father and grandfather were rectors before him and he knows our ways.'

'Quite so, Roper,' said Alleyn, and lit a cigarette.

'No. But the rector met his match in those two ladies, sir, and it's a marvel one of them hasn't snapped him up by this time. Likely he holds them off with holy conversation, but I've seen the hunted look in the man's eyes more than once.'

'I see,' said Alleyn. 'Do you think it generally known that Mr Jernigham kept this loaded automatic in the study?'

'I should say it was, sir. If I make so bold, sir, I'd say it was never squire that did this job. He's peppery, is Mr Jernigham, but I'd bet my last penny he's not a murderer. Flares up and forgets all about if the next minute. Very outspoken. Mr Henry, now, he's deeper. A nice young fellow but quiet-like. You never know what he's thinking. Still, he's got no call to kill anybody, and wouldn't if he had.'

'Who is Mrs Ross of Duck Cottage, Cloudyfold?'

'Stranger to these parts. She only came here last April.' Roper's blue eyes became hard and bright. 'Young?' asked Alleyn.

'Not what you'd say so very young. Thin. Pale hair, done very neat, and very neat in her dressing. Her clothes look different to most ladies. More like the females in the talkies only kind of simpler. Dainty. She's dressed very quiet, always, but you notice her.' Roper paused, six-foot-two of dim masculine appreciation. 'I reckon she's got It,' he said at last. 'It's not my place to say so, but I suppose a chap always knows her sort. By instinct.'

There was an odd little silence during which the other five men stared at Sergeant Roper.

'Dr Templett does, anyway,' he said at last.

'Oh,' said Alleyn. 'More local gossip?'

'The women-folk. You know what they are, sir. Given it a proper thrashing, they have. Well, there's a good deal of feeling on account of Mrs Templett being an invalid.'

'Yes, I suppose so. Let me see, that's all the cast of the play, isn't it? Except Miss Copeland.'

'Miss Dinah? She'll be in a taking-on, I make no doubt. After all the work she's given to this performance for it to go up, as you might say, in a cloud of dust. Still, she's courting, that'll be a kind of comfort to the maid. Mr Henry was watching over her after the tragedy, holding her hand for all to see. They're well-matched and we're hoping to hear it's a settled matter any time now. My missus says it'll be one in the eye for Miss Prentice.'

'Why on earth?'

'She won't be fancying another lady at Pen Cuckoo. I saw her looking blue murder at them even while deceased was lying you might say, a corpse at their feet. She's lucky it wasn't her. Should be thanking her Creator she's still here to make trouble.'

'Miss Prentice,' said Nigel, 'seems to be a very unpleasant cup of tea. Perhaps her sore finger was all a bluff and she rigged the tackle for the girl-friend.'

'Dr Templett said it was no bluff, Mr Bathgate,' said Fox. 'He said she held out till the last moment that she was going to play.'

'That's right enough, sir,' said Roper. 'I went round to the back to see Miss Dinah just after it had happened and there was Miss Prentice crying her eyes out with her finger looking that unwhole-some it'd turn your stomach, and Miss Dinah telling her she was ruining the paint on her face and the doctor saying, "I absolutely for-bid it. Your finger's in a very nasty state and if you weren't playing this part tonight," he said, "I'd open it up." Yes he threatened her with the knife, did doctor. Mr Henry says, "You'll make a mess of Mr Nevin's ecstasies." Her piece was composed by a chap of that sort name as you'll see in the programme. "You'll never stay the course, Cousin Eleanor," says Mr Henry. "I know it's hurting you like stink," says Mr Henry, "because you're crying," he says. But no, she would-n't give in till Miss Dinah fetched her father. "Come," he says, "we all know how you feel about it, but there are times when generosi-ty is better than heroism." She looked up at rector, then, and said, "If you say so, Father," and with that Miss Campanula says, "Now, who'll go get my music? Where's Gibson?" Which is the name of her chauffeur. So she give in, but very reluctant.'

'A vivid enough picture of the rival performances, isn't it?' said Alleyn. 'Well, there's the history of the case. It's getting on for three o'clock. I think, on second thoughts, Fox, we won't wait for the light of day. We'll make a night of it. This place must be over-hauled some time and it looks as though we'll have a busy day tomorrow. You can turn in if you like, Roper. Some one can relieve us at seven.'

'Are you going to search the premises, sir?'

'Yes.'

'Reckon I'd like to give a hand if it's agreeable to you.'

'Certainly. Fox, you and Thompson make sure we've missed nothing in the dressing-rooms and supper-room. Bailey, you can take Roper with you on the stage. Go over every inch of it. I'll tackle the hall and join you if I finish first.'

'Are you looking for anything in particular?' asked Nigel.

'The usual unconsidered trifles. Spare bits of Twiddletoy, for instance. Even a water pistol.'

'Not forgetting any kid's annuals that happen to be lying round,' added Fox.

'Poor things!' said Nigel. 'Back to childhood's day, I see. Is there a telephone here?'

'In a dressing-room,' said Alleyn. 'But it's only an extension.'

'I'll ring up the office from a pub, then. In the meantime, I may as well write up a pretty story.'

He took out his pad and settled himself at a table on the stage.

Police investigation is for the most part a dull business. Nothing could be more tedious than searching for things. Half a detective's life is spent in turning over dreary objects, finding nothing, and replacing them. Alleyn started in the entrance porch of the parish hall and began a meticulous crawl over dusty surfaces. He moved like a snail, across and across, between the rows of benches. He felt cold and dirty and he smelt nothing but dust. He could not allow his thoughts to dwell pleasantly on his own affairs, his coming marriage and the happiness that kept him company nowadays; because it is when his thoughts are abstracted from the business in hand that the detective misses the one small sign events have set in his path. Sometimes the men on the stage heard a thin whistling down the hall. Sergeant Roper's voice droned interminably. At intervals the church clock sweetly recorded the journey of the hours. Miss Campanula lay stealthily stiffening behind a red baize screen, and Nigel Bathgate recorded her departure in efficient journalese.

Alleyn had passed the benches and chairs and was grovelling about in the corner with an electric torch. Presently he uttered a soft exclamation. Nigel looked up from his writing and Bailey, who had the loose seat of a chair in his hands, shaded his eyes and peered down the corner.

Alleyn stood by the stage, on the audience's left. He held a small shining object between finger and thumb. His hand was gloved. One of his eyebrows was raised and his lips were pursed in a soundless whistle.

'Struck a patch, sir?' asked Bailey.

'Yes, I rather think so, Bailey.'

He walked over to the piano.

'Look.'

Bailey and Nigel came to the footlights.

The shining object Alleyn held in his hands was a boy's water-pistol.

II

'As you said yourself, Bathgate, back to childhood days.'

'What's the idea, sir?' asked Bailey.

'It seems to be a recurrent idea,' said Alleyn. 'I found this thing stuffed away in a sort of locker under the stage over there. It was poked in a dark corner, but there's little or no dust on it. The rest of the stuff in the locker's smothered in dirt. Look at the butt, Bailey. Do you see that shiny scratch? It's rather a super sort of water-pistol, isn't it? None of your rubber bulbs that you squeeze – but a proper trigger action. Fox!'

Fox and Thompson appeared from the direction of the supper-room.

Alleyn went to the small table where Bailey had placed the rest of the exhibits, lifted the covering cloth and laid his find beside the Colt automatic.

'The length is the same to within a fraction of an inch,' he said; 'and there's a mark on the butt of the Colt very much like the mark on the butt of the water-pistol. That, I believe, is where it was rammed in the piano, between the steel pegs where the strings are fastened.'

'But what the devil,' asked Nigel, 'is the explanation?'

Alleyn pulled off his gloves and fished in his pockets for his cigarette-case.

'Where's Roper?'

'Out at the back, sir,' said Bailey. 'He'll be back shortly with a new set of reminiscences. His super ought to issue a gag for that chap.'

'This is a rum go,' said Fox profoundly.

'"Jones Minor" all over it,' said Alleyn. 'You were right, Bailey, I believe, when you suggested the deathtrap in the piano was too elaborate to be true. It *is* only in books that murder is quite as fancy as all this. The whole thing carried the hall-mark of the booby-trap and the signature of the practical joker. It is somehow difficult to believe that a man or woman would, as Bailey has said, think up murder on these lines. But what if a man with murder in his heart came upon this booby-trap, this water-pistol aimed through a hole in the torn silk bib? What if this potential murderer thought of substituting a Colt for the water-pistol. It becomes less far-fetched, then, doesn't it? What's more, there are certain advantages. The murderer can separate himself from his victim and from the *corpus delicti*. The spadework has been done. All the murderer has to do is remove the water-pistol, jam in the Colt and tie the loose end of twine round the butt. It's not his idea, it's Jones Minor's.'

'He'd want to be sure the Colt was the same length,' said Fox.

'He could measure the water-pistol.'

'And then go home and check up his Colt?'

'Or somebody else's Colt,' said Bailey.

'One of the first points we have to clear up,' Alleyn said, 'is the accessibility of Jernigham's war souvenir. Roper says he thinks everybody knew about it, and apparently it was there in the study. They were there last night – Friday night, I mean. It's Sunday now, heaven help us.'

'If Dr Templett recognized the Colt,' observed Fox, 'he didn't let on.'

'No more he did.'

The back door banged and boots resounded in the supper-room.

'Here's Roper,' said Fox.

'Roper!' shouted Alleyn.

'Yes, sir?'

'Come here.'

Sergeant Roper stumbled up the steps and appeared on the stage.

'Come and have a look at this.'

'Certainly, sir.'

Roper placed his palm on the edge of the stage and vaulted deafeningly to the floor. He approached the table with an air of efficiency and contemplated the water-pistol.

'Know it?' asked Alleyn.

Roper reached out his hand.

'Don't touch it!' said Alleyn sharply.

''T, 't, 't!' said Fox and Bailey.

'Beg pardon, sir,' said Roper. 'Seeing that trifling toy, and recognizing it in a flash, I had a natural impulse, as you might say – '

'Your natural impulses must be mortified if you want to grow up into a detective,' said Alleyn. 'Whose water-pistol is this?'

'Mind,' said Roper warningly, 'there may be two of this class in the district, sir. Or more. I'm not taking my oath there aren't. But barring that eventuality, I reckon I can put an owner on it. And seeing he had the boldness to take a shot at me outside the Jernigham Arms, me being in uniform – '

'Roper,' said Alleyn, 'it is only about three hours to the dawn. Don't let the sun rise on your parentheses. Whose water-pistol is this?'

'Georgie Biggins,' said Roper.

CHAPTER 12

Further Vignettes

At twelve o'clock the Yard car dropped Alleyn and Fox at the Jernigham Arms.

The rain had stopped, but it was a dank, dreary morning, and so cloudy that only a mean thinning of the night, a grudging disclosure of vague, wet masses, gave evidence that somewhere beyond the Vale there was dawnlight.

Bailey and Thompson drove off for London. Alleyn stared after the tail-light of the car while Fox belaboured the front door of the Jernigham Arms.

'There's *somebody* moving about in there,' he grumbled.

'Here they come.'

It was the pot-boy, very tousled and peepy, and accompanied by a gust of stale beer. Alleyn thought that he looked like all pot-boys at dawn throughout time and space.

'Good-morning,' Alleyn said. 'Can you give us rooms for a day or two, and breakfast in an hour? There's a third man on his way here.'

'I'll aask Missus,' said the pot-boy. He gaped at them, blinked, and went off down a passage. They could hear him calling with the cracked uncertainty of adolescence:

'Missus! 'Be detec-er-tives from Lunnon, along of Miss Campanula's murder, likely. Mrs Pe-e-each! Missus!'

'The whole place buzzing with it,' said Alleyn.

II

At seven o'clock Henry found himself suddenly awake. He lay still, wondering for a moment why this day would be different from any other day. Then he remembered. He saw with precision a purple heap, the top of a head, the nape of a neck laced with dark, shining streaks. He saw a sheet of music, crumpled, pinned to the keys of a piano by the head. The picture was framed in aspidistras like a nightmarish valentine and across the lower margin was the top of a piano.

'I have looked down at a murdered woman.' And for a time his thoughts would not move beyond this sharp memory, so that he found himself anxiously re-tracing the pattern of the head, the neck, the white sheet of music, and the fatuous leaves. Then the memory of Dinah's cold fingers crept into his hands. He closed his hands on the memory, clenching them as he lay in bed, and the whole idea of Dinah came into his mind.

'If it had been Eleanor, there would have been an end to our troubles.'

He pushed this thought away from him, telling himself it was horrible, but it returned repeatedly, and at last he said, 'It is stupid to pretend otherwise. I do wish it had been Eleanor.' He began to think of all that happened after Idris Campanula died; of how his father went aside with Superintendent Blandish, and of the solemn, ridculous look on his father's face. He remembered Dr Templett's explanations and Miss Prentice's moans which had irritated them all very much. He remembered that when he looked at Mr Copeland he saw that his lips were moving, and realized, with embarrassment, that the rector was at prayer. He remembered Mrs Ross's almost complete silence and the way she and Templett had not spoken to each other. And again his thoughts returned to Dinah. He had walked to the rectory with Dinah and her father, and on the threshold he had kissed her openly, the rector seeming scarely aware of it. On the way home to Pen Cuckoo, the squire had not forgotten that, in the absence of Sir George Dillington, he was Chief Constable, and had discoursed solemnly on the crime, saying again and again that Henry was to treat everything he heard as confidential, and relating how, with Blandish, he had come to a decision to call in Scotland Yard. When they were indoors at last, Eleanor Prentice had fainted, and the squire had forced brandy down her throat with such an uncertain hand that he had half-asphyxiated her. They helped her to her room and Jocelyn, nervously assiduous, had knocked the bandaged finger so that she screamed with pain. Henry and his father had a solemn drink together in the dining-room, Jocelyn still discoursing on his responsibilities.

Henry went cold all over, his heart dropped like a plummet, and he faced the worst memory of all, the one that he had been pushing away ever since he woke.

It was when Jocelyn told him how, strong in his position of Acting Chief Constable, he had peered through the hole in the tucked silk front, and had seen the glimmer of a firearm.

'A revolver,' Jocelyn had said, 'or else an automatic.'

At that moment the picture of the box in the study had risen in Henry's imagination. He had hurried his father to bed, but when he was alone had been afraid to go into the study and lift the lid of the box. Now he knew that he must do it. Quickly, before the servants were up. He leapt out of bed, threw on his dressing-gown, and crept downstairs through the dark house. There was an electric torch in the hall. He found it and made his way to the study.

The box was empty. The notice 'LOADED' in block capitals lay at the bottom.

Henry turned away with panic in his heart, and a minute later he was knocking at his father's door.

III

Selia had been awake for a very long time. She was wondering when she could telephone to Dr Templett or whether it would be altogether too unsafe to get into touch with with. She knew the telephone rang at his bedside until eight o'clock in the morning, and that he slept far enough away from his wife's room for it not to disturb her. Mrs Ross wanted to ask him what he had done with the anonymous letter. She knew that he had put it in his wallet, and that he kept his wallet in his breast pocket. She remembered that after the catastrophe he had not changed back into his ordinary suit, and she was hideously afraid that the letter might still be in his coat at the hall. He was very forgetful and careless about such things, and had once left one of her letters, open, on his dressing-table, only remembering it later on in the day.

She had no knowledge of what the police would do. She had a sort of idea she had read in a criminal novel that they were not allowed to search through private houses without a permit of some kind. But did that apply to a public hall? And surely if the body of a murdered person was there, in the hall, they would hunt everywhere. What would they think if they found that letter? She wanted to warn Dr Templett to be ready with an answer.

But he himself was an official.

But he had almost certainly remembered the letter.

Would it be better to say he knew the author to be someone else – his wife, even? Anyone but one of those two women.

Her thoughts, needle-sharp, darted in and out of the fabric of her terror.

Perhaps if he went down early . . .

Perhaps she should have telephoned an hour ago.

She switched on her bedside lamp and looked at her clock. It was five minutes to eight.

Perhaps she was too late.

In a panic she reached for the telephone and dialled his number.

IV

Miss Prentice's finger had kept her awake, but it is doubtful if she would have slept even if it had not throbbed all night. Her thoughts were too hurried and busy, weaving backwards and forwards between the rector, herself and Idris Campanula, who was murdered. She thought of all sorts of things; of how when she first came to Pen Cuckoo she and Idris had been such friends, confiding the secrets of their bosoms to each other like schoolgirls. She

remembered all the delicious talks they had had together, talks full
of exciting conjectures about the behaviour of other people in the
village and the county. There would be nobody now who would
speak her language and discuss things and people in that way. They
had been so intimate until Idris grew jealous. That was the form
Miss Prentice gave to their differences: Idris grew jealous of her
friend's rising influence in the village and in church affairs.

She would not think yet of Mr Copeland. The memory of the
things he had said to her at confession must be thrust down into
oblivion, and that other memory, that other frightful revelation of
Idris's perfidy.

No. Better to remember the old friendly days and to think of
Idris's will. It had been a very simple will. A lot for Mr Copeland, a
little for the distant nephew, and seven thousand for Eleanor herself.
Idris had said she'd never had a real friend until Eleanor came, and
that if she died first she would be happy in the thought that she had
been able to do this. Eleanor even then rather resented her friend's
air of patronage.

But it was true that if she had this money she would no longer be
so dependent on Jocelyn.

Mr Copeland would be very well off indeed, for Idris was an
extremely rich woman.

Dinah would be an heiress.

She had not thought of that before. There would be no worldly
reason now why Dinah and Henry should not marry.

If she were to withdraw her opposition quickly, before the will
was known – would not that seem generous and kind? If she could
only stifle the reflection of that scene on Friday afternoon. Dinah
limp in Henry's arms, lost in rapture. It had nearly driven Eleanor
mad. How could she unsay all that she had said before she turned
away and stumbled up the lane, escaping from so much agony? But
with Dinah married to Henry, then her father would be lonely. A
rich lonely man fifty years old, and too dignified to look for a young
wife. Surely then!

Then! Then!

The first bell, calling the people to eight o'clock service roused her
from her golden plans. She rose, dressed, and went out into the dark
morning.

V

The rector was astir at seven. It was Sunday, and he would be in church in an hour. He dressed hurriedly, unable to lie thinking any longer of the events of the night that was past. All sorts of recollections flocked into his thoughts, and in all of them the murdered woman was present, turning them into nightmares. He felt as if he was dyed in guilt, as if he would never rid hmself of his dreadful memories. His thoughts were chaotic and quite uncontrollable.

Long before the warning bell sounded for early celebration, he stole out of the house and walked, as he had done every Sunday for twenty years, down the drive, through the nut walk and over the stile into the churchyard.

When he was alone inside the dark church he fell on his knees and tried to pray.

VI

Somewhere, a long way off, somebody was knocking at a door. Bang, bang, *bang*. Must be old Idris pounding away at that damned lugubrious tune. Blandish needn't have locked Eleanor up inside the piano. As Deputy Chief Constable, I object to that sort of thing; it isn't cricket. Let her out! If she knocks much louder she'll blow the place up, and then we'll have to get in the Yard. Bang, bang –

The squire woke with a sickening leap of his nerves.

'Wha-a-a?'

'Father, it's me! Henry! I want to speak to you.'

VII

When Dinah heard her father go downstairs long before his usual hour, she knew he hadn't slept, that he was miserable, and that he would go into church and pray. She hoped that he had remembered to wear a woollen cardigan under his cassock, because he seemed to catch cold more easily in the church than anywhere else. She knew last night that she was in for a difficult time with him. For some extraordinary reason, he had already begun to blame himself for the tragedy, saying that he had been weak and vacillating, not zealous enough in his duties as a parish priest.

Dinah was unable to follow her father's reasoning, and with a sinking heart she had asked if he suspected any one as the murderer of Idris Campanula. That was when they got home last night and she was fortified by Henry's kiss.

'Daddy, do you think you know?'

'No, darling, no. But I haven't helped them as I should. And then when I did try, it was too late.'

'But what do you mean?'

'You mustn't ask me, darling.'

And then she had realized that she was thinking of the confessional. What on earth had Idris Campanula told him on Friday? What had Eleanor Prentice told him? Something had upset him very much, Dinah was sure. Well, one of them was gone and wouldn't make mischief any more. It was no good trying to be sorry. She wasn't sorry, she was only frightened and filled with horror whenever she thought of the dead body. It was the first dead body Dinah had ever seen.

Of course it was obvious to everybody that the trap had been set for Eleanor Prentice. Her father must realize that. Who, then, had a motive to kill Eleanor Prentice?

Dinah sat up in bed, cold with terror. She remembered the meeting in the lane on Friday afternoon, the things Eleanor Prentice had said in a breathless whisper, and the answer Henry had made.

'If she tells them what he said,' thought Dinah, 'they'll say Henry had a motive.'

And with her whole soul she tried to send out a warning message to Henry.

But Henry, at that moment, was pounding his father's bedroom door, and into his startled mind there came no warning message from Dinah. There was no need for one, for already he was afraid.

VIII

Dr Templett was dreamlessly, and peacefully asleep when the telephone rang at his bedside. At once, and with the accuracy born of long practice, he reached out in the half light for the receiver.

'Dr Templett here,' he said, as he always did, when the telephone rang at an ungodly hour. He remembered that young Mrs Cartwright might now be in labour.

But it was Selia Ross.

'Billy? Billy, have you got that letter?'

'What!'

He lay there quite still, holding the receiver to his ear and listening to his own thumping heart.

'Billy! Are you there?'

'Yes,' he said, 'yes. It's all right. There's nothing to worry about. I'll look in some time today.'

'Do, for God's sake.'

'All right. Goodbye.'

He hung up the receiver and lay staring at the ceiling. What had he done with that letter?

CHAPTER 13

Sunday Morning

Alleyn and Fox were at breakfast and Nigel was still asleep when Superintendent Blandish walked in. He was blue about the chin and his eyes and nose were watery.

'You must wonder if there is anybody except that jabbering chap Roper in the Great Chipping Constabulary,' he said as he shook hands. 'I'm sorry to have neglected you like this; but we're in for a picnic, and no mistake with this case up at Moorton Park.'

'Damn' bad luck, the two cases cropping up at the same time,' said Alleyn. 'Of course, you'd have liked to handle our business yourself. Have you had breakfast?'

'Haven't taken a look at food since six o'clock yesterday.'

Alleyn went to the hatch and shouted:

'Mrs Peach! Another lot of eggs and bacon, if you can manage it.'

'Well, I won't say no,' said Blandish, and sat down. 'And I won't say I wouldn't have liked to try my hand at this business. But there you are: never rains but it pours, does it?'

'That's right,' agreed Fox. 'We get the same thing at the Yard. Though lately it's been quietish – hasn't it, Mr Alleyn?'

Blandish chuckled. 'Maybe that's why we've been honoured with the top-notchers,' he said, 'Well, Mr Alleyn, it will be quite an experience for us to see you working. Needless to say, we'll give you all the help we can.'

'Thank you,' said Alleyn. 'We'll need it. This is a remarkably rum business. You were in the audience, weren't you?'

'I was, and I can give you my word I got a fright. Thought the whole place had exploded. The old piano went on buzzing for Lord knows how long. By gum, it took all my self-control not to have a peep inside the lid before I went off to Moorton. But, "No," I thought. "You're handing over, and you'd better not meddle."'

'Extraordinarily considerate. We breathed our fervent thanks, didn't we, Fox? I suppose that conversation piece you've got for a sergeant has told you all about it?'

Blandish pulled an expressive grimace.

'I shut him up after the second recital,' he said. 'He wants sitting on, does Roper, but he's got his wits about him. I'd like to hear your account.'

While he devoured his eggs and bacon, Alleyn gave him the history of the night. When he came to the discovery of the message in Dr Templett's coat, Blandish laid down his knife and fork and stared at him.

'Glory!' he said.

'I know.'

'This is hell,' said Blandish. 'I mean to say, it's awkward.'

'Yes.'

'Not to put too fine a point on it, Mr Alleyn, it's bloody awkward.'

'It is.'

'By gum, I'm not so sure I do regret being out of it. It may not be anything, of course, but it can't be overlooked. And I've been associated with the doctor I don't know how many years.'

'Like him?' asked Alleyn.

'Do I like him? Well, now, yes, I suppose I do. We've always got on very pleasantly, you know. Yes, I – well, I'm accustomed to him.'

'You'll know the questions we're going to ask. In this sort of affair we have to batten on local gossip.'

Alleyn went to the corner of the dining-room, got his case and took from it the anonymous letter. It was flattened between two sheets of glass joined, at the edges, with adhesive tape. The corner, back and sides of the paper bore darkened impressions of fingers.

'There it is. We brought up three sets of latent prints. One of them corresponds with a print taken from a powder box in the dressing-room used by the victim and Miss Prentice. It has been identified as the victim's. A second has its counterpart on a new japanned make-up box, thought to be the property of Mrs Ross. The third is repeated on other papers in the wallet, and is obviously Dr Templett's.'

'Written by the deceased, sent to Mrs Ross and handed by her to the doctor?'

'It seems indicated. Especially as two of Mrs Ross's prints, if they are hers, appear to be superimposed on the deceased's prints, and one of Dr Templett's lies across two of the others. We'll get more definite results when Bailey develops his photographs.'

'This is an ugly business. You mentioned local gossip, Mr Alleyn. There's been a certain amount in this direction, no denying it, and the two ladies in question were mainly responsible, I fancy.'

'But is it a motive for murder?' asked Fox of nobody in particular.

'Well, Brer Fox, it might be. A doctor, in a country district especially, doesn't thrive on scandal. Is Templett a wealthy man, do you know, Blandish?'

'No, I wouldn't say he was,' said Blandish. 'They're an old Vale family, and the doctor's a younger son. His elder brother was a bit of a rip. Smart regiment before the war, and expensive tastes. It's always been understood the doctor came in for a white elephant when he got Chippingwood. I'd say he needs every penny he earns. He's a hunting man, too, and that costs money.'

'What about Mrs Ross?'

'Well, there you are! If you're to believe everything you hear, they are pretty thick. But gossip's not evidence, is it?'

'No, but it's occasionally based on some sort of foundation, more's the pity. Ah, well! It indicates a line and we'll follow the pointer. Now, about the automatic. It's Mr Jernigham's all right.'

'I've heard all about that, Mr Alleyn, and that's not too nice either, though I wouldn't believe, if I saw the weapon smoking in his hand, that the squire would shoot a woman, let alone plan to murder his own flesh and blood. Unlikely enough people have turned out to be murderers, as we all know, and I suppose that it is not beyond the possibilities that Mr Jernigham might kill his man in hot blood; but I've known him all my life, and I'd stake my reputation he's not the sort to do an underhand fantastic sort of job like this. The man's not got it in him. That's not evidence, either – '

'It's expert opinion, though,' said Alleyn, 'and to be respected as such.'

'The squire's acting Chief Constable while Sir George Dillington's away.'

'We seem to be on official preserves wherever we turn,' said Alleyn. 'I'll call at Pen Cuckoo later in the morning. The mortuary van came before it was light. Dr Templett's doing the post-mortem this afternoon. Either Fox or I will be there. I think our first job now is to call on Mr Georgie Biggins.'

'Young limb of Satan! You'll find him in the last cottage on the left, going out of Chipping. The station's in Great Chipping, you know – only five miles from here. Roper and a PC enjoy their mid-day snooze at a sub-station in this village. Both are at your service.'

'Is there a car of sorts I could hire for the time being? You'll need the official bus for your own work, of course.'

'As a matter of fact, I'm afraid we shall. It's a tidy stretch over to Moorton Park, and we'll be going backwards and forwards. No doubts about our men being Posh Jimmy & Co. Typical job. Funny how they stick to their ways, isn't it? About a car. As a matter of fact, the Biggins have got an old Ford they hire.'

'Splendid. An admirable method of approaching Mr Georgie. How old is he?'

'In years,' said Blandish, 'He's about thirteen. In sin he's a hundred. A limb, if ever there was one. Nerve of a rhinoceros.'

'Well see if we can shake it,' said Alleyn.

The superintendent departed, lamenting the amount of work that lay before him.

II

Alleyn and Fox lit their pipes and walked through Chipping. By daylight it turned out to be a small hamlet with a row of stone cottages on each side of the road, a general store, a post office, and the Jernigham Arms. Even the slope of Cloudyfold, rising steeply above it from the top of Pen Cuckoo Vale, did not rob Chipping of its upland character. It felt high in the world, and the cold wind blew strongly down the Vale road.

The Bigginses' cottage stood a little apart from the rest of the village, and had a truculent air. It was one of those bare-faced Dorset cottages, less picturesque than its neighbours, and more forbidding.

As Alleyn and Fox approached the front door, they heard a woman's voice:

'Whatever be the matter with you, then, mumbudgeting so close to my apron strings? Be off with you!'

Silence.

'To be sure,' continued the voice, 'if you wasn't so strong as a young foal, Georgie Biggins, I'd think something ailed you. Stick out your tongue.'

Silence.

'As clean as a whistle. Stick it in again, then. Standing there like you was simple Dick with your tongue lolling! I never see! What ails you?'

'Nuthun,' said a small voice.

'Nuthun killed nobody.'

Alleyn tapped on the door.

Another silence was broken by a sharp whispering and an unmistakable scuffle.

'Do what I tell you!' ordered the voice. 'Me in my working apron, and Sunday morning! Go *on* with you.'

There was a sound of rapid retreat and then the door opened three inches to disclose a pair of boot-button eyes and part of a very white face.

'Hullo,' said Alleyn. 'I've come to see if I can hire a car. This is Mr Biggins's house, isn't it?'

'Uh.'

'Have you got a car for hire?'

'Uh.'

'Well, how about opening the door a bit wider and we can talk about it?'

The door opened very slowly to another five inches. Georgie Biggins stood revealed in his Sunday suit. His moon-face was colourless and he had the look of a boy who may bolt without warning.

Alleyn said, 'Now, what about this car? Is your father at home?'

'Along to pub corner,' said Georgie in a stifled voice. 'Mum's comeun.'

The cinema has made all little boys familiar with the look of a detective. Alleyn kept a change of clothes in the Yard in readiness for sudden departures. His shepherd's plaid coat, flannel trousers and soft hat may have reassured Georgie Biggins, but when the boot-button eyes ranged farther afield and lit on Inspector Fox, in his dark suit, mackintosh and bowler, their owner uttered a yelp of pure terror, turned tail and charged into his mother, who had at that moment walked out of the bedroom. She was a large woman, and she caught her son with a practised hand.

'Now!' she said. 'That's enough and more, for sure. What's the meanings of these goings-on? You wait till your Dad comes home. I never see!'

She advanced to the door, bringing her son with her by the scruff of the neck.

'I'm sure I'm sorry to keep you waiting,' she said.

Alleyn asked about the car and was told he could have it. Mrs Biggins examined both of them with frank curiosity and led the way round the house to a dilapidated shed where they found a Ford car, six years old, but, as Alleyn cheerfully remarked, none the worse for that. He paid a week's rental in advance. Mrs Biggins kept a firm but absent-minded grip on her son's shirt-collar.

'I'll get you a receipt,' she said. 'Likely you're here on account of this terrible affair.'

'That's it,' said Alleyn.

'Are you from Scotland Yard, then?'

'Yes, Mrs Biggins, that's us.' Alleyn looked good naturedly at Master Biggins. 'Is this Georgie?' he asked. The next second, Master Biggins had left the best part of his Sunday collar in his mother's hand and had bolted like a rabbit, only to find himself held as if in a vice by the terrible man in the mackintosh and bowler.

'Now, now, now,' said Fox. 'What's all this?'

The very words he had so often heard on the screen.

'Georgie!' screamed Mrs Biggins in a maternal fury. Then she looked at her son's face and at the hands that held him.

'Here, you!' she stormed at Fox. 'What are you at, laying your hands on my boy?'

'There's nothing to worry about, Mrs Biggins,' said Alleyn. 'Georgie may be able to help us, that's all. Now look here, wouldn't it be better if we went indoors out of sight and sound of your neighbours?'

The shot went home.

'Mighty me!' said Mrs Biggins, still almost as white as her child, but rallying. 'Mighty me, it's true enough they spend most of the Lord's Day minding other folks' business and clacking their tongues. Georgie Biggins, if you don't hold your noise I'll have the skin off you. Do us go in, then.'

III

In a cold but stuffy parlour, Alleyn did his best with mother and son. Georgie was now howling steadily. Mrs Biggins's work-reddened hands pleated and repleated the folds of her dress. But she listened in silence.

'It's just this,' said Alleyn. 'Georgie is in no danger, but we believe he is in a position to give us extremely important information.'

Georgie checked a lamentable roar and listened.

Alleyn took the water-pistol from his pocket and handed it to Mrs Biggins.

'Do you recognize it?'

'For sure,' she said slowly. 'It's his'en.' Georgie burst out again.

'Young Biggins,' said Alleyn, 'is this your idea of being a detective? Come here.'

Georgie came.

'See here, now. How would you like to help the police bring a murderer to justice? How would you like to work with us? We're from Scotland Yard, you know. It's not often you'll get the chance to work with the Yard, is it?'

The black eyes fastened on Alleyn's and brightened.

'What are the other chaps going to think if you, if you' – Alleyn hunted for the right phrase – 'if you solve the problem that has baffled the greatest sleuths of all time?' He glanced at his colleague. Fox, looking remarkably bland, closed one eye.

'If you come in with us,' Alleyn continued, 'you'll be doing a man's job. How about it?'

A faintly hard-boiled expression crept over Georgie Biggins's undistinguished face.

'Okay,' he said in a treble voice still fuddled with tears.

'Good enough.' Alleyn took the water-pistol from Mrs Biggins. 'This is your gun, isn't it?'

'Yaas,' said Georgie; and, remembering James Cagney the week before last at Great Chipping Plaza, he added with a strong Dorset accent: 'Sure it's my gat.'

'You fixed that water-pistol in the piano at the hall, didn't you?'

'So what?' said Georgie.

This was a little too much for Alleyn. He contemplated the child for a moment and then said:

'Look here, Georgie, never you mind about the pictures. This is real. There's somebody about who ought to be locked up. You're an Englishman, a man of Dorset, and you want to see right done, don't you? You thought it would be rather fun if Miss Prentice got a squirt of water in the eye when she put her foot on the soft pedal. I'm afraid I agree. It would have been funny.'

Georgie grinned.

'But how about the music? You'd forgotten about that, hadn't you?'

'Nah, I had not. My pistol's proper strong pistol. 'Twould have bowled over the music, for certain, sure.'

'You may be right,' said Alleyn. 'Did you try it after you had fixed it up?'

'Nah.'

'Why not?'

''Cause something happened.'

'What happened?'

'Nuthin! Somebody made a noise. I went away.'

'Where did you get the idea?' said Alleyn after a pause. 'Come on, now.'

'I'll be bound I know, the bad boy,' interrupted his mother. 'If our Georgie's been up to such-like capers, it's out on one of the clap-trappery tales he's always at. Ay, only last week he tied an alarm clock under Father's chair, and set 'un for seven o'clock when he takes his nap, and there was the picture in this rubbish to give him away.'

'Was it out of a book, Georgie?'

'Yaas. Kind of.'

'I see. And partly out of your Twiddletoy model wasn't it?'

Georgie nodded.

'When did you do it?'

'Friday.'

'What time?'

'Afternoon. Two o'clock, about.'

'How did you get into the hall?'

'Was there with them girls and I stayed behind.'

'Tell me about it. You must have been pretty smart for them not to see what you were up to.'

Georgie it seemed, had slipped into a dark corner as the Friendly Young People left at about a quarter-past two. His idea had been to shoot at them with his water-pistol as they passed; but at the last moment a more amusing notion occurred to him. He remembered the diverting tale of a piano booby-trap which he had read with the greatest enjoyment in the last number of *Bingo Bink's Weekly*. He had some odds and ends of Twiddletoy in his pockets, and as soon as the front door slammed he got to work. First he silently examined the piano and made himself familiar with the action of the pedals. At this juncture his mother told Alleyn that Georgie was of a markedly mechanical turn of mind and had made many astonishing models from Twiddletoy all of which could be made to revolve or even pro-pel. Georgie had gone solidly to work. Stimulated by Alleyn's ardent attention, he described his handiwork. When it was finished he played a triumphant stanza or two of 'Chopsticks', taking care to use the loud pedal only.

'And nobody came?'

The devilish child turned white again.

'Nobody saw,' he muttered. 'They never saw nuthun. Only banged at door and shouted.'

'And you didn't answer? I see. Know who it was?'

'I never saw 'em.'

'All right. How did you leave?'

'By front door. I shut 'un behind me.'

There was a brief silence. Georgie's face suddenly twisted into a painful grimace, his upper lip trembled again, and he looked piteously at Alleyn.

'I never meant no harm,' he said. 'I never meant it to kill her.'

'That's all right,' said Alleyn. He reached out a hand and took the child by the shoulder.

'It's nothing to do with you, young Biggins,' said Alleyn.

But over the boy's head he saw the mother's stricken face and knew he could not help her so easily.

CHAPTER 14

According to the Jernighams

Alleyn went alone to Pen Cuckoo. He left Fox to visit Miss Campanula's servants, find out the name of her lawyers, and pick up any grain of information that might be the fruit of his well-known way with female domestics.

The Bigginses' car chugged doggedly up the Vale Road in second gear. It was a stiff grade. The Vale rises steeply above Chipping, mounting past Winton to Pen Cuckoo Manor and turning into Cloudyfold Rise at the head of the valley. It is not an obviously picturesque valley, but it has a charm that transcends mere prettiness. The lower slopes of Cloudyfold make an agreeable pattern, the groups of trees are beautifully disposed about the flanks of the hills, and the scattered houses, being simple, seem to have grown out of the country, as indeed they have, since they are built of Dorset stone. It is not a tame landscape, either. The four winds meet on Cloudyfold, and in winter the small lake in Pen Cuckoo grounds holds its mask of ice for days together.

Alleyn noticed that several lanes came down into the Vale Road. He could see that at least one of them led crookedly up to the Manor, and one seemed to be a sort of bridle path from the Manor down to the church. He drove on through the double gates, up the climbing avenue and out on the wide sweep before Pen Cuckoo house.

A flood of thin sunshine had escaped the heavy clouds, and Pen Cuckoo looked its wintry best, an ancient and gracious house, not very big, not at all forbidding, but tranquil. 'A happy house,' thought Alleyn, 'with a certain dignity.'

He gave his card to Taylor.

'I should like to see Mr Jernigham, if I may.'

'If you will come this way, sir.'

As he followed Taylor through the west wing, he thought: 'With any luck, it'll be the study.'

It was, and the study was empty.

As soon as the door had shut behind Taylor, Alleyn looked for the box described by Sergeant Roper. He found it on a table underneath one of the windows. He lifted the lid and saw that the box was empty. He looked closely at the notice 'LOADED,' which was painted in block capitals. Alleyn gently let fall the lid and walked over to the french windows. It was not locked. It looked across the end of the gravelled sweep and over the tops of the park trees right down Pen Cuckoo Vale in Chipping and beyond.

Alleyn was still tracing the course of the Vale Road as it wound through the valley when the squire walked in.

Jocelyn looked fresh and composed. Perhaps his eyes were a little more prominent than usual and his face a little less red, but he had the look of a man who has come to a decision, and there was a certain dignity and resolution in his manner.

'I'm glad to see you,' he said as he shook hands. 'Sit down, won't you? This is a terrible affair.'

'Yes,' said Alleyn. 'It's both terrible and bewildering.'

'Good God, I should think it was bewildering! It's the most damned complicated, incomprehensible business I ever want to come up against. I suppose Blandish has told you that in Dillington's absence I've got his job?'

'As Chief Constable? Yes, sir, he told me. That's partly my reason for calling on you.'

The squire stared solemnly into the fire and said, 'Quite.'

'Blandish says you were present when the thing happened.'

'Good God, yes. I don't know why it happened, though, or exactly how. As soon as we decided to call you in, Blandish was all for leaving things severely alone. Be damn' glad if you'd explain.'

Alleyn explained. Jocelyn listened with his eyes very wide open and his mouth not quite closed.

'Beastly, underhand, ingenious sort of thing,' he said. 'Sounds more like a woman's work to me. I don't mean to say I think women are particularly underhand, you know; but when they do turn nasty, in my opinion they are inclined to turn crooked-nasty.'

He laughed unexpectedly and uncomfortably.

'Yes,' agreed Alleyn.

'Sort of inverse ratio or something, what?' added the squire dimly.

'That's it, sir. Now, the first thing we've got to tackle is the ownership of the Colt. I don't know – '

'Wait a bit,' said Jocelyn. He stood up, drove his hands into his breeches pockets and walked over to the french windows.

'It's mine,' he said.

Alleyn did not answer. The squire turned and looked at him. Seeing nothing but polite attention in Allen's face, he made a slight inarticulate noise, strode to the table under the window and opened the box.

'See for yourself,' he said. 'It's been in that box for the last twenty years. It was there last week. Now it's gone.'

Alleyn joined him.

'Hellish unpleasant,' said Jocelyn, 'isn't it? I only found out this morning. My son was thinking about the business, it seems, and suddenly remembered that the Colt is always lying there, loaded. He came downstairs and looked, and then he came to my room and told me. I'm wondering if I ought not to resign my position as CC.'

'I shouldn't do that, sir,' said Alleyn. 'With any luck, we ought to able to clear up the disappearance of the automatic.'

'I feel pretty shaken up about it, I don't mind telling you.'

'Of course you do. As a matter of fact, I've brought the Colt up here to show you. May I just fetch it? I can slip out to the car this way.'

He went straight through the french windows and returned with his case, from which he took the automatic wrapped in a silk handkerchief.

'There's really no need for all these precautions,' said Alleyn as he unwrapped it. 'We've been all over it for prints and found none. My fingerprint man travels with half a laboratory in his kit. This thing's been dusted, peered at and photographed. It was evidently very thoroughly cleaned after it was put in position.'

He laid the automatic in the box. It exactly fitted the indentation in the green baize lining.

'Seems a true bill,' said Alleyn.

'How many rounds gone?' asked Jocelyn.

'Three,' answered Alleyn.

'I fired the first two in 1917,' said Jocelyn; 'but I swear before God I'd nothing to do with the third.'

'I hope you'll at least have the satisfaction of knowing who had,' said Alleyn. 'Did you write this notice, "Loaded", sir?'

'Yes,' said Jocelyn. 'What of it?'

Alleyn paused for a fraction of a second before he said, 'Only routine, sir. I was going to ask if it always lay on top of the Colt.'

'Certainly.'

'Do you mind, sir, if I take this box away with me? There may be prints; but I'm afraid your housemaids are too well trained.'

'I hope to God you find something. Do take it. I tell you, I'm nearly worried to death by the whole thing. It's a damned outrage that this blasted murderer – '

The door opened and Henry came into the room.

'This is my son,' said Jocelyn.

II

From an upstairs window Henry had watched the arrival of Alleyn's car. Ever since his visit to the study at dawn and his subsequent interview with the abruptly awakened Jocelyn, Henry had been unable to think coherently, to stay still, or do anything definite. It struck him that he was in very much the same condition as he had been last night while waiting in the wings for the curtain to go up. He had telephoned to Dinah and arranged to see her at the rectory. He had prowled miserably about the house. At intervals he had tried to reassure his father, who had taken the news well, but was obviously very shaken. He had wondered what they would do with Eleanor when she chose to appear. She had gone straight to her room on her return from church, and was reported to be suffering from a headache.

When Jocelyn went downstairs to meet Alleyn, Henry's condition became several degrees more uncomfortable. He imagined his father making a bad job of the automatic story, getting himself further and further involved, and finally losing his temper. The Yard man would probably be maddeningly professional and heavy handed. Henry pictured him seated on the edge of one of the study chair, staring at his father with sharp, inhuman eyes set in a massive policeman's face. 'He will carry his bowler in with him and his boots will be intolerable,' thought Henry. 'A mammoth of officialdom!'

At last his own idleness became insupportable, and he ran downstairs and made for the study.

He could hear his father's voice raised, as it seemed, in protest. He opened the door and walked in.

'This is my son,' said Jocelyn.

Henry's first thought was that this was some stranger, or perhaps a friend of Jocelyn's arrived with hideous inconvenience to visit them. He saw an extremely tall man, thin, and wearing good clothes, with an air of vague distinction.

'This is Mr Alleyn,' said Jocelyn, 'from Scotland Yard.'

'Oh,' said Henry.

He shook hands, felt suddenly rather young, and sat down. His next impression was that he had seen Mr Alleyn before. He found himself looking at Alleyn in terms of a pencil drawing. A drawing that might have been done by Durer with a sharp, hard pencil and then washed delicately with blue-blacks and ochres. 'A grandee turned monk,' thought Henry, 'but retaining some amusing memories.' And he sought to find a reason for this impression which seemed more like a recollection. The accents of the brows, the winged corners to the mouth and eyes, the sharp insistence of the skull – he had seen them all before.

'Henry!' said his father sharply.

Henry realized that Alleyn had been speaking.

'I'm so sorry,' he said. 'I'm afraid I didn't – I'm very sorry.'

'I was only asking,' said Alleyn, 'if you could help us with this business of the Colt. Your father says it was in its box last week. Can you get any nearer to it than that?'

'It was there on Friday afternoon at five,' said Henry.

'How d'you know?' demanded the squire.

'You'll scarcely credit it,' said Henry slowly, 'but I've only just remembered. It was before you came down. I was here with Cousin Eleanor waiting for the others to come in for Dinah's run-through for words. They all arrived together, or within two or three minutes of each other. Somebody, Dr Templett, I think, said something about the burglaries in Somerset last week. Posh Jimmy and his Boys, and all that. We wondered if they'd come this way. Miss Campanula talked about burglar alarms and what she'd do if she heard stealthy footsteps in the small hours. I told them about your war relic, Father, and we all looked at it. Mrs Ross said she didn't think it was safe to have a loaded firearm lying about. I showed her the safety catch was on. Then we talked about something else. You came in and we started the rehearsal.'

'That's a help,' said Alleyn. 'It narrows the time down to twenty-seven hours. That was Friday evening. Now, did either of you go to that hall on Friday afternoon?'

'I was hunting,' said Jocelyn. 'I didn't get back till five, in time for this run-through.'

Alleyn looked at Henry.

'I went for a walk,' said Henry. 'I left at about half-past two. I remember now. It was half-past two.'

'Did you go far?'

Henry looked straight before him.

'No. About half-way down to the church.'

'How long were you away?'

'About two hours.'

'You stopped somewhere, then?'

'Yes.'

'Did you speak to anybody?'

'I met Dinah Copeland.' Henry looked at his father. 'Not by appointment. We talked. For some time. Then my cousin, Eleanor Prentice, came up. She had been to church. If it's of any interest, I remember hearing the church clock strike three when she came up. After that Dinah went back to the rectory and I struck up a path to Cloudyfold. I came home by the hill path.'

'At what time did you get home?'

'Tea-time. About half-past four.'

'Thank you. Now for Friday at five, when the company met here and you showed them the automatic. Did they all leave together?'

'Yes,' said Henry.

'At what time?'

'Soon after six.'

'Nobody was alone in here at any time before they left?'

'No. We rehearsed in here. They all went out by the french windows. It saves trailing through the house.'

'Yes. Is it always unlocked?'

'During the day it is.'

'I lock it before we go to bed,' said Jocelyn, 'and fasten the shutters. Lock up the whole place.'

'You did this on Friday night, sir?'

'Yes. I was in here reading, all Friday evening.'

'Alone?'

'I was here part of the time,' Henry said. 'Something had gone wrong with one of Dinah's light plugs in the hall and I'd brought it up here to mend. I started in here, and then I went to my own room where I had a screwdriver. I tried to ring Dinah up, but our telephone was out of order. A branch had fallen across it in Top Lane.'

'I see. Now, how about yesterday? Any visitors?'

'Templett came up in the morning to borrow an old four-in-hand tie of mine,' said Jocelyn. 'He seemed to think he'd like to wear it in the play. He offered to look at my cousin's finger, but she wouldn't come down.'

'She was afraid he'd tell her she couldn't play her filthy "Venetian Suite",' said Henry. 'Do you admire the works of Ethelbert Nevin, Mr Alleyn?'

'No,' said Alleyn.

'They're gall and wormwood to me,' said Henry gloomily. 'And I suppose we'll have them here for the rest of our lives. Not that I like the bloody Prelude much better. Do you know what that Prelude is supposed to illustrate?'

'Yes, I think I do. Isn't it – '

'Burial,' said Henry. 'It's supposed to be a man buried alive. Bump, bump, bump on the coffin lid. Well, I suppose it's not so frightfully inappropriate.'

'Not so frightfully,' agreed Alleyn rather grimly. 'Now, about yesterday's visitors.'

But Henry and his father were rather vague about yesterday's visitors. The squire had driven into Great Chipping in the morning.

'And Miss Prentice?' asked Alleyn.

'Same thing. She went with us. She was in the hall all the morning. They were all there.'

'All?'

'Well, not Templett,' said Henry. 'He called in here as we've described, at about ten o'clock, and my father gave him the tie. And a pretty ghastly affair it is, I may add.'

'They were damn' smart at one time,' said the squire hotly. 'I remember I wore that tie – '

'Well, anyway,' said Henry, 'He got the tie. I didn't see him. I was hunting up my own clothes. We all went out soon after he'd gone. You saw him off, didn't you, Father?'

'Yes,' said the squire. 'Funny sort of fellow, Templett. First I knew about him was that Taylor told me he was in here and wanted the four-in-hand. I told Taylor to hunt it up and came down and found Templett. We talked for quite a long time and I'm blessed if, when I walked out with him to the car, poor little Mrs Ross wasn't sitting there. Damn' funny thing to do,' said Jocelyn, brushing up his moustache. ''Pon my word, I think the fellow wanted to keep her to himself.'

Alleyn looked thoughtfully at him.

'How was Dr Templett dressed?' he asked.

'What? I don't know. Yes, I think I do. Donegal tweed.'

'An overcoat?'

'No.'

'Bulging pockets?' asked Henry, with a grin at Alleyn.

'I don't think so. Why? Good Lord, you don't suppose he took my Colt, do you?'

'We've got to explore the possibilities, sir,' said Alleyn.

'My God,' said Jocelyn, 'I suppose they're all under suspicion! What?'

'Including us,' said Henry. 'You know,' he added, 'theoretically one wouldn't put it past Templett. Eleanor's been poisonous about his alleged – notice how I protect myself, Mr Alleyn – his alleged affair with Selia Ross.'

'Good God!' shouted Jocelyn angrily, 'haven't you got more sense than to talk like that, Henry? This is a damn' serious business, let me tell you, and you go blackening Mr – Mr Alleyn's mind against a man who – '

'I spoke theoretically, remember,' said Henry. 'I don't really suppose Templett is a murderer, and as for Mr Alleyn's mind – '

'It doesn't blacken very readily,' said Alleyn.

'And after all,' Henry continued, 'you might make out just as bad a case against me. If I thought I could murder Cousin Eleanor in safety I dare say I should undertake it. And I should think Mr Copeland would feel sorely tempted after the way she's – '

'*Henry!*'

'But, my dear Father, Mr Alleyn is going to hear all the local gossip if he hasn't done so already. Of course, Mr Alleyn will suspect each of us in turn. Even dear Cousin Eleanor herself is not above suspicion. She may have infected her finger in the approved manner with a not too deadly toxin. Or made it up to look septic. Why not? There were the grease paints. True, she overdid it a bit, but that may have been pure artistry.'

'Damn' dangerous twaddle,' shouted Jocelyn. 'It was hurting her like hell. I've known Eleanor since we were children, and I've never seen her cry before. She's a Jernigham.'

'A good deal of it was straight-out annoyance at not being able to perform the "Venetian Suite," if you ask me. Tears of anger, they were, and the only sort you'll ever wring from Eleanor's eyes. Did she cry when they yawked out her gall-bladder? No. She's a Jernigham.'

'Be quiet, sir,' stormed Jocelyn.

'As far as I can see, the only one of us who could *not* have set the trap is poor old Idris Campanula. Oh, God!'

Alleyn, watching Henry, saw him turn very white before he moved away to the window.

'All right,' Henry said to the landscape. 'One's got to do something about it. Can't go on all day thinking of an old maid with her brains blown out. Might as well be funny in our hard, decadent modern way.'

'I remember getting the same reaction in the war,' said Alleyn vaguely. 'As they say in vaudeville, "I had to laugh." It's not an uncommon rebound from shock.'

'I don't suppose I was being anything but excessively commonplace,' said Henry tartly.

III

'Then you don't know if anybody came while you were out yester-day morning?' asked Alleyn, after some considerable time spent in collecting the attention of the two Jernighams.

'I'll ask the servants,' said Jocelyn importantly, and rang for Taylor.

As Alleyn expected, the evidence of the servants was completely inconclusive. Nobody had actually rung the door bells, but on the other hand anybody might have walked into the study and done anything. They corroborated Jocelyn and Henry's statements about their own movements and Taylor remembered seeing Miss Prentice come in at four on Friday afternoon. When the last maid had gone Alleyn asked if they had all been at Pen Cuckoo for some time.

'Lord, yes,' said the squire. 'Out of the question they should have anything to do with this affair. No motive, no opportunity.'

'And not nearly enough sense,' added Henry.

'In addition to which,' said Alleyn, 'they have provided each other with alibis for the whole day until they all went down in a solid body to the church hall at seven-thirty.'

'I understand the entertainment provided,' said Henry, 'caused cook to vomit three times on the way home, and this morning, Father, I am told, the boot-boy heaved everything he had into the tops of your hunting boots.'

'Well, that's a nice thing!' began Jocelyn crossly.

Alleyn said, 'You told me it is out of the question that the auto-matic could have been substituted for the water-pistol during yester-day morning.'

'Unless it was done under the noses of a bevy of Friendly Young People and most of the company,' said Henry.

'How about the afternoon?'

'It was locked up then and the key, instead of being at the recto-ry as usual, was hidden, fancifully enough, behind the outside lava-tory,' said Henry. 'Dinah invented the place of concealment, and announced it at rehearsal. Cousin Eleanor was too put-out to object. Nobody but the members of the cast knew about it. As far as I know, only Templett and Mrs Ross called in during the afternoon.'

'What did you do?' asked Alleyn.

'I went for a walk on Cloudyfold. I met nobody,' said Henry, 'and I can't prove I was there.'

'Thank you,' said Alleyn mildly. 'What about you, sir?'

'I went round the stables with Rumbold, my agent,' said Jocelyn, 'and then I came in and went to sleep in the library. I was waked by my cousin at five. We had a sort of high tea at half-past six and went down to the hall at a quarter to seven.'

'All three of you?'

'Yes.'

'And now, if you please,' said Alleyn, 'I should like to see Miss Prentice.'

CHAPTER 15

Alleyn Goes to Church

Miss Prentice came in looking, as Henry afterwards told Dinah, as much like an early Christian martyr as her clothes permitted. Alleyn, who had never been able to conquer his proclivity for first impressions, took an instant dislike to her.

The squire's manner became nervously proprietary.

'Well, Eleanor,' he said, 'here you are. We're sorry to bring you down. May I introduce Mr Alleyn? He's looking into this business for us.'

Miss Prentice gave Alleyn a forbearing smile and a hand like a fish. She sat on the only uncomfortable chair in the room.

'I shall try not to bother you too long,' Alleyn began.

'It's only,' said Miss Prentice, in a voice that suggested the presence of Miss Campanula's body in the room, 'it's only that I hope to go to church at eleven.'

'It's a few minutes after ten. I think you'll have plenty of time.'

'I'll drive you down,' said Henry.

'Thank you dear, I think I should like to walk.'

'I'm going, anyway,' said Jocelyn.

Miss Prentice smiled at him. It was an approving, understanding sort of smile, and Alleyn thought it would have kept him away from church for the rest of his life.

'Well, Miss Prentice,' he said, 'we are trying to see daylight through a mass of strange circumstances. There is no reason why you shouldn't be told that Miss Campanula was shot by the automatic that is kept in a box in this room.'

431

'Oh, Jocelyn!' said Miss Prentice, 'how terrible! You know, dear, we *have* said it wasn't really quite advisable, haven't we?'

'You needn't go rubbing it in, Eleanor.'

'Why wasn't it advisable,' asked Henry. 'Had you foreseen, Cousin Eleanor, that somebody might pinch the Colt and rig it up in a piano as a lethal booby-trap?'

'Henry dear, please! We just said sometimes that perhaps it wasn't very wise.'

'Are you employing the editorial or the regal "we"?'

Alleyn said, 'One minute, please. Before we go any further I think, as a matter of pure police routine, I would like to see your finger, Miss Prentice.'

'Oh, dear! It's very painful. I'm afraid – '

'If you would rather Dr Templett unwrapped it – '

'Oh, no. No.'

'If you will allow me, I think I can do a fairly presentable bandage.'

Miss Prentice raised her eyes to Alleyn's and a very peculiar expression visited her face, a mixture of archness and submission. She advanced her swathed hand with an air of timidity. He undid the bandage very quickly and lightly and exposed the finger with a somewhat battered stall drawn over a closer bandage. He peeled off the stall and completely unwrapped the finger. It was inflamed, discoloured and swollen.

'A nasty casualty,' said Alleyn. 'You should have it dressed again. Dr Templett – '

'I do not wish Dr Templett to touch it.'

'But he could give you fresh bandages and a stall that has not been torn.'

'I have a first-aid box. Henry, would you mind, dear?'

Henry was despatched for the first-aid box. Alleyn redressed the finger deftly. Miss Prentice watched him with a sort of eager concentration, never lowering her gaze from his face.

'How beautifully you manage,' she said.

'I hope it will serve. You should have a sling, I fancy. Do you want the old stall?'

She shook her head. He dropped it in his pocket and was startled when she uttered a little coy murmur of protestation, for all the world as if he had taken her finger-stall from some motive of gallantry.

'You deserve a greater reward,' she said.

'Lummy!' thought Alleyn in considerable embarrassment. He said, 'Miss Prentice, I am trying to get a sort of timetable of everybody's movements from Friday afternoon until the time of the tragedy. Do you mind telling me where you were on Friday afternoon?'

'I was in church.'

'All the afternoon?'

'Oh, no,' said Eleanor softly.

'Between what hours were you there, please?'

'I arrived at two.'

'Do you know when the service was over?'

'It was not a service,' said Miss Prentice with pale forbearance.

'You were there alone?'

'It was confession,' said Henry impatiently.

'Oh, I see.' Alleyn paused. 'Was anybody else there besides yourself and – and your confessor?'

'No. I passed poor Idris on my way out.'

'When was that?'

'I think I remember the clock struck half-past two.'

'Good. And then?'

'I went home.'

'Directly?'

'I took the top lane.'

'The lane that comes out by the church?'

'Yes.'

'Did you pass the parish hall?'

'Yes.'

'You didn't go in?'

'No.'

'Was any one there, do you think?'

'The doors were shut,' said Miss Prentice. 'I think the girls only went in for an hour.'

'Were the keys in their place of concealment on Friday?' asked Alleyn.

Miss Prentice instantly looked grieved and shocked. Henry grinned broadly and said, 'There's only one key. I don't know it if was there on Friday. I think it was. Dinah would know about that.

Some of the committee worked there on Friday, as Cousin Eleanor
says, but none of us. They may have returned the key to the rectory.
I only went halfway down.'

'At what part of the top lane on Friday afternoon did you meet
Henry Jernigham and Miss Copeland, Miss Prentice?'

Alleyn heard her draw in her breath and saw her turn white. She
looked reproachfully at Henry and said:

'I'm afraid I don't remember.'

'I do,' said Henry. 'It was at the sharp bend above the foot-bridge.
You came round the corner from below.'

She bent her head. Henry looked as if he dared her to speak.

'There's something damned unpleasant about this,' thought Alleyn.

He said, 'How long did you spend in conversation with the others
before you went on to Pen Cuckoo?'

An unlovely red stained her cheeks.

'Not long.'

'About five minutes, I should think,' said Henry.

'And you arrived home, when?'

'I should think about half-past three. I really don't know.'

'Did you go out again on Friday, Miss Prentice?'

'No,' said Miss Prentice.

'You were about the house? I'm sorry to worry you like this, but
you see I really do want to know exactly what everybody did on
Friday.'

'I was in my room,' she said. 'There are two little offices that
Father Copeland has given us for use after confession.'

'Oh, I see,' said Alleyn, in some embarrassment.

II

Alleyn waded on. Miss Prentice's air of patient martyrdom
increased with every question, but he managed to get a good deal
of information from her. On Saturday, the day of the performance,
she had spent the morning in the parish hall with all the other
workers. She left when the others left, and, with Jocelyn and
Henry, returned to Pen Cuckoo for lunch. She had not gone
out again until the evening but had spent the afternoon in her

sitting-room. She remembered waking the squire at tea-time. After tea she returned to her room.

'During yesterday morning you were all at the hall?' said Alleyn. 'Who got there first?'

'Dinah Copeland, I should think,' said Jocelyn promptly. 'She was there when we arrived. She was always the first.'

Alleyn made a note of it and went on, 'Did any of you notice the position and appearance of the piano?'

They all looked very solemn at the mention of the piano.

'I think I did,' said Miss Prentice in a low voice. 'It was as it was for the performance. The girls had evidently arranged the drapery and pot-plants on Friday. I looked at it rather particularly as I was – I was to play it.'

'Good Lord!' ejaculated the squire, 'you were strumming on the damned thing. I remember now.'

'Jocelyn, dear, please! I did just touch the keys, I believe, with my right hand. Not my left,' said Miss Prentice with her most patient smile.

'This was yesterday morning, wasn't it?' said Alleyn, 'Now, please, Miss Prentice, try to remember. Did you use the soft pedal at all when you tried the piano?'

'Oh, dear, now I wonder. Let me see. I did sit down for a moment. I expect I did use the soft pedal. I always think soft playing is so much nicer. Yes, I should think almost without doubt I used the soft pedal.'

'Was anybody by the piano at the time?' asked Alleyn. Miss Prentice turned a reproachful gaze on him.

'Idris,' she whispered. 'Miss Campanula.'

'Here, wait a bit,' shouted Jocelyn. 'I've remembered the whole thing. Eleanor, you sat down and strummed about with your hand and she came up and asked you why you didn't try with your left to see how it worked.'

'So she did,' said Henry softly. 'And so, of course, she would.'

'And you got up and went away,' said the squire. 'Old Camp – well, Idris Campanula – gave a sort of laugh and dumped herself down and – '

'And away went the Prelude!' cried Henry. 'You're quite right, Father. Pom. *Pom!* POM!! And then down with soft pedal. That's it, sir,' he added, turning to Alleyn. 'I watched her. I'll swear it.'

'Right,' said Alleyn. 'We're getting on. This was yesterday morning. At what time?'

'Just before we packed up,' said Henry. 'About midday.'

'And – I know we've been over this before, but it's important – you all left together?'

'Yes,' said Henry. 'We three drove off in the car. I remember that I heard Dinah slam the back door just as we started. They were all out by then.'

'And none of you returned until the evening? I see. When you arrived at a quarter to seven you found Miss Copeland there.'

'Yes,' said Jocelyn.

'Where was she?'

'On the stage with her father, putting flowers in vases.'

'Was the curtain drawn?'

'Yes.'

'What did you all do?'

'I went to my dressing-room,' said the squire.

'I stayed in the supper-room and talked to Dinah,' said Henry. 'Her father was on the stage. After a minute or two I went to my dressing-room.'

'Here!' ejaculated Jocelyn, and glared at Miss Prentice.

'What, dear?'

'Those girls were giggling about in front of the hall. I wonder if any of them got up to any hanky panky with the piano.'

'Oh, my dear Father!' said Henry.

'They were strictly forbidden to touch the instrument,' said Miss Prentice. 'Ever since Cissie Drury did such damage.'

'How long was it before the others arrived? Dr Templett and Mrs Ross?' asked Alleyn.

'They didn't get down until half-past seven,' said Henry. 'Dinah was in a frightful stew and so were we all. She rang up Mrs Ross's cottage in the end. It took ages to get through. The hall telephone's an extension from the rectory and we rang for a long time before anybody at the rectory answered and at last, when it was connected with Mrs Ross's house, there was no reply, so we knew she'd left.'

'She came with Dr Templett?'

'Oh, yes,' murmured Miss Prentice.

'The telephone is in your dressing-room, isn't it, Mr Jernigham?'

'Mine and Henry's. We shared. We were all there round the telephone.'

'Yes,' said Alleyn. He looked from one face to another. Into the quiet room there dropped the Sunday morning sound of chiming bells. Miss Prentice rose.

'Thank you so much,' said Alleyn. 'I think I've got a general idea of the two days now. On Friday afternoon Miss Prentice went to church, Mr Jernigham hunted, Mr Henry Jernigham went for a walk. On her return from church, Miss Prentice met Mr Henry Jernigham and Miss Copeland, who had themselves met by chance in the top lane. That was at about three. Mr Henry Jernigham returned home by a circuitous route, Miss Prentice by the top lane. Miss Prentice went to her room. At five you had your reheasal for words in this room, and everybody saw the automatic. You all three dined at home and remained at home. It was also on Friday afternoon that some helpers worked for about an hour at the hall, but apparently they had finished at two-thirty when Miss Prentice passed that way. On Saturday (yesterday) morning Dr Templett and Mrs Ross called here for the tie. You all went down to the hall and you, sir, drove to Great Chipping. You all returned for lunch. By this time the piano was in position with the drapery and aspidistras on top. In the afternoon Mr Henry Jernigham walked up Cloudyfold and back. As far as we know, only Dr Templett and Mrs Ross visited the hall yesterday afternoon. At a quarter to seven you all arrived there for the performance.'

'Masterly, sir,' said Henry.

'Oh, I've written it all down,' said Alleyn. 'My memory's hopeless.'

'What about your music, Miss Prentice? When did you put it on the piano?'

'Oh, on Saturday morning, of course.'

'I see. You had it here until then?'

'Oh, no,' said Miss Prentice. 'Not *here*, you know.'

'Then, where?'

'In the hall, naturally.'

'It lives in the hall?'

'Oh, no,' she said opening her own eyes very wide, 'why should it?'

'I'm sure I don't know. When did you take it to the hall?'

'On Thursday night for the dress-rehearsal. Of course.'

'I see. You played for the dress-rehearsal?'

'Oh, no.'

'For the love of heaven!' ejaculated Jocelyn. 'Why the dickens can't you come to the point, Eleanor. She wanted to play on Thursday night but her finger was like a bad sausage,' he explained to Alleyn.

Miss Prentice gave Alleyn her martyred smile, shook her head slightly at the bandaged finger, and looked restlessly at the clock.

'H'm,' she said unhappily.

'Well,' said Alleyn. 'The music was in the hall from Thursday onwards and you put it in the rack yesterday morning. And none of you went into the hall before the show last night. Good.'

Miss Prentice said, 'Well – I think I shall just – Jocelyn, dear, that's the first bell, isn't it?'

'I'm sorry,' said Alleyn, 'but I should like, if I may, to have a word with you, Miss Prentice. Perhaps you will let me drive you down. Or if not – '

'Oh,' said Miss Prentice, looking very flurried, 'thank you. I think I should prefer – I'm afraid I really can't – '

'Cousin Eleanor,' said Henry. 'I will drive you down, Father will drive you down, or Mr Alleyn will drive you down. You might even drive yourself down. It is only twenty-five to eleven now and it doesn't take more than ten mintues to *walk* down, so you can easily spare Mr Alleyn a quarter of an hour.'

'I'm afraid I do fuss rather, don't I, but you see I like to have a few quiet moments before – '

'Now, look here, Eleanor,' said the squire warmly, 'this is an investigation into murder. Good Lord, it's your best friend that's been killed, my dear girl, and when we're right in the thick of it, damme, you want to go scuttling off to church.'

'*Jocelyn!*'

'Come on, Father,' said Henry. 'We'll leave Mr Alleyn a fair field.'

III

'– you see,' said Alleyn, 'I don't think you quite realize your own position. Hadn't it occurred to you that you were the intended victim?'

'It is such a dreadful thought,' said Miss Prentice.

'I know it is, but you've got to face it. There's a murderer abroad in your land and as far as one can see his first coup hasn't come off. It's been a fantastic and horrible failure. For your own, if not for the public's good, you must realize this. Surely you want to help us.'

'I believe,' said Miss Prentice, 'that our greatest succour lies in prayer.'

'Yes,' Alleyn said slowly, 'I can appreciate that. But my job is to ask questions, and I do ask you, most earnestly, if you believe that you have a bitter enemy among this small group of people.'

'I cannot believe it of any one.'

Alleyn looked at her with something very like despair. She had refused to sit down after they were alone, but fidgeted about in the centre of the room, looked repeatedly down the Vale, and was thrown into a fever of impatience by the call of the church bells.

A towering determined figure, he stood between Eleanor and the window, and concentrated his will on her. He thought of his mind as a pin-pointed weapon and he drove it into hers.

'Miss Prentice. Please look at me.'

Her glance wavered. Her pale eyes travelled reluctantly to his. Deliberately silent until he felt he had got her whole attention, he held her gaze with his own. Then he spoke. 'I may not try to force information from you. You are a free agent. But think for a moment of the position. You have escaped death by an accident. If you had persisted in playing last night you would have been shot dead. I am going to repeat a list of names to you. If there is anything between any one of these persons and yourself which, if I knew of it, might help me to see light, ask yourself if you should not tell me of it. These are the names:

'Mr Jocelyn Jernigham?

'His son, Henry Jernigham?

'The rector, Mr Copeland?'

'No!' she cried, 'no! Never! Never!'

'His daughter, Dinah Copeland?

'Mrs Ross?'

He saw the pale, eyes narrow a little.

'Dr Templett?'

She stared at him like a mesmerized rabbit.

'Well, Miss Prentice, what of Mrs Ross and Dr Templett?'

'I can accuse nobody. Please let me go.'

'Have you ever had a difference with Mrs Ross?'

'I hardly speak to Mrs Ross.'

'Or with Dr Templett?'

'I prefer not to discuss Dr Templett,' she said breathlessly.

'At least,' said Alleyn, 'he saved your life. He dissuaded you from playing.'

'I believe God saw fit to use him as an unworthy instrument.'

Alleyn opened his mouth to speak and thought better of it. At last he said, 'In your own interest, tell me this. Has Mrs Ross cause to regard you as her enemy?'

She wetted her lips and answered him with astounding vigour:

'I have thought only as every decent creature who sees her must think. Before she could silence the voice of reproach she would have to murder a dozen Christian souls.'

'Of whom Miss Campanula was one?'

She stared at him vacantly and then he saw she had understood him.

'That's why he wouldn't let me play,' she whispered.

On his way back, Alleyn turned off the Vale Road and drove up past the church to the hall. Seven cars were drawn up outside St Giles and he noticed a stream of villagers turning in at the lych-gate.

'Full house, this morning,' thought Alleyn grimly. And suddenly he pulled up by the hall, got out, and walked back to the church.

'The devil takes a holiday,' he thought, and joined in with the stream.

He managed to elude the solicitations of a sidesman and slip into a seat facing the aisle in the back row where he sat with his long hands clasped round his knee. His head looked remotely austere in the cold light from the open doors.

Winton St Giles is a beautiful church and Alleyn, overcoming that first depression inseparable from the ecclesiastical smell, and the sight of so many people with decorous faces, found pleasure in the tranquil solidity of stone shaped into the expression of devotion. The single bell stopped. The organ rumbled vaguely for three minutes, the congregation stood, and Mr Copeland followed his choir into church.

Like everybody else who saw him for the first time, Alleyn was startled by the rector's looks. The service was a choral Eucharist and he wore a cope, a magnificent vestment that shone like a blazon in the candle light. His silver hair, the incredible perfection of his features, his extreme pallor, and great height, made Alleyn think of an actor admirably suited for the performance of priestly parts. But when the time came for the short sermon, he found evidence of a simple and unaffected mind with no great sincerity. The rector spoke of prayers for the dead and told his listeners that there was nothing in the teaching of their church that forbade such prayers. He invited them to petition God for the peace of all souls departed in haste or by violence, and he commended meditation and a searching of their own hearts lest they should harbour anger or resentment.

As the service went on, Alleyn looking down the aisle, saw a dark girl with so strong a resemblance to the rector that he knew she must be Dinah Copeland. Her eyes were fixed on her father and in them Alleyn read anxiety and affection.

Miss Prentice was easily found, for she sat next the aisle in the front row. She rose and fell like a ping-pong ball on a water jet, sinking in solitary genuflexions and crossing herself like a sort of minor soloist. The squire sat beside her. The back of his neck wore an expression of indignation and discomfort, being both scarlet and rigid. Much nearer to Alleyn, and also next the aisle, sat a woman whom he recognized as probably the most fashionable figure in the congregation. Detectives are trained to know about clothes and Alleyn knew hers were impeccable. She wore them like a Frenchwoman. He could only see the thin curve of her cheek and an immaculate wing of straw-coloured hair, but presently, as if aware of his gaze, she turned her head and he saw her face. It was thinnish and alert, beautifully made-up, hard, but with a look of amused composure. The pale eyes looked into his and widened. She paused with unmistakable deliberation for a split second, and then turned away. Her luxuriously gloved hand went to her hair.

'That was once known as the glad eye,' thought Alleyn.

Under cover of a hymn he slipped out of church.

IV

He crossed the lane to the hall. Sergeant Roper was on duty at the gate and came smartly to attention.

'Well, Roper, how long have you been here?'

'I relieved Constable Fife an hour ago, sir. The super sent him along soon after you left. About seven-thirty, sir.'

'Anybody been about?'

'Boys,' said Roper, 'hanging round like wasps and as bold as brass with that young Biggins talking that uppish you'd have thought he was as good as the murderer, letting on as he was as full of inside knowledge as the Lord Himself, not meaning it in the way of blasphemy. I subdued him, however, and his mother bore him off to church. Mr Bathgate took a photograph of the building, and asked me to say, sir, that he'd look back in a minute or two in case you were here.'

'I dare say,' grunted Alleyn.

'And the doctor came along, too, in a proper taking on. Seems he left one of the knives for slashing open the body in the hall last night, and he wanted to fetch her out for to lay bare the youngest Cain's toe. I went in with the doctor but she was nowhere to be found, no not even in the pockets of his suit which seemed a strange casual spot for a naked blade, no doubt so deadly sharp as 'twould penetrate the very guts of a man in a flash. Doctor was proper put about by the loss and made off without another word.'

'I see. Any one else?'

'Not a living soul,' said Roper. 'I reckon rector will have brought this matter up in his sermon, sir. The man couldn't well avoid it, seeing it's his job to put a holy construction on the face of disaster.'

'He did just touch on it,' Alleyn admitted.

'A ticklish affair and you may be sure one that he didn't greatly relish, being a timid sort of chap.'

'I think I'll have a look round the outside of the hall, Roper.'

'Very good, sir.'

Alleyn wandered round the hall on the lane side, his eyes on the gravelled path. Roper looked after him wistfully until he disappeared at the back. He came to the rear door, saw nothing of interest, and turned to the outhouses. Here, in a narrow gap between two walls, he found a nail where he supposed the key had hung yesterday. He continued his search round the far side of the building and came at last to a window, where he stopped.

He remembered that they had shut this window last night before they left the hall. It was evidently the only one that was ever opened. The others were firmly sealed in accumulated grime. Alleyn looked at the wall underneath it. The surface of the weathered stone was grazed in many places, and on the ground he discovered fresh-ly detached chips. Between the gravelled path and the side of the building was a narrow strip of grass. This bore a rectangular impress that the night's heavy rain had softened but not obliterated. Within the margin of the impress he found traces of several large footprints and two smaller ones. Alleyn returned to a sort of lumber-shed at the back and fetched an old box. The edges at the open end bore traces of damp earth. He took it to the impression and found that it fitted exactly. It also covered the lower grazes on the wall. He exam-ined the box minutely, peering into the joints and cracks in the rough wood. Presently he began to whistle. He took a pair of tweez-ers from his pocket, and along the edge, from a crack where the wood had split, he pulled out a minute red scrap of some springy substance. He found two more shreds caught in the rough surface of the wood, and on a projecting nail. He put them in an envelope and sealed it. Then he replaced the box. He measured the height from the box to the window-sill.

'Good-morning,' said a voice behind him. 'You must be a detective.'

Alleyn glanced up and saw Nigel Bathgate leaning over the stone fence that separated the parish hall grounds from a path on the far side.

'What a fascinating life yours must be,' continued Nigel.

Alleyn did not reply. Inadvertently he released the catch on the steel tape. It flew back into the container.

'Pop goes the weasel,' said Nigel.

'Hold your tongue,' said Alleyn, mildly, 'and come here.'

Nigel vaulted over the wall.

'Take this tape for me. Don't touch the box if you can help it.'

'It would be pleasant to know why.'

'Five-foot-three from the box to the sill,' said Alleyn. 'Too far for Georgie, and in any case we know he didn't. That's funny.'

'Screamingly.'

'Go to the next window, Bathgate, and raise yourself by the sill. If you can.'

'Only if you tell me why.'

'I will in a minute. Please be quick. I want to get this over before the hosts of the godly are upon us. Can you do it?'

'Listen, Chief. This is your lucky day. Look at these biceps. Three months ago I was puny like you. By taking my self-raising course – '

Nigel reached up to the window sill, gave a prodigious heave, and cracked the crown of his head smartly on the sill.

'Great strength rings the bell,' said Alleyn. 'Now try and get a foothold.'

'Blast and damn you!' said Nigel, scraping at the wall with his shoes.

'That will do. I'm going into the hall. When I call out, I want you to repeat this performance. You needn't crack your head again.'

Alleyn went into the hall, forced open the second window two inches, and went over to the piano.

'Now!'

The shape of Nigel's head and shoulders rose up behind the clouded glass. His collar and tie appeared in the gap. Alleyn had a fleeting impression of his face.

'All right.'

Nigel disappeared and Alleyn rejoined him.

'Are you playing Peep Bo or what?' asked Nigel sourly.

'Something of the sort. I saw you all right. Yes,' continued Alleyn, examining the wall. 'The lady used the box. We will preserve the box. Dear me.'

'At least you might say I can come down.'

'I'm so sorry. Of course. And your head?'

'Bloody.'

'But unbowed, I feel sure. Now I'll explain.'

CHAPTER 16

The Top Lane Incident

Alleyn gave Nigel his explanation as they walked up Top Lane by the route Dinah had taken on Friday afternoon. They walked briskly, their heads bent, and a look of solemn absorption on their faces. In a few minutes they crossed a rough bridge and reached a sharp turn in the lane.

'It was here,' said Alleyn, 'that Henry Jernigham met Dinah Copeland on Friday afternoon. It was here that Eleanor Prentice found them on her return from the confessional. I admit that I am curious about their encounters, Bathgate. Miss Prentice came upon them at three, yet she left the church at half-past two. Young Jernigham says he was away two hours. He left home at two-thirty. It can take little more than five minutes to come down here from Pen Cuckoo. They must have been together almost half an hour before Miss Prentice arrived.'

'Perhaps they are in love.'

'Perhaps they are. But there is something that neither Miss Prentice nor Master Henry cares to remember when one speaks of this meeting. They turn pale. Henry becomes sardonic and Miss Prentice sends out waves of sanctimonious disapproval in the manner of a polecat.'

'What can you mean?'

'It doesn't matter. She left the church at three. She only spent five mintues here with the others and yet she did not reach Pen Cuckoo till after four. There seems to be a lot of time to spare. Henry struck up this path to the hilltop. Miss Copeland returned by the way we

have come, Miss Prentice went on to Pen Cuckoo. I have a picture
of three specks of humanity running together, exploding, and flying
apart.'

'There are a hundred explanations.'

'For their manner of meeting and parting? Yes, I dare say there
are, but not so many explanations for their agitation when the meeting is discussed. Say that she surprised them in an embrace, Master
Henry might feel foolish at the recollection, but why should Miss
Prentice go white and trembly?'

'She's an old maid, isn't she? Perhaps it shocked her.'

'It may have given her a shock.'

Alleyn was searching the wet lane.

'The rain last night was the devil. This great bough must have
been blown down quite recently. Master Henry told me that their
telephone was dumb on Friday night. He said it was broken by a
falling bough in Top Lane. There are the wires and it almost follows
as the night the day that this is the bough. It's protected the ground.
Wait, I believe we've struck a little luck.'

They moved the still unwithered bough.

'Yes. See here, Bathgate, here is where they stood. How much
more dramatic footprints can be than the prints of hands. Look, here
are Dinah Copeland's, if indeed they are hers, coming round the
bend into the protection of the bank. The ground was soft but not
too wet. Coming downhill we pick *his* prints up, as they march out
of the sodden lane into the lee of the bank and overlapping trees.
Surface water has seeped into them but there they are. And here,
where the bough afterwards fell, they met.'

'And what a meeting!' ejaculated Nigel, looking at the heavy
impressions of overlapping prints.

'A long meeting. Yes, and a lover's meeting. She looks a nice girl.
I hope Master Henry – '

He broke off.

'Here we are, by George. Don't come too far. Eleanor Prentice
must have rounded the corner, taken two steps or so, and stopped
dead. There are her feet planted side by side. She stood for some
time in this one place, facing the others and then – what happened?
Ordinary conversation? No, I don't think so. I'll have to try and get

it from the young ones. *She* won't tell me. Yes, there are her shoes, no doubt of it. Black-calf with pointed toes and low heels. Church hen's shoes. She was wearing them this morning.'

Alleyn squatted by the two solitary prints, reached out a long finger and touched the damp earth. Then he looked up at Nigel.

'Well, it's proved one thing,' he said.

'What?'

'If these are Eleanor Prentice's prints, and I think they are, it wasn't Eleanor Prentice who tried to see in at the window of the parish hall. Wait here, will you, Bathgate? I'm going down to the car for my stuff. We'll have a cast of these prints.'

II

At half-past twelve Alleyn and Nigel arrived at the Red House, Chipping. An elderly parlourmaid told them that Mr Fox was still there, and showed them into a Victorian drawing-room which, in the language of brassware and modernish silk Japanese panels, spoke unhappily of the late General Campanula's service in the East. It was an ugly room, over-furnished and unfriendly. Fox was seated at a writing desk in the window and before him were many neat stacks of papers. He rose and looked placidly at them over the tops of his glasses.

'Hullo, Brer Fox,' said Alleyn. 'How the hell are you getting on?'

'Fairly comfortably, thank you, sir. Good-morning, Mr Bathgate.'

'Good-morning, Inspector.'

'What have you got there?' asked Alleyn.

'A number of letters, sir, none of them very helpful.'

'What about that ominous wad of foolscap, you old devil? Come on, now; it's the will, isn't it?'

'Well, it is,' said Fox.

He handed it to Alleyn and waited placidly while he read it.

'This was a wealthy woman,' said Alleyn.

'How wealthy?' demanded Nigel, 'and what has she done with it?'

'Nothing that's for publication.'

'All right, all right.'

'She's left fifty thousand. Thirty of them go to the Reverend Walter Copeland of Winton St Giles in recognition of his work as a parish priest and in deep gratitude for his spiritual guidance and unfailing wisdom. Lummy! He is to use this money as he thinks best but she hopes that he will not give it all away to other people. Fifteen thousand to her dear friend, Eleanor Jernigham Prentice, four thousand to Eric Campanula, son of William Campanula, and second cousin to the testatrix. Last heard of in Nairobi, Kenya. A stipulation that the said four thousand be invested by Miss Campanula's lawyers, Messrs. Waterworth, Waterworth and Biggs, and the beneficiary to receive the interest at their hands. The testatrix adds the hope that the beneficiary will not spend the said interest on alcoholic beverages or women, and will think of her and mend his ways. One thousand to be divided among the servants. Dated May 21st, 1938.'

'There was a note enclosed dated May 21st of this year,' said Fox. 'Here it is, sir.'

Alleyn read aloud with one eyebrow raised:

'To all whom it may concern. This is my last Will and Testament so there's no need for anybody to go poking about my other papers for another. I should like to say that the views expressed in reference to the principal beneficiary are the views I hold at the moment. If I could add anything to this appreciation of his character to make it more emphatic, I would do so. There have been disappointments, and friends who have failed me, but I am a lonely woman and see no reason to alter my Will. Idris Campanula.'

'She seems to have been a very outspoken lady, doesn't she?' asked Fox.

'She does. That's a nasty jab in the eye for her dear friend, Eleanor Prentice,' said Alleyn.

'Well, now,' said Nigel briskly, 'do you think either of these two have murdered her? You always say, Alleyn, that money is the prime motive.'

'I don't say so in this instance,' Alleyn said. 'It may be, but I don't think it is. Well, there we are, Fox. We must get hold of the Waterworths and Mr Biggs, before they read about it in the papers.'

'I've rung them up, Mr Alleyn. The parlourmaid knew Mr Waterworth senior's private address.'

'Excellent, Fox. Anything else?'

'There's the chauffeur, Gibson. I think you might like to talk to him.'

'All right. Produce Gibson.'

Fox went out and returned with Miss Campanula's chauffeur. He wore his plum-coloured breeches and shining gaiters and had the air of having just crammed himself into his tunic.

'This is Gibson, sir,' said Fox. 'I think the Chief Inspector would like to hear about this little incident on Friday afternoon, Mr Gibson.'

'Good-morning,' said Alleyn. 'What's the incident?'

'It concerns deceased's visit to church at two-thirty, sir,' Fox explained. 'It seems that she called at the hall on her way down.'

'Really?' said Alleyn.

'Not to say called, sir,' said Gibson. 'Not in a manner of speaking, seeing she didn't go in.'

'Let's hear about it?'

'She used to go regular, you see, sir, to the confessing affair. About every three weeks. Well, Friday, she orders the car and we go down, getting there a bit early. She says, drive on to the hall, so I did and she got out and went to the front door. She'd been in a good mood all the morning. Pleased at going down to church and all, but soon as I saw her rattling the front door I knew one of her tantrums was coming on. As I was explaining to Mr Fox, sir, she was a lady that was given to tantrums.'

'Yes.'

'I watched her. Rattle, rattle, rattle! And then I heard her shouting. "Who's in there! Let me in!" I thought I could hear the piano, too. Off she goes round to the back. I turned the car. When I looked out again she had come round the other side, the one away from the lane. Her face was red, and, Gawd help us, I thought, here we go, and sure enough she starts yelling out for me to come. "There's someone in there behaving very suspicious," she says. "Take a look through that open window." I hauled myself up and there wasn't a blooming thing to be seen. "Where's the piano?" Well, I told her. The piano was there right enough down on the floor by the stage. I knew she was going to tell me to go to the rectory for the key, when I see Miss Prentice coming out of the church. So I drew her attention to Miss Prentice and she was off like a scalded cat, across the lane and down to the church. I followed along slow, it's only a couple of chain or so, and pulled up outside the church.'

'What about the box?'

'Pardon, sir?'

'Didn't you get a box out of the shed at the back of the hall for Miss Campanula to stand on in order to look through the window?'

'No, sir. No.'

Nigel grinned and whistled softly.

'All right,' said Alleyn. 'It's no matter. Anything else?'

'No, sir. Miss Prentice come out looking very upset, passed me, and went up the lane. I reckon she was going home by Top Lane.'

'Miss Prentice looked upset?'

'She did so, sir. It's my belief Mr Copeland had sent her off with a flea in her ear, if you'll excuse the liberty.'

'Did you watch her go? Look after her, I mean?'

'No, sir, I didn't like, seeing she was looking so queer.'

'D'you mean she was crying?'

'She wasn't actually that way, sir. Not shedding tears or anything, but she looked queer. Upset, very down in the mouth.'

'You don't know if she went to the hall?'

'No, sir, I can't say. I did have a look in the driving mirror and I saw her cross the road as soon as she'd gone a few steps, but she'd do that, anyway, sir, very likely.'

'Gibson, can you remember exactly how the piano looked? Describe it for me as accurately as you possibly can.'

Gibson scraped his jaw with his mechanic's hand.

'Down on the floor where it was in the evening, sir. Stool in front of it. No music on it. Er – let's see now. It wasn't quite the same. No, that's right. It *was* kind of different.'

Alleyn waited.

'I got it,' said Gibson loudly. 'Yes, by gum, I got it.'

'Yes?'

'Those pot plants was on the edge of the stage and the top of the piano was open.'

'Ah,' said Alleyn, 'I hoped so.'

III

'What's the inner significance of all that?' demanded Nigel when Gibson had gone. 'What about this box? Is it the one you had under the window?'

'It is.' Alleyn spoke to Fox. 'At some time since Gibson hauled himself up to look in at the window, somebody has put an open box there and stood on it. It's left a deep rectangular scar overlapping one of Gibson's prints. I found the box in the outhouse. It wasn't young Georgie. He used the door, and anyway the window would have been above his eye-level. The only footprints are Miss C.'s and some big ones, no doubt Gibson's. They trod on the turf. The box expert must have come later, perhaps on Saturday and only stood on the gravel. We'll try the box for prints, but I don't think we'll do any good. When I heard Gibson's story I expected we would find that Miss Campanula had used it. Evidently not. It's a tedious business but we'll have to clear it up. Have you said much to the maids?'

'It looks as if deceased was a proper tartar,' said Fox. 'I've heard enough to come to the conclusion. Mary, the parlourmaid, you saw just now, sir, seems to have acted as a kind of lady's-maid as well. Miss Campanula had a very open way with Mary when she was in the mood. Surprising some of the things she used to tell her.'

'For instance, Brer Fox?'

'Well, Mr Alleyn, to Mary's way of thinking, Miss C. was a bit queer on the subject of Mr Copeland. Potty on him is the way Mary puts it. She says that about the time the rector walks through the village of a morning, deceased used to go and hang about under one pretext or another until she could meet him.'

'Oh, Lord!' said Alleyn distastefully.

'Yes, it's kind of pitiful, sir, isn't it? Mary says she'd dress herself up, very particularly walk up to Chipping, and go into the little shop. She'd keep the woman there talking, while she bought some trifle or another, and all the time she'd be looking through the glass door. If the rector showed up, Miss Campanula would be off like lightning. She was a very uncertain tempered lady, and when things went wrong she used to scare the servants by the wild way she talked, saying she'd do something violent, and so on.'

'This is getting positively Russian,' said Alleyn, 'and remarkably depressing. Go on.'

'It wasn't so bad till Miss Prentice came. She had it her own way in the parish till then. But Miss Prentice seems to have put her in the shade, as you might say. Miss Prentice beat her to all the top places. She's president of this YPFC Affair and Miss C. was only secretary. Same sort of thing with the Girl Guides.'

'She's never a Girl Guide!' Alleyn ejaculated.

'Seems like it, and she beats Miss C. hands down, teaching the kids knots and camp cookery. Got herself decorated with badges and so on. Started at the bottom and swotted it all up. The local girls didn't fancy it much, but she kind of got round them; and when Lady Appleby gave up the Commissioner's job Miss Prentice got it. Same sort of thing at the Women's Circle and all the other local affairs. Miss P. was too smart for Miss C. They were as thick as thieves; but Mary says sometimes Miss C. would come back from a Friendly meeting or something of the sort, and the things she'd say about Miss Prentice were surprising.'

'Oh, Lord!'

'She'd threaten suicide and all the rest of it. Mary knew all about the will. Deceased often talked about it, and as short time back as last Thursday, when they had their dress rehearsal, she said it'd serve Miss Prentice right if she cut her out, but she was too charitable to do that, only she hoped if she did go first the money would be like scalding water on Miss Prentice's conscience. On Friday, Mary says, she had one of her good days. Went off to confession and came back very pleased. Same thing after the five o'clock affair at Pen Cuckoo, and in the evening she went to some Reading Circle or other at the rectory. She was in high feather when she left, but she didn't get back until eleven – very much later than usual. Gibson says she did-n't speak on the way back, and Mary says when she came in she had a scarf pulled round her face and her coat collar turned up and – '

'It wasn't her,' said Nigel. 'Miss Prentice had disguised herself in Miss C.'s clothes in order to have a look at the will.'

'Will you be quiet, Bathgate. Go on, Fox.'

'Mary followed her to her room; but she said she didn't want her, and Mary swears she was crying. She heard her go to bed. Mary took in her tea first thing yesterday morning, and she says Miss

Campanula looked shocking. Like an Aunt Sally that had been left out in the rain, was the way Mary put it.'

'Graphic! Well?'

'Well, she spent yesterday morning at the hall with the others, but when she came back she wrote a note to the lawyers and gave it to Gibson to post; but she stayed in all yesterday afternoon.'

'I knew you had something else up your sleeve,' said Alleyn. 'Where's the blotting paper?'

Fox smiled blandly.

'It's all right, as it turns out, sir. Here it is.'

He took a sheet of blotting paper from the writing-table and handed it to Alleyn. It was a clean sheet with only four lines of writing. Alleyn held it up to an atrocious mirror and read:

'De   S

              K dly   and   our   presentative to   ee me at
our earliest   on enience

                     ours faithfully
                    RIS C MP NULA.'

'Going to alter her will,' said Nigel over Alleyn's shoulder.

'Incubus!' said Alleyn. 'Miserable parasite! I wouldn't be surprised if you were right. Anything else, Fox?'

'Nothing else, sir. She seemed much as usual when she went down to the performance. She left here at seven. Not being wanted till the second act, she didn't need to be so early.'

'And they know of nobody, beyond the lawyers, whom she should inform?'

'Nobody, Mr Alleyn.'

'We'll have some lunch and then visit the rectory. Come on.'

When they returned to the Jernigham Arms they found that the representative of the *Chipping Courier* had been all too zealous. A crowd of young men wearing flannel trousers and tweed coats greeted Nigel with a sort of wary and suspicious cordiality, and edged round Alleyn. He gave them a concise account of the piano and its internal arrangements, said nothing at all about the water-pistol, told them the murder appeared to be motiveless, and besought them not to follow him about wherever he went.

'It embarrasses me and it's no use to you. I'll see that you get photographs of the piano.'

'Who's the owner of the Colt, Chief Inspector?' asked a pert
young man wearing enormous glasses.

'It's a local weapon, thought to have been stolen,' said Alleyn. 'If
there's anything more from the police, gentlemen, you shall hear of
it. You've got enough in the setting of the thing to do your screaming
worst. Off you go and do it. Be little Pooh Bahs. No corroborative
details required. The narrative is adequately unconvincing, and I
understand artistic verisimilitude is not your cup of tea.'

'Try us,' suggested the young man.

'*Pas si bête,*' said Alleyn. 'I want my lunch.'

'When are you going to be married, Mr Alleyn?'

'Whenever I get a chance. Good-morning to you.'

He left them to badger Nigel.

Alleyn and Fox finished their lunch in ten minutes, left the inn
by the back door, and were off, in Biggins's car before Nigel had
exhausted his flow of profanity. Alleyn left Fox in the village. He was
to seek out Friendly Young People, garner more local gossip, and
attend the postmortem. Alleyn turned up the Vale Road, and in five
minutes arrived at the rectory.

IV

Like most clerical households on Sunday, the rectory had a semi-public
look about it. The front door was wide open. On a hall table Alleyn
saw a neat stack of children's hymnbooks. A beretta lay beside them.
In a room some way down the hall they heard a female voice.

'Very well, Mr Copeland. Now the day is over.'

'I think so,' said the rector's voice.

'Through the night of doubt and sorrow,' added the lady brightly.

'Do they like that?'

'Aw, they love it, Mr Copeland.'

'Very well,' said the rector wearily. 'Thank you, Miss Wright.'

A large village maiden came out into the hall. She gathered the
hymn-books into a straw bag and bustled out, not neglecting to look
pretty sharply at Alleyn.

Alleyn rang the bell again, and presently an elderly maid appeared.

'May I see Mr Copeland?'

'I'll just see, sir. What name, please?'

'Alleyn. I'm from Scotland Yard.'

'Oh! Oh, yes, sir. Will you come this way, please?'

He followed her through the hall. She opened a door and said:

'Please, sir, the police.'

He walked in.

Mr Copeland looked as if he had sprung to his feet. At his side was the girl whom Alleyn had recognized as his daughter. They were indeed very much alike, and at this moment their faces spoke of the same mood: they looked startled and alarmed.

Mr Copeland, in his long cassock, moved forward and shook hands.

'I'm so sorry to worry you like this, sir,' said Alleyn. 'It's the worst possible day to badger the clergy, I know; but, unfortunately, we can't delay things.'

'No, no,' said the rector, 'we are only too anxious. This is my daughter. I'm afraid I don't – '

'Alleyn, sir.'

'Oh, yes. Yes. Do sit down. Dinah, dear?'

'Please go on Miss Copeland,' said Alleyn. 'I hope you may be able to help us.'

Evidently they had been sitting with the village maiden in front of the open fireplace. The chairs, drawn up in a semi-circle, were comfortably shabby. The fire, freshly mended with enormous logs, crackled companionably and lent warmth to the faded apple-green walls, the worn beams, the rector's agreeable prints, and a pot of bronze chrysanthemums from the Pen Cuckoo glasshouses.

They sat down, Dinah primly in the centre chair, Alleyn and the rector on either side of her.

Something of Alleyn's appreciation of this room may have appeared in his face. His hand went to his jacket pocket and was hurriedly withdrawn.

'Do smoke your pipe,' said Dinah quickly.

'That was very well observed,' said Alleyn. 'I'm sure you will be able to help us. May I, really?'

'Please.'

'It's very irregular,' said Alleyn; 'but I think I might, you know.'

And as he lit his pipe he was visited by a strange thought. It came into his mind that he stood on the threshold of a new relationship, that he would return to this old room and again sit before the fire. He thought of the woman he loved, and it seemed to him that she would be there, too, at this future time, and that she would be happy. 'An odd notion!' he thought, and dismissed it.

The rector was speaking: '– Terribly distressed. It is appalling to think that among the people one knows so well there should have been one heart that nursed such dreadful anger against a fellow creature.'

'Yes,' said Alleyn. 'The impulse to kill, I suppose, is dormant in most people; but when it finds expression we are so shockingly astonished. I have noticed that very often. The reaction after murder is nearly always one of profound astonishment.'

'To me,' said Dinah, 'the most horrible thing about this business is the grotesque side of it. It's like an appalling joke.'

'You've heard the way of it, then?'

'I don't suppose there's a soul within twenty miles who hasn't,' said Dinah.

'Ah,' said Alleyn. 'The industrious Roper.'

He lit his pipe and, looking over his thin hands at them, said, 'Before I forget, did either of you put a box outside one of the hall windows late on Friday or some time on Saturday?'

'No.'

'No.'

'I see. It's no matter.'

The rector said, 'Perhaps I shouldn't ask, but have you any idea at all of who – ?'

'None,' said Alleyn. 'At the moment, none. There are so many things to be cleared up before the case can begin to make a pattern. One of them concerns the key of the hall. Where was it on Friday?'

'On a nail between an outhouse and the main building,' said Dinah.

' I thought that was only on Saturday.'

'No. I left it there on Friday for the Friendly Circle members who worked in the lunch hour. They moved the furniture and swept up, and things. When they left at two o'clock they hung the key on the nail.'

'But Miss Campanula tried to get in at about half-past two and couldn't.'

'I don't think Miss Campanula knew about the key. I told the girls, and I think I said something about it at the dress rehearsal in case the others wanted to get in, but I'm pretty sure Miss Campanula had gone by then. We've never hung it there before.'

'Did you go to the hall on Friday?'

'Yes,' said Dinah. 'I went in the lunch hour to supervise the work. I came away before they had quite finished, and returned here.'

'And then you walked up Top Lane towards Pen Cuckoo?'

'Yes,' said Dinah, in surprise, and into her eyes came the same guarded look he had seen in Henry's.

'Was Georgie Biggins in the hall when you left at about two o'clock?'

'Yes. Making life hideous with his beastly water-pistol. He *is* a naughty boy, Daddy,' said Dinah. 'I really think you ought to exorcize Georgie. I'm sure he's possessed of a devil.'

'Then you haven't heard about Georgie?' murmured Alleyn. 'Roper has his points.'

'What about Georgie?'

Alleyn told them.

'I want,' he said, 'to make as little as possible of the obvious implication. There seems to be little doubt that Georgie, plus Twiddletoy, and his water-pistol made the bullets that the murderer subsequently fired. It's an unpleasant responsibility to lay on a small boy's shoulders, however bad he may be. I'm afraid it must come out in evidence, but as far as possibly I think we ought to try and avoid village gossip.'

'Certainly,' said the rector. 'At the same time, he knew he was doing something wrong. The terrible consequences – '

'Are disproportionately terrible, don't you think.'

'I do. I agree with you,' said Dinah.

Alleyn, seeing priest's logic in the rector's eye, hurried on.

'You will see,' he said, 'that the substitution of the Colt for the water-pistol must have taken place after two o'clock on Friday when George was flourishing his pistol. I know he stayed behind on Friday and rigged it up. He has admitted this. Miss Campanula's chauffeur, at her request, looked through the open window at two-thirty and saw the piano with the top open. His story leads us to believe that at that time Georgie was hiding somewhere in the building. Georgie did not tell me that at all willingly, and I confess I am afraid memory of Miss Campanula, banging at the doors and demanding admittance, is likely to become a childish nightmare. I don't pretend to understand child psychology.'

'The law,' said Dinah, 'in the person of her officer, seems to be surprisingly merciful.'

Alleyn disregarded this.

'So that give us two-thirty on Friday as a starting-off point. You, Miss Copeland, walked up Top Lane and by chance encountered Mr Henry Jernigham.'

'What!' the rector ejaculated. 'Dinah!'

'It's all right,' said Dinah in a high voice. 'It was by accident, Daddy. I did meet Henry and we did behave as you would have expected. Our promise was almost up. It's my fault. I couldn't help it.'

'Miss Prentice arrived some time later, I believe,' said Alleyn.

'Has she told you that?'

'Mr Henry Jernigham told me and Miss Prentice agreed. Do you mind, Miss Copeland, describing what happened at this triple encounter?'

'If they haven't told you,' said Dinah, 'I won't.'

CHAPTER 17

Confession from a Priest

'Won't you?' said Alleyn mildly. 'That's a pity. We shall have to do the Peer Gynt business.'

'What's that?'

'Go roundabout. Ask servants about the relationship between Miss Prentice and her young cousin. Tap the fabulous springs of village gossip – all that.'

'I thought,' flashed Dinah, 'that nowadays the CID was almost a gentleman's job.'

'Oh, no!' said Alleyn. 'You couldn't be more mistaken.'

Her face was scarlet. 'That was a pretty squalid remark of mine,' said Dinah.

'It was inexcusable, my dear,' said her father. 'I am ashamed that you have beeen capable of it.'

'I find no offence in it at all,' Alleyn said cheerfully. 'It was entirely apposite.'

But Mr Copeland's face was pink with embarrassment, and Dinah's still crimson with mortification. The rector addressed her as if she was a children's service. His voice became markedly more clerical, and in the movement of his head Alleyn recognized one of his pulpit mannerisms. He said, 'You have broken a solemn promise, Dinah, and to this fault you add a deliberate evasion and an ill-bred and entirely unjustifiable impertinence. You force me to make Mr Alleyn some sort of explanation.' He turned to Alleyn. 'My daughter and Henry Jernigham,' he said, 'have formed an attachment of which his father and I do not approve. Dinah suggested that they

should give their word not to meet alone for three weeks. Friday was
the final day of the three weeks. Miss Prentice was also of our mind
in this matter. If she came upon them at a moment when, as Dinah
has admitted, they had completely forgotten or ignored this promise, I am sure she was extremely disappointed and distressed.'

'She wasn't!' exclaimed Dinah, rallying a little. 'She wasn't a bit
like that. She was absolutely livid with rage and beastliness.'

'Dinah!'

'Oh, Daddy, *why* do you shut your eyes? You must know what
she's like – you of all people!'

'Dinah, I must insist – '

'No!' cried Dinah. 'No! First you say I've been underhand; and
then, when I go all upperhand and open, you don't like it any better. I'm sorry in a way that Henry and I didn't stay the course; but
we nearly did, and I *won't* think there was anything very awful
about Friday afternoon. I won't have Henry and me made seem
grubby. I'm sorry I was rude to Mr Alleyn and I – well, I mean it's
quite obvious it wasn't only rude, but silly. I mean, it's obvious from
the way he's taken it – I mean – oh, hell! Oh, Daddy, I'm sorry.'

Alleyn choked down a laugh.

The rector said, 'Dinah! Dinah!'

'Yes, well I *am* sorry. And now Mr Alleyn will think heaven
knows what about Friday afternoon. I may as well tell you, Mr
Alleyn, that in Henry's and my opinion Miss Prentice is practically
ravers. It's a well-known phenomenon with old maids. She's tried to
sublimate her natural appetites and – and – work them off in reli-
gion. I can't help it, Daddy, she *has*. And it's been a failure. She's only
repressed and repressed, and when she sees two natural, healthy
people making love to each other she goes off pop.'

'It is I,' said the rector, looking hopelessly at his child, 'who have
been a failure.'

'*Don't*. You haven't. It's just that you don't understand these
women. You're an angel, but you're not a modern angel.'

'I should be interested to know,' said Alleyn 'how an angel brings
himself up to date. Stream-lined wings, I suppose.'

Dinah grinned.

'Well, you know what I mean,' she said. 'And I'm right about
these two. If you had heard Miss Prentice! It was simply too shaming

and hideous. She actually shook all over and sort of gasped. And she said the most ghastly things to us. She threatened at once to tell you, Daddy, and the squire. She suggested – oh, she was beyond belief. What's more, she dribbles and spits.'

'Dinah, my dear!'

'Well, Daddy, she *does*. I noticed the front of her beastly dress, and it was *disgusting*. She either dribbles and spits, or else she spills her tea. Honestly! And, anyway, she was perfectly *septic*, the things she said.'

'Didn't either of you try to stop her?' asked Alleyn.

'Yes,' said Dinah. She turned rather white and added quickly: 'In the end she just blundered past us and went on up the lane.'

'What did you do?'

'I went home.'

'And Mr Jernigham?'

'He went up to Cloudyfold, I think.'

'By the steep path? He didn't walk down with you?'

'No,' said Dinah. 'He didn't. There's nothing in that.'

II

'I cannot see,' said the rector, 'that this unhappy story can have any bearing on the tragedy.'

'I think I can promise,' said Alleyn, 'that any information found to be irrelevant will be completely blotted out. We are, quite literally, not interested in any facts that cannot be brought into the pattern.'

'Well, that can't,' Dinah declared. She threw up her chin and said loudly:

'If you think, because Miss Prentice made us feel uncomfortable and embarrassed, it's a motive for murder, you're quite wrong. We're not in the least afraid of Miss Prentice or anything she might say or do. It can't make any difference to Henry and me.' Dinah's lower lip trembled and she added: 'We simply look at her from a detached analytical angle and are vaguely sorry for her. That's all.' She uttered a dry sob.

The rector said: 'Oh, my darling child, what nonsense,' and Dinah walked over to the window.

'Well,' said Alleyn mildly, 'let's go on being detached and analyt-ical. What did you both do on Saturday afternoon? That's yesterday.'

'We were both in here,' said Dinah. 'Daddy went to sleep. I went over my part.'

'What time did you get to the hall last evening?'

'We left here at half-past six,' answered Mr Copeland, 'and walked over by the path through our garden and wood.'

'Was anybody there?'

'Yes. Yes, Gladys Wright was there, wasn't she, Dinah? She is one of our best workers and was in charge of the programmes. She was in the front of the hall. I think the other girls were either there, or came in soon after we did.'

'Can you tell me exactly what you did up to the time of the catastrophe?'

'I can, certainly,' rejoined the rector, 'I saw that the copy of the play and the bicycle bell I had to ring were in their right places, and then I sat in an arm-chair on the stage to keep out of the way and see that nobody came in from the front of the hall. I was there until Dinah came for me to speak to Miss Prentice.'

'Did you expect Miss Prentice would be unable to play?'

'No, indeed. On the contrary, she told me her finger was much better. That was soon after she arrived.'

'Had you much difficulty in persuading Miss Prentice not to play?'

'Yes, indeed I had. She was most determined about it, but her fin-ger was really very bad. It was quite impossible, and I told her I should be very displeased if she persisted.'

'And apart from that time you never left the stage?'

'Oh! Oh, yes, I *did* go to the telephone before that, when they were trying to get Mrs Ross's house. That was at half-past seven. The telephone is an extension of ours and our maid, Mary, is deaf and takes a long time to answer.'

'We were all frantic,' said Dinah, from the window. 'The squire and Henry and Father and I were all standing round the telephone, with Miss Campanula roaring instructions, poor old thing. The squire hadn't got any trousers on, only pink woollen underpants. Miss Prentice came along, and when she saw him she cackled like a hen and flew away, but no one else minded about the squire's pants, not even Miss C. We were all in a flat spin about the others being late, you see. Father was just coming over to ring from here, when we got through.'

'I returned to the stage then,' said the rector.

'I can't tell you exactly what I did,' said Dinah. 'I was all over the place.' She peered through the window. 'Here's Henry now.'

'Why not go and meet him?' suggested Alleyn. 'Tell him how I bullied you.'

'You haven't, but I will,' said Dinah.

She opened the window and stepped out over the low sill into the garden.

'I'm so sorry,' said Alleyn, when the window had slammed.

'She's a good child, really,' said the rector sadly.

'I'm sure she is. Mr Copeland, you see what a strange position we are in, don't you? If Miss Prentice was the intended victim we must trace her movements, her conversation – yes, and if we could, even her thoughts during these last days. We are in the extraordinary position of having, apparently, a living victim in a case of homicide. There is even the possibility that the murderer may make a second attempt.'

'No! No! That's too horrible.'

'I am sure that, as your daughter says, you know a great deal about these two ladies – the actual and, as far as we know, the intended victim. Can you tell me anything, anything at all, that may throw a glint of light on this dark tangle of emotions?'

The rector clasped his hands and stared into the fire.

'I am very greatly troubled,' he said. 'I cannot see my way.'

'Do you mean that you have got their confidence, and that under ordinary circumstances you would never speak of your knowledge?'

'Let me make myself clear. As no doubt you already know, I have heard the confessions of many of my parishioners. Under no condition will I break the seal of the confessional. That goes without saying. Moreover, it would serve no purpose if I did. I tell you this lest you should think I hold a key to the mystery.'

'I recognize the position,' said Alleyn, 'and I shall respect it.'

'I'm glad of that. There are many people, I know, who regard the sacrament of confession in the Anglo-Catholic Church as an amateurish substitute for the Roman use. It is no such thing. The Romans say, "You must," the Protestant Nonconformists say, "You must not," the Catholic Church of England says, "You may!"'

But Alleyn was not there for doctrinal argument, and wouldn't have welcomed it under any circumstance.

He said, 'I realize that a priest who hears confession, no matter what faith he professes, must regard the confessional as inviolate. That, I take, is not what troubles you. Do you perhaps wonder if you should tell me something that you have heard from one of your penitents outside the confessional?'

The rector gave him a startled glance. He clasped his hands more tightly and said:

'It is not that I believe it would be any help. It's only that I am burdened with the memory and with a terrible doubt. You say that this murderer may strike again. I don't believe that is possible. I am sure it is not possible.'

'Why?' asked Alleyn in astonishment.

'Because I believe that the murderer is dead,' said the rector.

III

Alleyn turned in his chair and regarded Mr Copeland for some seconds before he answered.

At last he said: 'You think she did it herself?'

'I am sure of it.'

'Will you tell me why?'

'I suppose I must. Mr Alleyn, I am not, unfortunately, a man of strong character. All my life I have avoided unpleasantness. I know this very well and try to conquer my weakness. I have vacillated when I should have insisted; temporized when I should have taken definite action. Because of these veritable sins of omission I believe I am morally responsible, or at any rate in part responsible, for this terrible crime.'

He paused, still looking at the fire. Alleyn waited.

'On Friday night,' said Mr Copeland, 'the Reading Circle met in the rectory dining-room. It usually meets in St Giles Hall; but because of the preparations for the play they all came here instead. It was Miss Campanula's turn to preside. I went in for a short time. Dinah read a scene from *Twelfth Night* for them, and after that they went on with their book. It is G K Chesterton's *The Ball and the*

Cross, and Miss Campanula had borrowed my copy. When they had finished she came in here to return it. I was alone. It was about a quarter past ten.'

'Yes?'

'Mr Alleyn, it is very difficult and disagreeable for me to tell you of this incident. Really, I – I don't know quite how to begin. You may not be familiar with parochial affairs, but I think many clergy find that there is an unfortunately rather common type of church work-er who is always a problem to her parish priest. I don't know if you will understand me when I say that one finds this type among – dear me – among ladies who are not perhaps very young and who have no other interests.'

The rector was now very pink.

'I think I understand,' said Alleyn.

'Do you? Well, I am sorry to say poor Miss Campanula was real-ly an advanced – er – specimen of this type. Poor soul, she was lone-ly and she had a difficult temperament which I am sure she did her best to discipline, but a times I could not help thinking that she needed a doctor as well as a priest to help her. I have even suggested as much.'

'That was very wise advice, sir.'

'She didn't take it,' said the rector wistfully. 'She stuck to me, you see, and I'm afraid I failed her.'

'About Friday night?' Alleyn reminded him gently.

'Yes, I know. I'm coming to Friday night; but, really, it's *very* diffi-cult. There was a terrible scene. She – I think she had got it into her head that if Dinah married or went away again – Dinah is on the stage, you know – I should be as lonely as she was. She said as much. I was very much startled and alarmed and I was at a loss how to reply. I think she misunderstood my silence. I really can't quite remember the order of events. It was rather like a bad dream, and still is. She was trembling dreadfully and looking at me with such a desperate expression in her eyes that I – I – I – '

He shut his eyes tight and added in a great hurry: 'I patted her hand.'

'That was quite a natural thing to do, wasn't it?'

'You wouldn't have said so if you'd seen the result.'

'No?'

'No, indeed. The next moment she was, to be frank, in my arms. It was without any exception the most awful thing that has ever happened to me. She was sobbing and laughing at the same time. I was in agony. I couldn't release myself. We never draw our blinds in this room, and there was I in this appalling and even ludicrous situation. I was obliged actually to – to support her. And I was so sorry for her, too. It was so painfully evident that she had made a frightful mistake. I believe she was hysterically delighted. It makes me feel ashamed and, as we used to say when I was young, caddish to repeat all this.'

'It's beastly of you,' said Alleyn; 'but I'm sure you should tell me.'

'I would have preferred, before doing so, to take the advice of one of my brother clergy, but there is no one who – However, that is beside the point. You are being very patient.'

'How did it end?'

'Very badly,' said the rector, opening his eyes wide. 'It couldn't have ended worse. When she had quietened down a little – and it was a long time before she did – I hastened to release myself, and I am afraid the first thing I did was to draw the curtains. You see, some members of the Reading Circle might still have been about. Their young men come up to meet them. Worse than that, Miss Prentice rang up in the morning and said she wanted to speak to me that evening. While Miss Campanula was still with me she telephoned to say she was not coming. That was about 10.15. Dinah took the message and afterwards said she sounded upset. I – I'm afraid I had been obliged to be rather severe with her – I mean as her priest – that afternoon. I had given her certain instructions which would keep her at home, and in any case I think perhaps her finger was too painful. But at the time I expected her, and if she had seen, it would have been – well, really – '

The rector gulped and added quickly: 'But that is beside the point. I drew the curtains, and in my flurry I said something to Miss Campanula about expecting Miss Prentice. It turned out that I couldn't have said anything worse, because when I tried to tell this unfortunate soul that she was mistaken, she connected my explanation with Miss Prentice's visit.'

'Help!' said Alleyn.

'What did you say? Yes. Yes, indeed. She became quite frantic and I really can *not* repeat what she said, but she uttered the most dreadful abuse of Miss Prentice and, in a word, she suggested that Miss Prentice had supplanted her, not only in the affairs of the parish but in my personal regard. I became angry – justly angry, as I thought at the time. As her priest I ordered her to stop. I rebuked her and reminded her of the deadly sin of envy. I told her that she must drive out this wickedness from her breast by prayer and fasting. She became much quieter, but as she left she said one sentence that I shall never forget. She turned in the doorway and said, 'If I killed myself she would suffer for it; but if, as I stand here in this room, I could strike Eleanor Prentice dead, I'd do it!' And before I could answer her she had gone out and shut the door.'

IV

'Darling,' said Henry, 'I think I'd better tell him.'

'But *why?*'

'Because I believe Eleanor will if I don't.'

'How could she? It would be too shaming for her. She'd have to say how she behaved when she saw us.'

'No, she wouldn't. She'd just twist it round somehow so that it looked as if she found us in a compromising position and that you were covered with scarlet shame and I was furious and threatened to scrag her.'

'But, Henry, that would be a deliberate attempt to make him suspect you.'

'I wouldn't put it past her.'

'Well, I would. If you were tried for murder, it'd be a pretty good scandal, and she wouldn't care for that at all.'

'No, that's true enough. Perhaps I may as well keep quiet.'

'I should say you'd better.'

'Dinah,' said Henry, 'who do you think – ?'

'I *can't* think. It seems incredible that any of us should do it. It just isn't possible.'

'Daddy thinks she did it herself. He won't say why.'

'What, fixed it up for Eleanor and then at the last minute decided to take the count herself?'

'I suppose so. It must be something she said to him.'

'What do you think of Alleyn?' asked Henry abruptly.

'I like him. Golly, I was rude to him,' said Dinah, hurling another log of wood on the schoolroom fire.

'Were you, my sweet?'

'Yes. I implied he was no gent.'

'Well, that was a lie,' said Henry cheerfully.

'I know it was. He couldn't have been nicer about it. How I could! Daddy was livid.'

'Naturally. Honestly, Dinah!'

'I know.'

'I love you all the way to the Great Bear and round the Southern Cross and back again.'

'Henry,' said Dinah suddenly, 'don't let's ever be jealous.'

'All right. Why?'

'I keep thinking of those two. If they hadn't been jealous I don't believe this would have happened.'

'Good heavens, Dinah, you don't think Eleanor – '

'No. But I sort of feel as if the whole thing was saturated in their jealousy. I mean, it was only jealousy that made them so beastly to each other and to us and to that shifty beast, Mrs Ross.'

'Why do you call her a shifty beast?'

'Because I know in my bones she is,' said Dinah.

'I must say I wish my papa would restrain his middle-aged ardours when he encounters her. His antics are so damn' silly.'

'Daddy's completely diddled by her conversion to his ways. She's put her name down for the retreat in Advent.'

'That's not so bad as my parent's archness. I could wish she didn't respond in kind, I must say. Apart from that, I don't mind the lady.'

'You're a man.'

'Oh, nonsense,' said Henry, answering the implication.

'I wouldn't trust her,' said Dinah, 'as far as I could toss a grand piano.'

'Why bring pianos into it?'

'Well, I wouldn't. She's the sort that's always called a man's woman.'

'It's rather a stupid sort of phrase,' said Henry.

'It simply means,' said Dinah, 'that she's nice to men and would let a woman down as soon as look at her!'

'I should have thought it just meant that she was too attractive to be popular with her own sex.'

'Darling, that's simply a masculine cliché,' said Dinah.

'I don't think so.'

'There are tons of devastating woman who are enormously popular with their own sex.'

Henry smiled.

'Do you think she's attractive?' asked Dinah casually.

'Yes, very. I dare say she's rather a little bitch, but she is pleasing. For one thing, her clothes fit her.'

'Yes, they do,' said Dinah sombrely. 'They must cost the earth.'

Henry kissed her.

'I'm a low swine,' he muttered. 'I was being tiresome. You're my dear darling and I'm no more fit to love you than a sweep, but I do love you so much.'

'We must never be jealous,' whispered Dinah.

'Dinah!' called the rector in the hall below.

'Yes, Daddy?'

'Where are you?'

'In the schoolroom.'

'May I go up, do you think?' asked a deep voice.

'That's Alleyn,' said Henry.

'Come up here, Mr Alleyn,' called Dinah.

CHAPTER 18

Mysterious Lady

'Sit down, Mr Alleyn,' said Dinah. 'The chairs are all rather rickety in this room, I'm afraid. You know Henry, don't you?'

'Yes, rather,' said Alleyn. 'I'll have this, if I may.' He squatted on a stuffed footstool in front of the fire.

'I told Henry how rude I'd been,' said Dinah

'I was horrified,' said Henry. 'She's very young, poor girl.'

'You couldn't by any chance just settle down and spin us some yarns about crime?' suggested Dinah.

'I'm afraid not. It would be delightful to settle down, but you see we're not allowed to get familiar when we're on duty. It looks impertinent. I've got a monstrous lot of things to do before tonight.'

'Do you just collect stray bits of evidence,' asked Henry, 'and hope they'll make sense?'

'More or less. You scavenge and then you arrange everything and try and see the pattern.'

'Suppose there's no pattern?'

'There must be. It's a question of clearing away the rubbish.'

'Any sign of it so far?' asked Dinah.

'Not a great many signs.'

'Do you suspect either of us?'

'Not particularly.'

'Well, we didn't do it,' said Dinah.

'Good.'

'Cases of homicide,' said Henry, 'must be different from any other kind. Especially cases that occur in these sorts of surroundings. You're not dealing with the ordinary criminal classes.'

'True enough,' said Alleyn. 'I'm dealing with people like yourself who will be devastatingly frank up to a certain point – far franker than the practical criminal, who lies to the police from sheer force of habit – but who will probably bring a great deal more *savoir faire* to the business of withholding essentials. For instance, I know jolly well there's something more to that meeting you both had with Miss Prentice on Friday afternoon; but it's no good saying to you, as I would to Posh Jimmy: "Come on, now. It's not you I'm after. Tell me what I want to know and perhaps we'll forget all about that little job over at Moorton." Unfortunately, I've nothing against you.'

'That's exactly what I mean,' said Henry. 'Still, you can always go for my Cousin Eleanor.'

'Yes. That's what I'll have to do,' agreed Alleyn.

'Well, I hope you don't believe everything she tells you,' said Dinah, 'or you *will* get in a muddle. Where we're concerned she's as sour as a quince.'

'And anyway, she's practically certifiable,' added Henry. 'It's a question which was dottiest: Eleanor or Miss C.'

'Lamentable,' said Alleyn vaguely. 'Mr Jernigham, did you put a box outside one of the hall windows after 2.30 on Friday?'

'No.'

'What *is* this about a box?' asked Dinah.

'Nothing much. About the piano. When did those aspidistras make their appearance?'

'They were there on Saturday morning, anyway,' said Dinah. 'I meant to have them taken away. They must have masked the stage from the audience. I think the girls put them there after I left on Friday.'

'In which case Georgie moved them off to rig his pistol.'

'And the murderer,' Henry pointed out, 'must have moved them again.'

'Yes.'

'I wonder when,' said Henry.

'So do we. Miss Copeland, did you see Miss Campanula on Friday night?'

'Friday night? Oh, I saw her at the Reading Circle meeting in the dining-room.'

'Not afterwards?'

'No. As soon as I got out of the dining-room I came up here. She went into the study to see Daddy. I could just hear her voice scolding away as usual, I should think, poor thing.'

'The study is beneath this room, isn't it?'

'Yes. I wanted to have a word with Daddy, but I waited until I heard her and the other person go.'

Alleyn paused for a second before he said:

'The other person?'

'There was somebody else in the study with Miss C. I can't help calling her "Miss C." We all did.'

'How do you know there was someone else there?'

'Well, because they left after Miss C.,' said Dinah impatiently. 'It wasn't Miss Prentice, because she rang up from Pen Cuckoo just about that time. Mary called me to the telephone, so I suppose it must have been Glady's Wright. She's leader of the Reading Circle. She lives up the lane. She must have gone out by the window in the study, because I heard the lane gate give a squeak. That's how I knew she'd been here.'

Alleyn walked over to the window. It looked down on a gravelled path, a lawn, and a smaller earthen path that led to a rickety gate and evidently ran on beyond it through a small plantation to the lane.

'I suppose you always go that way to the hall?' asked Alleyn.

'Oh, yes. It's much shorter than going round the house from the front door.'

'Yes,' said Alleyn, 'it would be.'

He looked thoughtfully at Dinah and said, 'Did you hear this other person's voice?'

'Hi!' said Dinah. 'What *is* all this? No, I didn't. Ask Daddy. He'll tell you who it was.'

'Stupid of me,' said Alleyn. 'Of course he will.'

II

He didn't ask the rector, but before he left he crunched boldly round the gravel path and walked across the lawn to the gate. It certainly creaked very loudly. It was one of those old-fashioned gates that has a post stile beside it. The path was evidently used very often. There was no hope of finding anything useful on its hard but greasy surface. There had been too much rain since Friday night. 'Much too much rain,' sighed Alleyn. But just inside the gate he found two softened but unmistakable depressions. Horseshoe-shaped holes about two inches in diameter that had held water. 'Heels,' he thought, 'but not a hope of saying whose. Female. Stood there a long time facing the house.' He could see the rector crouched over the study fire. 'Oh, well,' he said, and plunged into the little wood. 'Nothing at all that's to the purpose. Nothing.'

He saw that the hall was only a little way up on the other side from where this path came out on the lane. He returned, circled the rectory, perfectly aware that Dinah and Henry watched him from the schoolroom window. As he got into the car Henry opened the window and leaned out.

'I say,' he shouted.

'Shut up,' said Dinah's voice behind him. *"Don't*, Henry.'

'What is it?' called Alleyn, squinting up through the driving-window.

'It's nothing,' said Dinah. 'He's gone ravers, that's all. Goodbye.'

Henry's head shot out of sight and the window slammed.

'Now I wonder,' thought Alleyn. 'If Master Henry has got the same idea as I have.'

He drove away.

At the Jernigham Arms he found Nigel, but no Fox. 'Where are you going?' Nigel demanded when Alleyn returned to the car.

'To call on a lady.'

'Let me come.'

'Why the devil?'

'I won't go in with you if you'd rather not.'

'Naturally. All right. I can do with some comic relief.'

'Oh, God, your only jig-maker,' said Nigel and got in. 'Now, who's the lady?' he said. 'Speak up, dearie.'

'Mrs Ross.'

'The mysterious stranger.'

'Why do you call her that?'

'It's the part she played in their show. I've got a programme.'

'So it is,' said Alleyn.

He turned the car up the Vale Road and presently he began to talk. He went over the history of the case from midday on Friday. As far as he could, he traced the movements of the murdered woman and each of her seven companions. He correlated their movements and gave Nigel a time-table he had jotted down in his notebook.

'I hate these damn' things,' Nigel grumbled. 'They shatter my interest; they remind me of a Bradshaw, and they are therefore completely unintelligible.'

'It's a pity about you,' said Alleyn drily. 'Look at the list at the bottom.'

Nigel looked and read:

'Piano. Drawing-pin holes. Automatic. Branch. Onion. Chopsticks. Key. Letter. Creaky gate. Window. Telephone.'

'Thank you,' said Nigel. 'Now, of course, I see the whole thing in a blinding flash. It's as clear as the mud in your eye. The onion is particularly obvious, and as for the drawing-pins – It's ludicrous that I didn't spot the exquisite reason of the drawing-pins.'

He returned the paper to Alleyn.

'Go on,' he continued acidly. 'Say it. "You have the facts, Bathgate. You know my methods, Bathgate. What of the little grey cells, Bathgate?" Sling in a quotation; add: "Oh, my dear chap," and vanish in a fog of composite fiction.'

'This is Cloudyfold,' said Alleyn. 'Cold, isn't it? They had twelve degrees of frost on the pub thermometer last night.'

'Oh, Mr Mercury, how you did startle me!'

'That must be Mrs Ross's cottage down there.'

'Can't I come in as your stenographer?'

'Very well. I may send you out on an errand into the village.'

Duck Cottage stands in a bend of the road before it actually reaches Cloudyfold Village. It is a typical Dorset cottage, plain fronted, well proportioned, cold-grey and weather-worn. Mrs Ross had smartened it up. The window sashes and sills and the front door were painted vermilion and a vermilion tub with a Noah's Ark tree stood on each side of the entrance which led straight off the road.

Alleyn gave a double rap on the shiny brass knocker.

The door was opened by a maid, all cherry-red and muslin. Mrs Ross was at home. The maid took Alleyn's card away with her and returned to usher them in.

Alleyn had to stoop his head under the low doorway, and the ceilings were not much higher. They walked through a tiny ante-room, down some uneven steps and into Mrs Ross's parlour. She was not there. It was a charming parlour looking out on a small formal garden. There were old prints on the walls, one or two respectable pieces of furniture, a deep carpet, some very comfortable chairs, and a general air of chintz, sparkle and femininity. It was a delicate little room. Alleyn looked at a bookcase filled with modern novels. He noticed one or two works by authors whose sole distinction had been conferred by the censor, and at three popular collections of famous criminal cases. They all had startling wrappers and photographic illustrations. Within their covers one would find the cases Brown and Kennedy, Bywaters, Seddon, and Stinie Morrison. Their style would be characterized by a certain arch taciturnity. Alleyn grinned to himself and took one of them from the shelf. He let it fall upon his hands and a discourse on dactylography faced him. The groove between the pages was filled with cigarette ash. A photograph of prints developed and enlarged from a letter illustrated the written matter. A woman's voice sounded. Alleyn returned the book to its place. The door opened and Mrs Ross came in.

She was the lady Alleyn had noticed in church. This did not surprise him much, but it made him feel wary. She greeted him with a sensible good-humoured air, shook hands and then gave him a slanting smile.

'This is Mr Bathgate,' said Alleyn. He noticed that Nigel's fingers had flown to his tie.

She settled them by the fire with the prettiest air in the world, and he saw her glance at the little cupid clock on the mantelpiece.

'I do think all this is too ghastly,' she said. 'That poor wretched old creature! How anybody could!'

'It's a bad business,' said Alleyn.

She offered them cigarettes. Alleyn refused and Nigel, rather unwillingly, followed suit. Mrs Ross took one and leaned towards Alleyn for a light.

'*Chanel, Numéro Cinq,*' thought Alleyn.

'I've never been "investigated" before,' said Mrs Ross. 'Dear me, that sounds rather peculiar, doesn't it? I don't mean what you mean.'

She chuckled. Nigel uttered rather a flirtatious laugh, caught Alleyn's eye and was silent.

Alleyn said, 'I shan't bother you for long, I hope. We've got to try and find out where everybody was from about midday Friday up to the moment of the disaster.'

'Heavens!' said Mrs Ross, 'I'll never be able to remember that; and if I do, it's sure to sound too incriminating for words.'

'I hope not,' said Alleyn sedately. 'We've got a certain amount of it already. On Friday you went to a short five o'clock rehearsal at Pen Cuckoo, didn't you?'

'Yes. Apart from that, I was at home all day.'

'And Friday evening?'

'Still at home. We aren't very gay in Cloudyfold, Mr Alleyn. I think I've dined out twice since I came here. The county is simply rushing me, as you see.'

'On Saturday evening I suppose you joined the others in the hall?'

'Yes. I carted down one or two things they wanted for the stage. We towed them in a trailer behind Dr Tem-plett's Morris.'

'Did you go straight to the hall?'

'No. We called at Pen Cuckoo. I'd quite forgotten that. I didn't get out of the car.'

'Dr Templett went into the study?'

'He went into the house,' she said lightly, 'I don't know which room.'

'He didn't return by the french window?'

'I don't remember.' She paused and then added: 'The squire, Mr Jernigham, came and talked to me. I didn't notice Dr Templett until he was actually at the car window.'

'Ah, yes. You came back here for lunch?'

'Yes.'

'And in the afternoon?'

'Saturday afternoon. That's only yesterday, isn't it? Heavens, it seems a lifetime! Oh, I took the supper down to the hall.'

'At what time?'

'I think it was about half-past three when I got there.'

'Was the hall empty?'

'Yes. No, it wasn't. Dr Templett was there. He arrived just after I did. He'd brought down his clothes.'

'How long did you stay there, Mrs Ross?'

'I don't know. Not long. It might have been half an hour.'

'And Dr Templett?'

'He left before I did. I was putting out sandwiches.'

'And cutting up onions?'

'*Onions!* Good Lord, why should I do that? No, thank you. I'm sick at the sight of one, and I have got some respect for my hands.'

They were luxurious little hands. She held them to the fire.

'I'm sorry,' said Alleyn. 'There was an onion in the supper-room.'

'I don't know how it got there. The supper-room was all scrubbed out on Friday.'

'It's no matter. Did you look at the piano on Saturday afternoon?'

'No, I don't think so. The curtain was down, so I suppose if any-thing had been out of order I shouldn't have noticed. I didn't go to the front of the hall. The one key opens both doors.'

'And only Dr Templett came in?'

'Yes.'

'Could anyone have come unnoticed into the front of the hall while you were in the supper-room?'

'I suppose they might have. No, No, of course they couldn't. We had the key and the front door was locked.'

'Did Dr Templett go into the auditorium at all?'

'Only to shut the window.'

'Which window was open?'

'It's rather odd,' she said quickly. 'I'm sure I shut it in the morning.'

III

'It's the window on the side away from the lane, nearest the front,' continued Mrs Ross after a pause. 'I remember that, just as we were leaving, I pulled it down in case the rain blew in. That was at midday.'

'Were you the last to leave at noon?'

'No. Well, we all left together; but I think Dr Templett and I actu-ally walked out first. The Copelands always leave by the back door.'

'So presumably someone reopened the window?'

'Presumably.'

'Were you on the stage when Dr Templett shut the window?'

'Yes.'

'What were you doing there?'

'We – I tidied it up and arranged one or two ornaments I'd brought.'

'Dr Templett helped you?'

'He – well, he looked on.'

'And all this time the window was open?'

'Yes, I suppose so. Yes, of course it was.'

'Did you tell him you thought you had shut it?'

'Yes.'

'You don't think somebody pushed it open from outside?'

'No,' she said positively. 'We were certain they didn't. The curtain was up. We'd have seen.'

'I thought you said the curtain was down.'

'Oh, how stupid of me. It was up when we got there, but we let it down. It was supposed to be down. I wanted to try the effect of a lamp I'd taken.'

'Did you lower the curtain before or after you noticed the window?'

'I don't remember. Oh. Yes, please, I think it was afterwards.'

She leaned forward and looked at Nigel, who had been making notes.

'It's simply petrifying to see all this going down,' she said to him. 'Do I read it over and sign it?'

'It would have to go into long-hand first,' said Nigel.

'Do let me see.'

He gave her his notes.

'They look exactly like journalists' copy,' said Mrs Ross.

'That's our cunning,' said Nigel boldly, but rather red in the face. She laughed and gave them back to him.

'Mr Alleyn thinks we're terribly flippant, I can see,' she said. 'Don't you, inspector?'

'No,' said Alleyn. 'I regard Bathgate as a zealous and serious-minded young officer.'

Nigel tried to look zealous and serious minded. He was a little shaken.

'You mustn't forget that telegram, Bathgate,' added Alleyn. 'I think you'd better go into Cloudyfold and send it. You can pick me up on the way back. Mrs Ross will excuse you.'

'Very good, sir,' said Nigel and left.

'What a very charming young man,' said Mrs Ross, with her air of casual intimacy. 'Are all your officers as Eton and Oxford as that?'

'Not quite all,' rejoined Alleyn.

What a curious trick she had of widening her eyes! The pupils actually seemed to dilate. It was as if she was aware of something, recognized it, and gave just that one brief signal. Alleyn read into it a kind of polite wantonness. 'She proclaims herself,' he thought, 'by that trick. She is a woman with a strong, determined appetite.' He knew very well that, for all her impersonal manner, she had made small practised signals to him, and he wondered if he should let her see he had recognized these signals.

He leaned forward in his chair and looked deliberately into her eyes.

'There are two more questions,' he said.

'Two more? Well?'

'Do you know whose automatic it was that shot Miss Campanula between the eyes and through the brain?'

She sat quite still. The corners of her thin mouth drooped a little. Her short blackened lashes veiled her light eyes.

'It was Jocelyn Jernigham's, wasn't it?' she said.

'Yes. The same Colt that Mr Henry Jernigham showed you on Friday evening.'

'That's awful,' she said and looked squarely at him. 'Does it mean that you suspect one of us?'

'By itself, it doesn't amount to so much. But it was his automatic that killed her.'

'*He'd* never do it,' she said contemptuously.

'Did you put a box outside one of the hall windows at any time, after 2.30 on Friday?' asked Alleyn.

'No. Why?'

'It's of no importance.'

Alleyn put his hand in the breast pocket of his coat and took out his note-book.

'Heavens!' said Selia Ross. 'What next?'

His long fingers drew out a folded paper. That trick with her eyes must after all be unconscious. She looked slantways at the paper and the lines of block capitals, painstakingly executed by Inspector Fox. She took it from Alleyn, raising her eyebrows, and handed it back.

'Can you tell me anything about this?' asked Alleyn.

'No.'

'I think perhaps I should tell you we regard it as an important piece of evidence.'

'I've never seen it before. Where did you find it?'

'It just cropped up,' said Alleyn.

Somebody had come into the adjoining room. There came the sound of stumbling feet on the uneven steps. The door burst open. Alleyn thought, 'Blast Bathgate!' and glanced up furiously.

It was Dr Templett.

CHAPTER 19

Statement from Templett

'Selia?' said Dr Templett, and stopped short.

The paper dangled from Alleyn's fingers.

'Hullo, chief inspector,' said Templett breathlessly. 'I thought I might find you here. I've just done the PM.'

'Yes?' said Alleyn. 'Anything unexpected?'

'Nothing.'

Alleyn held out the paper.

'Isn't this your letter?'

Templett stood absolutely still. He then shook his head, but the gesture seemed to repudiate the implication rather than the statement.

'Were you not looking for it this morning in the breast pocket of your coat?'

'Is it yours, Billy?' she said. 'Who's been writing comic letters to you?'

The skin of his face seemed to tighten. Two sharp little cords sprang up from his nostrils to the corners of his mouth. He turned to the fire and stooped as if to warm his hands. They trembled violently and he thrust them into his pockets. His face was quite without colour, but the fire-light dyed it crimson.

Alleyn waited.

Mrs Ross lit a cigarette.

'I think I'd like to speak to Mr Alleyn alone,' said Templett.

'Can you come back to Chipping with me?' asked Alleyn.

'What? Yes. Yes, I'll do that.'

Alleyn turned to Mrs Ross and bowed.

'Good-evening, Mrs Ross.'

'Is it so late? Goodbye. Billy, is anything wrong?'

Alleyn saw him look at her with a sort of wonder. He shook his head and walked out. Alleyn followed him.

Nigel was sitting in the Bigginses' car. Alleyn signalled quickly to him and followed Templett to his Morris.

'I'll come with you, if I may,' said Alleyn.

Templett nodded. They got in. Templett turned the car and accelerated violently. Cloudyfold Rise leapt at them. They crossed the hilltop in two mintues. It was already dusk and the houses in the Vale were lit. A cold mist hung about the hills.

'God damn it,' said Dr Templett, 'you needn't watch me like that! I'm not going to take cyanide.'

'Of course not.'

As they skidded round Pen Cuckoo corner, Templett said, 'I didn't do it.'

'All right.'

At the church lane turning the car skated twenty yards on the greasy road, and fetched up sideways. Alleyn held his peace and trod on imaginary brakes. They started off again more reasonably, but entered Chipping at forty miles an hour.

'Will you stop outside the Jernigham Arms for a minute?' asked Alleyn.

Templett did not slow down until they were within two hundred yards of the inn. They shot across the road and stopped with screaming brakes. The pot-boy came running out.

'Is Mr Fox there? Ask him to come out, will you?' called Alleyn cheerfully, 'And when Mr Bathgate arrives, send him on to the police station at Great Chipping. Ask him to bring my case with him.'

Fox came out, bare-headed.

'Pop in at the back, Brer Fox,' said Alleyn. 'We're going into Great Chipping. Dr Templett will take us.'

'Good-evening, doctor,' said Fox, and got in.

Dr Templett put in his clutch and was off before the door shut. Alleyn's arm hung over the back of the seat. He twiddled his long fingers eloquently.

They reached the outskirts of Great Chipping in ten minutes, and here Templett seemed to come to his senses. He drove reasonably enough through the narrow provincial streets and pulled up at the police station.

Blandish was there. A constable showed them into his office and stood inside the door.

'Good-evening, gentlemen,' said the superintendent, who seemed to be in superb form. 'Some good news for me, I hope? Glad to say we're getting on quite nicely with our little job, Mr Alleyn. I wouldn't surprised if we won't be able to give the City a bit of very sound information by tomorrow. The bird's flown to Bermondsey, and we ought to be able to pull him in. Very gratifying. Well, now, sit down, all of you. Smith! The chair by the door.'

He bustled hospitably, caught sight of Templett's face and was abruptly silent.

'I'll make a statement,' said Templett.

'I think perhaps I should warn you – ' said Alleyn.

'I know all that. I'll make a statement.'

Fox moved up to the table. Superintendent Blandish, very startled and solemn, shoved across a pad of paper.

II

'On Friday afternoon,' said Dr Templett, 'on my return from hunting, an anonymous letter came into my possession. I believe the police now have this letter. Inspector Alleyn has shown it to me. I attached very little importance to it. I do not know who wrote it. I put it in my pocket-book in the inside breast-pocket of my coat. I intended to destroy it. At five o'clock on Friday I attended a rehearsal at Pen Cuckoo. On my return home I was immediately called out on a difficult case. I did not get back until late night. I forgot all about the letter. Yesterday, Saturday, wearing the same suit, I left my house at about 8.30, having only just got up. I collected some furniture from Duck Cottage, called at Pen Cuckoo, went on to the hall, where I left the furniture. She was with me. The rest of Saturday was spent on my rounds. I was unusually busy. They gave me some lunch at the cottage hospital. In the afternoon I called at the hall. I was only there for about half an hour. I did not go near the piano and I didn't remember the letter. I was not alone at the hall at any time. I arrived there for the evening performance at half-past seven, or possibly later. I went straight to my dressing-room and changed, hanging up my coat on the wall. Henry Jernigham came in and helped me. After the tragedy I did not change until I got home. At no time did I remember the letter. The next time I saw it, was this afternoon when Inspector Alleyn showed it to me. That's all.'

Fox looked up.

Blandish said, 'Make a full transcript of Inspector Fox's notes, Smith.'

Smith went out with the notes.

Alleyn said, 'Before we go any further, Dr Templett, I think I should tell you that the letter I showed you was a copy of the original and made on identical paper. The original is in our possession and it is in my bag. Fox, do you mind seeing if Bathgate has arrived?'

Fox went out and in a minute returned with Alleyn's case.

'Have you,' Alleyn asked Templett, 'as far as your memory serves, given us the whole truth in the statement you have just made?'

'I've given you everything that's relevant.'

'I am going to put several questions to you. Would you like to wait until your lawyer is present?'

'I don't want a lawyer. I'm innocent.'

'Your answers will be taken down and – '

'And may be used in evidence. I know.'

'– And may be used in evidence,' Alleyn repeated.

'Well?' asked Templett.

'Have you shown the letter to anyone else?'

'No.'

'Did you receive it by post?'

'Yes.'

Alleyn nodded to Fox, who opened the case and took out the original letter between its two glass cover sheets.

'Here it is,' said Alleyn. 'You see, we have developed the prints. There are three sets – yours, the deceased's, and another's. I must tell you that the unknown prints will be compared with any that we find on the copy which Mrs Ross has held in her hands. You can see, if you look at the original, that one set of prints is superimposed on the other two. Those are your own. The deceased's prints are the undermost.'

Templett did not speak.

'Dr Templett, I am going to tell you what I believe to have happened. I believe that this letter was sent in the first instance to Mrs Ross. The wording suggests that it was addressed to a woman rather than a man. I believe that Mrs Ross showed it to you on Saturday, which was yesterday morning, and that you put it in your pocketbook. If this is so, you know as well as I do that you will be ill-advised to deny it. You have told us the letter came by post. Do you now feel it would be better to alter this statement?'

'It makes no difference.'

'It makes all the difference between giving the police facts instead of fiction. If we find what we expect to find from the fingerprints, you will not help matters by adding your misstatement to the one that was made at Duck Cottage.'

Alleyn paused and looked at the undistinguished, dogged face.

'You have had a great shock,' he said, and added in a voice so low that Blandish put his hand to his ear like a deaf rustic: 'It's no good trying to protect people who are ready at any sacrifice of loyalty to protect themselves.'

Templett laughed.

'So it seems,' he said. 'All right. That's how it was. It's no good denying it.'

'Mrs Ross gave you the letter on Saturday?'

'I suppose so. Yes.'

'Did you guess at the authorship?'

'I *guessed.*'

'Did you notice the smell of eucalyptus?'

'Yes. But I'm innocent. My God, I tell you I had no opportunity. I can give you an account of every moment of the day.'

'When you were at the hall with Mrs Ross, did you not leave her to go down to the auditorium?'

'Why should I?'

'Mrs Ross told me you shut one of the windows.'

'Yes. I'd forgotten. Yes, I did.'

'But if Mrs Ross says she had shut this window herself in the morning?'

'I know. We couldn't make it out.'

'You noticed the open window, shut it, returned to the stage, and lowered the curtain?'

'Did she tell you that!'

Templett suddenly collapsed into the chair behind him and buried his face in his hands. 'My God,' he said, 'I've been a fool. *What* a fool!'

'They say it happens once to most of us,' said Alleyn unexpectedly and not unkindly. 'Did Mrs Ross not mention at the time that she thought she had already shut the window?'

'Yes, yes, yes. She said so. But the window was *open*. It was opened about three inches. How can I expect you to believe it? You think I lowered the curtain, went to the piano, and fixed this bloody trap. I tell you I didn't.'

'Why did you lower the curtain?'

Templett looked at his hands.

'Oh, God,' he said. 'Have we got to go into all that?'

'I see,' said Alleyn. 'No, I don't think we need. There was a scene that would have compromised you both if anybody had witnessed it?'

'Yes.'

'Did you at any time speak about the letter?'

'She asked me if I'd found out – I may as well tell you. I've got a note somewhere from Miss Campanula. I thought I'd compare the paper. I'd been so rushed during the day I hadn't hadn't time. That's why I didn't destroy the thing.'

'When you opened the window did you look out?'

'What? Yes. Yes. I think I did.' There was a curious note of uncertainty in his voice.

'Have you remembered something?'

'What's the good! It sounds like something I've made up at the last moment.'

'Let's have it anyway.'

'Well, she caught sight of the window. She noticed it first; saw it over my shoulder, and got an impression that there was something that dodged down behind the sill. It was only a flash, she said. I thought it was probably one of those damned scouts. When I got to the window I looked out. There was nobody there.'

'Were you upset by the discovery of an eavesdropper?'

Templett shrugged his shoulders.

'Oh, what's the good!' he said. 'Yes, I suppose we were.'

'Who was this individual?'

'I can't tell you.'

'But didn't Mrs Ross say who it was? She must have had some impression.'

'Ask her if you must,' he said violently, 'I can't tell you.'

'When you looked out they had gone,' murmured Alleyn. 'But you looked out.'

He watched Dr Templett, and Blandish and Fox watched him. Fox realized that they had reached a climax. He knew what Alleyn's next question would be, he saw Alleyn raise one eyebrow and screw his mouth sideways before he asked his question.

'Did you look down?' asked Alleyn.

'Yes.'

'And you saw?'

'There was a box under the window.'

'Ah!' It was the smallest sigh. Alleyn seemed to relax all over. He smiled to himself and pulled out his cigarette case.

'That seemed to suggest,' said Templett, 'that somebody had stood there, using the box. It wasn't there when I got to the hall because I went round that way to get the key.'

Alleyn turned to Fox.

'Have you asked them about the box?'

'Yes, sir. Mr Jernigham, Miss Prentice, every kid in the village, *and* all the helpers. Nobody knows anything about it.'

'Good,' said Alleyn, heartily.

For the first time since they got there, Dr Templett showed some kind of interest.

'Is it important?' he asked.

'Yes,' said Alleyn. 'I think it's of the first importance.'

III

'You knew about this box?' asked Templett after a pause.

'Yes, why don't you smoke, Dr Templett?' Alleyn held out his case.

'Are you going to charge me?'

'No. Not on present information.'

Templett took a cigarette and Alleyn lit it for him.

'I'm in a hell of a mess,' said Templett. 'I see that.'

'Yes,' agreed Alleyn. 'One way and another you've landed your-self in rather a box.' But there was something in his manner that drove the terror out of Templett's eyes.

Smith came in with the transcript.

'Sergeant Roper's outside, sir,' he said. 'He came down with Mr Bathgate and wants to see you particularly.'

'He can wait,' said Blandish. 'He's wanted to see me particular about ten times a day ever since we got busy.'

'Yes, sir. Will I leave the transcript?'

'Leave it here,' said Blandish, 'and wait outside.'

When Smith had gone Blandish spoke to Dr Templett for the first time that evening.

'I'm very sorry about this, doctor.'

'That's all right,' said Templett.

'I think Mr Alleyn will agree with me that if it's got no bearing on the case we'll do our best to bury it.'

'Certainly,' said Alleyn.

'I don't care much what happens,' said Templett.

'Oh, come now, doctor,' said Blandish uncomfortably, 'you must-n't say that.'

But Alleyn saw a gay little drawing-room with a delicate straw-coloured lady, whose good nature did not stretch beyond a very definite point, and he thought he understood Dr Templett.

'I think,' he said, 'you had better give us a complete time-table of your movements from two-thirty on Friday up to eight o'clock last night. We shall check it, but we'll make the process an impersonal sort of business.'

'But for those ten minutes in the hall, I'm all right,' said Templett. 'God, I was with her all the time, until I shut the window! Ask her how long it took! I wasn't away two minutes over the business. Surely to God she'll at least bear me out in that. She's nothing to lose by it.'

'She shall be asked,' said Alleyn.

Templett began to give the names of all the houses he had visited on his rounds. Fox took them down.

Alleyn suddenly asked Blandish to find out how long the Pen Cuckoo telephone had been disconnected by the falling branch. Blandish rang up the exchange.

'From eight-twenty until the next morning.'

'Yes,' said Alleyn. 'Yes.'

Dr Templett's voice droned on with its flat recital of time and place.

'Yes, I hunted all day Friday. I got home in time to change and got to the five o'clock rehearsal. The servants can check that. When I got home again I found this urgent message . . . I was out till after midnight. Mrs Bains at Mill Farm. She was in labour twenty-four hours . . . yes – '

'May I interrupt?' asked Alleyn. 'Yesterday morning, at Pen Cuckoo, Mrs Ross did not leave the car?'

'No.'

'Were you shown into the study?'

'Yes.'

'You were there alone?'

'Yes,' said Templett, showing the whites of his eyes.

'Dr Templett, did you touch the box with the automatic?'

'Before God, I didn't.'

'One more question. Last night did you use all your powers of authority and persuasion to induce Miss Prentice to allow Miss Campanula to take her place?'

'Yes, but – she wouldn't listen to me.'

'Will you describe again how you found her?'

'I told you last night. I came in late. I thought Dinah would be worried and after I'd changed, I went along to the women's dressing-room to show her I was there. I heard some one snivelling and moaning, and through the open door I saw Miss Prentice in floods of tears, rocking backwards and forwards and holding her hand. I went in and looked at it. No doctor in his sense would have let her thump the piano. She *couldn't* have done it. I told her so, but she kept on saying, "I will do it. I will do it." I got angry and spoke my mind. I couldn't get any further with her. It was damned near time we started and I wasn't even made-up.'

'So you fetched Miss Copeland and her father, knowing the rector would possibly succeed where you had failed.'

'Yes. But I tell you it was physically impossible for her to use the finger. I could have told her that – '

He stopped short.

'Yes? You could have told her that, how long ago?' said Alleyn.

'Three days ago.'

IV

Smith returned.

'It's Sergeant Roper, sir. He says it's very particular indeed and he knows Mr Alleyn would want to hear it.'

'Blast!' said Blandish. 'All right, all right.'

Smith left the door open. Alleyn saw Nigel crouched over an anthracite stove and Roper, sweating and expectant, in the middle of the room.

'Right oh, Roper,' said Smith, audibly. Roper hurriedly removed his helmet, cleared his throat, and marched heavily into the room.

'Well, Roper?' said Blandish.

'Sir,' said Roper, 'I have a report.' He took his official note-book from a pocket in his tunic and opened it, bringing it into line with his nose. He began to read very rapidly in a high voice.

'This afternoon, November 28th, at 4 p.m. being on duty at the time outside the parish hall of Winton St Giles I was approached and accosted by a young female. She was well-known to me being by name Gladys Wright (Miss) of Top Lane, Winton. The following conversation eventuated. Miss Wright enquired of me if I was waiting for my girl or my promotion. Myself (PS Roper): I am on duty, Miss Wright, and would take it kindly if you would pass along the lane. Miss Wright: Look what our cat's brought in. PS Roper: And I don't want no lip or saucy boldness. Miss Wright: I could tell you something and I've come along to do it, but seeing you're on duty maybe I'll keep it for your betters. PS Roper: If you know anything, Gladys, you'd better speak up for the law comes down with majesty on them that aids and abets and withholds. Miss Wright: What will you give me? The succeeding remarks are not evidence and bear no connection with the matter in hand. They are therefore omitted.'

'What the hell did she tell you?' asked Blandish. 'Shut that damned book and come to the point.'

'Sir, the girl told me in her silly way that she came down to the hall at six-thirty on yesterday evening being one of them selected to usher. She let herself in and finding herself first to arrive, living nearby and not wishing to return home, the night being heavy rain with squalls and her hair being artificially twisted up with curls which to my mind – '

'What did she tell you?'

'She told me that at six-thirty she sat down as bold as brass and played "Nearer my Gawd to Thee" with the soft pedal on,' said Roper.

CHAPTER 20

According to Miss Wright

Sergeant Roper, sweating lightly, allowed an expression of extreme gratification to suffuse his enormous face. The effect of his statement on his superiors left nothing to be desired. Superintendent Blandish stared at his sergeant like a startled codfish, Detective-Inspector Fox pushed his glasses up his forehead and brought his hands down smartly on his knees. Dr Templett uttered in a whisper a string of amazing blasphemies. Chief Inspector Alleyn pulled his own nose, made a peculiar grimace, and said:

'Roper, you shall be hung with garlands, led through the village, and offered up at the Harvest Festival.'

'Thank you, sir,' said Roper.

'Where,' asked Alleyn, 'is Gladys Wright?'

Roper flexed his knees and pointed with his thumb over his shoulder.

'Stuck to her like glue, I have. I telephoned Fife from the hall to relieve me, keeping the silly maiden under observation the while. I brought her here, sir, on the bar of my bike, all ten stone of her, and seven mile if it's an inch.'

'Magnificent. Bring her in, Roper.'

Roper went out.

'I didn't get there till half-past seven,' whispered Dr Templett, shaking his finger at Alleyn. 'Not till half-past seven. You see! You see! The hall was full of people. Ask Dinah Copeland. She'll tell you I never went on the stage. Ask Copeland. He was sitting on the stage. I saw him through the door when I called him down. Ask any of them. My God!'

Alleyn reached out a long arm and gripped his wrist.

'Steady, now,' he said. 'Fox, there's the emergency flask in that case.'

He got Templett to take the brandy before Roper returned.

'Miss Gladys Wright, sir,' said Roper, flinging back the door and expanding his chest.

He shepherded his quarry into the room with watchful pride, handed her over, and retired behind the door to wipe his face down excitedly with the palm of his hand.

Miss Wright was the large young lady whom Alleyn had encountered in the rectory hall. Under a mackintosh she wore a plushy sort of dress with a hint of fur about it. Her head was indeed a mass of curls. Her face was crimson and her eyes black.

'Good-evening, Miss Wright,' said Alleyn. 'I'm afraid we've put you to a lot of trouble. Will you sit down?'

He gave her his own chair and sat on the edge of the desk.

Miss Wright backed up to the chair rather in the manner of a draught-horse, got half-way towards sitting on it, but thought better of this, and giggled.

'Sergeant Roper tells us you've got some information for us,' continued Alleyn.

'Aw him!' said Miss Wright. She laughed and covered her mouth with her hand.

'Now I understand that you arrived at the parish hall at half-past six last night. Is that right?'

'That's right.'

'Sure of the time?'

'Yass,' said Miss Wright. 'I heard the clock strike, see?'

'Good. How did you get in?'

'I got the key from outside and came in by the back door,' said Wright, and looked at the floor. 'Miss Dinah was soon after me.'

'Nobody else was in the hall. You switched on the light, I suppose?'

'Yass, that's right.'

'What did you do next?'

'Well, I looked round, like.'

'Yes. Have a good look round?'

'Aaw, yass. I suppose so.'

'Back and front of the stage, what? Yes. And then?'

'I took off my mac, and put out my programmes, like, and counted up my change, see, for selling.'

'Yes?'

'Aw deer,' said Wright, 'it does give me such a turn when I think about it.'

'I'm sure it does.'

'You know! When you think! What I was saying to Charley Roper, you never know. And look, I never thought of it till this afternoon at the Children's Service. I was collecting up hymn-books and it come all over me, so when I see Charley Roper hanging about outside the hall, I says, "Pardon me, Mr Roper," I says, "but I have a piece of information I feel it my duty to pass on."'

'Very proper,' said Alleyn with a glance at Roper.

'Yass, and I told him. I told him I might be laying where she is, seeing what I did!'

'What did you do?'

'I sat down and played a hymn on that rickety old affair. Aw, *well*!'

'Did you play loudly or softly?'

'Well, well, both, ackshully. I was seeing which pedal worked best on that shocking old affair, see?'

'Yes,' said Alleyn. 'I see. Did you put the pedal on suddenly and hard?'

'Aw no. Because one time the soft pedal went all queer because Cissie Dewry put her foot on it, so we always use it gentle-like. I didn't try it but the bare once. The loud one worked better,' said Miss Wright.

'Yes,' agreed Alleyn. 'I expect it would.'

'Well, it did,' confessed Miss Wright, and giggled again.

'But you did actually press the soft pedal down?' insisted Alleyn.

'Yass. Firm like. Not sharp.'

'Exactly. Was there a piece of music on the rack?'

'Oo yass, Miss Prentice's piece. I never touched it. Truly!'

'I'm sure you didn't. Miss Wright, suppose you were in a court of law, and someone put a Bible in your hand, and you were asked to swear solemnly in God's name that at about twenty to seven last night you put your foot firmly on the left pedal, would you swear it?'

Miss Wright giggled.

'It's very important,' said Alleyn. 'You see, there would be a pris-
oner in the court on trial for murder. Please think very carefully
indeed. Would you make this statement on oath?'

'Oh *yass,*' said Miss Wright.

'Thank you,' said Alleyn. He looked at Templett. 'I don't think we
need keep you, Dr Templett, if you are anxious to get home.'

'I – I'll drive you back,' said Templett.

'That's very nice of you – I shan't be long.' He turned back to
Gladys Wright. 'Did any one come in while you were playing?'

'I stopped when I heard them coming. Cissie Dewry come first
and then all the other girls.'

'Did you notice any of the performers?'

'No. We was all talking round the door, like.' She rolled her eyes
at Roper. 'That was when you come, Mr Roper.'

'Well, Roper?'

'They were in the entrance, sir, giggling and cackling in their
female manner, sure enough.'

'Oo you *are,*' said Miss Wright.

'And had any of the company arrived at that time?'

'Yes, sir,' said Roper. 'Miss Copeland was there ahead of me, but
she went to the back door same as all the performers, I don't doubt.
And the Pen Cuckoo party was there, sir, but I didn't know that till
I went round to back of stage when I found them bedizening their
faces in the Sunday-school rooms.'

'So that there was a moment when the ladies were at the front
door, talking, and the Pen Cuckoo party and Miss Copeland were
behind the scenes?'

'That's right, sir.'

'They were ringing and ringing at the telephone,' interjected Miss
Wright, 'all the time us girls was there.'

'And you say, Miss Wright, that none of the performers came into
the front hall.'

'Not one. Truly.'

'Sure?'

'Yass. Certain sure. We would have seen them. Soon after that the
doors were open and people started to come in.'

'Where did you stand?'

'Up top by the stage, ushering the two shillingses.'

'So if anybody had come down to the piano from the stage you would have seen them?'

'Nobody came down. Not ever. I'd take another Bible oath on that,' said Miss Wright, with considerable emphasis.

'Thank you,' said Alleyn. 'That's splendid. One other question. You were at the Reading Circle meeting at the rectory on Friday night. Did you go home by the gate into the wood. The gate that squeaks?'

'Oo *no*! None of us girls goes that way at night.' Miss Wright giggled, extensively. 'It's too spooky. Oo, I wouldn't go that way for anything. The others, they all went together, and my young gentleman, he took me home by lane.'

'So you're sure nobody used the gate?'

'Yass, for sure. They'd all gone,' said Miss Wright, turning scarlet, 'before us. And we used lane.'

'You passed the hall, then. Were there any lights in the hall?'

'Not in front.'

'You couldn't see the back windows, of course. Thank you so much, Miss Wright. We'll get you to sign a transcript of everything you have told us. Read it through carefully, first. If you wouldn't mind waiting in the outer office I think I can arrange for you to be driven home.'

'Oo well, thanks ever so,' said Miss Wright, and went out.

II

Alleyn looked at Templett.

'I ought to apologize,' he said, 'I've given you a damned bad hour.'

'I don't know why you didn't arrest me,' said Templett with a shaky laugh. 'Ever since I realized I'd left that bloody note in the dressing-room I've been trying to think how I could prove I hadn't rigged the automatic. There seemed to be no possible proof. Even now I don't see – Oh, well, it doesn't matter. Nothing much matters. If you don't mind, I'll wait outside in the car. I'd like a breath of fresh air.'

'Certainly.'

Dr Templett nodded to Blandish and went out.

'Will I shadow the man?' asked Roper, earnestly.

Blandish's reply was unprintable.

'You might ask Mr Bathgate to drive your witness home, Roper,' said Alleyn. 'Let her sign her statement first. Tell Mr Bathgate I'm returning with Dr Templett. And Roper, as tactfully as you can, just see how Dr Templett's getting on. He's had a shock.'

'Yes, sir.'

Roper went out.

'He's got about as much tact as a cow,' said Blandish.

'I know, but at least he'll keep an eye on Templett.'

'The lady let him down, did she?'

'With a thump that shook the crockery.'

'S-s-s-s!' said Blandish appreciatively. 'Is that a fact?'

'He's had two narrow escapes,' said Fox, 'and *that's* a fact. The lady's let him down with a jerk and he's lucky the hangman won't follow suit.'

'Fox,' said Alleyn, 'you have the wit of a Tyburn broadsheet, but there's matter in it.'

'I don't know where I am,' said Blandish. 'Are we any nearer to an arrest?'

'A good step,' said Alleyn. 'The pattern emerges.'

'What does that mean, Mr Alleyn?'

'Well,' said Alleyn, apologetically, 'I mean all these mad little things like the box, and the broken telephone, and the creaking gate – I'm not sure of the onion – '

'The onion!' cried Fox, triumphantly. 'I know all about the onion, Mr Alleyn. Georgie Biggins is responsible for that, the young limb. I saw him this afternoon and asked him, as well as every other youngster in the village, about the box. He's going round as pleased as Punch, letting on he's working at the case with the Yard. Answers me as cool as you please, and when I'm going he says, "Did you find an onion in the teapot, mister?" Well, it seems that they had a tea-party on the stage, with Miss Prentice and Miss Campanula quarrelling about which should pour out. If the young devil didn't go and put an onion in the pot. It seems they each had to take the lid off and look in the pot and this was another of Georgie's bright ideas. I suppose someone found it in time and threw it into the box on the floor, where you picked it up.'

'Dear little Georgie,' said Alleyn. 'Dear little boy! We've had red herrings before now, Fox, but never a Spanish onion. Well, as I was saying, all these mad little things begin to bear some sort of relationship.'

'That's nice, Mr Alleyn,' said Fox, woodenly. 'You're going to tell us you know who did it, I suppose?'

'Oh, yes,' said Alleyn looking at him in genuine surprise. 'I do *now*, Brer Fox. Don't you?'

III

When a man learns that his mistress, faced with putting herself in a compromising position, will quite literally see him hanged first, he is not inclined for conversation. Templett drove slowly back towards Chipping and was completely silent until the first cottage came into view. Then he said, 'I don't see how anyone could have done it. The piano was safe at six-thirty. The girl used the soft pedal. It was safe.'

'Yes,' agreed Alleyn.

'I suppose, putting the pedal down softly, the pressure wasn't enough to pull the trigger?'

'It's a remarkably light pull,' said Alleyn. 'I've tried.'

Templett brushed his hand across his eyes. 'I suppose my brain won't work.'

'Give the thing a rest.'

'But how could anybody fix that contraption inside the piano after half-past six when those girls were sky-larking about in the front of the house? It's impossible.'

'If you come down to the hall tomorrow night, I'll show you.'

'All right. Here's your pub. What time's the inquest? I've forgotten. I'm all to pieces.' He pulled up the car.

'Eleven o'clock tomorrow.'

Alleyn and Fox got out. It was a cold windy evening. The fine weather had broken again and it had begun to rain. Alleyn stood with the door open and looked at Templett. He leaned on the wheel and stared with blank eyes at the windscreen.

'The process of convalescence,' said Alleyn, 'should follow the initial shock. Take heart of grace, you will recover.'

'I'll go home,' said Templett. 'Good-night.'

'Good-night.'

He drove away.

They went upstairs to their rooms.

'Let's swap stories, Brer Fox,' said Alleyn. 'I'll lay my case, for what it's worth, on the dressing-table. I want a shave. You can open your little heart while I'm having it. I don't think we'll unburden ourselves to Bathgate just yet.'

They brought each other up-to-date before they went downstairs again in search of a drink.

They found Nigel alone in the bar parlour.

'I'm not going to pay for so much as half a drink and I intend to drink a very great deal. I've had the dullest afternoon of my life and all for your benefit. Miss Wright smells. When I took her to her blasted cottage she made me go in to tea with her brother who turns out to be the village idiot. Yes, and on the way back from Duck Cottage, your lovely car sprang a puncture. Furthermore – '

'Joe!' shouted Alleyn. 'Three whiskies-and-sodas.'

'I should damn' well think so. What are you ordering for yourselves?'

Nigel calmed down presently and listened to Alleyn's account of the afternoon. Mrs Peach, a large flowing woman, told them she had a proper juicy steak for their dinner and there was a fine fire in the back parlour. They moved in, taking their drinks with them. It was pleasant, when the curtains were drawn and the red-shaded oil lamp was lit, to hear the rain driving against the leaded windows and to listen to the sound of grilling steak beyond the kitchen slide.

'Not so many places left like this,' said Fox. 'Cosy, isn't it? I haven't seen one of those paraffin lamps for many a long day. Mrs Peach says old Mr Peach, her father-in-law, you know, won't have electricity in the house. He's given in as far as the tap-room's concerned but nowhere else. Listen to the rain! It'll be a wild night again.'

'Yes,' said Alleyn. 'It's strange, isn't it, to think of the actors in this silly far-fetched crime, all sitting over their fires, as we are now, six of them wondering what the answer is, and the seventh nursing it secretly in what used to be known as a guilty heart.'

'Oo-er,' said Nigel.

Mrs Peach's daughter brought in the steak.

'Are you going out again?' asked Nigel after an interval.

'I've got a report to write,' answered Alleyn. 'When that's done I think I might go up to the hall.'

'Whatever for?'

'Practical demonstration of the booby-trap.'

'I might come,' said Nigel. 'I can ring up the office from there.'

'You'll have to square up with the Copelands if you do. The hall telephone is on an extension from the rectory. Great hopping fleas!' shouted Alleyn, 'why the devil didn't I think of that before!'

'What!'

'The telephone.'

'Excuse him,' said Nigel to Fox.

IV

'We'll take half an hour's respite,' said Alleyn, when the cloth had been drawn and a bottle of port, recommended by old Mr Peach, had been set before them. 'Let's go over the salient features.'

'Why not?' agreed Nigel, comfortably.

Alleyn tried the port, raised an eyebrow, and lit a cigarette.

'It's respectable,' he said. 'An honest wine and all that. Well, as I see it, the salient features are these. Georgie Biggins rigged his booby-trap between two and three on Friday afternoon. Miss Campanula rattled on the door just before two-thirty. Georgie was in the hall, but must have hidden, because when Gibson looked through the window, the top of the piano was open and Georgie nowhere to be seen. Miss Campanula didn't know that the key was hung up behind the outhouse. The rest of the company were told but they are vague about it. Now Georgie didn't test his booby-trap because, as he says, "somebody came." I think this refers to Miss Campanula's onslaught on the door. I'm afraid Miss Campanula is a nightmare to Georgie. He won't discuss her. I'll have to try again. Anyway, he didn't test his booby-trap. But *somebody* did, because the silk round the hole made by the bullet was still damp last night. That means something was on the rack, possibly Miss Prentice's "Venetian Suite" which seems to have been down in the hall for the last week. It has a stain on the back which suggests that the jet of water hit it and splayed out, wetting the silk. Now, Georgie left the hall soon after the interruption, because he finished up by playing "Chop-sticks" with the loud pedal on, and Miss Campanula overheard this final performance. The next eighteen hours or so are still wrapped in mystery but, as far as we know, any of the company may have gone into the hall. Miss Prentice passed it on her way home from confession, the Copelands live within two minutes of the place. Master Henry says that after his meeting with Dinah Copeland he roamed the hills most of that unpleasantly damp afternoon. He may have come down to the hall. Jernigham senior seems to have hunted all day and so does Templett, but either of them may have come down in the evening. Miss Prentice says she spent the evening praying in her room, Master Henry says he tinkered with a light plug in his room, the squire says he was alone in the study. It takes about eight minutes to walk down Top Lane to the hall and perhaps fifteen to return. On Friday night the rector had an agonizing encounter in his own study. I'll tell you about it.'

Alleyn told them about it.

'Now the remarkable thing about this is that I believe he spoke the truth, but his story is made so much nonsense if Dinah Copeland was right in thinking there was a third person present. Miss C. would hardly make passionate advances and hang herself round the rector's neck, with a Friendly Helper to watch the fun. Dinah Copeland bases her theory on the fact that she heard the gate opposite the study window squeak, as if somebody had gone out that way. She tells us it couldn't have been Miss Prentice because Miss Prentice rang up a few minutes later to say she wasn't coming down. We know Miss Prentice was upset when she left confession that afternoon. The rector had ticked her off and given her a penance or something and he thinks that's why she didn't come. It wasn't any of the readers. Who the devil was it?'

'The rector himself,' said Nigel promptly, 'taking a short cut to the hall.'

'He says that after Miss C. left him he remained a wreck by his fireside.'

'That may not be true.'

'It may be as false as hell,' agreed Alleyn. 'There are one or two points about this business. I'll describe the layout and repeat the rector's story.'

When he had done this he looked at Fox.

'Yes,' said Fox. 'Yes, I think I get you there, Mr Alleyn.'

'Obviously, I'm right,' said Nigel, flippantly. 'It's the reverend.'

'Mr Copeland's refusing the money, Mr Bathgate,' said Fox. 'I was telling the chief, just now. I got that bit of information this afternoon. Mr Henry told the squire in front of the servants and it's all round the village.'

'Well, to finish Friday,' said Alleyn. 'Dr Templett spent the best part of the night on a case. That can be checked. Mrs Ross says she was at home. Tomorrow, Foxkin, I'll get you to use your glamour on Mrs Ross's maid.'

'Very good, sir.'

'Now then. Some time before noon yesterday, the water-pistol disappeared, because at noon Miss P. strummed with her right hand and used the soft pedal. Nothing happened.'

'Perhaps Georgie's plan didn't work,' suggested Nigel.

'We are going to see presently if Georgie's plan works. Whether it works or not, the fact remains that somebody found the water-pistol, removed and hid it, and substituted the Colt.'

'That must have been later still,' said Nigel.

'I agree with you, but not, I imagine, for the same reason. Dr Templett's story seems to prove that the box was placed outside the window while he and Mrs Ross were in the hall. He got the impression that someone dodged down behind the sill. Now this eavesdropper was not Miss Campanula because the servants agree that she didn't go out yesterday afternoon. Miss Prentice, the squire, Dinah Copeland and her father were all in their respective houses, but any of them could have slipped out for an hour. Master Henry was again roving the countryside. None of them owns to the box outside the window. Fox has asked every soul in the place and not a soul professes to know anything about the box.'

'That's right,' said Fox. 'I reckon the murderer was hanging about with the Colt and had a look in to see who was there. He'd see the cars in the lane but he'd want to find out if the occupants were in the hall or had gone that way into the vicarage. On the far side of the hall he'd have been out of sight, and he'd have plenty of time to dodge if they sounded as if they were coming round that way. He'd be safe enough. Or she,' added Fox with a bland glance at Nigel.

'That's how I read it,' agreed Alleyn. 'Now, look here.'

He took an envelope from his breast pocket, opened it, and, using tweezers, took out four minute reddish-brown scraps, which he laid on a sheet of paper.

'Salvage from the box,' he said.

Nigel prodded at them with the tweezers.

'Rubber,' said Nigel.

'Convey anything?'

'Somebody wearing goloshes. Miss Prentice, by gosh. I bet she wears goloshes. Or Miss C. herself. Good Lord,' said Nigel, 'perhaps the rector's right. Perhaps it is a case of suicide.'

'These bits of rubber were caught on a projecting nail and some rough bits of wood inside the box.'

'Well, she might have trodden inside the box before she picked it up.'

'You have your moments,' said Alleyn. 'I suppose she might.'

'Goloshes!' said Fox and chuckled deeply.

'Here!' said Nigel, angrily. 'Have you got a case?'

'The makings of one,' said Alleyn. 'We're not going to tell you just yet, because we don't want to lower our prestige.'

'We like to watch your struggles, Mr Bathgate,' said Fox.

'We are, as it might be,' said Alleyn, 'two experts on a watch-tower in the middle of a maze. "Look at the poor wretch," we say as we nudge each other, "there he goes into the same old blind alley. Jolly comical," we say, and then we laugh like anything. Don't we, Fox?'

'So we do,' agreed Fox. 'But never you mind, Mr Bathgate, you're doing very nicely.'

'Well, to hell with you anyway,' said Nigel. 'And moreover what about Gladys Wright putting her splay foot on the soft pedal an hour and a half before the tragedy?'

'Perhaps she wore goloshes,' said Fox, and for the first time in these records he broke into a loud laugh.

CHAPTER 21

According to Mr Saul Tranter

Alleyn finished his report by nine o'clock. At a quarter-past nine they were back in the Biggins' Ford, driving through pelting rain to the hall.

'I'll have to go up to the Yard before this case is many hours older,' said Alleyn. 'I telephoned the AC this morning but I think I ought to see him and there are a lot of odd things to be cleared up. Perhaps tomorrow night. I'd like to get to the bottom of that meeting between Master Henry, Dinah Copeland and Miss Prentice. I rather think Master Henry wishes to unburden himself and Miss Dinah won't let him. Here we are.'

Once more they crunched up the gravel path to the front door. The shutters had been closed and the windows were all locked. PC Fife was on duty. He let them in and being an incurious fellow retired thankfully when Alleyn said he would not be wanted for two hours.

'I'll ring up the Chipping station when we're leaving,' said Alleyn.

The hall smelt of dying evergreens and varnish. It was extremely cold. The piano still stood in its old position against the stage. The hole in the faded silk gaped mournfully. The aspidistras drooped a little in their pots. A fine dust had settled over everything. The rain drove down steadily on the old building and the wind shook the shutters and howled desperately under the eaves.

'I'm going to light these heaters,' said Nigel. 'There's a can of paraffin in one of the back rooms. This place smells of mortality.'

Alleyn opened his case and took out Georgie Biggins's water-pistol. Fox wedged the butt between steel pegs in the iron casing. The nozzle fitted a hole in the fretwork front. They had left the cord and pulleys in position.

'On Friday,' said Alleyn, 'there was only the long rent in the tucked silk. You see there are several of them. The material has rotted in the creases. No doubt Georgie arranged the silk tastefully behind the fretwork, so that the nozzle didn't catch the light. We'll have a practical demonstration from Mr Bathgate, Fox. Now, if you fix the *front* pulley, I'll tie the cord round the butt of the pistol. Hurry up. I hear him clanking in the background.'

They had just dropped a sheet of newspaper on the rack when Nigel reappeared with a large can.

'There's some fairly good beer in that room,' said Nigel. He began to fill the tank of the heater from his can. Alleyn sat down at the piano, struck two or three chords, and began to vamp '*Il était une Bergère*.'

'That's odd, Fox,' he said.

'What's wrong, Mr Alleyn?'

'I can't get the soft pedal to budge. You try. Don't force it.'

Fox seated himself at the piano and picked out 'Three Blind Mice,' with a stubby forefinger.

'That's right,' he said, 'It makes no difference.'

'What's all this?' demanded Nigel, and bustled forward. 'The soft pedal doesn't work.'

'Good Lord!'

'It makes no difference to the sound,' said Fox.

'You're not using it.'

'Yes, I am, Mr Bathgate,' lied Fox.

'Here,' said Nigel, 'let me try.'

Fox got up. Nigel took his place with an air of importance.

'Rachmaninoff's Prelude in C – Minor,' he said. He squared his elbows, raised his left hand and leant forward. The voice of the wind mounted in a thin wail and seemed to encircle the building. Down came Nigel's left hand like a sledge-hammer.

'Pom. *Pom*. POM!'

Nigel paused. A violent gust shook the shutters so impatiently that, for a second, he raised his head and listened. Then he trod on the soft pedal.

The newspaper fell forward on his hands. The thin jet of water caught him between the eyes like a cold bullet. He jerked backwards, uttered a scandalous oath, and nearly lost his balance.

'It does work,' said Alleyn.

But Nigel did not retaliate. Above all the uneasy clamour of the storm, and like an echo of the three pretentious chords, sounded a loud triple knock on the front door.

'Who the devil's that?' said Alleyn.

He started forward, but before he could reach the door it crashed open, and on the threshold stood Henry Jernigham with streaks of rain lacing his chalk-white face.

II

'What the hell's happening in here?' demanded Henry.

'Suppose you shut the door,' said Alleyn.

But Henry stared at him as if he had not heard. Alleyn walked past him, slammed the door, and secured the catch. Then he returned to Henry, took him by the elbow, and marched him up the hall.

Fox waited stolidly. Nigel wiped his face with his handkerchief and stared at Henry.

'Now what is it?' demanded Alleyn.

'My God!' said Henry, 'who played those three infernal chords?'

'Mr Bathgate. This is Mr Bathgate, Mr Jernigham, and this Detective-Inspector Fox.' Henry looked dimly at the other two and sat down suddenly.

'Oh, Lord,' he said.

'I say,' said Nigel. 'I'm most extraordinarily sorry if I gave you a shock, but I assure you I never thought – '

'I'd come into the lane,' said Henry, breathlessly, 'the rectory trees were making such a noise in the wind that you couldn't hear anything else.'

'Yes?' said Alleyn.

'Don't you see? I'd come up the path and just as I reached the door a great gust of wind and rain came screeching round the building like the souls of the damned. And then, when it dropped, those three chords on a cracked piano! My God, I tell you I nearly bolted.'

Henry put his hand to his face and then looked at his fingers.

'I don't know whether it's sweat or rain,' he said, 'and that's a fact. Sorry! Not the behaviour of a pukka sahib. No, by Gad, sir. Blimp wouldn't think anything of it.'

'I can imagine it was rather trying,' said Alleyn. 'What were you doing there, anyway?'

'Going home. I stayed on to supper at the rectory. Only just left. Mr Copeland's in such a hoo that he's forgotten all about choking me off. When I occurred at cold supper he noticed me no more than the High Church blancmange. I say, sir, I am sorry I made such an ass of myself. Honestly! How I could!'

'That's all right,' said Alleyn. 'But why did you turn in here?'

'I thought if that splendid fellow Roper held the dogwatch, I might say, "Stand ho! What hath this thing appeared?" and get a bit of gossip out of him.'

'I see.'

'Have a cigarette?' said Nigel.

'Oh, thank you. I'd better take myself off.'

'Would you like to wait and see a slight experiment?' asked Alleyn.

'Very much indeed, sir, if I may.'

'Before we begin, there's just one thing I'd like to say to you, as you are here. I shall call on Miss Prentice tomorrow and I shall use every means within the law to get her to tell me what took place on that encounter in Top Lane on Friday. I don't know whether you'd rather give me your version first.'

'I've told you already, she's dotty,' said Henry with nervous impatience. 'It's my belief she is actually and literally out of her senses. She looks like death and she won't leave her room except for meals, and then she's doesn't eat anything. She said at dinner tonight that she's in danger, and that in the end she'll be murdered. It's simply ghastly. God knows whom she suspects, but she suspects somebody, and she's half dead with fright. What sort of sense will you get out of a woman like that?'

'Why not give us a sane version first?'

'But it's nothing to do with the case,' said Henry, 'and if you feel like saying "tra-la," I'd be grateful if you'd restrain yourselves.'

'If it turns out to be irrelevant,' said Alleyn, 'it shall be treated as such. We don't use irrelevant statements.'

'Then why ask for them?'

'We like to do the winnowing ourselves.'

'Nothing happened in Top Lane.'

'You mean Miss Prentice stood two feet away from you both, stared into your face until her heels sank an inch into the ground, and then walked away without uttering a word?'

'It was private business. It was altogether our affair.'

'You know,' said Alleyn, 'that won't do. This morning at Pen Cuckoo, and this afternoon at the rectory, frankness was the keynote of your conversation. You have said that you wouldn't put it past Miss Prentice to do murder, and yet you boggle at repeating a single word that she uttered in Top Lane. It looks as though it's not Miss Prentice whom you wish to protect.'

'What do you mean?'

'Hasn't Miss Copeland insisted on your taking this stand because she's nervous on your account? What were you going to call out to me this afternoon when she stopped you?'

'Well,' said Henry unexpectedly, 'you're quite right.'

'See here,' said Alleyn, 'if you are innocent of murder, I promise you that you are not going the right way to make us think so. Remember that in a little place like this we are bound to hear of all the rifts and ructions and this thing only happened twenty-six hours ago. We've scarcely touched the fringe of local gossip, and already I know that Miss Prentice is opposed to your friendship with Miss Dinah Copeland. I know very well that to you police methods must seem odious and – '

'No, they don't,' said Henry. 'Of course, you've got to do it.'

'Very well, then.'

'I'll tell you this much, and I dare say it's no more than you've guessed; my cousin Eleanor was thrown into a dither by finding us there together, and our conversation consisted of a series of hysterical threats and embarrassing accusations on her part.'

'And did you make no threats?'

'She'll probably tell you I did,' said Henry; 'but, as I have said six or eight times already, she's mad. And I'm sorry, sir, but that's all I can tell you.'

'All right,' said Alleyn with a sigh. 'Let's get to work, Fox.'

III

They removed the water-pistol and set up the Colt in its place. Alleyn produced the 'Prelude' from his case and put it on the rack. Henry saw the hole blown through the centre and the surrounding ugly stains. He turned away and then, as if he despised this involuntary revulsion, moved closer to the piano and watched Alleyn's hands as they moved inside the top.

'You see,' said Alleyn, 'all the murderer had to do was exactly what I'm doing now. The Colt fits into the same place, and the loose end of cord which was tied round the butt of the water-pistol is tied round the butt of the Colt. It passes across the trigger. It is remarkably strong cord, rather like fishing line. I've left the safety catch on. Now look.'

He sat on the piano stool and pressed the soft pedal. The two pulleys stood out rigidly from their moorings, the cord tautened as the dampers moved towards the strings and checked.

'It's stood firm,' said Alleyn. 'Georgie made sure of his pulleys. Now.'

'By gum!' ejaculated Nigel, 'I never thought of – '

'I know you didn't.'

Alleyn reached inside and released the safety catch. Again he trod lightly on the soft pedal. This time the soft pedal worked. The cord tightened in the pulleys and the trigger moved back. They all heard the sharp click of the striker.

'Well, there you are for what it's worth,' said Alleyn lightly.

'Yes, but last night the top of the piano was smothered in bunting and six he-men aspidistras,' objected Henry.

'So you think it was done last night,' said Alleyn.

'I don't know when it was done, and I don't think it could have been done last night, unless it was before we all got to the hall.'

Alleyn scowled at Nigel, who was obviously pregnant with a new theory.

'It's perfectly true,' said Nigel defiantly. 'Nobody could have moved those pots after 6.30.'

'I do entirely agree with you,' said Alleyn. A bell pealed distantly. Henry jumped.

'That's the telephone,' he said and started forward.

'I'll answer it, I think,' said Alleyn. 'It's sure to be for me.'

He crossed the stage, found a light switch and made his way to the first dressing-room on the left. The old-fashioned manual telephone pealed irregularly until he lifted the receiver.

'Hullo?'

'Mr Alleyn? It's Dinah Copeland. Somebody wants to speak to you from Chipping.'

'Thank you.'

'Here you are,' said Dinah. The telephone clicked and the voice of Sergeant Roper said, 'Sir?'

'Hullo?'

'Roper, sir. I thought I should find you, seeing as how Fife is still asleep here. I have a small matter in the form of a recent arrest to bring before your notice, sir.'

'In *what* form?'

'By name Saul Tranter, and by employment as sly a poacher as ever you see; but we've cotched him very pretty, sir, and the man's sitting here at my elbow with guilt written all over him in the form of two fine cock-pheasants.'

'What the devil – ?' began Alleyn, and checked himself. 'Well, Roper what about it?'

'This chap says he's got a piece of information that'll make the court think twice about giving him the month's hard he's been asking for these last two years. He won't tell me, sir, but in his bold way he asks to be faced with you. Now, we've got to get him down to the lock-up some time and – '

'I'll send Mr Bathgate down, Roper. Thank you.' Alleyn hung up the receiver and stared thoughtfully at the telephone.

'I'll have to see about you,' he told it and returned to the front of the hall.

'Hullo,' he said, 'where's Master Henry?'

'Gone home,' said Fox. 'He's a funny sort of young gentleman, isn't he?'

'Rather a bumptious infant, I thought,' said Nigel.

'He's about the same age as you were when I first met you,' Alleyn pointed out, 'and not half as bumptious. Bathgate, I'm afraid you'll have to go into Chipping and get a poacher.'

'A poacher!'

'Yes. Treasure-trove of Roper's. Apparently the gentleman wishes to make a blunderbuss about his impending sentence. He says he's got a story to unfold. Bring Fife with him. Stop at the pub on the way back and get your own car, and let Fife drive the Ford here and he can use it afterwards to deliver this gentleman to the lock-up. We'll clear up this place tonight.'

'Am I representative of a leading London daily or your odd-boy?'

'You know the answer to that better than I do. Away you go.'

Nigel went, not without further bitter complaint. Alleyn and Fox moved to the supper-room.

'All this food can be thrown away tomorrow,' said Alleyn. 'There's something else I want to see down here, though. Look, there's the tea-tray ready to be carried on in the play. Mrs Ross's silver, I dare say. It looks like her. Modern, expensive and streamlined.'

He lifted the lid of the teapot.

'It reeks of onion. Dear little Georgie.'

'I suppose someone spotted it and threw it out. You found it lying on the floor here, didn't you, Mr Alleyn?'

'In that box over there. Yes, Bailey has found Georgie's and Miss P.'s prints in the pot, so presumably Miss P. hawked out the onion.'

He stooped down and looked under the table.

'You went all over here last night, didn't you, Fox? Last night! This morning! "Little Fox, we've had a busy day."'

'All over it, sir. You'll find the onion peel down there. Young Biggins must have skinned it and then put it in the teapot.'

'Did you find any powder in here?'

'Powder? No. No, I didn't. Why?'

'Or flour?'

'No. Oh, you're thinking of the flour on the onion.'

'I'll just get the onion.'

Alleyn fetched the onion. He had put it in one of his wide-necked specimen bottles.

'We haven't had time to deal with this as yet,' he said. 'Look at it, Fox, it's pinkish. That's powder, not flour.'

'Perhaps young Biggins fooled round with it in one of the dressing-rooms.'

They found that on each dressing-table there was a large box of theatrical powder. They were all new, and it looked as if Dinah

had provided them. The men's boxes contained a yellowish powder, the women's a pinkish cream. Mrs Ross, alone, had brought
her own in an expensive-looking French box. In the dressing-
room used by Miss Prentice and Miss Campanula, some of their
powder had been spilled across the table. Alleyn stooped and
sniffed at it.

'That's it,' he said. 'Reeks of onion.' He opened the box. 'But this
doesn't. Fox, ring up Miss Copeland and ask her when the powder
was brought into these rooms. It's an extension telephone. You just
turn the handle.'

Fox plodded away. Alleyn, in a sort of trance, stared at the top of
the dressing-table, shook his head thoughtfully and returned to the
stage. He heard a motor-horn, and in a minute the door opened.
Roper and Fife came in shepherding between them a pigmy of a man
who looked as if he had been plunged in a water-butt.

Mr Saul Tranter was an old man with a very bad face. His eyes
were no bigger than a pig's and they squinted, wickedly close together, on either side of his mean little nose. His mouth was loose and
leered uncertainly, and his few teeth were objects of horror. He smelt
very strongly indeed of dirty old man, dead birds and whisky. Roper
thrust him forward as if he was some fabulous orchid, culled at great
risk.

'Here he be, sir,' said Roper. 'This is Saul Tranter, sure enough,
with all his wickedness hot in his body, having been taken in the act
with two of squire's cock-pheasants and his gun smoking in his
hands. Two years you've dodged us, haven't you, Tranter, you old
fox? I thought I'd come along with Fife, sir, seeing I've got the hang
of this case, having brought my mind to bear on it.'

'Very good of you, Roper.'

'Now then, Tranter,' said Roper, 'speak up to the chief inspector
and let him have the truth – if so be it lies in you to tell it.'

'Heh, my sonnies!' said the poacher in a piping voice. 'Be that the
instrument that done the murder?' And he pointed an unspeakably
dirty hand at the piano.

'Never you mind that,' ordered Roper. 'That's not for your low
attention.'

'What have you got to tell us. Tranter?' asked Alleyn. 'Good Lord,
man, you're as wet at a water-rat!'

'Wuz up to Cloudyfold when they cotched me,' admitted Mr Tranter. He drew a little closer to the heater and began stealthily to steam.

'Ay, they cotched me,' he said. 'Reckon it do have to happen so soon or so late. Squire'll sit on me at court and show what a mighty man he be, no doubt, seeing it's his woods I done trapped and shot these twenty year. 'Od rabbit the man, he'd change his silly, puffed-up ways if he knew what I had up my sleeve for 'un.'

'That's no way to talk,' said Roper severely, 'you, with a month's hard hanging round your neck.'

'Maybe. Maybe not, Charley Roper.' He squinted up at Alleyn. 'Being I has my story to tell which will fix the guilt of this spring-gun on him as set it. I reckon the hand of the law did ought to be light on my ancient shoulders.'

'If your information is any use,' said Alleyn, 'we might put in a word for you. I can't promise. You never know. I'll have to hear it first.'

''Tain't good enough, mister. Promise first, story afterwards, is my motter.'

'Then it's not ours,' said Alleyn coolly. 'It looks as though you've nothing to tell, Tranter.'

'Is threats nothing? Is blasting words nothing? Is a young chap caught red-handed same as me, with as pretty a bird as ever flewed into a trap, nothing?'

'Well?'

Fox came down into the hall, joined the group round the heater and stared with a practised eye at Tranter. Nigel arrived and took off his streaming mackintosh. Tranter turned his head restlessly and looked sideways from one face to another. A trickle of brown saliva appeared at the corner of his mouth.

'Well?' Alleyn repeated.

'Sour, tight-fisted men be the Jernighams,' said Tranter. 'What's a bird or two to them! I'm up against all damned misers, and so be all my side. Tyrants they be, and narrow as the grave, father and son.'

'You'd better take him back, Roper.'

'Nay, then, I'll tell you. I'll tell you. And if you don't give me my dues, dang it, if I don't fling it in the faces of the JPs. Where be your pencils and papers, souls? This did oughter go down in writing.'

CHAPTER 22

Letter to Troy

'On Friday afternoon,' said Mr Tranter, 'I were up to Cloudyfold. Never mind why. I come down by my own ways, and proper foxy ways they be, so quiet as moonshine. I makes downhill to Top Lane. Never mind why.'

'I don't in the least mind,' said Alleyn. 'Do go on.'

Mr Tranter shot a doubtful glance at him and sucked in his breath.

'A'most down to Top Lane, I wuz, when I heard voices. A feymell voice and a man's voice, and raised in anger. "Ah," thinks I. "There's somebody down there kicking up Bob's-a-dying in the lane and, that being the case, the lane's no place for me, with never-mind-what under my arm and never-mind-what in my pockets, neither." So I worms my way closer, till at last I'm nigh on bank above lane. There's a great ancient beech tree a-growing there, and I lays down and creeps forward, so cunning as a serpent, till I looks down atwixt the green stuff into the lane. Yass. And what do I see?'

'What *do* you see?'

'Ah! I sees young Henry Jernigham, as proud as death and with the devil himself in his face, and rector's wench in his arms.'

'That's no way to talk,' admonished Roper. 'Choose your words.'

'So I will, and mind your own business, Charley Roper. And who do I see standing down in lane a-facing of they two with her face so sickly as cheese and her eyes like raging fires and her limbs trimbling like a trapped rabbit. Who do I see?'

'Miss Eleanor Prentice,' said Alleyn.

Mr Tranter, who was now steaming like a geyser and smelling like a polecat, choked and blinked his eyes.

'She's never told 'ee?'

'No. Go on.'

'Trimbling as if to take a fit, she was, and screeching feeble, but uncommon venomous. Threating 'em with rector, she was, and threating 'em with squire. She says she caught 'em red-handed in vice and she'd see every decent critter in parish heard of their goings-on. And more besides. You'd never believe that old maiden had the knowledge of sinful youth in her, like she do seem to have. Nobbut what she don't tipple.'

'Really?' Alleyn ejaculated.

'Aye. One of them hasty secret drinkers, she is. She'd sloshed her tipple down her bosom, as I clearly saw. No doubt that's what'd inflamed the old wench and caused her to rage and storm at 'em. She give it 'em proper hot and sizzling, did Miss Prentice. And when she was at the full blast of her fury, what does t' young spark do but round on 'er. Ave t' young toad! Grabs her by shoulders and hisses in 'er face. If she don't let 'em be, 'e says, and if she tries to blacken young maid's name in eyes of the world, he says, he'll stop her wicked tongue for good an' all. He were in a proper rage, more furious than her. Terrible. And rector's maid, she says, "Doan't, Henry, doan't!" But young Jernigham 'e take no heed of the wench, but hammer-and-tongs he goes to it, so white as a sheet and blazing like a furnace. Aye, they've all got murderous, wrathy, passionate tempers, they Jernighams, as is well known hereabouts; I've heard the manner of this bloody killing, and I reckon there's little doubt he set his spring-gun for t'one old hen and catched t'other. Now!'

II

'Damn!' said Alleyn, when Mr Tranter had been removed. 'What a *bloody* business this is.'

'Is it what you expected?' asked Nigel.

'Oh, I half expected it, yes. It was obvious that something pretty dramatic had happened on Friday afternoon. Miss Prentice and Henry Jernigham showed the whites of their eyes whenever it was mentioned, and the rector told me that he and the squire and Miss Prentice had all been opposed to this match. Why, the Lord knows. She seems a perfectly agreeable girl, rather a nice girl, blast it. And look at the way Master Henry responded to inquiry! Fox, did you ever know such a case? One cranky spinster is enough, heaven knows, and here we have two, each a sort of Freudian prize packet, and one a corpse on our hands.'

'The whole thing seems very unlikely sort of stuff to me, Mr Alleyn, and yet there it is. She *was* murdered. If that kid had never read his comic paper, and if he hadn't his Twiddletoy outfit, it wouldn't have happened.'

'I believe you're right there, Brer Fox.'

'I suppose, sir, that was what Miss Prentice wanted to see the rector about on Friday evening. The meeting in Top Lane, I mean.'

'Yes, I dare say it was. Oh, hell, we'll have to tackle Miss Prentice in the morning. What did Dinah Copeland say about the face-powder?'

'She brought it down with her last night. Georgie Biggins wasn't behind the scenes that night. He made such a nuisance of himself that they gave him the sack. He was call-boy at the dress rehearsal, but the tables and dressing-rooms have all been scrubbed out since then. That powder must have been split after half-past six last evening. And another thing: Miss Dinah Copeland never heard about the onion – or says she didn't.'

'That makes sense, anyway!'

'*Does it?*' said Nigel bitterly. 'I don't mind owning that I fail to see the faintest significance in anything you've been saying. Why this chat about an onion?'

'Why, indeed,' sighed Alleyn. 'Come on. We'll pack up and go home. Even a policeman must sleep.'

III

But before Alleyn went to sleep that night he wrote to his love:

> *The Jernigham Arms*
> *November 29*

My Darling Troy

What a chancey sort of lover you've got. A fly-by-night who speaks to you at nine o'clock on Saturday evening, and soon after midnight is down in Dorset looking at lethal pianos. Shall you mind this sort of thing when we are married? You say not, and I suppose and hope not. You'll turn that dark head of yours and find a husband gone from your side. 'Off again, I see,' you'll say, and fall to thinking of the picture you are to paint next day. My dear and my darling Troy, you shall disappear, too, when you choose, into the austerity of your work, and never, never, never shall I look sideways, or disagreeably, or in the manner of the martyred spouse. Not as easy a promise as you might think, but I make it.

This is a disagreeable and unlikely affair. You will see the papers before my letter reaches you, but in case you'd like to know the official version, I enclose a very short account written in Yard language, and kept as colourless as possible. Fox and I have come to a conclusion, but are hanging off and on, hoping for a bit more evidence to turn up before we make an arrest. You told me once that your only method in detection would be based on character: and a very sound method, too, as long as you've got a flair for it. Now, here are our seven characters for you. What do you make of them?

First, the squire, Jocelyn Jernigham of Pen Cuckoo, and Acting Chief Constable to make things more difficult. He's a reddish, baldish man, with a look of perpetual surprise in his rather prominent light eyes. A bit pomposo. You would always know from the tone of his voice whether he spoke to a man or a woman. I think he would bore you and I think you would frighten him. The ladies, you see, should be gay and flirtatious and winsome. You are not at all winsome, darling, are you? They should make a man feel he's a bit of a dog. He's not altogether a fool, though, and, I should think, has a temper of his own. I think his cousin, Eleanor Prentice, frightens him, but he's full of family pride, and probably considers that even half a Jernigham can't be altogether wrong.

Miss Eleanor Prentice is half a Jernigham. She's about forty-nine or fifty, and I think rather a horrid woman. She's quite colourless and she's got buck teeth. She disseminates an odour of sanctity. She smiles a great deal, but with an air of forbearance as if hardly anything was really quite nice. I think she's a religious fanatic, heavily focused on the rector. This morning when I interviewed her she was thrown into a perfect fever by the sound of the church bells. She could scarcely listen to the simplest question, much less return a reasonable answer, so ardent and impatient was her longing to go to church. Now, in your true religious that's understandable enough. If you believe in the God Christ preached, you must be overwhelmed by your faith, and in time of trouble turn, with a heart of grace, to prayer. But I don't think Eleanor Prentice is that sort of religious. God knows I'm no psycho-analyst, but I imagine she'd be meat and drink to any one who was. Does one talk about a sex-fixation? Probably not. Anyway, she's gone the way modern psychology seems to consider axiomatic with women of her age and condition. This opinion is based partly on the statements of Henry Jernigham and Dinah Copeland and partly on my own impression of the woman.

Henry Jernigham is a good-looking young man. He's dark, with a jaw, grey eyes and an impressive head. He adopts the conversational manner of the moment, ironic and amusing, and gives the impression that he says whatever comes . . . into his head. But I don't believe any one has ever done that. How deep are our layers of thought, Troy. So deep that the thought of thought is terrifying to most of us. After many years, or perhaps only a few years, you and I may sometimes guess at each other's thoughts before they are spoken; and how strange that will seem to us. 'A proof of our love!' we shall cry.

This young Jernigham is in love with Dinah Copeland. Why didn't we meet when I was his age and you were a solemn child? Should I have loved you when you were fourteen and I was twenty-three? In those days I seem to remember I had a passion for full-blown blondes. But, without doubt, I would have loved and you would have never noticed it. Well, Henry loves Dinah, who is a nice intelligent child and vaguely on the stage, as almost all of them seem to be nowadays. I long to drivel on about the damage that magnificent chap Irving did to his profession when he made it respectable. No art should be fashionable, Troy, should it? But Dinah is evidently a serious young actress and probably quite a good one. She adores Master Henry.

Dr Templett, as you will see, looks very dubious. He could have taken the automatic, he could have fixed it in position, he has a motive, and he used all his authority to bring about the change of pianists. But he didn't get down to the hall until the audience had arrived, and he was never alone from the time he arrived until the time of the murder. To meet, he's a commonplace enough fellow. Under ordinary circumstances. I think he'd be tiresomely facetious. There is no doubt that he was infected with a passion for Mrs Selia Ross, and woe betide the man who loves a thin straw coloured woman with an eye to the main chance. If she doesn't love him she'll let him down, and if she does love him she'll suck away his character like a leech. He'll develop anaemia of the personality. Mrs Ross as you will have gathered, *is* a thin, straw-coloured woman, with the sort of sex appeal that changes men's faces when they speak of her. Their eyes turn bright and at the same time guarded, and the muscle from the nostril to the corner of the mouth becomes accentuated. Do you think that a very humourless observation? It's very true, my girl, and if you ever want to draw a sensualist, draw him like that. Trust a policeman: old Darwin found it out in spite of those whiskers. Mrs Ross could have nipped out of the car and dodged through the french window into the squire's study while Templett was handing his hat and coat to the butler. Had you thought of that? But she came down to the hall with Templett for the evening performance.

The rector, Walter Copeland, B.A. Oxon: The first thing you think of is his head. He's an amazingly fine-looking fellow. Everything the photographer or the producer ordered for a magnificent cleric. Silver hair, dark eyebrows, saintly profile. It's like a head on a coin or a statue, and much too much like any magazine illustration of 'A Handsome Man.' He seems to be less startling than his looks, and appears, in fact like a conscientious priest, rather disinclined for difficult jobs, but capable, suddenly, of digging in his toes. He is High Church, and I am sure very sincerely so. I should say that, if his belief came into question, he could be obstinate and even ruthless, but the general impression is of gentle vagueness.

The murdered woman seems to have been an arrogant, lonely, hysterical spinster. She and Miss Prentice might be taken as the positive and negative poles of parochial fanaticism with the rector as the needle. Not a true analogy. The general opinion is that she was a tartar.

It's midnight. I didn't get to bed last night, so I must leave you now. Troy, shall we have a holiday cottage in Dorset? A small house with a stern grey front, not too picturesque, but high up in the world so that you could paint the curves of the hills and the solemn changing cloud shadows that hurry over Dorset? Shall we have one? I'm going to marry you next April, and I love you with all my heart.

Good-night,

R.

IV

Alleyn laid down his pen and stretched his cramped fingers.

He was, he supposed, the only waking being in the inn, and the silence of a country dwelling at night flowed in upon his mind. The wind had dropped again, and he realized that for some time there had been no sound of rain. The fire had fallen into a glow. The timbers of the inn crackled abruptly and startled him. He was suddenly weary. His body was a stranger to his mind and he looked at it in wonder. He stood as if in a trance, alarmed at meeting himself as a stranger, yet aware of this experience which was not new to him. As always, some part of his mind tried to step across the threshold of the unknown, but was unable to give purpose to his whole thought. He returned to himself and, rousing, lit his candle, turned out the lamp, and climbed the stairs to his room.

His window looked up the Vale. High above him he could see a light. 'They are late at bed at Pen Cuckoo,' he thought, and opened the window. The sound of water dripping from the eaves came into the room and the smell of wet grass and earth. 'Perhaps it will be fine tomorrow,' he thought, and went happily to bed.

CHAPTER 23

Frightened Lady

'– Let me remind you, gentlemen,' said the coroner, looking severely at Mr Prosser, 'that you are not concerned with theories. It is your duty to decide how this unfortunate lady met with her death. If you find you are able to do so, you must then make up your minds whether you are to return a verdict of accident, suicide or murder. If you are unable to arrive at this second decision, you must say so. Now, there is no difficulty in describing the manner of death. On Friday afternoon a small boy, after the manner of small boys, set an ingenious booby-trap. At some time before Saturday night, someone interfered with this comparatively harmless piece of mechanism. A Colt automatic was substituted for a water-pistol. You have heard that this automatic, the property of Mr Jocelyn Jernigham, was in a room which is accessible from outside all day and every day. You have heard that it was common knowledge that the weapon was kept loaded in this room. You realize, I am sure, that on Saturday it would have been possible for anybody to enter the room through the french window and take the automatic. You have listened to a lucid description of the mechanism of this death-trap. You have examined the Colt automatic. You have been told that at 6.30 Miss Gladys Wright used the left-hand pedal of the piano, and that nothing untoward occurred. You heard her say that from 6.30 until the moment of the catastrophe the front of the hall was occupied by herself, her fellow-helpers and, as they arrived, the audience. You have been shown photographs of the piano as it was at 6.30. The open top was covered in bunting which was secured to the sides by drawing-pins. On top of the piano and standing on the bunting, which stretched over the turned-back lid, were six pot plants. You realize that up to within fifteen minutes of the tragedy, every member of the company of performers, and every person in the audience, believed that it was Miss Prentice who was to play the overture. You may therefore have formed the opinion that Miss Prentice, and not Miss Campanula, was the intended victim. This need not affect your decision and, as a coroner's jury, does not actually concern you. If you agree that at eight o'clock Miss Campanula pressed the left-hand or soft pedal and was killed by a charge from the automatic and that somebody had put the automatic in the piano with felonious intent, in short with intent to murder, and if you consider there is no evidence to show who this person was – why, then, gentlemen, you may return a verdict to this effect.'

'O upright beak!' said Alleyn as Mr Prosser and the jury retired. 'O admirable and economic coroner! Slap, bang, and away they go. Slap, bang, and here they are again.'

They had indeed only gone into a huddle in the doorway, and returned looking rather as if they had all washed their faces in rectitude.

'Yes, Mr Prosser?'

'We are all agreed, sir.'

'Yes?'

'We return a verdict of murder,' said Mr Prosser, looking as if he feared he hadn't got it quite as it ought to be, 'against person or persons unknown.'

'Thank you. The only possible conclusion, gentlemen.'

'I should like to add,' said the smallest juryman, suddenly, 'that I think them water-pistols ought to be put down by law.'

II

Immediately after the inquest, Fox and Ford left for Duck Cottage. Alleyn's hand was on the door of Nigel's car, when he heard his name called. He turned and found himself face to face with Mrs Ross.

'Mr Alleyn – I'm so sorry to bother you, but may I come and see you? I've remembered something that I think you ought to know.'

'Certainly,' said Alleyn. 'Now, if it suits you.'

'You're staying at the Jernigham Arms, aren't you? May I come there in ten minutes?'

'Yes, of course. I shall drive straight there.'

'Thank you so much.'

Alleyn replaced his hat and climbed into the car.

'*Now*, what the devil?' he wondered. 'It's fallen out rather well, as it happens. Fox will have a longer session with the pretty housemaid.'

Nigel came out and drove him to the inn. Alleyn asked Mrs Peach if he could use the back parlour as an office for an hour. Mrs Peach was volubly agreeable.

Nigel was told to take himself off.

'Why should I? Who are you going to see?'

'Mrs Ross.'

'Why can't I be there?'

'Because I think she'll speak more freely if she sees me alone.'

'Well, let me sit in the next room with the slide a crack open.'

Alleyn looked thoughtfully at him.

'Very well,' he said, 'you may do that. Take notes. It can't be used in evidence, but it may be handy. Wait a second. You've got your camera?'

'Yes.'

'See if you can get a shot of her as she comes in. Careful about it. Get there quickly. She'll arrive in a second.'

Nigel was only just in time. In five minutes the pot-boy announced Mrs Ross, who came in looking much more like the Ritz than the Jernigham Arms.

'It *is* nice of you to see me,' she said. 'Ever since I remembered it, I've been worried about this thing. I felt very bold, accosting you outside the hall of justice or whatever it was. You must be rushed off your feet.'

'It's my job to listen,' said Alleyn.

'May I sit down?'

'Please. I think this is the most comfortable chair.'

She sat down with a pretty air of intimacy. She drew off her gloves, rummaged in her bag for her cigarettes, and then accepted one of his. Alleyn remained standing.

'You know,' said Mrs Ross, 'you're not a bit my idea of a detective.'

'No.'

'Not a *bit*. That enormous man who drives about with you looks much more the thing done at the Yard.'

'Perhaps you would rather see Inspector Fox?'

'No, I'd much rather see you. Don't snub me.'

'I'm sorry if I seemed to do that. What is it you would like to tell me?'

She leant forward. Her manner lost its flippancy and took on an air of practical concern, but also managed to suggest that she knew he would understand and sympathize with her motive in coming to him.

'You'll think I was such a fool not to remember it before,' she said; 'but the whole thing's been rather a shock. I suppose I simply had a blank moment or something. Not that I had any affection for the poor old thing; but, for all that, it was rather a shock.'

'I'm sure it was.'

'When you came to see me yesterday I had a ghastly headache and could hardly think. Did you ask me if I went out on Friday night?'

'Yes. You told me you were at home.'

'I *thought* I did. Honestly, I don't know what I could have been thinking about. I *was* at home practically all the evening, but I went out for about half an hour. I drove from here to post a letter. I quite forgot.'

'That's not very serious.'

'I'm extremely relieved to hear you say so,' she said, and laughed, 'I was afraid you'd be *angry* with me.'

She had a comical trick of over-emphasis, as if she parodied her own conversation. She drew on the word *angry*, making a grimace over it and opening her eyes very wide.

'Is that the whole story?' asked Alleyn.

'No, it's not,' she said flatly. 'The thing is, on my way down I came by Church Lane, past the hall. Church Lane goes on over the hills, you know, and comes out close to my cottage.'

'Yes.'

'Well, there was a light in one of the dressing-rooms.'

'What time was this?'

'It was eleven when I got back. Say about twenty to eleven. No, a little earlier.'

'Which dressing-room was it, do you know?'

'Yes. I've worked it out. It was too far away to be either of the women's rooms, and anyway they've got blinds. Miss Prentice, who is a very pure woman, thought it wasn't quite nice for us not to have blinds. The one Billy Templett uses has its window on the far side. It must have been the squire's. Mr Jernigham's. But the funny thing about it was that it only flashed on for a few seconds and then went out again.'

'Are you quite sure it wasn't the reflection of your headlights?'

'Absolutely positive. It was much too far to my right, and anyway it wasn't a bit like that. The glass is that thick stuff. No, a yellow square just popped up and popped out again.'

'I see.'

'It may not be anything at all, but it was on my conscience, so I thought I'd own up, and *come clean* and all that. I didn't think anything of it at the time. It might have been Dinah Copeland messing about over there, or any old thing; but as every moment after Friday seems important – '

'It's much better to let the police know of anything you remember that may have even the slightest significance,' said Alleyn.

'I hoped you'd say that. Mr Alleyn, I'm so terribly worried, and you're so human and unofficial, I wonder if I dare ask you something rather awkward.'

Alleyn's manner could scarcely have been more formal as he replied: 'I am here as a policeman, you know.'

'Yes, I know. Well, when in doubt, ask a policeman.' She grinned charmingly. 'No, but honestly I'm in a horrid – awful muddle. It's about Billy Templett. I'm sure you've already heard all the local gossip, amd you'll have found out for yourself that the charming people in this aristocratic part of the world have got minds like sinks and worse. No doubt they've told you all the local lies about Billy Templett and me. Well, we *are* great friends. He's the only soul in the entire district with an idea beyond hunting and other people's business, and we've got a lot in common. Of course, as a doctor, he's not supposed to look on women as anything but sets of insides and collections of complaints. I never dreamt it might actually do his

practice no good if he saw rather more of me than old Mrs Cain and
the oldest inhabitant. Oh, dear, this *is* difficult. May I have another
cigarette, please?'

Alleyn gave her another cigarette.

'I may as well choke it out before I lose my nerve altogether. Do
you suspect Billy of this beastly crime?'

'As the case stands,' said Alleyn, 'it appears to be quite impossible
that Dr Templett should have had any hand in it.'

'Is that true?' she asked, and her voice was as sharp as a knife.

'It is a very serious offence for a policeman to set traps or deliberately mislead his witnesses.'

'I'm sorry. I know that. It was just the relief. You remember that
letter you showed me yesterday? The anonymous letter?'

'Yes.'

'It was written to me.'

'Yes.'

'I knew I hadn't taken you in. You are a clever beast, aren't you?'
She laughed again. Alleyn wondered how many people had told her
she laughed like a gamine and whether she ever forgot it.

'Do you want to amend your statement about the letter?' he
asked.

'Yes, please. I want to explain. I showed the letter to Billy and we
discussed it and decided to take no notice. When you showed it to me
I supposed you'd picked it up somewhere in the hall, and as I knew
it had nothing to do with this murder, and I wanted to protect poor
old Billy. I said I didn't know anything about it. And then he came in
and I thought he'd take his cue from me and – well, it went wrong.'

'Yes,' said Alleyn, 'it went very wrong.'

'Mr Alleyn, what did he tell you last evening when he went away
with you? Was he – was he angry with me? He didn't realize I'd tried
to help him, did he?'

'I don't think so.'

'He might have known! It's one of those hideous things that turn
into a muddle.'

'I'm afraid your explanation has gone equally astray.'

'What do you mean?'

'I mean that you knew where Dr Templett put the letter and that
it is very unlikely we picked it up in the hall. I mean that yesterday

you spoke instinctively and with the object of getting out of an awkward position. You have since remembered that there is a fingerprint system, so you come to me with a story of altruistic motives. When I told you Dr Templett is not, on the evidence we have, a likely suspect you regretted that you had shown your hand. I think I know a frightened woman when I see one, and yesterday you were very frightened, Mrs Ross.'

She had let her cigarette burn down to her fingers. Her hand jerked and she dropped the butt on the floor. He picked it up and threw it in the fire.

'You're wrong,' she said. 'I did it for *him.*'

Alleyn made no answer.

She said, 'I thought she'd written it. The murdered woman. And I thought old Prentice was going to play.'

'Dr Templett didn't tell you on Saturday morning that it would be a physical impossibility for Miss Prentice to play?'

'We didn't discuss it. Billy didn't do it and neither did I. We didn't get to the place till nearly eight o'clock.'

'You arrived soon after 7.30,' Alleyn corrected her.

'Well, anyway, it was too late to do anything to the piano. The hall was packed. We were never alone.'

'Mrs Ross, when I asked you yesterday about the episode of the window, why did you not tell me you saw someone dodge down behind the sill?'

She seemed startled but not particularly alarmed at this. She looked at him, as he thought, speculatingly, as though she deliberately weighed his question and pondered the answer. At last she said:

'I suppose Billy told you that. It was only an impression through the thick glass. The window was only open about two inches.'

'I suggest that you were alarmed at the idea of an eavesdropper. I suggest that you noticed this shadow at the window only after you had been for some little time on the stage with Dr Templett, and that enough had taken place in that time for you to be seriously compromised. I suggest that you told Dr Templett to shut the window and that you lowered the curtain to ensure privacy.'

She tilted her head to one side and looked at him under her lashes.

'You really ought to join the Women's Circle. They'd adore that story at a tea-party.'

'I shall work,' said Alleyn, 'on the theory that you said nothing more to Dr Templett of this shadowy impression, as you did not wish to alarm him, but that it was not too shadowy or too fleeting for you to recognize the watcher at the window.'

That shot did go home. Her whole face seemed to sharpen and she made a quick involuntary movement of her hands. She waited for a moment, and he knew that she was mustering her nerves. Then in one swift movement she was on her feet, close to him, her hand on his coat.

'You don't believe I'd do anything like that, do you? You're not such a fool. I don't even understand how it worked, and I've never been able to tie a knot in my life. Mr Alleyn? Please?'

'If you are innocent you're in no danger.'

'Do you promise that?'

'Certainly.'

Before he could move she dropped her head against him and clung to his coat. She murmured broken phrases. Her hair was scented. He felt her uneven breathing.

'No, no,' he said, 'this won't do.'

'I'm sorry – you've frightened me. Don't be nervous, I'm not trying to seduce you. I'm only rather shaken. I'll be all right in a moment.'

'You're all right now,' said Alleyn. He took her wrists and held her away from him. 'That's better.'

She stood before him with her head bent down. She achieved a look of helpless captivity. Her whole posture seemed to proclaim her subjection. When she raised her face it wore a gamine grin.

'You're either made of dough,' she said, 'or else you're afraid I'll compromise you. Poor Mr Alleyn.'

'You would have been wiser to call on Mr Jernigham,' said Alleyn, 'He's Acting Chief Constable, you know.'

III

When she had been gone some minutes, Nigel looked cautiously into the back parlour.

'Hell knows no fury,' he said.

'An intensely embarrassing lady,' said Alleyn. 'Did you get a shot of her?'

'Yes. Ought to be all right. I got her as she came in.'

'Let me have the film or plate, or whatever it is.'

'Do explain all this, Alleyn.'

'It's as plain as daylight. She's got a genius for self-preservation. When I showed her the anonymous letter she was hell-bent on keeping out of suspicion, and on the spur of the moment denied all knowledge of it. She'd do her best for Templett up to a point, but a charge of homicide is definitely beyond that point. Yesterday she let him down with a thud. Now she's regretting it. I think she's probably as much in love with him as she could be with anybody. She's read a popular book on criminal investigation. She remembered that she'd handled the letter and realized we'd find her prints. So she hatched up this story. Now she knows we're not after Templett she'll try to get him back. But she's a sensible woman, and she wouldn't hang for him.'

'I wonder if he'll believe her,' said Nigel.

'Probably,' said Alleyn. 'If she gets a chance to see him alone.'

Fox came in.

'I've seen Mrs Ross's maid, sir. There's nothing much, except that Mrs Ross did go out on Friday night. It was the maid's night off, but her boy had a cold and it was raining, so she stayed in. She only mentioned this to Mrs Ross this morning.'

'And Mrs Ross mentioned it to me in case the maid got in first.'

'Is that a fact, sir?'

'It is, Brer Fox. You shall hear of our interview.'

Fox listened solemnly to the account of the interview.

'Well,' he said, 'she's come off worst in that bout, sir. What'll she do now?'

'I think she'd like to have a shot at old Jernigham. She's frightened and rattled. A shrewd woman, but not really clever.'

'Does she think you suspect her, Mr Alleyn?'

'She's afraid I might.'

'*Do* you suspect her?' asked Nigel.

'Of all sorts of things,' said Alleyn lightly. He sniffed at his coat. 'Blast the woman. I stink of Chanel No. 5.'

Nigel burst out laughing.

'Don't you think she's attractive?' he said. 'I do.'

'Fortunately I don't. I can see she might be; but she gives me housemaid's creeps. What do you think, Fox?'

'Well, sir, under more favourable conditions I dare say she'd be quite an experience in a way. There's something about her.'

'You licentious old article.'

'She's not very comfortable, if you know what I mean. More on the frisky side. I'd say she's one of these society ladies who, if they were born in a lower walk of life, would set up for themselves in a rather exclusive way, but well within the meaning of the act.'

'Yes, Fox.'

'What do we do now, Mr Alleyn?'

'We lunch. After lunch we have a word together. And tonight I think we play a forcing hand, Fox. We've got about as much information as we'll ever screw out of them by separate interviews. Let's see how we get on with a mixed bunch. There's a fast train from Great Chipping in an hour. I think I'll catch it. Will you see the telephone people? Have one more stab at the villagers for Saturday afternoon. The person who stood at the box and peeped through the window. Ask if any one saw anybody about the place. You won't get anything, but we've got to try. Arrange the meeting with Jernigham senior. I'd better see him myself beforehand. There are one or two things — Go carefully with him, Fox. And telephone to me at the Yard before half-past five.'

'I'll come up with you, if I may,' said Nigel.

'Do. There's a good train that gets to Great Chipping at 8.15. I'll return by that, and send a car ahead with two people and clanking chains, in case we feel like arresting somebody. All right?'

'Very good, sir,' said Fox.

'Then we'd better lunch.'

CHAPTER 24

The Peculiarity of Miss P.

'It's no good taking it like this, Eleanor,' said the squire, laying down his napkin and glaring at his cousin. 'How do you suppose we feel? You won't help matters by starving yourself.'

'I'm sorry, Jocelyn, but I cannot eat.'

'You can't go on like this, my dear girl. You'll get ill.'

'Would that matter very much?'

'Don't be an ass, Eleanor. Henry, give her some apple tart.'

'No, thank you, Henry.'

'What you want, Cousin Eleanor,' said Henry from the side table, 'is a good swinging whisky.'

'Please, dear. I'm sorry if I'm irritating you both. It would be better if I didn't come down to lunch.'

'Good Gad, woman,' shouted the squire. 'Don't talk such piffling drivel. We simply don't want you to kill yourself.'

'It's a pity,' said Miss Prentice stonily, 'that I wasn't killed. I realize that. It would have been a blessed release. They say poor Idris didn't feel anything. It's the living who suffer.'

'Cousin Eleanor,' said Henry, returning with a loaded plate, 'have you ever read *Our Mutual Friend*?'

'No, Henry.'

'Because you're giving a perfectly brilliant impersonation of Mrs R. W.'

'Was she very irritating?'

'Very.'

'That'll do, Henry,' said the squire. He darted an uncomfortable glance at Miss Prentice, who sat upright in her chair with her head bowed. At intervals she drew in her breath sharply and closed her eyes.

'Is your finger hurting you?' demanded Jocelyn after a particularly noticeable hiss from the sufferer. She opened her eyes and smiled palely.

'A little.'

'You'd better let Templett see it again.'

'I'm not likely to do that, Jocelyn.'

'Why not?' asked Henry. 'Do you think he's the murderer?'

'Oh, Henry, Henry,' said Miss Prentice. 'Some day you'll be sorry you have grieved me so much.'

'Upon my word,' said Henry, 'I can't for the life of me see why that should grieve you. One of us is a murderer. I only asked if you thought it might be Templett.'

'You are fortunate to be able to speak so lightly of this terrible, terrible tragedy.'

'We're as much worried as you are,' protested Jocelyn with an appealing glance at his son. 'Aren't we, boy?'

'Of course we are,' said Henry cheerfully.

'As a matter of fact, I've asked Copeland to come up here and talk the whole thing over.'

Miss Prentice clasped her hands and gave a little cry. A dull flush stained her cheeks and her eyes brightened.

'Is he coming? How wise of you, Jocelyn! He is so wonderful. He will help us all. It will all come out right. It will come out quite, quite all right.'

She laughed hysterically and clapped her hands.

'When is he coming?'

Jocelyn looked at her with positive terror.

'This evening,' he said. 'Eleanor, you're not well.'

'And is dear Dinah coming, too?' asked Miss Prentice shrilly.

'Hullo!' said Henry. 'Here's a change.' And he stared fixedly at his cousin.

'Henry,' said Miss Prentice very rapidly. 'Shall we forget our little differences? I have your happiness so much at heart, dear. If you had been more candid and straightforward with me – '

'Why should I?' asked Henry.

'– I think you would have found me quite understanding. Shall we let bygones be bygones? You see, dear, you have no mother to – '

'Will you excuse me, sir?' said Henry, 'I feel slightly sick.' And he walked out of the room.

'I thought,' said Miss Prentice, 'that I had been deeply enough injured already. So deeply, deeply injured. I am sorry I am rather excited, Jocelyn dear, but, you see, when someone is waiting down at St Giles to shoot you – *Jocelyn, is that somebody coming?*'

'What the devil's the matter, Eleanor?'

'It's that woman! It was her car! I saw it through the window. Jocelyn, I won't meet that woman. She'll do me an injury. She's wicked, wicked, wicked. A woman of Babylon. They're all the same. All bad, horrible creatures.'

'Eleanor, be quiet.'

'You're a man. You don't understand. *I will not meet her.*'

Taylor came in.

'Mrs Ross to see you, sir.'

'Damnation!' said the squire. 'All right. Take her to the study.'

II

The squire was worried about Eleanor. She was really very odd indeed, far odder than even these uncomfortable circumstances warranted. There was no knowing what she'd say next. If he didn't look out, she'd land him in a pretty tight corner with one of these extraordinary statements of hers. She'd got such a damned knowing look in her eye. When she thought he wasn't noticing her, she'd sit in a corner watching him, with an expression which could only be described as a leer. If she was going mad! Well, there was one thing: mad people couldn't give evidence. Perhaps the best thing would be to ask an alienist down for the weekend. He hoped to heaven she wouldn't take it in to her head to come raging into the study and go for poor little Mrs Ross. His thoughts raced through his head as he crossed the hall, passed through the library and entered his study. Anyway, it'd be a relief to talk to an attractive woman.

She did look very attractive. Pale-ish, but that was understandable. She wore her clothes like a Frenchwoman. He'd always liked
black. Damn' good figure and legs. He took the little hand in its
delicate glove and held it tightly.

'Well,' he said, 'this *is* nice of you.'

'I simply had to see you. You'll think me a most frightful bore,
coming at this time.'

'Now you knew that wasn't true before you said it.' The little
hand started in his.

'Have I hurt you?' asked the squire. 'I am a clumsy brute.'

'No. Not really. Only you are rather strong, aren't you? It's just
my ring.'

'I insist on investigating.'

He peeled back the glove and drew it down.

'Look at that! A red mark on the inside of your finger. Now, what
can be done about that?'

A subdued laugh. He separated the white fingers and kissed them.

'Ha-ha, my boy!' thought the squire, and led her to a chair.

'You've done me good already,' he said. 'Do you realize that,
madam?'

'Have I?'

'Don't you think you're rather an attractive little thing?'

'What am I supposed to say to that?'

'You know it damned well, so you needn't say anything. Ha, Ha,
ha!'

'Well, I *have* heard something like it before.'

'How often?' purred the squire.

'Never you mind.'

'Why are you so attractive?'

'Just made that way.'

'Little devil,' he said and kissed the hand again. He felt quite
excited. Everything was going like clockwork.

'Oh, dear,' whispered Mrs Ross. 'You're going to be simply livid
with me.'

'Simply furious?' he asked tenderly.

'Yes. Honestly. I don't want to tell you; but I must!'

'Don't look at me like that or I shall have to kiss you.'

'No, please. You must listen. Please.'

'If I listen I expect to be rewarded.'

'We'll see about that,' she said.

'Promise?'

'Promise.'

'I'm listening,' said the squire, rather feverishly.

'It's about this awful business. I want to tell you first of all, very, very sincerely that you've nothing to fear from me.'

'Nothing – ?'

He still held her hand, but his fingers relaxed.

'No,' she said, 'nothing. If you will just trust me – '

Her voice went on and on. Jocelyn heard her to the end, but when it was over he did not remind her of her promise.

III

When Alleyn left the assistant commissioner and returned to his own office, he found Bailey there.

'Well, Bailey?'

'Well, sir, Thompson's developed Mr Bathgate's film. He's got a couple of shots of the lady.'

He laid the still wet prints on the desk.

There was Mrs Ross in profile on the front step of the Jernigham Arms, and there she was again full face as she came up the path. Nigel must have taken his snapshots through the open window. Evidently she had not seen him. The pointed chin was set a little to one side, the under lip projected very slightly, and the thin mouth was drawn down at the corners. They were not flattering photographs.

'Any luck?' asked Alleyn.

With his normal air of mulish disapproval Bailey laid a card beside the prints. On it was mounted a double photograph. Sharp profile, thin mouth, pointed chin; and the front view showed the colourless hair drawn back in two immaculate shining wings, from the rather high forehead.

Alleyn muttered: 'Sarah Rosen. Age 33. Height 5 ft 5¼ins. Eyes, light blue. Hair, pale blonde. Very well dressed, cultured speech, usually poses as widow. Detained with Claude Smith on blackmailing charge, 1931. Subsequently released – insufficient evidence. Claude got ten years, didn't he?'

'That's right, sir. They stayed at the Ritz as brother and sister.'

'I remember. What about the prints?'

'They're good enough.'

'Blackmail,' said Alleyn thoughtfully.

'I've looked up the case. She was in the game all right, but they hadn't a thing on her. She seems to have talked her way out.'

'She would. Thank you, Bailey. I wish I'd known this a little earlier. Oh, well, no matter, it fits in very prettily.'

'Anything else, Mr Alleyn?'

'I'm going to my flat for half an hour. If Fox rings up before I'm back, tell him I'm there. The car ought to leave now. I'll fix that up. We'd better take a wardress, I suppose. All right, Bailey. Thank you.'

IV

Henry wondered what the devil Mrs Ross had to say to his father. He had watched, with extreme distaste their growing intimacy. 'How sharper than a serpent's tooth it is,' he thought, 'to have a prancing parent.' When Jocelyn spoke to Mrs Ross his habit of loud inexplicable laughter, his manner of leaning backwards, of making a series of mysterious little bows, the curious gesture he employed, the inclination his eyes exhibited towards protuberance, and the naked imbecility of his conversation, all vexed and embarrassed his son to an almost insupportable degree. If Jocelyn should marry her! Henry had no particular objection to Mrs Ross, but the thought of her as a stepmother struck dismay to his heart. His affection for his father was not weakened by Jocelyn's absurdities. He loved him deeply, he realized, and now the thought that his father might be making a fool of himself in there with that woman was more than he could endure. Miss Prentice had, no doubt, gone to her room; Dinah was out; there was nothing to do.

He wandered restlessly into the library, half-hoping that the door into the study would be open. It was closed. He could hear the murmur of a woman's voice. On and on. What the hell could she have to say? Then a baritone interjection in which he read urgency and vehemence. Then a long pause.

'My God!' thought Henry. 'If he has proposed to her!'

He whistled raucously, took an encyclopædia from the shelves, banged the glass door and slammed the book down on the table.

He heard his father exclaim. A chair castor squeaked and the voices grew more distant. They had moved to the far end of the room.

Henry flung himself into an arm-chair, and once again the conundrum of the murder beset him. Who *did* the police believe had tried to murder Eleanor Prentice? Which would they say had the greatest reason for wishing Eleanor dead? With the thud of fear that came upon him whenever he thought of this, he supposed that he himself had the most reason for wishing Eleanor out of the way. Was it possible that Alleyn suspected him? Whom *did* Alleyn suspect? Not Dinah, surely, not the rector, not his own father. Templett, then? Or – yes – Mrs Ross? But, Alleyn would surely reason, if Templett was the murderer, it was a successful murder since it was Templett who insisted that Eleanor shouldn't play the piano. Alleyn would wonder if Templett had told Mrs Ross he would not allow Eleanor to play. Did Dinah's tirade against Mrs Ross mean that Dinah suspected her? Had the police any idea who could have gone to the piano after there were people in the hall, and yet not be seen? Already the story of Gladys Wright had reached Pen Cuckoo. And as a final conjecture, perhaps they would ask themselves if Eleanor Prentice in some way had faked her finger and set the trap for her bosom enemy. Or might they agree with the rector and call it a case of attempted murder and suicide?

He leapt to his feet. There was no longer a sound of voices in the study. They must have gone out by the french window.

Henry opened the door and walked in. No. They were still there. Jocelyn Jernigham faced the door. When Henry saw Jocelyn he cried out: 'Father, what's the matter?'

Jocelyn said, 'Nothing's the matter.'

Mrs Ross said, 'Hullo! Good-afternoon.'

'Good-afternoon,' said Henry. 'Father, are you ill?'

'No. Don't come bursting into the room asking people if they're ill. It's ridiculous.'

'But your face! It's absolutely ashen.'

'I've got indigestion.'

'I don't believe it.'

'I thought he looked pale,' said Mrs Ross solicitously.

'He's absolutely green.'

'I'm nothing of the sort,' said Jocelyn angrily. 'Mrs Ross and I are talking privately, Henry.'

'I'm sorry,' said Henry stubbornly, 'but I know there's something wrong here. What is it?'

'There's nothing wrong, my dear boy,' she said lightly.

He stared at her.

'I'm afraid I still think there is.'

'Well, I very much hope you won't still think there is when we tell you all about it. At the moment I'm afraid it's a secret.' She looked up at Jocelyn. 'Isn't it?'

'Yes. Of course. Go away, boy, you're making a fool of yourself.'

'Are you sure,' Henry asked slowly, 'that nobody is making a fool of you?'

Taylor came in. He looked slightly disgruntled.

'Inspector Fox to see you, sir. I told him – '

'Good-afternoon, sir,' said a rumbling voice, and the bulk of Inspector Fox filled the doorway.

V

Henry saw the squire look quickly from the open window to Mrs Ross. Taylor stood aside and Fox walked in.

'I hope you'll excuse me coming straight in like this, sir,' said Fox. 'Chief Inspector Alleyn asked me to call. I took the liberty of following your butler. Perhaps I ought to have waited.'

'No, no,' said Jocelyn. 'Sit down, er – '

'Fox, sir. Thank you very much, sir.'

Fox placed his bowler on a near-by table. He turned to Henry.

'Good-afternoon, sir. We met last night, didn't we?'

'This is Inspector Fox. Mrs Ross,' said Henry.

'Good-afternoon, madam,' said Fox tranquilly. Then he sat down. As Alleyn once remarked to Nigel, there was a certain dignity about Fox.

Mrs Ross smiled charmingly.

'I must take myself off,' she said, 'and not interrupt Mr Fox. Don't move, anybody, please.'

'If it's not troubling you too much, Mrs Ross,' said Fox, 'I'd be obliged if you'd wait for a moment. There are one or two little routine questions for general inquiry, and it will save me taking up your time later on.'

'But I'm longing to stay, Mr Fox.'

'Thank you, madam.'

Fox took out his spectacles and placed them on his nose. He then drew his note-book from an inside pocket, opened it and stared at it.

'Yes,' he said. 'Now, the first item's a small matter, really. Did anybody present find the onion in the teapot?'

'*What!*' Henry ejaculated.

Fox fixed his eyes on him.

'The onion in the teapot, sir.'

'Which onion in what teapot?' demanded Jocelyn.

Fox turned to him.

'Young Biggins, sir, has admitted that he put a Spanish onion in the teapot used on the stage. We'd like to know who removed it.'

Mrs Ross burst out laughing.

'I'm so sorry,' she said, 'But it *is* rather funny.'

'It sounds a rather ridiculous sort of thing, doesn't it, madam?' agreed Fox gravely. 'Do you know anything about it?'

'I'm afraid not. I think Mr Alleyn has already accused me of an onion.'

'Did you happen to hear anything of it, sir?'

'Good Lord, no,' said Jocelyn.

'And you, Mr Henry?'

'Not I,' said Henry.

'The next matter,' said Fox, making a note, 'is the window. I understand you found it open on Saturday afternoon, Mrs Ross.'

'Yes. We shut it.'

'Yes. You'd already shut it once, hadn't you? At midday?'

'Yes, I had.'

'Who opened it?' inquired Fox, and he looked first at Jocelyn and then at Henry. They both shook their heads.

'I should think it was probably Miss Prentice. My cousin,' said Henry. 'She has a deep-rooted mania – ' He checked himself. 'She's a fresh-air fiend of the worst variety, and continually complained that the hall was stuffy.'

'I wonder if I might ask Miss Prentice?' said Fox. 'Is she at home, sir?'

The squire looked extremely uncomfortable.

'I think she's – ah – she's – ah – in. Yes.'

'Do you want me any longer, Mr Fox?' asked Mrs Ross.

'I think that will be all for the present, thank you, madam. The chief inspector would be much obliged if you could come down to the hall at about 9.15 this evening.'

'Oh? Yes, very well.'

'Thank you very much, madam.'

'I'll see you out,' said the squire hurriedly.

They went out by the french window.

Henry offered Fox a cigarette.

'No. Thank you very much, all the same, sir.'

'Mr Fox,' said Henry. 'What do you think of the rector's theory? I mean, the idea that Miss Campanula set the trap for my cousin, and that something happened to make her so miserable that when she was asked to play she thought: "Oh, well, this settles it. Here goes!"'

'Would you have said the deceased lady seemed very unhappy, sir?'

'Well, you know, I didn't notice her very much. But I've been thinking it over, and – yes – she was rather odd. She was damned odd. For one thing, she'd evidently had a colossal row with my cousin. Or rather my cousin seemed friendly enough, but Miss C. wouldn't say a word to her. She was a cranky old cup of tea, you know, and we none of us took much notice. Know what I mean?'

'I understand, sir,' said Fox, looking hard at Henry. 'Perhaps if I could just have a word with Miss Prentice,'

'Oh, Lord!' said Henry ruefully. 'Look here, Mr Fox, you'll find her pretty rum. You'll think we specialize in eccentric spinsters in this part of the world, but I promise you I think the shock of this business has pushed her off at the deep-end. She seems to think the murderer's made a mess of the first attempt, and sooner or later will have another go at her.'

'That's not unnatural, is it, sir? Perhaps the lady would feel more comfortable with police protection.'

'I pity the protector,' said Henry. 'Well, I suppose I'd better see if she'll come down.'

'If you wouldn't mind, sir,' said Fox comfortably.

In some trepidation, Henry mounted the stairs and tapped on Miss Prentice's door. There was no answer. He tapped again. The door opened suddenly and Miss Prentice was revealed with her fingers to her lips, like some mysterious buck-toothed sybil.

'What's happened!' she whispered.

'Nothing's happened, Cousin Eleanor. It's simply one of the men from Scotland Yard with a rather childish question to ask you.'

'Is that woman there? I won't meet that woman.'

'Mrs Ross has gone.'

'Henry, is that true?'

'Of course it's true.'

'Now, I've made you angry again. You're very unkind to me, Henry.'

'My dear cousin Eleanor!'

Her hand moved restlessly across the bosom of her dress.

'Yes, you are. So unkind. And I'm so fond of you. It's only for your own good. You're young and strong and handsome. All the Jernighams are very strong and beautiful. Don't listen to women like that, Henry. Don't listen to any woman. They'll do you harm. Except dear Dinah.'

'Will you come down and speak to Inspector Fox?'

'It's not a trap to make me meet that woman? Why is it a different man? Fox? Where's the other man? He was a gentleman. So tall! Taller than Father Copeland.'

He saw with astonishment that the movement of her hand traced a definite pattern on her bosom. She was crossing herself.

'This man is perfectly harmless,' said Henry. 'Do come.'

'Very well. My head's splitting. I suppose I must come.'

'That's better,' said Henry. He added awkwardly: 'Cousin Eleanor, your dress is undone.'

'Oh!' She blushed crimson and, to his horror, laughed shrilly and turned aside her head. Her fingers fumbled with the fastening of her dress. Then she shrank past him and, with a kind of coquettishness in her gait, hurried downstairs.

Henry followed with a sinking heart and escorted her to the study. His father had returned and stood before the fire. Jocelyn glared uncomfortably at Miss Prentice.

'Hullo, Eleanor, here you are. This is Inspector Fox.'

Miss Prentice offered her hand and, as soon as Fox touched it, snatched it away. Her eyes were downcast, her hands pleated a fold in her dress. Fox looked calmly at her.

'I'm sorry to trouble you, Miss Prentice, I only wanted to ask if you opened one of the hall windows as you left at noon on Saturday.'

'Oh, yes,' she whispered. 'Was that the unpardonable sin?'

'I beg your pardon, miss?'

'Did I let in it?'

'Let what in, Miss Prentice?'

'You know. But I only opened it the least little bit. A tiny crack. Of course it can make itself very small, can't it?'

Fox adjusted his spectacles and made a note.

'You did open the window?' he said.

'You shouldn't keep on asking. You know I did.'

'Miss Prentice, did you find anything in the teapot you were to use on the stage?'

'Is that where it hid?'

'Where what hid?'

'The unpardonable sin. You know. The thing she did!'

'You're talking nonsense, Eleanor,' said Jocelyn. He got behind her and made violent grimaces at Fox.

'I'm sorry if I irritate you, Jocelyn.'

'You don't know anything about an onion that a small boy put in the teapot, Miss Prentice?'

She opened her eyes very wide and shaped her mouth like an O. Then she slowly shook her head. Once started she seemed unable to leave off shaking her head, but went on and on until the movement lost all meaning.

'Well,' said Fox, 'I think that's all I need trouble you about, thank you, Miss Prentice.'

'Henry,' said Jocelyn. 'See your cousin upstairs.'

She went without another word. Henry hurried after her. Jocelyn turned to Fox.

'See how it is!' he said. 'The shock sent her out of her mind. There are no ways about it. See for yourself. Have to get a specialist. Better not believe a word she says.'

'She's never been like this before, sir?'

'Good God, no.'

'That's very distressing, sir, isn't it? The chief inspector asked me to speak to you, sir, about this evening. He thinks it would be a good idea to see, at the same time, all the people who were in the play, and he wonders if you would be good enough to send your party down to the hall.'

'I must say I don't quite see – As a matter of fact, I've asked the Copelands for dinner to talk things over.'

'That will fit in very nicely, then, won't it, sir? You can come on to the hall.'

'Yes, but I don't see what good it'll do.'

'The chief inspector will explain when he comes, sir. He asked me to say he'd be very much obliged if you would give the lead in this little matter. In view of your position in the county, sir, he thought you would prefer to come before the others. You've got two cars, haven't you, sir?'

'I suppose I'd better.' Jocelyn stared very hard at a portrait of his actress-ancestress and said, 'Have you got any idea who it is?'

'I couldn't say what the chief intends just at the moment, sir,' answered Fox so blandly that the evasion sounded exactly like a direct answer. 'No doubt he will report to you himself, sir. Would nine o'clock suit you at the hall, Mr Jernigham?'

'What? Oh, yes. Yes, certainly.'

'I'm much obliged, sir. I'll say good-afternoon.'

'Good-afternoon,' said Jocelyn restlessly.

VI

'This is Miss Bruce,' said the supervisor. 'She was on duty on Friday night, but I doubt if she'll be able to help you.'

Fox looked placidly at Miss Bruce and noted that she seemed a bright young person.

He said, 'Well, Miss Bruce, we'll be very pleased if you can put us right in this little matter. I understand you were on duty as an operator at ten o'clock on Friday evening.'

'Yes, that's right.'

'Yes. Now the call we're interested in came through somewhere round about 10.30. It was to the rectory, Winton St Giles. It's a party line with the old manual telephones and a long extension. Not many of those left, are there?'

'They'll be gone by this time next year,' said the supervisor.

'Is that a fact?' said Fox comfortably. 'Well, well. Now, Miss Bruce, can you help us?'

'I don't remember any calls on the rectory phone on Friday night,' said Miss Bruce. 'Chipping 10, the number is. I'm in the YPFC, so I know. We always have to ring a long time there, because the old housemaid Mary's a bit deaf, and Miss Dinah's room's away upstairs, and the rector never answers until he's fetched. It's a line that's used a lot, of course.'

'It would be.'

'Yes. Friday was Reading Circle night, and they're usually over at the hall, so everybody knows not to ring up on Friday, see, because they won't be in. Actually, last Friday it was at the rectory because of the play; but people wouldn't know that, see. They'd think: "Well, Friday. It's no use ringing on Friday."'

'So you're sure nobody rang?'

'Yes. Yes, I'm sure of it. I'd swear to it if that's what's wanted.'

'If the extension was used you wouldn't know, I suppose?'

'I wouldn't know a thing about that.'

'No,' agreed Fox. 'Well, thank you very much, miss. I'm greatly obliged. Good-afternoon.'

'Pleasure, I'm sure,' said Miss Bruce. 'Ta-ta.'

CHAPTER 25

Final Vignettes

The express from London roared into Great Chipping station. Alleyn, who had been reading the future in the murky window pane, rose hurriedly and put on his overcoat.

Fox was on the platform.

'Well, Brer Fox?' said Alleyn when they reached the Bigginses' Ford.

'Well, sir, the Yard car's arrived. They're to drive up quietly after we've all assembled. Allison can come into the supper-room with his two men and I'll wait inside the front door.'

'That'll be all right. I'd better give you all a cue to stand by, as Miss Copeland would say. Let's see. I'll ask Miss Prentice if she's feeling the draught. We'll sit on the stage round that table so there'll probably be a hell of a draught. How did you get on at Pen Cuckoo?'

'She was there.'

'Not?'

'Ross or Rosen. You had a lucky strike there, Mr Alleyn. Fancy her being Claude Smith's girl. We were on the Quantock case at that time, weren't we?'

'We weren't at the Yard, anyway. I've never seen her before this.'

'More've I. Well; she was there. Something up – between him and her – I should say.'

'Between who and her, Mr Fox?' asked Nigel. 'You're very dark and cryptic this evening.'

'Between Jernigham senior and Mrs Ross, Mr Bathgate. When I arrived he was looking peculiar, and Mr Henry seemed as if he thought something was up. She was cool enough, but I'd say the other lady was a case for expert opinion.'

'Miss Prentice?' murmured Alleyn.

'That's right, sir. Young Jernigham went and fetched her. She owned up to opening the window as sweet as you please, and then began to talk a lot of nonsense about letting in the unpardonable sin. I took it all down, but you'd be surprised how silly it was.'

'The unpardonable sin? Which one's that, I wonder?'

'Nobody owned to the onion,' said Fox gloomily.

'I think onions, in any form, the unpardonable sin,' said Nigel.

'I reckon you're right about the onion, Mr Alleyn.'

'I think so, Fox. After all, on finding onions in teapots, why not exclaim on the circumstance? Why not say, "Georgie Biggins for a certainty," and raise hell?'

'That's right, sir. Well, from the way they shaped up to the question, you'd say none of them had ever smelt one. Mr Jernigham's talking about getting a doctor in. Do you know what? I think he's sweet on her. On Rosen, I mean.'

Fox changed into second gear for Chipping Rise and said, 'The telephone's right. I told you that when I rang up, didn't I?'

'Yes.'

'And I've seen the four girls who helped Gladys Wright. Three of them are ready to swear on oath that nobody came down into the hall from the stage, and the fourth is certain nobody did, but wouldn't swear, as she went into the porch for a minute. I've re-checked the movements of all the people behind the scenes. Mr Copeland sat facing the floodlights from the time he got there until he went in to Mr Jernigham's room, when they tried to telephone to Mrs Ross. He went back to the stage and didn't leave it again until they all crowded round Miss Prentice.'

'I think it's good enough, Fox.'

'I think so, too. This Chief Constable business is awkward, isn't it, Mr Alleyn?'

'It is, indeed. I know of no precedent. Oh, well, we'll see what the preliminary interview does. You arranged that?'

'Yes, sir, that's all right. Did you dine on the train?'

'Yes, Fox. The usual dead fish and so on. Mr Bathgate wants to know who did the murder.'

'I do know,' said Nigel in the back seat; 'but I won't let on.'

'D'you want to stop at the pub, Mr Alleyn?'

'No. Let's get it over, Brer Fox, let's get it over.'

II

At Henry's suggestion, they had invited Dinah and the rector to dinner.

'You may as well take Dinah and me for granted, Father. We're not going to give each other up, you know.'

'I still think – however!'

And Henry, watching his father, knew that the afternoon visit of Miss Campanula's lawyers to the rectory, was Vale property. Jocelyn boggled and uttered inarticulate noises; but already, Henry thought, his father was putting a new roof on Winton. It would be better not to speak, thought Henry, of his telephone conversation with Dinah after Fox had gone. For Dinah had told Henry that her father felt he could not accept the fortune left by Idris Campanula.

Henry said, 'I don't suppose you suspect either the rector or Dinah, do you, even though they do get the money? They don't suspect us. Cousin Eleanor, who suspects God knows who, is in her room and won't appear until dinner.'

'She ought not to be alone.'

'One of the maids is with her. She's quietened down again and is quite normally long-suffering and martyred.'

Jocelyn looked nervously at Henry.

'What do you think's the matter with her?'

'Gone ravers,' said Henry cheerfully.

The Copelands accepted the invitation to dinner, sherry was served in the library, but Henry managed to get Dinah into the study, where he had made up a large fire and had secretly placed an enormous bowl of yellow chrysanthemums.

'Darling Dinah,' said Henry, 'there are at least fifty things of the most terrific importance to say to you, and when I look at you I can't think of one of them. May I kiss you? We're almost publicly betrothed, aren't we?'

'Are we? You've never really asked for my hand.'

'Miss Copeland – may I call you Dinah? – be mine. Be mine.'

'I may not deny, Mr Jernigham, that my sensibilities; nay, since I will not dissemble, my affections are touched by this declaration. I cannot hear you unmoved.'

Henry kissed her and muttered in her ear that he loved her very much.

'All the same,' said Dinah, 'I do wonder why Mr Alleyn wants us to go down to the hall tonight. I don't want to go. The place gives me the absolute horrors.'

'Me, too. Dinah, I made such a fool of myself last night.'

He told her how he had heard the three chords of the 'Prelude' as he came through the storm.

'I would have died of it,' said Dinah. 'Henry, *why* do they want us tonight? Are they – are they going to arrest someone?'

'Who?' asked Henry.

They stared solemnly at each other.

'Who indeed,' said Dinah.

III

'I tell you, Copeland, I'm pretty hard hit,' said the squire, giving himself a whisky-and-soda. 'It's so beastly uncomfortable. Have some more sherry? Nonsense, it'll do you good. You're not looking particularly happy yourself.'

'It's the most dreadful thing has ever happened to any of us,' said the rector listened with a steadily blanching face to Jocelyn's account of Miss Prentice.

'Poor soul,' he said, 'poor soul.'

'Yes, I know, but it's damned inconvenient. I'm sorry, rector, but it – well, it's – it's – Oh, God!'

'Would you like to tell me?' asked the rector, and if he spoke at all wearily Jocelyn did not notice it.

'No,' said Jocelyn, 'no. There's nothing to tell. I'm simply rather worried. What d'you suppose is the meaning of this meeting tonight?'

The rector looked curiously at him.

'I thought you probably knew. Your position, I mean – '

'As the weapon happens to be my property, I felt it better to keep right out of the picture. Technically, I'm a suspect.'

'Yes. Dear me, yes.' The rector sipped his sherry. 'So are we all, of course.'

'I wonder,' said the squire, 'what Alleyn is up to.'

'You don't think he's going to – to arrest anybody?'

They stared at each other.

'Dinner is served, sir,' said Taylor.

IV

'Good-night, dear,' said Dr Templett to his wife. 'I expect you'll be asleep when I get home. I'm glad it's been a good day.'

'It's been a splendid day,' said that steadfastly gallant voice. 'Good-night, my dear.'

Templett shut the door softly. The telephone pealed in his dressing-room at the end of the landing. The hospital was to ring before eight. He went to his dressing-room and lifted the receiver.

'Hullo?'

'Is that you, Billy?'

He sat frozen, the receiver still at his ear.

'Billy? Hullo? Hullo?'

'Well?' said Dr Templett.

'Then you are alive,' said the voice.

'I haven't been arrested, after all.'

'Nor, strangely enough, have I, in spite of the fact that I've been to Alleyn and taken the whole responsibility of the letter – '

'Selia! Not on the telephone!'

'I don't much care what happens to me now. You've let me down. Nothing else matters.'

'What do you mean? No, don't tell me! It's not true.'

'Very well. Goodbye, Billy.'

'Wait! Have you been told to parade at the hall this evening?'

'Yes. Have you?'

'Yes.' Dr Templett brushed his hand across his eyes. He muttered hurriedly: 'I'll call for you.'

'What?'

'If you like I'll drive you there.'

'I've got my own car. You needn't bother.'

'I'll pick you up at nine.'

'And drop me a few minutes later, I suppose?'

'That's not quite fair. What do you suppose I thought when – ?'

'You obviously don't trust me. That's all.'

'My God – !' began Dr Templett. The voice cut in coolly:

'All right. At nine. Why do you suppose he wants us in the hall? Is he going to arrest someone?'

'I don't know. What do you think?'

'I don't know.'

V

The church clock struck nine as the police car drew up outside the hall. Alleyn and Fox got out, followed by Detective-Sergeant Allison and two plain-clothes men. At the same moment, Nigel drove up in his own car with Sergeant Roper. They all went in through the back door. Alleyn switched on the stage lights and the supper-room light.

'You see the lie of the land, don't you,' he said. Two flights of steps from the supper-room to the stage. We'll have the curtain down, I think, Fox. You can stay on the stage. So can you, Bathgate, in the wings, and with not a word out of you. You know when to go down and what to do?'

'Yes,' said Nigel nervously.

'Good. Allison, you'd better move to the front door, and you others can go into the dressing-rooms. They'll come straight through the supper-room and won't see you. Roper, you're to go outside and direct them to the back door. Then come in. But quietly, if you don't want me to tear your buttons off and half-kill you. The rest of you can stay in the dressing-rooms until the company's complete. When it is complete, I'll slam both doors at the top of the steps. The piano's in position, isn't it, Fox? And the screens? Yes. All right, down with the curtain.'

The curtain came down in three noisy rushes, releasing a cloud of dust.

With the front of the hall shut out, the stage presented a more authentic appearance. Dinah's box set, patched and contrived though it was, resembled any touring company's stock scenery, while Mrs Ross's chairs and ornaments raised the interior to still greater distinction. The improvised lights shone bravely enough on chintz and china. The stage had taken on a sort of eerie half-life and an air of expectancy. On the round table Alleyn laid the anonymous letter, the 'Prelude in C Minor,' the 'Venetian Suite,' the pieces of rubber in their box, the onion, the soap-box and the teapot. He then covered this curious collection with a cloth.

Fox and Allison brought extra chairs from the dressing-rooms and put one of the paraffin lamps on the stage.

'Eight chairs,' counted Alleyn. 'That's right. Are we ready? I think so.'

'Nothing else, sir?'

'Nothing. Remember your cue. Leave on the supper-room lights. Here he comes, I think. Away you go.'

Fox walked over to the prompt corner. Nigel went through the opposite door and sat out of sight in the shadow of the proscenium. Allison went down to the auditorium, the two plain-clothes men disappeared into the dressing-rooms, and Roper, breathing stertorously, made for the back door.

'Shock tactics,' muttered Alleyn. 'Damn, I hate 'em. So infernally unfair, and they look like pure exhibitionism on the part of the police. Oh, well, can't be helped.'

'I don't hear a car,' whispered Nigel.

'It's coming.'

They all listened. The wind howled and the rain drummed on the shutters.

'I'll never think of this place,' said Nigel, 'without hearing that noise.'

'It's worse than ever,' said Fox.

'Here it is,' said Alleyn.

And now they all heard the car draw up in the lane. A door slammed. Boots crunched up the gravel path. Roper's voice could be heard. The back door opened. Roper, suddenly transformed into a sort of major-domo, said loudly:

'Mr Jernigham senior, sir.'

And the squire walked in.

CHAPTER 26

Miss Prentice feels the Draught

'So you see,' said Alleyn, 'I was led to wonder if, to speak frankly, the object of her visit was blackmail.'

The squire's face was drained of all its normal colour, but now it flushed a painful crimson.

'I cannot believe it.'

'In view of the record – '

The squire made a violent, clumsy gesture with his right hand. Standing in the centre of the stage under those uncompromising lights, he looked at once frightened and defiant. Alleyn watched him for a moment and then he said:

'You see, I think I know what she had to say to you.'

Jernigham's jaw dropped.

'I don't believe you,' he said hoarsely.

'Then let me tell what I believe to be her hold on you.'

Alleyn's voice went on and on, quietly, dispassionately. Jernigham listened with his gaze on the floor. Once he looked up as though he would interrupt, but he seemed to think better of this impulse and fell to biting his nails.

'I give you this opportunity,' said Alleyn. 'If you care to tell me now – '

'There is nothing to tell you. It's not true.'

'Mrs Ross did not come this afternoon with this story. She did not make these very definite terms with you?'

'I cannot discuss the matter.'

'Even,' said Alleyn, 'in view of this record?'

'I admit nothing.'

'Very well. I was afraid you would take this line.'

'In my position – '

'It was because of your position I gave you this opportunity. I can do no more.'

'I can't see why you want this general interview.'

'Shock tactics, sir,' said Alleyn.

'I – I don't approve.'

'If you wish, sir, I can hand my report in and you may make a formal complaint at the Yard.'

'No.'

'It would make no difference.' said Alleyn. 'I think the others have arrived. This is your last word?'

'I have nothing to say.'

'Very well, sir.'

Roper tapped at one of the supper-room doors.

'Hullo!' shouted Alleyn.

'Here they be, sir, every living soul, and all come together.'

'All right, Roper. Show them in.'

II

Miss Prentice came in first, followed by Dinah, the rector and Henry. Alleyn asked Miss Prentice to sit in the most comfortable chair, which he had placed on the prompt side of the table. When she dithered, he was so crisply polite that she was there before she realized it. She looked quickly towards the rector, who took the chair on her right. Dinah sat on her father's right with Henry beside her. The squire looked furtively at Alleyn.

'Will you sit down, sir?' invited Alleyn.

'What! Yes, yes,' said the squire convulsively, and sat beside Henry.

Mrs Ross came in. She was dressed in black and silver, a strange exotic figure in those surroundings. She said: 'Good-evening,' with her customary side-long smile, bowed rather more pointedly to Alleyn, and sat beside the squire. Templett, seeming ill at ease and shame-faced, followed her.

Miss Prentice drew in her breath and began to whisper:

'No, no, no! Never at the same table. I can't – !'

Alleyn sat on her left in the one chair remaining vacant and said, 'Miss Prentice – please!'

His voice had sufficeint edge to silence Miss Prentice and call the others to a sort of guarded alertness.

His long hands lay clasped before him on the table. He leant forward and looked with deliberation round the circle of attentive faces.

He said, 'Ladies and gentlemen, I shall not apologize for calling you together tonight. I am sure that most – not all, but most – of you are only too anxious that this affair should be settled, and I may tell you that we have now collected enough evidence to make an arrest. Each of you in turn has provided evidence; each of you has withheld evidence. From the information you have given, and from the significance of your several reticences, has emerged a pattern which, as we read it, has at its centre a single person: the murderer of Miss Idris Campanula.'

They sat as still as figures in a tableau, and the only sound, when Alleyn paused, was the sound of rain and the uneasy stirring of the wind outside.

'From the beginning, this strange affair has presented one particularly unusual problem: the problem of the murderer's intention. Was it Miss Idris Campanula for whom this trap was set, or was it Miss Eleanor Prentice? If it was indeed Idris Campanula, then the number of possible suspects was very small. If it was Miss Prentice, the field was a great deal wider. During most of yesterday and part of today my colleague, Inspector Fox interviewed the people have known and come into contact with both these ladies. He could find no motive for the murder of either of them, outside the circle of people we have found motive. Money, jealousy, love and fear are the themes most usually found behind homicide. All four appeared in this case if Miss Campanula was the intended victim: the last three, if the intended victim was Miss Prentice. The fact that on Friday evening at five o'clock Mr Henry Jernigham showed the automatic to all of you, except his father, who is the owner, was another circumstance that suggested one of you as the guilty person.'

Henry rested his head on his hand, driving his fingers through his hair. Templett cleared his throat.

'At the inquest this morning you all heard the story of the water-pistol. The booby-trap was ready at 2.30 on Friday. The water-pistol was no longer in position at noon on Saturday when Miss Prentice used the soft pedal. Yet some time between Friday at 2.30 and noon on Saturday, somebody sat at the piano and used the soft pedal and the booby-trap worked.'

Alleyn lifted the cloth from the table. Miss Prentice gave a nervous yelp. He took up the 'Venetian Suite' and pointed to the circular blister and discoloured splashes on the back.

'Five hours after the catastrophe, this was still damp. So was the torn silk round the hole in the front of the piano. Miss Prentice has told us that her music was left on the piano earlier in the week. All Saturday morning the hall was occupied. It seems, therefore, that the water-pistol was removed before Saturday morning, and presumably by the guilty person, since an innocent person would not have kept silent about the booby-trap. On Friday afternoon and evening the hall was deserted. At this stage I may say that Mr Jernigham and Dr Templett both have alibis for Friday afternoon, when they hunted up till a short time before the rehearsal-for-words at Pen Cuckoo. Dr Templett has an alibi for Friday and well into Saturday morning, during which time he was occupied with professional duties. It is hardly conceivable that he would enter the hall in the small hours of Saturday morning to play the piano. The helpers arrived soon after nine o'clock on Saturday, and by that time the pistol had been removed.

'Now for the automatic. If, as we suppose, the water-pistol was discovered on Friday, it is of course possible that the automatic was substituted before Saturday. This possibility we consider unlikely. It was known that the helpers would be in the hall all Saturday morning, and the murderer would have run the risk of discovery. It was only necessary for someone to disarrange the rotten silk in the front of the piano to reveal the nozzle of the Colt. True, this piece of music was on the rack; but it might have been removed. Somebody might have dusted the piano. It is also true that nobody was likely to look in the top, as the person who removed the water-pistol had taken pains to re-fasten the bunting with drawing-pins and to cover the top with heavy pot plants. Still, there would have been considerable risk. It seems more probable that the murderer would leave the setting of the automatic until as late as possible. Say about four o'clock on Saturday afternoon.'

Templett made a sudden movement, but said nothing.

'For four o'clock on Saturday afternoon,' said Alleyn, 'none of you has an alibi that would stand up to five minutes' cross-examination.'

'But – '

'I've told you – '

'I explained yesterday – '

'Do you want me to go into this? Wait a little and listen. At about half-past three, Mrs Ross arrived at the hall. Dr Templett got there a few minutes later. She had come to complete the supper arrangements, he to put his acting clothes in his dressing-room. They had both called at Pen Cuckoo in the morning. Mrs Ross tells us that while Dr Templett went into the house she remained in the car. I imagine there is no need to remind you all of the french window into the study at Pen Cuckoo.'

'I knew,' whispered Miss Prentice, 'I knew, I knew!'

'You're going beyond your duty, Mr Alleyn,' said Mrs Ross.

'No,' said Alleyn. 'I merely pause here to point out how easy it would have been for any of you to come up Top Lane and slip into the study. To return to the 3.30 visit to the hall. Dr Templett has given what I believe to be a true account of this visit. He has told us that he arrived to find Mrs Ross already there and occupied with the supper arrangements. After a time they came here on to this stage. They noticed that the last window on the right, near the front door, was a few inches open. Mrs Ross, who first noticed this, told Dr Templett that she saw someone dodge down behind the sill. To reach the window this onlooker used a box.'

He turned the cloth farther back and the dilapidated soap-box was revealed. Miss Prentice giggled and covered her mouth with her hand.

'This is the box. It fits into the marks under the window. Do you recognize it, Dr Templett?'

'Yes,' said Templett dully, 'I remember that splash of white on the top. I saw it as I looked down.'

'Exactly. I should explain that when Dr Templett reached the window he looked out to see if he could discover anybody. He saw nobody, but he noticed the box. He tells me it was not there when he arrived. Now Mrs Ross said that she did not recognize this person. But I have experimented, and have found that if one sees anybody at all under the conditions she has described, one stands a very good chance of recognizing them. One would undoubtedly know, for instance, whether it was a man or a woman whose image showed for a moment and disappeared behind the sill. It will be urged by the police that Mrs Ross did, in fact, recognize this person,' Alleyn turned to Templett.

'Mrs Ross did not tell you who it was?'

'I didn't know who it was,' said Mrs Ross.

'Dr Templett?'

'I believe Mrs Ross's statement.'

Alleyn looked at the squire.

'When you saw Mrs Ross alone this afternoon, sir, did she refer to this incident?'

'I can't answer that question, Alleyn,' muttered the squire. Henry raised his head and looked at his father with a sort of wonder.

'Very well, sir,' said Alleyn. 'I must remind you all that you are free to refuse answers to any questions you may be asked. The police may not set traps, and it is my duty to tell you that we have established the identity of the eavesdropper.' He took the lid from a small box.

'One of these fragments of rubber,' he said, 'was found on the point of a nail on the inside of the box. The others were caught behind projecting splinters also on the inside of the box.'

He opened an envelope and from it he shook a torn surgical finger-stall.

'The fragments of rubber,' he said, 'correspond with the holes in this stall.'

Miss Prentice electrified the company by clapping her hands with great violence.

'Oh, inspector,' she cried shrilly, 'how perfectly, perfectly wonderful you are!'

III

Alleyn turned slowly and met her enraptured gaze. Her prominent eyes bulged, her mouth was open, and she nodded her head several times with an air of ecstasy.

'Then you acknowledge,' he said, 'that you put this box outside the window on Saturday afternoon?'

'Of course!'

'And that you stood on it in order to look through the window?'

'Alas, yes!'

'Miss Prentice, why did you do this?'

'I was guided.'

'Why did you not admit you recognized the box when Inspector Fox asked you about it?'

With that unlovely air of girlishness she covered her face with her fingers.

'I was afraid he would ask me what I saw.'

'This is absolute nonsense!' said Templett angrily.

'And why,' continued Alleyn, 'did you tell me you were indoors all Saturday afternoon?'

'I was afraid to say what I'd done.'

'Afraid? Of whom?'

She seemed to draw herself inwards to a point of venomous concentration. She stretched out her arm across the table. The finger pointed at Mrs Ross.

'Of her. She tried to murder me. She's a murderess. I can prove it. I can prove it.'

'No!' cried the squire. 'No! Good God, Alleyn – '

'Is there any doubt in your mind, Mr Alleyn,' said Mrs Ross, 'that this woman is mad?'

'I can prove it,' repeated Miss Prentice.

'How?' asked Alleyn. 'Please let this finish, Mr Jernigham. We shall see daylight soon.'

'She knew I saw her. She tried to kill me because she was afraid.'

'You hear that, Mrs Ross? It is a serious accusation. Do you feel inclined to answer it? I must warn you, first, that Dr Templett has made a statement about this incident.'

She looked quickly at Templett.

He said, 'I thought you hadn't considered me over the other business. I told the truth.'

'You fool,' said Mrs Ross. For the first time she looked really frightened. She raised her hands to her thin neck and touched it surreptitiously. Then she hid her hands in her lap.

'I do not particularly want to repeat the gist of Dr Templett's statement,' said Alleyn.

'Very well.' Her voice cracked, she took a breath and then said evenly, 'Very well. I recognized Miss Prentice. I've nothing whatever to fear. One doesn't kill old maids for eavesdropping.'

'Mr Jernigham,' said Alleyn, 'did Mrs Ross tell you of this incident this afternoon?'

The squire was staring at Mrs Ross as if she was a sort of Medusa. Without turning his eyes, he nodded.

'She suggested that Miss Prentice had come down to the hall with the intention of putting the automatic in the piano?'

'So she had. I'll swear,' said Mrs Ross.

'Mr Jernigham?'

'Yes. Yes, she suggested that.'

'She told you, perhaps, that you could trust her?'

'Oh, my God!' said the squire.

'I arrived too late at this place,' said Mrs Ross, 'to be able to do anything to the piano.' She looked at Dinah. 'You know that.'

'Yes,' said Dinah.

'It was soon after that,' said Miss Prentice abruptly, 'that she began to set traps for me, you know. Then I saw it all in a flash. She must have seen me through a glass darkly, and because I witnessed the unpardonable sin she will destroy me. You understand, don't you, because it is very important. She is in league with The Others, and it won't be long before one of them catches me.'

Templett said, 'Alleyn, you must see. This has gone on long enough. It's perfectly obvious what's wrong here.'

'We will go on, if you please,' said Alleyn. 'Mr Copeland, you told me that on Friday night you expected Miss Prentice at the rectory.'

The rector, very pale, said, 'Yes.'

'She didn't arrive?'

'No. I told you. She telephoned.'

'At what time?'

'Not long after ten.'

'From Pen Cuckoo?'

'It was my hand, you know,' said Miss Prentice rapidly, 'I wanted to rest my hand. It was so *very* naughty. The blood tramped up and down my arm. Thump, thump, thump. So I said I would stay at home.'

'You rang from Pen Cuckoo?'

'I took the message, Mr Alleyn,' said Dinah, 'I told you.'

'And what do you say, Miss Copeland, if I tell you that on Friday night the Pen Cuckoo telephone was out of order from 8.20 until the following morning?'

'But – it couldn't have been.'

'I'm afraid it was.' He turned to Henry Jernigham. 'You agree?'

'Yes,' said Henry without raising his head.

'You can thank The Others for that,' said Miss Prentice in a trembling voice.

'The Others?'

'*The Others*, yes. They are always doing these sort of tricks; and she's the worst of the lot, that woman over there.'

'Well, Miss Copeland?'

'I took the message,' repeated Dinah. 'Miss Prentice said she was at home and would remain at home.'

'This contradiction,' said Alleyn, 'takes us a step further. Mrs Ross, on Friday night you drove down to Chipping by way of Church Lane?'

'Yes.'

'You have told me that you saw a light in this hall.'

'Yes.'

'You think it was in Mr Jernigham's dressing-room?'

'Yes.'

'The telephone is in that room, Miss Dinah, isn't it?'

'Yes,' whispered Dinah. 'Oh, yes.'

Alleyn took a card from his pocket and scribbled on it. He handed it over to Henry.

'Will you take Miss Dinah to the rectory?' he said. 'In half an hour I want you to ring through to here on the extension. Show this card to the man at the door and he will let you out.'

Henry looked fixedly at Alleyn.

'Very well, sir,' he said. 'Thank you.'

Henry and Dinah went out.

IV

'Now,' said Alleyn, 'we come to the final scene. I must tell you – though I dare say you have heard it all by now – that at 6.30 Miss Gladys Wright used the piano and pressed down the soft pedal.

Nothing untoward happened. Since it is inconceivable that anybody could remove the pot plants and rig the automatic after 6.30, we know that the automatic must have been already in position. The safety-catch, which Mr Henry Jernigham showed to all of you, and particularly to Mrs Ross, accounts for Gladys Wright's immunity. How, then, did the guilty person manage to release the safety-catch after Gladys Wright and her fellow-helpers were down in the front of the hall? I will show you how it could have been done.'

He went down to the footlights.

'You notice that the curtain falls on the far side of the improvised footlights and just catches on the top of the piano. Now, if you'll look.'

He stopped and pushed his hand under the curtain. The top of the piano, with its covering of green and yellow bunting, could be seen.

'This bunting is pinned down as it was on Saturday. It is stretched tight over the entire top of the piano. The lid is turned back, but of course that doesn't show. The pot plants stand on the inside of the lid. I take out the centre drawing-pin at the back and slide my hand under the bunting. I am hidden by the curtain, and the pot plants also serve as a mask for any slight movement that might appear from the front of the hall. My fingers have reached the space beyond the open lid. Inside the opening they encounter the cold, smooth surface of the Colt. Listen.'

Above the sound of rain and wind they all heard a small click.

'I have pushed over the safety-catch,' said Alleyn. 'The automatic is now ready to shoot Miss Campanula between the eyes.'

'Horrible,' said the rector violently.

'There is one sequence of events about which we can be certain,' said Alleyn. 'We know that the first person to arrive was Gladys Wright. We know that she entered the hall at 6.30, and was in front of the curtain down there with her companions until and after the audience came in. We know that it would have been impossible for anybody to come down from the stage into the front of the hall unnoticed. Miss Wright is ready to swear that nobody did this. We know that Miss Dinah Copeland arrived with her father soon after Gladys Wright, and was here behind the scenes. We know Mr Copeland sat on the stage until he made his announcement to the audience, only leaving it for a moment, to join the others at the telephone, and once again when he persuaded Miss Prentice not to play.

Mr Copeland, did you at any time see anybody stoop down to the curtain as I did just then?'

'No. No! I'm quite certain that I didn't. You see, my chair faced the exact spot.'

'Yes, therefore we know that unless Mr Copeland is the guilty person, the safety-catch must have been released during one of his two absences. But Mr Copeland believed, up to the last moment, that Miss Prentice was to be the pianist. We are satisfied that Mr Copeland is not the guilty person.'

The rector raised one of his large hands in a gesture that seemed to repudiate immunity. The squire, Miss Prentice, Mrs Ross and Templett kept their eyes fixed on Alleyn.

'Knowing the only means by which the safety-catch might be released, it seems evident that Miss Prentice was not the intended victim. Miss Prentice, you are cold. Do you feel a draught?'

Miss Prentice shook her head, but she trembled like a wet dog and looked not unlike one. There was a faint sound of movement behind the scenes. Alleyn went on:

'When you were all crowded round her and she gave in and con-sented to allow Miss Campanula to play, it would have been easy enough to come up here and put the safety-catch on again. Why run the risk of being arrested for the murder of the wrong person?'

Alleyn's level voice halted for a moment. He leant forward, and when he spoke again it was with extreme deliberation:

'No! The trap was set for Miss Campanula. It was set before Miss Prentice yielded her right to play, and it was set by someone who knew she would not play. The safety-catch was released at the only moment when the stage was empty. The moment when you were all crowded round the telephone. Then the murderer sat back and wait-ed for the catastrophe to happen. Beyond the curtain at this moment someone is sitting at the piano. In a minute you will hear the open-ing chords of the "Prelude" as you heard them on Saturday night. If you listen closely you will hear the click of the trigger when the soft pedal goes down. That will represent the report of the automatic. Imagine this guilty person. Imagine someone whose hand stole under the curtain while the hall was crowded and set that trap. Imagine someone who sat, as we sit now, and waited for those three fatal chords.'

Alleyn paused.

As heavy as lead and as loud as ever the dead hand had struck them out, in the empty hall beyond the curtain, thumped the three chords of Miss Campanula's 'Prelude.'

'Pom. *Pom.* POM!'

And very slowly, in uneven jerks, the curtain began to rise.

As it rose, so did Miss Prentice. She might have been pulled up by an invisible hand in her hair. Her mouth was wide open, but the only sound she made was a sort of retching groan. She did not take her eyes from the rising curtain, but she pointed her hand at the rector and waved it up and down.

'*It was for you,*' screamed Miss Prentice. '*I did it for you!*'

And Nigel, seated at the piano, saw Alleyn take her by the arm.

'Eleanor Prentice, I arrest you – '

CHAPTER 27

Case Ends

Henry and Dinah sat by the fire in the rectory study and watched the clock.

'*Why* does he want us to ring up?' said Dinah for perhaps the sixth time, 'I don't understand.'

'I think I do. I think the telephoning's only an excuse. He wanted us out of the way.'

'But why?'

Henry put his arm round her shoulders and pressed his cheek against her hair.

'Oh, Dinah,' he said.

'What, darling?'

Dinah looked up. He sat on the arm of the chair and she had to move a little in his embrace before she could see his eyes.

'Henry! What is it?'

'I think we're in for a bad spin.'

'But – isn't it Mrs Ross?'

'I don't think so.'

Without removing her gaze from his face she took his hand.

'I think it's Eleanor,' said Henry.

'*Eleanor!*'

'It's the only answer. Don't you see that's what Alleyn was driving at all the time?'

'But she *wanted* to play. She made the most frightful scene over not playing.'

'I know. But Templett said two days before that she'd never be able to do it. Don't you see, she worked it so that we should find her crying and moaning, and insist on her giving up?'

'Suppose we hadn't insisted.'

'She'd have left the safety-catch on or not used the soft pedal, or perhaps she'd have "discovered" the automatic and accused Miss C. of putting it there. That would have made a glorious scene.'

'I can't believe it.'

'Can you believe it of anyone else.'

'Mrs Ross,' said Dinah promptly.

'No, darling. I rather think Mrs Ross has merely tried to blackmail my papa. It is my cousin who is a murderess. Shall you enjoy a husband of whom every one will say: "Oh, yes, Henry Jernigham! Wasn't he the Pen Cuckoo murderess's nephew or son or something?"'

'I shall love my husband and I shan't hear what they say. Besides, you don't know. You're only guessing.'

'I'm certain of it. There are all sorts of things that begin to fit in. Things that don't fit any other way. Dinah, I know she's the one.'

'Anyway, my dear darling, she's mad.'

'I hope so,' said Henry. 'God, it's awful, isn't it?'

He sprang up and began to walk nervously up and down.

'I can't stand this much longer,' said Henry.

'It's time we rang up.'

'I'll do it.'

But as he reached the door they heard voices in the hall.

The rector came in, followed by Alleyn and the squire.

'Dinah! Where's Dinah?' cried the rector.

'Here she is,' said Henry. 'Father!'

The squire turned a chalk-white face to his son.

'Come here, old boy,' he said. 'I want you.'

'That chair,' said Alleyn quickly.

Henry and Alleyn put the squire in the chair.

'Brandy, Dinah,' said the rector. 'He's fainted.'

'No, I haven't,' said Jocelyn. 'Henry, old boy, I'd better tell you – '

'I know,' said Henry, 'It's Eleanor.'

Alleyn moved back to the door and watched them. He was now a detached figure. The arrest came like a wall of glass between himself and the little group that hovered round Jocelyn. He knew that most of his colleagues accepted these moments of isolation. Perhaps they were scarcely aware of them. But, for himself, he always felt a little like a sort of Mephistopheles, who looked on at his own handiwork. He didn't enjoy the sensation. It was the one moment when his sense of detachment deserted him. Now, as they remembered him, he saw in the faces turned towards him the familiar guarded antagonism of herded animals.

He said, 'If Mr Jernigham would like to see Miss Prentice, it shall be arranged. Superintendent Blandish will be in charge.'

He bowed, and was going when Jocelyn said loudly:

'Wait a minute.'

'Yes, sir?' Alleyn moved quickly to the chair. The squire looked up at him.

'I know you tried to prepare me for this,' he said. 'You guessed that woman had told me. I couldn't stand that until – until it was all up – I wouldn't admit it. You understand that.'

'Yes.'

'I'm all to blazes. Think what to do in the morning. Just wanted to say I appreciate the way you've handled things. Considerate.'

'I would have avoided the final scene, sir, if I had seen any other way.'

'I know that. Mustn't ask questions, of course. There are some things I don't understand – Alleyn, you see she's out of her mind?'

'Dr Templett, I'm sure, will advise you about an alienist, sir.'

'Yes. Thank you.'

The squire blinked up at him and then suddenly held out his hand.

'Good-night.'

'Good-night, sir.'

Henry said, 'I'll come out with you.'

As they walked to the door, Alleyn thought there were points about being a Jernigham of Pen Cuckoo.

'It's queer,' said Henry, 'I suppose this must be a great shock to us; but at the moment I feel nothing at all. Nothing. I don't realize that she's – Where is she?'

'The Yard car is on the way to Great Chipping. She'll need things from Pen Cuckoo. We'll let you know what they are.'

Henry stopped dead at the rectory door. His voice turned to ice.

'Is she frightened?'

Alleyn remembered that face with the lips drawn back from the projecting teeth, the tearless bulging eyes, the hands that opened and closed as if they had let something fall.

'I don't think she is conscious of fear,' he said. 'She was quite composed. She didn't weep.'

'She can't. Father often said she never cried as a child.'

'I remembered your father told me that.'

'I hated her,' said Henry. 'But that's nothing now; She's insane. It's strange, because there's no insanity in the family. What happens? I mean, when will they begin to try her. We – what ought we to do?'

Alleyn told him what they should do. It was the first time he had ever advised the relatives of a person accused of murder, and he said, 'But you must ask your lawyer's advice first of all. That is really all I may tell you.'

'Yes. Yes, of course. Thank you, sir.' Henry peered at Alleyn. He saw him against rods of rain that glinted in the light from the open door.

'It's funny,' said Henry jerkily. 'Do you know, I was going to ask you about Scotland Yard – how one began.'

'Did you think seriously of this?'

'Yes. I want a job. Hardly suitable for the cousin of the accused.'

'There's no reason why you shouldn't try for the police.'

'I've read your book. Good Lord, it's pretty queer to stand here and talk like this.'

'You're more shocked than you realize. If I were you I should take your father home.'

'Ever since yesterday, sir, I've had the impression I'd seen you before. I've just remembered. Agatha Troy did a portrait of you, didn't she?'

'Yes.'

'It was very good, wasn't it? Rather a compliment to be painted by Troy. Is she pleasant or peculiar?'

'I think her very pleasant indeed,' said Alleyn. 'I have persuaded her to say she will marry me. Good-night.'

He smiled, waved his hand and went out into the rain.

II

Nigel had driven his own car over to the rectory, and he took Alleyn to Great Chipping.

'The others have only just got away,' said Nigel. 'She fainted after you left, and Fox had to get Templett to deal with her. They're picking the wardress up at the substation.'

'Fainted, did she?'

'Yes. She's completely dotty, isn't she?'

'I shouldn't say so. Not completely.'

'Not?'

'The dottiness has only appeared since Saturday night. She's probably extremely neurotic. Unbalanced, hysterical, all that. In law, insanity is very closely defined. Her counsel will probably go for moral depravity, delusion, or halluncination. If he can prove a history of disturbances of the higher levels of thought, he may get away with it. I'm afraid poor old Copeland will have to relate his experiences. They'll give me fits for your performance on the piano, but I've covered myself by warning the listeners. I don't mind betting that even if lunacy is not proved, there'll be a recommendation for mercy. Of course, they may go all out for "not guilty" and get it.'

'You might give me an outline, Alleyn.'

'All right. Where are we? It's as dark as hell.'

'Just coming into Chipping. There's the police car ahead.'

'Ah, yes. Well, here's the order of events as we see it. On Friday, by 2.40, Georgie had set the booby-trap. Miss Campanula tried to get into the hall before he left it. He hid while the chauffeur looked through the window. When the chauffeur had gone, Georgie re-pinned the bunting over the open top of the piano, replaced the aspidistras and decamped. At a minute or two after half-past two, Miss C. passed Miss P. in the church porch. Miss P. was seen by Gibson. She crossed Church Lane and would pass the hall on her way to Top Lane. In Top Lane she met Dinah Copeland and Henry Jernigham at three o'clock.

'Apparently she had taken half an hour to walk a quarter of a mile. We did it yesterday in five mintues. Our case is that she'd gone into the hall in a great state of upset because the rector had ticked her off at confession. She must have sat at the piano, worked the booby-trap and got the jet of water full in the face. She removed the pistol, and probably the first vague idea of her crime came into her head, because she kept quiet about the booby-trap. Perhaps she remembered the Colt and wondered if it would fit. We don't know. We only know that at three o'clock she had the scene in Top Lane with Henry and Dinah, the scene that was watched and overheard by that old stinker, Tranter. Tranter and Dinah noticed that the bosom of her dress was wet. That, with the lapse in time, are the only scraps of evidence we've got so far to give colour to this bit of our theory, but I'd like to know how else the front of her bodice got wet, if not from the pistol. It wasn't raining, and anyhow rain wouldn't behave like that. And I'd like to know how else you can account for her arrival, as late as three, at a spot five minutes away.'

'Yes, it'll certainly take a bit of explaining.'

'The butler remembered she got back at four. At five Henry explained the mechanism of the Colt to the assembled company, stressing and illustrating the action of the safety-catch. Miss P. had told the rector she wanted to see him that evening. Of course, she wanted to give him a distorted and poisonous version of the meeting between Henry and his Dinah. She was to come to the rectory after the Reading Circle activities. About ten o'clock, that would be. Now, soon after ten, Miss C. flung herself into the rector's arms in the rectory study.'

'Christopher!'

'Yes. I hope for his sake we won't have to bring this out; but it's a faint hope. The curtains were not drawn, and anybody on the path to the hall could have seen. Round about 10.15, Miss Dinah heard the gate into the wood give its customary piercing shriek. She thought somebody had gone out that way and believed it was Miss C. We contend it was Miss Prentice in for her appointment. We contend she stood inside the gate transfixed by the tableau beyond the window, that she put the obvious interpretation on what she saw, and fell a prey to whatever furies visit a woman whose ageing heart is set on one man and whose nerves, desires and thoughts have been concentrated on the achievement of her hope. We think she turned, passed through the post-stile and returned to Church Lane. To help this theory we've got two blurred heel-prints, the statements that nobody else used the gate that night, and the fact that Miss P. rang up shortly afterwards from the hall.'

'How the devil d'you get that?'

'The telephone operator is prepared to swear nobody rang up the rectory. But Miss P. rang up and the old housemaid called Dinah Copeland, who went to the telephone. She evidently didn't notice it was an extension call. Miss P. said she was speaking from Pen Cuckoo. Miss P. has admitted she rang up. The hall telephone is an extension and doesn't register at the exchange. Mrs Ross saw a light in the hall telephone room, at the right moment. It's the only explanation. Miss P. didn't know the Pen Cuckoo telephone was out of order and thought she was safe enough to establish a false alibi. She probably got the water-pistol that night and took it away with her to see if the Colt was the same length. It was an eleventh of an inch shorter, which meant that the nozzle would fit in the hole without projecting. Now we come to Saturday afternoon. She told me she was in her room. Mrs Ross recognized her through the hall window, and we've got the scrapes of rubber to prove that she handled the box. She looked through the hall window to see if the coast was clear. I imagine Templett was embracing his dubious love, who saw the onlooker over his shoulder. Miss P. took to cover, leaving the box. When they'd gone, she crept into the hall and put the Colt in position. She'd had four emotional shocks in twenty-six hours. The rector had given her fits. She'd seen Henry making ardent love to Dinah. She'd seen Idris Campanula, apparently victoriously happy, in the rector's arms, and she'd watched Templett and Mrs Ross in what I imagine must have been an even more passionate encounter. And though I do *not* consider her insane in law, I do consider that these experiences drove her into an ecstasy of fury. Since it is the rector with whom she herself is madly and overwhelmingly in love, Idris Campanula was the object of her hatred. It was Idris who had robbed her of her hopes. Incidentally, it is Idris who left her a fortune. Georgie Biggins had shown her the way. It's worth noting here that she won a badge for tying knots, and taught the local Guides in this art. At half-past four she was back at Pen Cuckoo and waked the squire in time for tea. This account, too, sounds like conjecture, but the finger-stall proves she lied once, the telephone proves she lied twice, and the fingerprints in the teapot prove she lied three times.'

'In the teapot?'

'I'll explain in a minute.'

They reached the top of Great Chipping Rise, and the lights of the town swam brokenly beyond the rain.

'There's not much more,' said Alleyn. 'The prosecution will make the most of this last point. The only time the stage was deserted, after they arrived in the evening, was when all the others stood round the telephone trying to get through to Mrs Ross and Dr Templett. Only Miss Prentice was absent. She appeared for a moment, saw the squire in his under-pants, scuttled off to the stage and did her stunt with safety-catch. Our case really rests on this. We can check and double-check the movements of every one of them from half-past six onwards. The rector sat on the stage, and will swear nobody touched the piano from that side. Gladys Wright and her helpers were in the hall and will swear nobody touched it from that side. The only time the catch could have been moved was when they were all round the telephone, and Miss P. was absent. She is literally the only person who could have moved the catch.'

'By George,' said Nigel, 'she must be a cold-blooded creature! What a nerve!'

'It's given way a little since the event,' said Alleyn grimly. 'I think she found she wasn't as steady as she expected to be, so she allowed her hysteria to mount into the semblance of insanity. Her nerve had gone at the shock of her dear friend's death, you see. Now she's going to work the demented stuff for all it's worth. I wonder when she first began to be afraid of me. I wonder if it was when I put the finger-stall in my pocket. Or was it at the first tender mention of the onion?'

'The onion!' shouted Nigel. 'Where the devil does the onion come in?'

'Georgie Biggins put the onion in the teapot. We found it in a cardboard box in the corner of the supper-room. It had pinkish powder on it. There was pinkish powder on the table in Miss P.'s dressing-room. It smelt of onion. The dressing-rooms were locked while Georgie was in the hall, so he didn't drop the onion in Miss P.'s powder. My theory is that Miss P. found the onion in the teapot, which she had to use, took it to her dressing-room and put it down on the table amongst the spilt powder. The teapot has her prints on the inside, and hers and Georgie's on the outside.'

'But what the suffering cats did she want with an onion? She wasn't going to make Irish stew.'

'Haven't you heard that she had never been known to shed tears until Saturday night, when floods were induced by sheer pain and disappointment because she couldn't play the piano? She took a good sniff at the onion, opened her dressing-room door, swayed to and fro, moaned and wept and wept and wept until Dr Templett heard her and behaved exactly as she knew he would behave. Later on she chucked the onion into the débris in the supper-room. She ought to have returned it to the teapot.'

'I boggle at the onion.'

'Boggle away, my boy. If it was an innocent onion, why didn't she own to it? There are her powder and her prints. Nobody else extracted it from the teapot. But it doesn't matter. It's only another corroborative detail.'

'The whole thing sounds a bit like Pooh Bah.'

'It's a beastly business. I detest it. She's a horrible woman, not a generous thought in her make-up; but that doesn't make much odds. If Georgie Biggins hadn't set his trap she'd have gone on to the end of her days, most likely, hating Miss C., scheming, scratching, adoring. Everybody will talk psychiatry and nonsense. Her *ideé fixe* will be pitchforked about the studios of the intelligentsia. That old fool Jernigham, who's a nice old fool, and his son, who's no fool at all, will go through hell. The rector, who supplied the *ideé fixe*, will blame himself; and God knows he's not to blame. Templett will hover on the brink of professional odium, but he'll be cured of Mrs Ross.'

'What of Mrs Ross?'

'At least she's scored a miss in the Vale of Pen Cuckoo. No hope now of blackmailing old Jernigham into matrimony, or out of hard cash. We'll catch the Rosen sooner or later, please heaven, for she's a nasty bit of work, and that's a fact. She would have seen Templett in the dock before she'd have risked an eyelash to clear him, and yet I imagine she's very much attracted by

Templett. As soon as she knew we thought him innocent, she was all for him. Here we are.'

Nigel pulled up outside the police station.

'May I come in with you?' he asked.

'If you like, certainly.'

Fox met Alleyn in the door.

'She's locked up,' said Fox. 'Making a great old rumpus. The doctor's gone for a strait-jacket. Here's a letter for you, Mr Alleyn. It came this afternoon.'

Alleyn looked at the letter and took it quickly. The firm small writing of the woman he loved brought the idea of her into his mind.

'It's from Troy,' he said.

And before he went into the lighted building he looked at Nigel.

'If one could send every grand passion to the laboratory, do you suppose, in each resulting formula, we should find something of Dinah and Henry's young idyll, something of Templett's infatuation, something of Miss P.'s madness, and even something of old Jernigham's foolishness?'

'Who knows?' said Nigel.

'Not I,' said Alleyn.

Death at the Bar

For My Friends in the Dunedin Repertory Society

Contents

Cast of Characters

Luke Watchman, KC	
Sebastian Parish	*His cousin*
Norman Cubitt, RA	
Abel Pomeroy	*Proprietor, Plume of Feathers, Devon*
Will Pomeroy	*His son*
Mrs Ives	*Housekeeper at the Plume of Feathers*
The Hon Violet Darragh	*Of County Clare, Ireland*
Robert Legge	*Secretary and Treasurer to the Coombe Left Movement*
George Nark	*Farmer, of Ottercombe*
Decima Moore	*Of Cary Edge Farm and of Oxford*
Dr Shaw	*Police Surgeon, Illington*
Nicholas Harper	*Superintendent of Police, Illington*
Richard Oates, PC	*Of the Illington and Ottercombe Constabulary*
Dr Mordant	*Coroner for Illington*
Roderick Alleyn	*Chief Detective-Inspector, Criminal Investigation Department*
T. R. Fox	*Inspector, Criminal Investigation Department*
Colonel, The Honourable Maxwell Brammington	*Chief Constable*

CHAPTER 1

The Plume of Feathers

As Luke Watchman drove across Otterbrook Bridge the setting sun shone full in his eyes. A molten flood of sunlight poured towards him through the channel of the lane and broke into sequins across Otterbrook waters. He arched his hand over his eyes and peered through the spattered dazzle of the windscreen. Somewhere about here was the turning for Ottercombe. He lowered the window and leant out.

The warmth of evening touched his face. The air smelt of briar, of fern, and more astringently of the distant sea. There, fifty yards ahead, was the finger-post with its letters almost rubbed out by rain, 'Ottercombe, 7 miles.'

Watchman experienced the fufilment of a nostalgic longing and was content. Only now, when he was within reach of his journey's end, did he realize how greatly he had desired this return. The car moved forward and turned from the wide lane into the narrow. The curves of hills marched down behind hedgerows. There was no more sunlight. Thorns brushed the windows on each side, so narrow was the lane. The car bumped over pot-holes. The scent of spring-watered earth rose coldly from the banks.

'Downhill all the way now,' Watchman murmured. His thoughts travelled ahead to Ottercombe. One should always time arrivals for this hour when labourers turned homewards, when lamps were lit, when the traveller had secret glimpses into rooms whose thresholds he would never cross. At the Plume of Feathers, Abel Pomeroy would stand out in the roadway and look for incoming guests.

Watchman wondered if his two companions had got there before
him. Perhaps his cousin, Sebastian Parish, had set out on his evening
prowl round the village. Perhaps Norman Cubitt had already found
a subject and was down on the jetty dabbing nervously at a canvas.
This was the second holiday they had spent together in Ottercombe.
A curious trio when you came to think of it. Like the beginning of a
funny story. 'A lawyer, an actor, and a painter once went to a fishing village in Devon.' Well, he'd rather have Cubitt and Parish than
any of his own learned brethren. The law set too dead a seal on character, the very soul of a barrister took silk. And he wondered if he
had failed to escape the mannerisms of his profession, if he exuded
learned counsel, even at Ottercombe in South Devon.

The lane dived abruptly downhill. Watchman remembered
Decima Moore. Would she still be there? Did the Coombe Left
Movement still hold its meetings on Saturday nights, and would
Decima allow her arguments with himself to end as they had ended
that warm night nearly a year ago? He set his thoughts on the memory of the smell of seaweed and briar, and of Decima, trapped half-
way between resentment and fright, walking as if by compulsion
into his arms.

The hamlet of Diddlestock, a brief interlude of whitewash and
thatch, marked the last stage. Already, as he slid out of the shadow
of Ottercombe Woods, he fancied that he heard the thunder of the
sea.

Watchman checked his car, skidded, and changed into low gear.
Somewhere about here Diddlestock Lane crossed Ottercombe Lane,
and the intersection was completely masked by banks and
hedgerows. A dangerous turning. Yes, there it was. He sounded his
horn and the next second crammed on his brakes. The car skidded,
lurched sideways, and fetched up against the bank, with its right-
hand front bumpers locked in the left-hand rear bumpers of a baby
two-seater.

Watchman leant out of the driving window.

'What the hell do you think you're doing?' he yelled.

The two-seater leapt nervously and was jerked back by the
bumpers.

'Stop that!' roared Watchman.

He got out and stumbled along the lane to the other car.

It was so dark down there between the hedgerows that the driver's features, shadowed both by the roof of his car and the brim of his hat, were scarcely discernible. He seemed about to open the door when Watchman, bareheaded, came up to him. Evidently he changed his mind. He leant farther back in his seat. His fingers pulled at the brim of his hat.

'Look here,' Watchman began, 'you're a hell of a fellow, aren't you, bucketing about the countryside like a blasted tank! Why the devil can't you sound your horn? You came out of that lane about twenty times as fast as – What?'

The man had mumbled something.

'What?' Watchman repeated.

'I'm extremely sorry. Didn't hear you until – ' The voice faded away.

'All right. Well, we'd better do something about it. I don't imagine much damage has been done.' The man made no move and Watchman's irritation revived. 'Give me a hand, will you?'

'Yes, certainly. Of course.' The voice was unexpectedly courteous. 'I'm very sorry. Really, very sorry. It was all my fault.'

This display of contrition mollified Watchman.

'Oh well,' he said, 'no harm done, I dare say. Come on.'

The man got out on the far side and walked round to the back of his car. When Watchman joined him he was stooping over the locked bumpers.

'I can heave mine up if you don't mind backing an inch or two,' said the man. With large calloused hands he gripped the bumpers of his own car.

'All right,' agreed Watchman.

They released the bumpers without much trouble. Watchman called through his driving-window: 'All clear!' The man lowered his car and then groped uncertainly in his pockets.

'Cigarette?' suggested Watchman and held out his case.

'Very kind,' said the man. 'Coals of fire – ' He hesitated and then took a cigarette.

'Light?'

'I've got one, thanks.'

He turned aside and cupped his hands round the match, dipping his head with extravagant care as if a wind threatened the flame.

'I suppose you're going to Ottercombe?' said Watchman.

He saw a flash of teeth.

'Looks like it, doesn't it? I'm sorry I can't let you through till then.'

'I shan't be on your heels at the pace you travel,' grinned Watchman.

'No,' agreed the man, and his voice sounded remote as he moved away. 'I'll keep out of your way. Good-night.'

'Good-night.'

That ridiculous little car was as good as its driver's word. It shot away down the lane and vanished over the brow of a steep drop. Watchman followed more cautiously and by the time he rounded the hill the other car had turned a farther corner. He caught the distant toot of a horn. It sounded derisive.

II

The lane ran out towards the coast and straight for Coombe Rock, a headland that rose sharply from the downs to thrust its nose into the channel. A patch on the hillside seemed to mark an inconsequent end to the route. It was only when he drew closer to this patch that a stranger might recognize it as an entrance to a tunnel, the only gate into Ottercombe. Watchman saw it grow magically until it filled his range of vision. He passed a roadsign 'Ottercombe. Dangerous Corner. Change down,' and entered the mouth of the tunnel. He slowed down and switched on his lights. Dank walls closed about him, the sound of his progress echoed loudly and he smelt wet stones and seaweed. Before him, coldly and inkily blue, framed in black, was the sea. From within, the tunnel seemed to end in a shelf; actually it turned sharply to the left. Watchman had to stop and back his car before he could get round. There, down on his left and facing the sea, was Ottercombe.

Probably the alarming entrance into this village has saved it from becoming another Clovelly or Polperro. Ladies with Ye Olde Shoppe ambitions would hesitate to drive through Coombe Tunnel and very large cars are unable to do so. Moreover the village is not too picturesque. It is merely a group of houses whose whitewash is tarnished by the sea. There are no secret stairs in any of them, no ghosts walk Ottercombe Steps, no smugglers' cave looks out from Coombe Rock. For all that, the place has its history of grog-running and wrecking. There is a story of a fight in the tunnel between excisemen and the men of Coombe, and there are traces of the gate that once closed the tunnel every night at sunset. The whole of Ottercombe is the property of an irascible eccentric who keeps the houses in good repair, won't let one of them to a strange shopkeeper and breathes venom on the word 'publicity.' If a stranger cares to stay in Ottercombe he must put up at the Plume of Feathers, where Abel Pomeroy has four guest rooms, and Mrs Ives does the house-keeping and cooking. If the Coombe men like him, they will take him out in their boats and play darts with him in the evening. He may walk round the cliffs, fish off the rocks, or drive seven miles to Illington where there is a golf-course and a three-star hotel. These are the amenities of Ottercombe.

The Plume of Feathers faces the cobbled road of entrance. It is a square building, scrupulously whitewashed. It has no great height but its position gives it an air of dominance over the cottages that surround it. On the corner of the Feathers the road of approach splits and becomes a sort of inn yard off which Ottercombe Steps lead through the village and down to the wharf. Thus the windows of the inn on two sides, watch for the arrival of strangers. By the corner entrance is a bench, occupied on warm evenings by Abel Pomeroy and his cronies. At intervals Abel walks into the middle of the road and looks up towards Coombe Tunnel as his father and grandfather did before him.

As Watchman drove down, he could see old Pomeroy standing there in his shirt sleeves. Watchman flicked his headlights and Pomeroy raised his hand. Watchman sounded his horn and a taller figure, dressed in the slacks and sweater of some superb advertisement, came through the lighted doorway. It was Watchman's cousin, Sebastian Parish. Then the others *had* arrived.

He drew up and opened the door.

'Well, Pomeroy.'

'Well, Mr Watchman, we'm right down glad to see you again. Welcome to you.'

'I'm glad to get here,' said Watchman, shaking hands. 'Hallo, Seb. When did you arrive?'

'This morning, old boy,' answered his cousin. 'We stopped last night at Exeter with Norman's sister.'

'I was at Yeovil,' said Watchman. 'Where is Norman?'

'Painting down by the jetty. The light's gone. He'll be in soon. He's started a portrait of me on Coombe Rock. It's going to be rather wonderful. I'm wearing a red sweater and the sea's behind me. Very virile!'

'Good Lord!' said Watchman cheerfully.

'We'll get your things out for you, sir,' said old Pomeroy. 'Will!'

A tall fox-coloured man came through the doorway. He screwed up his eyes, peered at Watchman, and acknowledged his greeting without much show of enthusiasm.

'Well, Will.'

'Evening, Mr Watchman.'

'Bear a hand, my sonny,' said old Pomeroy.

His son opened the luggage carrier and began to haul out Watchman's suitcases.

'How's the Movement, Will?' asked Watchman. 'Still well on the left?'

'Yes,' said Will shortly. 'It's going ahead. Will these be all?'

'Yes, thanks. I'll take the car round, Seb, and join you in the bar. Is there a sandwich or so anywhere about, Abel?'

'We can do a bit better than that, sir. There's a fine lobster Mrs Ives has put aside, special.'

'By George, you're a host in a million. God bless Mrs Ives.'

Watchman drove round to the garage. It was a converted stable, a dark building that housed the memory of sweating horses rubbed down by stable lads with wisps of straw. When he stopped his engine Watchman heard a rat plop across the rafters. In addition to his own the garage held four cars. There was Norman Cubitt's Austin, a smaller Austin, a Morris and there, demure in the corner, a battered two-seater.

'You again!' said Watchman, staring at it. 'Well I'll be damned!'

He returned to the pub, delighted to hear the familiar ring of his own steps, to smell the tang of the sea and of burning driftwood. As he ran upstairs he heard voices and the unmistakable tuck of a dart in a cork board.

'Double twenty,' said Will Pomeroy, and above the general outcry came a woman's voice.

'Splendid, my dear. We win!'

'So, she *is* here,' thought Watchman as he washed his hands. 'And why, "my dear"? And who wins?'

III

Watchman, with his cousin for company, ate his lobster in the private taproom. There is a parlour at the Feathers but nobody ever uses it. The public and the private taprooms fit into each other like two L's, the first standing sideways on the tip of its short base, the second facing backwards to the left. The bar proper is common to both. It occupies the short leg of the Public, has a counter for each room and faces the short leg of the Private. The top of the long leg forms a magnificent ingle-nook flanked with settles and scented with three hundred years of driftwood smoke. Opposite the ingle-nook at the bottom angle of the L hangs a dart board made by Abel Pomeroy himself. There, winter and summer alike, the Pomeroys' chosen friends play for drinks. There is a board in the Public for the rank and file. If strangers to the Feathers choose to play in the Private, the initiates wait until they have finished. If the initiates invite a stranger to play, he is no longer a stranger.

The midsummer evening was chilly and a fire smouldered in the ingle-nook. Watchman finished his supper, swung his legs up on the settle, and felt for his pipe. He squinted up at Sebastian Parish, who leant against the mantelpiece in an attitude familiar to every West End playgoer in London.

'I like this place,' Watchman said. 'Extraordinarily pleasant, isn't it, returning to a place one likes?'

Parish made an actor's expressive gesture.

'Marvellous!' he said richly. 'To get away from everything! The noise! The endless racket! The artificiality! God, how I loathe my profession!'

'Come off it, Seb,' said Watchman. 'You glory in it. You were born acting. The gamp probably burst into an involuntary round of applause on your first entrance and I bet you played your mother right off the stage.'

'All the same, old boy, this good clean air means a hell of a lot to me.'

'Exactly,' agreed Watchman dryly. His cousin had a trick of saying things that sounded a little like quotations from an interview with himself. Watchman was amused rather than irritated by this mannerism. It was part and parcel, he thought, of Seb's harmless staginess, like his clothes which were too exactly what a gentleman, roughing it in South Devon, ought to wear. He liked to watch Seb standing out on Coombe Rock, bareheaded to the breeze, in effect waiting for the camera man to say 'OK for sound.' No doubt that was the pose Norman had chosen for his portrait of Sebastian. It occurred to him now that Sebastian was up to something. That speech about the artificiality of the stage was the introduction to a confidence, or Watchman didn't know his Parish. Whatever it was, Sebastian missed his moment. The door opened and a thin man with untidy fair hair looked in.

'Hallo!' said Watchman. 'Our distinguished artist.' Norman Cubitt grinned, lowered his painter's pack, and came into the ingle-nook.

'Well, Luke? Good trip?'

'Splendid! You're painting already?' Cubitt stretched a hand to the fire. The fingers were grimed with paint.

'I'm doing a thing of Seb,' he said. 'I suppose he's told you about it. Laying it on with a trowel, I am. That's in the morning. Tonight I started a thing down by the jetty. They're patching up one of the posts. Very pleasant subject, but my treatment of it so far is bloody.'

'Are you painting in the dark?' asked Watchman with a smile.

'I was talking to one of the fishing blokes after the light went. They've gone all politically-minded in the Coombe.'

'That,' said Parish, lowering his voice, 'is Will Pomeroy and his Left Group.'

'Will and Decima together,' said Cubitt. 'I've suggested they call themselves the Decimbrists.'

'Where are the lads of the village?' demanded Watchman. 'I thought I heard the dart game in progress as I went upstairs.'

'Abel's rat-poisoning in the garage,' said Parish. 'They've all gone out to see he doesn't give himself a lethal dose of prussic acid.'

'Good Lord!' Watchman ejaculated. 'Is the old fool playing around with cyanide?'

'Apparently. Why wouldn't we have a drink?'

'Why not indeed?' agreed Cubitt. 'Hi, Will!'

He went to the bar and leant over it, looking into the Public.

'The whole damn place is deserted. I'll get our drinks and chalk them up. Beer?'

'Beer it is,' said Parish.

'What form of cyanide has Abel got hold of?' Watchman asked.

'Eh?' said Parish vaguely. 'Oh, let's see now. I fetched it for him from Illington. The chemist hadn't got any of the stock rat-banes, but he poked round and found this stuff. I think he called it Scheele's acid.'

'Good, God!'

'What? Yes, that was it – Scheele's acid. And then he said he thought the fumes of Scheele's acid mightn't be strong enough, so he gingered it up a bit.'

'With what, in the name of all the Borgias?'

'Well – with prussic acid, I imagine.'

'You imagine! You imagine!'

'He said that was what it was. He said it was acid or something. I wouldn't know. He warned me in sixteen different positions to be careful. Suggested Abel wore a half-crown gas mask, so I bought it in case Abel hadn't got one. Abel's using gloves and everything.'

'It's absolutely monstrous!'

'I had to sign for it, old boy,' said Parish. 'Very solemn we were. God, he was a stupid man! Bone from the eyes up, but so, so kind.'

Watchman said angrily, 'I should damn well think he was stupid. Do you know that twenty-five drops of Scheele's acid will kill a man in a few minutes? Why, good Lord, in Rex v. Bull, if I'm not mistaken, it was alleged that accused gave only seven drops. I myself defended a medical student who gave twenty minims in error. Charge of manslaughter. I got him off but – how's Abel using it?'

'What's all this?' inquired Cubitt. 'There's your beer.'

'Abel said he was going to put it in a pot and shove it in a rathole,' explained Parish. 'I think he's filled with due respect for its deadliness, Luke, really. He's going to block the hole up and every-thing.'

'The chemist had no business to give you Scheele's, much less this infernal brew. He ought to be struck off the books. The pharmacopœial preparation would have been quite strong enough. He could have diluted even that to advantage.'

'Well, God bless us,' said Cubitt hastily, and took a pull at his beer.

'What happens, actually, when someone's poisoned by prussic acid?' asked Parish.

'Convulsion, clammy sweat, and death.'

'Shut up!' said Cubitt. 'What a filthy conversation!'

'Well – cheers, dear,' said Parish, raising his tankard.

'You do get hold of the most repellent idioms, Seb,' said his cousin. '*Te saluto.*'

'But not *moriturus,* I trust,' added Parish. 'With all this chat about prussic acid! What's it look like?'

'You bought it.'

'I didn't notice. It's a blue bottle.'

'Hydrocyanic acid,' said Watchman with his barrister's precision, 'is, in appearance, exactly like water. It is a liquid miscible with water and this stuff is a dilution of hydrocyanic acid.'

'The chemist,' said Parish, 'put a terrific notice on it. I remember I once had to play a man who'd taken cyanide. "Fool's Errand," the piece was; a revival with whiskers on it, but not a bad old drama. I died in a few seconds.'

'For once the dramatist was right,' said Watchman. 'It's one of the sudden poisons. Horrible stuff! I've got cause to know it. I was once briefed in a case where a woman took – '

'For God's sake,' interrupted Norman Cubitt violently, 'Shut up, both of you, I've got a poison phobia.'

'Have you really, Norman?' asked Parish. 'That's very interesting. Can you trace it?'

'I think so.' Cubitt rubbed his hair and then looked absent-mindedly at his paint-grimed hand. 'As a matter of fact, my dear Seb,' he said, with his air of secretly mocking at himself, 'you have named the root and cause of my affection. You have perpetrated a coincidence, Sebastian. The very play you mentioned just now, started me off on my Freudian road to the jim-jams. "Fool's Errand," and well named. It is, as you say, a remarkably naïve play. At the age of seven, however, I did not think so. I found it terrifying.'

'At the age of seven?'

'Yes. My eldest brother, poor fool, fancied himself as an amateur and essayed the principal part. I was bullied into enacting the small boy who, as I remember, perpetually bleated: "Papa, why is mamma so pale" and later on: "Papa, why is mamma so quiet? Where has she gone, papa?"'

'We cut all that in the revival,' said Parish. 'It was terrible stuff.'

'I agree with you. As you remember, papa had poisoned mamma. For years afterwards I had the horrors at the very word. I remember that I used to wipe all the schoolroom china for fear our Miss Tobin was a Borgian governess. I invented all sorts of curious devices in order that Miss Tobin should drink my morning cocoa and I hers. Odd, wasn't it? I grew out of it but I still dislike the sound of the word and I detest taking medicine labelled in accordance with the Pure Food Act.'

'Labelled what?' asked Parish with a wink at Watchman.

'Labelled poison, damn you,' said Cubitt.

Watchman looked curiously at him.

'I suppose there's something in this psycho-stuff,' he said. 'But I always rather boggle at it.'

'I don't see why you should,' said Parish. 'You yourself get a fit of the staggers if you scratch your finger. You told me once, you fainted when you had a blood test. That's a phobia, same as Norman's.'

'Not quite,' said Watchman. 'Lots of people can't stand the sight of their own blood. This poison scare's much more unusual. But you don't mean to tell me, do you, Norman, that because at an early age you helped your brother in a play about cyanide you'd feel definitely uncomfortable if I finished my story?'

Cubitt drained his tankard and set it down on the table.

'If you're hell-bent on your beastly story –' he said.

'It was only that I was present at the autopsy on this woman who died of cyanide poisoning. When they opened her up, I fainted. Not from emotion but from the fumes. The pathologist said I had a pronounced idiosyncrasy for the stuff. I was damned ill after it. It nearly did for me.'

Cubitt wandered over to the door and lifted his pack.

'I'll clean up,' he said, 'and join you for the dart game.'

'Splendid, old boy,' said Parish. 'We'll beat them tonight.'

'Do our damnedst anyway,' said Cubitt. At the doorway he turned and looked mournfully at Parish.

'She's asking about perspective,' he said.

'Give her rat-poison,' said Parish.

'Shut up,' said Cubitt and went out.

'What was he talking about?' demanded Watchman.

Parish smiled. 'He's got a girl-friend. Wait till you see. Funny chap! He went quite green over your story. Sensitive old beggar, isn't he?'

'Oh yes,' agreed Watchman lightly. 'I must say I'm sensitive in a rather different key where cyanide's concerned, having been nearly killed by it.'

'I don't know you could have a – what did you call it?'

'An idiosyncrasy?'

'It means you'd go under to a very small amount?'

'It does.' Watchman yawned and stretched himself full length on the settle.

'I'm sleepy,' he said. 'It's the sea air. A very pleasant state of being. Just tired enough, with the impressions of a long drive still floating about behind one's consciousness. Flying hedges, stretches of road that stream out before one's eyes. The relaxation of arrival setting in. Very pleasant!'

He closed his eyes for a moment and then turned his head to look at his cousin.

'So Decima Moore is still here,' he said.

Parish smiled. 'Very much so. But you'll have to watch your step, Luke.'

'Why?'

'There's an engagement in the offing.'

'What d'you mean?'

'Decima and Will Pomeroy.'

Watchman sat up.

'I don't believe you,' he said sharply.

'Well – why not?'

'Good Lord! A politically minded pot-boy.'

'Actually they're the same class,' Parish murmured.

'Perhaps; but she's not of it.'

'All the same – '

Watchman grimaced.

'She's a little fool,' he said, 'but you may be right,' and lay back again. 'Oh well!' he added comfortably.

There was a moment's silence.

'There's another female here,' said Parish, and grinned.

'Another? Who?'

'Norman's girl-friend of course. My oath!'

'Why? What's she like? Why are you grinning away like a Cheshire cat, Seb?'

'My dear soul,' said Parish, 'if I could get that woman to walk on the boards every evening and do her stuff exactly as she does it here – well, of course! I'd go into management and die a millionaire.'

'Who is she?'

'She's the Honourable Violet Darragh. She waters.'

'She *what?*'

'She does water-colours. Wait till you hear Norman on Violet.'

'Is she a nuisance?' asked Watchman apprehensively.

'Not exactly. Well, in a way. Pure joy to me. Wait till you meet her.'

Parish would say no more about Miss Darragh, and Watchman, only mildly interested, relapsed into a pleasant doze.

'By the way,' he said presently, 'some driving expert nearly dashed himself to extinction against my bonnet.'

'Really?'

'Yes. At Diddlestock Corner. Came bucketing out of the blind turning on my right, beat me by a split second, and hung his silly little stern on my front bumpers. Ass!'

'Any damage?'

'No, no. He heaved his pygmy up by the bottom and I backed away. Funny sort of fellow he is.'

'You knew him?' asked Parish in surprise.

'No.' Watchman took the tip of his nose between thumb and forefinger. It was a gesture he used in cross-examination. 'No, I don't know him, and yet – there was something – I got the impression that *he* didn't want to know *me*. Quite an educated voice. Labourer's hands. False teeth, I rather fancy.'

'You're very observant,' said Parish, lightly.

'No more than the next man, but there was something about the fellow. I was going to ask if you knew him. His car's in the garage.'

'Surely it's not – hallo, here are others.'

Boots and voices sounded in the public bar. Will Pomeroy came through and leant over the counter. He looked, not toward Watchman or Parish, but into a settle on the far side of the Private, a settle whose high back was towards them.

' 'Evening, Bob,' said Will cordially. 'Kept you waiting?'

'That's all right, Will,' said a voice from beyond the settle. 'I'll have a pint of bitter when you're ready.'

Luke Watchman uttered a stifled exclamation.

'What's up? asked his cousin.

'Come here.'

Parish strolled nearer to him and, in obedience to a movement of Watchman's head, stooped towards him.

'What's up?' he repeated.

'That's the same fellow,' muttered Watchman, 'he must have been here all the time. That's his voice.'

'Hell!' said Parish delightedly.

'D'you think he heard?'

'Of course he heard.'

'Blast the creature! Serves him right.'

'Shut up.'

The door into the private bar opened. Old Abel came in followed by Norman Cubitt. Cubitt took three darts from a collection in a pewter pot on the bar and moved in front of the dart board.

'I'll be there in a moment,' said a woman's voice from the passage. 'Don't start without me.'

Abel walked into the ingle-nook and put a bottle on the mantelpiece.

'Well, souls,' he said, 'reckon we'm settled the hash of they vermin. If thurr's not a corpse on the premises afore long, I'll be greatly astonished.'

CHAPTER 2

Advance by Watchman

The bottle was a small one and as Sebastian Parish had remarked it was conspicuously labelled. The word 'POISON' in scarlet on a white ground ran diagonally across on an attached label. It struck a note of interjection and alarm and focused the attention of the five men. Few who read that warning escape a sudden jolt of the imagination.

Parish said, 'Mr Watchman thinks you are a public danger, Abel. He's afraid we'll all be poisoned.'

'I'm afraid he'll poison himself,' said Watchman.

'Who, sir? Me?' asked Abel. 'Not a bit of it. I be mortal cautious sort of chap when it comes to this manner of murderous tipple, Mr Watchman.'

'I hope you are,' said Cubitt from the dart board.

'You're not going to leave it on the mantelshelf, father?' asked Will.

'No fear of that, sonny. I'll stow it away careful.'

'You'd much better get rid of it altogether,' said Watchman. 'Don't put it away somewhere. You'll forget all about it and some day someone will take a sniff at it to find out what it is. Let me take it back to the chemist at Illington. I'd very much like to have a word with that gentleman.'

'Lord love you,' said Abel, opening his eyes very wide, 'us've not finished with they bowldacious varmints yet, my sonnies. If so be they've got a squeak left in 'em us'll give 'em another powerful whiff and finish 'em off.'

'At least,' said Cubitt, throwing a dart into double-twenty, 'at least you might put it out of reach.'

'Mr Cubitt has a poison-phobia,' said Watchman.

'A what, sir?'

'Never mind about that,' said Cubitt. 'I should have thought anybody might boggle at prussic acid.'

'Don't fret yourselves, gentlemen,' said Abel. 'Thurr'll be none of this brew served out at the Feathers Tap.'

He mounted the settle and taking the bottle from the mantelpiece pushed it into the top shelf of a double cupboard in the corner of the ingle-nook. He then pulled off the old gloves he wore, threw them on the fire, and turned the key.

'Nobody can call me a careless man,' he said. 'I'm all for looking after myself. Thurr's my first-aid box in thurr, ready to hand, and if any of the chaps cuts themselves with a mucky fish-knife or any other infectious trifle of that sort, they gets a swill of iodine in scratch. Makes 'em squirm a bit and none the worse for that. I learnt that in the war, my sonnies. I was a surgeon's orderly and I know the mighty powers thurr be in drugs.'

He stared at the glass door. The label 'POISON' still showed, slightly distorted, in the darkness of the little cupboard.

'Safe enough thurr,' said Abel and went over to the bar.

With the arrival of the Pomeroys the private bar took on its customary aspect for a summer's evening. They both went behind the counters. Abel sat facing the Private and on Cubitt's order drew pints of draught beer for the company. A game of darts was started in the Public.

The man in the settle had not moved, but now Watchman saw his hand reach out for his pint. He saw the callouses, the chipped nails, the coarsened joints of the fingers. Watchman got up, stretched himself, grimaced at Parish, and crossed the room to the settle.

The light shone full in the face of the stranger. The skin of his face was brown, but Watchman thought it had only recently acquired this colour. His hair stood up in white bristles, his forehead was garnished with bumps that shone in the lamplight. The eyes under the bleached lashes seemed almost without colour. From the nostrils to the corners of the mouth ran grooves that lent emphasis to the fall of the lips. Without raising his head the man looked up at

Watchman, and the shadow of a smile seemed to visit his face. He got up and made as if to go to the door, but Watchman stopped him.

'May I introduce myself?' asked Watchman.

The man smiled more broadly. 'They *are* false teeth,' thought Watchman, and he added: 'We have met already this evening, but we didn't exchange names. Mine is Luke Watchman.'

'I gathered as much from your conversation,' said the man. He paused for a moment and then said: 'Mine is Legge.'

'I'm afraid I sounded uncivil,' said Watchman. 'I hope you'll allow me a little motorists' licence. One always abuses the other man, doesn't one?'

'You'd every excuse,' mumbled Legge, 'every excuse.' He scarcely moved his lips. His teeth seemed too large for his mouth. He looked sideways at Watchman, picked up a magazine from the settle, and flipped it open, holding it before his face.

Watchman felt vaguely irritated. He had struck no sort of response from the man and he was not accustomed to falling flat. Obviously, Legge merely wished to be rid of him and this state of affairs piqued Watchman's vanity. He sat on the edge of the table, and for the second time that evening offered his cigarette-case to Legge.

'No thanks – pipe.'

'I'd no idea I should find you here,' said Watchman, and noticed uncomfortably that his own voice sounded disproportionately cordial, 'although you did tell me you were bound for Ottercombe. It's a good pub, isn't it?'

'Yes, yes,' said Legge hurriedly. 'Very good.'

'Are you making a long visit?'

'I live here,' said Legge.

He pulled out his pipe and began to fill it. His fingers moved clumsily and he had an air of rather ridiculous concentration. Watchman felt marooned on the edge of the table. He saw that Parish was listening with a maddening grin, and he fancied that Cubitt's ears were cocked. 'Damn it,' he thought, 'I will not be put out of countenance by the brute. He *shall* like me.' But he could think of nothing to say and Mr Legge had begun to read his magazine.

From beyond the bar came the sound of raucous applause. Someone yelled: 'Double seventeen and we'm beat the Bakery.'

Norman Cubitt pulled out his darts and paused for a moment. He looked from Watchman to Parish. It struck him that there was a strong family resemblance between these cousins, a resemblance of character rather than physique. Each in his way, thought Cubitt, was a vain man. In Parish one recognized the ingenuous vanity of the actor. Off the stage he wooed applause with only less assiduity than he commanded it when he faced an audience. Watchman was more subtle. Watchman must have the attention and respect of every new acquaintance, but he played for it without seeming to do so. He would take endless trouble with a complete stranger when he seemed to take none. 'But he's getting no change out of Legge,' thought Cubitt maliciously. And with a faint smile he turned back to the dart board.

Watchman saw the smile. He took a pull at his tankard and tried again.

'Are you one of the dart experts?' he asked. Legge looked up vaguely and Watchman had to repeat his question.

'I play a little,' said Legge.

Cubitt hurled his last dart at the board and joined the others.

'He plays like the devil himself,' he said. 'Last night I took him on, 101 down. I never even started. He threw fifty, one, and the fifty again.'

'I was fortunate that time,' said Mr Legge with rather more animation.

'Not a bit of it,' said Cubitt. 'You're merely odiously accurate.'

'Well,' said Watchman, 'I'll lay you ten bob you can't do it again, Mr Legge.'

'You've lost,' said Cubitt.

'Aye, he's a proper masterpiece is Mr Legge,' said old Abel.

Sebastian Parish came across from the ingle-nook. He looked down good-humouredly at Legge. 'Nobody,' thought Cubitt, 'has any right to be as good-looking as Seb.'

'What's all this?' asked Parish.

'I've offered to bet Mr Legge ten bob he can't throw fifty, one, and fifty.'

'You've lost,' said Parish.

'This is monstrous,' cried Watchman. 'Do you take me, Mr Legge?'

Legge shot a glance at him. The voices of the players beyond the partition had quietened for the moment. Will Pomeroy had joined his father at the private bar. Cubitt and Parish and the two Pomeroys waited in silence for Legge's reply. He made a curious grimace, pursing his lips and screwing up his eyes. As if in reply, Watchman used that KC's trick of his and took the tip of his nose between thumb and forefinger. Cubitt, who watched them curiously, was visited by the fantastic notion that some sort of signal had passed between them.

Legge rose slowly to his feet.

'Oh yes,' he said. 'Certainly, Mr Watchman. I take you on.'

II

Legge moved, with a slovenly dragging of his boots, into a position in front of the board. He pulled out the three darts and looked at them.

'Getting a bit worn, Mr Pomeroy,' said Legge. 'The rings are loose.'

'I've sent for a new set,' said Abel. 'They'll be here tomorrow. Old lot can go into Public.'

Will Pomeroy left the public bar and joined his father. 'Showing 'em how to do it, Bob?' he asked.

'There's a bet on, sonny,' said old Pomeroy.

'Don't make me nervous, Will,' said Legge, with a grin.

He looked at the board, poised his first dart and, with a crisp movement of his hand flung it into the bullseye.

'Fifty,' said Will. 'There you are, gentlemen! Fifty!'

'Three-and-fourpence in pawn,' said Watchman.

'We'll put it into the CLM. if it comes off, Will,' said Legge.

'What's the CLM?' demanded Watchman.

Will stared straight in front of him and said, 'The Coombe Left Movement, Mr Watchman. We're a branch of the South Devon Left, now.'

'Oh Lord!' said Watchman.

Legge threw his second dart. It seemed almost to drop from his hand, but he must have used a certain amount of force since it went home solidly into the top right-hand division.

'And the one. Six-and-eight pence looking a bit off colour, Mr Watchman,' said Abel Pomeroy.

'He's stymied himself for the other double twenty-five, though,' said Watchman. 'The first dart's lying right across it.'

Legge raised his hand and, this time, took more deliberate aim. He threw from a greater height. For a fraction of a second the dart seemed to hang in his fingers before it sped downwards, athwart the first, into the narrow strip round the centre.

'And fifty it is!' said Will. 'There you are. Fifty. Good for you, comrade.'

A little chorus went up from Parish, Cubitt and old Abel.

'That man's a wizard.'

'Shouldn't be allowed!'

'You'm a proper masterpiece.'

'Well done, Bob,' added Will, as if determined to give the last word of praise.

Watchman laid a ten-shilling note on the table.

'I congratulate you,' he said.

Legge looked at the note.

'Thank you, Mr Watchman,' he said. 'Another ten bob for the fighting fund, Will.'

'Good enough, but it's straightout generous to give it.'

Watchman sat down again on the table-edge.

'All very nice,' he said. 'Does you credit, Mr Legge. I rather think another drink's indicated. With me, if you please. Loser's privilege.'

Will Pomeroy glanced uncomfortably at Legge. By Feathers etiquette, the winner of a bet at darts pays for the next round. There was a short silence broken by old Pomeroy who insisted that the next round should be on the house, and served the company with a potent dark ale, known to the Coombe as Treble Extra.

'We'll all play like Mr Legge with this inside us,' said Parish.

'Yes,' agreed Watchman, looking into his tankard, 'it's a fighting fund in itself. A very pretty tipple indeed.' He looked up at Legge.

'Do you know any other tricks like that one, Mr Legge?'

'I know a prettier one than that,' said Legge quietly, 'if you'll assist me.'

'I assist you?'

'Yes. If you'll stretch your hand out flat on the board I'll outline it with darts.'

'Really? You ought to be in the sawdust ring. No I don't think I trust you enough for that, you know. One would need a little more of Mr Pomeroy's Treble Extra.'

He stretched out his hand and looked at it.

'And yet, I don't know,' he said. 'I'd like to see you do it. Some other time. You know, Mr Legge, as a good Conservative, I feel I should deplore your gesture. Against whom is your fighting fund directed?'

But before Legge could speak, Will answered quickly, 'Against the capitalist, Mr Watchman, and all his side.'

'Really? So Mr Legge is also an ardent proletarian fan?'

'Secretary and treasurer for the Coombe Left Movement.'

'Secretary *and* treasurer,' repeated Watchman. 'Responsible jobs, aren't they?'

'Aye,' said Will, 'and it's a responsible chap that's taken 'em on for us.'

Legge turned away and moved into the ingle-nook. Watchman looked after him. Cubitt noticed that Watchman's good humour seemed to be restored. Any one would have thought that he had won the bet and that it had been for a much larger sum. And for no reason in the world Cubitt felt that there had been a passage of arms between Legge and Watchman, and that Watchman had scored a hit.

'What about you, Abel?' Watchman asked abruptly. 'Are you going to paint the Feathers red?'

'Me sir? No. I don't hold with Will's revolutionary ideas and he knows it, but us've agreed to differ. Does no harm, I reckon, for these young chaps to meet every Friday and make believe they're hashing up the laws and serving 'em out topsy-turvy – game in servants' hall and prunes and rice for gentry. Our Will was always a great hand for make-believe from the time he learned to talk. Used to strut about taproom giving orders to the furniture. "I be as good as Squire, now," he'd say in his little lad's voice and I reckon he's saying it yet.'

'You're blind to reason, father,' said Will. 'Blind-stupid and hidebound. Either you can't see or you won't. Us chaps are working for the good of all, not for ourselves.'

'Right enough, sonny. A fine noble ideal, I don't doubt, and when you've got us all toeing the line with no handicaps and nothing to run for – '

'The good of the State to run for. Each man equal – '

'And all coming in first. Damn' queer sort of race.'

'The old argument,' said Legge from the fireplace, 'and based as usual on a false analogy.'

'Is it a false analogy?' asked Watchman. 'You propose to kill private enterprise – '

'A chap,' said Will Pomeroy, 'will be as ambitious for the public good as he will for his own selfish aims. Give him the chance – that's all. Teach him to think. The people – '

'The people!' interrupted Watchman, looking at Legge's back. 'What do you mean by the people? I suppose you mean that vast collection of individuals whose wages are below a certain sum and who are capable of being led by the nose when the right sort of humbug comes along.'

'That's no argument,' began Will angrily. 'That's no more than a string of silly opinions.'

'That'll do, sonny,' said Abel.

'It's all right, Abel,' said Watchman, still looking at Legge. 'I invited the discussion. No offence, I should like to hear what Mr Legge has to say about private enterprise. As treasurer – '

'Wait a bit, Bob,' said Will as Legge turned from the fireplace. 'I don't like the way you said that, Mr Watchman. Bob Legge here is well-respected in the Coombe. He's not been long in these parts, ten months isn't it, Bob? But we've learned to know him and we've learned to like him. Reckon we've showed we trust him, too, seeing the position we've given him.'

'My dear Will,' said Watchman delicately, 'I don't dispute it for a moment. I think Mr Legge has done remarkably well for himself, in ten months.'

Will's face was scarlet under his thatch of fox-coloured hair. He moved forward and confronted Watchman, his tankard clenched in a great ham of a fist, his feet planted apart.

'Shut up, now, Luke,' said Sebastian Parish softly, and Cubitt murmured, 'don't heckle, Luke, you're on a holiday.'

'See here, Mr Watchman,' said Will, 'you can afford to sneer, can't you, but I'd like to know – '

'Will!' Old Abel slapped the bar with an open hand. 'That's enough. You'm a grown chap, not a lad, and what's more, the son of this house. Seems like I ought to give'ee light draught and lemonade till you learn to take a man's pint like a man. If you can't talk politics and hold your temper then you'll not talk politics at all. 'Be a job for you in Public here. 'Tend it.'

'I'm sorry, Will,' said Watchman. 'Mr Legge is fortunate in his friend.'

Will Pomeroy stood and looked under his brows from Watchman to Legge. Legge shrugged his shoulders, muttered something about moving into the public bar, and went out. Will turned on Watchman.

'There's something behind all this,' he said. 'I want to know what the game is, Mr Watchman, and damme, I'm going to find out.'

'Did I hear something about a game?' said a woman's voice. They all turned to look at the doorway. There they saw a short fat figure clad in a purple tweed skirt and a green jersey.

'May I come in?' asked the Hon. Violet Darragh.

III

Miss Darragh's entrance broke up the scene. Will Pomeroy turned, ducked under the flap of the private bar, and leant over the counter into the Public. Watchman stood up. The others turned to Miss Darragh with an air of relief, and Abel Pomeroy, with his innkeeper's heartiness, intensified perhaps by a feeling of genuine relief, said loudly, 'Come in then, Miss, company's waiting for you and you'm in time for a drink, with the house.'

'Not Treble Extra, Mr Pomeroy, if you don't mind. Sherry for me, if you please.'

She waddled over to the bar, placed her hands on the counter, and with an agility that astonished Watchman, made a neat little vault on to one of the tall stools. There she sat beaming upon the company.

She was a woman of perhaps fifty, but it would have been difficult to guess at her age since time had added to her countenance and figure merely layer after layer of firm wholesome fat. She was roundabout and compact. Her face was babyish, and this impression was heightened by the tight grey curls that covered her head. In repose she seemed to pout, and it was not until she spoke that her good humour appeared in her eyes, and was magnified by her spectacles. All fat people wear a look of inscrutability, and Violet Darragh was not unlike a jolly sort of sphinx.

Abel served her and she took the glass delicately in her small white paws.

'Well, now,' she said, 'is everybody having fun?' and then caught sight of Watchman. 'Is this your cousin, Mr Parish?'

'I'm sorry,' said Parish hurriedly. 'Mr Watchman, Miss Darragh.'

'How d'ye do?' said Miss Darragh.

Like many Irishwomen of her class she spoke with such a marked brogue that one wondered whether it was inspired by a kind of jocularity that had turned into a habit.

'I've heard about you, of course, and read about you in the papers, for I dearly love a good murder and if I can't have me murder I'm all for arson. That was a fine murder case you defended last year, now, Mr Watchman. Before you took silk, 'twas you did your best for the poor scoundrel.'

Watchman expanded.

'I didn't get him off, Miss Darragh.'

'Ah well, and a good job you didn't, for we'd none of us have been safe in our beds. And there's Mr Cubitt come from his painting down by the jetty, in mortal terror, poor man, lest I plague him with me perspective.'

'Not at all,' said Cubitt, turning rather pink.

'I'll leave you alone now. I know very well I'm a trouble to you, but it's good for your character, and you may look upon me as a kind of holiday penance.'

'You're a painter too, Miss Darragh?' said Watchman.

'I'm a raw amateur, Mr Watchman, but I've a kind of itch for ut. When I see a little peep I can't rest till I'm at ut with me paints. There's Mr Cubitt wincing as if he had a nagging tooth, when I talk of a pretty peep. You've a distinguished company in your house, Mr Pomeroy,' continued Miss Darragh. 'I thought I was coming to a quiet little village, and what do I find but a galaxy of the talents. Mr

Parish who's turned me heart over many a time with his acting; Mr Cubitt, down there painting within stone's throw of meself, and now haven't we the great counsel to add to our intellectual feast. I wonder now, Mr Watchman, if you remember me poor cousin Bryonie's case?'

'I – yes,' said Watchman, greatly disconcerted. 'I – I defended Lord Bryonie. Yes.'

'And didn't he only get the mere eighteen months due entirely to your eloquence? Ah, he's dead now, poor fellow. Only a shadow of himself, he was when he came out. It was a terrible shock to 'um.'

'Undoubtedly.'

' 'Twas indeed. He never had many brains, poor fellow, and it was an unlucky day for the family when he took it into his head to dabble in business. Where's Miss Moor? I thought I heard you speak of a game of darts.'

'She's coming,' said Cubitt.

'And I hope you'll all play again for I found it a great entertainment. Are you a dart player too, Mr Watchman?'

'I try,' said Watchman.

Footsteps sounded on the stairs.

'Here is Decima,' said Cubitt.

IV

A tall young woman came into the room and stood, very much at her ease, screwing her eyes up a little in the glare of the lights.

'I'm so sorry if I've kept you waiting,' said Decima Moor. 'Good-evening, every one.'

They all greeted her. There was a second's pause and then Watchman moved into the centre of the room.

'Good-evening,' said Watchman.

She faced him and met his gaze.

'So you have arrived,' she said. 'Good-evening.'

She touched his outstretched hand, walked over to the bar, and settled herself on one of the tall stools. She wore a fisherman's jersey and dark blue slacks. Her hair was cut like a poet's of the romantic period and was moulded in short locks about her head and face.

She was good-looking with a classic regularity of beauty that was given an individual quirk by the blackness of her brows and the singular intensity of her eyes. She moved with the kind of grace that only just escapes angularity. She was twenty-four years of age.

If an observant stranger had been at the Feathers that evening, he might have noticed that on Decima's entrance the demeanour of most of the men changed. For Decima owned that quality which Hollywood has loudly defined for the world. She owned a measure of attraction over which she herself had little governance. Though she must have been aware of this, she seemed unaware, and neither in her manner nor in her speech did she appear to exercise conscious charm. Yet from the moment of her entrance the men when they spoke to each other, looked at her, and in each of them was the disturbance of Decima's attraction reflected. Watchman's eyes brightened, he became more alert, and he spoke a little louder. Parish expanded as if in a spotlight and he exuded gallantry. Cubitt's air of vague amiability contracted to a sharp awareness. Abel Pomeroy beamed upon Decima. Will, still flushed from his passage with Watchman, turned a deeper red. He answered her greeting awkwardly and was very much the solemn and self-conscious rustic.

Decima took a cigarette from Parish and looked round the taproom.

'Has the dart game begun?' she asked.

'We're waiting for you, my angel,' said Parish. 'What have you been doing with yourself all this time?'

'Washing. I've attended a poison party. I hope you didn't spill prussic acid about the garage, you two Pomeroys.'

'You're not 'feared, too, are you Miss Dessy?' asked Abel. 'A fine, bold, learned, female like you.'

Decima laughed.

'A revolting picture,' she said. 'What do you think Will?'

She leant across the bar and looked beyond Abel into the Public. Will's back was towards her. He turned and faced Decima. His eyes devoured her, but he said nothing. Decima raised her tankard and drank to him. He returned the gesture clumsily, and Cubitt saw Watchman's eyebrows go up.

'Well,' said Decima suddenly, 'what have you all been talking about? You're very silent now, I must say.'

Before any of the others could reply, Watchman said: 'We've been arguing, my dear.'

'Arguing?' She still looked at Will. Watchman drained his tankard, moved up to the bar, and sat on the stool next hers.

'Yes,' he said. 'Until Miss Darragh came in we did nothing else.'

'And why should I stop you?' asked Miss Darragh. She slipped neatly off her high stool and toddled into the ingle-nook. 'I've a passion for argument. What was it about, now? Art? Politics? Love?'

'It was about politics,' said Watchman, still looking at Decima. 'The State, the People, and – private enterprise.'

'You?' Decima said. 'But you're hopeless. When our way of things comes round, you'll be one of our major problems.'

'Really? Won't you need any barristers?'

'I wish I could say no,' said Decima.

Watchman laughed.

'At least,' he said, 'I may hold a watching brief for you.'

She didn't answer and he insisted: 'Mayn't I?'

'You're talking nonsense,' said Decima.

'Well,' said Parish suddenly, 'how about a Round-the-Clock contest to enliven the proceedings?'

'Why not, indeed?' murmured Cubitt.

'Will you play?' Watchman asked Decima.

'Of course. Let's all play. Coming, Will?'

But Will Pomeroy jerked his head towards the public taproom where two or three new-comers noisily demanded drinks.

'Will you play, Miss Darragh?' asked Decima.

'I will not, thank you my dear. I've no eye at all for sport. When I was a child, didn't I half-blind me brother Terence with an apple intended to strike me brother Brian? I'd do you some mischief were I to try. Moreover, I'm too fat. I'll sit and watch the fun.'

Cubitt, Parish and Decima Moore stood in front of the dart-board. Watchman walked into the ingle-nook. From the moment when Will Pomeroy had taken up cudgels for him against Watchman, Legge had faded out. He had taken his drink, his pipe, and his thoughts, whatever they might be, into the public bar.

Presently a burst of applause broke out, and Will Pomeroy shouted that Legge was a wizard and invited Decima and Cubitt to look at what he had done. The others followed, peered into the public bar.

A colossal red-faced man stood with his hand against the public dart-board. His fingers were spread out, and in the gaps between darts were embedded, with others outside the thumb and the little finger.

'Look at that!' cried Will. 'Look at it!'

'Ah,' said Watchman. 'So Mr Legge has found another victim. A great many people seem to have faith in Mr Legge.'

There was a sudden silence. Watchman leant over the private bar and raised his voice.

'We are going to have a match,' he said. 'Three-a-side. Mr Legge, will you join us?'

Legge took his pipe out of his mouth and said, 'What's the game?'

'Darts. Round-the-Clock.'

'Round-the-Clock?'

'Yes. Haven't you played that version?'

'A long time ago. I've forgotten – '

'You have to get one dart in each segment in numerical sequence, ending on a double,' explained Cubitt.

'In fact,' said Watchman very pleasantly, 'you might call it "Doing Time." Haven't you ever done time, Mr Legge?'

'No,' said Legge, 'But I'll take you on. I'll be there in a minute.'

'Right. And if you beat me at this I'm damned if tomorrow night I don't let you take a pot at my hand.'

'Thank you,' said Legge. 'I'll remember.'

CHAPTER 3

Further Advance by Watchman

'The chief fault in Luke,' said Sebastian Parish, 'is that he is quite incapable of letting well alone.'

Norman Cubitt tilted his hat over his eyes, peered from Parish to his canvas, and began to scuffle among his tubes of paint. He uttered a short grunt.

'More than that,' added Parish, 'he glories in making bad a good deal worse. Do you mind my talking, old boy?'

'No. Turn the head a little to the right. Too much. That's right. I won't keep you much longer. Just while the sun's on the left side of the face. The shoulders are coming too far round again.'

'You talk like a doctor about my members – "*the*" head, "*the*" face, "*the*" shoulders.'

'You're a vain fellow, Seb. Now, hold it like that, do. Yes, there's something persistently impish in Luke. He jabs at people. What was he up to last night with Will Pomeroy and Legge?'

'Damned if I know. Funny business, wasn't it? Do you think he's jealous of Will?'

'Jealous?' repeated Cubitt. With his palette-knife he laid an unctuous stroke of blue beside the margin of the painted head. 'Why, jealous?'

'Well – because of Decima.'

'Oh nonsense! And yet I don't know. He's not your cousin for nothing, Seb. Luke's got his share of the family vanity.'

'I don't know why you say I'm vain, damn you. I don't think I'm vain at all. Do you know I get an average of twelve drivelling letters a day from females in front? And do they mean a thing to me?'

607

'You'd be bitterly disappointed if there was a falling off. Don't move your shoulders. But you may be right about Luke.'

'I'd like to know,' said Parish, 'just how much last year's little flirtation with Decima added up to.'

'Would you? I don't think it's relevant.'

'Well,' said Parish, 'she's an attractive wench. More "It" to the square inch than most of them. It's hard to say why. She's got looks, of course, but not the looks that usually get over that way. Not the voluptuous type. Her – '

'Shut up,' said Cubitt violently and added: 'I'm going to paint your mouth.'

His own was set in an unusually tight line. He worked for a time in silence, stood back, and said abruptly:

'I don't really think Will Pomeroy was his objective. He was getting at Legge, and why the devil he should pick on a man he'd never seen in his life until last night is more than I can tell.'

'I thought he seemed to be sort of probing. Trying to corner Legge in some way.'

Cubitt paused with his knife over the canvas.

'Yes,' he said slowly. 'That's perfectly true. I thought so too. Trick of the trade perhaps. Counsels curiosity. Almost one expected him to put his foot on the seat of a chair and rest his elbow on his knee. Now I come to think of it, I believe he did hitch his coat up by the lapels.'

'Characteristic,' pronounced Parish seriously. He himself had used these touches several times in trial scenes.

Cubitt smiled. 'But he sounded definitely malicious,' he added.

'He's not malicious,' said Parish uncomfortably.

'Oh yes, he is,' said Cubitt coolly. 'It's one of his more interesting qualities. He can be very malicious.'

'He can be very generous too.'

'I'm sure he can. I like Luke, you know. He interests me enormously.'

'Apparently, he likes you,' said Parish. 'Apparently.'

'Hallo!' Cubitt walked back from his canvas and stood squinting at it. 'You said that with a wealth of meaning, Seb. What's in the air? You can rest a minute if you like.'

Parish moved off the boulder where he had been sitting, stretched himself elaborately, and joined Cubitt. He gazed solemnly at his own portrait. It was a large canvas. The figure in the dull red sweater was three-quarter life-size. It was presented as a dark form against the lighter background which was the sea and sky. The sky appeared as a series of paling arches, the sea as a simple plane broken by formalized waves. A glint of sunlight had found the cheek and jawbone on the right side of the face.

'Marvellous, old boy,' said Parish. 'Marvellous!'

Cubitt, who disliked being called 'old boy,' grunted.

'Did you say you'd show it in this year's Academy?' asked Parish.

'I didn't, Seb, but I will. I'll stifle my æsthetic conscience, prostitute my undoubted genius, and send your portrait to join the annual assembly of cadavers. Do you prefer "Portrait of an Actor", "Sebastian Parish, Esq"! or simply "Sebastian Parish"?'

'I think I would like my name,' said Parish seriously. 'Not, I mean, that everybody wouldn't know – '

'Thank you. But I see your point. Your press agent would agree. What were you going to say about Luke? His generosity, you know, and his apparently liking me so much?'

'I don't think I ought to tell you, really.'

'But of course, you are going to tell me.'

'He didn't actually say it was in confidence,' said Parish.

Cubitt waited with a slight smile.

'You'd be amazed if you knew,' continued Parish.

'Yes?'

'Yes. Oh, rather. At least I imagine you would be. I was. I never expected anything of the sort, and after all I am his nearest relation. His next-of-kin.'

Cubitt turned and looked at him in real astonishment.

'Are you by any chance,' he asked, 'talking about Luke's will?'

'How did you guess?'

'My dear, good Seb – '

'All right, all right. I suppose I did give it away. You may as well hear the whole thing. Luke told me the other day that he was leaving his money between us.'

'Good Lord!'

'I know. I happened to look him up after the show one evening, and found him browsing over an official-looking document. I said something, chaffingly you know, about it, and he said: "Well, Seb, you'll find it out some day, so you may as well know now." And then he told me.'

'Extraordinarily nice of him,' said Cubitt uncomfortably, and he added: 'Damn! I wish you hadn't told me.'

'Why on earth?'

'I don't know. I enjoy discussing Luke and now I'll feel he's sort of sacrosanct. Oh well, he'll probably outlive both of us.'

'He's a good bit older than I am,' said Parish. 'Not, I mean, that I don't hope with all my heart he will. I mean – as far as I'm concerned – '

'Don't labour it, Seb,' said Cubitt kindly. 'I should think Luke will certainly survive me. He's strong as a horse and I'm not. You'll probably come in for the packet.'

'I hate talking about it like that.'

Parish knocked his pipe out on a stone. Cubitt noticed that he was rather red in the face.

'As a matter of fact,' he muttered, 'it's rather awkward.'

'Why?'

'Well I'm plaguily hard up at the moment and I'd been wondering – '

'If Luke would come to the rescue?' Parish was silent.

'And in the light of this revelation,' Cubitt added, 'you don't quite like to ask. Poor Seb! But what the devil do you do with your money? You ought to be rolling. You're always in work. This play you're in now is a record run, isn't it, and your salary must be superb.'

'That's all jolly fine, old man, but you don't know what it's like in the business. My expenses are simply ghastly.'

'Why?'

'Why, because you've got to keep up a standard. Look at my house. It's ruinous, but I've got to be able to ask the people that count to a place they'll accept and, if possible, remember. You've got to look prosperous in this game, and you've got to entertain. My agent's fees are hellish. My clubs cost the earth. And like a blasted fool I backed a show that flopped for thousands last May.'

'What did you do that for?'

'The management are friends of mine. It looked all right.'

'You give money away, Seb, don't you? I mean literally. To out-of-luck actors? Old-timers and so on?'

'I may. Always think "there but for the grace of God!" It's such a damn' chancy business.'

'Yes. No more chancy than painting, my lad.'

'You don't have to show so well if you're an artist. People expect you to live in a peculiar way.'

Cubitt looked at him, but said nothing.

Parish went on defensively: 'I'm sorry, but you know what I mean. People expect painters to be Bohemians and all that.'

'There was a time,' said Cubitt, 'when actors were content to be Bohemians, whatever that may mean. I never know. As far as I am concerned it means going without things you want.'

'But your pictures sell.'

'On an average I sell six pictures a year. Their prices range from twenty pounds to two hundred. It usually works out at about four hundred. You earn that in as many weeks, don't you?'

'Yes, but – '

'Oh, I'm not grumbling. I've got a bit of my own and I could make more, I dare say, if I took pupils or had a shot at commercial art. I've suited myself and it's worked out well enough until – '

'Until what?' asked Parish.

'Nothing. Let's get on with the work, shall we? The light's no good after about eleven.'

Parish walked back to the rock and took up his pose. The light wind whipped his black hair from his forehead. He raised his chin and stared out over the sea. He assumed an expression of brooding dominance.

'That right?' he asked.

'Pretty well. You only want a pair of tarnished epaulettes and we could call it "Elba."'

'I've always thought I'd like to play Napoleon.'

'A fat lot you know about Napoleon.'

Parish grinned tranquilly.

'Anyway,' he said, 'I'd read him up a bit if I had to. As a matter of fact Luke looks rather like him.'

'The shoulders should come round,' said Cubitt. 'That's more like it. Yes, Luke is rather the type.'

He painted for a minute or two in silence, and then Parish suddenly laughed.

'What's up?' asked Cubitt.

'Here comes your girl.'

'What the devil do you mean?' demanded Cubitt angrily and looked over his shoulder. 'Oh – I see.'

'Violet,' said Parish. 'Who did you think it was?'

'I thought you'd gone dotty. Damn the woman.'

'Will *she* paint me too?'

'Not if I know it.'

'Unkind to your little Violet?' asked Parish.

'Don't call her that.'

'Why not?'

'Well damn it, she's not very young and she's – well, she may be a pest, but she's by way of being a lady.'

'Snob!'

'Don't be so dense, Seb. Can't you see – oh Lord, she's got all her gear. She *is* going to paint. Well, I've just about done for today.'

'She's waving.'

Cubitt looked across the headland to where Miss Darragh, a droll figure against the sky, fluttered a large handkerchief.

'She's put her stuff down,' said Parish. 'She's going to sketch. What is there to paint, over there?'

'A peep,' said Cubitt. 'Now, hold hard and don't talk. There's a shadow under the lower lip – '

He worked with concentration for five minutes, and then put down his palette.

'That'll do for today. We'll pack up.'

But when he'd hitched his pack on his shoulders and stared out to sea for some seconds, he said suddenly:

'All the same, Seb, I wish you hadn't told me.'

II

It was understood among the three friends that each should go his own way during the weeks they spent at Ottercombe. Watchman had played with the notion of going out in the dawn with the fishing boats. He woke before it was light and heard the tramp of heavy boots on cobble-stones and the sound of voices down on Ottercombe

Steps. He told himself comfortably that here was a link with the past. For hundreds of years the Coombe men had gone down to their boats before dawn. The children of Coombe had heard them stirring, their wives had fed them and seen them go, and for centuries their voices and the sound of their footsteps had roused the village for a moment in the coldest hour of the night. Watchman let the sounds die away, snuggled luxuriously down in bed, and fell asleep.

He woke again at half-past nine and found that Parish had already breakfasted and set out for Coombe Rock.

'A mortal great mammoth of a picture Mr Cubitt be at,' said Abel Pomeroy, as Watchman finished his breakfast. 'Paint enough to cover a wall, sir, and laid on so thick as dough. At close quarters it looks like one of they rocks covered in shell-fish, but 'od rabbit it, my sonnies, when you fall away twenty feet or more, it's Mr Parish so clear as glass. Looking out over the Rock he be, looking out to sea, and so natural you'd say the man was smelling the wind and thinking of his next meal. You might fancy a stroll out to the Rock, sir, and take a look at Mr Cubitt flinging his paint left and right.'

'I feel lazy, Abel. Where's Will?'

'Went out along with the boats, sir.' Abel rasped his chin, scratched his head, and re-arranged the objects on the bar.

'He's restless, is Will,' he said suddenly. 'My own boy, Mr Watchman, and so foreign to me as a changeling.'

'Will is?' asked Watchman, filling his pipe.

'Ah, Will. What with his politics and his notions he's a right down stranger to me, is Will. A very witty lad too, proper learned, and so full of arguments as a politician. He won't argufy with me, naturally, seeing I'm not his equal in the way of brains, nor anything like it.'

'You're too modest, Abel,' said Watchman lightly.

'No, sir, no. I can't stand up to that boy of mine when it comes to politics and he knows it and lets me down light. I'm for the old ways, a right down Tory, and for why? For no better reason than it suits me, same as it suited my forebears.'

'A sound enough reason.'

'No, sir, not according to my boy. According to Will it be a damn' fool reason and a selfish one into the bargain.'

'I shouldn't let it worry you.'

'More I do, Mr Watchman. It's not our differences that worry me. It's just my lad's restless mumbudgetting ways. You saw how he was last night. Speaking to you that fashion. Proper 'shamed of him, I was.'

'It was entirely my fault, Abel, I baited him.'

'Right down generous of you to put it like that, but all the same he's not himself these days. I'd like him to settle down. Tell you the truth, sir, it's what's to become of the Feathers that troubles me, and it troubles me sore. I'm nigh on seventy, Mr Watchman. Will's my youngest. 'Tother two boys wurr took in war, and one girl's married and in Canada, and 'tother in Australia. Will'll get the Feathers.'

'I expect,' said Watchman, 'that Will'll grow out of his red ideas and run the pub like any other Pomeroy.'

Old Abel didn't answer and Watchman added: 'When he marries and settles down.'

'And when will that be, sir? Likely you noticed how 'tis between Will and Miss Dessy? Well now, that's a funny state of affairs, and one I can't get used to. Miss Dessy's father, Jim Moore up yurr to Carey Edge Farm, is an old friend of mine. Good enough. But what happens when Dessy's a lil' maid no higher than my hand? 'Od rabbit it, if old Jim don't come in for a windfall. Now his wife being a ghastly proud sort of a female and never tired of letting on she came down in society when she married, what do they do but send young Dessy to a ladies' school where she gets some kind of free pass into a female establishment at Oxford.'

'Yes. I know.'

' 'Ess and comes home at the end of it a dinky lil' chit, sure enough, and husband-high; but speaking finniky-like and the equal of all the gentlefolks in the West Country.'

'Well?' said Watchman.

'Well, sir, that's fair enough. If she fancies our Will above the young sparks she meets in her new walk of life, good enough. I'm proper fond of the maiden, always have been. Good as a daughter to me, and just the same always, no matter how ladylike she'm grown.'

Watchman stood up and stretched himself.

'It all sounds idyllic, Abel. A charming romance.'

'Wait a bit, sir, wait a bit. 'Baint so simple as all that. These yurr two young folks no sooner mets again than my Will sets his heart, burning strong and powerful, on Decima Moore. Eaten up with love from time he sets eyes on her, was Will, and hell-bent to win her. She come back with radical notions, same as his own, and that's a bond a'tween 'em from the jump. Her folks don't fancy my Will, however, leastways not her mother, and they don't fancy her views neither, and worst of all they lays blame on Will. Old Jim Moore comes down yurr and has a tell with me, saying life's not worth living up to farm with Missus at him all day and half night to put his foot down and stop it. That's how 'twurr after you left last year, sir, and that's how 'tis still. Will burning to get tokened and wed, and Dessy – '

'Yes?' asked Watchman as Abel paused and looked fixedly at the ceiling. 'What about Decima?'

'That's the queerest touch of the lot, sir,' said Abel.

Watchman, lighting his pipe, kept his eye on his host and saw that he now looked profoundly uncomfortable.

'Well?' Watchman repeated.

'It be what she says about wedlock,' Abel muttered.

'What does she say?' asked Watchman sharply.

'Be shot if she haven't got some new-fangled notion about wedlock being no better than a name for savagery. Talks wild trash about freedom. To my way of thinking the silly maiden don't know what she says.'

'What,' asked Watchman, 'does Will say to all this?'

'Don't like it. The chap wants to be tokened and hear banns read, like any other poor toad, for all his notions. He wants no free love for his wife or himself. He won't talk to me, not a word, but Miss Dessy does, so open and natural as a daisy. Terrible nonsense it be, I tells her, and right down dangerous into bargain. Hearing her chatter, you might suppose she's got some fancy-chap up her sleeve. Us knows better of course, but it's an uncomfortable state of affairs and seemingly no way out. Tell you what, sir, I do blame this Legge for the way things are shaping. Will'd have settled down, he *was* settling down, afore Bob Legge come yurr. But now he've stirred up all their revolutionary notions again, Miss Dessy's along with the rest. I don't fancy Legge. Never have. Not for all he'm a masterpiece with darts. My way of thinking, he'm a cold calculating chap and powerful bent on having his way. Well, thurr 'tis, and talking won't mend it.'

Watchman walked to the door and Abel followed him. They stood looking up the road to Coombe Tunnel.

'Daily-buttons!' exclaimed Abel, 'talk of an angel and there she be. That's Miss Dessy, the dinky little dear. Coming in to do her marketing.'

'So it is,' said Watchman. 'Well, Abel, on second thoughts I believe I'll go and have a look at that picture.'

III

But Watchman did not go directly to Coombe Rock. He lingered for a moment until he had seen Decima Moore go in at the post-office door, and then he made for the tunnel. Soon the darkness swallowed him, his footsteps rang hollow on the wet stone floor, and above him, a luminous disc, shone the top entry. Watchman emerged, blinking, into the dust and glare of the high road. To his left, the country rolled gently away to Illington, to his right, a path led round the cliffs to Coombe Rock, and then wound inland to Cary Edge Farm where the Moores lived.

He arched his hand over his eyes and on Coombe Head could make out the shape of canvas and easel with Cubitt's figure moving to and fro, and beyond a tiny dot which must be Sebastian Parish's head. Watchman left the road, climbed the clay bank, circled a clump of furze and beneath a hillock from where he could see the entrance to the tunnel, he lay full length on the short turf. With the cessation of his own movement the quiet of the countryside engulfed him. At first the silence seemed complete, but after a moment or two the small noises of earth, and sky welled up into his consciousness. A lark sang above his head with a note so high that it impinged upon the outer borders of hearing and at times soared into nothingness. When he turned and laid his ear to the earth it throbbed with the far-away thud of surf against Coombe Rock, and when his fingers moved in the grass it was with a crisp stirring sound. He began to listen intently, lying so still that no movement of his body could come between his senses and more distant sound. He closed his eyes and to an observer he would have seemed to sleep. Indeed his face bore that look of inscrutability which links sleep in our minds with death. But he was not asleep. He was listening: and presently his ears caught a new rhythm, a faint hollow beat. Someone was coming up through the tunnel.

Watchman looked through his eyelashes and saw Decima Moore step into the sunlight. He remained still, while she mounted the bank to the cliff path. She rounded the furze-bush and was almost upon him before she saw him. She stood motionless.

'Well, Decima,' said Watchman and opened his eyes.

'You startled me,' she said.

'I should leap to my feet, shouldn't I? And apologize?'

'You needn't trouble. I'm sorry I disturbed you. Goodbye.'

She moved forward.

Watchman said: 'Wait a moment, Decima.'

She hesitated. Watchman reached out a hand and seized her ankle.

'Don't do that,' said Decima. 'It makes us both look silly. I'm in no mood for dalliance.'

'Please say you'll wait a moment and I'll behave like a perfect little gent. I've something serious to say to you.'

'I don't believe it.'

'I promise you. Of the first importance. Please.'

'Very well,' said Decima.

He released her and scrambled to his feet.

'Well, what is it?' asked Decima.

'It'll take a moment or two. Do sit down and smoke a cigarette. Or shall I walk some of the way with you?'

She shot a glance at the distant figures on Coombe Head and then looked at him. She seemed ill at ease, half-defiant, half-curious.

'We may as well get it over,' she said.

'Splendid. Sit down now, do. If we stand here, we're in full view of anybody entering or leaving Ottercombe, and I don't want to be interrupted. No, I've no discreditable motive. Come now.'

He sat down on the hillock under the furze-bush and after a moment's hesitation she joined him.

'Will you smoke? Here you are.'

He lit her cigarette, dug the match into the turf, and then turned to her.

'The matter I wanted to discuss with you,' he said, 'concerns this Left Movement of yours.'

Decima's eyes opened wide.

'That surprises you?' observed Watchman.

'It does rather,' she said. 'I can't imagine why you should suddenly be interested in the CLM'

'I've no business to be interested,' said Watchman, 'and in the ordinary sense, my dear Decima, I am not interested. It's solely on your account – no, do let me make myself clear. It's on your account that I want to put two questions to you. Of course if you choose you may refuse to answer them.'

Watchman cleared his throat, and pointed a finger at Decima.

'Now in reference to this society – '

'Dear me,' interrupted Decima with a faint smile. 'This green plot shall be our court, this furze-bush our witness-box; and we will do in action as we will do it before the judge.'

'A vile paraphrase, and if we are to talk of midsummernight's dreams, Decima – '

'We certainly won't do that,' she said, turning very pink. 'Pray continue your cross-examination, Mr Watchman.'

'Thank you, my lord. First question: is this body – society, club, movement, or whatever it is – an incorporated company?'

'What does that mean?'

'It means among other things that the books would have to be audited by a chartered accountant.'

'Good Heavens, no. It's simply grown up, largely owing to the efforts of Will Pomeroy and myself.'

'So I supposed. You've a list of subscribing members.'

'Three hundred and forty-five,' said Decima proudly.

'And the subscription?'

'Ten bob. Are you thinking of joining us?'

'Who collects the ten bobs?'

'The treasurer.'

'*And* secretary. Mr Legge?'

'Yes. What are you driving at? What were you at last night, baiting Bob Legge?'

'Wait a moment. Do any other sums of money pass through his hands?'

'I don't see why I should tell you these things,' said Decima.

'There's no reason, but you have my assurance that I mean well.'

'I don't know what you mean.'

'And you may be sure I shall regard this conversation as strictly confidential.'

'All right,' she said uneasily. 'We've raised sums for different objects. We want to start a Left Book Club in Illington and there are one or two funds – Spanish, Czech and Austrian refugees and the fighting fund and so on.'

'Yes. At the rate of how much a year. Three hundred for instance?'

'About that. Quite that, I should think. We've some very generous supporters.'

'Now look here, Decima. Did you inquire very carefully into this man Legge's credentials?'

'I – no. I mean, he's perfectly sound. He's secretary for several other things. Some philatelic society and a correspondence course, and he's agent for one or two things.'

'He's been here ten months, hasn't he?'

'Yes. He's not strong, touch of TB, I think, and some trouble with his ears. His doctor told him to come down here. He's been very generous and subscribed to the movement himself.'

'May I give you a word of advice? Have your books audited.'

'Do you know Bob Legge? You can't make veiled accusations – '

'I have made no accusations.'

'You've suggested that – '

'That you should be business-like,' said Watchman. 'That's all.'

'Do you know this man? You must tell me.'

There was a very long silence and then Watchman said:

'I've never known anybody of that name.'

'Then I don't understand,' said Decima.

'Let us say I've taken an unreasonable dislike to him.'

'I'd already come to that conclusion. It was obvious last night.'

'Well, think it over.' He looked fixedly at her and then said suddenly:

'Why won't you marry Will Pomeroy?'

Decima turned very white and said: 'That, at least is entirely my own business.'

'Will you meet me here tonight?'

'No.'

'Do I no longer attract you, Decima?'

'I'm afraid you don't.'

'Little liar, aren't you?'

'The impertinent lady-killer stuff,' said Decima, 'doesn't wear very well. It has a way of looking merely cheap.'

'You can't insult me,' said Watchman. 'Tell me this. Am I your only experiment?'

'I don't want to start any discussion of this sort. The thing's at an end. It's been dead a year.'

'No. Not on my part. It could be revived; and very pleasantly. Why are you angry? Because I didn't write?'

'Good Lord, no!' ejaculated Decima.

'Then why – '

He laid his hand over hers. As if unaware of his touch, her fingers plucked at the blades of grass beneath them.

'Meet me here tonight,' he repeated.

'I'm meeting Will tonight at the Feathers.'

'I'll take you home.'

Decima turned on him.

'Look here,' she said, 'we'd better get this straightened out. You're not in the least in love with me, are you?'

'I adore you.'

'I dare say, but you don't love me. Nor do I love you. A year ago I fell for you rather heavily and we know what happened. I can admit now that I was – well, infatuated. I can even admit that what I said just then wasn't true. For about two months I *did* mind your not writing. I minded damnably. Then I recovered in one bounce. I don't want any recrudescence.'

'How solemn,' muttered Watchman. 'How learned, and how young.'

'It may seem solemn and young to you. Don't flatter yourself I'm the victim of remorse. I'm not. One has to go through with these things, I've decided. But don't let's blow on the ashes.'

'We wouldn't have to blow very hard.'

'Perhaps not.'

'You admit that, do you?'

'Yes. But I don't want to do it.'

'Why? Because of Pomeroy?'

'Yes.'

'Are you going to marry him, after all?'

'I don't know. He's ridiculously class-conscious about sex. He's completely uneducated in some ways, but – I don't know. If he knew about last year he'd take it very badly, and I can't marry him without telling him.'

'Well,' said Watchman suddenly, 'don't expect me to be chivalrous and decent. I imagine chivalry and decency don't go with sex-education and freedom anyway. Don't be a fool, Decima. You know you think it would be rather fun.'

He pulled her towards him. Decima muttered, 'No, you don't,' and suddenly they were struggling fiercely. Watchman thrust her back till her shoulders were against the bank. As he stooped his head to kiss her, she wrenched one hand free and struck him clumsily but with violence, across the mouth.

'You – ' said Watchman.

She scrambled to her feet and stood looking down at him.

'I wish to God,' she said savagely, 'that you'd never come back.'

There was a moment's silence.

Watchman, too, had got to his feet. They looked into each other's eyes; and then, with a gesture that, for all its violence and swiftness suggested the movement of an automaton, he took her by the shoulders and kissed her. When he had released her they moved apart stiffly with no eloquence in either of their faces or figures.

Decima said, 'You'd better get out of here. If you stay here it'll be the worse for you. I could kill you. Get out.'

They heard the thud of footsteps on turf, and Cubitt and Sebastian Parish came over the brow of the hillock.

CHAPTER 4

The Evening in Question

Watchman, Cubitt and Parish lunched together in the taproom. Miss Darragh did not appear. Cubitt and Parish had last seen her sucking her brush and gazing with complacence at an abominable sketch. She was still at work when they came up with Watchman and Decima. At lunch, Watchman was at some pains to tell the others how he and Decima Moore met by accident, and how they had fallen to quarrelling about the Coombe Left Movement.

They accepted his recital with, on Parish's part, rather too eager alacrity. Lunch on the whole, was an uncomfortable affair. Something had gone wrong with the relationship of the three men. Norman Cubitt, who was acutely perceptive in such matters, felt that the party had divided into two, with Parish and himself on one side of an intangible barrier, and Watchman on the other. Cubitt had no wish to side, however, vaguely, with Parish against Watchman. He began to make overtures, but they sounded unlikely and only served to emphasize his own discomfort. Watchman answered with the courtesy of an acquaintance. By the time they had reached the cheese, complete silence had overcome them.

They did not linger for their usual post-prandial smoke. Cubitt said he wanted to get down to the jetty for his afternoon sketch, Parish said he was going to sleep, Watchman, murmuring something about writing a letter, disappeared upstairs.

They did not see each other again until the evening when they met in the private taproom for their usual cocktail. The fishing boats had come in, and at first the bar was fairly full. The three friends joined in local conversation and were not thrown upon their own resources until the evening meal which they took together in the ingle-nook. The last drinker went out saying that there was a storm hanging about, and that the air was unnaturally heavy. On his departure complete silence fell upon the three men. Parish made one or two halfhearted attempts to break it but it was no good, they had nothing to say to each other. They finished their meal and Watchman began to fill his pipe.

'What's that?' said Parish suddenly. 'Listen!'

'High tide,' said Watchman. 'It's the surf breaking on Coombe Rock.'

'No, it's not. Listen.'

And into the silence came a vague gigantic rumble.

'Isn't it thunder?' asked Parish.

The others listened for a moment but made no answer.

'What a climate!' added Parish.

The village outside the inn seemed very quiet. The evening air was sultry. No breath of wind stirred the curtains at the open windows. When, in a minute or two, somebody walked round the building, the footsteps sounded unnaturally loud. Another and more imperative muttering broke the quiet.

Cubitt said nervously:

'It's as if a giant, miles away on Dartmoor, was shaking an iron tray.'

'That's exactly how they work thunder in the business,' volunteered Parish.

'*The business*,' Watchman said with violent irritation. 'What business? Is there only one business?'

'What the hell's gone wrong with you?' asked Parish.

'Nothing. The atmosphere,' said Watchman.

'I hate thunder-storms,' said Cubitt quickly. 'They make me feel as if all my nerves were on the surface. A loathsome feeling.'

'I rather like them,' said Watchman.

'And that's the end of *that* conversation,' said Parish with a glance at Cubitt.

Watchman got up and moved into the window. Mrs Ives came in with a tray.

'Storm coming up?' Parish suggested.

' 'Ess, sir. Very black outside,' said Mrs Ives.

The next roll of thunder lasted twice as long as the others and ended in a violent tympanic rattle. Mrs Ives cleared the table and went away. Cubitt moved into the ingle-nook and leant his elbows on the mantelpiece. The room had grown darker. A flight of gulls, making for the sea, passed clamorously over the village. Watchman pulled back the curtains and leant over the window-sill. Heavy drops of rain had begun to fall. They hit the cobble-stones in the inn yard with loud slaps.

'Here comes the rain,' said Parish, unnecessarily.

Old Abel Pomeroy came into the Public from the far door. He began to shut the windows and called through into the Private.

'We'm in for a black storm, souls.'

A glint of lightning flickered in the yard outside. Parish stood up scraping his chair-legs on the floor-boards.

'They say,' said Parish, 'that if you count the seconds between the flash and the thunder it gives you the distance – '

A peal of thunder rolled up a steep crescendo.

'– the distance away in fifths of a mile,' ended Parish.

'Do shut up, Seb,' implored Watchman, not too unkindly.

'Damn it all,' said Parish. 'I don't know what the hell's the matter with you. Do you, Norman?'

Abel Pomeroy came through the bar into the taproom.

'Be colder soon, I reckon,' he said. 'If you'd like a fire gentlemen – '

'We'll light it, Abel, if we want it,' said Cubitt.

'Good enough, sir.' Abel looked from Cubitt and Parish to Watchman, who still leant over the window-sill.

'She'll come bouncing and teeming through that window, Mr Watchman, once she do break out. Proper deluge she'll be.'

'All right, Abel. I'll look after the window.'

A livid whiteness flickered outside. Cubitt and Parish had a momentary picture of Watchman, in silhouette against the background of inn-yard and houses. A second later the thunder broke in two outrageous claps. Then, in a mounting roar, the rain came down.

'Yurr she comes,' said Abel.

He switched on the light and crossed to the door into the passage.

'Reckon Legge'll bide tonight after all,' said Abel.

Watchman spun round.

'Is Legge going away?' he asked.

'He'm called away on business, sir, to Illington. But that lil' car of his leaks like a lobster-pot. Reckon the man'd better wait till tomorrow. I must look to the gutters or us'll have the rain coming in through upstairs ceilings.'

He went out.

The evening was now filled with the sound of rain and thunder. Watchman shut the window and came into the room. His head was wet.

He said: 'It's much colder. We might have that fire.'

Cubitt lit the fire and they watched the first flames rise uncertainly among the driftwood.

'The rain's coming down the chimney,' said Parish. 'Hallo! Who's this?'

The taproom door opened slowly. There, on the threshold, stood the Hon. Violet Darragh, dripping like a soused hen. Her cotton dress was gummed to her person with such precision that it might as well have melted. Her curls were flattened into streaks, and from the brim of her hat poured little rivers that rushed together at the base of her neck, and, taking the way of least resistance, streamed centrally to her waist where they deployed and ran divergently to the floor. With one hand she held a canvas hold-all, with the other a piece of paper that still bore streaks of cobalt-blue and veridian across its pulpy surface. She might have been an illustration from one of the more Rabelaisian pages of *La Vie Parisienne*.

'My dear Miss Darragh!' ejaculated Watchman.

'Ah, look at me!' said Miss Darragh. 'What a pickle I'm in, and me picture ruined. I was determined to finish it and I stayed on till the thunder and lightning drove me away in terror of me life, and when I emerged from the tunnel didn't it break over me like the entire contents of the ocean. Well, I'll go up now and change, for I must look a terrible old sight.'

She glanced down at herself, gasped, cast a comical glance at the three men, and bolted.

Will Pomeroy and two companions entered the Public from the street door. They wore oilskin hats and coats, and their boots squelched on the floor-boards. Will went into the bar and served out drinks. Parish leant over the private bar and gave them good-evening.

'You seem to have caught it in the neck,' he observed.

'That's right, Mr Parish,' said Will. 'She's a proper masterpiece. The surface water'll be pouring through the tunnel if she keeps going at this gait. Here you are chaps, I'm going to change.'

He went through the Private into the house, leaving a wet trail behind him. They heard him at the telephone in the passage. He had left the door open and his voice carried above the sound of the storm.

'That you, Dessy? Dessy, this storm's a terror. You'd better not drive that old car over tonight. Tunnel'll be a running stream. It's not safe.'

Watchman began to whistle under his breath. Abel returned and took Will's place in the bar.

'I'd walk over myself,' Will was saying, 'only I can't leave father single-handed. We'll have a crowd in, likely, with this weather.'

'I'm going to have a drink,' said Watchman suddenly.

'Walk?' said Will. 'You're not scared of lightning, then. Good enough, and nobody better pleased than I am. I'll lend you a sweater and, Dessy, you'd better warn them you'll likely stay the night. Why not? So I do, then and you'll find it out, my dear. I'll come a fetch along the way to meet you.'

The receiver clicked. Will stuck his head round the door.

'Dessy's walking over, Dad. I'll go through the tunnel to meet her. Have you seen Bob Legge?'

'He said he'd be up to Illington tonight, sonny.'

'He'll never make it. Has he left?'

'In his room yet, I fancy.'

'I'll see,' said Will. 'I've told Dessy she'd better stay the night.'

'Very welcome, I'm sure. Ask Mrs Ives to make room ready.'

'So I will, then,' said Will, and disappeared.

'Walking over!' said Abel. 'A matter of two miles it is, from yurr to Cary Edge. Wonderful what love'll do, gentlemen, 'baint it?'

'Amazing,' said Watchman. 'Is nobody else going to drink?'

II

By eight o'clock the public tap was full and the private nearly so. Decima Moore and Will had looked in, but at the moment were closeted upstairs with Mr Legge who had apparently decided not to go to Illington. Miss Darragh came down in dry clothes with her curls rubbed up, and sat writing letters by the fire.

Two of Abel's regular cronies had come in: Dick Oates, the Ottercombe policeman, and Arthur Gill, the grocer. A little later they were joined by Mr George Nark, an elderly bachelor-farmer whose political views chimed with those of the Left Movement, and who was therefore a favourite of Will Pomeroy's. Mr Nark had been a great reader of the Liberal Literature of his youth, and had never got over the surprise and excitement that he had experienced thirty years ago on reading Winwood Reade, H G Wells, and the *Evolution of Man*. The information that he had derived from these and other serious works had, with the passage of time, become transmitted into simplified forms which though they would have astonished the authors, completely satisfied Mr Nark.

The rain still came down in torrents and Mr Nark reported the Coombe Tunnel was a running stream.

'It's a crying shame,' he said, gathering the attention of the Private. 'Bin going on for hundreds of years and no need for it. We can be flooded out three times a year and capitalistic government only laughs at us. Science would have druv a class-A highroad into the Coombe if somebody had axed it. But does a capitalistic government ax the advice of Science? Not it. It's afraid to. And why? Because Science knows too much for it.'

'Ah,' said Mr Gill.

'That's capitalism for you,' continued Mr Nark. 'Blind-stupid and arrogant. Patching up where it should pitch-in and start afresh. What can you expect, my sonnies, from a parcel of wage-slaves and pampered aristocrats that don't know the smell of a day's work. So long as they've got their luxuries for themselves – '

He stopped and looked at Miss Darrah.

'Axing your pardon, Miss,' said Mr Nark. 'In the heat of my discourse I got carried off my feet with the powerful rush of ideas and forgot your presence. This'll be all gall and wormwood to you, doubtless.'

'Not at all, Mr Nark,' said Miss Darragh cheerfully. 'I'm myself a poor woman, and I've moods when I'm consumed with jealousy for anybody who's got a lot of money.'

This was not precisely the answer Mr Nark, who was a prosperous farmer, desired.

'It's the government,' he said, 'that does every man jack of us out of our scientific rights.'

'As far as that goes,' said PC Oates, 'I reckon one government's as scientific as the other. Look at sewage for instance.'

'Why?' demanded Mr Nark, 'should we look at sewage? What's sewage got to do with it? We're all animals.'

'Ah,' said Mr Gill, 'so we are, then.'

'Do you know, Dick Oates,' continued Mr Nark, 'that you've got a rudimentary tail?'

'And if I have, *which* I don't admit – '

'Ask Mr Cubitt, then. He's an artist and no doubt has studied the skeleton of man in its present stage of evolution. The name escapes me for the moment, but we've all got it. Isn't that correct, sir?'

'Yes, yes,' said Norman Cubitt hurriedly. 'Quite right, Mr Nark.'

'There you are,' said Mr Nark. 'Apes, every manjack of us, and our arms have only grown shorter through us knocking off the habit of hanging from limbs of trees.'

'What about our tongues?' asked Mr Oates.

'Never mind about them,' answered Mr Nark warmly, 'do you know that an unborn child's got gills like a fish?'

'That doesn't make a monkey of it, however.'

'It goes to show, though.'

'What?'

'You want to educate yourself. In a proper government the State 'ud educate the police so's they'd understand these deep matters for themselves. They know all about that in Russia. Scientific necessity that's what it is.'

'I don't see how knowing I've got a bit of a tail and once had a pair of gills is going to get me any nearer to a sergeant's stripe,' reasoned Mr Oates. 'What I'd like is a case. You know how it happens in these crime stories, chaps,' he continued, looking round the company. 'I read a good many of them, and it's always the same thing. The keen young PC happens to be on the spot when there's a homicide. His super has to call in the Yard and before you know where you are, the PC's working with one of the Big four and getting praised for his witty deductions. All I can say is I wish it happened like that in the Illington and Ottercombe Riding. Well, I'd best go round the beat, I reckon Down the Steps and up again, is about all this drownded hole'll see of me tonight. I'll look in again, chaps.'

Mr Oates adjusted his helmet, fastened his mackintosh, looked to his lamp, and went out into the storm.

'Ah, the poor fellow!' murmured Miss Darragh comfortably from inside the ingle-nook settle.

'In a properly conducted state – ' began Mr Nark.

His remark was drowned in a clap of thunder. The lights wavered and grew so dim that the filaments in the bulbs were reduced to luminous threads.

'Drat they electrics,' said old Abel. 'That's the storm playing bobs-a-dying with the wires somewhere. Us'll be in darkness afore closing time, I dare say.' And he raised his voice to a bellow.

'Will! Oi, Will!'

Will's voice answered from above. The lights brightened. After a minute or two, Decima and Will came downstairs and into the Private. Each carried an oil lamp.

'Guessed what you were hollowing for,' said Will, with a grin. 'Here's the lamps. We'll put 'em on the two bars, Dessy, and match-es handy. Bob Legge's fetching the other, Dad. Ceiling in his room's sprung a leak and the rain's coming in pretty heavy. The man was sitting there, so lost in thought he might have drowned. I've fixed up a bucket to catch it, and told him to come down.'

Will stared for a second at Watchman, and added rather trucu-lently: 'We told Bob we missed his company in the Private, didn't we, Dess?'

'Yes,' said Decima.

Watchman looked at her. She turned her back to him and said something to Will.

'Let us by all means have Mr Legge among us,' Watchman said. 'I hope to beat him – all round the clock.'

And in a minute or two, Mr Legge came in with the third unlit lamp.

III

On the day following the thunderstorm, the patrons of the Plume of Feathers tried very hard to remember in some sort of order, the events of the previous evening; the events that followed Mr Legge's entrance into the private taproom. For one reason and another their stories varied, but no doubt the principal reason for their variation might be found in the bottle of Courvoisier '87 that Abel Pomeroy had brought up from the cellar. That was after Mr Gill had gone home, and before Mr Oates returned from a somewhat curtailed beat round the village.

It was Watchman who started the discussion on brandy. Watchman apparently had got over whatever unfriendly mood had possessed him earlier in the evening and was now as communicative as he had been silent. He began to tell legal stories and this he did very well indeed, so that in a minute or two he had the attention of both bars; the patrons of the public taproom leaning on the bar counter and trying to see into the other room. He told stories of famous murder trials, of odd witnesses, and finally of his biggest case before he took silk. He did not give the names of the defendants, only describing them as the embezzling experts of the century. He had led for the defence of one of them and had succeeded in shifting most of the blame to the other who got, he said, a swingeing big sentence. He became quite exalted over it all.

Sebastian always said that his cousin would have made an actor. He was certainly an excellent mimic. He gave a character sketch of the judge and made a living creature of the man. He described how, after the verdict, when the defendant's house was sold up, he had bought three dozen of brandy from the cellar.

'Courvoisier '87,' said Watchman. 'A superb year.'

'Me cousin Byronie,' said Miss Darragh, looking round the corner of her settle, 'had the finest cellar in County Clare, I believe. Before the disaster of course.'

Watchman started and stared at Miss Darragh in confusion.

'Dear me, Mr Watchman,' she said composedly, 'what is the matter with you? Had you forgotten I was here?'

'I – it sounds very ungallant, but I believe I had.'

'What brandy did you say, sir?' asked Abel, and when Watchman repeated mechanically, "Courvoisier '87," Abel said placidly that he believed he had three bottles in his own cellar.

'I picked 'em up when old Lawyer Payne over to Diddlestock died and was sold up,' said Abel. 'Half-dozen, thurr was, and squire split 'em with me. I think that's the name. It's twelve month or more since I looked at 'em.'

Watchman had already taken three glasses of Treble Extra and, although sober, was willing to be less so. Parish, suddenly flamboyant, offered to bet Abel a guinea that the brandy was not Courvoisier '87 and on Abel shaking his head, said if it was Courvoisier '87, damn it, they'd kill a bottle of it there and then. Abel took a candle and went off to the cellar. The three men in the public taproom went away. Will Pomeroy left the public bar and came to the private one. He had shown little interest in Watchman's stories. Legge had gone into the ingle-nook where he remained reading a book on the Red Army in Northern China. Watchman embarked on a discussion with Cubitt on the subject of capital punishment. Soon it became a general argument with Decima, Cubitt and Parish on one side; and Watchman, dubiously supported by Mr Nark, on the other.

'It's a scientific necessity,' said Mr Nark. 'The country has to be purged. Cast out your waste material is what I say and so does Stalin.'

'So does Hitler if it comes to that,' said Cubitt. 'You're talking of massed slaughter, aren't you?'

'You can slaughter in a righteous manner,' said Mr Nark, 'and you can slaughter in an unrighteous manner. It's all a matter of revolution. Survival of the fittest.'

'What on earth's that to say to it?' asked Cubitt.

'We're talking about capital punishment in this country aren't we?' Decima asked.

Throughout the discussion, though she had launched several remarks at Watchman, she had not spoken directly to him. In each instance Watchman had answered exactly as if the conversation was between those two alone. He now cut in quickly.

'I thought so,' said Watchman. 'My learned friend is a little confused.'

'I regard it,' Decima continued, always to Cubitt, 'as a confession of weakness.'

'I think it's merely barbaric and horrible,' said Parish.

'Terrible,' murmured Miss Darragh drowsily. 'Barbarous indeed! If we can't stop men from killing each other by any better means than killing in turn then they'll persist in it till their dying day.'

Cubitt, with some difficulty, stifled a laugh.

'Quite right, Miss Darragh,' he said. 'It's a concession to the savage in all of us.'

'Nonsense,' said Watchman. 'It's an economic necessity.'

'Ah,' said Mr Nark with the air of one clutching at a straw, 'ah, now you're talking.'

Abel came back with a bottle in his hands.

'There you are gentlemen,' he said. 'It's Mr Watchman's brandy and no doubt about it. See for yourself, sir.'

Watchman looked at the bottle.

'By God, you're right, Abel.'

'This is magnificent,' cried Parish. 'Come on. We'll open it. Have you any brandy glasses? Never mind, tumblers'll do. It's a bit cold, but we'll humour it.'

Abel opened the bottle.

'This,' said Watchman, 'is my affair. Shut up, Seb, I insist. Abel, you and Will must join us.'

'Well, thank you very much, sir, I'm sure,' said Abel.

'I'm afraid,' said Decima, 'that I really dislike brandy. It'd be wasted on me.'

'What will you have then?'

'I'm sorry to be so tiresome, but I'd really rather not have a drink.'

'My poor girl,' said Watchman.

'Dessy'll have a stone-ginger with me,' said Will Pomeroy suddenly.

'With me,' said Watchman. 'Eight brandies, two stone-gingers, Abel, and kill the bottle.'

'Good Lord, Luke,' expostulated Cubitt, 'you'll have us rolling.'

'None for me, thank you, Mr Watchman,' said Miss Darragh. 'I'm afraid that I, too, am a Philistine.'

'You'll have a drink, though?'

'I shall join you,' said Miss Darragh, 'in the non-alcoholic spirit.'

'Six brandies, Abel,' amended Watchman. 'The first half now, and the second hereafter.'

Abel poured out the brandy. They watched him in silence.

The rain still poured down, but the thunder sounded more distantly.

Watchman took the first tot to Legge and put it on a table at his elbow.

'I hope you'll join us, Mr Legge,' he said.

Legge looked at the brandy and then directly at Watchman.

'It's very kind of you,' he said. 'As a matter of fact I've some work to do and – '

'"Let other hours be set apart for business,"' quoted Watchman. Today it is our pleasure to be drunk. Do you like good brandy, Mr Legge?'

'This,' said Legge, 'is the vintage of my choice.'

He took the glass and nursed it between those calloused hands.

'An exquisite bouquet,' said Mr Legge.

'I knew you'd appreciate it.'

'Your health,' said Legge and took a delicate sip.

The others, with the exception of Mr Nark, murmured self-consciously and sipped. Mr Nark raised his glass.

'Your very good health, sir. Long life and happiness,' said Mr Nark loudly and emptied his glass at one gulp. He drew in his breath with a formidable whistle, his eyes started from his head and he grabbed at the air.

'You'm dashed at it too ferocious, George,' said Abel.

Mr Nark shuddered violently and fetched his breath.

'It's a murderous strong tipple,' he whispered. 'If you'll pardon me, Mr Watchman, I'll break it down inwardly with a drop of water.'

But presently Mr Nark began to smile and then to giggle, and as he giggled so did Cubitt, Parish and Watchman. By the time the first tot of Courvoisier '87 had been consumed, there was much laughter in the private bar, and a good deal of rather loud, aimless conversation. Watchman proposed that they have a round-the-clock competition on the dart-board.

Parish reminded him of Legge's trick with the darts.

'Come on, Luke,' cried Parish. 'If you let him try it on you, damme if I won't let him try it on me.'

Mr Legge was understood to say he was willing.

Watchman pulled the darts out of the board.

'Come on now,' he said. 'I'm equal to the lot of you. Even Mr Legge. Round-the-clock it is, and if he beats me this time, we'll have the other half and he can do his circus trick with my hand. Is it a bargain, Mr Legge?'

'If you're not afraid,' said Legge indistinctly, 'I'm not. But I'd like a new set of darts.'

'Afraid? With a brandy like this on board, I'd face the devil himself.'

'Good old Luke,' cried Parish.

Abel fished under the shelves and brought up a small package which he clapped down on the bar counter.

'Brand new set o'darts, my sonnies,' said Abel. 'Best to be bought and come this evening from London. I'll fix the flights in 'em while you play round-the-clock with the old 'uns. Bob Legge can christen 'em with this masterpiece of an exhibition.'

He broke the string and opened the package.

'Come now, Mr Legge,' said Watchman. 'Is it a bargain?'

'Certainly,' said Legge. 'A bargain it is.'

CHAPTER 5

Failure by Mr Legge

PC Oates had gone as far as the tunnel, had returned, and had descended the flight of stone steps that leads to the wharf from the right-hand side of the Feathers. He had walked along the passage called Fish Lane, flashing his lamp from time to time on streaming windows and doorways. Rain drummed on Oates's mackintosh cape, on his helmet, on cobble-stones, and on the sea that, only a few feet away, in the darkness, lapped at the streaming waterfront. The sound of the rain was almost as loud as the sound of thunder and behind both of these was the roar of surf on Coombe Rock. A ray of lamplight from a chink in a window-blind shone obliquely on rods of rain, and by its suggestion of remote comfort made the night more desolate.

Far above him, dim and forlorn, the post-office clock told a quarter past nine.

Oates turned at the end of Fish Lane and shone light on the second flight of Ottercombe Steps. Water was pouring down them in a series of miniature falls. He began to climb, holding tightly to the handrail. If anyone could have seen him abroad in the night, lonesome and dutiful, his plodding figure might have suggested a progression into the past when the night-watchman walked through Ottercombe to call the hours to sleeping fishermen. Such a flight of fancy did not visit the thoughts of Mr Oates. He merely told himself that he was damned if he'd go any farther, and when the red curtains of the Plume of Feathers shone through the rain he mended his pace and made for them.

But before he had gone more than six steps he paused. Some noise that had not reached him before threaded the sound of the storm. Someone was calling out – shouting – yelling. He stopped and listened.

'O-o-oates! Hallo! Dick! Di-i-ick! Oo-o-oates!'

'Hallo!' yelled Oates and his voice sounded very desolate.

'Hallo! Come – back – here.'

Oates broke into a lope. The voice had come from the front of the pub. He crossed the yard, passed the side of the house and the door into the Public, and came in sight of the front door. A tall figure, shading its eyes, was silhouetted against the lighted entry. It was Will Pomeroy. Oates strode out of the night into the entry.

'Here!' he said, 'what's up?' And when he saw Will Pomeroy's face: 'What's happened here?'

Without speaking Will jerked his thumb in the direction of the private tap. His face was the colour of clay, and one corner of his mouth twitched.

'Well, what *is* it?' demanded Oates impatiently.

'In there. Been an accident.'

'*Accident*. What sort of an accident?'

But before Will could answer Decima Moore came out of the taproom, closing the door behind her.

'Here's Dick,' said Will.

'Will,' said Decima, 'there's no doubt about it. He's dead.'

'My Gawd, who's dead!' shouted Oates.

'Watchman.'

II

Oates looked down at the figure on the settle. He had remembered to remove his helmet, but the water dripped off his cape in little streams. When he bent forward three drops fell on the blind face. Oates dabbed at them with his finger and glanced round apologetically.

He said, 'What happened?'

Nobody answered. Old Pomeroy stood by the bar, his hands clasped in front of him. His face spoke only of complete bewilderment. He looked from one to another of the men as if somewhere there was some sort of explanation which had been withheld from him. Sebastian Parish and Norman Cubitt stood together in the ingle-nook. Parish's face was stained with tears. He kept smoothing back his hair with a nervous and meaningless gesture of the right hand. Cubitt's head was bent down. He seemed to be thinking deeply. Every now and then he glanced up sharply from under his brows. Mr Nark sat on one of the bar-stools, clenching and unclenching his hands, and struggling miserably with intermittent but profound hiccoughs. Legge, as white as paper, bit his fingers and stared at Oates. Decima and Will stood together in the doorway. Miss Darragh sat just outside the ingle-nook on a low chair. Her moonlike face was colourless but she seemed composed.

Watchman lay on a settle near the dart-board and opposite the bar. His eyes were wide open. They seemed to stare with glistening astonishment at the ceiling. The pupils were wide and black. His hands were clenched; the right arm lay across his body, the left dangled, and where the knuckles touched the floor they, like the back of the hand, were stained red.

'Well,' repeated Oates violently, 'can't any of you speak? What happened? Where's your senses? Have you sent for a doctor?'

'The telephone's dead,' said Will Pomeroy. 'And he's past doctoring, Dick.'

Oates picked up the left wrist.

'What's this? Blood?'

'He got a prick from a dart.'

Oates looked at the clenched hand and felt the wrist. In the third finger there was a neat puncture on the outside, below the nail. It was stained brown. The nails were bluish.

'I did that,' said Legge suddenly. 'It was my dart.'

Oates laid the hand down and bent over the figure. A drop of water fell from his coat on one of the staring eyes. He fumbled inside the shirt, looking over his shoulder at Will Pomeroy.

'We'll have to fetch a doctor, however,' he said.

'I'll go,' said Cubitt. 'Is it Illington?'

'Doctor Shaw, sir. Main road in, and the last corner. It's on the left after you pass police station. He's police-surgeon. I'd be obliged if you'd stop at the station and report.'

'Right.'

Cubitt went out.

Oates straightened up and unbuttoned his cape.

'I'll have to get some notes down,' he said, and felt in the pocket of his tunic. He stepped back and his boots crunched excruciatingly.

'There's glass all over the floor,' said Will.

Decima Moore said, 'Can't we – cover him up?'

'It would be better, don't you think?' said Miss Darragh, speaking for the first time.

'Can I – '

Will said, 'I'll get something,' and went out.

Oates looked round the group and at last addressed himself to Sebastian Parish.

'How long ago was this, sir?' he asked.

'Only a few minutes. It happened just before you came in.'

Oates glanced at his watch.

'Half-past nine,' he said and noted it down.

'Let's hear what happened,' he said.

'But it's not a case for the police,' said Parish. 'I mean, because he died suddenly – '

'You called me in, sir,' said Oates. 'It's no doubt a case for the doctor. Leave it, if you wish, sir, till he comes.'

'No, no,' said Parish, 'I don't mean that I object. It's only that your notebook and everything – it's so awful somehow.' He turned to Abel Pomeroy. 'You tell him.'

'It was like this, Dick,' said old Abel. 'Mr Legge here, had told us how he could throw the darts like a circus chap between the fingers of a man's hand stretched out on a board. You heard him. Mr Watchman, in his bold way, said he'd hold his hand out and Mr Legge was welcome to have a shot at it. 'Twouldn't do no great damage, Mr Watchman said, if he did stick him. Us all said it was a silly rash kind of trick. But Mr Watchman was hell-bent on it.'

'He insisted,' said Will.

'So he did, then. And up goes his hand. Mr Legge throws the first three as pretty as you please, outside little finger, a'tween little and third, a'tween third and middle. Then he throws the fourth and 'stead of going a'tween middle and first finger it catches middle finger. "Got me," says Mr Watchman.'

'And then – then what?' asked Abel.

'It was curious,' said Miss Darragh, slowly. 'He didn't move his hand at once. He kept it there, against the board. The blood trickled down his finger and spread like veins in a leaf over the back of his hand. One had time to wonder if the dart had gone right through and he was, in a way crucified.'

'He turned mortal ghastly white,' said Abel.

'And then pulled the dart out,' said Parish, 'and threw it down on the floor. He shuddered, didn't he?'

'Yes,' said Abel. 'He shuddered violent.'

'He always turned queer at the sight of his own blood, you know,' said Parish.

'Well, what next?' asked Oates.

'I think he took a step towards the settle,' said Parish.

'He sat on the settle,' said Decima. 'Miss Darragh said. "He's feeling faint, give him a sip of brandy." Mr Legge said he looked ill and could he have lockjaw? Someone else, Mr Pomeroy I think, said he ought to have iodine on his finger. Anyhow Mr Pomeroy got the first-aid box out of the bottom cupboard. I looked for a glass with brandy in it but they were all empty. I got the bottle. While I was doing that – pouring out the brandy, I mean – Mr Pomeroy dabbed iodine on the finger. Mr Watchman clenched his teeth and cried out. He jerked up his arms.'

She stopped short and closed her eyes.

Will Pomeroy had come back with a sheet. He spread it over Watchman and then turned to Decima.

'I'll take you out of this,' he said. 'Come upstairs to Mrs Ives, Dessy.'

'No, I'll finish.'

'No need.'

Will put his arm across Decima's shoulder and turned to Oates.

'I'll tell you. Mr Parish, here, said Mr Watchman couldn't stand the sight of blood. Father said something about iodine, like Dessy told you, and he got the first-aid box out of the cupboard. He took out the bottle and it was nearly empty. Father tipped it up and poured some on Mr Watchman's finger and then got out a bandage. Then Dessy gave him his brandy. He knocked the glass out of her hand.'

'Miss Darragh was just going to tie his finger up,' said Abel, 'when lights went out.'

'Went out?'

' 'Ess. They'd been upping and downing ever since thunder set in and this time they went out proper for about a minute.'

'It was frightful,' said Parish rapidly. 'We could hear him breathing. We were all knocking against each other with broken glass everywhere and – those awful noises. Nobody thought of the oil lamps, but Legge said he'd throw some wood on the fire to make a blaze. He did, and just then the lights went up.'

'Hold hard, if you please, sir,' said Oates. 'I'll get this down in writing.'

'But, look here – '

Parish broke off and Will began again.

'When the lights went on again we all looked at Mr Watchman. He was in a kind of fit, seemingly. He thrashed about with his arms and legs and then fell backwards on settle, where he is now. His breathing came queer for a bit and then – didn't come at all. I tried to get doctor, but the wires must be down. Then I came out and called you.'

Will turned Decima towards the door.

'If you want me, Father,' he said, 'I'll be up along. Coming, Dessy?'

'I'm all right,' said Decima.

'You'll be better out of here.'

She looked at him confusedly, seemed to hesitate, and then turned to Miss Darragh.

'Will you come, too?' asked Decima.

Miss Darragh looked fixedly at her and then seemed to make up her mind.

'Yes, my dear, certainly. We're better out of the way now, you know.'

Miss Darragh gathered up her writing block and plodded to the door. Decima drew nearer to Will, and obeying the pressure of his hand, went out with him.

Legge walked across and looked down at the shrouded figure.

'My God,' he said, 'do you think it was the dart that did it? My God, I've never missed before! He moved his finger. I swear he moved his finger. My God, I shouldn't have taken that brandy!'

'Where is the dart?' asked Oates, still writing.

Legge began hunting about the floor. The broken glass crackled under his boot.

'If it's all the same to you, Abel,' said Oates suddenly, 'I reckon we'd better leave this end of the room till doctor's come. If it's all the same to you, I reckon we'll shift into the Public.'

'Let's do that, for God's sake,' said Parish.

Mr Nark was suddenly and violently ill.

'That settle's it,' said old Abel. 'Us'll move.'

III

'Steady,' said the doctor. 'There's no particular hurry, you know. It's no joke negotiating Coombe Tunnel on a night like this. We must be nearly there.'

'Sorry,' said Cubitt. 'I can't get it out of my head you might – might be able to do something.'

'I'm afraid not from your account. Here's the tunnel, now. I should change down to first, really I should.'

Cubitt changed down. 'I expect you wish you'd driven yourself,' he said grimly.

'If it hadn't been for that slow puncture – there's the turning. Can you do it in one in this car? Splendid. I must confess I don't enjoy driving into the Coombe, even on clear nights. Now the road down. Pretty steep, really, and it's streaming with surface water. Shameful state of repair. Here we are.'

Cubitt put on his brakes and drew up with a sidelong skid at the front door of the Feathers. The doctor got out, reached inside for his bag, and ducked through the rain into the entry. Cubitt followed him.

'In the private bar, you said?' asked Dr Shaw.

He pushed open the door and they walked in.

The private bar was deserted but the lights were up in the Public beyond, and they heard a murmur of voices.

'Hallo!' called Dr Shaw.

There was a scuffling of feet and Will Pomeroy appeared on the far side of the bar.

'Here's doctor,' said Will, over his shoulder.

'Just a minute, Will,' said the voice of Mr Oates. 'I'll trouble you to stay where you are, if you please, gentlemen.'

He loomed up massively, put Will aside, and reached Dr Shaw by way of the tap proper, ducking under both counters.

'Well, Oates,' said Dr Shaw, 'what's the trouble?'

Cubitt, stranded inside the door, stayed where he was. Oates pointed to the settle. Dr Shaw took off his hat and coat, laid them with his bag on a table, and then moved to the shrouded figure. He drew back the sheet and, after a moment's pause, stooped over Watchman.

Cubitt turned away. There was a long silence.

At last Dr Shaw straightened up and replaced the sheet.

'Well,' he said, 'let's have the whole story again. I've had it once from Mr Cubitt, but he says he was a bit confused. Where are the others?'

'In here, doctor,' said Abel Pomeroy. 'Will you come through?'

Oates and Will held up the counter-flap and Dr Shaw went into the public bar. Parish, Mr Nark and Abel had got to their feet.

Dr Shaw was not the tallest man there but he dominated the scene. He was pale and baldish and wore glasses. His intelligence appeared in his eyes which were extremely bright and a vivid blue. His lower lip protruded. He had an unexpectedly deep voice, a look of serio-comic solemnity, and a certain air of distinction. He looked directly and with an air of thoughtfulness, at each of the men before him.

'His relations must be told,' he said.

Parish moved forward. 'I'm his cousin,' he said, 'and his nearest relation.'

'Oh, yes,' said Dr Shaw. 'You're Mr Parish?'

'Yes.'

'Yes. Sad business, this.'

'What was it?' asked Parish. 'What happened? He was perfectly well. Why did he – I don't understand.'

'Tell me this,' said Dr Shaw. 'Did your cousin become unwell as soon as he received this injury from the dart?'

'Yes. At least he seemed to turn rather faint. I didn't think much of it because he's always gone like that at the sight of his own blood.'

'Like what? Can you describe his appearance?'

'Well, he – O God, what did he do, Norman?'

Cubitt said, 'He just said "Got me," when the dart stuck, and then afterwards pulled it out and threw it down. He turned terribly pale. I think he sort of collapsed on that seat.'

'I've seen a man with tetanus,' said Legge suddenly. 'He looked just the same. For God's sake, doctor, d'you think he could have taken tetanus from that dart?'

'I can't tell you that off-hand, I'm afraid. What happened next?'

Dr Shaw looked at Cubitt.

'Well, Abel here – Mr Pomeroy – got a bandage and a bottle of iodine and put some iodine on the finger. Then Miss Darragh, a lady who's staying here, said she'd bandage the finger, and while she was getting out the bandage Miss Moore gave him brandy.'

'Did he actually take the brandy?'

'I think he took a little but after she'd tipped the glass up he clenched his teeth and knocked it out of her hand.'

'Complain of pain?'

'No. He looked frightened.'

'And then? After that?'

'After that? Well, just at the moment, really, the lights went out, and when they went up again he seemed much worse. He was in a terrible state.'

'A fit,' said Mr Nark, speaking for the first time. 'The man had a fit. Ghastly!' He belched uproariously.

'There's a very strong smell of brandy,' said Dr Shaw.

'It spilt,' explained Mr Nark hurriedly. 'It's all over the floor in there.'

'Where's the dart, Oates? asked Dr Shaw.

'In there, sir. I've put it in a clean bottle and corked it up.'

'Good. I'd better have it. You'll have to leave the room in there as it is, Mr Pomeroy, until I've had a word with the superintendent. The body may be removed in the morning.'

'Very good, sir.'

'And I'm afraid, Mr Parish, that under the circumstances I must report this case to the coroner.'

'Do you mean there'll have to be an inquest?'

'If he thinks it necessary.'

'And – and a post-mortem?'

'If he orders it.'

'Oh God!' said Parish.

'May I have your cousin's full name and his address?'

Parish gave them. Dr Shaw looked solemn and said it would be a great loss to the legal profession. He then returned to the private bar. Oates produced his note-book and took the floor.

'I'll have all your names and addresses, if you please, gentlemen,' he said.

'What's the use of saying that?' demanded Mr Nark, rallying a little. 'You know 'em already. You took our statements. We've signed 'em, and whether we should in law is a point I'm not sure of.'

'Never mind if I know 'em or don't, George Nark,' rejoined Oates. 'I know my business and that's quite sufficient. What's your name?'

He took all their names and addresses and suggested that they go to bed. They filed out through a door into the passage. Oates then joined Dr Shaw in the private bar.

'Hallo, Oates,' said the doctor. 'Where's that dart?'

'Legge picked the dart off the floor,' Oates said.

He showed it to Dr Shaw. He had put it into an empty bottle and sealed it.

'Good,' said Dr Shaw, and put the bottle in his bag.

'Now the remains of the brandy glass. They seem to have tramped it to smithereens. We'll see if we can gather up some of the mess. There's forceps and an empty jar in my bag. Where did the iodine come from?'

'Abel keeps his first-aid outfit in that corner cupboard, sir. He's a great one for iodine. Sloshed it all over Bob Legge's face today when he cut himself with his razor.'

Dr Shaw stooped and picked up a small bottle that had rolled under the settle.

'Here it is, I suppose.' He sniffed at it. 'Yes, that's it. Where's the cork?'

He hunted about until he found it.

'Better take this too. And the brandy bottle. Good heavens, they seem to have done themselves remarkably proud. It's nearly empty. Now where's the first-aid kit?'

Dr Shaw went to the cupboard and stared up at the glass door.

'What's that bottle in there?' he said sharply.

Oates joined them.

'That, sir? Oh yes, I know what that is. It's some stuff Abel got to kill the rats in the old stables. He mentioned it earlier this evening.'

Oates rubbed his nose vigorously.

'Seems more like a week ago. There was the deceased gentleman standing drinks and chaffing Abel, not much more than a couple of hours ago. And now look at him. Ripe for coroner as you might say.'

'Did Abel say what this rat-poison was?'

'Something in the nature of prussic acid, I fancy, sir.'

'Indeed?' said Dr Shaw. 'Get my gloves out of my overcoat pocket will you, Oates.'

'Your gloves, sir?'

'Yes, I want to open the cupboard.'

But when Oates brought the gloves, Dr Shaw still stared at the cupboard door.

'Your gloves, sir.'

'I don't think I'll use 'em. I don't think I'll open the door, Oates. There may be fingerprints all over the shop. We'll leave the cupboard door, Oates, for the expert.'

CHAPTER 6

Inquest

The Illington coroner was James Mordant Esq., M.D. He was sixty-seven years old and these years sat heavily upon him for he suffered from dyspepsia. He seemed to regard his fellow men with breeding suspicion, he sighed a great deal, and had a trick of staring despondently at the merest acquaintances. He had at one time specialized in bacteriology and it was said of him that he saw human beings as mere playgrounds for brawling micrococci. It was also said that when Dr Mordant presided over an inquest, the absence in court of the corpse was not felt. He sat huddled behind his table and rested his head on his hand with such a lack-lustre air that one might have thought he scarcely listened to the evidence. This was not the case, however. He was a capable man.

On the morning of the inquest on Luke Watchman, the third day after his death, Dr Mordant, with every appearance of the deepest distrust, heard his jury sworn and contemplated the witnesses. The inquest was held in the town hall and owing to the publicity given to Watchman's death in the London papers, was heavily attended by the public. Watchman's solicitor, who in the past had frequently briefed him, had come down from London. So had Watchman's secretary and junior and a London doctor who had attended him recently. There was a fair sprinkling of London pressmen. Dr Mordant, staring hopelessly at an old man in the front row, charged the jury to determine how, when, where, and by what means, the deceased came by his death, and whether he died from criminal, avoidable, or natural causes. He then raised his head and stared at the jury.

'Is it your wish to view the body?' he sighed.

The jury whispered and huddled, and its foreman, an auctioneer, said they thought perhaps under the circumstances they *should* view the body.

The coroner sighed again and gave an order to his officer. The jury filed out and returned in a few minutes looking unwholesome. The witnesses were then examined on oath by the coroner.

PC Oates gave formal evidence of the finding of the body. Then Sebastian Parish was called and identified the body. Everybody who had seen his performance of a bereaved brother in a trial scene of a famous picture, was now vividly reminded of it. But Parish's emotion, thought Cubitt, could not be purely histrionic unless, as he had once declared, he actually changed colour under the stress of a painful scene. Sebastian was now very pale indeed and Cubitt wondered uneasily what he thought of this affair, and how deeply he regretted the loss of his cousin. He gave his evidence in a low voice but it carried to the end of the building, and when he faltered at the description of Watchman's death, at least two of the elderly ladies in the public seats were moved to tears. Parish wore a grey suit, a soft white shirt and a black tie. He looked amazingly handsome and on his arrival, had been photographed several times.

Cubitt was called next and confirmed Parish's evidence.

Then Miss Darragh appeared. The other witnesses exuded discomfort and formality but Miss Darragh was completely at her ease. She took the oath with an air of intelligent interest. The coroner asked her if she had remembered anything that she hadn't mentioned in her first statement or if there was any point that had been missed by the previous witness.

'There is not,' said Miss Darragh. 'I told the doctor, Dr Shaw 'twas, all I had seen; and when the policeman, Constable Oates 'twas, came up on the morning after the accident, I told 'um all I knew all over again. If I may be allowed to say so it is my opinion that the small wound Mr Watchman had from the dart had nothing whatever to do with his death.'

'What makes you think, that, Miss Darragh?' asked the coroner with an air of allowing Miss Darragh a certain amount of latitude.

'Wasn't it a small paltry prick from a brand new dart that couldn't hurt a child? As Mr Parish said at the time, he was but frightened at the sight of his own blood. That was my own impression. 'Twas later that he became so ill.'

'When did you notice the change in his condition?'

'Later.'

'Was it after he had taken the brandy?'

'It was. Then or about then or after.'

'He took the brandy after Mr Pomeroy put iodine on his finger?'

'He did.'

'You agree for the rest with the previous statements?'

'I do.'

'Thank you, Miss Darragh.'

Decima Moore came next. Decima looked badly shaken but she gave her evidence very clearly and firmly. The coroner stopped her when she came to the incident of the brandy. He had a curious trick of prefacing many of his questions with a slight moan, rather in the manner of a stage parson.

'N-n-n you say, Miss Moore, that the deceased swallowed some of the brandy?'

'Yes,' said Decima.

'N-n-n you are positive on that point?'

'Yes.'

'Yes. Thank you. What happened to the glass?'

'He knocked it out of my hand on to the floor.'

'Did you get the impression that he did this deliberately?'

'No. It seemed to be involuntary.'

'And was the glass broken?'

'Yes.' Decima paused. 'At least – '

'N-n-n – yes?'

'It was broken, but I don't remember whether that happened when it fell, or afterwards when the light went out. Everybody seemed to be treading on broken glass after the lights went out.'

The coroner consulted his notes.

'And for the rest, Miss Moore, do you agree with the account given by Mr Parish, Mr Cubitt and Miss Darragh?'

'Yes.'

'In every particular?'

Decima was now very white indeed. She said, 'Everything they said is quite true, but there is one thing they didn't notice.'

The coroner sighed.

'What is that, Miss Moore?' he asked.

'It was after I gave him the brandy. He gasped and I thought he spoke. I thought he said one word.'

'What was it?'

'Poisoned,' said Decima.

And a sort of rustling in the room seemed to turn the word into an echo.

The coroner added to his notes.

'You are sure of this?' he asked.

'Yes.'

'Yes. And then?'

'He clenched his teeth very hard. I don't think he spoke again.'

'Are you positive that it was Mr Watchman's own glass that you gave him?'

'Yes. He put it on the table when he went to the dart-board. It was the only glass there. I poured a little into it from the bottle. The bottle was on the bar.'

'Had anyone but Mr Watchman touched the glass before you gave him the brandy?'

Decima said: 'I didn't notice anyone touch it.'

'Quite so. Have you anything further to tell us? Anything that escaped the notice of the previous witnesses?'

'Nothing,' said Decima.

Her deposition was read to her, and, like Parish and Cubitt, she signed it.

Will Pomeroy took the oath with an air of truculence and suspicion, but his statement differed in no way from the others, and he added nothing material to the evidence. Mr Robert Legge was the next to give evidence on the immediate circumstances surrounding Watchman's death.

On his appearance there was a tightening of attention among the listeners. The light from a high window shone full on Legge. Cubitt looked at his white hair, the grooves and folds of his face, and the calluses on his hands. He wondered how old he was and why Watchman had baited him, and exactly what sort of background he had. It was impossible to place the fellow. His clothes were good; a bit antiquated as to cut perhaps, but good. He spoke like an educated man and moved like a labourer. As he faced the coroner he straightened up and held his arms at his sides almost in the manner of a private soldier. His face was rather white and his fingers twitched, but he spoke with composure. He agreed that the account given by the previous witnesses was correct. The coroner clasped his hands on the table and gazed at them with an air of distaste.

'About this n-n-n experiment with the darts, Mr Legge,' he said, 'when was it first suggested?'

'I believe on the night of Mr Watchman's arrival. I mentioned, I think, that I had done the trick and he said something to the effect that he wouldn't care to try. I think he added that he might, after all, like to see me do it.' Legge moistened his lips. 'Later on that evening I did the trick in the public taproom and he said that if I beat him at round-the-clock he'd let me try it on him.'

'What,' asked the coroner, drearily, 'is round-the-clock?'

'You play into each segment of the dart-board beginning at number one. As soon as you miss a shot the next player has his turn. You have three darts, that is three chances to get a correct opening shot, but after that you carry on until you miss. You have to finish with fifty.'

'You all played this game?'

Legge hesitated: 'We were all in it except Miss Darragh. Miss Moore began. When she missed, Mr Cubitt took the next turn, then I came.'

'Yes?'

'I didn't miss.'

'You mean you – ran out in one turn?'

'Yes.'

'And then?'

'Mr Watchman said he believed he would trust me to do the hand trick.'

'And did you do it?'

'No, I was not anxious to do it, and turned the conversation. Later, as I have said, I did it in the public room.'

'But the following night, last Friday, you attempted it on the deceased?'

'Yes.'

'Will you tell us how this came about?'

Legge clenched his fingers and stared at an enlargement of a past mayor of Illington.

'In much the same circumstances. I mean, we were all in the private bar. Mr Watchman proposed another game of round-the-clock and said definitely that if I beat him I should try the trick with the hand. I did win and he at once insisted on the experiment.'

'Were you reluctant?'

'I – no. I have done the trick at least fifty times and I have only failed once before. On that occasion no harm was done. The dart grazed the third finger but it was really nothing. I told Mr Watchman of this incident, but he said he'd stick to his bargain, and I consented.'

'Go on please, Mr Legge.'

'He put his hand against the dart-board with the fingers spread out as I suggested. There were two segments of the board showing between the fingers in each instance.' Legge paused and then said: 'So you see it's really easier than round-the-clock. Twice as easy.'

Legge stopped and the coroner waited.

'Yes?' he said to his blotting paper.

'I tried the darts, which were new ones, and then began. I put the first dart on the outside of the little finger and the next between the little and third fingers, and the next between the third and middle.'

'It was the fourth dart, then, that miscarried?'

'Yes.'

'How do you account for that?'

'At first I thought he had moved his finger. I am still inclined to think so.'

The coroner stirred uneasily.

'Would you not be positive on this point if it was so? You must have looked fixedly at the fingers.'

'At the space between,' corrected Legge.

'I see.' Dr Mordant looked at his notes.

'The previous statements,' he said, 'mention that you had all taken a certain amount of a vintage brandy. Exactly how much brandy, Mr Legge, did you take?'

'Two nips.'

'How large a quantity? Mr William Pomeroy states that a bottle of Courvoisier '87 was opened at Mr Watchman's request and that the

contents were served out to everyone but himself, Miss Darragh and
Miss Moore. That would mean a sixth of a bottle to each of the persons who took it.'

'Er – yes. Yes.'

'Had you finished your brandy when you threw the dart?'

'Yes.'

'Had you taken anything else previously?'

'A pint of beer,' said Legge unhappily.

'N-n-n – yes. Thank you. Now where did you put the darts you
used for this experiment?'

'They were new darts. Mr Pomeroy opened the package and suggested – ' Legge broke off and wetted his lips. 'He suggested that I
should christen the new darts,' he said.

'Did you take them from Mr Pomeroy?'

'Yes. He fitted the flights while we played round-the-clock and
then gave them to me for the experiment.'

'No one else handled them?'

'Mr Will Pomeroy and Mr Parish picked them up and looked at
them.'

'I see. Now for the sequel, Mr Legge.'

But again Legge's story followed the others. His deposition was
read to him and he signed it, making rather a slow business of writing his name. The coroner called Abel Pomeroy.

II

Abel seemed bewildered and nervous. His habitual cheerfulness had
gone and he gazed at the coroner as at a recording angel of peculiar
strictness. When they reached the incident of the brandy, Dr
Mordant asked Abel if he had opened the bottle. Abel said he had.

'And you served it, Mr Pomeroy?'

' 'Ess sir.'

'Will you tell us from where you got the glasses and how much
went into each glass?'

' 'Ess sir. I got glasses from cupboard under bar. They was the best
glasses. Mr Watchman said we would kill the bottle in two halves,
sir. So I served half-bottle round. 'Twas about two fingers each. Us

polished that off and then they played round-the-clock, sir, and then us polished off 'tother half. 'Least, sir, I didn't take my second tot. Tell the truth, sir, I hadn't taken no more than a drop of my first round and that was enough for me. I'm not a great drinker,' said old Abel innocently, 'and I mostly bides by beer. But I just took a drain to please Mr Watchman. I served out for the rest of the company 'cepting my Will and Miss Darragh and Miss Dessy – Miss Moore, sir. But I left fair drain in bottle.'

'Why did you do that?'

Abel rubbed his chin and glanced uncomfortably at the other witnesses.

'Seemed like they'd had enough, sir.'

'This was before the experiment with the deceased's hand, of course,' said the coroner to the jury. 'Yes, Mr Pomeroy. How much was in the glasses on the second round?'

' 'Bout a finger and half, sir I reckon.'

'Did you hand the drinks round yourself?'

Abel said: 'I don't rightly remember. Wait a bit though, I reckon Mr Watchman handed first round to everyone.' Abel looked anxiously at Will who nodded. ' 'Ess, sir. That's how 'twas.'

'You must not communicate with other persons, Mr Pomeroy, before giving your answers,' said Dr Mordant darkly. 'And the second round?'

'Ah. I poured it out and left glasses on bar,' said Abel thoughtfully. 'Company was fairly lively by then. There was a lot of talk. I reckon each man took his own, second round. Mr Watchman carried his over to table by dart-board.'

'Would you say that at this juncture the men who had taken brandy were sober?'

'Not to say sober, sir, and not to say proper drunk. Bosky-eyed, you might say, 'cepting old George Nark and he was proper soaked. 'Ess, he was so drunk as a fish was George Nark.'

Two of the jury men laughed at this and several of the public. The coroner looked about him with an air of extreme distaste and silence set in immediately.

'Is it true,' said the coroner, 'that you have been poisoning rats in your garage, Mr Pomeroy?'

Old Abel turned very white and said, 'Yes.'

'What did you use?'

' 'Twas some stuff from the chemist.'

'Yes. Did you purchase it personally?'

'No sir. It was got for me.'

'By whom?'

'By Mr Parish, sir. I axed him and he kindly fetched it. I would like to say, sir, that when he give it to me 'twas all sealed up chemist fashion.'

'N-n yes. Do you know the nature of this poison?'

'I do believe, sir, it was in the nature of prussic acid. It's not marked anything but poison.'

'Please tell the jury how you used this substance and when?'

Abel wetted his lips and repeated his story. He had used the rat poison on Thursday evening, the evening of Watchman's arrival. He had taken great care and used every precaution. A small vessel had been placed well inside the mouth of the rat hole and some of the fluid poured into it. The hole was plugged up with rags and the bottle carefully corked. No waste drops of the fluid had escaped. Abel had worn old gloves which he afterwards threw on the fire. He had placed the bottle in a corner cupboard in the ingle-nook. It had stood alone on the shelf and the label 'Poison' could be seen through the glass door. Every one in the house was aware of the bottle and its contents.

'We have heard that the iodine was taken from a cupboard in the ingle-nook. Was this the same cupboard?'

' 'Ess fay,' said Abel quickly, 'but 'twasn't same shelf, sir. 'Twas in a tin box in another shelf and with a different door, but same piece of furniture.'

'You fetched the iodine?'

'So I did, then, and it was snug and tight in first-aid tin same as it always is. And, axing your pardon, sir, I used a dab of that same iodine on Bob Legge's chin only that evening and there the man is as fit as a flea to bear witness.'

'Quite. Thank you, Mr Pomeroy. Call Bernard Noggins, chemist of Illington.'

Mr Bernard Noggins could have been called nothing else. His eyes watered, his face was pink, his mouth hung open, and he suffered from hay fever. He was elderly and vague, and he obviously went in great terror of the coroner. He was asked if he remembered Mr Parish's visit to his shop. He said he did.

'Mr Parish asked you for a rat-poison?'

'Yes. Yes, he did.'

'What did you supply?'

'I – er – I no proprietary rat-bane in stock,' began Mr Noggins miserably, 'and no arsenic. So I suggested that the fumes of a cyanide preparation might prove beneficial.'

'Might prove *what?*'

'Efficacious. I suggested Scheele's acid.'

'You sold Mr Parish Scheele's acid?'

'Yes. No – I – actually – I diluted – I mean I added – I mean I produced a more concentrated solution by adding HCN. I – er – I supplied a 50% solution. Yes.'

The coroner dropped his pen and gazed at Mr Noggins, who went on in a great hurry.

'I warned Mr Parish. He will agree I warned him most carefully and he signed the register – every formality and precaution – most particular. Full instructions. Label.'

The coroner said: 'Why did you make this already lethal fluid so much more deadly?'

'Rats,' said Mr Noggins. 'I mean Mr Parish said it was for rats, and that Mr Pomeroy had tried a commercial rat-bane without success. Mr Parish suggested – suggested – I should – '

'Should what, Mr Noggins?'

'That I should ginger it up a bit as he put it.' Mr Noggins in the excess of his discomfort uttered a mad little laugh. The coroner turned upon him a face sickly with disapprobation and told him he might stand down. Dr Mordant then addressed the jury.

'I think, gentlemen, we have heard enough evidence as to fact and circumstance surrounding this affair and may now listen to the medical evidence. Dr Shaw, if you please!'

Dr Shaw swore himself in very briskly and, at the coroner's invitation, described the body as it was when he first saw it. The coroner's attitude of morbid introspection increased but he and Dr Shaw seemed to understand each other pretty well.

'The eyes were wide open and the pupils widely dilated, the jaws tightly clenched – ' Dr Shaw droned on and on. Parish and Cubitt who had remained in court both looked rather sick. Legge eyed Dr Shaw with a sort of mesmerized glare. Will Pomeroy held Decima's hand and old Abel stared at his boots. Mr Nark, who had expected to be called, looked alternately huffy and sheepish. A large bald man who looked as if he ought to be in uniform seemed to prick up his ears. He was Superintendent Harper of the Illington Police Force.

'You have performed an autopsy?' asked the coroner.

'Yes.'

'What did you find?'

'I found the blood much engorged and brilliant in colour. I found nothing unusual in the condition of the stomach. I sent the contents to be analysed however and the report has reached me. Nothing unexpected has been found. I also sent a certain quantity of the blood to be analysed.'

Dr Shaw paused.

'N-n – yes?'

'In the case of the sample of blood the analyst has found definite traces of hydrocyanic acid. These traces point to the presence of at least a grain and a half of the acid in the blood stream.'

'And the fatal dose?'

'One may safely say less than a grain.'

'Did you send the brandy bottle and the iodine bottle which was found under the bench to the analyst?'

'Yes.'

'What was the result, Dr Shaw?'

'The test was negative. The analyst can find no trace of hydrocyanic acid in either bottle.'

'And the dart?'

'The dart was also tested for traces of hydrocyanic acid.' Dr Shaw looked directly at the coroner and said crisply. 'Two tests were used. The first was negative. The second positive. Indications of a very slight trace of hydrocyanic acid were found upon the dart.'

III

There was only one other witness, a representative of the firm that made the darts. He stated with considerable emphasis that at no

stage of their manufacture did they come in contact with any form
of cyanide and that no cyanic preparation was to be found in the
entire factory.

The coroner summed up at considerable length and with com-
mendable simplicity. His manner suggested that the jury as a whole
was certifiable as mentally unsound but that he knew his duty and
would perform it in the teeth of stupidity. He surveyed the circumstances surrounding Watchman's death. He pointed out that the
only word spoken by the deceased, the word 'poisoned' overheard
by one witness alone, should not weigh too heavily in the minds of
the jury. In the first place the evidence might be regarded as hearsay
and therefore inadmissable at any other court. In the second there
was nothing to show why the deceased had uttered this word or
whether his impression had been based on any actual knowledge.
They might attach considerable importance to the point that the
post-mortem analysis gave positive signs of the presence of some
kind of cyanide in the blood. They might, while remembering the
presence of a strong solution of hydrocyanic acid in the room, also
note the assurance given by several of the witnesses that all reasonable precaution had been taken in the use and disposal of the bottle. They would very possibly consider that the use for domestic
purposes of so dangerous a poison was extremely ill-advised. He
reminded them of Watchman's idiosyncrasy for the acid. He delivered a short address on the forms in which this, the most deadly of
the cerebral depressants, was usually found. He said that since
hydrogen cyanide is excessively volatile the fact that none was
found in the stomach did not preclude the possibility that the
deceased had taken it by the mouth. He reminded them again of the
expert evidence. No cyanide had been found in the brandy bottle or
the iodine bottle. The fragments of the broken brandy-glass had also
given a negative result in the test for cyanide but they might
remember that as those fragments were extremely minute the test
in this instance could not be considered conclusive. They would of
course note that the point of the dart had yielded a positive result
in the second test made by the analyst. This dart was new but had
been handled by three persons before Mr Legge used it. He wound
up by saying that if the jury came to the conclusion that the
deceased died of cyanide poisoning but that there was not enough

evidence to say positively how he took the poison, they might return a verdict to this effect.

Upon this hint the jury retired for ten minutes and came back to deliver themselves, as well as they could remember them in Dr Mordant's own words. They added a shocked and indignant remark on the subject of prussic acid in the home.

The inquest on Luke Watchman was ended and his cousin was free to bury his body.

CHAPTER 7

Complaint from a Publican

'Summer,' said Chief Detective-Inspector Alleyn moodily, 'is a-comyng in and my temper is a-going out. Lhude sing cuccu. I find that the length of my patience, Fox, fluctuates in an inverse ratio with the length of the days.'

'Don't you like the warm weather?' asked Detective-Inspector Fox.

'Yes, Fox, but not in London. Not in the Yard. Not in the streets where one feels dirty half an hour after one has bathed. Not when one is obliged to breathe the fumes of petrol and the body-odour of those who come to make statements and remain to smell. That creature who has just left us stank abominably. However, the case is closed, which is a slight alleviation. But I don't like summer in London.'

'Ah well,' said Fox shifting his thirteen stone from one leg to the other, 'chacun à son goût.'

'Your French improves.'

'It ought to, Mr Alleyn. I've been sweating at it for two years now but I can't say I feel what you might call at home with it. Give me time and I can see my way with the stuff but that's not good enough. Not nearly good enough.'

'Courage, Fox. Dogged as does it. What brought you up here?'

'There's a chap came into the waiting-room an hour ago with rather a rum story, sir. They sent him along to me. I don't know that there's much in it, but I thought you might be interested.'

'Why?' asked Alleyn apprehensively.

'I nearly sent him off,' continued Fox who had his own way of imparting information. 'I did tell him it was nothing to do with us and that he'd better go to the local Super, which is, of course, what he'll have to do anyway if there's anything in it.'

'Fox,' said Alleyn, 'am I a Tantalus that you should hold this beaker, however unpalatable, beyond my reach? What was this fellow's story? What prevented you from following the admirable course you have outlined? And why have you come in here?'

'It's about the Watchman business.'

'Oh?' Alleyn swung round in his chair. 'What about it?'

'I remembered you'd taken an interest in it, Mr Alleyn, and that deceased was a personal friend of yours.'

'Well – an acquaintance.'

'Yes. You mentioned that there were one or two points that were not brought out at the inquest.'

'Well?'

'Well, this chap's talking about one of them. The handling of the darts.'

Alleyn hesitated. At last he said. 'He must go to the local people.'

'I thought you might like to see him before we got rid of him.'

'Who is he?'

'The pub-keeper.'

'Has he come up from Devon to see us?'

'Yes, he has. He says the Super at Illington wouldn't listen to him.'

'None of our game.'

'I thought you might like to see him,' Fox repeated.

'All right, blast you. Bring him up.'

'Very good, sir,' said Fox and went out.

Alleyn put his papers together and shoved them into a drawer of his desk. He noticed with distaste that the papers felt gritty and that the handle of the drawer was sticky. He wished suddenly that something important might crop up somewhere in the country, somewhere, for preference, in the South of England and his thoughts switched back to the death of Luke Watchman in Devon. He called to mind the report of the inquest. He had read it attentively.

Fox returned and stood with his hand on the door.

'In here, if you please, Mr Pomeroy,' said Fox.

Alleyn thought his visitor would have made a very good model for the portrait of an innkeeper. Abel's face was broad, ruddy, and amiable. His mouth looked as if it had only just left off smiling and was ready to break into a smile again, for all that, at the moment, he was rather childishly solemn. He wore his best suit and it sat uneasily upon him. He walked half-way across the floor and made a little bow.

'Good afternoon, sir,' said Abel.

'Good afternoon, Mr Pomeroy. I hear you've come all the way up from the West Country to see us.'

'I have so, sir. First time since Coronation and not such a pleasant errand. I bide home-along mostly.'

'Lucky man. Sit down, Mr Pomeroy.'

'Much obliged, sir.'

Abel sat down and spread his hands on his knees.

'This gentleman,' he said, looking at Fox, 'says it do be none of your business here, sir. That's a bit of a facer. I got no satisfaction along to Illington, and I says to myself, "I'll go up top. I'll cut through all their pettifogging, small-minded ways, and lay my case boldly before the witty brains of those masterpieces at Scotland Yard." Seems like I've wasted time and money.'

'That's bad luck,' said Alleyn. 'I'm sorry, but Inspector Fox is right. The Yard only takes up an outside case at the request of the local superintendent, you see. But if you'd care to tell me, unofficially, what the trouble is, I think I may invite you to do so.'

'Better than nothing, sir, and thank you very kindly.' Abel moistened his lips and rubbed his knees. 'I'm sore troubled,' he said. 'It's got me under the weather. First time anything of a criminal nature has ever come my way. The Feathers has got a clean sheet, sir. Never any trouble about after-hours in my house. Us bides by the law and now it seems as how the law don't bide by we.'

'A *criminal* nature?' said Alleyn.

'What else am I to think of it, sir? 'Twasn't accident! 'Twasn't neglect on my part for all they're trying to put on me.'

'Suppose,' said Alleyn, 'we begin at the beginning, Mr Pomeroy. You've come to see us because you've information – '

Abel opened his mouth but Alleyn went on: '– information or an opinion about the death of Mr Luke Watchman.'

'Opinion!' said Abel. 'That's the word.'

'The finding at the inquest was death by cyanide poisoning, with nothing to show exactly how it was taken.'

'And a proper fidgeting suspicioning verdict it was,' said Abel warmly. 'What's the result? Result is George Nark, so full of silly blusteracious nonsense as an old turkeycock, going round 't Coombe with a story as how I killed Mr Watchman along of criminal negligence with prussic acid. George Nark axing me of an evening if I've washed out glasses in my tap, because he'd prefer not to die in agony same as Mr Watchman. George Nark talking his ignorant blusteracious twaddle to any one as is stupid enough to listen to him.'

'Very irritating,' said Alleyn. 'Who is Mr Nark?'

'Old fool of a farmer, sir, with more long words than wits in his yed. I wouldn't pay no attention, knowing his tongue's apt to make a laughing-stock of the man, but other people listen and it's bad for trade. I know,' said Abel steadily, 'I know as certain-sure as I know anything in this life, that it was no fault of mine Mr Watchman died of poison in my private tap. Because why? So soon as us had done with that stuff in my old stables, it was corked up proper. For all there wasn't a drop of wetness on the bottle, I wiped it thorough and burned the rag. I carried it in with my own hands, sir, and put it in the cupboard. Wearing gas mask and gloves, I was, and I chucked the gloves on the fire and washed my hands afterwards. And thurr that bottle stood, sir, for twenty-four hours and if any drop of stuff came out of it, 'twas by malice and not by accident. I've axed my housekeeper and the li'l maid who works for us and neither on 'em's been near cupboard. Too mortal scared they wurr. Nor has my boy Will. And what's more, sir, the glasses Mr Watchman and company drank from that ghastly night, was our best glasses, and I took 'em special out of cupboard under bar. Now, sir, could this poison, however deadly, get itself out of stoppered bottle, through glass door, and into tumbler under my bar? Could it? I ax you?'

'It sounds rather like a conjuring trick,' agreed Alleyn with a smile.

'So it do.'

'What about the dart, Mr Pomeroy?'

'Ah!' said Abel. 'Thicky dart! When George Nark don't be saying I did for the man in his cups, he be swearing his soul away I mused up thicky dart with prussic acid. Mind this, sir, the darts wurrn't arrived when us brought in poison on Thursday night, and they wurr only unpacked five minutes before the hijus moment itself. Now!'

'Yes, they were new darts, weren't they? I seem to remember – '

''Ess fay, and never used till then. I opened 'em up myself while company was having their last go round-the-clock. I opened 'em up on bar counter. Fresh in their London wrappings, they wurr. Mr Parish and my boy Will, they picked 'em up and looked at 'em casual like, and then Bob Legge, he scooped 'em up and took a trial throw with the lot. He said they carried beautiful. Then he had his shot at Mr Watchman's hand. They wurr clean new, they darts.'

'And yet,' said Alleyn, 'the analyst found a trace of cyanide on the dart that pierced Mr Watchman's finger.'

Abel brought his palms down with a smack on his knees.

''Od rabbit it,' he shouted, 'don't George Nark stuff that thurr chunk of science down my gullet every time he opens his silly face? Lookee yurr, sir! 'Twas twenty-four hours and more, since I put bottle o' poison in cupboard. I'd washed my hands half a dozen times since then. Bar had been swabbed down. Ax yourself, how could I infectorite they darts?'

Alleyn looked at the sweaty earnest countenance before him and whistled soundlessly.

'Yes,' he said at last, 'it seems unlikely.'

'Unlikely. It's slap down impossible.'

'But – '

'If poison got on thicky dart,' said Abel, ''twasn't by accident not yet by carelessness. 'Twas by malice. 'Twas with murderacious intent. Thurr!'

'But how do you account – '

'Account? Me?' asked old Abel agitatedly. 'I don't. I leaves they intellectual capers to Superintendent Nicholas Harper and a pretty poor fist he do be making of it. That's why – '

'Yes, yes,' said Alleyn hurriedly. 'But remember that Mr Harper may be doing more than you think. Policemen have to keep their own counsel, you see. Don't make up your mind that because he doesn't say very much – '

'It's not what he don't say, it's the silly standoffishness of what he do say. Nick Harper! Damme, I was to school with the man, and now he sits behind his desk and looks at me as if I be a fool. "Where's your facts?" he says. "Don't worry yourself," he says, "if there's anything fishy us'll fish for it." Truth of the matter is the man's too small and ignorant for a murderous matter. Can't raise himself above the level of motor licences and after-hour trade, and more often than not he makes a muck of them. What'll come to the Feathers if this talk goes on? Happen us'll have to give up the trade, after a couple of centuries.'

'Don't you believe it,' said Alleyn. 'We can't afford to lose our old pubs, Mr Pomeroy, and it's going to take more than a week's village gossip to shake the trade at the Plume of Feathers. It is just a week since the inquest, isn't it? It's fresh in Mr George Nark's memory. Give it time to die down.'

'If this affair dies down, sir, there'll be a murderer unhung in the Coombe.'

Alleyn raised his brows.

'You feel like that about it?'

''Ess, I do. What's more, sir, I'll put a name to the man.'

Alleyn lifted a hand but old Abel went on doggedly.

'I don't care who hears me, I'll put a name to him and that there name's Robert Legge. Now!'

II

'A very positive old article,' said Alleyn when Fox returned from seeing Abel Pomeroy down the corridor.

'I can't see why he's made up his mind this chap Legge is a murderer,' said Fox. 'He'd only known deceased twenty-four hours. It sounds silly.'

'He says Watchman gibed at Legge,' said Alleyn. 'I wonder if he did. And why.'

'I've heard him in court often enough,' said Fox. 'He was a prime heckler. Perhaps it was a habit.'

'I don't think so. He was a bit malicious though. He was a striking sort of fellow. Plenty of charm and a good deal of vanity. He always seemed to me to take unnecessary trouble to be liked. But I didn't know him well. The cousin's a damn good actor. Rather like Watchman, in a way. Oh well, it's not our pidgin, thank the Lord. I'm afraid the old boy's faith in us wonderful police has been shaken.'

'D'you know the Super at Illington, Mr Alleyn?'

'Harper? Yes, I do. He was in on that arson case in South Devon in '37. Served his apprenticeship in L Division. You must remember him.'

'Nick Harper?'

'That's the fellow. Devon, born and bred. I think perhaps I'd better write and warn him about Mr Pomeroy's pilgrimage.'

'I wonder if old Pomeroy's statement's correct. I wonder if he did make a bloomer with the rat poison, and is simply trying to save his face.'

'His indignation seemed to me to be supremely righteous. I fancy he thinks he's innocent.'

'Somebody else may have mucked about with the bottle and won't own up,' Fox speculated.

'Possible. But who'd muck about with hydrocyanic acid for the sheer fun of the thing?'

'The alternative,' said Fox, 'is murder.'

'Is it? Well, you bumble off and brood on it. You must be one of those zealous officers who rise to the top of the profession.'

'Well, sir,' said Fox, 'it's funny. On the face of it, it's funny.'

'Run away and laugh at it, then. I'm going home, Br'er Fox.'

But when Fox had gone Alleyn sat and stared at the top of his desk. At last he drew a sheet of paper towards him and began to write.

'*Dear Nick*, – It's some time since we met and you'll wonder why the devil I'm writing. A friend of yours has just called on us, Abel Pomeroy of the Plume of Feathers, Ottercombe. He's in a state of injury and fury and is determined to get to the bottom of the Luke Watchman business. I tried to fob him off with fair words but it wasn't a howling success and he's gone away with every intention of making things hum until you lug a murderer home to justice. I thought I'd just warn you, but you'll probably hear from him before this reaches you. Don't, for the love of Mike, think we want to butt in. How are you? I envy you your job, infuriated innkeepers and all. In this weather we suffocate at C1.

Yours ever,

Roderick Alleyn'

Alleyn sealed and stamped this letter. He took his hat and stick from the wall, put on one glove, pulled it off again, cursed, and went to consult the newspaper files for the reports on the death of Luke Watchman.

An hour passed. It is significant that when he finally left the Yard and walked rapidly down the Embankment, his lips were pursed in a soundless whistle.

CHAPTER 8

Alleyn at Illington

Superintendent Nicholas Harper to Chief Detective-Inspector Alleyn:

> 'Illington Police
> Station,
> South Devon,
> 8th August.

Dear Mr Alleyn, – Yours of the 6th inst. to hand for which I thank you. As regards Mr Abel Pomeroy I am very grateful for information received as per your letter as it enabled me to deal with Pomeroy more effectively, knowing the action he had taken as regards visiting C1. For your private information we are working on the case which presents one or two features which seem to preclude possibility of accident. Well Mr Alleyn – Rory, if you will pardon the liberty – it was nice to hear from you. I have not forgotten that arson case in '37 nor the old days in L Division. A country Super gets a bit out of things.

With kind regards and many thanks,

> Yours faithfully,
> *N. W. Harper, Superintendent.*'

Part of a letter from Colonel the Hon. Maxwell Brammington, Chief Constable of South Devon, to the Superintendent of the Central Branch of New Scotland Yard:

'– and on the score of the deceased's interests and activities being centred in London, I have suggested to Superintendent Harper that he consult you. In my opinion the case is somewhat beyond the resources and experience of our local force. Without wishing for a moment to exceed my prerogative in this matter, I venture to suggest that as we are already acquainted with Chief Detective-Inspector Alleyn of C1, we should be delighted if he was appointed to this case. That, however, is of course entirely for you to decide.

I am,

Yours faithfully,

Maxwell Brammington, CC.'

'Well, Mr Alleyn,' said the Superintendent of C1, staring at the horseshoe and crossed swords that garnished the walls of his room, 'you seem to be popular in South Devon.'

'It must be a case, sir,' said Alleyn, 'of sticking to the ills they know.'

'Think so? Well, I'll have a word with the AC. You'd better pack your bag and tell your wife.'

'Certainly, sir.'

'You knew Watchman, didn't you?'

'Slightly, sir. I've had all the fun of being turned inside out by him in the witness-box.'

'In the Davidson case?'

'And several others.'

'I seem to remember you were equal to him. But didn't you know him personally?'

'Slightly.'

'He was a brilliant counsel.'

'He was indeed.'

'Well, watch your step and do us proud.'

'Yes, sir.'

'Taking Fox?'

'If I may.'

'That's all right. We'll hear from you.'

Alleyn returned to his room, collected his emergency suitcase and kit, and sent for Fox.

'Br'er Fox,' he said, 'this is a wish-fulfilment. Get your fancy pyjamas and your toothbrush. We catch the midday train for South Devon.'

II

The branch-line from Exter to Illington meanders amiably towards the coast. From the train windows Alleyn and Fox looked down on sunken lanes, on thatched roofs and on glossy hedgerows that presented millions of tiny mirrors to the afternoon sun. Alleyn let down the window and the scent of hot grass and leaves drifted into the stuffy carriage.

'Nearly there, Br'er Fox. That's Illington church spire over the hill and there's the glint of sea beyond.'

'Very pleasant,' said Fox, dabbing at his enormous face with his handkerchief. 'Warm though.'

'High summer, out there.'

'You never seem to show the heat, Mr Alleyn. Now I'm a warm man. I perspire very freely. Always have. It's not an agreeable habit, though they tell me it's healthy.'

'Yes, Fox.'

'I'll get the things down, sir.'

The train changed its pace from slow to extremely slow. Beyond the window, a main road turned into a short-lived main street with a brief network of surrounding shops. The word 'Illington' appeared in white stones on a grassy bank, and they drew into the station.

'There's the super,' said Fox. 'Very civil.'

Superintendent Harper shook hands at some length. Alleyn, once as touchy as a cat, had long ago accustomed himself to official handclasps. And he liked Harper who was bald, scarlet-faced, blue-eyed, and sardonic.

'Glad to see you, Mr Alleyn,' said Harper. 'Good afternoon. Good afternoon, Mr Fox. I've got a car outside.'

He drove them in a police Ford down the main street. They passed a Woolworth store, a departmental store, a large hotel, and a row of small shops amongst which Alleyn noticed one labelled 'Bernard Noggins, Chemist'.

'Is that where Parish bought the cyanide?'

'You haven't lost any time, Mr Alleyn,' said Harper who seemed to hover on the edge of Alleyn's christian name and to funk it at the last second. 'Yes, that's it. He's a very stupid sort of man, is Bernie Noggins. There's the station. The colonel will be along presently. He's in a shocking mood over this affair, but you may be able to cope with him. I thought that before we moved on to Ottercome, you might like to see the files and have a tell,' said Harper whose speech still held a tang of West Country.

'Splendid. Where are we to stay?'

'That's as you like, of course, Mr Alleyn, but I've told that old blatherskite Pomeroy to hold himself in readiness. I thought you might prefer to be on the spot. I've warned him to say nothing about it and I think he'll have the sense to hold his tongue. No need to put anybody on the alert, is there? This car's at your service.'

'Yes, but look here – '

'It's quite all right, Mr Alleyn. I've a small two-seater we can use here.'

'That sounds perfectly splendid,' said Alleyn and followed Harper into the police station.

They sat down in Harper's office while he got out his files. Alleyn looked at the photographs of past superintendents, at the worn linoleum and varnished wood-work, and he wondered how many times he had sat in country police stations waiting for the opening gambit of a case that, for one reason or another, had been a little too much for the local staff. Alleyn was the youngest chief-inspector at the Central Branch of New Scotland Yard, but he was forty-three. 'I'm getting on,' he thought without regret. 'Old Fox must be fifty, he's getting quite grey. We've done all this so many times together.' And he heard his own voice as if it was the voice of another man, uttering the familiar phrases.

'I hope we won't be a nuisance to you, Nick. A case of this sort's always a bit tiresome isn't it? Local feeling and so on.'

Harper clapped a file down on his desk, threw his head back and looked at Alleyn from under his spectacles.

'Local feeling?' he said. 'Local stupidity! I don't care. They work it out for themselves and get a new version every day. Old Pomeroy's not the worst, not by a long chalk. The man's got something to complain about or thinks he has. It's these other experts, George Nark and Co, that make all the trouble. Nark's written three letters to the Illington *Courier*. The first was about finger-printing. He called it the Bertillion system, of course, ignorant old ass, and wanted to know if we'd printed everyone who was there when Watchman died. So I got him round here and printed him. So he wrote another letter to the paper about the liberty of the subject and said the South Devon constabulary were a lot of Hitlers. Then Oates, the Coombe PC, found him crawling about outside Pomeroy's garage with a magnifying class and kicked him out. So he wrote another letter saying the police were corrupt. Then the editor, who ought to know better, wrote a damn-fool leader, and then three more letters about me appeared. They were signed, "Vigilant", "Drowsy" and "Moribund". Then all the pressmen who'd gone away came back again. I don't care. What of it? But the CC began ringing me up three times a day and I got fed up and suggested he asked you and he jumped at it. There's the file.'

Alleyn and Fox hastened to make sympathetic noises.

'Before we see the file,' Alleyn said, 'we'd very much like to hear your own views. We've looked up the report on the inquest so we've got the main outline or ought to have it.'

'My views?' repeated Mr Harper moodily. 'I haven't got any. I don't think it was an accident.'

'Don't you, now!'

'I don't see how it could have been. I suppose old Pomeroy bleated about his injuries when he went screeching up to the Yard. I think he's right. Far as I can see the old man did take reasonable precautions. Well, perhaps not that, the stuff ought never to have been left on the premises. But I don't see how, twenty-four hours after he'd stowed the bottle away in the cupboard, he could have infected that dart accidentally. We've printed the cupboard. It's got his prints on it and nobody else's.'

'Oh,' said Alleyn, 'then it isn't a case of somebody else having tampered with the bottle and been too scared to own up.'

'No.'

'How many sets of Pomeroy's prints are on the cupboard door?'

'Several. Four good ones on the knob. And he turned the key in the top cupboard when he put the cyanide away. His print's on the key all right and you can't do the pencil trick, for I've tried. It's a fair teaser.'

'Any prints on the bottle?'

'None. But he explained he wore gloves and wiped the bottle.'

'The cupboard door's interesting.'

'Is it? Well, when he opened the parcel of darts he broke the seals. I got hold of the wrapping and string. The string had only been tied once and the seals have got the shop's mark on them.'

'Damn good, Nick,' said Alleyn. Mr Harper looked a little less jaundiced.

'Well, it goes to show,' he admitted. 'The dart was OK when old Pomeroy unpacked it. Then young Will and Parish handled the darts, and then Legge tried them out. Next thing – one of 'em sticks into deceased's finger and in five minutes he's a corpse.'

'The inference being – ?'

'God knows! They found cyanide on the dart but how the hell it got there's a masterpiece. I suppose old Pomeroy's talked Legge to you.'

'Yes.'

'Yes. Well, Legge had his coat off and his sleeves rolled up. Cubitt and young Pomeroy swear he took the darts with his left hand and held them point outward in a bunch while he tried them. They say he didn't wait any time at all. Just threw them into the board, said they were all right, and then waded in with his trick. You see, they were all watching Legge.'

'Yes.'

'What about the other five, Super?' asked Fox. 'He used six for the trick, didn't he?'

'Meaning one of them might have contrived to smear cyanide on one dart, while they looked at the lot?'

'It doesn't make any sort of sense,' said Alleyn. 'How was Cubitt or young Pomeroy to know Legge was going to pink Watchman?'

'That's right,' agreed Harper, relapsing. 'So it must be Legge but it couldn't be Legge; so it must be accident but it couldn't be accident. Funny, isn't it?'

'Screamingly.'

'The iodine bottle's all right and so's the brandy bottle.'

'The brandy glass was broken?'

'Smashed to powder except the bottom and that was in about thirty pieces. They couldn't find any cyanide.'

'Whereabouts on the dart was the trace of cyanide?'

'On the tip and half-way up the steel point. We've printed the dart, of course. It's got Legge's prints all over it. They've covered

Abel's or anybody else's who touched it except Oates, and he kept his head and only handled it by the flight. The analyst's report is here. And all the exhibits.'

'Yes. Have you fished up a motive?'

'The money goes to Parish and Cubitt. Two-thirds to Parish and one-third to Cubitt. That's excepting one or two small legacies. Parish is the next-of-kin. It's a big estate. The lawyer was as close as an oyster, but I've found out it ought to wash up at something like fifty thousand. We don't know much beyond what everybody knows. Reckon most folks have seen Sebastian Parish on the screen, and Mr Cubitt seems to be a well-known artist. The CC expects the Yard to tackle that end of the stick.'

'Thoughtful of him! Anyone else?'

'They've found a bit already. They've found Parish's affairs are in a muddle and he's been to the Jews. Cubitt had money in that Chain Stores Unlimited thing, that bust the other day. There's motive there all right.'

'Anyone else? Pomeroy's fancy? The mysterious Legge?'

'Him? Motive? You've heard Pomeroy, Mr Alleyn. Says deceased behaved peculiar to Legge. Chaffed him like. Well, what is there in that? It seems there was a bit of a collision between them, the day Mr Watchman drove into the Coombe. Day before the fatality that was. Legge's a bad driver anyway. Likely enough Mr Watchman felt kind of irritated, and let Legge know all about it when they met again. Likely, Legge's views irritated Mr Watchman.'

'His views?'

'He's an out-and-out communist is Legge. Secretary and treasurer of the Coombe Left Movement and in with young Will and Miss Moore. Mr Watchman seems to have made a bit of a laughing stock of the man but you don't do murder because you've been made to look silly.'

'Not very often I should think. Do you know anything about Legge? He's a newcomer, isn't he?'

Harper unhooked his spectacles and laid them on his desk.

'Yes,' he said, 'he's foreign to these parts. We've followed up the usual routine, Mr Alleyn, but we haven't found much. He says he came here for his health. He's opened a small banking account at Illington, three hundred and fifty pounds. He came to the Feathers ten months ago. He gets a big lot of letters, and writes a lot to all parts of the West Country and sends away a number of small packages. Seems he's agent for some stamp collecting affair. I got the name, "Phillips Philatelic Society", and got one of our chaps to look up the headquarters in London. Sure enough, this chap Legge's the forwarding agent for the west of England. Well, he chummed up with young Will, and about three months ago they gave him this job with the Coombe Left business. I don't mind saying I don't like the looks of the man. He's a funny chap. Unhealthy, I'd say. Something the matter with his ears. We've searched all their rooms and I found a chemist's bottle and a bit of a squirt in his. Had it tested, you bet, but it's only some muck he squirts into his beastly lug. So I returned it. Cubitt's room was full of his painting gear. We found oil, and turpentine and varnish. Went through the lot. Of course we didn't expect to find anything. Parish,' said Harper in disgust, 'uses scent. Well, not to say scent, but some sort of toilet water. No, I don't mind saying I don't like the looks of Legge, but there again Miss Moore says Mr Watchman told her he'd never set eyes on the man before.'

'Well,' said Alleyn, 'let's go through the list while we're at it. What about young Pomeroy?'

'Will? Yes. Yes, there's young Will.' Harper opened the file and stared at the first page, but it seemed to Alleyn that he was not reading it. 'Will Pomeroy,' said Harper, 'says he didn't like Mr Watchman. He makes no bones about it. Mr Parish says they quarrelled on account of this chap Legge. Will didn't like the way Mr Watchman got at Legge, you see, and being a hot-headed loyalist kind of fellow, he tackled Mr Watchman. It wasn't much of an argument, but it was obvious Will Pomeroy had taken a scunner on Mr Watchman.'

'And – what is the lady's name? Miss Decima Moore. What about her?'

'Nothing. Keeps company with Will. She's a farmer's daughter. Old Jim Moore up to Cary Edge. Her mother's a bit on the classy side. Foreigner to these parts and can't forget she came down in society when she married Farmer Moore. Miss Decima was educated at Oxford and came home a red leftist. She and deceased used to argufy a bit about politics, but that's all.'

Alleyn counted on his long thin fingers.

'That's five,' he said, 'six counting old Pomeroy. We're left with the Honourable Violet Darragh and Mr George Nark.'

'You can forget 'em,' rejoined Harper. 'The Honourable Violet's a rum old girl from Ireland, who takes views in paints. She was there writing letters when it happened. I've checked up on her and she's the genuine article. She'll talk the hind leg off a donkey. So'll George Nark. He's no murderer. He's too damned silly to kill a woodlouse except he treads on it accidental.'

'How many of these people are still at Ottercombe?'

'All of 'em.'

'Good Lord!' Alleyn exclaimed, 'didn't they want to get away when it was all over? I'd have thought – '

'So would anybody,' agreed Harper. 'But it seems Mr Cubitt had started off on several pictures down there and wants to finish them. One's a likeness of Mr Parish so he's stayed down-along too. They waited for the funeral which was here. Deceased had no relatives nearer than Mr Parish and Mr Parish said he thought his cousin would have liked to be put away in the country. Several legal gentlemen came down from London and the flowers were a masterpiece. Well, they just stopped on, Mr Cubitt painting as quiet as you please. He's a cool customer, is Mr Cubitt.'

'How much longer will they be here?'

'Reckon another week. They came for three. Did the same thing last year. It's a fortnight tonight since this case cropped up. We've kept the private bar shut up. Everything was photographed and printed. There was nothing of interest in deceased's pockets. He smoked some outlandish kind of cigarettes. Daha – something, but that's no use. We've got his movements taped out. Arrived on Thursday night and didn't go out. Friday morning, went for a walk, but don't know exactly where, except it was through the tunnel. Friday afternoon, went upstairs after lunch and was in his room writing letters. Seen in his room by Mrs Ives, the housekeeper, who went up at 3.30 to shut windows and found him asleep on his bed. Also seen at four o'clock by Mr Cubitt who looked in on his way back from painting down on the wharf. Came downstairs at 5.15 or thereabouts and was in the private bar from then onwards till he died. I don't think I missed anything.'

'I'm sure you didn't.'

'You know,' said Harper warming a little, 'it's a proper mystery, this case. Know what I mean, most cases depend on routine. Boil 'em down and it's routine that does the trick as a general rule. May do it here, but all the same this is a teaser. I'm satisfied it wasn't accident but I can't prove it. When I'm told on good authority that there was cyanide on that dart, and that Mr Watchman died of cyanide in his blood, I say "well, there's your weapon," but alongside of this there's six people, let alone my own investigation, that prove to my satisfaction nobody could have tampered with the dart. But the dart was poisoned. Now, the stuff in the rat hole was in a little china jar. I've left it there for you to see. I got another jar of the same brand. They sell some sort of zinc ointment in them and Abel had several; he's mad on that sort of thing. Now the amount that's gone from the bottle, which Noggins says was full, is a quarter of an ounce more than the amount the jar holds and Abel swears he filled the jar. The jar was full when we saw it.'

'Full?' said Alleyn sharply. 'When did you see it?'

'The next morning.'

'Was the stuff in the jar analysed?'

Harper turned brick-red.

'No,' he said. 'Abel swore he'd filled it and the jar's only got his prints on it. And, I tell you, it *was* full.'

'Have you got the stuff?'

'Yes. I poured it off and kept it. Seeing there's a shortage the stuff on the dart must have come from the bottle.'

'For how long was the bottle uncorked?'

'What? Oh, he said that when he used it he uncorked the bottle and put it on the shelf above the hole, with the cork beside it. He was very anxious we should know he'd been careful, and he said he didn't want to handle the cork more than was necessary. He said he was just going to pour the stuff in the jar when he thought he'd put the jar in position first. He did that and then filled it, holding the torch in his other hand. He swears he didn't spill any and he swears nobody touched the bottle. The others were standing in the doorway.'

'So the bottle may have been uncorked for a minute or two?'

'I suppose so. He plugged up the hole with rag before he did anything else. He had the bottle on the floor beside him.'

'And then?'

'Well, then he took up the bottle and corked it. I suppose,' said Harper, 'I should have had the stuff analysed but we've no call to suspect Abel Pomeroy. There was none missing from the jar and there are only his prints on it, and there's the extra quarter ounce missing from the bottle. No, it's gone from the bottle. Must have. And, see here, Mr Alleyn, the stuff was found on the dart and nowhere else. What's more, if it was the dart that did the trick and it's murder, then Legge's our bird because only Legge controlled the flight of the dart.'

'Silly sort of way to kill a man,' said Fox, suddenly. 'It'd be asking for a conviction, Super, now wouldn't it?'

'Maybe he reckoned he'd get a chance to wipe the dart,' said Harper.

'He had his chance,' said Alleyn quickly. 'Wasn't it brought out that Legge helped the constable – Oates isn't it? – to find the dart? He had his chance, then, to wipe it.'

'And if he was guilty, why didn't he?' ended Fox.

'You're asking *me*,' said Superintendent Harper. 'Here's the colonel.'

III

The chief constable was an old acquaintance of Alleyn's. Alleyn liked Colonel Brammington. He was a character, an oddity, full of mannerisms that amused rather than irritated Alleyn. He was so unlike the usual county-minded chief constable that it was a matter for conjecture how he ever got the appointment, for he spent half his life in giving offence and was amazingly indiscreet. He arrived at Illington Police Station in a powerful racing car that was as scarred as a veteran. It could be heard from the moment it entered the street and Harper exclaimed agitatedly:

'Here he comes! He knows that engine's an offence within the meaning of the Act and he doesn't care. He'll get us all into trouble one of these days. There are complaints on all sides. On all sides!'

The screech of heavy tyres and violent braking announced Colonel Brammington's arrival and in a moment he came in. He was a vast red man with untidy hair, prominent eyes, and a loud voice. The state of his clothes suggested that he'd been dragged by the heels through some major disaster.

He shouted an apology at Harper, touched Alleyn's hand as if it was a bomb, stared at Fox, and then hurled himself into a seagrass chair with such abandon that he was like to break it.

'I should have been here half an hour ago,' shouted Colonel Brammington, 'but for my car, my detestable, my abominable car.'

'What was the matter, sir?' asked Harper.

'My good Harper, I have no notion. Fortunately I was becalmed near a garage. The fellow thrust his head among her smoking entrails, uttered some mumbo-jumbo, performed suitable rites with oil and water, and I was enabled to continue.'

He twisted his bulk in the creaking chair and stared at Alleyn.

'Perfectly splendid that you have responded with such magnificent celerity to our *cri du coeur*, Alleyn. We shall now resume, thankfully, the upholstered leisure of the not too front, front stall.'

'Don't be too sure of that, sir,' said Alleyn. 'It looks as if there's a weary grind ahead of us.'

'O God, how insupportably dreary! What, hasn't the solution been borne in upon you in a single penetrating flash? Pray expect no help from me. Have you got a cigarette, Harper?'

Alleyn offered his case.

'Thank you. I haven't even a match, I'm afraid. Ah, thank you.' Colonel Brammington lit his cigarette and goggled at Alleyn. 'I suppose Harper's given you the whole tedious rigmarole,' he said.

'He's given me the file. I suggest that Fox and I take it with us to Ottercombe and digest it.'

'O Lord! Yes, do. Yes, of course. But you've discussed the case?'

'Yes, sir. Mr Harper has given me an excellent survey of the country.'

'It's damned difficult country. Now, on the face of it, what's your opinion, accident or not?'

'On the face of it,' said Alleyn, 'not.'

'O Lord!' repeated Colonel Brammington. He got up with surprising agility from his tortured chair, and moved restlessly about the room. 'Yes,' he said, 'I agree with you. The fellow was murdered. And of all the damned unconscionable methods of despatching a man! An envenom'd stuck, by God! How will you hunt it home to this fellow?'

'Which fellow, sir?'

'The murderer, my dear man. Legge! A prating soapbox orator of a fellow, I understand; some squalid little trouble-hatcher. Good God, my little Alleyn, of course he's your man! I've said so from the beginning. There was cyanide on the dart. He threw the dart. He deliberately pinked his victim.'

'Harper,' said Alleyn with a glance at the superintendent's shocked countenance, 'tells me that several of the others agree that Legge had no opportunity to anoint the dart with cyanide or anything else.'

'Drunk!' cried Colonel Brammington. 'Soaked in a damn' good brandy, the lot of 'em. My opinion.'

'It's possible, of course.'

'It's the only answer. My advice, for what it's worth is, haul him in for manslaughter. Ought to have been done at first only that drooling old pedagogue Mordant didn't put it to the jury. However, you must do as you think best.'

'Thank you, sir,' said Alleyn gravely. Brammington grinned.

'The very pineapple of politeness,' he quoted. 'Come and dine with me tomorrow. Both of you.'

'May I ring up?'

'Yes, yes,' said Colonel Brammington impatiently. 'Certainly.'

He hurried to the door as if overcome by an intolerable urge to move on somewhere. In the doorway he turned.

'You'll come round to my view,' he said, 'I'll be bound you will.'

'At the moment, sir,' said Alleyn, 'I have no view of my own.'

'Run him in on the minor charge,' added Colonel Brammington, raising his voice to a penetrating shout as he disappeared into the street, 'and the major charge will follow as the night the day.'

A door slammed and in a moment the violence of his engines was reawakened.

'Well now,' said Alleyn. 'I wonder.'

CHAPTER 9

Alleyn at the Feathers

The sun had nearly set when Alleyn and Fox drove down Ottercombe Road towards the tunnel. As the car mounted a last rise they could see Coombe Head, a quarter of a mile away across open hills. So clear was the evening that they caught a glint of gold where the surf broke into jets of foam against the sunny rocks. Alleyn slowed down and they saw the road sign at the tunnel entrance.

'Ottercombe. Dangerous corner. Change down.'

'So I should think,' muttered Alleyn, as the sheer drop appeared on the far side. He negotiated the corner and there, at the bottom of the steep descent, was the Plume of Feathers and Ottercombe.

'By George,' said Alleyn, 'I don't wonder Cubitt comes here to paint. It's really charming, Fox, isn't it? A concentric design with the pub as its axis. And there, I fancy, is our friend Pomeroy.'

'On the lookout, seemingly,' said Fox.

'Yes. Look at the colour of the sea, you old devil. Smell that jetty-tar-and-iodine smell, blast your eyes. Fox, murder or no murder, I'm glad we came.'

'As long as you're pleased, sir,' said Fox, dryly.

'Don't snub my ecstasies, Br'er Fox. Good evening, Mr Pomeroy.'

Abel hurried forward and opened the door.

'Good evening, Mr Alleyn, sir. We'm glad to see you. Welcome to the Feathers, sir.'

He used the same gestures, almost the same words as those with which he had greeted Watchman fourteen days ago. And Alleyn, if he had realized it, answered as Watchman had answered.

'We're glad to get here,' he said.

'Will!' shouted old Abel. 'Will!'

And Will, tall, fox-coloured, his eyes screwed up in the sunlight, came out and opened the back of the car. He was followed by a man whom Alleyn recognized instantly. He was nearly as striking off the stage as on it. The walk was unmistakable; the left shoulder raised very slightly, the long graceful stride, imitated, with more ardour than discretion, by half the young actors in London.

The newcomer glanced at Alleyn and Fox and walked past the car.

'Another marvellous evening, Mr Pomeroy,' he said airily.

'So 'tis, then, Mr Parish,' said Abel.

Alleyn and Fox followed Will Pomeroy into the Feathers. Abel brought up the rear.

'Show the rooms, sonny. There are the gentlemen we're expecting. They're from London. From Scotland Yard,' said Abel.

Will Pomeroy gave them a startled glance.

'Move along, sonny,' said Abel. 'This way, sir. Us'll keep parlour for your private use, Mr Alleyn, in case so be you fancy a bit of an office like.'

'That sounds an excellent arrangement,' said Alleyn.

'Have you had supper, sir?'

'Yes, thank you, Mr Pomeroy. We had it with Mr Harper.'

'I wonder,' said Abel unexpectedly, 'that it didn't turn your stomachs back on you, then.'

'This way, please,' said Will.

They followed Will up the steep staircase. Abel stood in the hall looking after them.

The Feathers, like all old buildings, had its own smell. It smelt of wallpaper, driftwood smoke, and very slightly of beer. Through the door came the tang of the waterfront to mix with the house-smell. The general impression was of coolness and seclusion. Will showed them two small bedrooms whose windows looked over Ottercombe Steps and the chimney-tops of Fish Lane, to the sea. Alleyn took the first of these rooms and Fox the second.

'The bathroom's at the end of the passage,' said Will from Alleyn's doorway. 'Will that be all?'

'We shall be very comfortable,' said Alleyn, and as Will moved away he added: 'You're Mr Pomeroy's son?'

'Yes,' said Will stolidly.

'I expect Mr Harper has explained why we are here.'

Will nodded and said nothing.

'I'd be very glad,' added Alleyn, 'if you could spare me a minute or two later on.'

Will said, 'I'll be serving in the bar all the evening.'

'I'll see you there, then. Thank you.'

But Will didn't move. He stared at the window and said, 'This affair's upset my father. He takes it to heart, like; the talk that goes on.'

'I know.'

'I reckon he's right about it being no accident.'

'Do you?'

'Yes. Nobody touched the bottle by mistake – 'tisn't likely.'

'Look here,' said Alleyn, 'can you spare a moment now to show me the rat-hole in the garage?'

Will's eyelashes flickered.

'Yes,' he said, 'reckon I can do that.' He shifted his weight from one foot to the other, and added with a kind of truculence. 'Reckon when the police come in, there's not much use in refusing. Not unless you've got a pull somewhere.'

'Oh come,' Alleyn said mildly, 'we're not as corrupt as all that, you know.'

Will's face turned scarlet but he said doggedly, 'It's not the men, it's the system. It's the way everything is in this country.'

'One law,' suggested Alleyn amiably, 'for the rich, and so on?'

'It's true enough.'

'Well, yes. In many ways I suppose it is. However, I'm not open to any bribery at the moment. We always try to be honest for the first few days, it engenders confidence. Shall we go down to the garage?'

'It's easy enough,' Will said, 'to make the truth look silly. A man never seems more foolish-like than he does when he's speaking his whole mind and heart. I know that.'

'Yes,' agreed Alleyn, 'that's quite true. I dare say the apostles were as embarrassing in their day, as the street-orator with no audience is in ours.'

'I don't know anything about that. They were only setting up a superstition. I'm dealing with the sober truth.'

'That's what I hope to do myself,' said Alleyn. 'Shall we join the rats?'

Will led Alleyn across the yard to the old stables. A small evening breeze came in from the sea, lifting Alleyn's hair and striking chill through his tweed coat. Gulls circled overhead. The sound of men's voices drifted up from the waterfront.

'It'll be dark in-along,' said Will.

'I've got a torch.'

'The rat-hole's not in the proper garage, like. It's in one of the old loose-boxes. It's locked and we haven't got the key. Harper's men did that.'

'Mr Harper gave me the key,' said Alleyn.

The old loose-box doors had been padlocked, and sealed with police tape. Alleyn broke the tape and unlocked them.

'I wonder,' he said, 'if you'd minding asking Mr Fox to join me. He's got a second torch. Ask him to bring my case.'

'Yes,' said Will, and after a fractional pause, 'sir.'

Alleyn went into the stable. It had been used as an extra garage but there was no car in it now. Above the faint reek of petrol oozed another more disagreeable smell, sweetish and nauseating. The cyanide, thought Alleyn, had evidently despatched at least one rat. The place was separated from the garage-proper, an old coach-house, by a semi-partition; but the space between the top of the partition and the roof had recently been boarded up, and Alleyn awarded Harper a good mark for attention to detail. Harper, he knew had also taken photographs of the rat-hole and tested the surrounding walls and floors for prints. He had found dozens of these.

Alleyn flashed his torch round the bottom of the walls and discovered the rat-hole. He stooped down. Harper had removed the rag and jar, tested them for prints, and found Abel's. He had then drained off the contents of the jar and replaced it. There was the original rag stuffed tight in the hole. Alleyn pulled it out and the smell of dead rat became very strong indeed. The ray of light glinted on a small jar. It was less than an inch in diameter and about half an inch deep.

Fox loomed up in the doorway. He said:

'Thank you, Mr Pomeroy, I'll find my way in.'

Will Pomeroy's boots retreated across the cobble-stones.

'Look here, Br'er Fox,' said Alleyn.

A second circle of light flickered on the little vessel. Fox peered over Alleyn's shoulder.

'And it was full,' said Fox.

'Yes,' said Alleyn. 'That settles it, I fancy.'

'How d'you mean, sir.'

'It's a case of murder.'

II

The parlour of the Feathers is the only room in the house that is generally uninhabited. For the usual patrons, the private tap is the common room. The parlour is across the side passage and opposite the public taproom. It overlooks Ottercombe Steps and beneath its windows are the roofs of the Fish Lane houses. It has a secret and deserted life of its own. Victoria's Jubilee and Edward the Seventh's wedding face each other across a small desert of linoleum and plush. Above the mantelpiece hangs a picture of two cylindrical and slug-like kittens. Upon the mantelpiece are three large shells. A rag-rug, lying in front of the fireplace, suggests that in a more romantic age Harlequin visted the Feathers and sloughed his skin before taking a leap up the chimney.

For Alleyn's arrival the parlour came to life. Someone had opened the window and placed a bowl of flowers on the plush-covered table. Abel Pomeroy hurriedly added a writing pad, a pencil, a terrible old pen and a bottle of ink. He surveyed the arrangements with an anxious smile, disappeared for a minute, and returned to ask Alleyn if there was anything else he needed.

'Two pints of beer, Mr Pomeroy,' said Alleyn, 'will set me up for the rest of the evening.'

Abel performed a sort of slow-motion trick with his right hand drawing away his apron to reveal a thickly cobwebbed bottle.

'I wonder, sir,' he said, 'if you'd pleasure me by trying a drop of this yurr tipple. 'Twurr laid down by my old Dad, many a year back. Sherry 'tis. 'Montillady. I did use to call 'er Amadillo afore I knew better.'

'But my dear Mr Pomeroy,' said Alleyn, 'this is something very extra indeed. It's a wine for the gods.'

'Just what the old colonel said, sir, when I told him us had it. It would pleasure the Feathers, sir, if you would honour us.'

'It's extraordinarily nice of you.'

'You wurr 'straordinary nice to me, sir, when I come up to London. If you'll axcuse me, I'll get the glasses.'

'It should be decanted, Mr Pomeroy.'

'So it should, then. I'll look out a decanter tomorrow, sir, and in the meanwhile us'll open the bottle.'

They opened the bottle and took a glass each.

'To the shade of Edgar Allan Poe,' murmured Alleyn, and raised his glass.

'The rest is yours, gentlemen,' said Abel. ''Twill be set aside special. Thurr's a decanter in the Private. If so be you bain't afeard, same as George Nark, that all my bottles is full of pison, tomorrow I'll decant this yurr tipple in your honour.'

Alleyn and Fox murmured politely.

'Be thurr anything else I can do, gentlemen?' asked Abel.

'We'll have a look at the private bar, Mr Pomeroy, if we may.'

'Certainly, sir, certainly, and terrible pleased us'll be to have her opened up again. 'Tis like having the corpse itself on the premises, with Private shuttered up and us chaps all hugger-mugger of an evening in Public. Has His Royal Highness the Duke of Muck condescended to hand over the keys, sir?'

'What? Oh – yes I have the keys.'

'Nick Harper!' said Abel, 'with his fanciful blown-up fidgeting ways. Reckon the man laces his boots with red tape. This way if you please, gentlemen, and watch yourselves for the step. "Dallybuttons, Nick," I said to him, "You've aimed your camera and blowed thicky childish li'l squirter over every inch of my private tap, you've lain on your belly and scraped the muck off the floor. What do 'ee want," I said! "Do 'ee fancy the corpse will hant the place and write murderer's name in the dust?" I axed him. This is the door, sir.'

Alleyn produced his bunch of keys and opened the door.

The private tap had been locked up by Oates a fortnight ago, and reopened by Harper and his assistants only for purposes of investigation. The shutter over the bar counter had been drawn down and locked. The window shutters also were fastened. The place was in complete darkness.

Abel switched on the light.

It was a travesty of the private tap that Alleyn saw. The comfort and orderliness of its habitual aspect were quite gone. It had suffered such a change as might overtake a wholesome wench turned drab in a fortnight. Dust covered the tables, settles, and stools. The butt ends of cigarettes strewed the floor, tobacco ash lay everywhere in small patches and trails. The open hearth was littered with ashes of the fire that had warmed Watchman on the night he died. Five empty tumblers were stained with the dregs of Courvoisier '87, two with the dregs of the ginger-beer. Of the eighth glass such powdered fragments as had escaped Harper's brush, crunched jarringly underfoot. The room smelt indescribably stale and second-rate.

'It do gall me uncommon,' said Abel, 'for my private taproom to display itself in thicky shocking state.'

'Never mind, Mr Pomeroy,' said Alleyn, 'we're used to it, you know.'

He stood just inside the door with Fox at his shoulder. Abel watched them anxiously but it is doubtful if he remarked the difference in their attitudes. Fox's eyes, light grey in colour, brightened and sharpened as he looked about the room. But Alleyn might have been a guest in the house, and with no more interest than politeness might allow his gaze shifted casually from one dust-covered surface to another.

After a few minutes, however, he could have given a neat drawing, with nice attention to detail, of the private taproom. He noticed the relative positions of the dart-board, the bar and the settle. He paid attention to the position of the lights, and remarked that the spot, chalked on the floor by Oates, where Legge had stood when he threw the darts, was immediately under a strong lamp. He saw that there was a light switch inside the door and another by the mantelpiece. He walked over to the corner cupboard.

'Nick Harper,' said Abel, 'took away that theer cursed pison bottle. He took away the bits of broken glass and brandy bottle and iodine bottle. He took away the new darts, all six of 'em. All Nick Harper left behind is dirt and smell. Help yourself to either of 'em.'

'Don't go just yet,' said Alleyn. 'We want your help, Mr Pomeroy, if you'll give it to us.'

'Ready and willing,' Abel said with emphasis. 'I'm ready and willing to do all I can. By my way of thinking you two gentlemen are here to clear my name, and I be mortal set on that scheme.'

'Right. Now will you tell me, as well as you can remember, where everybody stood at the moment when you poured out the second round of brandies. Can you remember? Try to call up the picture of this room as it was a fortnight ago tonight.'

'I can call it to mind right enough,' said Abel slowly. 'I been calling it to mind every night and a mighty number of times every night, since that ghassley moment. I was behind bar – '

'Let's have those shutters away,' said Alleyn.

Fox unlocked the shutters and rolled them up. The private tap proper was discovered. A glass door, connecting the two bars, was locked and through it Alleyn could see into the Public. Will Pomeroy was serving three fishermen. His shoulder was pressed against the glass door. He must have turned his head when he heard the sound of the shutters. He looked at Alleyn through his eyelashes and then turned away.

Alleyn examined the counter in the private tap. It was stained with dregs fourteen days old. Abel pointed to a lighter ring.

'Thurr's where brandy-bottle stood,' he said. ''Ess fay, thurr's where she was, sure enough.'

'Yes. Now, where were the people? You say you stood behind the bar?'

''Ess, and young Will was in corner 'twixt bar and dart-board. Rest of 'em had just finished round-the-clock. Bob Legge had won. They used the old darts and when he ran home he put 'em back in that thurr wooden rack by board. Yurr they be. Nick Harper come over generous,' said Abel with irony, 'and left us they old darts. He collared the new 'uns.'

'Ah yes,' said Alleyn hurriedly. 'What about the rest of the party?'

'I'm telling you, sir. Chap Legge'd won the bout. Mr Watchman says, "By God it's criminal, Legge. Men have been jailed for less," he says in his joking way. "Come on," he says, "Us'll have t'other half," he says, "and then, be George, if I don't let 'ee have a go at my hand." He says it joking, sir, but to my mind Mr Watchman knew summat about Legge and to my mind Legge didn't like it.'

Abel glanced through the glass door at Will, but Will's back was turned. The three customers gaped shamelessly at Alleyn and Fox.

'Well now,' Abel went on, lowering his voice, 'Legge paid no 'tention to Mr Watchman 'cept to say casual-like "I'll do it all right, but don't try it if you feel nervous," which wurr very wittest manner of speech the man could think of to egg on Mr Watchman, to set his fancy hellbent on doing it. ''Ess, Legge egged the man on, did Legge. That's while he was putting away old darts. Then he moved off, tantalizing, to t'other end of room. T'other ladies and gentlemen was round bar, 'cepting Miss Darragh, who was setting with her writing in ingle-nook. Thurr's her glass on 't old settle, sir. Stone-ginger, she had. Miss Dessy, that's Miss Moore, sir, she was setting on the bar, in the corner yurr swinging her legs. That'll be her glass on the ledge thurr. Stone-ginger. The three gentlemen, they wurr alongside bar. Mr Cubitt next Miss Dessy, then Mr Watchman and then Mr Parish. I 'member that, clear as daylight, along of Miss Darragh making a joke about 'em. "Three graces," she called 'em, being a fanciful kind of middle-aged lady.'

'That leaves Mr George Nark.'

'So it does then, the silly old parrot. ''Ess. George Nark wurr setting down by table inside of door, laying down the law as is the foolish habit of the man. Well now, I poured out the second tots beginning with Mr Cubitt. Then Mr Watchman and then Mr Parish. Then George Nark brings his glass over with his tongue hanging out and insults t'murdered gentleman by axing for soda in this masterpiece of a tipple, having nigh-on suffercated hisself with first tot, golloping it down ferocious. No sooner does he swallow second tot than he's proper blind tipsy. 'Ess, so soused as a herring wurr old George Nark. Lastly, sir, Mr Watchman gets Legge's glass from mantelshelf and axes me to pour out the second tot.'

'Leaving his own glass on the bar between Mr Parish and Mr Cubitt?'

''Ess. Legge wurr going to wait till after he'd done his trick. Us knows what wurr in the evil thoughts of the man. He wanted to keep his eye in so's he could stick Mr Watchman with thicky murderous dart.'

'Mr Pomeroy,' said Alleyn, 'I must warn you against making statements of that sort. You might land yourself in a very pretty patch of trouble, you know. What happened next? Did you pour out Mr Legge's brandy for him?'

''Ess, I did. And Mr Watchman tuk it to him saying he'd have no refusal. Then Mr Watchman tuk his own dram over to table by dartboard. He drank 'er down slow and then says he, "Now for it!" '

'And had Mr Legge been anywhere near Mr Watchman's glass?'

Abel looked mulish. 'No, sir, no. Not azacly. Not at all. He drank his over in ingle-nook opposite Miss Darragh. 'Twasn't then the mischief wurr done, Mr Alleyn.'

'Well,' said Alleyn, 'we shall see. Now for the accident itself.'

The story of those few minutes, a story that Alleyn was to hear many times before he reached the end of this case, was repeated by Abel and tallied precisely with all the other accounts in Harper's file, and with the report of the inquest.

'Very well,' said Alleyn. He paused for a moment and caught sight of Will's three customers staring with passionate interest through the glass door. He moved out of their range of vision.

'Now we come to the events that followed the injury. You fetched the iodine from that cupboard?'

'Sure enough, sir, I did.'

'Will you show me what you did?'

'Certainly. Somebody – Legge 'twas – out of the depths of his hypocrisy, says, "put a drop of iodine on it," he says. Right. I goes to thicky cupboard which Nick Harper has played the fool with, mucking round with his cameras and squirts of powder. I opens bottom door this way, and thurr on shelf is my first-aid box.'

Alleyn and Fox looked at the cupboard. It was a double corner cabinet, with two glass doors one above the other. Abel had opened the bottom door. At the back of the shelf was a lidless tin, containing the usual first-aid equipment, and a very nice ship's decanter. Abel removed the decanter.

'I'll scald and scour 'er out,' he said. 'Us'll have your sherry in this yurr, gentlemen, and I'll join you tomorrow in fust drink to show there's no hanky-panky.'

'We'll be delighted if you'll join us, Mr Pomeroy, but I don't think we need feel any qualms.'

'Ax George Nark,' said Abel bitterly. 'Have a tell with George Nark and get your minds pisened. I'll look after your stomachs.'

Alleyn said hurriedly: 'And that's the first-aid equipment?'

'That's it, sir. Bottle of iodine was laying in empty slot yurr,' Abel explained. 'I tuk it out and I tuk out bandage at same time.'

'You should keep your first-aid box shut up, Mr Pomeroy,' said Alleyn absently.

'Door's airtight, sir.'

Alleyn shone his torch into the cupboard. The triangular shelf forming the roof of the lower cupboard and the floor of the top one was made of a single piece of wood and fitted closely.

'And the bottle of prussic acid solution was in the upper cupboard?' asked Alleyn.

''Ess, tight-corked. Nick Harper's taken – '

'Yes, I know. Was the upper door locked?'

'Key turned in lock same as it be now.'

'You said at the inquest that you had used the iodine earlier in the evening.'

'So I had, then. Bob Legge had cut hisself with his razor. He said he wurr shaving hisself along of going to Illington. When storm came up – it wurr a terror that thurr storm – us told Legge he'd better bide home-along. I reckon that's the only thing I've got to blame myself for. Howsumdever the man came in for his pint at five o'clock, and I give him a lick of iodine and some sticking plaster.'

'Are you certain, Mr Pomeroy? It's important.'

'Bible oath,' said Abel. 'Thurr y'are, sir. Bible oath. Ax the man hisself. I fetched out my first-aid box and give him the bottle. Ax him.'

'Yes, yes. And you're certain it was at five o'clock?'

'Bob Legge,' said Abel, 'has been into tap for his pint *at* five o'clock every day 'cepting Sunday fur last ten months. Us opens at five in these parts and when I give him the iodine I glanced at clock and opened up.'

'When you put the bottle in the top cupboard on the Thursday night you wore gloves. Did you take them off before you turned the key?'

''Ess fay, and pitched 'em on fire. Nick Harper come down off of his high horse furr enough to let on my finger marks is on key. Don't that prove it?'

'It does indeed,' said Alleyn.

Fox, who had been completely silent, now uttered a low growl.

'Yes, Fox?' asked Alleyn.

'Nothing, Mr Alleyn.'

'Well,' said Alleyn, 'we've almost done. We now come to the brandy Miss Moore poured out of the Courvoisier bottle into Watchman's empty glass. Who suggested he should have brandy?'

'I'm not certain-sure, sir. I b'lieve Mr Parish first, and then Miss Darragh, but I wouldn't swear to her.'

'Would you swear that nobody had been near Mr Watchman's glass between the time he took his second nip and the time Miss Moore gave him the brandy?'

'Not Legge,' said Abel thoughtfully. And then with that shade of reluctance with which he coloured any suggestion of Legge's innocence, 'Legge wurr out in middle o' floor afore dart-board. Mr Watchman stood atween him and table wurr t' glass stood. Mr Parish walked over to look at Mr Watchman spreading out his fingers. All t'others stood hereabouts behind Legge. No one else went anigh t' glass.'

'And after the accident? Where was everybody then?'

'Crowded round Mr Watchman. Will stepped out of corner. I come through under counter. Miss Darragh stood anigh us and Dessy by Will. Legge stood staring where he wurr. Reckon Mr Parish did be closest still to glass, but he stepped forward when Mr Watchman flopped down on settle. I be a bit mazed-like wurr they all stood. I disremember.'

'Naturally enough. Would you say anybody could have touched that glass between the moment when the dart struck and the time Miss Moore poured out the brandy?'

'I don't reckon anybody could,' said Abel, but his voice slipped a half-tone and he looked profoundly uncomfortable.

'Not even Mr Parish.'

Abel stared over Alleyn's head and out of the window. His lower lip protruded and he looked as mulish as a sulky child.

'Maybe he could,' said Abel, 'but he didn't.'

CHAPTER 10

The Tumbler and the Dart

'We may as well let him have this room,' said Alleyn, when Abel had gone. 'Harper's done everything possible in the way of routine.'

'He's a very thorough chap, is Nick Harper.'

'Yes,' agreed Alleyn. 'Except in the matter of the rat-hole jar. However, Fox, we'll see if we can catch him out before we let the public in. Let's prowl a bit.'

They prowled for an hour. They kept the door locked and closed the bar shutters. Dim sounds of toping penetrated from the public taproom. Alleyn had brought Harper's photographs and they compared these with the many chalk marks Harper had left behind him. A chalk mark under the settle showed where the iodine bottle had rolled. The plot of the bottle of Scheele's Acid was marked in the top cupboard. The shelves of the corner cupboard were very dusty and the trace left by the bottle showed clearly. Alleyn turned to the fireplace.

'He hasn't sifted the ashes, Br'er Fox. We may as well do that, I think.'

Fox fetched a small sieve from Alleyn's case. The ashes at first yielded nothing of interest, but in the last handful they found a small misshapen object which Alleyn dusted and took to the light.

'Glass,' he said. 'They must have had a good fire. It's melted and gone all bobbly. There's some more. Broken glass half melted by the fire.'

'They probably make the fire up on the old ashes,' said Fox. 'It may have lain there through two or three fires.'

'Yes, Fox. And then again it may not. I wonder if those fragments of the brandy glass were complete. This has been a thickish piece, I should say.'

'A bit of the bottom?'

'We'll have to find out. You never know. Where was the broken glass?'

The place where most of the broken glass had been found was marked on the floor.

'O careful Mr Harper!' Alleyn sighed. 'But it doesn't get us much farther, I'm afraid. Fox, I'm like to get in a muddle over this. You must keep me straight. You know what an ass I can make of myself. No'; as Fox looked amiably sceptical. 'No, I mean it. There are at least three likely pitfalls. I wish to heaven they hadn't knocked over that glass and trampled it to smithereens.'

'D'you think there was cyanide in the glass, Mr Alleyn?'

'God bless us, Fox, I don't know. I don't know, my dear old article. How can I? But it would help a lot if we *could* know one way or the other. Finding none on those tiny pieces isn't good enough.'

'At least,' said Fox, 'we know there was cyanide on the dart. And knowing that, sir, and ruling out accident, I must say I agree with old Pomeroy. It looks like Legge.'

'But how the devil could Legge put prussic acid on the dart with eight people all watching him? He was standing under the light, too.'

'He felt the points,' said Fox without conviction.

'Get along with you, Foxkins. Prussic acid is extremely volatile. Could Legge dip his fingers in the acid and then wait a couple of hours or so – with every hope of giving himself a poisoned hand? He'd have needed a bottle of the stuff about him.'

'He may have had one. He may be a bit of a conjurer. Legerdemain,' added Fox.

'Well – he may. We'll have to find out.'

Alleyn lit a cigarette and sat down.

'Let's worry it out,' he said. 'May I talk? And when I go wrong, Fox, you stop me.'

'It's likely then,' said Fox, dryly, 'to be a monologue. But go ahead, sir, if you please.'

Alleyn went ahead. His pleasant voice ran on and on and a kind of orderliness began to appear. The impossible, the possible, and the probable were sorted into groups, and from the kaleidoscopic jumble of evidence was formed a pattern.

'Imperfect,' said Alleyn, 'but at least suggestive.'

'Suggestive, all right,' Fox said. 'And if it's correct the case, in a funny sort of way, still hinges on the dart.'

'Yes,' agreed Alleyn. 'The bare bodkin. The feathered quarrel and all that. Well, Fox, we've wallowed in speculation and now we'd better get on with the job. I think I hear Pomeroy senior in the public bar so presumably Pomeroy junior is at liberty. Let's remove to the parlour.'

'Shall I get hold of young Pomeroy?'

'In a minute. Ask him to bring us a couple of pints. You'd better not suggest that he joins us in a drink. He doesn't like us much, and I imagine he'd refuse, which would not be the best possible beginning.'

Alleyn wandered into the ingle-nook, knocked out his pipe on the hearthstone and then stooped down.

'Look here, Fox.'

'What's that, sir?'

'Look at this log-box.'

Fox bent himself at the waist and stared into a heavy wooden box in which Abel kept his pieces of driftwood and the newspaper used for kindling. Alleyn pulled out a piece of paper and took it to the light.

'It's been wet,' observed Fox.

'Very wet. Soaked. It was thrust down among the bits of wood. A little pool has lain in the pocket. Smell it.'

Fox sniffed vigorously. 'Brandy?' he asked.

'Don't know. Handle it carefully, Br'er Fox. Put it away in your room and then get Pomeroy junior.'

Alleyn returned to the parlour, turned on the red-shaded lamp and settled himself behind the table.

Fox came in followed by Will Pomeroy. Will carried two pint pots of beer. He set them down on the table.

'Thank you,' said Alleyn. 'Can you spare us a moment?'

'Yes.'

'Sit down, won't you?'

Will hesitated awkwardly, and then chose the least comfortable chair and sat on the extreme edge. Fox took out his notebook and Will's eyes flickered. Alleyn laid three keys on the table.

'We may return these now, I think,' he said. 'I'm sure you'll be glad to see the Plume of Feathers set right again.'

'Thanks,' said Will. He stretched out his hand and took the keys.

'The point we'd like to talk about,' said Alleyn, 'is the possibility of the dart that injured Mr Watchman being tainted with the stuff used for rat poison – the acid kept in the corner cupboard of the private tap. Now, your father – '

'I know what my father's been telling you,' interrupted Will, 'and I don't hold with it. My father's got a damn' crazy notion in his head.'

'What notion is that?' asked Alleyn.

Will looked sharply at him, using that trick of lowering his eyelashes. He did not answer.

'Do you mean that your father's ideas about Mr Robert Legge are crazy.'

'That's right. Father's got his knife into Bob Legge because of his views. There's no justice nor sense in what he says. I'll swear, Bible oath, Bob Legge never interfered with the dart. I'll swear it before any judge or jury in the country.'

'How can you be so positive?'

'I was watching the man. I was in the corner between the dartboard and the bar. I was watching him.'

'All the time? From the moment the darts were unpacked until he threw them?'

'Yes,' said Will doggedly. 'All the time.'

'Why?'

'Eh?'

'Why did you watch him so closely?'

'Because of what the man was going to do. We all watched him.'

'Suppose,' said Alleyn, 'that for the sake of argument I told you we knew positively that Mr Legge, while he held the darts in his left hand, put his right hand in his pocket for a moment – '

'I'd say it was a lie. He didn't. He never put his hand in his pocket.'

'What makes you so positive, Mr Pomeroy?'

'For one thing he was in his shirt sleeves.'

'What about his waistcoat and trousers' pockets?'

'He hadn't a waistcoat. His sleeves was rolled up and I was watching his hands. They never went near his trousers' pockets. He held the darts in his left hand and I was watching the way he felt the points, delicate like, with the first finger of his other hand. He was saying they was right-down good darts; well made and well balanced.' Will leant forward and scowled earnestly at Alleyn.

'Look 'ee here, sir,' he said. 'If Bob Legge meant any harm to they darts would he have talked about them so's we all looked at the damn' things? Would he, now?'

'That's a very sound argument,' agreed Alleyn. 'He would not.'

'Well, then!'

'Right. Now the next thing he did was to throw all six darts, one after the other, into the board. He had six, hadn't he?'

'Yes. There were six new 'uns in the packet. Usual game's only three, but he took all six for this trick.'

'Exactly. Now, what did he do after he'd thrown them?'

'Said they carried beautiful. He'd thrown the lot round the centre very pretty. Mr Watchman pulled 'em out and looked at 'em. Then Mr Watchman spread out his left hand on the board and held out the darts with his right. "Fire ahead," he says, or something like that.'

Alleyn uttered a short exclamation and Will looked quickly at him.

'That wasn't brought out at the inquest,' said Alleyn.

'Beg pardon? What wasn't?'

'That Mr Watchman pulled out the darts and gave them to Mr Legge.'

'I know that, sir. I only thought of it today. I'd have told Mr Harper next time I saw him.'

'It's a little odd that you should not remember this until a fortnight after the event.'

'Is it then?' demanded Will. 'I don't reckon it is. Us didn't think anything at the time. Ask any of the others. Ask my father. They'll remember all right when they think of it.'

'All right,' said Alleyn. 'I suppose it's natural enough you should forget.'

'I know what it means,' said Will quickly. 'I know that, right enough. Mr Watchman handled those darts, moving them round in his hands like. How could Bob Legge know which was which after that?'

'Not very easily, one would suppose. What next?'

'Bob took the darts and stepped back. Then he began to blaze away with 'em. He never so much as glanced at 'em, I know that. He played 'em out quick.'

'Until the fourth one stuck into the finger?'

'Yes,' said Will doggedly, 'till then.'

Alleyn was silent. Fox, notebook in hand, moved over to the window and stood looking over the roofs of Ottercombe to the sea.

'I'll tell you what it is,' said Will suddenly.

'Yes?' asked Alleyn.

'I reckon the poison on those darts's a blind.'

He made this announcement with an air of defiance, and seemed to expect it would bring some sort of protest from the other two. But Alleyn took it very blandly.

'Yes,' he said, 'that's possible, of course.'

'See what I mean?' said Will eagerly. 'The murderer had worked it out he'd poison Mr Watchman. He'd worked it out he'd put the stuff in his drink, first time he got a chance. Then when Bob Legge pricks him by accident, the murderer says to himself, "There's a rare chance." He's got the stuff on him. He puts it in the brandy glass and afterwards, while we're all fussing round Mr Watchman, he smears it on the dart. The brandy glass gets smashed to pieces but they find poison on the dart. That's how I work it out. I reckon whoever did this job tried, deliberate, to fix it on Bob Legge.'

Alleyn looked steadily at him.

'Can you give us anything to support this theory?'

Will hesitated. He looked from Alleyn to Fox, made as if to speak, and then seemed to change his mind.

'You understand, don't you,' said Alleyn, 'that I am not trying to force information. On the other hand if you do know of anything that would give colour to the theory you have yourself advanced it would be advisable to tell us about it.'

'I know Bob Legge didn't interfere with the dart.'

'After it was all over and the constable looked for the dart, wasn't it Legge who found it?'

'Sure-ly! And that goes to show. Wouldn't he have taken his chance to wipe the dart if he'd put poison on it?'

'That's well reasoned,' said Alleyn. 'I think he would. But your theory involves the glass. Who had an opportunity to put prussic acid in the glass?'

Will's fair skin reddened up to the roots of his fox-coloured hair.

'I've no wish to accuse anybody,' he said. 'I know who's innocent and I speak up for him. There won't be many who'll do that. His politics are not the colour to make powerful friends for him when he's in trouble. I know Bob Legge's innocent but I say nothing about the guilty.'

'Now, look here,' said Alleyn amiably, 'you've thought this thing out for yourself and you seem to have thought it out pretty thoroughly. You must see that we can't put a full stop after your pronouncement on the innocence of Mr Legge. The best way of establishing Legge's innocence is to find where the guilt lies.'

'I don't know anything about that.'

'Really?'

'Yes, sir,' said Will. 'Really.'

'I see. Well, can you tell us if Mr Legge stood anywhere near the brandy glass before he threw the darts?'

'He was nowhere near it. Not ever. It was on the table by the board. He never went near it.'

'Do you remember who stood near that table?'

Will was silent. He compressed his lips into a hard line.

'For instance,' Alleyn paused, 'was Mr Sebastian Parish anywhere near the table?'

'He might have been,' said Will.

II

'And now, Fox,' said Alleyn, 'we'll have a word with Mr Sebastian Parish, if he's on the premises. I don't somehow think he'll have strayed very far. See if you can find him.'

Fox went away. Alleyn took a long pull at his beer and read through the notes Fox had made during the interview with Will Pomeroy. The light outside had faded and the village had settled down for the evening. Alleyn could hear the hollow sounds made by men working with boats, the tramp of heavy boots on stone, a tranquil murmur of voices, and, more distantly, the thud of breakers. Within the house he heard sounds of sweeping and of quick footsteps. The Pomeroys had lost no time cleaning up the private bar. In the public bar, across the passage, a single voice seemed to drone on and on as if somebody made a speech to the assembled topers. Whoever it was it came to an end. A burst of conversation followed and then a sudden silence. Alleyn recognized Fox's voice. Someone answered clearly and resonantly, 'Yes, certainly.'

'That's Parish,' thought Alleyn.

The door from the public taproom into the passage was opened and shut. Sebastian Parish and Fox came into the parlour.

The evening was warm and Parish was clad in shorts and a thin blue shirt. He wore these garments with such an air that the makers might well have implored him to wear their shorts and shirts, free of cost, in and out of season for the rest of his life. His legs were olive brown and slightly glossy, the hair on his olive brown chest was golden brown. He looked burnished and groomed to the last inch. The hair on his head, a darker golden brown, was ruffled, for all the world as if his dresser had darted after him into the wings, and run a practised hand through his locks. There was something almost embarrassing in so generous a display of masculine beauty. He combined in his appearance all the most admired aspects of a pukka sahib, a Greek god, and a wholesome young Englishman. Fox came after him like an anti-climax in good serviceable worsted.

'Ah, good evening, Inspector,' said Parish.

'Good evening,' said Alleyn. 'I'm sorry to worry you.'

Parish's glance said, a little too plainly: 'Hallo, so you're a gentleman.' He came forward and, with an air of manly frankness, extended his hand.

'I'm very glad to do anything I can,' he said.

He sat on the arm of a chair and looked earnestly from Alleyn to Fox.

'We hoped for this,' he said. 'I wish to God they'd called you in at once.'

'The local men,' Alleyn murmured, 'have done very well.'

'Oh, they've done what they could, poor old souls,' said Parish. 'No doubt they're very sound at bottom, but it's rather a long way before one strikes bottom. Considering my cousin's position I think it was obvious that the Yard should be consulted.'

He looked directly at Alleyn and said: 'But I know you!'

'Do you?' said Alleyn politely. 'I don't think – '

'I know you!' Parish repeated dramatically. 'Wait a moment. By George, yes, of course. You're the – I've seen your picture in a book of famous trials.' He turned to Fox with the air of a Prince Regent.

'What *is* his name?' demanded Parish.

'This is Mr Alleyn, sir,' said Fox, with the trace of a grin at his superior.

'Alleyn! My God, yes, of course; Alleyn!'

'Fox,' said Alleyn austerely, 'be good enough to shut the door.' He waited until this was done and then addressed himself to the task of removing the frills from the situation.

'Mr Parish,' Alleyn said, 'we have been sent down here to make inquiries about the death of your cousin. The local superintendent has given us a very full and explicit account of the circumstances surrounding his death but we are obliged to go over the details for ourselves.'

Parish made an expressive gesture, showing them the palms of his hands. 'But, of course,' he said.

'Yes. Well, we thought that before we went any further we should ask to see you.'

'Just a moment,' interrupted Parish. 'There's one thing I must know. Mr Alleyn, was my cousin murdered?'

Alleyn looked at his hands which were joined together on the table. After a moment's thought he raised his eyes.

'It is impossible to give you a direct answer,' he said, 'but as far as we have gone we can find no signs of accident.'

'That's terrible,' said Parish, and for the first time his voice sounded sincere.

'Of course something that will point to accident may yet come out.'

'Good God, I hope so.'

'Yes. You will understand that we want to get a very clear picture of the events leading up to the moment of the accident.'

'Have you spoken to old Pomeroy?'

'Yes.'

'I suppose he's talked about this fellow Legge?'

Alleyn disregarded the implication and said: 'About the position of everybody when Mr Legge threw the darts. Can you remember – '

'I've thrashed the thing out a hundred times a day. I don't remember particularly clearly.'

'Well,' said Alleyn, 'let's see how we get on.'

Parish's account followed the Pomeroys' pretty closely, but he had obviously compared notes with all the others.

'To tell you the truth,' he said, 'I'd had a pint of beer and two pretty stiff brandies. I don't say I've got any very clear recollection of the scene. I haven't. It seems more like a sort of nightmare than anything else.'

'Can you remember where you stood immediately before Mr Legge threw the darts?'

Alleyn saw the quick involuntary movement of those fine hands and he thought there was rather too long a pause before Parish answered.

'I'm not very certain, I'm afraid.'

'Were you, for instance, near the table that stands between the dart-board and the settle?'

'I may have been. I was watching Legge.'

'Try to remember. Haven't you a clear picture of Legge as he stood there ready to throw the darts?'

Parish had a very expressive face. Alleyn read in it the reflection of a memory. He went on quickly.

'Of course you have. As you say, you were watching him. Only in the medley of confused recollections that picture was, for a time, lost. But, as you say, you were watching him. Did he face you?'

'He – yes.'

Alleyn slid a paper across the table.

'Here, you see, is a sketch plan of the private bar.' Parish looked at it over his shoulder. 'Now there's the dart-board, fairly close to the bar counter. Legge must have stood there. There isn't room for more than one person to stand in the corner by the bar counter, and Will Pomeroy was there. So to face Legge you must have been by the table.'

'All right,' said Parish restively. 'I don't say I wasn't, you know. I only say I'm a bit hazy.'

'Yes, of course, we understand that perfectly. But what I'm getting at is this. Did you see Legge take the darts after the trial throw?'

'Yes. My cousin pulled them out of the board and gave them to Legge. I remember that.'

'Splendid,' said Alleyn. 'It's an important point and we're anxious to clear it up. Thank you. Now standing like that as we've agreed you were standing, you would see the whole room. Can you remember the positions of the other onlookers?'

'I remember that they were grouped behind Legge. Except Abel who was behind the bar counter. Oh, and Will. Will was in the corner as you've said. Yes.'

'So that it would have been impossible, if any of the others came to the table, for their movement to escape your notice?'

'I suppose so. Yes, of course it would. But I can't see why it matters.'

'Don't you remember,' said Alleyn gently, 'that Mr Watchman's glass was on that table? The glass that was used afterwards when Miss Moore gave him the brandy?'

III

Parish was not a rubicund man but the swift ebbing of what colour he had was sufficiently startling. Alleyn saw the pupils of his eyes dilate; his face was suddenly rather pinched.

'It was the dart that was poisoned,' said Parish. 'They found that out. It was the dart.'

'Yes. I take it nobody went to the table?'

'I don't think anybody – Yes, I suppose that's right.'

'And after the accident?'

'How d'you mean?'

'What were your positions?'

'Luke – my cousin – collapsed on the settle. I moved up to him. I mean I stooped down to look at him. I remember I said – oh, it does-n't matter.'

'We should like to hear, if we may.'

'I told him to pull himself together. You see I didn't think any-thing of it. He's always gone peculiar at the sight of his own blood. When we were kids he used to faint if he scratched himself.'

'Did anybody but yourself know of this peculiarity?'

'I don't know. I should think Norman knew. Norman Cubitt. He may not have known but I rather think we've talked about it quite recently. I seem to remember we did.'

'Mr Parish,' said Alleyn, 'will you focus your memory on those few minutes after your cousin collapsed on the settle. Will you tell us everything you can remember?'

Parish got to his feet and moved restlessly about the room. Alleyn had dealt with people of the theatre before. He had learnt that their movements were habitually a little larger than life, and he knew that in many cases this staginess was the result of training and instinct and that it was a mistake to put it down to deliberate artifice. He knew that, in forming an opinion of the emotional integrity of actors, it was almost impossible to decide whether their outward-seeming was conscious or instinctive; whether it expressed their sensibility or merely their sense of theatre. Parish moved restlessly as though some dramatist had instructed him to do so. But he may not, thought Alleyn, know at this moment how beautifully he moves.

'I begin to see it,' said Parish suddenly. 'Really it's rather as if I tried to recall a dream, and a very bad dream, at that. You see the lights kept fading and wobbling, and then one had drunk rather a lot, and then afterwards all that happened makes it even more confused. I'm trying to think about it as a scene on the stage, a scene of which I've had to memorize the positions.'

'That's a very good idea,' said Alleyn.

The door opened and a tall man with an untidy head looked in.

'I beg your pardon. Sorry!' murmured this man.

'Mr Cubitt?' asked Alleyn. Parish had turned quickly. 'Do come in, please.'

Cubitt came in and put down a small canvas with its face to the wall. Parish introduced him.

'I'd be glad if you'd stay,' said Alleyn. 'Mr Parish is going to try and recall for us the scene that followed the injury to Mr Watchman's hand.'

'Oh,' said Cubitt and gave a lopsided grin. 'All right. Go ahead, Seb. Sorry I cut in.'

He sat on a low chair near the fireplace and wound one thin leg mysteriously round the other. 'Go ahead,' he repeated.

Parish, at first, seemed a little disconcerted, but he soon became fortified by his own words.

'Luke,' he said, 'is lying on the settle. The settle against the left-hand wall.'

'Actors' left or audience's left?' asked Cubitt.

'Audience's left. I'm deliberately seeing it as a stage setting, Norman.'

'So I understand.'

'– and Inspector Alleyn knows the room. At first nobody touches Luke. His face is very white and he looks as if he'll faint. I'm standing near his head. Legge's still out in front of the dart-board. He's saying something about being sorry. I've got it now. It's strange, but thinking of it like this brings it back to me. You, Norman, and Decima, are by the bar. She's sitting on the bar in the far corner. Will has taken a step out into the room and Abel's leaning over the bar. Wait a moment. Miss Darragh is farther away near the ingle-nook, and is sitting down. Old George Nark, blind tight, is teetering about near Miss Darragh. That's the picture.'

'Go on, please,' said Alleyn.

'Well, the lights waver. Sometimes it's almost dark, and then the figures all show up again. Or – ' Parish looked at Cubitt.

'No,' said Cubitt. 'That wasn't the brandy, Seb. You're quite right.'

'Well, I can't go any further,' said Parish petulantly. 'The rest's still a filthy nightmare. Can you sort it out?'

'Please do, if you can, Mr Cubitt,' said Alleyn.

Cubitt was filling his pipe. His fingers, blunt-ended, were stained as usual with oil paint.

'It's as everybody described it at the inquest,' he said. 'I think Seb and I both had the same idea, that Watchman was simply upset at the sight of his own blood. It's true about the lights. The room seemed to – to sort of pulse with shadows. I remember Luke's right hand. It groped about his chest as if he felt for a handkerchief or something. Legge said something like "My God! I'm sorry. Is it bad?" Something like that. And then Legge said something more. "Look at his face! My God, it's not lockjaw, is it?" And you, Seb, said, "Not it," and trotted out the old story about Luke's sensibilities.'

'How was I to know? You make it sound – '

'Of course you weren't to know. I agreed with you, but Legge was very upset and, at the mention of lockjaw, Abel went to the cupboard and got out the iodine and a bandage. Miss Darragh came to life and took the bandage from Abel. Abel dabbed iodine on the finger and Luke sort of shuddered like you do with the sting of the stuff. Miss Darragh said something about brandy. Decima Moore took the bottle off the bar and poured some into Luke's glass. His glass was on the table.'

'The table by the dart-board close to Mr Parish?'

Cubitt looked up from his pipe.

'That's it,' he said. 'Decima gave Luke the brandy. He seemed to get worse just about then. He had a sort of convulsion.' Cubitt paused. 'It was beastly,' he said and his voice changed. 'The glass went flying. Miss Darragh pressed forward with the bandage and then – then the lights went out.'

'That's very clear,' said Alleyn. 'I take it that, from the time Abel Pomeroy got the iodine and bandage until Mr Watchman died, you were all gathered round the settle?'

'Yes. We didn't really change positions much, not Legge, or Will, or Seb here, or me. Abel and the two women came forward.'

'And when the lights went up again,' said Alleyn, 'were the positions the same?'

'Pretty much. But – '

'Yes?'

Cubitt looked steadily at Alleyn. His pipe was gripped between his teeth. He felt in his pockets.

'There was a devil of a lot of movement while the lights were out,' said Cubitt.

CHAPTER 11

Routine

'What sort of movement?' asked Alleyn.

'I know what you mean,' said Parish, before Cubitt could answer. 'It was Luke. He must have had a sort of attack after the lights went out. It was appalling.'

'I don't mean that,' said Cubitt. 'I know Luke made a noise. His feet beat a sort of tattoo on the settle. He flung his arms about and – he made other noises.'

'For God's sake,' Parish burst out, 'don't talk about it like that! I don't know how you can sit there and discuss it.'

'It looks as if we've got to,' said Cubitt.

'I'm afraid it does,' agreed Alleyn. 'What other movements did you notice, beyond those made by Mr Watchman?'

'Somebody was crawling about the floor,' Cubitt said.

Parish made a gesture of impatience. 'My dear old Norman,' he said, ' "Crawling about the floor!" You're giving Mr Alleyn a wrong impression. Completely wrong! I've no doubt one of us may have stooped down in the dark, knelt down perhaps, to try and get hold of Luke.'

'I don't mean that at all,' said Cubitt calmly. 'Someone was literally crawling about the floor. Whoever it was banged his head against my knees.'

'Where were you standing?' asked Alleyn.

'By the foot of the settle. I had my back to the settle. The backs of my knees touched it.'

'How do you know it was a head?' demanded Parish. 'It might have been a foot.'

'I can distinguish between a foot and a head,' said Cubitt, 'even in the dark.'

'Somebody feeling round for the brandy glass,' said Parish.

'It was after the brandy glass was broken.' Cubitt looked at Alleyn. 'Somebody trod on the glass soon after the lights went out. There's probably nothing in it, anyway. I've no idea at all whose head it was.'

'Was it Legge's head?' demanded Parish suddenly.

'I tell you, Seb,' said Cubitt quite mildly, 'I don't know whose head it was. I merely know it was there. It simply butted against my knees and drew away quickly.'

'Well, of course!' said Parish. 'It was Abel.'

'Why Abel?'

Parish turned to Alleyn.

'Abel dropped the bottle of iodine just before the lights went out. I remember that. He must have stooped down to try and find it.'

'If it was Abel he didn't succeed,' said Alleyn. 'The bottle was found under the settle, you know.'

'Well, it was dark.'

'So it was,' agreed Alleyn. 'Why did you think it might be Mr Legge's head?'

Parish at once became very solemn. He moved to the hearthrug. He thrust his hands into the pockets of his shorts, pulled in his belly, and stuck out his jaw.

'God knows,' he began. 'I don't want to condemn any man, but Norman and I have talked this thing over.'

'Come off it, Seb,' said Cubitt. 'We haven't a blessed thing against the fellow, you know. Nothing that would be of any interest to Mr Alleyn. I'm very well aware that my own ideas are largely self-protective. I suppose you know, Mr Alleyn, that Watchman left me some of his money.'

'Yes,' said Alleyn.

'Yes. It's as good a motive as any other. Better than most. I don't fancy I'm in a position to make suggestions about other people.'

He said this with a sort of defiance, looking out of the window and half-smiling.

'This sort of thing,' added Cubitt, 'finds out the thin patches in one's honesty.'

'If you can admit as much,' said Alleyn quickly, 'perhaps they are not so very thin.'

'Thanks,' said Cubitt dryly.

'Well,' began Parish with the air of running after the conversation. 'I don't altogether agree with you, Norman. I make no secret about dear old Luke leaving the rest of his money to me. In a way it was the natural thing for him to do. I'm his next-of-kin.'

'But I,' said Cubitt, 'am no relation at all.'

'Oh, my dear old boy!' cried Parish in a hurry, 'you were his best friend. Luke said so when he – ' Parish stopped short.

'To revert,' said Alleyn, 'to Mr Legge. You were going to talk about Mr Legge, weren't you?'

'I was,' said Parish. 'I can't help what you think, Norman, old boy. It seems to me that Legge's hand in this ghastly business is pretty obvious. Nobody but Legge could have known the poisoned dart would take effect. I must say I don't see that there's much mystery about it.'

'And the motive?' asked Cubitt.

Alleyn said, 'I understand your cousin told you that he and Mr Legge were strangers to each other.'

'I know he did,' said Parish, 'but I don't believe it was true. I believe Luke recognized Legge. Not at first, perhaps, but later. During that first evening in the bar. I suppose you know that Legge smashed into my cousin's car before ever he got here? That's a bit funny, too, when you come to think of it.'

'What,' asked Cubitt, 'is the dark inference, Seb? Why was it funny? Do you suppose that Legge lurked round Diddlestock corner in a two-seater, and that every time he heard a powerful car coming down Ottercombe Road, he hurled his baby out of cover in the hopes of ramming Luke?'

'Oh, don't be an ass. I simply mean it was a coincidence.'

'About the first evening in the bar?' suggested Alleyn, who had decided that there was a certain amount to be said for allowing Parish and Cubitt plenty of rein.

'Yes. Well, I was going to tell you,' said Parish. 'I talked to Luke while he had his supper in the bar. He told me about this business with the cars and rather let off steam on the subject of the other driver. Well, it turned out that Legge was sitting in the settle – the

– actually it was the settle where Luke – where it happened. When Luke realized Legge must have heard he went across and sort of made the *amende honorable*, if you know what I mean. He didn't make much headway. Legge was rather stuffy and up-stage.'

'Was all this while the poison-party was going on in the stable?'

'What? Yes. Yes, it was.'

'So that Mr Legge did not attend the party in the stables?'

'I suppose not. But he knew all about it. When Abel came in he warned everybody in the place about what he'd done.'

Parish hesitated. 'It's hard to describe,' he said. 'But if you'd known my cousin you'd understand. He seemed to be getting at Legge. Even you'll agree to that, Norman.'

'Yes,' said Cubitt. 'I put it down to Luke's vanity.'

'His vanity?' asked Alleyn.

'Parish doesn't agree with me,' said Cubitt with a faint smile, 'on the subject of Watchman's vanity. I've always considered he attached importance to being on good terms with people. It seemed to me that when Legge snubbed his advances Watchman was at first disconcerted and put out of countenance, and then definitely annoyed. They had a bet on that first night about Legge's dart-throwing and Legge won. That didn't help. Then, Watchman chipped Legge about his politics and his job. Not very prettily, I thought. It was then, or about then, that the trick with the darts was first mentioned.'

'By Legge,' Parish pointed out.

'I know, but Luke insisted on the experiment.'

'Mr Cubitt,' said Alleyn, 'did you not get the impression that these two men had met before?'

Norman Cubitt rumpled his hair and scowled.

'I don't say that,' he said. 'I wondered. But I don't think one should attach too much importance to what Watchman said.' And like Parish, he added, 'if you'd ever met him you'd understand.'

Alleyn did not think it necessary to say that he had met Watchman. He said, 'Can you remember anything definite that seemed to point to recognition?'

'It was more the way Luke spoke than what he actually said,' explained Parish. 'He kept talking about Legge's job and sort of suggesting he'd done pretty well for himself. Didn't he, Norman?'

'I seem to remember a phrase about leading the people by the nose,' said Cubitt, 'which sounded rather offensive. And the way Luke invited Legge to play round-the-clock was not exactly the glass of fashion *or* the mould of form. He asked Legge if he'd ever done time.'

'Oh,' said Alleyn.

'But it all sounds far too solemn and significant when you haul it out and display it like this.'

'Any one would think,' said Parish, 'that you were trying to protect Legge. I thought it was all damned odd.'

'I'm not trying to protect Legge but I've no particular wish to make him sound like a man of mystery. "Who is Mr X?" As far as we know Mr X is a rather dreary little Soviet fan who combines philately with communism and is pretty nippy with the darts. And what's more I don't see how he could have infected the dart. In fact I'm prepared to swear he didn't. I was watching his hands. They're ugly hands and he's a clumsy mover. Have you noticed he always fumbles and drops his money when he pays for his drinks? He's certainly quite incapable of doing any sleight-of-hand stuff with prussic acid.'

Alleyn looked at Fox. 'That answers your question,' he said.

'What question?' asked Cubitt. 'Or aren't we supposed to know?'

'Fox wondered if Mr Legge could be an expert at legerdemain,' said Alleyn.

'Well, you never know. That's not impossible,' said Parish. 'He might be.'

'I'll stake my oath he's not,' said Cubitt. 'He's no more likely to have done it than you are – '

Cubitt caught his breath and for the first time looked profoundly uncomfortable.

'Which is absurd,' he added.

Parish turned on Cubitt. His poise had gone and for a moment he looked as though he both hated Cubitt and was afraid of him.

'You seem very sure of yourself, Norman,' he said. 'Apparently my opinion is of no value. I won't waste any more of Mr Alleyn's time.'

'My dear old Seb – ' Cubitt began.

Alleyn said, 'Please, Mr Parish! I'm sure all this business of questions that seem to have neither rhyme nor reason is tedious and exasperating to a degree. But you may be sure that we shall go as carefully as we go slowly. If there is any link between this man and your cousin I think I may promise you that we shall discover it.'

'I suppose so,' said Parish, not very readily. 'I'm sorry if I'm unreasonable, but this thing has hit me pretty hard.'

'Oh dear,' thought Alleyn, 'he *will* speak by the book!' And aloud he said, 'Of course it has. I've nearly done for the moment. There are one or two more points. I think you looked at the new darts before they were handed to Mr Legge.'

Parish froze at that. He stood there on the dappled hearthrug and stared at Alleyn. He looked like a frightened schoolboy.

'I only picked them up and looked at them,' he said. 'Anyone will tell you that.' And then with a sudden spurt of temper. 'Damnation, you'll be saying I killed my cousin next!'

'I wasn't going to say that,' said Alleyn peacefully. 'I was going to ask you to tell me who handled the darts before and after you did.'

Parish opened his mouth and shut it again. When he did speak it was with a kind of impotent fury.

'If you'd said at first – you've got me all flustered.'

Cubitt said, 'I think I can tell you that, Alleyn. Abel unpacked the darts and laid them on the counter. Parish simply picked two or perhaps three of them up and poised them. That's right, isn't, Seb?'

'I don't know,' said Parish sullenly. 'Have it your own way. *I* don't know. Why should I remember?'

'No reason in the world,' said Alleyn cheerfully.

'Well,' said Cubitt, 'Sebastian put them down and Will Pomeroy took them up. I remember that Will turned away and held them nearer the light. He said something about the way they were made with the weight in the brass point and not in a lead band. He said that the card flights were better than feathers. Abel fitted the darts with card flights.' Cubitt hesitated and then added, 'I don't suppose it's relevant but I'm prepared to say definitely that Parish did nothing more than pick them up and put them down.'

'Thank you, Norman,' said Parish. 'Is that all, Mr Alleyn?'

'My last question for the moment – did you see Miss Moore pour out the brandy for Mr Watchman?'

Dead silence. And then Parish, wrinkling his forehead, looking half-peevish, half-frightened, said, 'I didn't watch her, but you needn't go probing into all that. Decima Moore had nothing to do with – '

'Seb,' interrupted Cubitt quietly, 'you would do better to answer these questions as they are put to you. Mr Alleyn will meet Decima. He will find out for himself that, as far as this affair is concerned, she is a figure of no importance. You must see that he's got to ask about these things.' He turned to Alleyn with his pleasant lop-sided grin, 'I believe the word is "routine",' said Cubitt. 'You see I know my detective fiction.'

'Routine it is,' said Alleyn. 'And you're perfectly correct. Routine is the very fibre of police investigation. Your novelist too has now passed the halcyon days when he could ignore routine. He reads books about Scotland Yard, he swots up police manuals. He knows that routine is deadly dull and hopelessly poor material for a thriller; so, like a wise potboiler, he compromises. He heads one chapter "Routine", dismisses six weeks of drudgery in as many phrases, cuts the cackle and gets to the 'osses. I wish to the Lord we could follow his lead.'

'I'll be bound you do,' said Cubitt. 'Well, if it's any help, I didn't notice much when Decima poured out the brandy except that she was very quick about it. She stood with the rest of us round the settle, someone suggested brandy, she said something about his glass being empty, and went to the bar for the bottle. I got the impression that she simply slopped some brandy in the glass and brought it straight to Watchman. If I may, I should like to add that she was on the best of terms with Watchman and, as far as I know, had no occasion in the world to wish him dead.'

'Good God!' said Parish in a hurry, 'Of course not. Of course not.'

'Yes,' said Alleyn. 'I see. Thank you so much. Now then, Mr Parish until the accident stood by the table where Mr Watchman had left his empty glass. I take it that Mr Parish would have noticed, would have been bound to notice, if anyone came near enough to interfere with the glass. He tells me that the rest of the party were grouped behind Legge. Do you agree to that, Mr Cubitt?'

'Yes. Except Will. Will was in the corner beyond the dart-board. He couldn't have got at the glass. Nobody – ' Again Cubitt caught his breath.

'Yes?'

'In my opinion,' said Cubitt, 'nobody touched the glass, could have touched it, either before or after Decima fetched the brandy bottle. Nobody.'

'Thank you very much,' said Alleyn. 'That's all for the moment.'

II

'What's the time, Fox?' asked Alleyn, looking up from his notes.

'Half-past nine, sir.'

'Has Legge come in yet?'

'Not yet, Mr Alleyn,' said Fox. He stooped slightly and closed the parlour door. Fox always closed doors like that, inspecting the handle gravely as if the turning of it was a delicate operation. He then straightened up and contemplated his superior.

'Legge,' said Fox, advancing slowly, 'is only here on sufferance as you might put it. I've just had one in the public tap. They're not opening the Private till tomorrow. So I had one in the Public.'

'Did you, you old devil!'

'Yes. This chap Nark's in there and I must say he suits his name.'

'In the Australian sense? A fair nark?'

'That's right, sir. I don't wonder old Pomeroy hates the man. He wipes out his pint-pot with a red cotton handkerchief before they draw his beer. To be on the safe side, so he says. And talk!'

'What's he talk about?'

'The law,' said Fox with an air of the deepest disgust. 'As soon as he knew who I was he started on it, and a lot of very foolish remarks he made. You ought to have a chat with him, Mr Alleyn, he'd give you the pip.'

'Thanks,' said Alleyn. 'About Legge. Why's he here on sufferance?'

Fox sat down.

'Because of old Pomeroy,' he said. 'Old Pomeroy thinks Legge's a murderer and wanted him to look for other lodgings, but young Pomeroy stuck to it and they let him stay on, and got his way. However, Legge's given notice and has found rooms in Illington. He's moving over on Monday. He seems to be very well liked among the chaps in the bar, but they're a simple lot, taking them by and large. Young Oates, the Ottercombe PC's in there. Very keen to see you.'

'Oh! Well, I'll have to see him sooner or later. While we're wait-ing for Legge, why not? Bring him in.'

Fox went out and returned in half a minute.

'PC Oates, sir,' said Fox.

PC Oates was brick-red with excitement and as stiff as a poker from a sense of discipline. He stood inside the door with his helmet under his arm and saluted.

'Good evening, Oates,' said Alleyn.

'Good evening, sir.'

'Mr Harper tells me you were on duty the night Mr Watchman died. Are you responsible for the chalk marks in the private tap-room?'

PC Oates looked apprehensive.

'Furr some of 'em, sir,' he said. 'Furr the place where we found the dart, like, and the marks on the settle, like. I used the chalk off the scoring-board, sir.'

'Is it your first case of this sort?'

''Ess, sir.'

'You seem to have kept your head.'

Wild visions cavorted through the brain of PC Oates. He saw in a flash all the keen young PCs of his favourite novels and each of them, with becoming modesty, pointed out a tiny detail that had escaped the notice of his superiors. To each of them did the Man from Higher Up exclaim, 'By thunder, my lad, you've got it,' and upon each of them was rapid promotion visited, while chief consta-bles, the Big Four, yes, the Man at the Top himself, all told each other that young Oates was a man to be watched. For each of these PCs was the dead spit and image of PC Oates himself.

'Thank you, sir,' said Oates.

'I'd like to hear about your appearance on the scene,' said Alleyn.

'In my own words, sir?'

'If you please, Oates,' said Alleyn.

Dick Oates took a deep breath, mustered his wits, and began.

'On the night of Friday, August 2nd,' he began, and paused in horror. His voice had gone into the top of his head and had turned soprano on the way. It was the voice of a squeaking stranger. He uttered a singular noise in his throat and began again.

'On the night of Friday, August 2nd, at approximately 9.16 p.m.,' said Oates in a voice of thunder, 'being on duty at the time, I was proceeding up South Ottercombe Steps with the intention of completing my beat. My attention was aroused by my hearing the sound of my own name, viz, Oates, being called repeatedly from a spot on my left, namely the front door of the Plume of Feathers, public-house, Abel Pomeroy, proprietor. On proceeding to the said front door, I encountered William Pomeroy. He informed me that there had been an accident. Miss Decima Moore came into the entrance from inside the building. She said, "There is no doubt about it, he is dead." I said, to the best of my knowledge and belief, "My Gawd, who is dead?" Miss Moore then said, "Watchman." I then proceeded into the private taproom.'

Oates paused. Alleyn said, 'Yes, Oates, that's all right, but when I said your own words I meant your own words. This is not going to be taken down and used in evidence against you. I want to hear what sort of an impression you got of it all. You see, we have already seen your formal report in the file.'

''Ess, sir,' said Oates, breathing rather hard through his nostrils.

'Very well, then. Did you get the idea that these men were tight, moderately tight, or stone-cold sober?'

'I received the impression, sir, that they had been intoxicated but were now sobered.'

'All of them?'

'Well, sir, when I left the tap at nine o'clock, sir, to proceed – to go round the beat, they was not to say drunk but bosky-eyed like. Merry like.'

'Including Mr Legge?'

'By all means,' said Oates firmly. 'Bob Legge, sir, was sozzled. Quiet like, but muddled. Well, the man couldn't find his way to his mouth with his pipe, not with any dash as you might say.'

'He was still pretty handy with the darts, though,' observed Fox.

'So he was then, sir. But I reckon, sir, that's second nature to the man, drunk or sober. He smelt something wonderful of tipple. And after I left, sir, he had two brandies. He must have been drunk.'

'But sobered by shock?' suggested Alleyn.

'That's what I reckoned, sir.'

'Did you notice anything in Legge's manner or in the manner of any of the others that led you to think the thing wasn't an accident?'

Oates flexed his knees in the classic tradition and eased his collar.

'Legge,' he said, 'was rather put about. Well, sir, that's natural, he having seemingly just killed a man and got over a booze in one throw of a dart if you want to put it fanciful. Yes, he was proper put out, was Bob Legge. White as a bogey and trembling. Kept saying the deceased gentleman had taken tetanus. Now that,' said Oates, 'might of been a blind, but it looked genuine to me. That's Legge. There wasn't anything unusual in Abel Pomeroy. Worried, but there again, who isn't with a fresh corpse on the premises? Young Will had his eye on Miss Dessy Moore. Natural again. She's so pretty as a daisy and good as promised to Will. Staring at him, with eyes like saucers, and ready to swoon away. Kind of frightened. Bore up all right, till she'd told me how she give the deceased brandy, and then seemed, in a manner of speaking, to cave in to it, and went off with Will, scared-like and looking at him kind of bewildered. Will give me the clearest answers of the lot, sir. Kept his head, did Will.'

'And the two friends?'

'Two gentlemen, sir? Mr Parish looked scared and squeamish. Very put out, he was, and crying too, something surprising. Answered by fits and starts. Not himself at all. Mr Cubitt the straight out opposite. Very white and didn't go near the body while I was there. Wouldn't look at it, I noticed. But cool and collected, and answered very sensible. It was Mr Cubitt fetched the doctor. I got the idea he wanted to get out into the open air, like. Seemed to me, sir, that Mr Parish kind of let himself go and Mr Cubitt held himself in. Seemed to me that likely Mr Cubitt was the more upset.'

'Yes,' said Alleyn. 'I see. Go on.'

'The rest, sir? I didn't see The Honourable Darragh till the morning. The Honourable Darragh, sir, behaved very sensible. Not but what she wasn't in a bit of a quiver, but being a stout lady, you noticed it more. Her cheeks jiggled something chronic when she talked about it, but she was very sensible. She's a great one for talking, sir, and it's my belief that when she got over the surprise she fair revelled in it.'

'Really? And now we're left as usual with Mr George Nark.'

'Nothing but vomit and hiccough, sir. Drunk as an owl.'

'I see. Well, Oates, you've given us a clear enough picture of the actors. Now for the dart. Where was the dart when you found it?'

'Legge found it, sir. I asked for it almost immediate, sir, but they was all that flustered they paid no heed to me. 'Cepting Legge who had been going on about, "was it the dart that did it?" and, "had he killed the man?" and, "wasn't it lockjaw?" and, "he must have shifted his finger," and so forth; and so soon as I asked for the dart he stooped down and peered about and then he says, "there it is!" and I saw it and he picked it up from where it had fallen. It was stained and still looked damp, sir. Blood. And I suppose, sir, the poison.'

Oates paused and then said, 'If I may take the liberty, sir.'

'Yes, Oates?'

'They all says, sir, that Mr Watchman threw that there dart down, sir. They say he threw it down 'tother side of the table.'

'Yes.'

'Well, now, sir, *it was laying on the floor.*'

'What?' exclaimed Fox.

'It was,' repeated Oates, '*a-laying* on the floor. I saw it. Ax Legge, he'll bear me out.'

'Whereabouts?' asked Alleyn sharply.

'Behind the table, sir, like they said, and well away from where they had been standing. The table was betwixt the settle and the board.'

'I see,' said Alleyn. And then the wildest hopes of Dick Oates was realized. The words with which he had soothed himself to sleep, the words that he heard most often in his dearest dreams, were spoken unmistakably by the Man from Higher Up.

'By George,' said Chief Detective-Inspector Alleyn, 'I believe you've got it!'

CHAPTER 12

Curious Behaviour of Mr Legge

On that first night in Ottercombe, from the time Oates left them until half-past eleven, Alleyn and Fox thrashed out the case and debated a plan of action. Alleyn was now quite certain that Watchman had been murdered.

'Unless there's a catch, Br'er Fox, and I can't spot it if there is. The rat hole, the dart, the newspaper, and the general evidence ought to give us "who", but we're still in the dark about "how". There are those bits of melted glass, now.'

'I asked old Pomeroy. He says the fireplace was cleared out the day before.'

'Well, we'll have to see if the experts can tell us if it's the same kind as the brandy glass. Rather, let us hope they can say definitely that it's not the same. Oh Lord!'

He got up, stretched himself, and leant over the window-sill. The moon was out, and the sleeping roofs of Ottercombe made such patterns of white and inky black as woodcut draughtsmen love. It was a gull's-eye view Alleyn had from the parlour window, a setting for a child's tale of midnight wonders. A cat was sitting on one of the crooked eaves. It stared at the moon and might have been waiting for an appointment with some small night-gowned figure that would presently lean, dreaming, from the attic window. Alleyn had a liking for old fairy tales and found himself thinking of George Macdonald and the Back of the North Wind. The Coombe was very silent in the moonlight.

'All asleep,' said Alleyn, 'except us, and Mr Robert Legge. I wish he'd come home to bed.'

'There's a car now,' said Fox, 'up by the tunnel.'

It was evidently a small car and an old one. With a ramshackle clatter it drew nearer the pub, and then the driver must have turned his engine off and coasted down to the garage. There followed the squeak of brakes. A door slammed tinnily. Someone dragged open the garage door.

'That's him,' said Fox.

'Good,' said Alleyn. 'Pop into the passage, Fox, and hail him in.'

Fox went out, leaving the door open. Alleyn heard slow steps plod across the yard to the side entrance. Fox said, 'Good evening, sir. Is it Mr Legge?'

A low mumble.

'Could you spare us a moment, sir? We're police officers. Chief Inspector Alleyn would be glad to have a word with you.'

A pause, another mumble, and then approaching steps.

'This way, sir,' said Fox, and ushered in Mr Robert Legge.

Alleyn saw a medium-sized man who stooped a little. He saw a large head, white hair, a heavily-lined face and a pair of callused hands. Legge, blinking in the lamplight, looked a defenceless, a rather pathetic figure.

'Mr Legge?' said Alleyn. 'I'm sorry to bother you so late in the evening. Won't you sit down?'

Fox moved forward a chair and, without uttering a word, Legge sat in it. He was under the lamp. Alleyn saw that his clothes, which had once been good, were darned and faded. Everything about the man seemed bleached and characterless. He looked nervously from Alleyn to Fox. His lips were not quite closed and showed his palpably false teeth.

'I expect,' said Alleyn, 'that you have guessed why we are here.'

Legge said nothing.

'We're making inquiries about the death of Mr Luke Watchman.'

'Oh, yes?' said Legge breathlessly.

'There are one or two points we would like to clear up and we hope you will be able to help us.'

The extraordinarily pale eyes flickered.

'Only too pleased,' murmured Legge and looked only too wretched.

'Tell me,' said Alleyn, 'have you formed any theory about this affair?'

'Accident.'

'You think that's possible?'

Legge looked at Alleyn as if he had said something profoundly shocking.

'Possible? But of course it's possible. Dreadfully possible. Such a way to do things! They should have bought traps. The chemist should be struck off the rolls. It's a disgrace.'

He lowered his voice and became conspiratorial.

'It was a terrible, virulent poison,' he whispered mysteriously. 'A shocking thing that they should have it here. The coroner said so.'

He spoke with a very slight lisp, a mere thickening of sibilants caused, perhaps, by his false teeth.

'How do you think it got on the dart you threw into Mr Watchman's finger?'

Legge made a gesture that disconcerted and astonished Alleyn. He raised his hand and shook a finger at Alleyn as if he gently admonished him. If his face had not spoken of terror he would have looked faintly waggish.

'You suspect me,' he said. 'You shouldn't.'

Alleyn was so taken aback by this old-maidish performance that for a moment he could think of nothing to say.

'You shouldn't,' repeated Legge. 'Because I didn't.'

'The case is as wide open as the grave.'

'He's dead,' whispered Legge, 'and buried. *I* didn't do it. I was the instrument. It's not a very pleasant thing to be the instrument of death.'

'No. You should welcome any attempt to get to the bottom of the affair.'

'So I would,' muttered Legge eagerly, 'if I thought they would get to the truth. But I'm not popular here. Not in some quarters. And that makes me nervous, Chief Inspector.'

'It needn't,' said Alleyn. 'But we're being very unorthodox, Mr Legge. May we have your full name and address?'

Fox opened his notebook. Legge suddenly stood up and, in an uncertain sort of fashion, came to attention.

'Robert Legge,' he said rapidly, 'care of the Plume of Feathers, Ottercombe, South Devon. Business address: Secretary and Treasurer, The Combe Left Movement, GPO Box 119, Illington.'

He sat down again.

'Thank you, sir,' said Fox.

'How long have you been here, Mr Legge?' asked Alleyn.

'Ten months. My chest is not very good. Nothing serious, you know. I needn't be nervous on *that* account. But I was in very low health altogether. Boils. Even in my ears. Very unpleasant and painful. My doctor said it would be as well to move.'

'Ah, yes. From where?'

'From Liverpool. I was in Liverpool. In Flattery Street, South, Number 17. Not a very healthy part.'

'That was your permanent address?'

'Yes. I had been there for some little time. I had one or two secretaryships. For a time I was in vacuums.'

'What!'

'In vacuum cleaners. But that did not altogether agree with my chest. I got very tired and you wouldn't believe how rude some women can be. Positively odious! So I gave it up for stamps.'

His voice, muffled and insecure though it was, seemed the voice of an educated man. Alleyn wondered if he had been born to vacuum cleaners and philately.

'How long were you in Liverpool, Mr Legge?'

'Nearly two years.'

'And before that?'

'I was in London. In the City. I was born in London. Why do you ask?'

'Routine, Mr Legge,' said Alleyn and thought of Cubitt. 'What I was going to ask you was this. Had you ever met Mr Watchman before he arrived at Ottercombe?'

'Yes, indeed.'

Alleyn looked up.

'Do you mind telling us where you met him? You need not answer any of these questions, of course, if you don't want to.'

'I don't in the least object, Chief Inspector. I met him in a slight collision at Diddlestock corner. He was very nice about it.'

Alleyn stared at him and he blinked nervously. Fox, Alleyn noticed, was stifling a grin.

'Was that the first time you saw him?'

'Oh, no. I'd *seen* him before. In court.'

'What?'

'I used to go a great deal to the courts when I was in London. I always found it very absorbing. Of course, Mr Watchman didn't know *me*.'

'I see.'

Alleyn moved Abel's best inkpot from one side of the table to the other and stared thoughtfully at it.

'Mr Legge,' he said at last, 'how much did you have to drink on that Friday night?'

'Too much,' said Legge quickly. 'I realize it now. Not so much as the others, but too much. I have a good head as a rule, a very good head. But unless he moved his finger, which I still think possible, I must have taken too much.' He gave Alleyn a sidelong glance.

'I usually play my best,' said Mr Legge, 'when I am a little intoxicated. I must have overdone it. I shall never forgive myself, never.'

'How long was it,' Alleyn asked, 'before you realized what had happened?'

'Oh, a very long time. I thought it must be tetanus. I've seen a man with tetanus. You see, I had forgotten about that dreadful stuff. I had forgotten that Mr Pomeroy opened the cupboard that afternoon.'

'That was for – '

'I know what you're going to say,' Legge interrupted, again with that gesture of admonishment. 'You're going to remind me that he opened it to get the iodine for my face. Do you suppose that I can ever forget that? I was doubly the instrument. That's what upsets me so dreadfully. He must have done something then, and accidentally got it on his fingers. I don't know. I don't pretend it's not a mystery.' His face twitched dolorously. 'I'm wretchedly unhappy,' he whispered. 'Miserable!'

People with no personal charm possess one weapon, an occasional appeal to our sense of pathos. There was something intolerably pitiable in Legge; in his furtiveness, his threadbare respectability, his obvious terror, and his little spurts of confidence. Alleyn had a violent desire to get rid of him, to thrust him away as something indecent and painful. But he said, 'Mr Legge, have you any objections to our taking your fingerprints?'

The chair fell over as Legge got to his feet. He backed towards the door, turning his head from side to side and wringing his hands. Fox moved to the door but Legge seemed unaware of him. He gazed like a trapped animal at Alleyn.

'O God!' he said. 'O dear! O dear me! O God, I *knew* you'd say that!' and broke into tears.

II

'Come now, Mr Legge,' said Alleyn at last, 'you mustn't let the affair get on your nerves like this. If, as you think, Mr Watchman's death was purely accidental, you have nothing to fear. There's nothing very terrible in having your fingerprints taken.'

'Yes, there is,' contradicted Legge in a sort of fury. 'It's a perfectly horrible suggestion. I resent it. I deeply resent it. I most strongly object.'

'Very well, then,' said Alleyn placidly, 'we won't take them.'

Mr Legge blew his nose violently and looked over the top of his handkerchief at Alleyn.

'Yes,' he said, 'that's all very well, but I know what tricks you'll get up to. You'll get them by stealth, I know. I've heard of the practices that go in the police. I've studied the matter. It's like everything else in a state governed by capitalism. Trickery and intimidation. You'll give me photographs to identify and take my fingerprints from them.'

'Not now you've warned us,' said Alleyn.

'You'll get them against my will and then you'll draw false conclusions from them. That's what you'll do.'

'What sort of false conclusions?'

'About me,' cried Legge passionately, 'about me.'

'You know that's all nonsense,' said Alleyn quietly. 'You will do yourself no good by talking like this.'

'I won't talk at all. I will not be trapped into making incriminating statements. I will not be kept in here against my will!'

'You may go whenever you wish,' said Alleyn. 'Fox, will you open the door?'

Fox opened the door. Legge backed towards it, but on the threshold he paused.

'If only,' he said with extraordinary intensity, 'if only you'd have the sense to see that I couldn't have done anything even if I'd wanted to. If only you'd realize that and leave me in peace. You don't know *what* damage you may do, indeed you don't. If only you would leave me in peace!'

He swallowed noisily, made a movement with his hands that was eloquent of misery and defeat, and went away.

Fox stopped with his hand on the door knob.

'He's gone back to the garage,' said Fox. 'Surely he won't bolt.'

'I don't think he'll bolt, Fox. Not in that car.'

Fox stood and listened, looking speculatively at Alleyn.

'Well,' he said, 'that was a rum go, Mr Alleyn, wasn't it?'

'Very rum indeed. I suppose you're thinking what I'm thinking?'

'He's been inside,' said Fox. 'I'll take my oath that man's done his stretch.'

'I think so too, and what's more he had that suit before he went in. It was made by a decent tailor about six years ago, or more, and it was made for Mr Legge. It fits him well enough and he's too odd a shape for reach-me-downs.'

'Notice his hands?'

'I did. And the hair, and the walk, and the eyes. I thought he was going to sob it all out on my bosom. Ugh!' said Alleyn, 'it's beastly, that furtive, wary look they get. Fox, ring up Illington and ask Harper to send the dart up to Dabs. It's got his prints. Not very nice ones, but they'll do to go on with.'

Fox went off to the telephone, issued cryptic instructions, and returned.

'I wonder,' said Fox, 'who he is, and what they pulled him in for.'

'We'll have to find out.'

'He behaved very foolish,' said Fox austerely. 'All that refusing to have his prints taken. We're bound to find out. We'll have to get his dabs, sir.'

'Yes,' agreed Alleyn, 'on the sly, as he foretold.'

'I wonder what he's *doing* out there,' said Fox.

'Wait a moment,' said Alleyn. 'I'll have a look.'

He stole into the passage. Legge had left the side door ajar and Alleyn could see the yard outside, flooded with moonshine. He slipped out and moved like a cat, across the yard and into the shadow of the garage door. Here he stopped and listened. From inside the garage came a rhythmic whisper interrupted at intervals by low thuds and accompanied by the sound of breathing. A metal door opened and closed stealthily, a boot scraped across stone. The rhythmic whisper began again. Alleyn stole away and recrossed the yard, his long shadow going fantastically before him.

When he rejoined Fox in the parlour, he was grinning broadly.

'What's he up to?' asked Fox.

'Being one too many for the infamous police,' said Alleyn. 'He's polishing his car.'

'Well, I'll be blooming well blowed,' said Fox.

'He must have nearly finished. Switch off the light, Fox. It'd be a pity to keep him waiting.'

Fox switched off the light. He and Alleyn sat like shadows in the bar parlour. The Ottercombe town clock struck twelve and, a moment later, the same dragging footsteps sounded in the yard. The side door was shut and the steps went past the parlour. The staircase light clicked and a faint glow showed underneath the door.

'Up he does,' whispered Alleyn.

Legge went slowly upstairs, turned the light off, and moved along the passage above their heads. A door closed.

'Now then,' said Alleyn.

They went upstairs in the dark and slipped into Alleyn's room, the first on the top landing. The upstairs passage was bright with moonlight.

'His is the end one,' murmured Alleyn. 'He's got his light on. Do you suppose he'll set to work and wipe all the untensils in his room.'

'The thing's silly,' whispered Fox. 'I've never known anything like it. What's the good of it? We'll *get* his blasted dabs.'

'What do you bet me he won't come down to breakfast in gloves?'

'He's capable of anything,' snorted Fox.

'Sssh! He's coming out.'

'Lavatory?'

'Possibly.'

Alleyn groped for the door and unlatched it.

'What are you doing, sir?' asked Fox rather peevishly.

'Squinting through the crack,' Alleyn whispered. 'Now he's come out of the lavatory.'

'I can hear that.'

'He's in his pyjamas. He doesn't look very delicious. Good Lord!'

'What?'

'He's crossed the passage,' breathed Alleyn, 'and he's stooping down at another door.'

'What's he up to?'

'Can't see – shadow. Now he's off again. Back to his own room. Shuts the door. Light out. Mr Legge finished for the night.'

'And not before it was time,' grumbled Fox. 'They've got a nice sort of chap as secretary and treasurer for their society. How long'll we give him, Mr Alleyn? I'd like to have a look what he's been up to.'

'I'll give him ten minutes and then go along the passage.'

'Openly?'

'Yes. Quickly but not stealthily, Fox. It's the room on the right at the end. It looked almost as if he was shoving a note under the door. Very odd.'

'What age,' asked Fox, 'is the Honourable Violet Darragh?'

'What a mind you have! It was probably young Pomeroy's door.'

'I hadn't thought of that, sir. Probably.'

Alleyn switched on the light and began to unpack his suitcase. Whistling soundlessly he set his room in order, undressed, and put on his pyjamas and dressing-gown.

'Now then,' he said. He picked up his towel and sponge-bag and went out.

Fox waited, his hands on his knees. He heard a tap turned on. Water pipes gurgled. In a distant room someone began to snore in two keys. Presently Fox heard the pad of feet in the passage and Alleyn returned.

His towel was round his neck. His hair was rumpled and damp and hung comically over his eyes. He looked like a rather distinguished faun who had chosen to disguise himself in pyjamas and a dressing-gown. Between thumb and forefinger he held a piece of folded paper.

'Crikey, Fox!' said Alleyn.

'What have you got there, sir?'

'Lord knows. A threat? A *billet dowx*? Find my case, please, Fox, and get out a couple of tweezers. We'll open it carefully. At least it may have his prints. Thank the Lord I brought that camera.'

Fox produced the tweezers. Alleyn dropped his paper on the glass top of the washstand. Using the tweezers, he opened it delicately. Fox looked over his shoulder and read ten words written in pencil.

'Implore you usual place immediately. Most important. *Destroy at once.*'

'Crikey again,' said Alleyn. 'An assignation.'

'Where did you get it, Mr Alleyn?'

'Under the door. I fished for it with a hairpin I found in the bathroom. Luckily there was a good gap.'

'Will Pomeroy's door?'

'Does Will Pomeroy wear high-heeled shoes, size four and a half, made by Rafferty, Belfast?'

'Lor',' said Fox. 'The Honourable Violet.'

CHAPTER 13

Miss Darragh Stands firm

The summer sun shines early on the Coombe, and when Alleyn looked out of his window at half-past five it was at a crinkled and sparkling sea. The roofs of Fish Lane were cleanly pale. A column of wood smoke rose delicately from a chimney-pot. Someone walked, whistling, down Ottercombe Steps.

Alleyn had been dressed for an hour. He was waiting for Mr Robert Legge. He supposed that the word 'immediately' in the note for Miss Darragh might be interpreted as 'the moment you read this', which no doubt would be soon after Miss Darragh awoke.

Fox and Alleyn had been very industrious before they went to bed. They had poured iodine into a flat dish and they had put Mr Legge's letter into the dish but not into the iodine. They had covered the dish and left it for five minutes, and then set up an extremely expensive camera by whose aid they could photograph the note by lamplight. They might have spared themselves the trouble. There were no fingerprints on Mr Legge's note. Fox had gone to bed in high dudgeon. Alleyn had refolded the note and pushed it under Miss Darragh's door. Four minutes later he had slipped peacefully into sleep.

The morning smelt fresh. Alleyn leant over the window-sill and glanced to his left. At the same moment three feet away Fox leant over his window-sill and glanced to his right. He was fully dressed and looked solidly prepared to take up his bowler hat and go anywhere.

'Good morning, sir,' said Fox in a whisper. 'Pleasant morning. He's just stirring, I fancy.'

'Good morning to you, Br'er Fox,' rejoined Alleyn. 'A very pleasant morning. I'll meet you on the stairs.'

He stole to the door of his room and listened. Presently the now familiar footsteps sounded in the passage. Alleyn waited for a few seconds and then slipped through the door. Fox performed a similar movement at the same time.

'Simultaneous comedians,' whispered Alleyn. 'Come on.'

Keeping observation is one of the most tedious of a detective officer's duties. Laymen talk of shadowing. It is a poetic term for a specialized drudgery. In his early days at Scotland Yard, Alleyn had hated keeping observation and had excelled at it, a circumstance which casts some light on his progress as a detective. There are two kinds of observation in the police sense. You may tail a man in such a manner that you are within his range of vision but unrecognized or unremarked by him. You may also be obliged to tail a man in circumstances that forbid his seeing you at all. In a deserted hamlet, at half-past five on a summer's morning, Mr Legge could scarcely fail to recognize his tormentors of the previous evening. Alleyn and Fox wished to follow him without being seen.

They reached the entrance lobby of the pub as Mr Legge stepped into the street. Alleyn moved into the private tap and Fox into a sort of office on the other side of the front entrance. Alleyn watched Mr Legge go past the window of the private tap and signalled to Fox. They hurried down the side passage in time to see Mr Legge pass the garage and make for the South Steps. Alleyn nodded to Fox who strolled across the yard, and placed himself in a position where he could see the South Steps, reflected handily in a cottage window. When the figure of Mr Legge descended the steps and turned to the left, Fox made decent haste to follow his example.

Alleyn opened the garage and backed the police Ford into the yard. He then removed his coat and hat, let a good deal of air out of his spare tyre and began, in a leisurely manner to pump it up again. He had inflated and replaced the spare tyre and was peering into the engine, when Miss Darragh came out of the pub.

Alleyn had not questioned the superintendent at all closely about Miss Darragh, nor was her appearance dwelt upon in the files of the case. He was therefore rather surprised to see how fat she was. She was like a pouter-pigeon in lavender print. She wore an enormous straw hat, and carried a haversack and easel. Her round face was quite inscrutable but Alleyn thought she looked pretty hard at him. He dived farther inside the bonnet of the car and Miss Darragh passed down the South Steps.

Alleyn gave her a good start and then put on his coat and hat.

When he reached the foot of the steps he looked cautiously round the corner of the wall to the left. Miss Darragh had reached the south end of Fish Lane and now plodded along a stone causeway to the last of the jetties. Alleyn crossed Fish Lane and followed under the lee of the houses. At the end of Fish Lane he behaved with extreme caution, manoeuvring for a vantage point. There was nobody about. The fishing fleet had gone out at dawn and the housewives of Ottercombe were either in bed or cooking breakfast. Alleyn paused at Mary Yeo's shop on the corner of Fish Lane and the causeway. By peering diagonally through both windows at once, he had a distorted view of the jetty and of Miss Darragh. She had set up a camp-stool and had her back to Ottercombe. Alleyn saw her mount her easel. A sketching block appeared. Presently Miss Darragh began to sketch.

Alleyn walked down an alley towards the jetty, and took cover in an angle of one of the ramshackle cottages that sprawled about the waterfront. This is the rough quarter of Ottercombe. Petronella Broome has a house of ill-repute, four rooms, on the south water-front; and William Glass's tavern was next door until Superintendent Harper made a fuss and had the licence cancelled. This stretch of less than two hundred yards is called the South Front. At night it takes on a sort of glamour. Its lamps are reflected redly in the water. Petronella's gramophone advertises her hospitality, bursts of laugh-ter echo over the harbour, and figures move dimly to and fro across the lights. But at ten to six in the morning it smells of fish and squalor.

Alleyn waited for five minutes before Legge appeared from behind a bollard at the far end of the jetty. Legge crossed the end of the jetty and stood behind Miss Darragh who continued to sketch.

'Damn,' said Alleyn.

The tide was out and three dinghies were beached near the jetty. A fourth was made fast to the far end and seemed to lie, bobbing complacently, directly under Miss Darragh. Alleyn thought the water looked fairly shallow for at least half-way down the jetty. He groaned and with caution, moved towards the front. Miss Darragh did not turn, but from time to time Legge glanced over his shoulder. Alleyn advanced to the foreshore under cover of boats, fishing gear, and the sea wall. To an observer from one of the windows, he would have seemed to be hunting for lost property. He reached the jetty.

For half-way along the jetty the water was about two feet deep. Alleyn, cursing inwardly, rolled up his trousers and took to it, keeping under the jetty. The water was cold and the jetty smelt. Abruptly the bottom shelved down. Alleyn could now hear the faintest murmur of voices and knew that he was not so very far from his objective. The dinghy was hidden by posts but he could hear the glug-glug of its movement and the hollow thud it made when it knocked against the post to which it was made fast. Just beyond it was a flight of steps leading up to the jetty. Alleyn mounted a crossbeam. It was slimy and barnacled but he found handholds to the end. If he could reach the dinghy! His progress was hazardous, painful, and maddeningly slow, but at last he grasped the post. He embraced it with both arms, straddled the crossbeams and wriggled round until he reached the far side.

Underneath him was the dinghy and lying full-length in the dinghy was Inspector Fox. His notebook lay open on his chest.

Fox winked at his superior and obligingly moved over. Alleyn pulled the dinghy closer, and not without difficulty lowered himself into the bows.

'Two minds with but a single thought,' he whispered. 'Simultaneous comedy again.'

He took out his notebook and cocked his ears.

From the jetty above, the voices of Miss Darragh and Mr Legge sounded disembodied and remote. For a second or two Alleyn could hear nothing distinctly, but, as his concentration sharpened, words and phrases began to take form. Miss Darragh was speaking. She spoke in little bursts of eloquence broken by pauses that fell oddly until he realized that while she talked she painted.

'– and haven't I gone sufficiently far, coming down here, to meet you? I go no farther at all. I'm sorry for the nasty pickle you're in . . . terribly cruel the way . . . haunts you . . . compromised myself . . . can't expect . . . ' Her voice died into a mysterious murmur. Alleyn raised his eyebrows and Fox shook his head. Miss Darragh droned on. Suddenly she said very distinctly, 'It's no good at all asking, for I'll not do ut.'

Legge began to mumble quite inaudibly. She interrupted him with a staccato, 'Yes, yes, I realize all that.' And a moment later, 'Don't think I'm not sorry. I am.' And then, incisively, 'Of course, I know you're innocent of ut, but I can't – '

For the first time Mr Legge became intelligible.

'My blood be on your head,' said Mr Legge loudly.

'Ah, don't say that. Will you be quiet, now? You've nothing to fear.'

Legge's voice dropped again but Alleyn's hearing was now attuned to it. He heard isolated phrases. 'Hounded to death . . . just when I was . . . expiated my fault . . . God knows . . . never free from it.'

Footsteps padded across the beams overhead, and when Miss Darragh spoke, it was from a different place. She had moved, perhaps to look at the sketch, and now stood near the edge of the jetty. Her voice, seeming very close, was startlingly clear.

'I promise you,' she said, 'that I'll do my best, but I'll not commit perjury – '

'Perjury!' said Legge irritably. He had followed her.

'Well, whatever it is. I'll do my best. I've no fear at all of their suspecting you, for they'll have their wits about them and will soon see it's impossible.'

'But don't you see – they'll think – they'll tell every one – '

'I can see it's going to be hard on you and I've got my – you know well enough why I feel bound to help you. That'll do now. Rest easy, and we'll hope for the best.'

'Don't forget how I came to my trouble.'

'I do not and I will not. Be off, now, for it's getting late. I've finished me little peep and it's nothing better than a catastrophe; me mind was not on ut. We'd best not be seen walking back together.'

'I'm at your mercy,' said Legge. And they heard him walk away.

II

Alleyn and Fox breakfasted in the dining-room. Cubitt and Parish were nowhere to be seen, but Miss Darragh sat at a corner table and gave them good morning as they came in. Alleyn knew that from behind the paper she watched them pretty closely. He caught her at it twice, but she did not seem to be at all embarrassed and the second time twinkled and smiled at him.

'I see you've no paper,' said Miss Darragh. 'Would you like to have a look at the Illington *Courier*?'

'Thank you so much,' said Alleyn, and crossed over to the table.

'You're Mr Roderick Alleyn are ye not?'

Alleyn bowed.

'Ah, I knew you from your likeness to your brother George,' said Miss Darragh.

'I am delighted that you knew me,' said Alleyn, 'but I've never thought that my brother George and I were much alike.'

'Ah, there's a kind of a family resemblance. And then, of course, I knew you were here, for the landlord told me. You're a good deal better-looking than your brother George. He used to stay with me cousins, the Sean O'Darraghs for Punchestown. I met 'um there. I'm Violet Darragh so now you know who 'tis that's so bold with you.'

'Miss Darragh,' said Alleyn, 'would you spare us a moment when you have finished your breakfast?'

'I would. Is it about this terrible affair?'

'Yes.'

'I'll be delighted. I'm a great lover of mysteries myself, or I was before this happened. They're not such grand fun when you're in the middle of 'um. I'll be in the private taproom when you want me. Don't hurry now.'

'Thank you,' said Alleyn. Miss Darragh rose and squeezed past the table. Alleyn opened the door. She nodded cheerfully and went out.

'Cool,' said Fox, when Alleyn joined him. 'You'd never think she had anything up her sleeve, sir, now would you?'

'No, Fox, you wouldn't. I wonder what line I'd better take with her. She's as sharp as a needle.'

'I'd say so,' agreed Fox.

'I think, Fox, you had better ask her, in your best company manners, to walk into our parlour. It looks more official. I must avoid that friend of the family touch – ' Alleyn stopped short and rubbed his nose. 'Unless, indeed, I make use of it,' he said. 'Dear me, now, I wonder.'

'What's the friend-of-the-family touch, sir?'

'Didn't you hear? She has met my brother George who is physically as unlike me as may be. Mentally, too, I can't help hoping. But perhaps that's vanity. What do you think?'

'I haven't had the pleasure of meeting Sir George, Mr Alleyn.'

'He's rather an old ass, I'm afraid. Have you finished?'

'Yes, thank you, sir.'

'Then I shall remove to the parlour. My compliments to Miss Darragh, Foxkin, and I shall be grateful if she will walk into my parlour. Lord, Lord, I hope I don't make a botch of this.'

Alleyn went to the parlour. In a minute or two Fox came in with Miss Darragh.

Ever since he entered the detective service, Alleyn has had to set a guard against a habit of instinctive reactions to new acquaintances. Many times has he repeated to himself the elementary warning that roguery is not incompatible with charm. But he has never quite overcome certain impulses towards friendliness, and his austerity of manner is really a safeguard against this weakness, a kind of protective colouring, a uniform for behaviour.

When he met Violet Darragh he knew that she would amuse and interest him, that it would be easy to listen to her and pleasant to strike up a sort of friendship. He knew that he would find it difficult to believe her capable of double-dealing. He summoned the discipline of a system that trains its servants to a high pitch of objective watchfulness. He became extremely polite.

'I hope you will forgive me,' he said, 'for suggesting that you should come in here. Mr Pomeroy has given us this room as a sort of office, and as all our papers – '

'Ah, don't worry yourself,' said Miss Darragh. She took the armchair that Fox wheeled forward, wriggled into the deep seat, and tucked her feet up.

'It's more comfortable here,' she said, 'and I'm a bit tired. I was out at the crack of dawn at me sketching. Down on the front, 'twas, and those steps are enough to break your heart.'

'There must be some very pleasant subjects down there,' murmured Alleyn. 'At the end of the jetty, for instance.'

'You've a good eye for a picture,' said Miss Darragh. 'That's where I was. Or perhaps you saw me there?'

'I think,' said Alleyn, 'that you passed me on your way out. I was in the garage yard.'

'You were. But the garage yard does not overlook the jetty.'

'Oh, no,' said Alleyn vaguely. 'Now, Miss Darragh, may we get down to what I'm afraid will be, for you, a very boring business. It's about the night of this affair. I've seen your statement to the police, and I've read the report of the inquest.'

'Then,' said Miss Darragh, 'I'm afraid you'll know all I have to tell you and that's not much.'

'There are one or two points we'd like to go over with you if we may. You told the coroner that you thought the wound from the dart had nothing to do with Mr Watchman's death.'

'I did. And I'm positive it hadn't. A little bit of a puncture no bigger than you'd take from a darning-needle.'

'A little bigger than that surely?'

'Not to make any matter.'

'But the analyst found cyanide on the dart.'

'I've very little faith in 'um,' said Miss Darragh.

'In the analyst? It went up to London, you know. It was the very best analyst,' said Alleyn with a smile.

'I know 'twas, but the cleverest of 'um can make mistakes. Haven't I read for myself how delicate these experiments are with their fractions of a grain of this and that and their acid tests, and their heat tests and all the rest of it? I've always thought it's blown up with their theories and speculations these fine chemists must be. When they're told to look for prussic acid they'll be determined to find it. Ah, well, maybe they did find poison on the dart, but that makes no difference at all to me theory, Mr Alleyn. If there was prussic acid or cyanide, or somebody's acid on the dart (and why, for pity's sake, can't they find one name for ut and be done with ut), then 'twas put on in the factory or the shop, or got on afterwards for 'twas never there at the time.'

'I beg your pardon?' asked Alleyn apologetically. 'I don't quite – '

'What I mean is this, Mr Alleyn. Not a soul there had a chance to play the fool with the darts, and why should they when nobody could foretell the future?'

'The future? You mean nobody could tell that the dart would puncture the finger?'

'I do.'

'Mr Legge,' said Alleyn, 'might have known, mightn't he?'

'He might,' said Miss Darragh coolly, 'but he didn't. Mr Alleyn, I never took my eyes off 'um from the time he took the darts till the time he wounded the poor fellow, and that was no time at all, for it passed in a flash. If it's any help I'm ready to make a sworn statement, an affidavit, isn't it? that Legge put nothing on the dart.'

'I see,' said Alleyn.

'Even Mr Pomeroy who is set against Mr Legge, and Mr Parish too, will tell you he had no chance to infect the dart.'

Miss Darragh made a quick nervous movement with her hands, clasping them together and raising them to her chin.

'I know very well,' she said, 'that there are people here will make things black for Mr Legge. You will do well to let 'um alone. He's a delicate man and this affair's racking his nerves to pieces. Let 'um alone, Mr Alleyn, and look elsewhere for your murderer, if there's murder in ut.'

'What's your opinion of Legge?' asked Alleyn abruptly.

'Ah, he's a common well-meaning little man with a hard life behind 'um.'

'You know something of him? That's perfectly splendid. I've been trying to fit a background to him and I can't.'

For the first time Miss Darragh hesitated, but only for a second. She said, 'I've been here nearly three weeks and I've had time to draw my own conclusions about the man.'

'No more than that?'

'Ah, I know he's had a hard time and that in the end he's come into harbour. Let 'um rest there, Mr Alleyn, for he's no murderer.'

'If he's no murderer he has nothing to fear.'

'You don't know that. You don't understand.'

'I think perhaps we are beginning to understand. Miss Darragh, last night I asked Mr Legge if, as a matter of routine, he would let us take his fingerprints. He refused. Why do you suppose he did that?'

'He's distressed and frightened. He thinks you suspect 'um.'

'Then he should welcome my procedure that is likely to prove our suspicions groundless. He should rather urge us to take his prints than burst into a fit of hysterics when we ask for them.'

A faint line appeared between Miss Darragh's eyes. Her brows were raised and the corners of her mouth turned down. She looked like a disgruntled baby.

'I don't say he's not foolish,' she said. 'I only say he's innocent of murder.'

'There's one explanation that sticks out a mile,' Alleyn said. 'Do you know the usual reason for withholding fingerprints?'

'I do not.'

'The knowledge that the police already have them.'

Miss Darragh said nothing.

'Now if that should be the reason in this case,' Alleyn continued, 'it is only a matter of time before we arrive at the truth. If, to put it plainly, Legge has been in prison, we shall very soon trace his record. But we may have to arrest him for manslaughter to do it.'

'All this,' exclaimed Miss Darragh with spirit, 'all this to prove he didn't kill Watchman. All this disgrace and trouble! And who's to pay the cost of ut? 'Twould ruin him entirely.'

'Then he would be well advised to make a clean breast and tell us of his record, before we find it out for ourselves.'

'How do you know that he has a record?'

'I think,' said Alleyn, 'I must tell you that I was underneath the south jetty at six o'clock this morning.'

She opened her eyes very wide indeed, stared at him, clapped her fat little hands together, and broke into a shrill cackle of laughter.

'Ah, what an old fule you've made of me,' said Miss Darragh.

III

But although she took Alleyn's disclosure in good part she still made no admissions. She was amused and interested in his exploit of the morning, didn't in the least resent it, and exclaimed repeatedly that it was no use trying to keep out of his clutches. But she did elude him, nevertheless, and he began to see her as a particularly slippery pippin, bobbing out of reach whenever he made bite at it.

Alleyn was on difficult ground and knew it. The notes that he and Fox had made of the conversation on the jetty were full of gaps

and, though they pointed in one direction, contained nothing conclusive.

Detective officers are circumscribed by rules which, in more than
one case, are open to several interpretations. It is impossible to
define exactly the degrees of pressure in questions put by the detective. Every time an important case crops up he is likely enough to
take risks. If he is lucky his departure from rule of thumb comes off,
but at the end of every case, like a warning bogey, stands the figure
of defending counsel, ready to pounce on any irregularity and shake
it angrily before the jury.

Miss Darragh had not denied the suggestion that Legge had a
police record, and Alleyn decided to take it as a matter of course that
such a record existed and that she knew about it.

He said, 'It's charming of you to let me down so lightly.'

'For what, me dear man?'

'Why, for lying on my back in a wet dinghy and listening to your
conversation.'

'Isn't it your job? Why should I be annoyed? I'm only afraid
you've misinterpreted whatever you heard.'

'Then,' said Alleyn, 'I shall tell you how I have interpreted it, and
you will correct me if I am wrong.'

'So you say,' said Miss Darragh good-humouredly.

'So I hope. I think that Legge has been to gaol, that you know it,
that you're sorry for him, and that as long as you can avoid making
a false statement you will give me as little information as possible. Is
that right?'

'It's right in so far as I'll continue to hold me tongue.'

'Ugh!' said Alleyn with a rueful grin. 'You *are* being firm with me,
aren't you? Well, here we go again. I think that if Mr Legge had not
been to gaol you would laugh like mad and tell me what a fool I
was.'

'You do, do you?'

'Yes. And what's more I do seriously advise you to tell me what
you know about Legge. If you won't do that, urge Legge to come out
of the thicket, and tell me himself. Tell him that we've always got the
manslaughter charge up our sleeves. Tell him that his present line of
behaviour is making us extremely suspicious.' Alleyn paused and
looked earnestly at Miss Darragh.

'You said something to this effect this morning, I know,' he added. 'Perhaps it's no good. I don't see why I should finesse. I asked Legge to let me take impressions of his fingerprints. Good prints would have been helpful but they're not essential. He picked up the dart, it has been tested and we've got results. I asked him for impressions because I already suspected he had done time and I wanted to see how he'd respond. His response convinced me that I was right. We've asked the superintendent at Illington to send the dart to the Fingerprint Bureau. Tomorrow they will telephone the result.'

'Let 'um,' said Miss Darragh cheerfully.

'You know, you're withholding information. I ought to be very stiff with you.'

'It's not meself I mind,' she said. 'I'm just wishing you'd leave the poor fellow alone. You're wasting your time, and you're going to do 'um great harm in the end. Let 'um alone.'

'We can't,' said Alleyn. 'We can't let any of you alone.'

She began to look very distressed and beat the palms of her hands together.

'You're barking up the wrong tree,' she said. 'I'll accuse no one; but look farther and look nearer home.'

And when he asked her what she meant she only repeated very earnestly, 'Look farther and look nearer home. I'll say no more.'

CHAPTER 14

Crime and Mr Legge

'Fox,' said Alleyn, 'get your hat. We'll walk to Cary Edge Farm and call on Miss Moore. Miss Darragh says it's a mile and a quarter over the downs from the mouth of the tunnel. She says we shall pass Cubitt painting Parish on our way. An eventful trip. Let us take it.'

Fox produced the particularly rigid felt hat that appears when his duties take him into the country. Will Pomeroy was in the front passage and Alleyn asked him if he might borrow one of a collection of old walking-sticks behind the door.

'Welcome,' said Will shortly.

'Thank you so much. To get to Cary Edge Farm we turn off to the right from the main road, don't we?'

'Cary Edge?' repeated Will and glared at them.

'Yes,' said Alleyn. 'That's where Miss Moore lives, isn't it?'

'She won't be up-along this morning.'

'What's that, sonny?' called old Abel from the private taproom. 'Be the gentlemen looking for Miss Dessy? She's on her way over by this time for Saturday marketing.'

Will moved his shoulders impatiently.

'You know everyone's business, Father,' he muttered.

'Thank you, Mr Pomeroy,' called Alleyn. 'We'll meet her on the way, perhaps.'

''Less she do drive over in old car,' said Abel, coming to the door. 'But most times her walks.'

He looked apprehensively at Will and turned back into the bar.

'We'll risk it,' said Alleyn. 'Back to lunch, Mr Pomeroy.'

'Thank 'ee, sir.'

Alleyn and Fox walked up to the tunnel mouth. When they reached it Alleyn glanced back at the Plume of Feathers. Will stood in the doorway looking after them. As Alleyn turned, Will moved back into the pub.

'He will now telephone Cary Edge in case Miss Moore has not left yet,' observed Alleyn. 'No matter. She'll have been expecting us to arrive sooner or later. Come on.'

They entered the tunnel.

'Curious, Fox, isn't it?' said Alleyn, and his voice rang hollow against the rock walls. 'Ottercombe must have been able to shut itself up completely on the landward side. I bet some brisk smuggling went forward in the old days. Look out, it's slippery. Miss Moore must be an intrepid driver if she motors through here in all weathers.'

They came out into the sunshine. The highway, a dusty streak, ran from the tunnel. On each side the downs rolled along the coast in a haze of warmth, dappled by racing cloud shadows. Farther inland were the hills and sunken lanes, the prettiness of Devon; here was a sweep of country where Englishmen for centuries had looked coastwards, while ships sailed across their dreams and their thoughts were enlarged beyond the seaward horizon.

'Turn to the right,' said Alleyn.

They climbed the bank and rounded a furze bush in a sunken hollow.

'Good spot for a bit of courting,' said Fox, looking at the flattened grass.

'Yes, you old devil. You may invite that remarkably buxom lady who brought our breakfast to stroll up here after hours.'

'Mrs Ives?'

'Yes. You'll have to get in early, it's a popular spot. Look at those cigarette butts, squalid little beasts. Hallo!'

He stooped and picked up two of them.

'The cigarette butt,' he said, 'has been derided by our detective novelists. It has lost caste and now ranks with the Chinese and datura. No self-respecting demi-highbrow will use it. That's because old Conan Doyle knew his job and got in first. But you and I Br'er Fox, sweating hacks that we are, are not so superior. This cigarette was a

Dahabieh, an expensive Egyptian. Harper said they found some
Egyptian cigarettes in Watchman's pockets. Not many Dahabieh-
smokers in Ottercombe, I imagine. Parish and Cubitt smoke
Virginians. This one has lipstick on it. Orange-brown.'

'Not Miss Darragh,' said Fox.

'No, Fox. Nor yet Mrs Ives. Let's have a peer. There's been rain
since the Dahabiehs were smoked. Look at those heelmarks.
Woman's heels. Driven into the bank.'

'She must have been sitting down,' said Fox. 'Or lying. Bit of a
struggle seemingly. What had the gentleman been up to?'

'What indeed? What did Miss Darragh mean by her "look further
and look nearer home"? We've no case for a jury yet, Fox. We must-
n't close down on a theory. Can you find any masculine prints? Yes.
Here's one. Not a very good one.'

'Watchman's?'

'We may have to find out. May be nothing in it. Wait a bit,
though. I'm going back to the pub.'

Alleyn disappeared over the ridge and was away for some minutes. He returned with two stones, a bit of an old box, and a case.

'Better,' he said, 'in your favourite phrase, Br'er Fox, to be sure
than sorry.'

He opened the case. It contained a rubber cup, a large flask of
water, some plaster-of-Paris, and a spray-pump. Alleyn sprayed the
footprints with shellac, and collected twigs from under the furze
bushes, while Fox mixed plaster. They took casts of the four clearest
prints, reinforcing the plaster with the twigs and adding salt to the
mixture. Alleyn removed the casts when they had set, covered the
footprints with the box, weighted it with stones, and dragged
branches of the furze bush down over the whole. The casts he
wrapped up and hid.

'You never know,' he said. 'Let's move on.'

They mounted the rise and away on the headland saw Cubitt, a
manikin, moving to and fro before his easel.

'We'll have to join the infamous company of gapers,' said Alleyn.
'Look, he's seen us. How eloquent of distaste that movement was!
There's Parish beyond. He's doing a big thing. I believe I've heard
Troy speak of Norman Cubitt's work. Let's walk along the cliffs, shall
we?'

They struck out to the right and hadn't gone many yards before they came to a downward slope where the turf was trampled. Alleyn stooped and examined it.

'Camp-stool,' he muttered. 'And here's an empty tube. Water-colour. The Darragh spoor, I imagine. An eventful stretch of country, this. I wonder if she was here on that Friday. You can't see the other place from here, Fox. You might hear voices, though.'

'If they were raised a bit.'

'Yes. Angry voices. Well, on we go.'

As they drew nearer Cubitt continued to paint, but Parish kept turning his head to look at them. When they came within earshot, Cubitt shouted at them over his shoulder.

'I hope to God you haven't come here to ask questions. I'm busy.'

'All right,' said Alleyn. 'We'll wait.'

He walked beyond them, out of sight of the picture. Fox followed him. Alleyn lay on the lip of the headland. Beneath them, the sea boomed and thudded against a rosy cliff. Wreaths of seaweed endlessly wove suave patterns about Coombe Rock. A flight of gulls mewed and circled in and out of the sunlight.

'What a hullabaloo and a pother,' said Alleyn. 'How many thousands of times before they come adrift, do these strands of seaweed slither out and swirl and loop and return? Their gestures are so beautiful that it is difficult to realize they are meaningless. They only show us the significance of the water's movements but for themselves they are helpless. And the sea is helpless too, and the winds it obeys, and the wider laws that rule the winds, themselves ruled by passive rulers. Dear me, Fox, what a collection of ordered inanities. Rather like police investigations. I can't look over any more, I've no head for heights.'

'Here comes Mr Cubitt, sir,' said Fox.

Alleyn rolled over and saw Cubitt, a vast figure against the sky.

'We're resting now,' said Cubitt. 'Sorry to choke you off, but I was on a tricky bit.'

'We are extremely sorry to bother you,' said Alleyn. 'I know it is beyond a painter's endurance to be interrupted at a critical moment.'

Cubitt dropped down on the grass beside him.

'I'm trying to keep a wet skin of paint all over the canvas,' he said. 'You have to work at concert pitch for that!'

'Good Lord!' Alleyn exclaimed. 'You don't mean you paint right through that surface in three hours?'

'It keeps wet for two days. I've got a new brand of slow-drying colours. Even so, it's a bit of an effort.'

'I should think so, on a thing that size.'

Parish appeared on the brow of the hill.

'Aren't you coming to see my portrait?' he cried.

Cubitt glanced at Alleyn and said, 'Do, if you'd like to.'

'I should, enormously.'

They walked back to the easel.

The figure had come up darkly against the formalized sky. Though the treatment was one of extreme simplification, there was no feeling of emptiness. The portrait was at once rich and austere. There was no bravura in Cubitt's painting. It seemed that he had pondered each brushmark gravely and deeply, and had then laid it down on a single impulse and left it so.

'Lord, it's good,' said Alleyn. 'It's grand, isn't it?'

Parish stood with his head on one side and said, 'Do you like it?' But Cubitt said, 'Do you paint, Alleyn?'

'No, not I. My wife does.'

'Does she exhibit at all?'

'Yes,' said Alleyn. 'Her name is Troy.'

'O God!' said Cubitt. 'I'm sorry.'

'She's good, isn't she?' said Alleyn humbly.

'To my mind,' answered Cubitt, 'the best we've got.'

'Do you think it's like me?' asked Parish. 'I tell Norman he hasn't quite got my eyes. Judging by my photographs, you know. Not that I don't like it. I think it's marvellous, old boy, you know that.'

'Seb,' said Cubitt, 'your price is above rubies. So long as you consider it a pretty mockery of nature, I am content.'

'Oh,' said Parish, 'I'm delighted with it, Norman, really. It's only a suggestion about the eyes.'

'How long have you been at it?' asked Alleyn.

'This is the sixth day. I had two mornings before the catastrophe. We shelved it for a bit after that.'

'Naturally,' added Parish solemnly. 'We didn't feel like it.'

'Naturally,' agreed Cubitt dryly.

'Tell me,' said Alleyn, 'did you ever pass Mr Watchman on your way to or from this place?'

Cubitt had laid a streak of blue across his palette with the knife. His fingers opened and the knife fell into the paint. Parish's jaw dropped. He looked quickly at Cubitt as if asking him a question.

'How do you mean?' asked Cubitt. 'He was only here one day. He died the night after he got here.'

'That was the Friday,' said Alleyn. 'Did you work here on the Friday morning?'

'Yes.'

'Well, was Mr Watchman with you?'

'Oh, no,' said Cubitt quickly, 'he was still in bed when we left.'

'Did you see him on the way home?'

'I don't think we did,' said Parish.

'In a little hollow this side of a furze bush and just above the main road.'

'I don't think so,' said Parish.

'No,' said Cubitt, a little too loudly. 'We didn't. Why?'

'He was there some time,' said Alleyn vaguely.

Cubitt said, 'Look here, do you mind if I get going again? The sun doesn't stand still in the heavens.'

'Of course,' said Alleyn quickly.

Parish took up the pose. Cubitt looked at him and filled a brush with the colour he had mixed. He raised the brush and held it poised. Alleyn saw that his hand trembled.

'It's no good,' said Cubitt abruptly, 'we've missed it. The sun's too far round.'

'But it's not ten yet,' objected Parish.

'Can't help it,' said Cubitt and put down his palette.

'For pity's sake,' said Alleyn, 'don't go wrong with it now.'

'I'll knock off, I think.'

'We've been a hell of a nuisance. I'm sorry.'

'My dear chap,' said Parish, 'you're nothing to the modest Violet. It's a wonder she hasn't appeared. She puts up her easel about five yards behind Norman's and brazenly copies every stroke he makes.'

'It's not as bad as that, Seb.'

'Well, personally,' said Parish, 'I've had quite as much as I want of me brother Terence and me brother Brian and me unfortunate cousin poor Bryonie.'

'What!' exclaimed Alleyn.

'She has a cousin who is a noble lord and got jugged for something.'

'Bryonie,' said Alleyn. 'He was her cousin, was he?'

'So it seems. Do you remember the case?'

'Vaguely,' said Alleyn. 'Vaguely. Was Miss Darragh anywhere about on that same morning?'

'She was over there,' said Parish. 'Back in the direction you've come from. She must have stayed there for hours. She came in, drenched to the skin and looking like the wrath of heaven, late in the afternoon.'

'An enthusiast,' murmured Alleyn. 'Ah, well, we mustn't hang round you any longer. We're bound for Cary Edge Farm.'

Something in the look Cubitt gave him reminded Alleyn of Will Pomeroy.

Parish said, 'To call on the fair Decima? You'll be getting into trouble with Will Pomeroy.'

'Seb,' said Cubitt, 'pray don't be kittenish. Miss Moore is out on Saturday mornings, Alleyn.'

'So Will Pomeroy told us, but we hoped to meet her on her way to Ottercombe. Good luck to the work. Come along, Fox.'

II

A few yards beyond the headland they struck a rough track that led inland and over the downs.

'This will take us there, I expect,' said Alleyn. 'Fox, those gentlemen lied about Watchman and the furze bush.'

'I thought so, sir. Mr Cubitt made a poor fist of it.'

'Yes. He's not a good liar. He's a damn' good painter. I must ask Troy about him.'

Alleyn stopped and thumped the point of his stick on the ground.

'What the devil,' he asked, 'is this about Lord Bryonie?'

'He's the man that was mixed up in the Montague Thringle case.'

'Yes, I know. He got six months. He was Thringle's cat's-paw. By George, Fox, d'you know what?'

'What, sir?'

'Luke Watchman defended Bryonie. I'll swear he did.'

'I wouldn't remember.'

'Yes, you would. You must. By gum, Fox, we'll look up that case. Watchman defended Bryonie, and Bryonie was Miss Darragh's cousin. Rum. Monstrous rum.'

'Sort of fetched her into the picture by another route.'

'It does. Well, come on. We've lots of little worries. I wonder if Miss Moore uses orange-brown lipstick. I tell you what, Fox, I think Cubitt is catched with Miss Moore.'

'In love with her?'

'Deeply, I should say. Did you notice, last night, how his manner changed when he talked about her? The same thing happened just now. He doesn't like our going to Cary Edge. Nor did Will Pomeroy. I wonder what she's like.'

He saw what Decima was like in thirty seconds. She came swinging over the hilltop. She wore a rust-coloured jumper and a blue skirt. Her hair was ruffled, her eyes were bright, and her lips were orange-brown. When she saw the two men she halted for a second and then came on towards them.

Alleyn took off his hat and waited for her.

'Miss Moore?'

'Yes.'

She stopped, but her pose suggested that it would be only for a moment.

'We hoped that we might meet if we were too late to find you at home,' said Alleyn. 'I wonder if you can give us a minute or two. We're police officers.'

'Yes.'

'I'm sorry to bother you, but would you mind – ?'

'You'd better come back to the farm,' said Decima. 'It's over the next hill.'

'That will be a great bore for you, I'm afraid.'

'It doesn't matter. I can go into the Coombe later in the morning.',

'We shan't keep you long. There's no need to turn back.'

Decima seemed to hesitate.

'All right,' she said at last. She walked over to a rock at the edge of the track and sat on it. Alleyn and Fox followed her.

She looked at them with the kind of assurance that is given to women who are unusually lovely and sometimes to women who are emphatically plain. She was without self-consciousness. Nobody had told Alleyn that Decima was beautiful and he was a little surprised. 'It's impossible,' he thought, 'that she can be in love with young Pomeroy.'

'I suppose it's about Luke Watchman,' said Decima.

'Yes, it is. We've been sent down to see if we can tidy up a bit.'

'Does that mean they think it was murder?' asked Decima steadily, 'or don't you answer that sort of question?'

'We don't,' rejoined Alleyn, smiling, 'answer that sort of question.'

'I suppose not,' said Decima.

'We are trying,' continued Alleyn, 'to trace Mr Watchman's movements from the time he got here until the time of the accident.'

'Why?'

'Part of the tidying-up process.'

'I see.'

'It's all pretty plain sailing except for Friday morning.'

Alleyn saw her head turn so that for a second she looked towards Ottercombe Tunnel. It was only for a second and she faced him again.

'He went out,' said Alleyn, 'soon after breakfast. Mr Pomeroy saw him enter the tunnel. That was about ten minutes before you left Ottercombe. Did you see Mr Watchman on your way home?'

'Yes,' she said, 'I saw him.'

'Where, please.'

'Just outside the top of the tunnel by some furze bushes. I think he was asleep.'

'Did he wake as you passed him?'

She clasped her thin hands round her knees.

'Oh, yes,' she said.

'Did you stop, Miss Moore?'

'For a minute or two, yes.'

'Do you mind telling us what you talked about?'

'Nothing that could help you. We – we argued about theories.'

'Theories?'

'Oh, politics. We disagreed violently over politics. I'm a red rebel, as I suppose you've heard. It rather annoyed him. We only spoke for a moment.'

'I suppose it was apropos of the Coombe Left Movement?' murmured Alleyn.

'Do you?' asked Decima.

Alleyn looked apologetic. 'I thought it might be,' he said, 'because of your interest in the movement. I mean it would have been a sort of natural ingredient of a political argument, wouldn't it?'

'Would it?' asked Decima.

'You're quite right to snub me,' said Alleyn ruefully. 'I'm jumping to conclusions and that's a very bad fault in our job. Isn't it, Fox?'

'Shocking, sir,' said Fox.

Alleyn pulled out his notebook.

'I'll just get this right, if I may. You met Mr Watchman at about what time?'

'Ten o'clock.'

'At ten o'clock or thereabouts. You met him by accident. You think he was asleep. You had a political argument in which the Coombe Left Movement was not mentioned.'

'I didn't say so, you know.'

'Would you mind saying so or saying not so? Just for my notes?' asked Alleyn, with such a quaint air of diffidence that Decima suddenly smiled at him.

'All right,' she said, 'we did argue about the society, though it's nothing to do with the case.'

'If you knew the numbers of these books that I've filled with notes that have nothing whatever to do with the case you'd feel sorry for me,' said Alleyn.

'We'll manage things better when we run the police,' said Decima.

'I hope so,' said Alleyn gravely. 'Was your argument amicable?'

'Fairly,' said Decima.

'Did you mention Mr Legge?'

Decima said, 'Before we go any further there's something I'd like to tell you.'

Alleyn looked up quickly. She was frowning. She stared out over the downs, her thin fingers were clasped together.

'You'd better leave Robert Legge alone,' said Decima. 'If Watchman was murdered it wasn't by Legge.'

'How do you know that, Miss Moore?'

'I watched him. He hadn't a chance. The others will have told you that. Will, Norman Cubitt, Miss Darragh. We've compared notes. We're all positive.'

'You don't include Mr Parish?'

'He's a fool,' said Decima.

'And Mr Abel Pomeroy?'

She blushed unexpectedly and beautifully.

'Mr Pomeroy's not a fool but he's violently prejudiced against Bob Legge. He's a ferocious Tory. He thinks we – he thinks Will and I are too much under Bob's influence. He hasn't got a single reasonable argument against Bob. He simply would rather it was Bob than any-one else and has hypnotized himself into believing he's right. It's childishly obvious. Surely you must see that. He's an example in ele-mentary psychology.'

Alleyn raised an eyebrow. She glared at him.

'I'm not disputing it,' said Alleyn mildly.

'Well, then – '

'The camp seems to be divided into pro-Leggites and anti-Leggites. The funny thing about the pro-Leggites is this: they protest his innocence and, I am sure, believe in it. You'd think they'd wel-come our investigations. You'd think they'd say, "Come on, then, look into his record, find out all you like about him. He's a decent citizen and an innocent man. He'll stand up to any amount of inves-tigation." They don't. They take the line of resenting the mildest form of question about Legge. Why's that, do you suppose? Why do you warn us off Mr Legge?'

'I don't – '

'But you do,' insisted Alleyn gently.

Decima turned her head and stared searchingly at him.

'You don't look a brute,' she said doubtfully.

'I'm glad of that.'

'I mean you don't look a complete robot. I suppose, having once committed yourself to a machine, you have to tick over in the appointed manner.'

'Always providing someone doesn't throw a spanner in the works.'

'Look here,' said Decima. 'Bob Legge had an appointment in Illington that evening. He was just going; he would have gone if Will hadn't persuaded him not to. Will told him he'd be a fool to drive through the tunnel with the surface water pouring through it.'

She was watching Alleyn and she said quickly, 'Ah! You didn't know that?'

Alleyn said nothing.

'Ask Will. Ask the man he was to meet in Illington.'

'The local police have done that,' said Alleyn. 'We won't question the appointment. We only know Mr Legge didn't keep it.'

'He couldn't. You can't drive through that tunnel when there's a stream of surface water pouring down it.'

'I should hate to try,' Alleyn agreed. 'We're not making much of an outcry over Mr Legge's failure to appear. It was you, wasn't it, who raised the question?'

'I was only going to point out that Bob didn't know there would be a thunderstorm, did he?'

'Unless the pricking of his thumbs or something – '

'If this was murder I suppose it was premeditated. You won't deny that?'

'No. I don't deny that.'

'Well, then! Suppose he was the murderer. He didn't know it would rain. It would have looked pretty fishy for him to put off his appointment for no reason at all.'

'It would. I wonder why he didn't tell me this himself.'

'Because he's so worried that he's at the end of his tether. Because you got hold of him last night and deliberately played on his nerves until he couldn't think. Because – '

'Hallo!' said Alleyn. 'You've seen him this morning, have you?'

If Decima was disconcerted she didn't show it. She blazed at Alleyn:

'Yes, I've seen him, and I scarcely recognized him. He's a mass of overwrought nerves. His condition's pathological. The next thing will be a confession of a crime he didn't commit.'

'How about the crime he did commit?' asked Alleyn. 'It would be more sensible.'

And that did shake her. She caught her breath in a little gasping sigh. Her fingers went to her lips. She looked very young and very guilty.

'So you knew all the time,' said Decima.

CHAPTER 15

Love Interest

Alleyn had expected that Decima would hedge, rage, or possibly pretend to misunderstand him. Her sudden capitulation took him by surprise and he was obliged to make an embarrassingly quick decision. He plumped for comparative frankness.

'We expect,' he said, 'a report on his fingerprints. When that comes through we shall have official confirmation of a record that we suspected from the first and of which we are now certain.'

'And you immediately put two and two together and make an absurdity.'

'What sort of absurdity?'

'You will say that because he didn't come forward and announce "I'm a man with a police record", he's a murderer. Can't you see how he felt? Have you the faintest notion what it's like for a man who's been in prison to try to get back, to try to earn a miserable pittance? Have you ever thought about it at all or wondered for two seconds what becomes of the people you send to gaol? To their minds? I know you look after their bodies with the most intolerable solicitude. You are there always. Every employer is warned. There is no escape. It would be better, upon my honour, I believe it would be better, to hang them outright than – than to tear their wings off and let them go crawling out into the sun.'

'That's a horrible analogy,' said Alleyn, 'and a false one.'

'It's a true analogy. Can't you see why Legge was so frightened? He's only just stopped having to report. Only now has he got his thin freedom. He thought, poor wretch, that we wouldn't keep him on if we knew he'd been to gaol. Leave him alone! Leave him alone!'

'How long have you known this about him?' asked Alleyn.

She stood up abruptly, her palm against her forehead as though her head ached.

'Oh, for some time.'

'He confided in you? When?'

'When he got the job,' said Decima flatly.

Alleyn did not believe this, but he said politely, 'That was very straightforward, wasn't it?' And as she did not answer he added, 'Do you know why he went to prison?'

'No. I don't want to know. Don't tell me. He's wiped it out, God knows, poor thing. Don't tell me.'

Alleyn reflected, with a certain amount of amusement, that it was as well she didn't want to know what Legge's offence had been. Some image of this thought may have appeared in his face. He saw Decima look sharply at him and he said hurriedly: 'All this is by the way. What I really want to ask you is whether, on the morning you encountered Mr Watchman by the furze bush, you were alone with him all the time.'

He saw that now she was frightened for herself. Her eyes widened, and she turned extremely pale.

'Yes. At least – I – no. Not at the end. I rather think Norman Cubitt and Sebastian Parish came up.'

'You rather think?'

'They did come up. I remember now. They did.'

'And yet,' said Alleyn, 'when I asked them if they saw Watchman that morning, they said definitely that they did not.'

'They must have forgotten.'

'Please! You can't think I'll believe that. They must have been over every word that was spoken by Watchman during the last hours of his life. They have told me as much. Why, they must have walked back to the inn with him. How could they forget?'

Decima said, 'They didn't forget.'

'No?'

'It was for me. They are being little gents.'

Alleyn waited.

'Well,' she said, 'I won't have it. I won't have their chivalry. If you must know, they surprised their friend in a spirited attempt upon my modesty. I wasn't pleased and I was telling him precisely what I thought of him. I suppose they were afraid you would transfer your attentions from Bob Legge to me.'

'Possibly,' agreed Alleyn. 'They seem to think I am a sort of investigating chameleon.'

'I imagine,' said Decima in a high voice, 'that because I didn't relish Mr Watchman's embraces and told him so, it doesn't follow that I set to work and murdered him.'

'It's not a strikingly good working hypothesis. I'm sorry to labour this point but we've no sense of decency in the force. Had he shown signs of these tricks before?'

The clear pallor of Decima's face was again flooded with red. Alleyn thought, 'Good Lord, she's an attractive creature. I wonder what the devil she's like.' He saw, with discomfort, that she could not look at him. Fox made an uneasy noise in his throat and stared over the downs. Alleyn waited. At last Decima raised her eyes.

'He was like that,' she murmured.

Alleyn now saw a sort of furtiveness in Decima. She was no longer tense, her pose had changed and she offered him no challenge.

'I suppose he couldn't help it,' she said, and then with a strange look from Alleyn to Fox she added, 'It's nothing. It doesn't mean anything. You needn't think ill of him. I was all right.'

In half a minute she had changed. The educational amenities provided by that superior mother had fallen away from her. She had turned into a rustic beauty, conscious of her power of provocation. The rumoured engagement to Will Pomeroy no longer seemed ridiculous. And, as if she had followed Alleyn's thought, she said, 'I'd be very glad if you wouldn't say anything of this to Will Pomeroy. He knows nothing about it. He wouldn't understand.'

'I'll sheer off it if it can be done. It was not the first time you'd had difficulty with Watchman?'

She paused and then said, 'We hadn't actually – come to blows before.'

'Blows? Literally?'

'I'm afraid so.'

She stood up. Alleyn thought she mustered her self-assurance. When she spoke again it was in a different key, ironically and with composure.

'Luke,' she said, 'was amorous by habit. No doubt it was not the first time he'd miscalculated. He wasn't in the least disconcerted. He – wasn't in the least in love with me.'

'No?'

'It's merely a squalid little incident which I had rather hoped to forget. It was, I suppose, very magnificent of Seb and Norman to lie about it, but the gesture was too big for the theme.'

'Now she's being grand at me,' thought Alleyn. 'We are back in St Margaret's Hall.'

He said: 'And Watchman had never made himself objectionable before that morning?'

'I did not usually find him particularly objectionable.'

'I intended,' said Alleyn, 'to ask you if he had ever made love to you before?'

'I have told you he wasn't in the least in love with me.'

'I'm unlucky in my choice of words, I see. Had he ever kissed you, Miss Moore?'

'This is very tedious,' said Decima. 'I have tried to explain that my acquaintance with Luke Watchman was of no interest or significance to either of us, or, if you will believe me, to you.'

'Then why,' asked Alleyn mildly, 'don't you give me an answer and have done with it?'

'Very well,' said Decima breathlessly. 'You can have your answer. I meant nothing to him and he meant less to me. Until last Friday he'd never been anything but the vaguest acquaintance.' She turned on Fox. 'Write it down. You'll get no other answer. Write it down.'

'Thank you, miss,' said Fox civilly. 'I don't think I've missed anything. I've got it down.'

II

'Well, have you finished?' demanded Decima, who had succeeded in working herself up into a satisfactory temper. 'Is there anything else you want to know? Do you want a list in alphabetical order of my encounters with any other little Luke Watchmans who have come my way?'

'No,' said Alleyn. 'No. We limit our impertinences to the police code. Our other questions are, I hope, less offensive. They concern the brandy you gave Mr Watchman, the glass into which you poured it, and the bottle from which it came.'

'All right. What about them?'

'May we have your account of that particular phase of the business?'

'I told Oates and I told the coroner. Someone suggested brandy. I looked round and saw Luke's glass on the table, between the settle where he lay and the dart-board. There wasn't any brandy left in it. I saw the bottle on the bar. I was very quick about it. I got it and poured some into the glass. I did not put anything but brandy in the glass. I can't prove I didn't, but I didn't.'

'But perhaps we can prove it. Was anyone near the table? Did anyone watch you pour the brandy?'

'Oh, God!' said Decima wearily, 'how should I know? Sebastian Parish was nearest to the table. He may have noticed. I don't know. I took the glass to Luke. I waited for a moment while Abel Pomeroy put iodine on Luke's finger, and then I managed to pour a little brandy between his lips. It wasn't much. I don't think he even swallowed it, but I suppose you won't believe that.'

'Miss Moore,' said Alleyn suddenly, 'I can't tell you how pathetically anxious we are to accept the things people tell us.' He hesitated and then said, 'You see, we spend most of our working life asking questions. Can you, for your part, believe that we get a kind of sixth sense and sometimes feel very certain indeed that a witness is speaking the truth, or, as the case may be, is lying? We're not allowed to recognize our sixth sense, and when it points a crow's flight towards the truth we may not follow it. We must cut it dead and follow the dreary back streets of collected evidence. But if they lead us anywhere at all it is almost always to the same spot.'

'Eminently satisfactory,' said Decima. 'Everything for the best in the best of all possible police forces.'

'That wasn't quite what I meant. Was it after you had given him the brandy that Mr Watchman uttered the single word "poisoned"?'

'Yes.'

'Did you get the impression that he spoke of the brandy?'

'No. I don't know if your sixth sense will tell you I'm lying, but it seemed to me he *tried* to take the brandy, and perhaps did swallow a little, and that it was when he found he couldn't drink that he said – that one word. He said it between his clenched teeth. I had never seen such a look of terror and despair. Then he jerked his hand. Miss Darragh was going to bandage it. Just at that moment the lights went out.'

'For how long were they out?'

'Nobody knows. It's impossible to tell. I can't. It seemed an age. Somebody clicked the switch. I remember that. To see if it had been turned off accidentally, I suppose. It was a nightmare. The rain sounded like drums. There was broken glass everywhere – crunch, crunch, squeak. And his voice. Not like a human voice. Like a cat mewing. And his heels, drumming on the settle. And everybody shouting in the dark.'

Decima spoke rapidly and twisted her fingers together.

'It's funny,' she said, 'I either can't talk about it at all, or I can't stop talking about it. Once you start, you go on and on. It's rather queer. I suppose he was in great pain. I suppose it was torture. As bad as the rack, or disembowelling. I've got a terror of physical pain. I'd recant anything first.'

'Not,' said Alleyn, 'your political views?'

'No,' agreed Decima, 'not those. I'd contrive to commit suicide or something. Perhaps it was not pain that made him cry like that and drum with his heels. Perhaps it was only reflex something. Nerves.'

'I think,' said Alleyn, 'that your own nerves have had a pretty shrewd jolt.'

'What do you know about nerves?' demanded Decima with surprising venom. 'Nerves! These things are a commonplace to you. Luke Watchman's death-throes are so much data. You expect me to give you a neat statement about them. Describe in my own words the way he clenched his teeth and drew back his lips.'

'No,' said Alleyn. 'I haven't asked you about those things. I have asked you two questions of major importance. One was about your former relationship with Watchman and the other about the brandy you gave him before he died.'

'I've answered you. If that's all you want to know you've got it. I can't stand any more of this. Let me – '

The voice stopped as if someone had switched it off. She looked beyond Alleyn and Fox to the brow of the hillock. Her eyes were dilated.

Alleyn turned. Norman Cubitt stood against the sky.

'Norman!' cried Decima.

He said, 'Wait a bit, Decima,' and strode down towards her. He stood and looked at her and then lightly picked up her hands.

'What's up?' asked Cubitt.

'I can't stand it, Norman.'

Without looking at Alleyn or Fox he said, 'You don't have to talk to these two precious experts if it bothers you. Tell 'em to go to hell.' And then he turned her round and, over her shoulder, grinned, not very pleasantly, at Alleyn.

'I've made a fool of myself,' whispered Decima.

She was looking at Cubitt as though she saw him for the first time. He said, 'What the devil are you badgering her for?'

'Just,' said Alleyn, 'out of sheer wanton brutality.'

'It's all right,' said Decima. 'He didn't badger, really. He's only doing his loathsome job.'

Her eyes were brilliant with tears, her lips not quite closed, and still she looked with a sort of amazement into Cubitt's face.

'Oh, Norman!' she said, 'I've been so inconsistent and fluttery and feminine. Me!'

'You!' said Cubitt.

'In a moment,' thought Alleyn, 'he'll kiss her.' And he said, 'Thank you so much, Miss Moore. I'm extremely sorry to have distressed you. I hope we shan't have to bother you again.'

'Look here, Alleyn,' said Cubitt, 'if you do want to see Miss Moore again I insist on being present, and that's flat.'

Before Alleyn could answer this remarkable stipulation Decima said, 'But, my dear man, I'm afraid you can't insist on that. You're not my husband, you know.'

'That can be attended to,' said Cubitt. 'Will you marry me?'

'Fox,' said Alleyn, 'what are you staring at? Come back to Ottercombe.'

III

'Well, Mr Alleyn,' said Fox when they were out of earshot, 'we see some funny things in our line of business, don't we? What a peculiar moment now, for him to pick on for a proposal. Do you suppose he's been courting her for a fair while, or did he spring it on her sudden?'

'Suddenish, I fancy, Fox. Her eyes were wet and that, I suppose, went to his head. I must say she's a very lovely creature. Didn't you think so?'

'A very striking young lady,' agreed Fox. 'but I thought the super said she was keeping company with young Pomeroy?'

'He did.'

'She's a bit on the classy side for him, you'd think.'

'You would, Fox.'

'Well, now, I wonder what she'll do. Throw him over and take Mr Cubitt? She looked to me to be rather inclined that way.'

'I wish she'd told the truth about Watchman,' said Alleyn.

'Think there'd been something between them, sir? Relations? Intimacy?'

'Oh Lord, I rather think so. It's not a very pleasant thought.'

'Bit of a *femme fatale*,' said Fox carefully. 'But there you are. They laugh at what we used to call respectability, don't they? Modern women – '

Alleyn interrupted him.

'I know, Fox, I know. She is very sane and intellectual and modern, but I don't mind betting there's a strong dram of rustic propriety that pops up when she least expects it. I think she's ashamed of the Watchman episode, whatever it was, and furious with herself for being ashamed. What's more, I don't believe she knew until Friday that Legge was an old lag. All guesswork. Let's forget it. We'll have an early lunch and call on Dr Shaw. I want to ask him about the wound in the finger. Come on.'

They returned by way of the furze bush, collecting the casts and Alleyn's case. As they disliked making entrances with mysterious bundles, they locked their gear in the car and went round to the front of the Feathers. But here they walked into a trap. Sitting beside Abel Pomeroy on the bench outside the front door was an extremely thin and tall man with a long face, a drooping moustache, and foolish eyes. He stared very fixedly at Fox, who recognized him as Mr George Nark and looked the other way.

'Find your road all right, gentlemen?' asked Abel.

'Yes, thank you, Mr Pomeroy,' said Alleyn.

'It's a tidy stretch, sir. You'll be proper warmed up.'

'We're not only warm but dry,' said Alleyn.

'Ripe for a pint, I dessay, sir?'

'A glorious thought,' said Alleyn.

Mr Nark cleared his throat. Abel threw a glance of the most intense dislike at him and led the way into the private bar.

''Morning,' said Mr Nark, before Fox could get through the door.

''Morning, Mr Nark,' said Fox.

'Don't know but what I wouldn't fancy a pint myself,' said Mr Nark firmly, and followed them into the Private.

Abel drew Alleyn's and Fox's drinks.

''Alf-'n-'alf, Abel,' said Mr Nark grandly.

Somewhat ostentatiously Abel wiped out a shining pint-pot with a spotless cloth. He then drew the mild and bitter.

'Thank 'ee,' said Mr Nark. 'Glad to see you're acting careful. Not but what, scientifically speaking, you ought to bile them pots. I don't know what the law has to say on the point,' continued Mr Nark, staring very hard at Alleyn. 'I'd have to look it up. The law may touch on it, and it may not.'

'Don't tell us you're hazy on the subject,' said Abel bitterly. 'Us can't believe it.'

Mr Nark smiled in an exasperating manner and took a pull at his beer. He made a rabbit-like noise with his lips, snapping them together several times with a speculative air. He then looked dubiously into his pint-pot.

'Well,' said Abel tartly, 'what's wrong with it? You'm not pisoned this time, I suppose?'

'I dessay it's all right,' said Mr Nark. 'New barrel bain't it?'

Abel disregarded this inquiry. The ship's decanter that they had been seen in the cupboard now stood on the bar counter. It was spotlessly clean. Abel took the bottle of Amontillado from a shelf above the bar. He put a strainer in the neck of the decanter and began, carefully, to pour the sherry through it.

'What jiggery-pokery are you up to now, Abel?' inquired Mr Nark. 'Why, Gor'dang it, that thurr decanter was in the pison cupboard.'

Abel addressed himself exclusively to Alleyn and Fox. He explained the various methods used by Mrs Ives to clean the decanter. He poured himself out a glass of the sherry and invited them to join him. Under the circumstances they could scarcely refuse. Mr Nark watched them with extraordinary solicitude and remarked that they were braver men than himself.

'Axcuse me for a bit if you please, gentlemen,' said Abel elaborately to Alleyn and Fox. 'I do mind me of summat I've got to tell Mrs Ives. If you'd be so good as to ring if I'm wanted.'

'Certainly, Mr Pomeroy,' said Alleyn.

Abel left them with Mr Nark.

'Fine morning, sir,' said Mr Nark.

Alleyn agreed.

'Though I suppose,' continued Mr Nark wooingly, 'all weathers and climates are one to a man of your calling. Science,' continued Mr Nark, drawing closer and closer to Alleyn, 'is a powerful high-handed mistress. Now, just as a matter of curiosity, sir, would you call yourself a man of science?'

'Not I,' said Alleyn, good-naturedly. 'I'm a policeman, Mr Nark.'

'Ah! That's my point. See? That's my point. Now, sir, with all respect you did ought to make a power more use of the great wonders of science. I'll give in your fingerprints. There's an astonishing thing, now! To think us walks about unconscious-like, leaving our pores and loops all over the shop for science to pick up and have the laugh on us.'

It was a peculiarity of Mr Nark's conversational style that as he drew nearer to his victim he raised his voice. His face was now about twenty inches away from Alleyn's and he roared like an infuriated auctioneer.

'I'm a reader,' shouted Mr Nark. 'I'm a reader and you might say a student. How many printed words would you say I'd absorbed in my life? At a guess, now?'

'Really,' said Alleyn. 'I don't think I could possibly – '

'Fifty-eight million!' bawled Mr Nark. 'Nigh on it. Not reckoning twice overs. I've soaked up four hundred words, some of 'em as much as five syllable, mind you, every night for the last forty years. Started in at the age of fifteen. "Sink or swim," I said, "I'll improve my brain to the tune of four hundred words per day till I passes out or goes blind!" And I done it. I don't suppose you know a piece of work called *The Evvylootion of the Spices*?'

'Yes.'

'There's a tough masterpiece of a job. Took me a year and more, that did. Yes, I've tackled most branches of science. Now the last two years I've turned my eyes in the direction of crime. Trials of famous criminals, lives of murderers, feats of detection, all the whole biling of 'em. Can't get enough of 'em. I'm like that. Whole hog or nothing. Reckon I've sucked it dry.'

Mr Nark emptied his pint-pot and, perhaps as an illustrative gesture, sucked his moustache. He looked at Alleyn out of the corners of his eyes.

'This is a very pretty little case now,' he said. 'I don't say there's much in it but it's quite a pretty bit of an affair in its way. You'll be counting on knocking it off in a day or two, I suppose?'

'I don't know about that, Mr Nark.'

'I was a witness.'

'At the inquest? I thought – '

'Not at the inquest,' interrupted Mr Nark in a great hurry. 'No. Superintendent Nicholas Gawd-Almighty Harper had the running of the inquest. I was a witness to the event. More than that I've made a study of the affair and I've drew my own deductions. I don't suppose they'd interest you. But I've drew 'em.'

Alleyn reflected that it was extremely unlikely that Mr Nark's deductions would be either intelligible or interesting, but he made an agreeable noise and invited him to have another drink. Mr Nark accepted and drew it for himself.

'Ah,' he said. 'I reckon I know as much as anybody about this affair. There's criminal carelessness done on purpose, and there's criminal carelessness done by accident. There's motives here and there's motives there, each of 'em making 'tother look like a fool, and all of 'em making the biggest fool of Nicholas Harper. Yes. Us chaps takes our lives in our hands when we calls in at Feathers for a pint. Abel knows it. Abel be too mortal deathly proud to own up.'

'Carelessness, you said? How did it come about?'

If Mr Nark's theory of how cyanide got on the dart was ever understood by himself he had no gift for imparting it to others. He became incoherent, and defensively mysterious. He dropped hints and, when pressed to explain them, took fright and dived into obscurities. He uttered generalizations of bewildering stupidity, assumed an air of huf-finess, floundered into deep water, and remained there blowing like a grampus. Alleyn was about to leave him in this plight when, perhaps as a last desperate bid for official approval, Mr Nark made a singular statement.

'The Garden of Eden,' he said, 'as any eddicated chap knows, is bunk. You can't tell me there's any harm in apples. I grow 'em. Us started off as a drop of jelly. We've come on gradual ever since, working our way up through slime and scales and tails to where we are. We had to *have* a female to do the job. Us knows that. Biological necessity. But she's been a poisonous snare and a curse to us as even the ignorant author of Genesis had spotted and noted down in his foolish fashion, under cover of a lot of clap-trap. She's wuss than a serpent on her own, and she's mostly always at the back of our troubles. Searchy la fem as the French detectives say and you ought to bear in mind. This ghastly affair started a year ago and there's three alive now that knows it. There was four.'

Alleyn realized with a sinking heart that he would have to pay attention to Mr Nark. He saw in Mr Nark a desire for fame struggling with an excessive natural timidity. Mr Nark hungered for the admiring attention of the experts. He also dreaded the law, to which he seemed to accord the veneration and alarm of a neophyte before the altar of some tricky and fickle diety. Alleyn decided that he must attempt to speak to him in his own language.

He said, 'That's very interesting, Mr Nark. Strange, isn't it, Fox? Mr Nark has evidently – ' he fumbled for the magic word – 'evidently made the same deductions as we have from the evidence in hand.'

Fox gave his superior a bewildered and disgusted glance. Alleyn said rather loudly, 'See what I mean, Fox?'

Fox saw. 'Very striking, sir,' he said. 'We'll have to get you into the force, Mr Nark.'

Mr Nark buttoned his coat.

'What'll you take, gentlemen?' he asked.

But it was heavy going. To get any sense out of him Alleyn had to flatter, hint, and cajole. A direct suggestion threw him into a fever of incoherence, at a hint of doubt he became huffy and mysterious. As she seemed to be the only woman in the case, Alleyn attempted to crystalize on Decima.

'Miss Moore,' he said at last, 'is naturally very much upset by Mr Watchman's death.'

'Ah,' said Mr Nark. 'Is she? She may be. P'raps! I don't know anything about women. She may be. Huh!'

Alleyn achieved a knowing laugh in which Fox joined.

'You look below the surface, I see,' said Alleyn.

'I base my deductions on facts. Take an example,' said Mr Nark. His third drink, a Treble Extra, had begun to have a mellowing effect. His native burr returned to his usually careful utterance and he smiled knowingly. 'Take an example. I don't say it's true to natur'. It's an illustration. A parrible. If I take a stroll up along Apple Lane of a warm night and hears a courting couple 'tother side of hedge in old Jim Moore's orchard, I draws my own conclusions. Doan't I?'

'No doubt.'

''Ess. And *ef*,' said Mr Nark, '*ef* I do bide thurr not with idea of eavesdropping but only to reflect and ponder in my deep bitter manner on the wiles of females in gineral, and *ef* I yurrs a female voice I axpects to yurr, and a maskeline voice I doan't axpects to yurr, and *ef*,' continued Mr Nark fighting his way to the end of his sentence, 'I says "Hallo!" to myself and passes on a step, and *ef* I meets the owner of the maskuline voice I did axpect to yurr, standing sly and silent in hedge: what do I say? Wait a bit. Doan't tell me. I'll tell you. I says "Durn it!" I says, "thurr'll be bloodshed along of this yurr if us doan't look out." And *ef* I bides a twelve month or more and nothing happens and then something does happen, bloody and murderous, what do I say then?'

Mr Nark raised his hand as a signal that this question also was rhetorical and paused for so long that Fox clenched both his fists and Alleyn had time to light a cigarette.

'I sez,' said Mr Nark loudly, 'not a damn' thing.'

'What!' ejaculated Alleyn.

'Not a damn' thing. But I thinks like a furnace.'

'What do you think, Mr Nark?' asked Alleyn with difficulty.

'I thinks 'tis better to yold my tongue ef I want to keep breath in my body. And I yolds it. 'Ess fay, I be mum and I stays mum.'

Mr Nark brought off a mysterious gesture with his right forefinger, leered knowingly at Alleyn, and tacked rapidly towards the door. Once there, he turned to deliver his last word.

'Doan't you go calling my words statements,' he said, 'they're a nallegory, and a nallegory's got nothing to do with the law. You doan't trip me up thicky fashion. I know natur' of an oath. Searchy la fem.'

CHAPTER 16

Alleyn Exceeds His Duty

After they had lunched Alleyn brought his report up to date and Fox, sitting solemnly at the parlour table, typed it in duplicate. Alleyn had a brief interview with Abel Pomeroy and returned with three tumblers. One of these he smashed to splinters with the poker, keeping the pieces together, and emptying them into a tin. The other two he wrapped up and placed, with a copy of his report, in his case. He also spent some time throwing down darts and finding that they stuck in the floor. These employments at an end, they drove to Illington. The day had turned gloomy, heavy rain was falling, and the road was slimy.

Alleyn dropped Fox at Woolworth's and went on to Dr Shaw's house at the end of the principal street. He was shown into a surgery that smelt of leather, iodine, and ether. Here he found Dr Shaw. He had an air of authority and a pleasing directness of manner.

'I hope I'm not an infernal nuisance, coming at this hour,' said Alleyn. 'Your patients – '

'That's all right. Surgery doesn't start till two. Old trot sitting out there in the waiting-room. *Malade imaginaire*. Do her good to wait a bit, she plagues my life out. Sit down. What do you want to talk about?'

'Principally about the wound and the dart. I've read the police report of the inquest.'

'Thought it rather full of gaps? So it is. Mordant, the coroner, you know, is a dry old stick, but he's got his wits about him. Respectable bacteriologist in his day. He and Harper got their heads together, I

767

imagine, and decided just how much would be good for the jury. What about the wound?'

'Were there any traces of cyanide, prussic acid, or whatever the blasted stuff is?'

'No. We got a man from London, you know. One of your tame experts. Good man. Mordant and I were both there when he made his tests. We didn't expect a positive result from the wound.'

'Why not?'

'Two reasons. He'd bled pretty freely and, if the stuff was introduced on the dart, what wasn't absorbed would be washed away by blood. Also, the stuff's very volatile.'

'They found the trace on the dart.'

'Yes. Oates kept his head and put the dart into a clean soda-water bottle and corked it up. Couldn't do that with the finger.'

'Even so, wouldn't you expect the stuff to evaporate on the dart.'

Dr Shaw uttered a deep growl and scratched his cheek.

'Perfectly correct,' he said, 'you would. Puzzling.'

'Doesn't it look as if the Scheele's acid, or rather the fifty per cent prussic acid solution, must have been put on the dart a very short time before Oates bottled it up?'

'It does. Thought so all along.'

'How long was it, after the event, that you got there?'

'Within half an hour after his death.'

'Yes. Now, look here. For private consumption only, would you expect a cyanide solution, however concentrated, to kill a man after that fashion?'

Dr Shaw thrust his hands in his pockets and stuck out his lower lip.

'I'm not a toxicologist,' he said. 'Mordant is, and we've taken the king-pin's opinion. Watchman, on his own statement, had a strong idiosyncrasy for cyanide. He told Parish and Cubitt about this the night before the tragedy.'

'Yes. I saw that in the files. It's good enough, you think?'

'We've got no precedent for the affair. The experts seem to think it good enough. That dart was thrown with considerable force. It penetrated to the bone, or rather, it actually entered the finger at such an angle that it must have lain along the bone. It's good enough.'

'There was no trace of cyanide in the mouth?'

'None. But that doesn't preclude the possibility of his having taken it by the mouth.'

'O Lord!' sighed Alleyn, 'nor it does. Did the room stink of it?'

'No, it stank of brandy. So did the body. Brandy, by the way, is one of the antidotes given for cyanide poisoning. Along with artificial respiration, potassium permanganate, glucose, and half a dozen other remedies none of which is much use if the cyanide has got into the bloodstream.'

'Have you a pair of scales?' asked Alleyn abruptly. 'Chemical scales or larger but accurate scales?'

'What? Yes. Yes, I have. Why?'

'Fox, my opposite number, will be here in a minute. He's calling at the police station for the fragments of broken tumbler. I've got a rather fantastic notion. Nothing in it, I dare say. We've a pair of scales at the pub, but I thought you might be amused if we did a bit of our stuff here.'

'Of course I would. Wait a moment while I get rid of that hypochondriacal crone. Shan't be long. Don't move. She only wants a flea in her ear.'

Dr Shaw went into the waiting-room. Alleyn could hear his voice raised in crisp admonishment.

'– pull yourself together, you know. . . . sound as a bell . . . take up a hobby . . . your own physician ... be a sensible woman.'

A doorbell rang and in a moment Fox and Superintendent Harper were shown into the surgery.

'Hallo, hallo!' said Harper. 'What's all this I hear? Thought I'd come along. Got an interesting bit of news for you.' He dropped his voice. 'I sent a chap up to London by the milk train. He's taken the dart to Dabs and they've just rung through. The prints are good enough. What do you think they've found?'

'I can see they've found something, Nick,' said Alleyn, smiling.

'You bet they have. Those prints belong to Mr Montague Thringle who did four years for embezzlement and came out of Broadmoor twenty-six months ago.'

'Loud cheers,' said Alleyn, 'and *much* laughter.'

'Eh? Yes, and that's not the best of it. Who do you think defended one of the accused and shifted all the blame on to Thringle?'

'None other than Luke Watchman, the murdered KC?'

'You're right. Legge's a gaolbird who owes, or thinks he owes, his sentence to Watchman. He's just dug himself in pretty, with a nice job and a lot of mugs eating out of his hand, and along comes the very man who can give him away.'

'Now I'll tell you something you don't know,' said Alleyn. 'Who do you think was implicated with Montague Thringle and got off with six months?'

'Lord Bryonie. Big scandal it was.'

'Yes. Miss Darragh's unfortunate cousin, the Lord Bryonie.'

'You don't tell me that. Miss Darragh! I'd put her right out of the picture.'

'She holds a watching-brief for Thringle-alias-Legge, I fancy,' said Alleyn, and related the morning's adventure.

'By gum!' cried Harper, 'I think it's good enough. I reckon we're just about right for a warrant. With the fact that only Legge could have known the dart would hit – what d'you think? Shall we pull him in?'

'I don't think we'll make an arrest just yet, Nick.'

'Why not?'

'Well, I think the result would be what the high-brows call a miscarriage of justice. I'll tell you why.'

II

But before he had finished telling them why, an unmistakable rumpus in the street announced the arrival of Colonel Brammington's car. And presently Colonel Brammington himself came charging into the room with Dr Shaw on his heels.

'I saw your car outside,' he shouted. 'A galaxy of all the talents with Aesculapius to hold the balance. Aesculapius usurps the seat of justice, poetic justice with her lifted scale.'

Dr Shaw put a small pair of scales on the table and grinned. Colonel Brammington took one of Alleyn's cigarettes and hurled himself into a chair.

'Curiosity,' he said, 'was praised by the great Doctor as one of the permanent and certain characteristics of a vigorous intellect. His namesake, the rare Ben, remarked that he did love to note and to observe. With these noble precedents before me I shall offer no excuse, but, following the example of Beatrice, shall like a lapwing run, close to the ground, to hear your confidence. An uncomfortable feat and one for which my great belly renders me unfit. Have you any matches? Ah, thank you.'

Harper, with his back to the chief constable, turned his eyes up for the edification of Fox. He laid a tin box on the table.

'Here you are, Mr Alleyn.'

'Good.' Alleyn weighed the box speculatively in his hands and then emptied its contents into the scale.

'What is that?' demanded Colonel Brammington. 'Glass? Ah, the orts and fragments of the brandy-glass, perhaps?'

'That's it, sir,' said Alleyn.

'And pray why do you put them on the scales?'

'Sir,' murmured Alleyn politely, 'to find out their weight.'

Colonel Brammington said mildly, 'You mock me, by heaven. And what do they weigh?'

'Two ounces, forty-eight grains. That right, Dr Shaw?'

'That's it.'

Alleyn returned the fragments to their box and took a second box from his pocket.

'In this,' he said, 'are the pieces of an identically similar glass for which I gave Mr Pomeroy one and sixpence. They are his best glasses. Now then.'

He tipped the second shining heap into the scales.

'Yes, by George,' said Alleyn softly. 'Look. Two ounces, twenty-four grains.'

'Here!' exclaimed Harper. 'That's less. It must be a lighter glass.'

'No,' said Alleyn. 'It's the same brand of glass. Abel took the glasses for the brandy from a special shelf. I've borrowed two more, unbroken. Let's have them, Fox.'

Fox produced two tumblers. Each of them weighed two ounces, twenty-four grains.

'But look here,' objected Harper. 'We didn't get every scrap of that glass up. Some of it had been ground into the boards. Watchman's glass should, if anything, weigh less than the others.'

'I know,' said Alleyn.

'Well, then – '

'Some other glass must have fallen,' said Colonel Brammington. 'They were full of distempering draughts, red-hot with drinking. One of them may have let fall some other glass. A pair of spectacles. Didn't Watchman wear an eyeglass?'

'It was round his neck,' said Dr Shaw, 'unbroken.'

'There seems to have been no other glass broken, sir,' said Alleyn. 'I've asked. Did you find all the pieces in one place, Harper?'

'Like you'd expect, a bit scattered and trampled about. I dare say there were pieces in the soles of their boots. Damn it all,' cried Harper in exasperation, 'it *must* weigh lighter.'

He weighed the glass again, peering suspiciously at the scales. The results was exactly the same. The fragments of Watchman's glass weighed twenty-four grains heavier than the unbroken tumbler.

'This is rather amusing,' said Colonel Brammington.

Alleyn sat at the table and spread the broken glass over a sheet of paper. Fox gave him a pair of tweezers and he began to sort the pieces into a graduated row. The other men drew closer.

'It's the same tumbler,' said Colonel Brammington. 'There, you see, are the points of one of those loathsome stars.'

Alleyn took a jeweller's lens from his pocket.

'Ah!' muttered Colonel Brammington, staring at him with a bulging and raffish eye. 'He peers, he screws a glass into his orb and with enlarged vision feeds his brain.'

'We always feel rather self-conscious about these things,' said Alleyn, 'but they have their uses. Here, I think, are three, no, four small pieces of glass that *might* be different from – well, let's weigh them.'

He put them in the scales.

'Thirty-one grains. That, Harper, leaves a margin of eleven grains for the bits you missed. Any good?'

'Do you think these bits are a different class of stuff, Mr Alleyn?' asked Harper.

'I think so. There's a difference in colour and if you look closely you can see they're a bit thicker.'

'He has written a monograph on broken tumblers,' cried Colonel Brammington delightedly. 'Let me look through your lens.'

He crouched over the table.

'They are different,' he said. 'You are quite right, my dear Alleyn. What can it mean? The iodine bottle? No, it was found unbroken beneath the settle.'

'What did you discover at Woolworth's, Fox?' asked Alleyn.

'Nothing much, Mr Alleyn. I tried all the other places as well. They haven't sold any and they say there's very little shop-lifting in Illington.'

'Veil after veil will lift,' remarked Colonel Brammington, 'but there will be veil upon veil behind. What is this talk of shop-lifting?'

'I'll explain, sir,' began Alleyn.

'On second thoughts, pray don't. I prefer, Alleyn, to be your Watson. You dine with me tonight? Very good. Give me the evidence, and let me brood.'

'But don't you wish to hear Mr Alleyn's case, sir?' asked Harper in a scandalized voice. 'Your position – '

'I do not. I prefer to listen to voices in the upper air nor lose my simple faith in mysteries. I prefer to take the advice of the admirable Tupper and will let not the conceit of intellect hinder me from worshipping mystery. But nevertheless give me your plain plump facts. I will sing, with Ovid, of facts.'

'You will not have Ovid's privilege of inventing them,' rejoined Alleyn. 'I have brought a copy of my report on the case. It's up to date.'

Colonel Brammington took the file and seemed to become the victim of an intolerable restlessness. He rose, hitched up his shapeless trousers and said rapidly in a high voice, 'Well, goodbye, Shaw. Come to dinner tonight.'

'Oh, thank you very much, sir,' said Dr Shaw. 'I'd like to. Black tie?'

'As the fancy takes you. I shall make some gesture. Broadcloth and boiled linen. You come, Harper?'

'Thank you, sir, I'm afraid I can't. I've got to – '

'All right. I see. Three then. You, Alleyn, Shaw, and – ah – '

'Fox,' said Alleyn.

'Ah, yes. Splendid. Well, *au revoir*.'

'I was going to ask you, sir – ' began Harper.

'O God! What?'

'It doesn't matter, sir, if you're in a hurry,' Harper opened the door with emphasized politeness. 'Good afternoon, sir.'

'Oh, goodbye to you, Harper, goodbye,' said Colonel Brammington impatiently, and plunged out.

'If that,' said Harper sourly, 'is the modern idea of a chief constable it's not mine. You wouldn't credit it, would you, that when that gentleman's brother dies, he'll be a Lord? A Lord, mind you! Bawling hurricane. Where's he get the things he says, Doctor? Out of his head or out of books?'

'Not having his brains, his memory, or his library, I can't tell you,' said Dr Shaw.

III

Alleyn, Fox and Harper went to the police station. Here they had a long reiterative conversation. They compared Alleyn's casts with the shoes Watchman wore on the day of his death, and found that they tallied exactly. They went over the case step by step. Alleyn expounded, the others listened. They laid their collection of oddments on Harper's table; the brandy-bottle, the broken glass, the iodine bottle, the stained newspaper, the small china vessel from the rat-hole and the bottle of Scheele's Acid. Harper gave Alleyn a stoppered bottle.

'Ah,' said Alleyn, 'that's the stuff out of the rat-hole jar. I want you to get it analysed. Perhaps Dr Mordant would do it. No, I suppose that would be too unofficial. It had better go up to London.'

'You think our murderer got the stuff from the garage?' asked Harper.

'I do.'

'But the thing was full.'

'Because it was full,' said Alleyn.

'You reckon that was water,' asked Harper slowly.

'Yes, Nick.'

'I see,' said Harper.

'The poison-party,' said Alleyn, 'was attended by Abel, who put the prussic acid in the china pot and stopped the hole; by Will, by Miss Moore, by Legge, who only looked in for a moment, and by a couple of fishermen who were on their way to the public bar and who don't come into the picture. Subsequently Abel warned everybody in the place about what he had done, so that the actual attendance at the poison-party may not give us our answer. On the other hand it is possible that one of them lagged behind and pinched the poison. They all profess to have forgotten in what order they left. Now prussic acid in Mr Noggins' fifty per cent solution is a highly volatile liquid. Judging by the stench, its fumes have accounted for at least one rat, so probably it was not removed immediately. On the other hand it seems it would evaporate considerably in something under an hour. I'm not sure on this point. We'll experiment. The experts say in their report, under an hour. Very good. My contention is that the murderer must have nipped into the garage, within an hour after Abel left it, and taken the poison which would be kept in a tightly-corked bottle until it was needed.'

'But how the hell would he get it? The jar had Abel's prints. It hadn't been touched.'

'Do you remember – ?'

'By God!' shouted Harper. 'Don't tell me. I've got it.'

He broke into a stream of oaths through which his enlightenment struggled for expression.

'That's it,' said Alleyn. 'Looks like it, doesn't it?'

'Looks like it!' ejaculated Harper. 'It blasted well shrieks of it. I'm a hell of a detective I am! Look at me! I missed the point about that evaporation business! Took Abel in to look at the pot and he said it was just the amount he'd poured in. Well, the damn thing was full. I never thought it might be water. I took photographs and sealed the place up just as it was. I did pour off this stuff and keep it. I'll say that for myself. I made sure the poison had come out of the bottle in the cupboard. Blast it!'

'Abel's prints,' Alleyn said, 'were still on the key of the cupboard and on the knob. You can't open the door without turning the key and the knob. Dr Shaw saw that, when he looked at the cupboard and waited until it had been tested for prints. If anyone else had been to the cupboard they would either have left their own prints, used gloves and smeared Abel's prints, or else wiped them off entirely. Nobody could have been to the cupboard.'

'I knew that, but all the same – Well, I suppose I thought they might have got at the bottle while – oh, hell!'

'Anybody might have missed it, Mr Harper,' said Fox. 'I didn't pick it till Mr Alleyn pointed it out.'

'And I was lucky,' said Alleyn. 'I'd read Taylor on the cyanides during our trip down.'

'Well,' said Harper, 'the coroner and Dr Shaw missed the point. Oates gave evidence of discovery of the stuff in the rat-hole. Old Pomeroy deposed it was the same amount he'd poured in. Nobody said anything about evaporation.'

'Oates,' Alleyn pointed out, 'saw it the first night with Dr Shaw, before they knew the exact nature of the poison. Not much more than twenty-six hours after it was put there.'

'He might have just dipped the dart in the stuff,' said Harper. 'I did think of that. But now – '

'Now we know the dart must have been doctored a very short time before Oates sealed it up. You see where we're heading?'

'Yes,' said Harper unwillingly. 'I see, all right. But suppose Legge had the stuff on him and put it on the dart just before he threw it – '

'He didn't,' said Alleyn. 'Believe me, he didn't. He's a clumsy man. He fumbles. His hands are coarse and his fingers are thick. To get cyanide on that dart with seven pairs of eyes watching him, he'd need the skill and the hands of a conjurer. Even Abel Pomeroy, who thinks or wants to think Legge did the job, can't offer an idea of how he did it. Parish who has thrown Legge in my teeth every time I've seen him, hasn't an argument to offer. And on the other side we've got Will, Miss Moore, Miss Darragh and Cubitt all ready to swear with, I believe, perfect truth, that Legge, as he stood there under the light, had no chance of anointing the fourth or any other dart.'

'But we can't explain the poison in any other way.'

'Oh, yes,' said Alleyn, 'I think we can. This is our case – '

IV

Five o'clock had struck and they were still at the police station. Alleyn had gone over every word of his report with Harper. He had described each interview and had sorted the scraps of evidence into two groups, the relevant and the irrelevant. He had poured prussic

acid solution into Abel's little jar and, to reproduce rat-hole conditions, had placed it in a closed drawer. At the end of forty-six minutes half had evaporated.

'So you see,' said Alleyn, 'if the liquid you found in the tin is
water, as I believe it is, it looks as if the murderer must have visited
the garage within forty-six minutes. Now on that night – the night
on which Watchman chipped Legge and Will Pomeroy lost his temper – Legge gave an exhibition of dart-throwing which lasted only a
few seconds. This took place a few minutes after Abel had set the
poison in the garage. The argument followed. Legge went into the
public bar where he brought off the trick with the darts. He then
returned and joined the others in a game of Round-the-Clock – '

'There you are,' interrupted Harper. 'He could – sorry. Go on.'

'I know he could, Nick, but wait a bit. According to your report
they all, with the exception of Miss Darragh, who had gone to bed,
stayed in the private taproom until closing time. Our forty-five minutes have gone.'

'I suppose,' said Harper, 'one of them might have gone out for a
few minutes without being noticed.'

'Yes, and that is a point that will be urged by counsel. All we can
prove here is opportunity – possibility. We can't bring anything
home. May we have the stuff you took from the rat-hole, Nick? Fox,
would you get my bag? Mr Noggins was generous with his prussic
acid and there are at least three ounces of the water, if it is water.
The analyst can lend us half. Let's poach on his preserves and find
out for ourselves.'

Fox opened Alleyn's bag. From it he took two open-mouthed vessels about two inches high, two watch-glasses, and a small bottle.
Alleyn squinted at the bottle.

'Silver nitrate. That's the stuff. Can you produce some warm
water, Nick? Well, well, I *am* exceeding my duty to be sure.'

Harper went out and returned with a jug of water and a photographic dish. Alleyn poured a little water into the dish, half-filled
one of his tiny vessels with the fluid found in the rat-hole, and the
other with acid from Abel's bottle. He wetted the underside of the
watch-glasses with nitrate solution and placed them over the vessels.
He then stood the vessels, closed by the watch-glasses, in the warm
water.

'Fox now says the Lord's Prayer backwards,' he explained. 'I emit a few oddments of ectoplasm and Hi Cockalorum the spell is wound up! Take a look at that, Nick.'

They stared at the dish. On the surface of the prussic acid a little spiral had risen. It became denser, it flocculated and the watch-glass was no longer transparent but covered with an opaque whiteness.

'That's cyanide, that was,' said Alleyn. 'Now, look at the other. A blank, my lord. It's water, Br'er Fox, it's water. Now let's pour them back into their respective bottles and don't give me away to the analyst.'

'I suppose,' said Harper, as Alleyn tidied up. 'I suppose this means we needn't worry ourselves about the cupboard. The cupboard doesn't come into the blasted affair.'

Alleyn held on the palm of his hand the three pieces of glass he had separated from the fragments of the broken brandy tumbler, and the small misshapen lumps he had found in the ashes of the fire.

'Oh, yes,' he said. 'Yes. We're not home yet, not by a long march, but the cupboard still comes into the picture. Think.'

Harper looked from the pieces of glass to Alleyn's face and back again.

'Yes,' he said slowly, 'yes. But you'll have the devil of a job to prove it.'

'I agree,' said Alleyn. 'Nevertheless, Nick, I hope to prove it.'

CHAPTER 17

Mr Fox Takes Sherry

Parish came downstairs singing 'La Donna è Mobile'. He had a pleasant baritone voice which had been half-trained in the days when he had contemplated musical comedy. He sang stylishly and one could not believe that he sang unconsciously. He swung open the door of the private tap and entered on the last flourish of that impertinent, that complacently debonair refrain.

'Good evening, sir,' said Abel from behind the bar. ''Tis again.'

Parish smiled wistfully.

'Ah, Abel,' he said with a slight sigh, 'it's not as easy as it sounds; but my cousin would have been the last man to want long faces, poor dear old fellow.'

'So he would, then,' rejoined Abel heartily, 'the very last.'

'Ah,' said Mr Nark, shaking his head. Norman Cubitt looked over the top of his tankard and raised his eyebrows. Legge moved into the ingle-nook where Miss Darragh sat knitting.

'What'll you take, Mr Parish?' asked Abel.

'A Treble Extra. I need it. Hallo, Norman, old man,' said Parish with a sort of brave gaiety. 'How's the work going?'

'Nicely, thank you, Seb.' Cubitt glanced at the clock. It was a quarter past seven. 'I'm thinking of starting a big canvas,' he said.

'Are you? What subject?'

'Decima,' said Cubitt. He put his tankard down on the bar. 'She has very kindly said she'll sit for me.'

'How'll you paint her?' asked Parish.

'I thought on the downs by Cary Edge. She's got a red sweater thing. It'll be life size. Full length.'

'Ah, now,' exclaimed Miss Darragh from the ingle-nook, 'you've taken my advice in the latter end. Haven't I been at you, now, ever since I got here to take Miss Moore for your subject? I've never seen a better. Sure the picture'll be your masterpiece for she's a lovely young creature.'

'But, my dear chap,' objected Parish, 'we're off in a day or two. You'll never finish it.'

'I was going to break it gently to you, Seb. If you don't object I think I'll stay on for a bit.'

Parish looked slightly hurt.

'That's just as you like, of course,' he said. 'Don't ask me to stay. The place is too full of memories.'

'Besides,' said Cubitt dryly, 'you start rehearsals on today week, don't you?'

'As a matter of fact I do.' Parish raised his arms and then let them fall limply to his sides. 'Work!' he said. 'Back to the old grind. Ah well!' And he added with an air of martyrdom, 'I can go back by train.'

'I'll drive you into Illington, of course.'

'Thank you, old boy. Yes, I'd better get back to the treadmill.'

'Keep a stiff upper lip, Seb,' said Cubitt with a grin.

The door opened and Alleyn came in. He wore a dinner jacket and stiff shirt. Someone once said of him that he looked like a cross between a grandee and a monk. In evening clothes the grandee predominated. Parish gave him a quick appraising glance, Mr Nark goggled, and Miss Darragh looked up with a smile. Cubitt rumpled his hair and said: 'Hallo! Here comes the county!'

Mr Legge shrank back into the ingle-nook. Upon all of them a kind of weariness descended. They seemed to melt away from him and towards each other. Alleyn asked for two glasses of the special sherry and told Abel that he and Fox would be out till latish.

'May we have a key, Mr Pomeroy?'

'Us'll leave side-door open,' said Abel. 'No need fur key, sir. Be no criminals in this neighbourhood. Leastways – ' He stopped short and looked pointedly at Legge.

'That's splendid,' said Alleyn. 'How far is it to Colonel Brammington's?'

''Bout eight mile, sir. Shankley Court. A great masterpiece of a place, sir, with iron gates and a deer-park. Carry on four miles beyond Illington and turn left at The Man of Devon.'

'Right,' said Alleyn. 'We needn't leave for half an hour.'

Cubitt went out.

Alleyn fidgeted with a piece of rag round his left hand. It was clumsily tied and fell away, disclosing a trail of red.

He twitched the handkerchief out of his breast pocket, glanced at it and swore. There was a bright red spot on the handkerchief.

'Blast that cut,' said Alleyn. 'Now I'll have to get a clean one.'

'Hurt yurrself, sir?' asked Abel.

'Tore my hand on a rusty nail in the garage.'

'In the garage!' ejaculated Mr Nark. 'That's a powerful dangerous place to get a cut finger. Germs galore, I dessay, and as like as not some of the poison fumes still floating about.'

'Aye,' said Abel angrily, 'that's right, George Nark. All my premises is stiff with poison. Wonder 'tis you come anigh 'em. Here, Mr Alleyn, sir, I'll get 'ee a dressing fur that thurr cut.'

'If I could have a bit of rag and a dab of peroxide or something.'

'Doan't you have anything out of that fatal cupboard,' said Mr Nark. 'Not if you value the purity of your bloodstream.'

'You know as well as I do,' said Abel, 'that thur cupboard's been scrubbed and fumigated. Not that thurr's anything in it. Thurr baint. Nicholas Harper made off with my first-aid set, innocent though it wurr.'

'And the iodine bottle,' pointed out Mr Nark, 'so you can't give the inspector iodine, lethal or otherwise.'

'Thurr's another first-aid box upstairs,' said Abel. 'In bathroom cupboard. Will!' He looked into the public bar. 'Will! Get 'tother box out of bathroom cupboard, my sonny. Look lively.'

'It doesn't matter, Mr Pomeroy,' said Alleyn. 'Don't bother. I'll use this handkerchief.'

'No trouble, sir, and you'll need a bit of antiseptic in that cut if you took it off of a rusty nail. I'm a terror fur iodine, sir. I wurr a surgeon's orderly in France, Mr Alleyn, and learned hospital ways.

Scientific ideas baint George Nark's private property though you might think they wurr.'

Will Pomeroy came downstairs and into the private tap. He put a small first-aid box on the counter and returned to the public bar. Abel opened the box.

''Tis spandy-new,' he said. 'I bought it from a traveller only couple of days afore accident. Hallo! Yurr, Will!'

'What's up?' called Will.

'Iodine bottle's gone.'

'Eh?'

'Where's iodine?'

'I dunno. It's not there,' shouted Will.

'Who's had it?'

'I dunno. I haven't.'

'It really doesn't matter, Mr Pomeroy,' said Alleyn. 'It's bled itself clean. If I may have a bit of this lint and an inch of the strapping. Perhaps there wasn't any iodine?'

''Course there wurr,' said Abel. 'Yurr's lil' bed whurr it lay. Damme, who's been at it? *Mrs Ives!*'

He stumped out and could be heard roaring angrily about the back premises.

Alleyn put a bit of lint over his finger and Miss Darragh stuck it down with strapping. He went upstairs, carrying his own glass of sherry and Fox's. Fox was standing before the looking-glass in his room knotting a sober tie. He caught sight of Alleyn in the glass.

'Lucky I brought my blue suit,' said Fox, 'and lucky you brought your dress clothes, Mr Alleyn.'

'Why didn't you let me tell Colonel Brammington that we'd neither of us change, Foxkin?'

'No, no, sir. It's the right thing for you to dress, just as much as it'd be silly for me to do so. Well, it'd be an affected kind of way for me to act, Mr Alleyn. I never get a black coat and boiled shirt on my back except at the Lodge meetings and when I'm on a night-club job. The colonel would only think I was trying to put myself in a place where I don't belong. Did you find what you wanted, Mr Alleyn?'

'Abel bought another first-aid set, two days before Watchman died. The iodine has been taken. He can't find it.'

'Is that so?'

Fox brushed the sleeves of his coat and cast a final searching glance at himself in the glass. 'I washed that razor blade,' he said.

'Thank you, Fox. I was a little too free with it. Bled all over Abel's bar. Most convincing. What's the time? Half-past seven. A bit early yet. Let's think this out.'

'Right oh, sir,' said Fox. He lifted his glass of sherry. 'Good luck, Mr Alleyn,' he said.

II

Decima had promised to come to Coombe Head at eight o'clock. Cubitt lay on the lip of the cliff and stared at the sea beneath him, trying, as Alleyn had tried, to read order in the hieroglyphics traced by the restless seaweed. The sequence was long and subtle, unpausing, unhurried. Each pattern seemed significant but all melted into fluidity, and he decided, as Alleyn had decided, that the forces that governed these beautiful but inane gestures ranged beyond the confines of his imagination. He fell to appraising the colour and the shifting tones of the water, translating these things into terms of paint, and he began to think of how, in the morning, he would make a rapid study from the lip of the cliff.

'But I must fix one pattern only in my memory and watch for it to appear in the sequence, like a measure in some intricate saraband.'

He was so intent on this project that he did not hear Decima come and was startled when she spoke to him.

'Norman?'

Her figure was dark and tall against the sky. He rose and faced her.

'Have you risen from the sea?' he asked. 'You are lovely enough.'

She did not answer and he took her hand and led her a little way over the headland to a place where their figures no longer showed against the sky. Here they faced each other again.

'I am so bewildered,' said Decima. 'I have tried since this morning to feel all sorts of things. Shame. Compassion for Will. Anxiety. I can feel none of them. I can only wonder why we should so suddenly have fallen in love.'

'It was only sudden for you,' said Cubitt. 'Not for me.'

'But – ? Is that true. How long – ?'

'Since last year. Since the first week of last year.'

Decima drew away from him.

'But, didn't you know? I thought last year that you had guessed.'

'About Luke? Yes, I guessed.'

'Everything?'

'Yes, my dear.'

'I wish very much that it hadn't happened,' said Decima. 'Of that I am ashamed. Not for the orthodox reason but because it made such a fool of me; because I pretended to myself that I was sanely satisfying a need, whereas in reality I merely lost my head and behaved like a dairymaid.'

'Hallo!' said Cubitt. 'You're being very county. What's wrong with dairymaids in the proletariat?'

'Brute,' muttered Decima and, between laughter and tears, stumbled into his arms.

'I love you very much,' whispered Cubitt.

'You'd a funny way of showing it. Nobody ever would have dreamt you thought anything about me.'

'Oh, yes, they would. They did.'

'Who?' cried Decima in terror. 'Not Will?'

'No. Miss Darragh. She as good as told me so. I've seen her eyeing me whenever you were in the offing. God knows I had a hard job to keep my eyes off you. I've wanted like hell to do this.'

But after a few moments Decima freed herself.

'This is going the wrong way,' she said. 'There mustn't be any of this.'

Cubitt said, 'All right. We'll come back to earth. I promised myself I'd keep my head. Here, my darling, have a cigarette, for God's sake, and don't look at me. Sit down. That's right. Now, listen. You remember the morning of that day?'

'When you and Sebastian came over the hill?'

'Yes. Just as you were telling Luke you could kill him. Did you?'

'No.'

'Of course you didn't. Nor did I. But we made a botch of things this morning. Seb and I denied that we saw Luke as we came back from Coombe Head, and I think Alleyn knew we were lying. I got a nasty jolt when he announced that he was going to see you. I didn't know what to do. I dithered round and finally followed him, leaving Seb to come home by himself. I was too late. You'd told him?'

'I told him that Luke and I quarrelled that morning because Luke had tried – had tried to make love to me. I didn't tell him – Norman, I lied about the rest. I said it hadn't happened before. I was afraid. I was cold with panic. I didn't know what you and Sebastian had told him. I thought, if he found out that I had been Luke's mistress and that we'd quarrelled, he might think – They say poison's a woman's weapon, don't they? It was like one of those awful dreams. I don't know what I said. I lost my head. And that other man, Fox, kept writing in a book. And then you came and it was as if – oh, as if instead of being alone in the dark and terrified I had someone beside me.'

'Why wouldn't you stay with me when they'd gone?'

'I don't know. I wanted to think. I was muddled.'

'I was terrified you wouldn't come here tonight, Decima.'

'I shouldn't have come. What are we to do about Will?'

'Tell him.'

'He'll be so bewildered,' said Decima, 'and so miserable.'

'Would you have married him if this hadn't happened?'

'I haven't said I would marry you.'

'I have,' said Cubitt.

'I don't know that I believe in the institution of marriage.'

'You'll find that out when you've tried it, my darling.'

'I'm a farmer's daughter. A peasant.'

'The worst of you communists,' said Cubitt, 'is that you're such snobs. Always worrying about class distinctions. Come here.'

'Norman,' said Decima presently, 'who do you think it was?'

'I don't know. I don't know.'

Cubitt pressed her hands against him and, after a moment, spoke evenly. 'Did Will ever guess about you and Luke?'

She moved away from him at arm's length. 'You can't think Will would do it?'

'Did he guess?'

'I don't think I – '

'I rather thought he had guessed,' said Cubitt.

III

When Alleyn had gone out, the atmosphere of the taproom changed. Parish began to talk to Abel, Miss Darrah asked Legge when he was moving into Illington, Mr Nark cleared his throat and, by the simple expedient of shouting down every one else, won the attention of the company.

'Ah,' he said. 'Axing the road to Shankley Court, was he? Ah. I expected it.'

Abel gave a disgruntled snort.

'I expected it,' repeated Mr Nark firmly. 'I had a chat with the chief inspector this morning.'

'After which, in course,' said Abel, 'he knew his business. All he's got to do is to clap handcuffs on somebody.'

'Abel,' said Mr Nark, 'you're a bitter man. I'm not blaming you. A chap with a tumble load on his conscience, same as what you've got, is scarcely responsible for his words.'

'On his conscience!' said Abel angrily. 'What the devil do you mean? Why doan't 'ee say straight out I'm a murderer?'

'Because you're not, Abel. Murder's one thing and negligence is another. Manslaughter is the term for your crime. If proper care had been took, as I told the chief inspector – though, mind you, I'm not a chap to teach a man his own business – '

'What sort of a chap did you say you wasn't?'

Miss Darragh intervened.

'I'm sure,' she said, 'we all must hope for the end of this terrible affair. Whether 'twas accident, or whether 'twas something else, it's been a dreadful strain and an anxiety for us all.'

'So it has then, Miss,' agreed Abel. He looked at Legge who had turned his back and was engaged, with the assistance of a twisted handkerchief, on an unattractive exploration of his left ear. 'Sooner they catch the murderer the happier all of us'll be.'

Parish caught Abel's eyes and he too looked at Legge.

'I can't believe,' said Parish, 'that a crime like this can go unpunished. I shall not rest content until I know my cousin is avenged.'

'Ah now, Mr Parish,' said Miss Darragh, 'you must not let this tragedy make the bitter man of you. Sure, you're talking like the Count of Monte Cristo if 'twas he was the character I call to mind.'

'Do I sound bitter?' asked Parish in his beautiful voice. 'Perhaps I do. Perhaps I am.'

A shadow of something that might have been a twinkle flitted across Miss Darragh's face.

'A little too bitter,' she said, and it was impossible to tell whether or not she spoke ironically.

On the floor above them there was a sudden commotion. A man's voice spoke urgently. They heard a scuffle of feet and then someone ran along the upstairs passage.

'What's wrong with the sleuths?' asked Parish.

No one answered. Miss Darragh took up her knitting. Mr Nark picked his teeth. Parish finished his beer.

'We all want to see the man caught,' said Legge suddenly. He spoke in his usual querulous, muffled voice. He looked ill and he seemed extremely nervous. Miss Darragh glanced at him and said soothingly:

'Of course.'

'Their behaviour,' said Legge, 'is abominable. Abominable! I intend writing a letter to the Commissioner of Scotland Yard. It is disgraceful.'

Parish planted his feet apart, put his head on one side, and looked at Legge with the expression he used in films of the Bulldog Drummond type. His voice drawled slightly.

'Feelin' nervous, Legge?' he asked. 'Now isn't that a pity.'

'Nervous! I am not nervous, Mr Parish. What do you mean by – '

'Gentlemen,' said old Abel.

There was a brief silence broken by an urgent clatter of footsteps on the stairs.

The door into the private tap swung open. Alleyn stood on the threshold. When Miss Darragh saw his face she uttered a sharp cry that was echoed, oddly, by Parish.

Alleyn said:

'Nobody is to move from this room. Understand? What's Dr Shaw's telephone number?'

Abel said, 'Illington 579, sir.'

Alleyn kicked the door wide open and moved to the wall telephone just outside. He dialled a number and came into the doorway with the receiver at his ear.

'You understand,' he said, 'none of you is to move. Where's Cubitt?'

'He's gone out,' said Parish. 'What's the matter, Mr Alleyn, for God's sake.'

Alleyn was speaking into the receiver.

'Dr Shaw? At once, please, it's the police.' He eyed them all as he waited.

'There has been an accident,' he said. 'Where's that decanter of sherry?'

'Here, sir,' said Abel.

'Take it by the end of the neck, lock it in the cupboard behind you, and bring the key to me. That you, Shaw? Alleyn. Come at once. Same trouble as last time. I've given an emetic. It's worked, but he's half-collapsed. I'll do artificial respiration. For God's sake be quick.'

He clicked the receiver and took the key Abel brought him. He dialled another number and spoke to Abel as he dialled it.

'Lock the shutters and all the doors. Both bars. Bring the keys here. Illington Police Station? Oates? Inspector Alleyn. I want Mr Harper and yourself at once at the Plume of Feathers. Jump to it.'

He hung up the receiver. Abel was clattering round the public bar. Alleyn slammed the shutters in the private bar.

'If any one opens these shutters or tries to leave this room,' he said, 'there will be an arrest on a charge of attempted murder. Bring those others through here.'

'But, look here – ' said Parish.

'Quiet!' said Alleyn and was obeyed. Abel shepherded a couple of astonished fishermen into the private bar. Will Pomeroy followed. Abel slammed down the bar shutter and locked it. He came to Alleyn and gave him the keys. Alleyn pushed him outside, slammed the door and locked it.

'Now,' he said, 'come up here.'

He ran up the stairs, taking three at a stride. Abel followed, panting. The door of Alleyn's room was open. Fox sat on the bed with the wash-hand basin at his feet. His face was curiously strained and anxious. When he saw Alleyn he tried to speak, but something had gone wrong with his mouth. He kept shutting his jaw with a sharp involuntary movement and his voice was thick. He jerked his hand at the bowl.

'Thank God,' said Alleyn. 'Can you do yet another heave, old thing?'

Fox jerked his head sideways and suddenly pitched forward. Alleyn caught him. 'Move that basin,' he ordered. 'I want to get him on the floor.'

Abel moved the basin and together he and Alleyn lowered Fox. Alleyn had wrenched open Fox's collar and tie. He now loosened his clothes. Somewhere in the background of his conscious thoughts was an impression that it was strange to be doing these things to Fox whom he knew so well. He began the movements of resuscitation, working hard and rhythmically. Abel quietly cleared an area round Fox.

'When you'm tiring, sir,' said Abel, 'I'll take a turn.'

But Alleyn scarcely knew he had a body of his own. His body and breath, precariously and dubiously, belonged to Fox. His thoughts were visited by hurrying pictures. He saw a figure that shoved and sweated and set the wheels of a great vehicle in motion. A figure turned and turned again at a crank handle. He was aware, at moments most vividly, of his own glass of untouched sherry on the dressing-table. Fox's arms were heavy and stiff. Presently his eyes opened. The pupils had widened almost to the rim of the iris, the eyes had no expression. Alleyn's own eyes were half-blinded with sweat. Suddenly the body on the floor heaved.

'That's better,' said Abel, stooping to the basin, 'he'm going to vomit again.'

Alleyn turned Fox on his side. Fox neatly and prolifically made use of the basin.

'Brandy,' said Alleyn. 'In a bag in the wardrobe.'

He watched Abel fetch the flask. Alleyn unscrewed the top, smelt at the contents, and took a mouthful. He squatted on his haunches with the brandy in his mouth. The brandy was all right. He swallowed it, poured some into the cap of the flask, and gave it to Fox.

Downstairs the telephone was pealing.

'Go and answer it,' said Alleyn.

Abel went out.

'Fox,' said Alleyn. 'Fox, my dear old thing.'

Fox's lips moved. Alleyn took his handkerchief and wiped that large face carefully.

'Very inconvenient,' said a voice inside Fox. 'Sorry.'

'You b – old b – ,' said Alleyn softly.

CHAPTER 18

Mr Legge Commits a Misdemeanour

'I'm better,' said Fox presently. 'I'd like to sit up.'

Alleyn propped him against the bed.

A car pulled outside and in a moment Alleyn heard a clatter of steps and the sound of voices. Abel came in.

'Yurr be doctor,' Abel said, 'and Nick Harper with police. And colonel's on telephone roaring like proper grampus.'

'O Lord!' Alleyn ejaculated. 'Abel, tell him what's happened. He'll probably want to come over here. Apologize for me. Where's the doctor?'

'Here,' said Dr Shaw, and walked in. 'What's the trouble? Hallo!' He went to Fox.

'I'm better, doctor,' said Fox. 'I've vomited.'

Dr Shaw took his pulse, looked at his eyes, and nodded.

'You'll do,' he said, 'but we'll make a job of it. Come into the bathroom. You'd better keep that matter in the basin, Alleyn.'

He opened his bag, took out a tube, and jerked his head at Fox.

'Here!' said Fox resentfully, eyeing the tube.

'How did it happen?' asked Dr Shaw.

Harper came in.

'I've left Oates and another man downstairs,' said Harper. 'What's up?'

'Fox drank a glass of sherry,' said Alleyn. 'There's the glass. We'll detain all the crowd downstairs. You too, Mr Pomeroy. Go down and join them.'

'Move along, Abel,' said Harper.

'I yurrd, I yurrd,' grunted Abel irritably, and went out.

'You'd better go down with them, Nick,' said Alleyn. 'Tell Oates to watch our man like a lynx. Abel will show you a decanter. Bring it up here. Here's the key. Use my gloves. You'd better search them. You won't find anything but you'd better do it. Leave Miss Darragh for the moment.'

Harper went out.

'Did you take any sherry, Alleyn?' asked Dr Shaw sharply.

'I? No.'

'Sure?'

'Perfectly. Why?'

'You look a bit dicky.'

'I'm all right.'

'Mr Alleyn has just saved my life for me,' whispered Fox.

'You come along,' said Dr Shaw, and led him out.

Alleyn took an envelope from his pocket and put it over the glass from which Fox had drunk. He weighted the envelope with the saucer from his wash-hand stand. He got his bag and took out an empty bottle and a funnel. He smelt the sherry in his own glass and then poured it into the bottle, stoppered it, and wrote on the label. He was annoyed to find that his hands shook. His heart thumped intolerably. He grimaced and took another mouthful of brandy.

Harper came back.

'Oates and my other chap are searching them,' said Harper. 'They made no objections.'

'They wouldn't. Sit down, Nick,' said Alleyn, 'and listen. Put Fox's sick out of the way first, for the Lord's sake. Give it to Shaw. I've got palsy or something.'

Harper performed this office and sat down.

'Yesterday evening,' said Alleyn, 'Abel Pomeroy opened a bottle of a very sound sherry. Fox and I had a glass each. At a quarter to one today Abel decanted the sherry. He, Fox and I had a glass each after it was decanted. George Nark was in the bar. Later on, Miss Darragh, Legge, Parish, Cubitt, and Will Pomeroy came in and we talked about the sherry. They all knew it was for our private use. Some forty minutes ago, Abel poured out two glasses. Fox drank his and within half a minute he was taken very ill. The symptoms were those of cyanide poisoning. I'll swear Abel didn't put anything in the glasses. There's

Fox's glass. We'll do our stuff with what's left. I've covered it but we'd better get the dregs into an airtight bottle. You'll find one in my bag there. There's a funnel on the dressing-table. D'you mind doing it? Clean the funnel out first. I used it for the stuff in my glass.'

Harper did this.

'It's a bad blunder,' he said. 'What good would it do him? Suppose you'd both been killed? I mean, it's foolish. Is it panic or spite or both?'

'Neither, I imagine. I see it as a last attempt to bolster up the accident theory. The idea is that in the same mysterious way as cyanide got on the dart so it got into the decanter. The decanter, you see, was brought out from the corner cupboard. Mrs Ives had washed it in about two dozen changes of boiling water. I don't think anybody but Nark and Abel were aware of this. We were no doubt supposed to think the decanter was tainted by being in the cupboard.'

Superintendent Harper uttered a vulgar and incredulous word.

'I know,' agreed Alleyn. 'Of course it was. But if Fox and (or) I had popped off, you'd have had a devil of a job proving it was murder. Oh, it's a blunder, all right. It shows us two things. The murderer must have kept a bit of cyanide up his sleeve and he must have visited the private bar after Abel decanted the sherry at a quarter to one this afternoon. We will now search their rooms. We won't find anything, but we'd better do it. I'll just see how Fox is getting on.'

Fox, white and shaken, was sitting on the edge of the bath. Dr Shaw was washing his hands.

'He'll do all right now,' said Dr Shaw. 'Better go to bed and take it easy.'

'I'm damned if I do,' said Fox. 'Excuse me, sir, but I'm damned if I do.'

Alleyn took him by the elbow.

'Blast your eyes,' he said, 'you'll do as you're told. Come on.'

Fox consented with a bad grace to lying on his bed. Alleyn and Harper searched the rooms.

II

At first Harper said that the rooms, in all essentials, were as he had found them on the day after Watchman's death. In Cubitt's they found an overwhelming smell of studio and the painting gear that had engendered it. There were bottles of turpentine and oil, half-finished works, Cubitt's paint-box, and boxes of unopened tubes. Alleyn smelt the bottles and shook his head.

'We needn't take them,' he said, 'their stink is a lawful stink. You can't put turpentine or oil into vintage sherry and get away with it.'

'What about prussic acid? It smells strong enough.'

'Of almonds. A nutty flavour. Do you remember the account of the murder of Rasputin?'

'Can't say I do,' said Harper.

'Youssoupoff put cyanide in the wine. Rasputin drank several glasses, apparently with impunity.'

'But – '

'The theory is that the sugar in the wine took the punch out of the poison. That may account for Fox's escape. No doubt the sherry had a fine old nutty aroma. By God, I'll get this expert.'

'What are we looking for?'

'For anything that could have held the stuff he put in the decanter. Oh, he'll have got rid of it somehow, of course. But you never know.'

They went into the bathroom. In a cupboard above the hand-basin they found Abel's second first-aid outfit. Alleyn asked Harper if there had been a bottle of iodine there on the day after the murder. Harper said no. He had checked the contents of the cupboard. They separated and took the rest of the rooms between them, Alleyn going to Legge's and Parish's, Harper to the others. Alleyn took a small empty bottle from Parish's room. It had held pills and smelt of nothing at all. On Legge's dressing-table he found a phial half-full of a thick pinkish fluid that smelt of antiseptic. Mr Legge's ear lotion. He kept it and searched all the drawers and pockets but found nothing else of interest. Abel's room was neat and spotless, Will's untidy and full of books. The wearisome and exacting business went on. Down below, in the private bar, Oates and his mate kept company with the patrons of the Plume of Feathers. They were very quiet. Occasionally Alleyn heard the voices of Parish and of Mr Nark. Ottercombe clock struck ten, sweetly and slowly. There was a moment of complete quiet broken by a violent eruption of noise down in the bar. Alleyn and Harper met in the passage.

'Somebody cutting up rough,' said Harper.

A falsetto voice screamed out an oath. A table was overturned and there followed a great clatter of boots. Harper ran downstairs and Alleyn followed. Inside the private bar they found Legge, mouthing and gibbering, between Oates and a second uniformed constable.

'What's all this?' asked Harper.

'Misdemeanour, sir,' said Oates whose nose was bleeding freely. 'Assault *and* battery.'

'I don't care what it is,' screamed Legge. 'I can't stand any more of this – '

'Shut up, you silly chap,' admonished Oates. 'He tried to make a breakaway, sir. Sitting there as quiet as you please, and all of a sudden makes a blind rush for the door and when we intercepts him he wades in and assaults and batters the pair of us. Won't give over, sir. You're under arrest, Robert Legge, and it is my duty to warn you that you needn't say anything, but what you do say may be used in evidence. Stop that.'

'Persecuted,' whispered Legge. 'Persecuted, spied upon, driven and badgered and maddened. I know what it means. Let me go. Damn you, let me go!'

He kicked Oates on the shin. Oates swore and twisted Legge's arm behind his back. Legge screamed and went limp.

'You'll have to be locked up,' said Harper sadly. 'Now, are you going to behave or have we got to put the bracelets on you? Be a sensible chap.'

'I'll resist,' said Legge, 'till you kill me.'

'Oh, take him away,' said Harper. 'Put him in a room, upstairs, both of you.'

Legge, struggling and gasping horridly, was taken out.

'Ah, it's at his wits' end he is, poor wretch,' said Miss Darragh.

Cubitt said, 'Look here, this is ghastly. If he's not guilty why the hell – ?'

Parish said, 'Not guilty! I must say that for an innocent man his behaviour is pretty fantastic'

Will Pomeroy crossed the room and confronted Alleyn and Harper.

'Why's he arrested?' demanded Will.

'Assaulting a constable and interfering with the police in the execution of their duty,' said Harper.

'My God, he was drove to it! If this is justice the sooner there's a revolution in the country the better. It's enough to send the man mad, the way you've been pestering him. Haven't you the sense to see the state he's got into? Damme if I'm not nigh-ready to take on the lot of you myself. Let that man go.'

'That'll do, Will,' said Harper.

' "That'll do!" The official answer for every blasted blunder in the force. Bob Legge's my comrade – '

'In which case,' said Alleyn, 'you'll do well to think a little before you speak. You can hardly expect Mr Harper to set up constables in rows for your comrade Legge to bloody their noses. While his mood lasts he's better in custody. You pipe down like a sensible fellow.' He turned to Harper. 'Stay down here a moment, will you? I'll take a look at Fox and rejoin you.'

He ran upstairs and met Oates in the landing.

'My mate's put Legge in his own room, sir,' said Oates.

'Good. He'd better stay with him and you'd better dip your nose in cold water before you resume duty. Then come and relieve Mr Harper.'

Oates went into the bathroom. Alleyn opened Fox's door and listened. Fox was snoring deeply and rhythmically. Alleyn closed the door softly and returned to the taproom.

III

It was the last time that he was to see that assembly gathered together in the private taproom of the Plume of Feathers. He had been little over twenty-four hours in Ottercombe but it seemed more like a week. The suspects in a case of murder become quickly and strangely familiar to the investigating officer. He has an aptitude for noticing mannerisms, tricks of voice and of movement. Faces and figures make their impression quickly and sharply. Alleyn expected, before he saw them, Cubitt's trick of smiling lop-sidedly, Parish's habit of sticking out his jaw, Miss Darragh's look of inscrutability, Will Pomeroy's mulish blushes, and his father's way of opening his eyes very widely. The movement of Nark's head, slanted conceitedly, and his look of burning self-importance, seemed to be memories of a year rather than of days. Alleyn felt a little as if they were marionettes, obeying a few simple jerks of their strings and otherwise inert and stupid. He felt wholeheartedly bored with the lot of them, the thought of another bout of interrogation was almost intolerable. Fox might have been killed. Reaction had set in, and Alleyn was sick at heart.

'Well,' he said crisply, 'you may as well know what has happened. Between a quarter to one and five past seven somebody put poison in the decanter of sherry that was kept for our use. You will readily understand that we shall require a full account from each one of you of your movements after a quarter to one. Mr Harper and I will see you in turn in the parlour. If you discuss the matter among yourselves it will be within hearing of Constable Oates who will be on duty in this room. We'll see you first if you please, Mr Cubitt.'

But it was the usual exasperating job that faced him. None of them had a complete alibi. Each of them could have slipped unseen into the taproom and come out again unnoticed. Abel had locked the bar shutter during closing hours, but every one knew where he kept his keys, and several times when the bar was open it had been deserted. Cubitt said he was painting from two o'clock until six when he returned for his evening meal. He had been one of the company in the taproom when Alleyn came in for the sherry but had left immediately to meet Decima Moore on Coombe Head. The others followed with similar stories, except old Pomeroy who frankly admitted he had sat in the taproom for some time, reading his paper. Each of them denied being alone there at any time after Abel had decanted the sherry. An hour's exhaustive inquiry failed to prove or disprove any of their statements. Last of all, Mr Legge was brought down in a state of the profoundest dejection and made a series of protestations to the effect that he was being persecuted. He was a pitiful object, and Alleyn's feeling of nausea increased as he watched him. At last Alleyn said:

'Mr Legge, we only arrived here last evening but, as you must realize, we have already made many inquiries. Of all the people we have interviewed, you alone have objected to the way we set about our job. Why?'

Legge looked at Alleyn without speaking. His lower lip hung loosely, his eyes, half-veiled, in that now familiar way by his white lashes, looked like the eyes of a blind man. Only his hands moved restlessly. After a moment's silence he mumbled something inaudible.

'What do you say?'

'It doesn't matter. Everything I say is used against me.'

Alleyn looked at him in silence.

'I think,' he said at last, 'that it is my duty to tell you that a dart bearing your fingerprints was sent to the bureau early this morning. They have been identified and the result has been telephoned to us.'

Legge's hands moved convulsively.

'They have been identified,' Alleyn repeated, 'as those of Montague Thringle. Montague Thringle was sentenced to six years imprisonment for embezzlement, a sentence that was afterwards reduced to four years and was completed twenty-six months ago.' He paused. Legge's face was clay-coloured. 'You must have known we'd find out,' said Alleyn. 'Why didn't you tell me last night who you were?'

'Why? Why?' demanded Legge. 'You know why. You know well enough. The very sight and sound of the police! Anathema! Questions, questions, questions! At me all the time. Man with a record. Hound him out. Tell everybody. Slam every door in his face. And you have the impertinence to ask me why I was silent. My God!'

'All right,' said Alleyn, 'we'll leave it at that. How did you spend your afternoon?'

'There you go!' cried Legge, half-crying but still with that curious air of admonishment. 'There you go, you see! Straight off. Asking me things like that. It's atrocious.'

'Nonsense,' said Alleyn.

'Nonsense!' echoed Legge, in a sort of fury. He shook his finger in Alleyn's face. 'Don't you talk like that to me, sir. Do you know who I am? Do you know that before my misfortune I was the greatest power in English finance? Let me tell you that there are only three men living who fully comprehended the events that brought about the holocaust of '29 and '30, and I am one of them. If I had not put my trust in titled imbeciles, if I had not been betrayed by a skulking moron, I should be in a position to send for you when I wished to command your dubious services, or dismiss them with a contemptuous fiddle-de-dee.'

This astonishing and ridiculous word was delivered with such venom that Alleyn was quite taken aback. Into his thoughts, with the appropriate logic of topsy-turvy, popped the memory of a jigging line:

> 'To shirk the task were fiddle-de-dee.
> To shirk the task were fiddle-de, fiddle-de – '

He pulled himself together, cautioned and tackled Mr Legge, and at last got a statement from him. He had spent the afternoon packing his books, papers and effects, and putting them in his car. He had intended to take the first load into his new room that evening. He had also written some letters. He offered frantically to show Alleyn the letters. Alleyn had already seen them and they amounted to nothing. He turned Legge over to Oates whose nose was now plugged with cotton-wool.

'You'd better take him to the station,' said Alleyn.

'I demand bail,' cried Legge in a trembling voice.

'Mr Harper will see about that,' said Alleyn. 'You're under arrest for a misdemeanour.'

'I didn't kill him. I know what you're up to. It's the beginning of the end. I swear – '

'You are under arrest for assaulting police officers,' said Alleyn wearily. 'I will repeat the caution you have already heard.'

He repeated it and was devoutly thankful when Legge, in a condition of hysterical prostration, was led away. Harper, with Oates and his mate, was to drive him to Illington and lodge him in the police station.

'The colonel's at the station,' said Harper acidly. 'That was him on the telephone while you were upstairs. His car's broken down again. Why, in his position and with all his money, he doesn't – oh, well! He wants me to bring him back here or you to come in. Which'll it be? The man'll talk us all dotty, wherever he is.'

'I'll have another look at Fox,' said Alleyn. 'If he's awake, I'll get him into bed and then follow you into Illington. I'd like the doctor to see him again.'

'There'll be no need for that, sir, thank you.'

Alleyn spun round on his heel to see Fox, fully dressed and wearing his bowler hat, standing in the doorway.

CHAPTER 19

The Chief Constable as Watson

'I've reported for duty, if you please, Mr Alleyn,' said Fox.

'You unspeakable old ninny,' said Alleyn, 'go back to bed.'

'With all respect, sir, I'd rather not. I've had a very pleasant nap and am quite myself again. So if you'll allow me – '

'Br'er Fox,' said Alleyn, 'are we to have a row?'

'I hope not, sir, I'm sure,' said Fox tranquilly. 'Six years I think it is now, and never a moment's unpleasantness, thanks to your tact and consideration.'

'Damn you, go to bed.'

'If it's all the same to you, sir, I'd rather – '

'Mr Fox,' Alleyn began very loudly and stopped short. They stared at each other. Harper coughed and moved to the door. Alleyn swore violently, seized Fox by the arm, and shoved him into an armchair. He then knelt on the harlequin rug and lit the fire.

'I'd be obliged, Nick,' said Alleyn over his shoulder, 'if you'd bring Colonel Brammington here. Would you explain that circumstances over which I appear to have no control oblige me to remain at the Plume of Feathers?'

'I'm quite able to drive – ' Fox began.

'You shut up,' said Alleyn warmly.

Harper went out.

'Offences against discipline,' said Alleyn, 'are set forth in the Police Regulations under seventeen headings, including neglect of duty and disobedience to orders, together with a general heading covering discreditable conduct.' He looked up from the fire. 'Discreditable conduct,' he repeated.

Fox was shaken with a soundless subterranean chuckle.

'I'm going into the taproom,' said Alleyn. 'If you move out of that chair I'll damn well serve you with a Misconduct Form. See Regulation 13.'

'I'll get the super in as my witness, sir,' said Fox. 'See Regulation 17.' And at this pointless witticism he went off into an ecstasy of apoplectic mirth.

Alleyn returned to the taproom where Oates still kept guard. Miss Darragh was knitting in the ingle-nook, Parish stood near the shuttered windows, Cubitt was drawing in the battered sketch-book he always carried in his pocket. Abel Pomeroy sat disconsolately in one of his own settles. Will glowered in a corner. Mr Nark wore the expression of one who has been made to feel unpopular.

Alleyn said, 'You may open up again if you wish, Mr Pomeroy. I'm sorry to have kept you all so long. Until you and your rooms had been searched, we had no alternative. Tomorrow, you will be asked to sign the statements you have made to Mr Harper. In the meantime, if you wish, you may go to your rooms. You will not be allowed to leave the premises until further orders. Mr Nark may go home.'

From the stairs came the sound of heavy steps. Harper and the second constable came down with Legge between them. Alleyn had left the taproom door open. Six pairs of eyes turned to watch Legge go out.

Miss Darragh suddenly called out, 'Cheer up, now. It's nothing at all, man. I'll go bail for you.'

Will started forward.

'I want to speak to him.'

'Certainly,' said Alleyn.

'I'm sorry it has turned out this way, mate,' said Will. 'Damned injustice and nothing less. It won't make any difference with the Party. You know that. We'll stick by you. Wish I'd bloodied 'tother nose and gone to clink along with you.'

'They've got a down on me,' said Legge desolately.

'I know that. Good luck!'

'Come along now,' said Harper. 'Get a move on. Ready, Oates?'

Oates went out to them and Alleyn shut the door.

'Well,' said Parish. 'I call that a step in the right direction, Mr Alleyn.'

'For God's sake, Seb, hold your tongue,' said Cubitt.

'What d'you mean by that, Mr Parish?' demanded Will. 'You'd better be careful what you're saying, hadn't you?'

'That's no way to speak, sonny,' said Abel.

'While I've a tongue in my head – ' began Will.

'You'll set a guard on it, I hope,' said Alleyn. 'Good night, gentlemen.'

They filed out one by one. Parish was the only one who spoke. With his actor's instinct for an effective exit he turned in the doorway.

'I imagine,' he said, looking steadily at Alleyn, 'that I shan't be run in for contempt if I venture to suggest that this gentleman's departure marks the beginning of the end.'

'Oh, no,' said Alleyn politely. 'We shan't run you in for that, Mr Parish.'

Parish gave a light laugh and followed the others upstairs.

Only Miss Darragh remained. She put her knitting into a large chintz bag, took off her spectacles and looked steadily at Alleyn.

'I suppose you had to take that poor fellow in charge,' she said. 'He behaved very foolishly. But he's a mass of nerves, you know. It's a doctor he's needing, not a policeman.'

'Who? Mr Montague Thringle?' asked Alleyn vaguely.

'So the cat's out of the bag is ut?' said Miss Darragh placidly. 'Ah, well, I suppose 'twas bound to be. I've kept my end of the bargain.'

'I'd very much like to know what it was,' said Alleyn.

'Didn't you guess?'

'I wondered if by any chance Lord Bryonie's family had promised to keep an eye on Mr Thringle.'

'Ah, you'll end in a cocked hat with a plume in ut,' said Miss Darragh, 'if 'tis cocked hats they give to chief commissioners. That's it, sure enough. Me poor cousin Bryonie always felt he'd been responsible for the crash. He was very indiscreet, it seems, and might have helped to patch things up if he'd kept his wits about 'um. But he didn't. He'd no head for business and he only half-suspected there was anything illegal going on. But he said he'd only learned one kind of behaviour and, when it didn't fit in with finance, he was entirely at sea and thought maybe he'd better hold his peace. But it wasn't in his nature not to talk and that was the downfall of 'um. The jury saw that he'd been no more than a cat's-paw, but when he got off with the lighter sentence there was a great deal of talk that 'twas injustice and that his position saved him. Thringle felt so himself and said so. Me cousin never lost his faith in Thringle who seemed to have cast a kind of spell over 'um, though you wouldn't think it possible, would you, to see Thringle now? But in those days he was a fine-looking fellow. Dark as night, he was, with a small imperial, and his own teeth instead of those dreadful china falsehoods they gave 'um in prison. It's no wonder at all you didn't know 'um from Adam when you saw 'um. Well, the long and short of ut 'twas that before he died the family promised poor Bryonie they'd look after Mr Thringle when he came out of gaol. He was on their conscience, and I won't say he didn't know ut and make the most of ut. We kept in touch with 'um, and he wrote from here saying he'd changed his name to Legge and that he needed money. We've not much of that to spare but we had a family conference and, as I was planning a little sketching jaunt anyway, I said I'd take ut at Ottercombe and see for meself how the land lay. So that was what I did. Don't ask me to tell you the nature of our talks for they were in confidence and had nothing to say to the case. I wish with all me heart you could have left 'um alone but I see 'twas impossible. He fought those two big policemen like a Kilkenny cat, silly fellow. But if it's a question of bailing him out I'll be glad to do ut.'

'Thank you,' said Alleyn, 'I'll see that the right people are told about it. Miss Darragh, have you done any sketching along the cliffs from the tunnel to Coombe Head?'

Miss Darragh looked at him in consternation. 'I have,' she said.

'In the mornings?'

''Twas in the mornings.'

'You were there on the morning after Mr Watchman arrived in Ottercombe?'

She looked steadily at him. 'I was,' said Miss Darragh.

'We saw where you had set up your easel. Miss Darragh, did you, from where you were working, overhear a conversation between Miss Moore and Mr Watchman?'

Miss Darragh clasped her fat little paws together and looked dismally at Alleyn.

'Please,' said Alleyn.

'I did. I could not avoid it. By the time I'd decided I'd get up and show meself above the sky-line, it had gone so far I thought I had better not.'

She gave him a quick look and added hurriedly, 'Please, now, don't go thinking all manner of dreadful things.'

'What am I to think? Do you mean it was a love-scene?'

'Not in – no. No, the reverse.'

'A quarrel?'

'It was.'

'Was it of that scene you were thinking when you told me this morning, to look further and look nearer home?'

'It was. I wasn't thinking of her. God forbid. Don't misunderstand me. I was not the only one who heard them. And that's all I'll say.'

She clutched her bag firmly and stood up.

'As regards this searching,' added Miss Darragh, 'the superintendent let me off. He said you'd attend to ut.'

'I know,' said Alleyn. 'Perhaps you won't mind if Mrs Ives goes up with you to your room.'

'Not the least in the world,' said Miss Darragh.

'Then I'll send for her,' said Alleyn.

II

While he waited for Harper and the chief constable, Alleyn brought his report up to date and discussed it with Fox who remained, weakly insubordinate, in his chair by the fire.

'It's an ill wind,' said Fox, 'that blows nobody any good. I take it that I've had what you might call a thorough spring-clean with the doctor's tube taking the part of a vacuum cleaner, if the idea's not too fanciful. I feel all the better for it.'

Alleyn grunted.

'I don't know but what I don't fancy a pipe,' continued Fox.

'You'll have another spring-clean if you do.'

'Do you think so, Mr Alleyn? In that case I'll hold off. I fancy I hear a car, sir. Coming through the tunnel, isn't it?'

Alleyn listened.

'I think so. We'll get the CC to fix up a warrant. Well, Br'er Fox, it's been a short, sharp go this time, hasn't it?'

'And you were looking forward to a spell in the country, sir.'

'I was.'

'We'll be here yet awhile, with one thing and another.'

'I suppose so. Here they are.'

A car drew up in the yard. The side door opened noisily, and Colonel Brammington's voice sounded in the passage. He came in with Harper and Oates at his heels. The colonel was dressed in a dinner suit. He wore a stiff shirt with no central stud. It curved generously away from his person and through the gaping front could be seen a vast expanse of pink chest. Evidently he had at some earlier hour wetted his hair and dragged a comb through it. His shoelaces were untied and his socks unsupported. Over his dinner jacket he wore a green tyrolese bicycling cape.

'I can't apologize enough, sir,' Alleyn began, but the chief constable waved him aside.

'Not at all, Alleyn. A bore, but it couldn't be helped. I am distended with rich food and wines. Strong meat belongeth to them that are of full age. I freely confess I outdid the meat, outdid the frolic wine. It was, I flatter myself, a good dinner, but I shall not taunt you with a recital of its virtues.'

'I am sure it was a dinner in a thousand,' said Alleyn. 'I hope you didn't mind coming here, sir. Fox was still – '

'By heaven!' interrupted Colonel Brammington, 'this pestilent poisoner o'er tops it, does he not? The attempt, I imagine, was upon you both. Harper has told me the whole story. When will you make an arrest, Alleyn? May we send this fellow up the ladder to bed, and that no later than the Quarter Sessions! Let him wag upon a wooden nag. A pox on him! I trust you are recovered, Fox? Sherry, wasn't it? Amontillado, I understand. Double sacrilege, by the Lord!'

Colonel Brammington hurled himself into a chair and asked for a cigarette. When this had been given him, he produced from his trousers' pocket a crumpled mass of typescript which Alleyn recognized as the carbon copy of his report.

'I have been over the report, Alleyn,' said Colonel Brammington, 'and while you expended your energies so happily in resuscitating the poisoned Fox (and by the way, our murderer carries the blacker stigma of a fox-poisoner!) I read this admirable digest. I congratulate you. A masterly presentation of facts, free from the nauseating redundancies of most bureaucratic documents. I implored you to allow me to be your Watson. You consented. I come, full of my theory, ready to admit my blunders. Is there by any chance some flask of fermented liquor in this house to which cyanide has not been added? May we not open some virgin bottle?'

Alleyn went into the bar, found three sealed bottles of Treble Extra, chalked them up to himself and took them with glasses into the parlour.

'We should have a taster,' said Colonel Brammington. 'Some Borgian attendant at our call. What a pity the wretched Nark is not here.'

'There are times,' said Alleyn, 'when I could wish that Mr Nark had been the corpse in the case. I don't think we need blench at the Treble Extra and I washed the glasses.'

He broke a paper seal, drew the cork, and poured out the beer.

'Really,' said Colonel Brammington, 'I do feel a little timid about it, I must say. Some fiendish device – '

'I don't think so,' said Alleyn and took a pull at his beer. 'It's remarkably good.'

'You show no signs of stiffening limb or glassy eye. It is, as you say, good beer. Well, now, Alleyn, I understand from Harper that you have all arrived at a decision. I, working independently, have also made up my mind. It would delight me to find we were in agreement and amuse me to learn that I was wrong. Will you indulge me so far as to allow me to unfold the case as I see it?'

'We should be delighted, sir,' said Alleyn, thinking a little of his bed.

'Excellent,' said Colonel Brammington. He flattened out the crumpled report and Alleyn saw that he had made copious notes in pencil all over the typescript. 'I shall relate my deductions in the order in which they came to me. I shall follow the example of all Watsons and offer blunder after blunder, inviting your compassionate scorn and remembering the observation that logic is only the art of going wrong with confidence. Are you all ready?'

'Quite ready, sir,' said Alleyn.

III

'When first this case turned up,' said Colonel Brammington, 'it seemed to me to be a moderately simple affair. The circumstances were macabre, the apparent weapon unlikely, but I accepted the weapon and rejoiced in the circumstances. It was an enlivening murder.'

He turned his prominent eyes on Harper who looked scandalized.

'After all,' said Colonel Brammington, 'I did not know the victim and I frankly confess I adore a murder. Pray, Mr Harper, do not look at me in that fashion. I want the glib and oily art to speak and purpose not. I enjoy a murder and I enjoyed this one. It seemed to me that Legge had anointed the dart with malice aforethought and prussic acid, had prepared the ground with exhibitions of skill, and had deliberately thrown awry. He had overheard Watchman's story of his idiosyncrasy for the cyanide. He had seen Pomeroy put the bottle in the cupboard. Cyanide had been found on the dart. What more did we need? True, the motive was lacking, but when I learnt that you suspected Legge of being a gaolbird, a sufficient motive appeared. Legge had established himself in this district in a position of trust, he handled monies, he acquired authority. Watchman, by his bantering manner, suggested that he recognized Legge. Legge feared he would be exposed. Legge therefore murdered Watchman. That was my opinion until this afternoon.'

Colonel Brammington took a prodigious swig of beer and flung himself back in his tortured chair.

'This afternoon,' he said, 'I was astonished at your refusal to arrest Legge, but when I took the files away and began to read them I changed my opinion. I read the statements made by the others and I saw how positive each was that Legge had no opportunity to anoint the dart. I was impressed by your own observation that his hands were clumsy, that he was incapable of what would have amounted to an essay in legerdemain. Yet cyanide was found on the dart. Who had put it there. It is a volatile poison, therefore it must have been put on the dart not long before Oates sealed it up. I wondered if, after all, the whole affair was an accident, if there was some trace of poison on Abel Pomeroy's clothes or upon the bar where he unpacked the darts. It was a preposterous notion and it was smashed as squat as a flounder by the fact that the small vessel in the rat-hole had been filled up with water. I was forced to believe the cyanide had been taken from the rat-hole immediately, or soon after, old Pomeroy put it there. Any of the suspects might have done this. But only four of the suspects had handled the darts; Legge, the Pomeroys, and Parish. Only Legge controlled the flight of the darts. Watchman took them out of the board after the trial throw and gave them to Legge. Now here,' said Colonel Brammington with an air of conscious modesty, 'I fancy I hit on something new. Can you guess what it was?'

'I can venture to do so,' Alleyn rejoined. 'Did you reflect that all the darts had been thrown into the board on the trial, and that if cyanide was on any one of them, it would have been effectively cleaned off?'

'Good God!' ejaculated the chief constable.

He was silent for some time, but at last continued with somewhat forced airiness.

'No. No, that was not my point, but by Jupiter it supports my case. I was going to say that since Watchman removed the darts and handed them to Legge, it would have been quite impossible for Legge to know which dart was tainted. This led me to an alternative. Either all the darts were poisoned or else, or else, my dear Alleyn, the dart that wounded Watchman was tainted after, and not before, the accident.' He glanced at Alleyn.

'Yes, sir,' said Alleyn. 'One or the other.'

'You agree? You had thought of it?'

'Will Pomeroy suggested the second alternative,' said Alleyn.

'Damn! However! Legge, I had decided, was not capable of anointing one, much less six darts during the few seconds he held them in his hand before doing his trick. Legge would scarcely implicate himself by anointing the dart after he had seen Watchman die. Therefore someone had tried to implicate Legge. I was obliged to bow to your wisdom, my dear Alleyn. I dismissed Legge. I finished your report and I considered the other suspects. Who, of these seven persons, for they are seven if we include Miss Darragh and Miss Moore, could most easily have taken cyanide from the small vessel in the rat-hole? One of the Pomeroys, since their presence in or about the outhouses would not be remarked. Abel Pomeroy's fingerprints and only his were found on the small vessel. Who of the seven had an opportunity to smear cyanide on the dart? Abel Pomeroy, since he unpacked the darts. Who, in the first instance, had cyanide brought into the premises? Abel Pomeroy. Putting motive on one side, I felt that Abel Pomeroy was my first choice. My second fancy – and don't look so wryly upon me, Harper, a chief constable may have fancies as well as the next man – my second fancy fell upon Will Pomeroy. Your interview with the unspeakable Nark, my dear Alleyn, was not barren of interest. Amidst a plethora of imbecilities, Nark seemed to make one disclosure of interest. He said, or rather from your report I understood him to hint, that he had, on the occasion of Watchman's first visit to Ottercombe, overheard an amorous encounter between Watchman and Miss Moore. He hinted, moreover, that as he crept farther along Apple Lane he came upon Will Pomeroy, lurking and listening in the hedge. Now, thought I, if this were true, here is the beginning of motive; for, in the interim, the courtship between young Pomeroy and Miss Moore ripened. Suppose, on Watchman's return, that the rustic lover thought he saw a renewal of attentions. Suppose Parish or Cubitt hinted at the scene they interrupted by the furze bushes? But ignoring motive, what of opportunity? Will Pomeroy handled the darts after they were unpacked by his father. Could he have had a phial of cyanide-solution in his pocket? Nobody watched Will Pomeroy with the close attention that they all gave to Legge. Your observation on the trial throw shatters this theory. Do I see another bottle of this superb beer? Thank you.

'On the whole I preferred Pomeroy senior. There seemed no reason to doubt young Pomeroy's violent defence of Legge. He would not have thrown suspicion on Legge and then vehemently defended him. Old Pomeroy, on the other hand, detests Legge and has, from the first, accused him of the murder. But I was determined to look with an equal eye upon the field of suspects. I turned, with I hope becoming reluctance, to the ladies. On Miss Darragh I need not dwell. Harper has told me of your discovery of her link with Legge, and it is obvious that she merely took what may be described as a family interest in him. The family tree in this instance being unusually shady. Ha! But Miss Moore, if Nark is to be believed, cannot be so dismissed. There had been amorous passages between Miss Moore

and Watchman. Miss Moore denied this in the course of your interview. Could love have turned into the proverbial hatred? What happened when those ambiguous heelmarks were printed in the turf
behind the furze bush? A quarrel? Was she afraid her lover would
betray her to her fiancé? And opportunity? Could she have introduced poison into the glass? Who better, since she poured out the
brandy? But here, as with young Pomeroy, I had to pause. Whoever
poisoned Watchman took peculiar pains to implicate Legge, but, ever
since the investigation began, Miss Moore has been ardent to the
point of rashness in her defence of Legge. She has braved everything
for Legge, and there is a ring of urgency in her defence that bears the
very tinct of sincerity. I dismissed Miss Moore. I turned, at last, to
Sebastian Parish and Norman Cubitt. Here it was impossible to
ignore motive. Motive in the form of handsome inheritances was an
conspicuous as a pitchfork in Paradise. What of fact? Cubitt did not
handle the darts but, on my second alternative, he could have tainted the poisoned dart after Watchman threw it down. But if the dart
was a blind and didn't kill Watchman, what did? The brandy? We
are told that criminals repeat the manner of their crimes and this
attempt upon you and Fox supports the theory. The murderer had
killed Watchman by the method of putting cyanide in his brandy?
The murderer hoped to kill you by putting cyanide in your sherry?
To return. The fingerprint and rat-hole objection applies to Cubitt
and Parish as it does to everyone but Pomeroy senior. Of course it is
possible that the murderer drew the poison off with some instrument and without touching the vessel. This brings me to Parish.'

Colonel Brammington darted a raffish glance at Alleyn and
accepted a fresh cigarette.

'To Parish,' he repeated. 'And here we must not ignore a point
that I feel is extremely important. Parish purchased the cyanide solution. It was he who suggested, to the certifiable Noggins, that it
should be gingered up, as he put it. It was he who carried it back to
the inn. Old Pomeroy said that the wretched Noggins' sealing-wax
was unbroken when Parish gave him the bottle. It is possible to substitute one drop of sealing-wax by another? And if this had been
done, why the interference with the rat-hole? But suppose the
wrapping and seal were intact. Suppose that Parish made sure of
obtaining a strong enough poison, delivered the bottle, sealed as he

had received it, and later went to the rat-hole; why then he would
be acting more wisely, he would be removing suspicion one step
away from himself. His defence would be: "If I had intended to use
this damnable poison surely I would have taken the opportunity to
extract it from the bottle when it was actually in my hands." I began
to think I had got on the trail at last. I inspected the notes made by
our man, Oates, when the memory of the night's events were still
fresh, or as fresh as the aftermath of Courvoisier would allow. It was
Parish, equally with Watchman, who suggested they should have
the brandy, Parish who applauded and encouraged the suggestion
that Legge should try the experiment with the darts. I began to wonder if this was an opportunity Parish had awaited, if he had the
cyanide concealed about him in readiness for use. Could he have
reasoned that Legge, full of brandy, was likely to make a blunder in
throwing the darts and that, if he did blunder, here was Parish's
opportunity to bring off his plan? This was purely conjectural, my
dear Alleyn, but before long I came upon a thumping fact. Up to the
moment when Miss Moore poured out the brandy that failed to
restore Watchman, Parish, and only Parish, had an opportunity of
putting anything in Watchman's glass. Parish knew that if Legge
wounded Watchman, Watchman would turn queasy. Parish encouraged the brandy-drinking and dart-throwing. Parish stood near the
glass until it was used.'

Colonel Brammington thumped the arm of his chair and pointed
a hairy finger at Alleyn.

'Above all,' he shouted, 'Parish has done nothing but murmur
against Legge. Suspicions, Bacon remarked, that are artificially nour-
ished by the tales and whisperings of others, have stings. This, Parish
foresaw. This he hoped would prove true. My case against Parish is
that he took cyanide from the rat-hole as soon as he could after Abel
Pomeroy put it there. Or, I offer it as an alternative, that he took
cyanide from the original bottle, replaced the small amount with
water, and contrived to rewrap and seal the bottle; and, as a blind,
upset the vessel in the rat-hole without disturbing Pomeroy's prints,
and filled it with water. This suggests a subtlety of reasoning which
may or may not appeal to you. But to the burden of my tale. Parish
had, that very evening, heard of Watchman's idiosyncrasy for
cyanide, he had been reminded of Watchman's habit of turning faint

at the sight of his own blood, he had heard Watchman baiting Legge and Legge's offer to perform his trick with Watchman's hand, he had heard Watchman half-promise to let him try. The following night, when the brandy was produced and drunk, he saw his chance. He encouraged the drinking and the projected experiment. When Legge wounded Watchman and Watchman turned faint, Parish stood near the glass. He had the cyanide about him. Brandy was suggested. Parish put his poison in the glass. The lights went out. Parish groped on the floor, bumped his head against Cubitt's legs, found the dart and infected it. He then ground whatever phial he had about him into powder together with the broken tumbler on the floor, and finding a more solid piece under his heel threw it into the fire. And from then onwards, gentlemen, I maintain that everything the fellow did or said is consistent with the theory that he murdered his cousin. I plump for Parish.'

Colonel Brammington stared about him with an unconvincing air of modesty tinged with a hint of anxiety.

'Well,' he said, 'there you are. An essay in Watsoniana. Am I to be set down? Shall I perceive my mentor wafting his eyes to the contrary and a falling lip of much contempt?'

'No, indeed,' said Alleyn. 'I congratulate you, sir. A splendid marshalling of facts and a magnificent sequence of deductions.'

If so large and red a man could be said to simper, Colonel Brammington simpered.

'Really,' he said. 'I have committed no atrocious blunder? My deductions march with yours?'

'Almost all the way. We shall venture to disagree on one or two points.'

'I make no claim to infallibility,' said the chief constable. 'What are the points? Let us have them.'

'Well,' said Alleyn apologetically and with an uncomfortable glance at Harper and at Fox, 'there's only one point of any importance. I – in our view of the case you've – you've hit on the wrong man.'

CHAPTER 20

Conjecture into Fact

For a second or two Alleyn wondered if there would be an explosion
or, worse, a retreat into heavy silence. Fearing that the expression of
gloating delight upon Harper's face might turn the scales, Alleyn had
placed himself between the chief constable and his superintendent.
But Colonel Brammington behaved admirably. He goggled for a
moment, he became rather more purple in the face, and he made a
convulsive movement that caused his shirt-front to crackle sharply,
but finally he spoke with composure.

'Your manners, my dear Alleyn,' he said, 'are, as always, worthy
of a Chesterfield. I am pinked on the very point of a compliment.
The wrong man? Indeed? Then I must be ludicrously at fault. I have
made some Gargantuan error. My entire sequence of deductions – '

'No, no, sir. Your case against Parish is supported by facts, but not
by all the facts. Parish might so nearly have murdered Watchman, by
either of the two methods you've described.'

'Then – Well?'

'The circumstance that excludes Parish, excluded his only means
of murder. If he did it, it was by poisoning the brandy, and he could-
n't tell which glass would be used. Not possibly. But we'll come to
that in a minute. Our case, and I'm afraid it's a dubious one at the
moment, is that there are one or two scraps of evidence that only fit
into the pattern if they are allowed to point in one direction, and
that is not towards Parish.'

'What are they? More beer, I implore you.'

'To begin with,' said Alleyn, filling Colonel Brammington's glass, 'the two iodine bottles.'

'What!'

'Shall we take them, sir, as they turn up?'

'Let us, for God's sake.'

'You, sir, ended with Sebastian Parish. I shall begin with him. If Parish was a murderer how lucky he was! How all occasions did inform against Watchman and favour Parish! It was on the evening after his decision that the brandy was produced, so *that* was pure luck. He didn't know Legge would wound Watchman, he only hoped that under the influence of brandy, he might miss his mark. When it so fell out, he had to make up his mind very rapidly and plan a series of delicate and dangerous manoeuvres. And how oddly he behaved! He risked his own immunity by handling the darts, and this, when his whole object was that Legge should seem to be the poisoner. After the accident, instead of putting cyanide in the brandy glass and moving away from it, he stood beside it, in a position that was likely to be remembered. And again, how could he tell that Miss Moore would use that glass? There were seven other glasses about the room. She might have taken a clean glass. Parish made no attempt to force that glass upon her. She chose it. More stupendous luck. Now, with the exception of Miss Moore, this objection applies to the supposition that any of them put cyanide in the brandy-glass. They couldn't be sure it would be used. Only Miss Moore could be sure of that for she chose it.'

'You surely don't – Go on,' said Colonel Brammington.

'I entirely agree that, ruling out Legge and assuming that the whole arrangement of the business was an attempt to implicate Legge; Cubitt, Miss Darragh, Will Pomeroy, and Miss Moore, must be counted out, since they have all declared that Legge was unable to meddle with the darts. Our case rests on a different assumption.'

'Here, wait a bit,' cried the colonel. 'No. All right. Go on.'

'Abel Pomeroy and Parish were the only ones openly to accuse Legge. Abel Pomeroy was particularly vehement in his insistence that Legge deliberately killed Watchman. He came up to London to tell me about it.'

'Old Pomeroy was my earlier choice.'

'Yes, sir. To return to the brandy. For the reason I have given you, and for reasons that I hope to make clear, we are certain that cyanide was put on the dart after, and not before, it pierced Watchman's finger. Otherwise it would have been removed by the trial throw into the cork board or, if there was any trace left, possibly washed off by the blood that flowed freely from Watchman's finger and with which the dart was greatly stained. The cyanide was found on the point of the dart. Watchman, we think, was poisoned, not by the dart nor by the brandy. How, then?'

'But, my dear fellow, there was no cyanide in the iodine bottle. They found the bottle. There was no cyanide.'

'None. Now here, sir, we have a bit of evidence that is new to you. I feel sure that if you'd had it earlier today it would have made a difference to your view of the case. We have found out that within a few hours of the murder, a bottle of iodine disappeared from the bathroom cupboard upstairs.'

Colonel Brammington stared a little wildly at Alleyn, made as if to speak, and evidently thought better of it. He waved his hand.

'The bottle of iodine that was originally in the downstairs first-aid box,' Alleyn continued, 'was an entirely innocent bottle, with Abel's prints on it and only his. Legge's prints were added when he borrowed this bottle to doctor a cut on his chin. Abel gave it to him. Now that innocent and original bottle is, I consider, the one that was found under the settle. All that is left of the bottle Abel Pomeroy used when he poured iodine into Watchman's wound, is represented, or so we believe, by the surplus amount of glass Mr Harper swept up from the floor and by the small misshapen fragments we found in the ashes.'

'Hah!' ejaculated the colonel. 'Now I have you. A lethal bottle, taken from the bathroom and infected, was substituted for the innocent bottle in the first-aid box. Only Abel Pomeroy's prints were found on the cupboard door and so on. Abel Pomeroy himself took the bottle from the box and himself poured the iodine into the wound. Splendid!'

'Exactly, sir,' said Alleyn.

'Well, Alleyn, I readily abandon my second love. I return, chastened, to my first love. How will you prove it?'

'How indeed! We hope that an expert will be able to tell us that the fragments of glass are, in fact, of the same type as that used for iodine bottles. That's not much but it's something and we *have* got other strings to our bow.'

'What's his motive?'

'Whose motive, sir?'

'Old Pomeroy's.'

Alleyn looked at him apologetically.

'I'm sorry, sir. I hadn't followed you. Abel Pomeroy had no motive, as far as I know, for wishing Watchman dead.'

'What the hell d'you mean?'

'I didn't think Abel Pomeroy was strictly your first love, sir. May I go on? You see, once we accept the iodine theory, we must admit that the murderer knew Watchman would be wounded by the dart. Nobody knew that, sir, but Legge.'

II

It took the second half of the last bottle of Treble Extra to mollify the chief constable, but he was mollified in the end.

'I invited it,' he said, 'and I got it. In a sense, I suppose I committed the unforgivable offence of failing to lead trumps. Legge was trumps. Go on, my dear Alleyn. Expound. Is it Locke who says that it is one thing to show a man he is in error and another to convince him of the truth? You have shown me my error. Pray reveal the whole truth.'

'From the first,' said Alleyn, 'it seemed obvious that Legge was our man. Mr Harper realized that, and so, sir, did you. This afternoon I told Harper that Fox and I had arrived at the same conclusion. You asked me not to give you our theory, but before and after you came into Illington we discussed the whole thing. Harper was for arresting him there and then, and I, mistakenly perhaps, thought that we should give him more rope. I thought that on our evidence, which rests so much upon conjecture, we would not establish a *prima facie* case.'

'What is your evidence beyond the tedious – well, go on.'

'As we see it,' said Alleyn, 'Legge planned the whole affair to look like an accident. No doubt he hoped that it would go no further than the inquest. His behaviour has been consistent with the theory of accident. He has shown us a man overwrought by the circumstance of having unwittingly killed someone. That describes his behaviour after Watchman died, at the inquest, and subsequently. He chanced everything on the accident theory. It is easy, now, to say he took an appalling risk, but he very nearly got away with it. If old Abel hadn't raised such a dust about the good name of his public-house, and if Mr Nark and others had not driven Harper, here, to fury, you might very well have got no further. Legge's motive was the one we have recognized. It harks back to the days when he was Montague Thringle and stood his trial for large-sized embezzlement, and all the rest of it. At least three of the enormous number of people he ruined committed suicide. There was the usual pitiful list of old governesses and retired clerks. A shameful affair. Now, in defending Lord Bryonie, Watchman was able to throw almost the entire blame on Legge, or Thringle as I suppose we must learn to call him. Let him be Legge for the moment. Watchman made a savage attack on Legge, and it was in no small measure due to him that Legge got such a heavy sentence. He had an imperial and moustaches in those days and had not turned grey. His appearance was very greatly changed when he came out of gaol. After various vicissitudes in Liverpool and London, he came down here suffering from a weak chest and some complaint of the ear, for which he uses a lotion and a dropper. Harper found the dropper when he searched Legge's room on the morning after Watchman died. It's not there now.'

'That's right,' said Harper heavily.

'Legge got on well in Illington and Ottercombe. He'd got his philatelic job, and he was treasurer to a growing society. We shall inspect the books of the Coombe Left Movement. If he has not yet fallen into his old ways on a smaller scale, it is, I am sure, only because the funds at his disposal are not yet large enough. All was going like clockwork until, out of a clear sky, came Watchman in his car. That collision of theirs must have given Legge an appalling shock. Watchman didn't recognize him, though, and later while Legge sat unseen in the taproom, he overheard Watchman tell Parish of the collision and say, as Parish admitted he said, that he did not know the man who ran into him. But before Legge could go out that night, Watchman came across and tried to make friends with him. Legge doesn't seem to have been very responsive but he stuck it out. The

rat-poisoning party returned and Legge's skill with darts was discussed. Legge took up Watchman's bet and won. I think it must have
amused him to do that. Now, it was soon after this that Watchman
began to twit Legge about his job and his political opinions. I've gone
over the events of this first evening with the witnesses. Though they
are a bit hazy, they agree that Watchman's manner was offensive. He
ended by inviting Legge to a game of round-the-clock and the manner of the invitation was this: he said, "Have you ever done time,
Mr Legge?" I think that throughout the whole evening Watchman,
having recognized Legge, played cat-and-mouse with him. I knew
Watchman. He had a curious feline streak of cruelty in him. I think
it must have been then that Legge made up his mind Watchman had
recognized him. Legge went into the public bar for a time. I believe
he also went into the garage and sucked up cyanide in the little
dropper he used for his ear lotion. Just, as they say, in case.'

'Damned ingenious,' said Colonel Brammington, 'but conjectural.'

'I know. We are only half-way through the case. It has changed
its complexion with Oates's arrest of Legge for assault. We've only
been here some thirty hours, you see. If we can check the time Legge
appeared in the public bar with the time he left the private one, and
all that deary game, we shall be a step nearer. But dismiss all this
conjecture and we still have the facts. We still know that only Legge
controlled the flight of the dart.'

'Yes.'

'The next day was the fatal one. Legge stayed out of sight all day.
Late in the afternoon, he left it as late as possible, and just before the
others came in, he went down to the bar with a razor-cut on his chin
and asked Abel for some iodine. Abel got the box out of the corner
cupboard and gave it to Legge. Legge returned it a few minutes later.
He had dabbed iodine on his chin. He had also substituted for the
iodine bottle in the box, the iodine bottle he had taken from the
bathroom. This he had doctored with prussic acid from the rat-hole.
By this really neat manoeuvre he got Abel to do the dirty work and
accounted for any prints of his own that might afterwards be found
on the bottle. In the evening Legge had a perfectly genuine appointment in Illington. At about five o'clock the storm broke, and I think
that like a good villain Mr Legge made plans to the tune of thunder

off-stage. The storm was a fair enough reason for staying indoors. The failing lights were propitious. The Pomeroys both told him he couldn't get through the tunnel. When Will Pomeroy went up to Legge's room in the evening, he found him rather thoughtful. However, he came down and joined the party in the bar. I think he had made up his mind that, if Watchman suggested the trick should be done that night, he would wound Watchman. Abel, so keen on antiseptic, would produce the first-aid set from the cupboard. So it worked out. Two points are interesting. The first is the appearance and the consumption of the brandy. That was an unexpected development but he turned it to good account. He sat in the ingle-nook and appeared to get quietly and thoroughly soaked. That would account nicely for his missing with the tricks. In the wood-basket beside his seat we found a newspaper into which liquid had been poured. The newspaper had been there since that night. Fox and I think we can detect a trace of the fruitful vine in the stains. But he must have watched the others anxiously. Would they be too tight to remember he had no chance to monkey with the darts? Luckily for him, Will, Abel, Miss Darragh, and Miss Moore, all remained sober. That brings us to the second point. Legge's great object was to provide himself with an alibi for doctoring the darts. That was why he fell in with Abel's suggestion that he should use the new darts. Legge stood under the central light and waited for the darts to be handed to him. He was in his shirt sleeves and they were rolled back like a conjurer's. Parish, Will, Abel, and Watchman, all handled the darts. When Legge got them he at once threw them one by one into the board, as a trial. That was his first mistake but it would have looked odd for him not to do it. Then Watchman pulled them out and gave them to him. Watchman spread out his hand and the sequel followed. There were six people ready to swear Legge had done nothing to the darts.'

Alleyn paused.

'I'm afraid this is heavy going,' he said. 'I won't be much longer. Watchman, when hit, pulled out the dart and threw it into the floor. When Oates called for the dart Legge obligingly found it on the floor behind the table but not before Oates, who's a sharp fellow, Nick, had, as he says, spotted it a-lying there. You throw these darts down as often as you like and I'll guarantee they stick in. And moreover we've statements from them all that it *did* stick in. All right. The lights had been wavering on and off throughout the evening. Before Watchman died they went off. There was a horrid interval during which Watchman made ghastly noises, everybody tramped about on broken glass, and Cubitt felt somebody's head butt against his legs. Miss Moore, she told me, heard somebody click the light to see if it would go on. Not very bright of Miss Moore. Legge clicked the light to make sure it would stay off. He then dived down to find the tell-tale iodine bottle and plant the innocent one under the bench. He must, as you say, have found the bottom of the bottle hard to smash and have thrown it in the fire. You remember he called out that he would throw wood on the fire in order to get a little light. Just as he did that the lights went on. There's a second switch in the ingle-nook, you know. He'd done another job of work in the dark. He'd picked up the dart and infected it with cyanide. The dart was sticking in the floor, well away from the others. He had only to feel for the table and then find the dart. Here he made the fatal mistake of adding a fancy-touch. We've proved that the dart was infected *after* the accident. Legge's fingerprints are all over it. If anyone else had pulled it out of the floor they would either have left prints of their own or smudged his. He should have left the dart alone, and we would have concluded that if it was ever poisoned the stuff was washed off by blood or had evaporated.'

'I cannot conceive,' said the colonel, 'why he'd wanted to anoint the dart. Why implicate himself? Why?'

'In order that we should think exactly what we did think. "Why," we cried, "there was Legge, finding the dart, with every opportunity to wipe it clean and he didn't! It couldn't be Legge!" Legge's plan, you see, depended on the theory of accident. He made it clear that he could have done nothing to the dart beforehand.'

'Then,' said the colonel, 'if the rest of this tarradiddle, forgive me, my dear fellow, is still in the air, we yet catch him on the point of the dart.'

'I think so. I explained to Harper this afternoon that I thought it better not to make an arrest at once. We realized that our case rested on a few facts and a mass of dubious conjecture. Fox and I pretend to despise conjecture, and we hoped to collect many more bits of evidence before we fired point-blank. We still hope to get them before Legge comes up for assault and battery. We hope, in a word, to turn conjecture into fact. Until this evening I also hoped to get more from Legge himself, and, by George, I nearly got a dose of prussic acid. He must have slipped into the taproom and put his last drop of poison in the decanter. He must also have had that last drop hidden away in a bottle somewhere ever since he murdered Watchman. Not on his person, for he was searched, and not in his room. Perhaps in his new room at Illington, perhaps in a *cache* somewhere outside the pub. Some time after Harper had searched his room, Legge got rid of a small glass dropper with a rubber top. If he used it to draw prussic acid from the rat-hole, he must have cleaned it and filled it with his lotion, emptied it and restored it to its place on his dressing-table. If he also used it to do his work with the decanter, he got rid of it this afternoon together with whatever vessel housed the teaspoonful of prussic acid. We'll search for them both.'

Alleyn paused and looked round the circle of attentive faces. He raised a long finger.

'If we could find so much as the rubber top of that dropper,' he said, 'hidden away in some unlikely spot, then it would be goodbye conjecture and welcome fact.'

III

'A needle,' cried Colonel Brammington after a long pause, 'a needle in a haystack of gigantic proportions.'

'It's not quite so bad as that. It rained pretty heavily during the lunch-hour. Legge hasn't changed his shoes and he hasn't been out in them. They're slightly stained and damp. He crossed the yard several times, but he didn't get off cobble stones. The paths and roads outside the pub are muddy. He's therefore either thrown the bottle and dropper from the window or got rid of them in the house or garage.'

'Lavatory,' said Fox gloomily.

'Possibly, Br'er Fox. We may have to resort to plumbing. His whole object would be to get rid of them immediately. He didn't know when we mightn't take a glass of sherry. Now there's a valuable axiom which you, Colonel, have pointed out. The criminal is very prone to repetition. How did Legge get rid of the iodine bottle. He smashed it and threw the thick pieces into the fire. When he had more glass to get rid of in a hurry, wouldn't he at once think of his former method? He's a very unusual criminal if he didn't. There was no fire here, but during the afternoon he made several trips to the garage. He was packing some of his books in the car. I think our first move is to search the car and the garage. It's full of junk so it will be a delightful task.'

Alleyn turned to Oates.

'Would you like to begin, Oates?'

'Yes, sir, thank you, sir.'

'Search the car and garage thoroughly. I'll join you in ten minutes.'

'Methodical, now,' said Harper, 'remember what I've told you.'

'Yes, sir.'

Oates went out.

'I think Mrs Ives is still about,' said Alleyn. 'She works late.'

'I'll see if I can find her, sir,' said Fox.

'You'll stay where you are. I'll go,' said Alleyn.

Mrs Ives had gone to her room but had got no further than her first row of curling pins. Alleyn interviewed her in Legge's room. She'd taken a cup of tea up to him in the afternoon when he was packing his books. She couldn't say exactly when, but knew it was after three and before four o'clock. She had noticed the ear-lotion and dropper on top of his dressing-table.

'Particular, I noticed it,' said Mrs Ives, 'along of it being wet and marking wood. Usually, of a morning, it's all mucky with that pink stuff he puts in his ears. "About time you washed that thing," I said, "and I see you've done it." He seemed quite put-about. Well, you know, put-about, like, at my noticing.'

'And did you go away soon after that, Mrs Ives?'

'Well, sir, seeing I was not welcome,' said Mrs Ives, bridling a little, 'I went. I offered to help him with his books but he seemed like he didn't fancy it, so I went on with my work upstairs. Polishing floor, I was.'

'Which floor did you polish when you left Mr Legge?'

'Passage, sir, and I might of saved myself the trouble, seeing he come and went to and fro from yard half a dozen times, stepping round me and dropping muck from his papers and passels.'

'Did he go into the bathroom or any other room upstairs?'

Mrs Ives blushed. 'He didn't, then. He made two or three trips and after last trip he went into private tap. The gentlemen were down there, Mr Parish and Mr Cubitt. You come up here soon after that to change your clothes.'

Alleyn thanked her, spent an uncomfortable quarter of an hour on the roof outside Legge's window, and returned to the parlour.

'We're in luck,' he said, and gave them Mrs Ives' story of the ear-dropper.

'That's why he didn't fill it with lotion again and leave it. He'd just washed it when Mrs Ives walked in, and when she noticed it, he lost his nerve and decided to get rid of it.'

'The dropper,' said Harper, 'had a rubber top.'

'It'd float,' said Fox.

'He didn't go there, Br'er Fox. Mrs Ives would have seen him. And there isn't one downstairs. It's the garage or the yard. Hallo, here's Oates!'

Oates came in. He was slightly flushed with triumph.

'Well?' said Harper.

'In accordance with instructions, sir,' said Oates, 'I proceeded to search the premises – '

'A truce to these vain repetitions,' began Colonel Brammington with some violence.

'Never mind all that, Oates,' said Harper. 'Have you found anything?'

'Smashed glass, sir. Powdered to scatters and under a bit of sacking. The sacking's been newly shifted, sir.'

'We'll look at it,' said Alleyn. 'Anything else?'

'I searched the car, sir, without success. I noted she was low in water, sir, and I took the liberty of filling her up. When she was full, sir, this come up to the top.'

He opened his great hand.

Lying on the palm was a small wet indiarubber cap such as is used on chemist's lotion droppers for the eye or ear. 'Goodbye conjecture,' said Alleyn, 'and welcome fact.'

May 3rd, 1939,
    New Zealand.

The Figure Quoted

The Figure Quoted appeared in the Christchurch evening newspaper, *The Sun,* in December 1927, and was reprinted in an anthology, *New Zealand Short Stories,* in 1930. Recently rediscovered, this intriguing tale is the earliest known example of Ngaio Marsh's published fiction.

Mr Batey (Batey and Burt, Auctioneers) stood in the middle of those ill-lit, indescribably dreary business premises of his and looked unenthusiastically at the 'lots' which he hoped to sell in the course of the next two hours.

This was a remnant day. All the hopelessly impossible oddments of former sales were massed together, with one or two attractions thrown in to arouse the desirable gambling spirit in the heart of that peculiar public which waited upon Mr Batey's arts as an auctioneer. There were neat little lots of china, three cotton gabardine dresses of no character, an ancient gramophone, which in response to the solicitations of Mr Batey's clerk was even now giving tongue to a hopelessly ancient fox-trot; there were piles of dreadful old music sheets and collections of second-hand books. Hanging disconsolately on the dirty wall were three oil-paintings. One of them presented some indecently-pink flamingos standing in a pool which at first glance appeared to be afflicted with floating kidneys. A closer examination showed these objects to be the leaves of water-lilies. The other two works were landscapes of terrifying gloom.

In the middle of all this decorous and depressing jumble stood the marble basin that was attracting Mr Batey's attention at the moment. It was unbelievably lovely and Mr Batey despised it from the depths of his heart. Its shape was perfect. The pure Greek outline of a shallow vessel with outward-curving, generous base and exquisitely-tilted lip. Beneath the rim was a band of fruit and leaves enclosed between two garlands that a Doric shepherd might have woven one day in spring. Inside the rim was a little flattened platform where once upon a time a stone nymph must have sat, dabbling her feet in the water and looking down slantways at the faun who still crouched on the pedestal. But the nymph had gone.

'What are you to do with a thing like that?' asked Mr Batey of his assistant. 'I dunno what you were thinking of, Ern . . . a good quid . . . and what I mean to say is . . . who's going to buy it?'

'I kind of liked it,' said Ern.

'Well, I can't say I see what took your fancy.'

If Ern had moved in other circles he might have returned the inevitable answer of the layman: 'I don't know anything about it, but I do know what I like.' However, he was unacquainted with this formula and merely said combatively: 'What's wrong with it? It's pretty.'

'It's that big you might have a bath in it,' returned Mr Batey inconsequentially, 'and that affair sitting down at the bottom with sheep's legs . . . I mean to say!'

The customers began to drift in and inspect the lots . . .

It would be difficult to say from what section of the public Mr Batey drew his patrons. For the most part they were women in overcoats of varying degrees of dilapidation. Half a dozen men hung about the entrance and cracked a dispirited joke or two. It was the usual weekly afternoon auction and the usual crowd attended it, poking, examining . . . dubious faces thrust forward to reject, or to appraise with pursed lips of covetousness, some dingy object, which, heaven knows why, attracted their ineradicable acquisitiveness.

A little group collected round the stone basin.

'Look very nice in the front garden, Mrs Clark,' said Mr Batey jovially.

'What's it for?' inquired the lady he had spoken to.

'It's . . . well, you see what it is . . . it's an ornamental urn, in a manner of speaking.'

'Ow!'

'Very fine thing.'

A dealer pushed his way through the crowd and looked at it disinterestedly.

'Didn't know you went in for that sort of thing,' he remarked.

Mr Batey detected a sneer, and without replying, majestically mounted his desk and, putting on his pince-nez, surveyed his audience with a practised eye. Suddenly and vehemently, he attacked it with his professional manner.

'Now then, ladies and gentlemen.' He paused effectively, and the crowd settled itself on benches, chairs, packing-cases, and on the flight of stairs that ran up the back wall of the room. Mr Batey, in a few well-chosen words, enlarged on the excellence of a coal-scuttle which Ern, cynically staring about him, held up for everyone to see.

'Now then,' repeated Mr Batey, 'it's a beautiful thing. Good as new. Worth a couple of quid. How much have you got for it, ladies? Start me with something.'

This phrase was a convention. Nobody ever started Mr Batey with any bid, however lowly, but the use of the convention enabled him to proceed along the usual lines and in five minutes the coal-scuttle, 'worth a couple of quid', was knocked down for eight shillings. It was quickly succeeded by a meat dish and a set of the works of Lord Byron.

Mr Batey was apparently on the top of his form, attacking vigorously, uttering an occasional quip, and inquiring pathetically, 'What's the matter with it, ladies?' yet, in his heart, he was ill at ease. That stone basin . . . ridiculously fancied by Ern . . . had really almost taken hold of Mr Batey's imagination; an experience which, as he himself would have said, was as unusual as it was 'undesirable'. He was not keen on his imagination at any time. It was a quality of his mind in which he was not interested, and to have it aroused by a tuppenny-ha'penny bit of masonry was very fidgeting. He wished that the long shaft of sunlight coming in at the top of the stairs had not fallen so exactly on the little stone faun as he crouched on his furry haunches at the foot of the pedestal. Mr Batey's eyes, try as he would to fix them on his audience, would keep turning toward the empty platform inside the rim of the bowl, at which the faun so fixedly stared. Better put the thing up at once and get it off his mind. He knocked Lord Byron down to a dealer for three-and-six, and said hastily:

'Lot 5. Ornamental Urn.'

At this flamboyant description of himself, Ern gave a sudden start. ''Ow much?' he ejaculated.

'Not you. That,' said Mr Batey.

Ern, covered in confusion, came down from his table to the accompaniment of a subdued titter from the crowd. Mr Batey was glad of the laugh. It gave him time, like a comedian who is uncertain of his lines, to gather himself together for his opening sally. It was all very tiresome, though why he should be so fussed about it he could not have said.

Nobody would bid and the thing would fall back on his hands; which was exactly what he did not want. The fountain, basin, urn, whatever it was, was a 'rum affair', and he wouldn't wonder if there wasn't something uncanny about it. Come, come.

'Now, ladies and gentlemen, I have got something particularly fine to offer you. A really classy bit of masonry. Put it on the front lawn and your residence would be at once exclusive and genteel. Now, how much will you start me at?'

He paused, entirely without expectation, when to his utter amazement a man's voice said very placidly:

'Three pounds.'

Mr Batey kept his head admirably. His eyes, perhaps, turned a little glassy, but he actually managed to ejaculate coldly:

'Well, ladies and gentlemen, I suppose I must start somewhere, so I'll take three pounds as a bid. Three pounds I've got . . .' and lowering his voice he went on quacking in the orthodox manner. Three pounds I got – three pounds – three quid I got – three quid.'

There was some sort of disturbance going on at the head of the stairs. That single shaft of sunlight prevented Mr Batey from seeing clearly in this direction. Vague, drab figures jostled each other behind a screen of gold-dust. Suddenly a clear and extraordinary youthful voice called out something that he could not catch.

'Is that a bid up there?' asked Mr Batey. The same voice made the same bird-like exclamation.

'Three-ten,' said Mr Batey on the off-chance, and not being contradicted drew breath to quack again.

'Four,' said the man's voice.

'Four,' said Mr Batey. A little pale hand and a bare arm shot up on the other side of the shaft of light. Odd!

'Five,' said Mr Batey.

'Ten,' said the first bidder. The insane idea that Ern had taken it upon himself to 'trot' his fancy visited Mr Batey's confused and harried soul, but he held on nobly.

'That's better, gentlemen – thank you, sir. Ten quid I got. Ten for this highly-ornamental urn. Ten quid.'

He turned his head automatically toward the spot from which the voice of his female bidder seemed to come and nearly fainted.

From out of the confused jumble of vague figures at the head of the stairs emerged, all too clearly to be seen, a lovely girl. She floated, rather than walked, to the banister head, which in area was about the same size as the empty platform inside the stone bowl. On this banister post she seated herself, cupping her chin in her hand and looking down slantways at the faun who was so far below. Mr Batey's first wild desire was to heave in her direction one of his cotton gabardine dresses.

She was wearing nothing at all.

The grateful sun shone directly upon her, and so pale she was and so still she sat that she looked for all the world as if she were carved out of stone. Her appearance acted upon Mr Batey exactly like a severe concussion following a blow on the head. His voice and limbs and even his brain went on functioning, but unnaturally . . . they were prone at any moment to peter out altogether. He continued to quack. She nodded. He took her bid and quacked again. He could now see the gentleman who had first called the running, a scholarly-looking, elderly person, leaning against the front door post. 'Fifteen,' said this man, calmly, without so much as glancing at the head of the stairs.

Mr Batey glanced. Poor Mr Batey, victim of circumstances and of his trade, continued to take bids from a completely-undressed lady whom nobody else appeared to notice. That was the queer part about it. There were all those elderly and respectable ladies round her, paying no more attention to her than if she had been as fully clad as they themselves. Was she a mad woman? Was everyone mad, wondered Mr Batey, or was he himself insane? A cold sweat burst out on his brow.

'Twenty. Thank you, madam,' he shouted, wildly averting his gaze from her as she gently inclined her head toward him. 'Come on, sir, it's against you . . . twenty pounds . . . cheap y'know.'

'Twenty-five.'

'Twenty-five I've got.' Gosh, there she was nodding at him again! Thirty. Thirty pounds . . . thirty quid . . . come on, ladies and gentlemen, what's the matter with it?' (What, indeed!) 'Thirty I've got!'

'Wait a moment,' said the gentleman quietly. 'Shouldn't there be a second figure?'

'Another!' screamed Mr Batey, almost unmanned by this final irregularity. '*Another figure!* How many more?' He clutched at the rail of his desk and glared quite dreadfully into the middle distance.

'I believe there has been, at some time, a female figure seated on the platform inside the basin. Have you this figure? Is it detachable?'

Mr Batey had almost reached the end of his tether. The whole of his everyday business had become pagan and improper. What was all this chat about figures? This unblushing demand and all-too-ready supply? What were they taking him for?

'If you want figgers!' he suddenly bawled in the astonished gentleman's face – ''Ow about that!' and he pointed wildly but dramatically at his offensive visitor. The gentleman put up his glasses and gazed across the room.

'H'm,' he said.

'What d'you mean, "H'm"?' roared Mr Batey. 'I should think it was "H'm".'

'Before we go any further,' said the gentleman, 'I should like to look at this separate piece . . .'

'"Piece" is right.'

'. . . presumably it goes with the fountain?'

'Perzoomably . . . !' Mr Batey was inarticulate. The shameless man was now approaching the girl on the banister head. She took no notice of him, but remained as if frozen, her chin in her hand, a slanting smile on her lips. This smile, the gentleman's face, as if it were a mirror, faintly reflected. Then glancing at Ern, who was looking a little dazed, he murmured, 'May we not re-enthrone her?' and before Mr Batey's galvanized eyes, they toppled her over, bore her down the stairs, and set her up inside the stone basin. There she sat, lost behind an age of antiquity, sun-warmed, but quite, quite still.

'Forty . . . for the whole thing,' said the gentleman. It was Mr Batey's swan song, but he managed it.

'Any advance on forty for the whole concern?' he gabbled, insanely beating the air with his hammer. There was no advance. 'Away she goes,' gasped Mr Batey. 'That's all, thank you, ladies and gentlemen.'

The crowd, surprised at the short duration of the sale, drifted away. The man who had bought . . . 'goodness knows what he has bought,' thought Mr Batey . . . gave his cheque and address to Ern and with a nod towards Mr Batey walked briskly away.

Mr Batey and Ern behaved very much like simultaneous comedians. They watched the customer disappear; they turned their heads sharply toward each other, and in perfect unison asked each other:

'Where did it come from?'

'Where did it come from?'

'What!'

'What!'

'The figger.'

'The figger.'

'Don't *you* know?' gasped Mr Batey.

'I thought you'd bought it,' said Ern. Mr Batey became glassy.

'Who run 'im up to forty?' asked Ern. 'I couldn't see her. Who was she, anyway?'

'Not . . . not much to look at.'

'Well-dressed sorter dame?'

'Dressed?' repeated Mr Batey with extreme difficulty; 'I wouldn't say well-dressed.'

'Well, Mr Batey, I wasn't so far wrong after all,' suggested Ern, 'when I said it was a bit of good stuff.'

'I still consider it an unwarranted speculation,' said Mr Batey, 'in . . . ah . . . in consideration of . . . the figure quoted.'

'I don't get you,' said Ern.

'You wouldn't,' said Mr Batey, profoundly.